T0359680

Also by
Linda Lael Miller

NO.1 *NEW YORK TIMES* BESTSELLING AUTHOR

LINDA LAEL
MILLER

The McKettricks

TATE & GARRETT

THE MCKETTRICKS: TATE & GARRETT © 2024 by Harlequin Books S.A.

MCKETTRICKS OF TEXAS: TATE
© 2010 by Linda Lael Miller
Australian Copyright 2010
New Zealand Copyright 2010

First Published 2010
Third Australian Paperback Edition 2024
ISBN 978 1 038 92190 1

MCKETTRICKS OF TEXAS: GARRETT
© 2010 by Linda Lael Miller
Australian Copyright 2010
New Zealand Copyright 2010

First Published 2010
Third Australian Paperback Edition 2024
ISBN 978 1 038 92190 1

This is a work of fiction. Names, characters, places, and incidents are either the
product of the author's imagination or are used fictitiously, and any resemblance
to actual persons, living or dead, business establishments, events, or locales is
entirely coincidental.

Published by
Mills & Boon
An imprint of Harlequin Enterprises (Australia) Pty Limited
(ABN 47 001 180 918), a subsidiary of HarperCollins
Publishers Australia Pty Limited (ABN 36 009 913 517)
Level 19, 201 Elizabeth Street
SYDNEY NSW 2000
AUSTRALIA

MIX
Paper | Supporting
responsible forestry
FSC
www.fsc.org FSC® C001695

® and ™ (apart from those relating to FSC®) are trademarks of Harlequin
Enterprises (Australia) Pty Limited or its corporate affiliates. Trademarks indicated
with ® are registered in Australia, New Zealand and in other countries.
Contact admin_legal@Harlequin.ca for details.

Printed and bound in Australia by McPherson's Printing Group

CONTENTS

McKettricks Of Texas: Tate

Dear Reader,

I'm delighted to see this new edition of the McKettrick trilogy—one of my all-time favorite series. These three modern-day McKettrick men are irrepressible and larger-than-life, and I believe you'll fall in love with them just like I did.

Tate, Garrett and Austin are three Texas-bred brothers who find their matches in the Remington sisters. Meet oldest brother Tate first. When he sets his sights on his old high school sweetheart, Libby Remington, the town of Blue River, Texas, will never be the same!

I'm sure you already know how I feel about Western fiction, especially Western romance. I love it! And I feel that way about the West itself, in all its grandeur and diversity. I've set stories in Texas, of course (like these three), Montana (the Painted Pony Creek and Big Sky books), Arizona (my Mojo Sheepshanks series) and Wyoming (my newest series, the Brides of Bliss County).

Another thing I want to mention, but that I'm sure you already know, is how I feel about animals and our responsibility to care for them. This is a cause that's near and dear to my heart. I want to emphasize that we should all support our local shelters! And we all need to keep our pets safe—neutered, vaccinated and identified with microchips and/or tags—and to encourage others to do the same. Pets (or companion animals, as many prefer to call them) bring us so much unconditional love, so much joy. And that's what they deserve from us, too.

Happy trails!

With love,

For Leslee Borger, my fellow cowgirl,
with love and appreciation.

PROLOGUE

Silver Spur Ranch
Blue River, Texas

SPRING THUNDER EXPLODED OVERHEAD, fit to cleave the roof right down the middle and blow out every window on all three floors.

Tate McKettrick swore under his breath, while rain pelted the venerable walls like machine-gun fire.

Like as not, the creek would be over the road by now, and he'd have to travel overland to get to town. He was running late—again. And Cheryl, his ex-wife, would blister his ears with the usual accusations, for sure.

He didn't give a damn, she'd say, about their delicate twin daughters, because he'd wanted boys, as rough-and-tumble as he and his brothers had been. That was her favorite dig. She'd never know—because he wasn't about to let on—how that particular remark never failed to sear a few layers off his heart. He would literally have died for Audrey and Ava—the twins were the only redeeming features of a marriage that should never have taken place in the first place.

Since one good jab was never enough for Cheryl, she'd most likely go on to say that being late for their daughters' dance recital was his way of spiting *her*, their mother. He'd *used* his own

children, she'd insist—he *knew* she hated it when he was late—
yada, yada, yada.

Blah, blah, blah.

Tate didn't have to "use" the twins to get under Cheryl's hide—
he'd done that in spades after the divorce by forcing her to live in
Blue River, so they could share custody. Audrey and Ava alter-
nated between their mother's place in town and the ranch, a week
there, a week here, with the occasional scheduling variation. As
soon as he picked them up on the prescribed days, Cheryl was
off to some hot spot to hobnob with her fancy friends and all but
melt her credit cards.

Tight-jawed with resignation, Tate plunked down on the edge
of his bed and reached for the boots he'd polished before shedding
his rain-soaked range clothes to take a hasty shower. Clad in stiff
new jeans and the requisite long-sleeved white Western shirt, the
cowboy version of a tux, he listened with half an ear to the rodeo
announcer's voice, a laconic drone spilling from the speakers of
the big flat-screen TV mounted on the wall above the fireplace.

He was reaching for the remote to shut it off when he caught
his brother's name.

The hairs on Tate's nape bristled, and something coiled in the
pit of his stomach, snakelike, fixing to spring.

"...Austin McKettrick up next, riding a bull named Buzzsaw..."

Tate's gaze—indeed, the whole of his consciousness—swung
to the TV screen. Sure enough, there was his kid brother, in high-
definition, living color, standing on the catwalk behind the chute,
pacing a little, then shifting from one foot to the other, eager for
his turn to ride.

The shot couldn't have lasted more than a second or two—
another cowboy had just finished a ride and his score was about
to be posted on the mega-screen high overhead—but it was long
enough to send a chill down Tate's spine.

The other cowboy's score was good, the crowd cheered, and
the camera swung back to Austin. He'd always loved cameras, the
damn fool, and they'd always loved him right back.

The same went for women, kids, dogs and horses.

He crouched on the catwalk, Austin did, while down in the
chute, the bull was ominously still, staring out between the rails,

biding his time. The calm ones were always the worst, Tate reflected—Buzzsaw was a volcano, waiting to blow, saving all his whup-ass for the arena, where he'd have room to do what he'd been bred to do: wreak havoc.

Break bones, crush vital organs.

A former rodeo competitor himself, though his event had been bareback bronc riding, Tate knew this bull wasn't just mean; it was two-thousand pounds of cowboy misery, ready to bust loose.

Austin had to have picked up on all that and more. He'd begun his career as a mutton-buster when he was three, riding sheep for gold-stamped ribbons at the county fair, progressed to Little Britches Rodeo and stayed with it from then on. He'd taken several championships at the National High School Rodeo Finals and been a star during his college years, too.

It wasn't as if he didn't know bulls.

Austin looked more cocky than tense; in any dangerous situation, his mantra was "Bring it on."

Tate watched as his brother adjusted his hat again, lowered himself onto the bull's back, looped his hand under the leather rigging and secured it in a "suicide wrap," essentially tying himself to the animal. A moment later, he nodded to the gate men.

Tate stared, unable to look away. He felt an uncanny sensation like the one he'd experienced the night their mom and dad had been killed; he'd awakened, still thrashing to tear free of the last clammy tendrils of a nightmare, his flesh drenched in an icy sweat, the echo of the crash as real as if he'd witnessed the distant accident in person.

He'd known Jim and Sally McKettrick were both gone long before the call came—and he felt the same soul-numbing combination of shock and dread now.

A single, raspy word scraped past his throat. *"No."*

Of course, Austin couldn't hear him, wouldn't have paid any heed if he had.

The bull went eerily still, primal forces gathering within it like a storm, but as the chute gate swung open, the animal erupted from confinement like a rocket from a launchpad, headed skyward.

Buzzsaw dove and then spun, elemental violence unleashed.

Austin stayed with him, spurring with the heels of his boots, right hand high in the air, looking as cool as if he were idling in the old tire-swing that dangled over the deepest part of the swimming hole. Four long seconds passed before he even lost his hat.

Tate wanted to close his eyes, but the message still wasn't making it from his brain to the tiny muscles created for that purpose. He'd had differences with his youngest brother—and some of them were serious—but none of that mattered now.

The clock on the screen seemed to move in slow motion; eight seconds, as all cowboys know, can be an eternity. For Tate, the scene unfolded frame by frame, in a hollow, echoing void, as though taking place one dimension removed.

Finally, the bull made his move and arched above the ground like a trout springing from a lake and then rolling as if determined to turn his belly to the ceiling of that arena, and sent Austin hurtling to one side, but not clear.

The pickup men moved in, ready to cut Austin free, but that bull was a hurricane with hooves, spinning and kicking in all directions.

The bullfighters—referred to as clowns in the old days—were normally called on to distract a bull or a horse, lead it away from the cowboy so he'd have time to get to the fence and scramble over it, to safety.

Under these circumstances, there wasn't much anybody could do.

Austin bounced off one side of that bull and then the other, still bound to it, his body limp. Possibly lifeless.

Fear slashed at Tate's insides.

Finally, one of the pickup men got close enough to cut Austin free of the rigging, curve an arm around him before he fell, and wrench him off the bull. Austin didn't move as the pickup man rode away from Buzzsaw, while the bullfighters and several riders drove the animal out of the arena.

Tate's cell phone, tucked into the pocket of the sodden denim jacket he'd worn to work cattle on the range that day, jangled. He ignored its shrill insistence.

Paramedics were waiting to lower Austin onto a stretcher. The announcer murmured something, but Tate didn't hear what it was because of the blood pounding in his ears.

The TV cameras covered the place in dizzying sweeps. In the stands, the fans were on their feet, pale and worried, and most of the men took their hats off, held them to their chests, the way they did for the Stars and Stripes.

Or when a hearse rolled by.

Behind the chutes, other cowboys watched intently, a few lowering their heads, their lips moving in private prayer.

Tate stood stock-still in the middle of his bedroom floor, bile scalding the back of his throat. His heart had surged up into his windpipe and swollen there, beating hard, fit to choke him.

Both phones were ringing now—the cell and the extension on the table beside his bed.

He endured the tangle of sound, the way it scraped at his nerves, but made no move to answer.

On-screen, the rodeo faded away, almost instantly replaced by a commercial for aftershave.

That broke Tate's paralysis; he turned, picked up his discarded jacket off the floor, ferreted through its several pockets for his briefly silent cell phone. It rang in his hand, and he flipped it open.

"Tate McKettrick," he said automatically.

"Holy Christ," his brother Garrett shot back, "I thought you'd never answer! Listen, Austin just tangled with a bull, and it looks to me like he's hurt bad—"

"I know," Tate ground out, trying in vain to recall what city Austin had been competing in that week. "I was watching."

"Meet me at the airstrip," Garrett ordered. "I have to make some calls. I'll be there as soon as I can."

"Garrett, the weather—"

"Screw the weather," Garrett snapped. Nothing scared him—except commitment to one woman. "If you're too chickenshit to go up in a pissant rainstorm like this one, just say so right now and save me a trip to the Spur, okay? *I'm* going to find out where they're taking our kid brother and get there any way I have to, because, goddamn it, this might be goodbye. Do you *get* that, cowboy?"

"I get it," Tate said, after unlocking his jawbones. "I'll be waiting when you hit the tarmac, Top Gun."

Garrett, calling on a landline, had the advantage of hanging up with a crash. Tate retrieved his wallet from the dresser top and his battered leather bomber jacket from the walk-in closet, shrugging into it as he headed for the double doors separating the suite from the broad corridor beyond.

With generations of McKettricks adding wings to the house as the family fortune doubled and redoubled, the place was ridiculously large, over eighteen thousand square feet.

Tate descended one of the three main staircases trisecting the house, the heels of his dress boots making no sound on the hand-loomed runner, probably fashioned for some sultan before the first McKettrick ever set foot in the New World.

Hitting the marble-floored entryway, he cast a glance at the antique grandfather's clock—he hadn't worn a watch since his job with McKettrickCo had evaporated in the wake of the IPO of the century—and shook his head when he saw the time.

Four-thirty.

Audrey and Ava's dance recital had started half an hour ago.

Striding along a glassed-in gallery edging the Olympic-size pool, with its retractable roof and floating bar, he opened his cell phone again and speed-dialed Cheryl.

She didn't say "Hello." She said, "*Where the hell are you,* Tate? Audrey and Ava's big number is *next,* and they keep peeking around the curtain, hoping to see you in the audience and—"

"Austin's been hurt," Tate broke in, aching as he imagined his daughters in their sequins and tutus, watching for his arrival. "I can't make it tonight."

"But it's your week and I have plans...."

"Cheryl," Tate bit out, "did you hear what I said? Austin's hurt."

He could just see her, curling her lip, arching one perfectly plucked raven eyebrow.

"So help me God, Tate, if this is an excuse—"

"It's no excuse. Tell the kids there's been an emergency, and I'll call them as soon as I can. *Don't* mention Austin, though. I don't want them worrying."

"Austin is hurt?" For a lawyer, Cheryl could be pretty slow on the uptake at times. "What happened?"

Tate reached the kitchen, with its miles of glistening granite counters and multiple glass-fronted refrigerators. Cheryl's question speared him in a vital place, and not just because he wasn't sure he'd ever see Austin alive again.

Suppose it was too late to straighten things out?

What if, when he and Garrett flew back from wherever their crazy brother was, Austin was riding in the cargo hold, in a box?

Tate's eyes burned like acid as he jerked open the door leading to the ten-car garage.

"He drew a bad bull," he finally said, forcing the words out, as spiky-sharp as a rusty coil of barbed wire.

Cheryl drew in a breath. "Oh, my God," she whispered. "He isn't going to—to die?"

"I don't know," Tate said.

Austin's beat-up red truck, one of several vehicles with his name on the title, was parked in its usual place, next to the black Porsche Garrett drove when he was home. The sight gave Tate a pang as he jerked open the door of his mud-splattered extended-cab Silverado and climbed behind the wheel, then pushed the button to roll up the garage door behind him.

"Call when you know anything," Cheryl urged. "Anything at all."

Tate ground the keys in the ignition, and backed out into the rain with such speed that he nearly collided with one of the ranch work-trucks parked broadside behind him.

The elderly cowpuncher at the wheel got out of the way, pronto.

Tate didn't stop to explain.

"I'll call," he told Cheryl, cranking the steering wheel. He begrudged her that promise, but he couldn't reach his daughters except through his ex-wife.

Cheryl was crying. "Okay," she said. "Don't forget."

Tate shut the phone without saying goodbye.

At the airstrip, he waited forty-five agonizing minutes in his truck, watching torrents of rain wash down the windshield, remembering his kid brother at every stage of his life—the new baby he and Garrett had soon wanted to put up for adoption, the mutton-buster, the high school and college heartthrob.

The man Cheryl swore had seduced her one night in Vegas, when she was legally still Tate's wife.

When the jet, a former member of the McKettrickCo fleet,

landed, he waited for it to come to a stop before shoving open the truck's door and making a run for the airplane.

Garrett stood in the open doorway, having lowered the steps with a hydraulic whir.

"He's in Houston," he said. "They're going to operate as soon as he's stable."

Tate pushed past him, dripping rainwater. "What's his condition?"

Garrett raised the steps again, shouldered the door shut and set the latch. "Critical," he said. "According to the surgeon I spoke to, his chances aren't too good."

Tate moved toward the cockpit, using the time his back was turned to Garrett to rub his burning eyes with a thumb and forefinger. "Let's go."

Minutes later, they were in the air, the plane bucking stormy air currents as it fought for every foot of altitude. Lightning flashed, seeming to pass within inches of the wings, the nose, the tail.

Eventually, though, the skies cleared.

When they landed at a private field outside of Houston, an SUV Garrett had rented before leaving the capital waited on the hot, dry asphalt. The key was in the ignition; Garrett took the wheel, and they raced into the city.

They were all too familiar with the route to the best private hospital in Texas. Their parents had died there, a decade before, after an eighteen-wheeler jumped the median and crashed head-on into their car.

A nurse and two administrators met Tate and Garrett in the lobby, all unwilling to meet their eyes, let alone answer their questions.

When they reached the surgical unit, they found Austin lying on a gurney outside a state-of-the-art operating suite, surrounded by a sea of people clad in green scrubs.

Tate and Garrett pushed their way through, then stood on either side of their brother.

Austin's face was so swollen and discolored they wouldn't have recognized him if he hadn't crooked up one side of his mouth in a grin that could only have belonged to him.

"That was one bad-ass bull," he said.

"You're going to be all right," Garrett told Austin, his face grim.

"Hell, yes, I'm going to be all right," Austin croaked out. His eyes, sunken behind folds of purple flesh, arched to Tate. "Just in case, though, there's one thing I need you to know for sure, big brother," he added laboriously, his voice so low that Tate had to bend down to hear him. "I never slept with your wife."

CHAPTER ONE

Three months later

CHERYL'S RELATIVELY SMALL backyard was festooned with streamers and balloons and crowded with yelling kids. Portable tables sagged under custom-made cakes and piles of brightly wrapped presents, while two clowns and a slightly ratty Cinderella mingled with miniature guests, all of them sugar-jazzed. Austin's childhood pony, Bamboozle, trucked in from the Silver Spur especially for the birthday party, provided rides with saintlike equanimity.

Keeping one eye on the horse and the other on his daughters, six years old as of 7:52 that sunny June morning, Tate counted himself a lucky man, for all the rocky roads he'd traveled. Born almost two months before full term, the babies had weighed less than six pounds put together, and their survival had been by no means a sure thing. Although the twins were fraternal, they looked so much alike that strangers usually thought they were identical. Both had the striking blue eyes that ran in the McKettrick bloodline, and their long glossy hair was nearly black, like Cheryl's and his own. His girls were healthy now, thank God, but Tate still worried plenty about them, on general principle. They seemed so fragile to him, too thin, with their long, skinny legs, and Ava wore glasses and a hearing aid that was all but invisible.

Cheryl startled Tate out of his reflections by jabbing him in the ribs with a clipboard. Today, her waist-length hair was wound into a braided knot at the back of her neck. "Sign this," she ordered, sotto voce.

Tate had promised himself he'd be civil to his ex-wife, for the twins' sake. Looking down into Cheryl's green eyes—she'd been a beauty queen in her day—he wondered what he'd been drinking the night they met.

Gorgeous as Cheryl was, she flat-out wasn't his type, and she never had been.

He glanced at the paper affixed to the clipboard and frowned, then gave all the legalese a second look. It was basically a permission slip, allowing Audrey and Ava to participate in something called the Pixie Pageant, to be held around the time school started, out at the Blue River Country Club. Under the terms of their custody agreement, Cheryl needed his approval for any extracurricular activity the children took part in. It had cost him plenty to get her to sign off on that one.

"No," he said succinctly, tucking the clipboard under one arm, since Cheryl didn't look like she intended to take it back.

The former Mrs. McKettrick, once again using her maiden name, Darbrey, rolled her eyes, patted her sleek and elegant hair. "Oh, for God's sake," she complained, though he had to give her points for keeping her voice down. "It's just a harmless little pageant, to raise money for the new tennis court at the community center—"

Tate's mind flashed on the disturbing film clips he'd seen of kids dolled up in false eyelashes, blusher and lipstick, like Las Vegas showgirls, prancing around some stage. He leaned in, matching his tone to hers. "They're *six*, Cheryl," he reminded her. "Let them be little girls while they can."

His former wife folded her tanned, gym-toned arms. She looked good in her expensive daffodil-yellow sundress, but the mean glint in her eyes spoiled the effect. "*I* was in pageants from the time I was five," she pointed out tersely, "and I turned out okay." Realizing too late that she'd opened an emotional pothole and then stepped right into it, she made a slight huffing sound.

"Debatable," Tate drawled, plastering a smile onto his mouth because some of the moms and nannies were looking in their direction, and they'd stirred up enough gossip as it was.

Cheryl flushed, toyed with one tasteful gold earring. "Bastard," she whispered, peevish. "Why do you have to be so damn pigheaded about things like this?"

He laughed. Hooked his thumbs through the belt loops of his jeans. Dug in his heels a little—both literally and figuratively. "If other people want to let their kids play Miss This-That-and-the-Other-Thing, that's their business. It's probably harmless fun, but *mine* aren't going to—not before they're old enough to make the choice on their own, anyhow. By that time, I hope Audrey and Ava will have more in their heads than makeup tips and the cosmetic uses of duct tape."

Eyes flashing, Cheryl looked as though she wanted to put out both hands and shove him backward into the koi pond—or jerk the clipboard from under his arm and bash him over the head with it. She did neither of those things—she didn't want a scene any more than he did, though her reasons were different. Tate cared about one thing and one thing only: that his daughters had a good time at their birthday party. Cheryl, on the other hand, knew a public dustup would make the rounds of the country club and the Junior League before sundown.

She had her image to consider.

Tate, by contrast, didn't give a rat's ass what anybody thought—except for his daughters, that is, and a few close friends.

So they glared at each other, he and this woman he'd married years ago, squaring off like two gunfighters on a dusty street. And then Ava slipped between them.

"Don't fight, okay?" she pleaded anxiously, the hot Texas sunlight glinting on the smudged lenses of her glasses. "It's our *birthday,* remember?"

Tate felt his neck pulse with the singular heat of shame. So much for keeping the ongoing hostilities between Mommy and Daddy under wraps.

Cheryl smiled wickedly and rested a manicured hand on Ava's shoulder, left all but bare by the spaghetti strap holding up her dress—a miniature version of her mother's outfit. Audrey's getup was the same, except blue.

"Your daddy," Cheryl told the child sweetly, "doesn't want you and Audrey to compete in the Pixie Pageant. I was trying to change his mind."

Good luck with that, Tate thought, forcibly relaxing the muscles in his jaws. He tried for a smile, for Ava's sake, but the effort was a bust.

"That stuff is dumb anyway," Ava said.

Audrey appeared on the scene, as though magnetized by an opinion at variance with her own. "No, it *isn't,*" she protested, with her customary spirit. "Pageants are good for building self-confidence and making friends, and if you win, you get a banner and a trophy *and* a tiara."

"I see you've been coaching them to take the party line," Tate told Cheryl.

Cheryl's smile was dazzling. He'd spent a fortune on those pearly whites of hers. Through them, she said, "Shut up, Tate."

Ava, always sensitive to the changing moods of the parental units, started to cry, making a soft, sniffly sound that tore at Tate's heart. "We're only going to be six *once,*" she said. "And everybody's looking!"

"Thank heaven we're only going to be six once," Audrey interjected sagely, folding her arms Cheryl-style. "I'd rather be forty."

Tate bent his knees, scooped up Ava in the crook of one arm and tugged lightly at Audrey's long braid with his free hand. Ava buried her face in his shoulder, bumping her glasses askew. He felt tears and mucus moisten the fabric of his pale blue shirt.

"Forty?" she said, voice muffled. "Even *Daddy* isn't that old!"

"You're such a baby," Audrey replied.

"Enough," Tate told both children, but he was looking at Cheryl as he spoke. "When is this shindig supposed to be over?"

They'd opened presents, devoured everything but the cakes and competed for prizes a person would expect to see on a TV game show. What else was there to do?

"Why can't you just stop fighting?" Ava blurted.

"We're *not* fighting, darling," Cheryl pointed out quietly, before turning to sweep her watchful friends and the nannies up in a benign smile. "And stop carrying on, Ava. It isn't becoming— or ladylike."

"Can we go out to the ranch, Daddy?" Ava asked him plaintively, ignoring her mother's comment. "I like it better there, because nobody fights."

"Me, too," Tate agreed. It was his turn to take the kids, and he'd been looking forward to it since their last visit. Giving them back was always a wrench.

"Nobody fights at the ranch?" Audrey argued, sounding way too bored and way too sophisticated for a six-year-old. Yeah, she was a prime candidate for the Pixie Pageant, all right, Tate thought bitterly—bring on the mascara and enough hairspray to rip a new hole in the ozone layer, and don't forget the feather boas and the fishnet stockings.

Audrey drew a breath and went right on talking. "I guess you don't remember the day Uncle Austin came home from the hospital after that bull hurt him so bad, before he started rehab in Dallas, and how he told Daddy and Uncle Garrett to stay out of his part of the house unless they wanted a belly full of buckshot."

Cheryl arched one eyebrow, triumphant. For all their land, cattle, oil shares and cold, hard cash, the McKettricks were just a bunch of Texas rednecks, as far as she was concerned. She'd grown up in a Park Avenue high-rise, a cherished only child, after all, her mother an heiress to a legendary but rapidly dwindling fortune, her father a famous novelist, of the literary variety.

But, please, nobody mention that dear old Mom snorted coke and would sleep with anything in pants, and Dad ran through the last of his wife's money and then his surprisingly modest earnings as the new Ernest Hemingway.

Cheryl had never gotten over the humiliation of having to wait tables and take out student loans to put herself through college and law school.

"I wonder what my attorney would say," Cheryl intoned, "if I told him the children are exposed to *guns,* out there on the wild and wooly Silver Spur."

While Tate couldn't argue that there weren't firearms on the ranch—between the snakes and all the other dangers inherent to the land, firepower might well prove to be a necessity at any time—it was a stretch to say the girls were "exposed" to them.

Every weapon was locked up in one of several safes, and the combinations changed regularly.

"I wonder what *mine* would say," Tate retorted evenly, the fake smile aching on his face, "if he knew about your plans for this week."

"Stop," Ava begged.

Tate sighed, kissed his daughter smartly on the forehead, and set her on her feet again. "Sorry, sweetheart," he said. "Say goodbye and thanks to your friends. The party's over."

"They haven't even sung the song I taught them," Cheryl said.

Ava leaned against Tate's hip. "We're not good singers at all," she confided.

Somewhat to Tate's surprise, it was Audrey, the performer in the family, who turned on one sandaled heel, faced the assemblage and announced cheerfully, "You can all go home now—my dad says the party's over."

Cheryl winced.

The kids—and the pony—seemed relieved. So did the nannies, though the proper term, according to Cheryl, was *au pairs*. The mothers, many of whom Tate had known since kindergarten and dated in high school between all-too-frequent breakups with Libby Remington, the great love of his youth, if not his entire life, hid bitchy little smiles with varying degrees of success.

"The girls are a little tired," Cheryl explained, with convincing sincerity. "All this excitement—"

"Can we ride horses when we get to the ranch?" Audrey called, from halfway across the yard. "Can we swim in the pool?"

Tate made damn sure he didn't smile at this indication of how "tired" his daughters were, but it was hard.

Ava remained at his side, both arms clenched around his waist now.

"Their suitcases," Cheryl said tightly, "are in the hall."

"Let's load Bamboozle in the trailer," Tate told Ava, gently easing out of her embrace. "Then we'll get your stuff and head for the ranch."

Ava peeled herself away from Tate, walked over and took Bamboozle by the bridle strap, patiently waiting to lead the elderly animal to the trailer hitched to the back of Tate's truck. Audrey had disappeared into the house, on some mission all her own.

"Don't help," Cheryl snapped, out of one side of her mouth. "You've already done enough, Tate McKettrick."

"I live to delight you in every possible way, Cheryl."

Audrey poked her head out between the French doors standing a little ajar between the living room and the patio. "Can we stop at the Perk Up on the way out of town, Dad?" she wanted to know, as calmly as if the backyard weren't full of dismissed guests. "Get some of those orange smoothie things, like before?"

Tate grinned. "Sure," he told his daughter, even though the thought of stopping at Libby's coffee shop made the pit of his stomach tighten. He'd only gone in there the last time because he'd known Libby was out of town, and her sister, Julie, was running the show.

Which was ridiculous. They'd managed to avoid each other for years now, no mean trick in such a small town, but it was getting to be too damn much work.

"Just what they need—more sugar," Cheryl muttered, shaking her head as she walked away, her arms still crossed in front of her chest, only more tightly now.

Tate held his tongue. *He* hadn't been the one to serve cake and ice cream and fruit punch by the wheelbarrow load all afternoon.

Cheryl kept walking.

Tate and Ava led the pony into the horse trailer, which, along with his truck, took up at least three parking spaces on the shady street in front of Cheryl's house. He'd bought the place for her as a part—a *small* part—of their divorce settlement.

"Boozle might get lonely riding in this big trailer all by himself," Ava fretted, standing beside the pony while he slurped up water from a bucket. "Maybe I should ride back here with him, so he'd have some company."

"Not a chance," Tate said affably, dumping a flake of hay into the feeder for the pony to munch on, going home. "Too dangerous."

Ava adjusted her glasses. "Audrey really wants to be in that Pixie Pageant," she said, her voice small. "She's going to nag you three ways from Sunday about it, too."

Tate bit back a grin. "I think I can handle a little nagging," he said lightly. "Let's go get your stuff and hit the road, Shortstop."

"I probably wouldn't win anyway," Ava mused wistfully, stopping her father cold.

"Win what?" Tate asked.

Ava giggled, but it was a strained sound, like she was forcing it. "The *Pixie Pageant,* Dad. Keep up, will you?"

Tate's throat went tight, but he managed a chuckle. "Sure, you'd win," he said. "And that's another reason I won't let you enter in the first place. Just think how bad all those other little girls would feel."

"Audrey could be Miss Pixie," Ava speculated thoughtfully, a small, light-rimmed shadow standing there in the horse trailer. "She can twirl a baton and everything. I keep on dropping mine."

"Audrey isn't entering," Tate said. Bamboozle was between them; he removed the pony's saddle and blanket, ran a hand along his sweaty back. "She'll just have to content herself with being Miss *McKettrick,* at least for the foreseeable future."

Ava mulled that over for a few moments, chewing her lower lip. "Do you think I'll be pretty when I grow up, Dad?"

Tate moved to the back of the trailer, jumped down, turned and held out his arms for Ava, even though she could have walked down the ramp. "No," he said, as she came within reach. "I think you'll be beautiful, like you are right now."

Ava felt featherlight as he swung her to the ground, and it gave him a pang. Was it his fault that the girls had been born too soon? Was there something he could have done to prevent all the struggles they'd faced just getting through infancy?

"You're only saying that because you're my dad."

"I'm saying it because it's true," Tate said.

Ava stepped back while he slid the ramp into place under the trailer, then shut and latched the doors. "Mommy says it's never too soon to think about becoming a woman," she ventured. "Things we do now could affect our whole, *entire* lives, you know."

Tate kept his back to the child, so she wouldn't see the fury in his face. He spoke in the most normal tone he could summon. "You'll only be a little girl for a few years," he answered carefully. "Just concentrate on that for now, okay? Because 'becoming a woman' will take care of itself."

Wasn't it only yesterday that the twins were newborns, making a peeping sound instead of squalling, like most babies, hooked up to tubes and wires, dwarfed by their incubators at the hospital in Houston? Now, suddenly, they were six. He'd be walking them down the aisle at their weddings before he knew what hit him, he thought bleakly.

He shoved one hand through his hair, longing to get back to the ranch and pull on battered jeans that had never known the heat of an iron. Shed the spiffy shirt, so fresh from the box that the starch in the fabric chafed his skin.

On the ranch, he could breathe, although he'd seriously considered moving out of the mansion, taking up residence in the old bunkhouse or a simple single-wide down by one of the bends in the creek.

Mothers and nannies streamed past, herding grouchy children toward various cars and minivans. A few of the women spoke to Tate, most of them cordial, while a few others wished Ava a happy birthday in subdued tones and ignored him completely.

Tate wasn't much for chatting, but he was friendly enough. When somebody spoke to him, he spoke back.

A scraping sound alerted him to Audrey, dragging her suitcase down the front walk on its wheels. He went to take the bag from her, stowed it in the front seat, on the passenger side, where his dog, Crockett, used to ride. Crockett had died of old age more than a year before, but Tate still forgot he wasn't around sometimes and stood with the truck door open, waiting to hoist his sidekick aboard.

"You got your bag packed?" he asked Ava, when she scrambled into the backseat, with Audrey. They both had those special safety rigs, booster chairs with straps and hooks.

"I've got plenty of clothes at the ranch," Ava responded, with a shake of her head. One of the pink barrettes holding her bangs out of her face had sprung loose, and her braid was coming undone. "Let's go before Mom makes us come back and sing."

Tate laughed, rounded the front of the truck and got behind the wheel.

"Beauty-Shop Betsey," Audrey scoffed. "What possessed Jeffrey's mom to buy us doll heads with curlers?" She'd been talking like a grown-up since she was two.

"Hey," Tate said, starting up the engine, waiting for the flock of departing vans and Volvos to thin out a little. God only knew when Blue River, official population 8,472, had last seen a traffic snarl like this. "If somebody goes to all the trouble of buying you a birthday present, you ought to appreciate it."

"Mom said we could exchange the stuff we don't want," Audrey informed him, with a touch of so-there in her tone. "Everybody included gift receipts."

Tate figured it was high time to change the subject. "How about those orange smoothies?" he asked.

TATE MCKETTRICK, LIBBY REMINGTON thought, watching as he drew his truck and horse trailer to a stop in front of her shop, got out and strode purposefully toward the door.

It bothered her that after all this time the sight of him still made her heart flutter and her stomach jump. Damn the man, with his dark, longish hair, ink-blue eyes, and that confident, rolling way he moved, as though he'd greased his hip sockets.

Although it was growing, with a population now of almost 9,000, Blue River wasn't exactly a metropolis, and that meant she and Tate ran into each other from time to time. Whenever they did, they'd nod and quickly head in separate directions, but they'd *never* sought each other out.

Poised to turn the "Open" sign to "Closed," Libby closed her eyes for a moment, hoping he was a mirage. A figment of her fevered imagination.

He wasn't, of course.

When she looked again, he was standing just on the other side of the glass door, peering through the loop in the *P* in *Perk Up,* grinning.

A McKettrick—a pedigree in that part of the country—Tate was used to getting what he wanted, including service on a Sunday afternoon, when the store closed early.

Libby sighed, turned the dead bolt, and opened the door.

"Two orange smoothies," he said, without preamble. "To go."

Libby looked past him, saw his twin daughters in the backseat of his fancy truck. An old grief rose up within her, one she'd worked hard to lay to rest. From the time she'd fallen for Tate, back in second grade, she'd planned on marrying him when they both grew up, been bone-certain *she'd* be the one to have his babies.

"Where's Crockett?" she asked, without intending to.

Sadness moved in Tate's impossibly blue eyes. "Had to have him put down a while back," he said. "He was pretty old, and then he got sick."

"I'm sorry," Libby said, because she was. For the dog.

"Thanks," he answered.

She stepped back to let Tate in, against her better judgment. "I'm fostering a couple of mixed breeds, because the shelter is full again. Want one—or, better yet, both?"

Tate shook his head. Light caught in his ebony hair, where the comb ridges still showed. "Just a couple of those smoothie things. Orange. Light on the sugar, if that's an option."

Libby stepped behind the counter, more because she wanted to put some kind of solid barrier between herself and Tate than to mix the drinks he'd requested. Her gaze strayed to the kids waiting in the truck again. They both looked like their father. "Will there be anything else?"

"No," Tate said, taking out his beat-up wallet. "How much?"

Libby told him the price of two orange smoothies, with tax, and he laid the money on the countertop. There were at least three drive-through restaurants on the outskirts of town; he'd pass them coming and going from the Silver Spur. So why had he stopped at her store, on Blue River's narrow main street, with a horse trailer hitched to his huge phallic symbol of a truck?

"You're sure you don't want something for yourself?" she asked lightly, and then wished she'd kept her mouth shut.

Tate's grin tilted to one side. He smelled of sun-dried laundry and aftershave and pure *man*. A look of mischief danced in his eyes.

When he spoke, though, he said, "It's their birthday," accompanied by a rise and fall of his powerful shoulders. His blue shirt was open at the throat, and she could see too much—and not quite enough—of his chest.

Libby whipped up the drinks, filling two biodegradable cups

from a pitcher, attached the lids and set them next to the cash register. "Then maybe you'd like to give them a dog or two," she replied, with an ease she didn't feel. Being in such close proximity to Tate rattled her, but it probably didn't show. "Since it's their birthday."

"Their mother would have a fit," he said, reaching for the cups. His hands were strong, calloused from range work. Despite all that McKettrick money, he wasn't afraid to wade into a mudhole to free a stuck cow, set fence posts in the ground, buck bales or shovel out stalls.

It was one of the reasons the locals liked him so much, made them willing to overlook the oil wells, now capped, and the ridiculously big house and nearly a hundred thousand acres of prime grassland, complete with springs and creeks and even a small river.

He was one of them.

Of course, the *locals* hadn't been dumped because he'd gotten some other woman pregnant just a few months after he'd started law school.

No, that had happened to *her*.

She realized he was waiting for her to respond to his comment about his ex-wife. *Their mother would have a fit.*

Can't have that, Libby thought, tightening her lips.

"The ice is melting in those smoothies," she finally said. Translation: *Get out. It hurts to look at you. It hurts to remember how things were between us before you hooked up with somebody you didn't even love.*

Tate grinned again, though his eyes looked sad, and then he turned sideways, ready to leave. "Maybe we'll stop by your place and have a look at those dogs after all," he said. "Would tomorrow be good?"

He'd stayed with Cheryl-the-lawyer for less than a year after the twins were born. As soon as the babies began to thrive, he'd moved Cheryl and his infant daughters into the two-story colonial on Oak Street.

The gossip had burned like a brush fire for months.

"That would be fine," Libby said, back from her mental wanderings. Tate McKettrick might have broken her heart, but he'd loved his ancient, arthritic dog, Davy Crockett. And she needed to find homes for the pair of pups.

Hildie, her adopted black Lab, normally the soul of charity, was starting to resent the canine roommates, growling at them when they got too near her food dish, baring her teeth when they tried to join her on the special fluffy rug at the foot of Libby's bed at night. The newcomers, neither more than a year old, seemed baffled by this reception, wagging their tails uncertainly whenever they ran afoul of Hildie, then launching right back into trouble.

They would be very happy out there on the Silver Spur, with all that room to run, Libby thought.

A rush of hope made the backs of her eyes burn as she watched Tate move toward the door.

"Six?" she said.

Tate, shifting the cups around so he could open the door, looked back at her curiously, as though he'd already forgotten the conversation about the dogs, if not Libby herself.

"I close at six," Libby said, fanning herself with a plastic-coated price list even though the secondhand swamp cooler in the back was working fine, for once. She didn't want him thinking the heat in her face had anything to do with him, even though it did. "The shop," she clarified. "I close the shop at six tomorrow. You could stop by the house and see the dogs then."

Tate looked regretful for a moment, as though he'd already changed his mind about meeting the potential adoptees. But then he smiled in that way that made her blink. "Okay," he said. "See you a little after six tomorrow night, then."

Libby swallowed hard and then nodded.

He left.

She hurried to lock the door again, turned the "Closed" sign to the street, and stood there, watching Tate stride toward his truck, so broad-shouldered and strong and confident.

What was it like, Libby wondered, to live as though you owned the whole world?

On the off chance that Tate might glance in her direction again, once he'd finished handing the cups through the window of his truck to the girls, Libby quickly turned away.

She took the day's profits from the till—such as they were—and tucked the bills and checks into a bank deposit bag. She'd hide them in the usual place at home, and stop by First Cattleman's in the morning, during one of the increasingly long lulls in business.

The house she'd lived in all her life was just across the alley, and Hildie and the pups were in the backyard when she approached the gate, Hildie lying in the shade of the only tree on the property, the foster dogs playing tug-of-war with Libby's favorite blouse, which had either fallen or been pulled from the clothesline.

Seeing her, the pups dropped the blouse in the grass—the lawn was in need of mowing, as usual—and yipped in gleefully innocent greeting. Libby didn't have the heart to scold them, and they wouldn't have understood anyway.

With a sigh, she retrieved the blouse from the ground and stayed bent long enough to acknowledge each of the happy-eyed renegades with a pat on the head. "You," she said sweetly, "are very, *very* bad dogs."

They were ecstatic at the news. A matched set, they both had golden coats and floppy ears and big feet. While Hildie looked on, nonplussed, they barked with joy and took a frenzied run around the yard, knocking over the recycling bin in the process.

Hildie finally rose from her nest under the oak, stretched and ambled slowly toward her mistress.

Libby leaned to ruffle Hildie's ears and whisper, "Hang in there, sweet girl. With any luck at all, those two will be living the high life out on the Silver Spur by tomorrow night."

Hildie's gaze was liquid with adoration as she looked up at Libby, panting and swinging her plume of a tail.

"Suppertime," Libby announced, to all and sundry, straightening again. She led the way to the back door, the three dogs trailing along behind her, single file, Hildie in the lead.

The blouse proved unsalvageable. Libby flinched a little, tossing it into the rag bag. The blue fabric had flattered her, accentuating the color of her eyes and giving her golden brown hair some sparkle.

Easy come, easy go, she thought philosophically, although, in truth, nothing in her life had *ever* been easy.

The litany unrolled in her head.

She'd paid $50 for that blouse, *on sale*.

The economy had taken a downturn and her business reflected that.

Marva was back, and she was more demanding every day.

And as if all that weren't enough, Libby had two dogs in dire need of good homes—she simply couldn't afford to keep them—and she'd already pitched the pair to practically every other suitable candidate in Blue River with no luck. Jimmy-Roy Holter was eager to take them, but he wanted to name them Killer and Ripper, *plus* he lived in a camper behind his mother's house, surrounded by junked cars, and had bred pit bulls to sell out of the back of his truck, along a busy stretch of highway, until an animal protection group in Austin had forced him to close down the operation.

Libby washed her hands at the sink, rubbed her work-chafed hands down the thighs of her blue jeans since she was out of paper towels and all the cloth ones were in the wash.

No, as far as placing the pups in a good home was concerned, Tate McKettrick was her only hope. She'd have to deal with him.

Damn her lousy-assed luck.

CHAPTER TWO

BY THE TIME they got to the ranch, Audrey and Ava were streaked pale orange from the smoothie spills and had developed dispositions too reminiscent of their mother's for Tate's comfort. The minute he brought the truck to a stop alongside the barn, they were out of their buckles and car seats and hitting the ground like storm troopers on a mission, pretty much set on pitching a catfight, right there in the dirt.

Tate stepped between them before the small fists started flying and loudly cleared his throat. The eldest of three brothers, he'd had some practice at keeping the peace—though he'd been an instigator now and again himself. "One punch," he warned, *"just one,* and nobody rides horseback or uses the pool for the whole time you're here."

"What about kicks?" Audrey demanded, knuckles resting on her nonexistent hips. "Is kicking allowed?"

Tate bit back a grin. "Kicks are as bad as punches," he said. "Equal punishment."

Both girls looked deflated—he guessed they had that Mc-Kettrick penchant for a good brawl. If their features and coloring hadn't told the story, he'd have known they were his just by their tempers.

"Let's put Bamboozle back in his stall and make sure the other horses are taken care of," Tate said, when neither of his daughters spoke. "Then you can shower—in separate parts of the house—and we'll hit the pool."

"I'd rather hit Ava," Audrey said.

Ava started for her sister, mad all over again, and once more, Tate interceded deftly. How many times had he hauled Garrett and Austin apart, in the same way, when *they* were kids?

"You couldn't take me anyhow," Audrey taunted Ava, and then she stuck out her tongue and the battle was on again. The girls skirted him and went for each other like a pair of starving cats after the same fat canary.

Tate felt as if he were trying to herd a swarm of bees back into a hive, and he might not have untangled the girls before they did each other some harm if Garrett hadn't sprinted out of the barn and come to his aid.

He got Audrey around the waist from behind and hoisted her off her feet, and Tate did the same with Ava. And both brothers got the hell kicked out of their knees, shins and thighs before the twin-fit finally subsided.

There was a grin in Garrett's eyes, which were the same shade of blue as Tate's and Audrey's and Ava's, as he looked at his elder brother over the top of his niece's head. "Well," he drawled, as the twins gasped in delight at his mere presence, "*this* is a fine how-do-you-do. And after I drove all the way from Austin to be here, too. Why, I have half a mind to send your birthday present right back to Neiman Marcus and pretend this is just any old day of the week, nothing special."

Simultaneously, Tate and Garrett set their separate charges back on their sandaled feet.

Audrey smoothed her crumpled sundress and her hair—females of all ages tended to preen when Garrett was around—and asked, with hard-won dignity, "What did you get us, Uncle Garrett?"

Last year, Tate remembered with a tightening along his jaw-line, it had been life-size porcelain dolls, custom-made by some artist in Austria, perfect replicas of the twins themselves. He was glad the things were at Cheryl's—they gave him the creeps, staring blankly into space. He'd have sworn he'd seen them breathe.

"Why don't you go around to the kitchen patio and find out?"

Garrett suggested mysteriously. "Then you'll know whether it's worth behaving yourselves for or not."

Hostilities forgotten—for the time being anyway—the girls ran squealing for the wide sidewalk that encircled the gigantic house.

Whatever Garrett had bought for Audrey and Ava, it was sure to make Tate's offering—a croquet set from Wal-Mart—look puny and ill-thought-out by comparison.

Not that he put a lot of stock in comparison.

"I thought you were in the capital, fetching and carrying for the senator," Tate said, taking his brother's measure in a sidelong glance.

Garrett chuckled and slapped him—a little too hard—on one shoulder. "Sorry I missed the shindig in town," he said, ignoring the remark about his employer. "But I managed to get here, in spite of meetings, a press conference and at least one budding scandal neatly avoided. That's pretty good."

Tate sucked in a breath, let it out. Jabbed at the dirt with the heel of one boot. Garrett was a generous uncle and a good brother, for the most part, but he was living the wrong kind of life for a Texas McKettrick, and he didn't seem to know it. "I don't know what gets into those two," Tate said, shoving a hand through his hair. As far as he knew, he hadn't been in smoothie-range on the ride home, but he felt sticky all over just the same.

Whoops of delight echoed from the distant patio and Esperanza, the middle-aged housekeeper who had worked in that house since their parents' wedding day, could be heard chattering in happy Spanish.

"They'll be fine," Garrett said lightly. Easy for an uncle to say, not so simple for a father.

"What the hell did you get them this time?" Tate asked, starting in the direction of the hoopla. His mood was shifting again, souring a little. He kept thinking about that damn croquet set. "Thoroughbred racehorses?"

Garrett kept pace, grinning. He usually enjoyed Tate's discomfort—unless someone else was causing it. He was no fan of Cheryl's, that was for sure. "Now, why didn't I think of that?"

"Garrett," Tate warned, "I'm serious. Audrey and Ava are six years old. They have more toys than they could use in ten lifetimes, and I'm trying not to raise them like heiresses—"

"They *are* heiresses," Garrett pointed out, just as, a beat late, Tate had realized he would. "Over and above their trust funds."

"That doesn't mean they ought to be spoiled, Garrett."

"You're just too damn serious about everything," Garrett replied.

Just then, Ava ran to meet them, glasses sticky-lensed and askew, her grubby face flushed with excitement. "It's our very own *castle!*" she whooped. "Esperanza says some men brought it on a flatbed truck and it took them *all day* to put the pieces together!"

"Christ," Tate muttered.

"A crew will be here next week sometime, to dig the moat," Garrett told Ava. He might have been promising her a dress for one of her dolls, the way he made it sound.

"The *moat?*" Tate growled. "You're kidding, right?"

Garrett laughed. Would have given Tate another whack on the back if Tate hadn't sidestepped him in time. "What's a castle without a moat?"

Ava danced with excitement, as spindly legged as a spring deer. "There are *turrets,* Dad, and each one has a banner flying from the top. One says 'Audrey' and one says 'Ava'! There are stairs and rooms and there's even a plastic fireplace that lights up when you flip a hidden switch—"

Man, Tate thought grimly, that croquet set was going to be the clinker gift of the century. Damned if he was about to shop again, though, and he hadn't set foot in Neiman Marcus since he was sixteen, when his mother dragged him there to pick out a suit for the junior prom.

He'd endured that only because Libby Remington was his date, and he'd wanted to impress her.

Tate rustled up a grin for his daughter, but his swift glance at Garrett was about as friendly as a splash of battery acid. "A castle with turrets and flags and a prospective moat," he drawled. "Every kid in America ought to have one."

"You think *I* overdid it?" Garrett teased. "Austin had a line on a retired circus elephant—rehab is boring him out of his ever-lovin' mind, so he cruises the internet on his laptop a lot—until

I talked him out of it. Trust me, you could have done a lot worse than a *castle,* big brother."

Right up until he rounded the last corner of the house before the kitchen patio and the acre of lawn abutting it, Tate hoped the thing would turn out to be no bigger than your average dollhouse.

No such luck. It dwarfed the equipment shed where he kept the field tractor, a couple of horse trailers, several riding lawn mowers and four spare pickup trucks. Set on rock slabs, the castle itself was made of some resin-type material, resembling chiseled stone, and stood so tall that it blotted out part of the sky.

Audrey, wearing a pointed princess hat with glittered-on stars and moons and a tinsel tassel trailing from it, waved happily from an upper window.

Tate turned to Garrett, one eyebrow raised. "What? No drawbridge?"

"That would have been a little over the top," Garrett said modestly.

"Ya think?" Tate mocked.

Esperanza, beaming, flapped her apron, resembling a portly bird with only one wing as she inspected the monstrosity from all sides.

Tate waited until Princess Audrey had descended from the tower to fling herself at Garrett in a fit of gratitude—soon to be joined by Ava—before giving one wall a hard shove with the flat of his right hand.

The structure seemed sound, though he'd want to inspect every inch of it, inside and out, to make sure.

"Am I the only one who thinks this is ridiculous?" he asked. "An obscene display of conspicuous consumption?"

"The plastic is all recycled," Garrett avowed, all but reaching around to pat himself on the back.

Tate rolled his eyes and walked away, leaving Garrett and Esperanza and the girls to admire McKettrick Court and returning to the trailer to unload poor old Bamboozle. He settled the pony in his stall, gave him hay and a little grain, and moved to the corral fence to look out over the land, where the horses and cattle grazed in their separate pastures.

At least there was one consolation, he thought; Austin hadn't sent the elephant.

The sound of an arriving rig made him turn around, look toward the driveway. It was a truck, pulling a gleaming trailer behind it.

A headache thrummed between Tate's temples. Maybe he'd been too quick to dismiss the pachyderm possibility.

Audrey and Ava, having heard the arrival, came bounding around the house, their shiny tassels trailing in the blue beginnings of twilight. Both of them were glitter-dappled from the pointed hats.

Tate and his daughters collided just as the driver was getting down out of the truck cab. A stocky older man, balding, the fella grinned and consulted his clipboard with a ceremonious flourish bordering on the theatrical.

"I'm looking for Miss Audrey and Miss Ava McKettrick," he announced. Tate almost expected him to unfurl a scroll or blow a long brass horn with a velvet flag hanging from it.

Tate was already heading for the back of the trailer, his headache getting steadily worse.

Somehow, despite his bulk, the driver beat him there, blocked him bodily from opening the door and taking a look inside.

By God, Tate thought, *if Austin had sent his kids an elephant...*

"If you wouldn't mind, Mr.—?" the driver said. His name, stitched on his khaki workshirt, was "George."

"McKettrick," Tate replied, through his teeth.

"The order specifically says I'm to deliver the contents of this trailer to the recipients and no one else."

Tate swore under his breath, stepped back and, with a sweeping motion of one arm, invited George to do the honors.

"Who placed this order," Tate asked, with exaggerated politeness, "if that information isn't privileged or anything?"

George lowered a ramp, then climbed it to fling up the trailer's rolling door.

No elephant appeared in the gap.

The suspense heightened—Audrey and Ava were huddled close to Tate on either side by then, fascinated—as George duly checked his clipboard.

"Says here, it was an A. McKettrick. Internet order. We don't get many of those, given the nature of the—er—items."

The twins were practically jumping up and down now, and Esperanza and Garrett had come up behind, hovering, to watch the latest drama unfold.

George disappeared into the shadowy depths, and a familiar clomping sound solved the mystery before two matching Palomino ponies materialized out of the darkness, shining like a pair of golden flames. Their manes and tails were cream-colored, brushed to a blinding shimmer, and each sported a bridle, a saddle and a bright pink bow the size of a basketball.

"Damn," Garrett muttered, "the bastard one-upped me."

"Yeah?" Tate replied, after pulling the girls back out of the way so George could unload the wonder horses. "Wait till you see what *I* got them."

LIBBY HAD EATEN SUPPER—salad and soup—watched the evening news, checked her email, brought the newspaper in from its plastic box by the front gate and done two loads of laundry when the telephone rang.

Damn, she hoped it wasn't the manager at Poplar Bend, the town's one and only condominium complex, calling to complain that Marva was playing her CDs at top volume again, and refused to turn down the music.

In the six months since their mother had suddenly turned up in Blue River in a chauffeur-driven limo and taken up residence in a prime unit at Poplar Bend, Libby and her two younger sisters, Julie and Paige, had gotten all sorts of negative feedback about Marva's behavior.

None of them knew precisely what to do about Marva.

Picking up the receiver, she almost blurted out what she was thinking—"It's not my week to watch her. Call Julie or Paige"—and by the time she had a proper "Hello" ready, Tate had already spoken.

No one else's voice affected her in the visceral way his did.

"I need those dogs," he said, almost furtively. "Tonight."

Libby blinked. "I beg your pardon."

"I need the dogs," Tate repeated. Then, after a long pause that probably cost him, he added, "Please?"

"Tate, what on earth—? Do you realize what time it is?" She squinted at the kitchen clock, but the room was dark and since she'd just been passing through with a basket of towels from the dryer, she hadn't bothered to flip on a light switch.

"Eight?" Tate said.

"Oh," Libby said, mildly embarrassed. The hours since she'd left the Perk Up had dragged so that she thought surely it must be at least eleven.

"You know I'll give them a good home," Tate went on. "The dogs, I mean."

Libby suppressed a sigh. The pups were curled up together on the hooked rug in the living room, sound asleep. Faced with the prospect of actually giving them up, she knew she was going to miss them—a lot.

"Yes," she agreed. "I know. You can pick them up anytime tomorrow. Just stop by the shop and I'll—"

"It has to be tonight, and—well—if you could deliver them—"

"Deliver them?"

"Look, it's a lot to ask, I know that," Tate said, "and I can't explain right now, and I can't leave, either, even though Garrett and Esperanza are both here, because it's the girls' birthday and everything."

"And you want to give them the dogs for a present after all?"

"Something like that. Lib, I know it's an imposition, but I'd really appreciate it if you could bring them out here right about now."

"But you haven't even seen them—"

"Dogs are dogs," Tate said. "They're all great. And I figure you wouldn't have suggested I adopt them if they weren't good around kids."

"It's normally not the best idea to give pets as gifts, Tate. Too much fuss and excitement isn't good for the animal or the child." What was she *saying?*

She'd been the one to suggest the adoption in the first place, and with good reason—the poor creatures needed the kind of home Tate could give them. With him, they would have the best of everything, and, more important, Tate was a dog person. He'd proved that with Crockett and a lot of other animals, too.

"We're not talking about dyed chicks and rabbits at Easter here, Lib," Tate replied. He was nearly whispering.

"What about kibble—and, well—things they'll need?"

"They can survive on ground sirloin until I can get to the store and pick up dog chow tomorrow," Tate reasoned. "I'm in a fix, Libby. I need your help."

The pups had risen from the hooked rug and stood shoulder to shoulder in the doorway now, ears perked, tails wagging. Her heart sank a little at the sight.

"Okay," Libby heard herself say. "We'll be there as soon as I can load them into my car and make the drive."

Tate let out a long breath. "Great," he said. "I owe you, big-time."

You can say that again, buster, Libby thought. *How about fixing me up with a new heart, since you broke the one I've got?*

The call ended.

"You're going to be McKettrick dogs now," Libby told the guys, with a sniffle in her voice. "Best of the best. You'll probably have your own bedrooms and separate nannies."

They wagged harder. It was impossible, of course, but Libby would have sworn they knew they were headed for a place where they could settle in and belong, for good.

"Heck," she added, on a roll, "you'll even get names."

More wagging.

Libby found her purse and, after considerably more effort, her car keys. Since she lived across the alley from her café and walked everywhere but to the supermarket, she tended to misplace them.

If her aging, primer-splotched Impala would start, they were on their way.

"Want to come along for the ride?" she asked Hildie, resting on a rug of her own, in front of the couch.

Hildie yawned, stretched and went back to sleep.

"Guess that's a 'no,'" Libby said.

The pups were always ready to go when they heard the car keys jingle, and she almost tripped over them twice crossing the kitchen to the back door.

After loading the adoptees into the backseat of the rust-mobile, parked in her tilting one-car garage on the alley, she slid behind the wheel, closed her eyes to offer a silent prayer that the engine would start, stuck the key into the ignition and turned it.

The Impala's motor caught with a huffy roar, the exhaust belching smoke.

Libby backed up slowly and drove with her headlights off until she'd passed Chief of Police Brent Brogan's house at the end of the block. The chief had already warned her once about emissions standards—she was clearly in violation of said standards—and she'd made an appointment at the auto shop to get the problem fixed, twice. The trouble was, she'd had to cancel both times, once because Marva was acting up and neither Julie nor Paige was anywhere to be found, and once because a water pipe at the shop had burst and she'd been forced to call in a plumber, thereby blowing the budget.

All she needed now was a ticket.

She caught a glimpse of the chief through his living-room window as she pulled onto the street. His back was to her, and it looked as though he were playing cards or a board game with his children.

Still, Libby didn't flip on her headlights until she reached the main street. Only when she'd passed the city limits did she give the Impala a shot of gas, and she kept glancing at the rearview mirror. Brent took his job seriously.

He was also one of Tate McKettrick's best friends. If by some chance he'd seen her sneaking out of the alley in a cloud of illegal exhaust fumes, she would simply explain that she was delivering these two dogs to the Silver Spur because Tate wanted them *tonight*.

She bit her lower lip. Tate had said he owed her big-time. Well, then, he could just get her out of trouble with Brent, if she got into any.

But Libby made it all the way out to the Silver Spur without incident, and Tate must have been watching for her, because he was standing in the big circular driveway, with its hotel-size fountain, when she pulled in.

The dogs went wild in the backseat, scrabbling at the doors and rear windows, yipping to be set free.

Tate's grin lit up the night.

He came to the car, opened the back door on the driver's side and greeted the pair with ear-rufflings and the promise of sirloin for breakfast.

The dogs leaped to the paving stones and carried on like a pair of groupies finding themselves backstage at a rock concert.

Frankly, Libby had expected a little more pathos when it came time to part, since she'd been caring for these rascals for over two months, but evidently, the reluctance was all on her side.

"Hey, Lib," Tate said, just when she'd figured he was planning to ignore her completely. "You saved my life. Want to come inside for some birthday cake?"

Lib. It wasn't the first time he'd called her by the old nickname, even recently. He'd used it over the phone earlier, conning her into bringing the dogs out to his ranch that very night. Hearing it now, though, in person instead of over a wire, caused a deep emotional ache in her, a sort of yearning, as though she'd missed the last train or bus or airplane of a lifetime, and would now live out her days wandering forsaken in some wilderness.

"I shouldn't," Libby said.

Tate crouched to give the dogs the attention they continued to clamor for, but his face was turned upward, toward Libby, who was still sitting in her wreck of a car. Lights from the enormous portico over the front doors played in his hair. "Why not?" he asked.

"It's late and Hildie's home alone."

"Hildie?"

"My dog," she said.

"Is she sick?"

Libby shook her head.

"Old?"

Again, a shake.

That deadly grin of his—it should have been registered somewhere, like an assault weapon—crooked up the corner of his mouth. "Will she eat the curtains in your absence? Order pizza and smoke cigars? Log on to the internet and cruise X-rated websites?"

Libby laughed. "No," she said. Once, they'd been so close, she and Tate. She'd known his dog, Crockett, well enough to grieve almost as much over not seeing him anymore as she had over losing his master. It seemed odd, and somehow wrong, that Tate had never made Hildie's acquaintance. "She's a good dog. She'll behave."

"Then come in and have some birthday cake."

Libby looked up at the front of that great house, and she remembered stolen afternoons in Tate's bed, the summer after high school especially. Traveling further back in time, she recalled the night his parents came home early from a weekend trip and caught them swimming naked in the pool.

Mrs. McKettrick had calmly produced a bath sheet for Libby, bundled her into a pink terrycloth bathrobe, and driven her home with Libby, shivering, though the weather was hot and humid at the time.

Mr. McKettrick had ordered Tate to the study as she was leaving with Tate's mom. "We're going to have ourselves a *talk,* boy," the rancher had said.

So much had changed since then.

Tate's mom and dad were gone.

Her own father had long since died of cancer, after a lingering and painful decline.

Tate had married Cheryl, and they'd had twins together.

On the one hand, Libby really wanted to go inside and join the party.

On the other, she knew there would be too many other memories waiting to ambush her—mostly simple, ordinary ones, as it happened, like her and Tate doing their homework together, playing pool in the family room, watching movies and sharing bowls of popcorn. But it was the ordinary memories, she'd learned after losing her dad, that had the most power, the most poignancy.

With all her other problems, Libby figured she couldn't handle so much poignancy just then.

"Not this time," she said quietly, and shifted the Impala into Reverse.

"You need to get that exhaust fixed," Tate told her. The smile was gone; his expression was serious. Moments before, she'd been convinced he'd only invited her inside to be polite, wanted to repay her in some small way for bringing the dogs to him on such short notice. Now she wondered if it actually *mattered* to him, that she accept his invitation. Was it possible that he was disappointed by her refusal?

She nodded. "It's on the agenda. Good night, Tate."

He looked down at the dogs, still frolicking around him as eagerly as if he'd stuffed raw T-bone steaks into each of his jeans pockets. "What are their names?"

"They don't have any," Libby said. "I call them 'the dogs.'"

Tate chuckled. "That's creative," he replied. His body was half turned, as though the house and the people inside it were drawing him back, and she supposed they were. Garrett and Austin were both wild, in their different ways, but Tate had been born to be a family man, like his father. "You're sure you won't come in?"

"I'm sure."

One of the big main doors opened, and the twins bounded out, dressed in identical pink cotton pajamas.

Libby's heart lurched at the sight of them, and she put the Impala back in Park.

"Puppies!" they cried in unison, rushing forward.

Libby sat watching as the pups and the little girls immediately bonded, knowing all the while that she had to go.

"Happy birthday," Tate told his daughters, with a tenderness Libby had never heard in his voice before. He glanced back at her, mouthed the word, "Thanks."

Libby's vision was blurred. She blinked rapidly and was about to suck it up, back out of that spectacular driveway and head on home, where she belonged, when suddenly one of the children, the one with glasses, ran to the side of her car and peered inside.

"Hi," she said. "We have a castle. Would you like to see it?"

Libby looked up at the front of the house. "Not tonight, sweetheart, but thank you."

"My name is Ava. You're Libby Remington, aren't you? You own the Perk Up Coffee Shop."

Although Libby couldn't recall actually meeting the girls, Blue River wasn't a big place, and practically everybody knew everybody else. "Yes, I'm Libby. I hope you're having a happy birthday."

"We *are*," the child said. "Uncle Garrett bought us our very own castle from Neiman-Marcus, and Uncle Austin sent us ponies. But *Dad* gave us what we *really* wanted—puppies!"

"Take these rascals inside and give them some water," Tate told his daughters. He lingered, while the "rascals" followed the twins into the house without so much as a backward glance at Libby.

Libby's throat tightened, partly because this was goodbye for her and the dogs, partly because of the little girls' obvious joy and partly for reasons she could not have identified to save her life.

"I actually bought them a croquet set," Tate confessed.

Libby frowned. In the old days, she and Julie and Paige had played a lot of backyard croquet with their dad, and she cherished the recollection. She'd been proud that when other daddies were on the golf course with their friends and business associates, hers had chosen to spend the time with her and her sisters. "What's wrong with that?"

He sighed, stood with his arms folded, his head tilted back. He'd always loved looking at the stars, said that was why he'd never be happy in a big city. "Nothing," he admitted. "But I kind of lost my head after the castle and the ponies were delivered. Call it male ego."

"You're not going to change your mind about the dogs, are you?" Libby asked, worried all over again.

Tate gripped the edge of her open window and bent to look in at her. His face was mere inches from hers, and for one terrible, wonderful, wildly confusing moment, she thought he was going to kiss her.

He didn't, though.

"I'm not going to change my mind, Lib," he said. "The mutts will have a home as long as I do."

"You wouldn't send them to town to live with your wife?"

"*Ex*-wife," Tate said. "No, Cheryl's not a dog person. Like the ponies, they'll live right here on the Silver Spur for the duration."

"Okay," Libby said, now almost desperate to be gone.

And oddly, *equally* desperate to stay.

Tate straightened, smiled down at her. Half turned again, toward the house. Toward his daughters and the dogs that were already loved and would soon be named, toward his brother Garrett and Esperanza, the housekeeper.

But then he turned back.

"I don't suppose you'd like to have dinner with me some night?" he asked, sounding as shy as he had that long-ago day when he'd asked her to the junior prom. "Soon?"

CHAPTER THREE

"I CAN'T PAY YOU," Libby warned, the next morning, when her sister Julie showed up at the shop, all set to bake scones and chocolate-chip cookies, her four-year-old son Calvin in tow. Clad in swim trunks and flip-flops, with a plastic ring around his waist, Libby's favorite—and *only*—nephew had clearly made up his mind to take advantage of the first body of water to present itself.

He adjusted his horn-rimmed glasses, with the chunk of none-too-clean tape holding the bridge together, and climbed onto one of three stools lining the short counter.

Libby ruffled his hair. "Hey, buddy," she said. "Want an orange smoothie?"

"No, thanks," Calvin replied glumly.

Julie, twenty-nine, with long, naturally auburn hair that fell to the middle of her back in spiral curls—also natural—and a figure that would do any exercise maven proud, wore jeans and a royal blue long-sleeved T-shirt. Thus her hazel eyes, which tended to reflect whatever color she was wearing that day, were the pure azure of a clear spring sky. She grinned at Libby and headed for the tiny kitchen in the back of the shop.

"You could take my week troubleshooting with Marva," she sang. "Instead of paying me wages, I mean."

"Not a chance," Libby said, but the refusal was rhetorical, and Julie knew that as well as she did. The three sisters rotated, week by week, taking responsibility for their mother, which meant visiting regularly, settling the problems Marva invariably caused with neighbors and hunting her down when she decided to take off on one of her hikes into the countryside and got lost. Marva was always up to something.

"Mom doesn't have anything better to do anyway," Calvin confided solemnly. He was precocious for his age, and he'd already been reading for a year. Julie, a high school English and drama teacher, was off for the summer, and her usual fill-in job at the insurance agency had fallen through for some unspecified reason. "You might as well let her make scones."

Libby chuckled and couldn't resist planting a smacking kiss on Calvin's cheek. "The community pool is closed for maintenance this week," she reminded him. "So what's with the trunks and the plastic inner tube?"

Calvin's eyes were a pale, crystalline blue, like those of his long-gone father, a man Julie had met while she was student teaching in Galveston, after college. As close as she and Julie were, Libby knew very little about Gordon Pruett, except that he'd owned a fishing boat and was a lot better at going away than coming back. He'd stayed around long enough to pass his unique eye color on to his son and name him Calvin, for his favorite uncle, but soon enough he'd felt compelled to move on.

Gordon didn't visit, but he wasn't completely worthless. He remembered birthdays, mailed his son a box of awkwardly wrapped presents every Christmas, and sent Julie a few hundred dollars in child support each month.

Most of the time, the checks even cleared the bank.

Calvin pushed his everyday glasses up his nose—he had better ones for important occasions. "I *know* the pool is closed for maintenance, Aunt Libby," he said, "but the kid next door to us— Justin?—well, his mom and dad bought him a swimming pool, the kind you blow up with a bicycle pump. His dad filled it with a garden hose this morning, but Justin's mom said we can't swim until the sun heats the water up. I just want to be ready."

Julie chuckled as she came out of the kitchen. She'd already managed to get flour all over the front of her fresh apron. "Hey,

Mark Spitz," she said to her son, "how about going next door for a five-pound bag of sugar? Give you a nickel for your trouble."

Almsted's, probably one of the last surviving mom-and-pop grocery stores in that part of Texas, was something of a local institution, as much a museum as a place of business.

"You can't buy anything for a nickel," Calvin scoffed, but he climbed down from the stool and held out one palm, reporting for duty.

Libby gave him a few dollars from the till to pay for the sugar, and Calvin marched himself out onto the sidewalk, headed next door.

Julie immediately stationed herself at a side window, in order to keep an eye on him. No child had ever gone missing from Blue River, but a person couldn't be too careful.

"We've already *got* plenty of sugar," Libby said.

"I know," Julie answered, watching as her son went into Almsted's, with its peeling, green-painted wooden screen door. "I have something to tell you, and I don't want Calvin to hear."

Libby, busy getting ready for the Monday-morning latte rush, went still. "Is something wrong?"

"Gordon emailed me," Julie said, still keeping her careful vigil. "He's married and he and his wife pass through town often, on the way to visit his parents in Tulsa, and now Gordon and the little woman want to stop by sometime soon, and get acquainted with Calvin."

"That sounds harmless," Libby observed, though she felt a prickle of uneasiness at the news.

"I don't like it," Julie replied firmly. She smiled, which meant Calvin had reappeared, lugging the bag of sugar, and stepped back so he wouldn't see her. "What if Gordon decides to be an actual, step-up father, now that he's married?"

"Julie, he *is* Calvin's father—"

Julie made a throat-slashing motion with one hand, and Calvin struggled through the front door, might have been squashed by it if he hadn't been wearing the miniature inner tube with the goggle-eyed frog-head on the front.

"Here," he said, holding the bag out to his mother. "Where's my nickel?"

Julie paid up, casting a warning glance in Libby's direction as she did so. There was to be no more talk of Gordon Pruett's impending visit while Calvin was around.

"I'm bored," Calvin soon announced. "I want to go to playschool over at the community center."

"You should have thought of that when you insisted on wearing swimming trunks and the floaty thing with the frog-head," Julie responded lightly, heading back toward the kitchen with the unnecessary bag of sugar. "You're not dressed for playschool, kiddo."

"There's a dress code?" Libby asked. She generally took Calvin's side when there was a difference of opinion.

"No," Julie conceded brightly, "but I'd be willing to bet nobody else is wearing a bathing suit."

Two secretaries came in then, for their double nonfat lattes, following by Jubal Tabor, a lineman for the power company. In his midforties, with a receding hairline and a needy personality, Jubal always ordered the Rocket, a high-caffeine concoction with ginseng and a lot of sugar. Said it got him through the morning.

"Expectin' a flood, kid?" he asked Calvin, who was back on his stool, shoulders hunched, frog-head slightly askew.

Calvin rolled his eyes.

Hiding a smile, Libby served the secretaries' drinks, took their money and thanked them.

Meanwhile, Julie made sure she stayed in the kitchen. Jubal asked her to the movies nearly every time their paths crossed, and even now he was standing on tiptoe trying to catch a glimpse of her while the espresso for his Rocket steamed out of the steel spigot.

"He's not so bad," Libby had said once, when Julie had sent Jubal away with another carefully worded rejection.

"Julie and Jubal?" her sister had said, her eyes green that day because she was wearing a mint-colored blouse. "Our names alone are reason enough to steer clear—we'd sound like second cousins to the Bobbsey twins. Besides, he's too old for me, he wears white socks and he always calls Calvin 'kid.'"

The admittedly comical ring of their names, Jubal's age and the white socks might have been overlooked, in Libby's opinion, but the gruff way he said "kid" whenever he spoke to Calvin bugged her, too. So she'd stopped reminding her sister that there was a shortage of marriageable men in Blue River.

"Scones aren't ready yet?" Jubal asked, casting a disapproving eye toward the virtually empty plastic bakery display case beside the cash register. "Out at Starbucks, they've *always* got scones."

Libby refrained from pointing out to Jubal that he never bought scones anyway, no matter how good the selection was, and set his drink on the counter. "You been cheating on me, Jubal?" she teased. "Buying your jet fuel from the competition?"

Jubal looked at her and blinked once, hard, as though he'd never seen her before. "You want to go to the movies with me tonight?" he asked.

Calvin made a rude sound, which Jubal either missed or pretended not to hear.

"I'm sorry," Libby said, with a note of kind regret in her voice. "I promised Tate McKettrick I'd have dinner with him."

Julie dropped something in the kitchen, causing a great clatter, and out of the corner of her eye, Libby saw Calvin watching her with renewed interest. Since he'd been born long after the breakup, he couldn't have registered the implications of his aunt's statement, but that well-known surname had a cachet all its own.

Even among four-year-olds, it seemed.

"Well," Jubal groused, "far be it from me to compete with a *McKettrick*."

Libby merely smiled. "Thanks for the business, Jubal," she told him. "You have yourself a good day, now."

Jubal paid up, took his Rocket and left.

The instant his utility van pulled away from the curb, Julie peeked out of the kitchen. "Did I hear you say you're going to dinner with Tate?" she asked.

Libby tried to act casual. "He asked me last night. I said maybe."

"That isn't what you told Mr. Tabor," Calvin piped up. "You lied."

"I didn't lie," Libby lied. First, she'd driven her car without the emissions repair, single-handedly destroying the environment, to hear her conscience tell it, and now *this*. She was setting a really bad example for her nephew.

"Yes, you did," Calvin insisted.

"Sometimes," Julie said carefully, resting a hand on Calvin's small, bare shoulder, "we say things that aren't *precisely* true so we don't hurt other people's feelings."

Calvin held his ground. "If it's not the truth, then it's a lie. That's what you always tell *me,* Mom."

Libby sighed. "If Tate asks me out again," she told Calvin, "I'll say yes. That way, I won't have fibbed to anybody."

"I can't believe you didn't say 'yes' in the first place," Julie marveled. "Elisabeth Remington, are you *crazy?*"

Libby cleared her throat, slanted a glance in Calvin's direction to remind her sister that the conversation would have to wait.

"Can I go to playschool if I put on clothes?" Calvin asked, looking so woeful that Julie mussed his hair and ducked out of her floury apron.

"Sure," she said. "Let's run home so you can change." She turned to Libby. "I put the first batch of scones in the oven a couple of minutes ago," she added. "When you hear the timer ding, take them out."

"Are you coming back?" Libby asked, as equally invested in a "no" as she was in a "yes." Once she and her sister were alone again, between customers, Julie would grill her about Tate. If Julie *didn't* return, the first batch of scones would sell out in a heartbeat, as always, and there wouldn't be any more for the rest of the day, because Libby always burned everything she baked, no matter how careful she was.

"Only if you promise to take my turn babysitting Marva so I can—" Julie paused, cleared her throat "—leave town for a few days."

"We're going somewhere?" Calvin asked, immediately excited. On a teacher's salary, with the child support going into a college account, he and Julie didn't take vacations.

"Yes," Julie answered, passing Libby an arch look. "If your aunt Libby will agree to look after Gramma while we're gone, that is."

Calvin sagged with disappointment. "Nobody," he said, "wants to spend any more time with *Gramma* than they have to."

"Calvin Remington," Julie replied, without much sternness to her tone, "that was a terrible thing to say."

"You say it all the time."

"It's still terrible, all right?" Julie turned to Libby. "Deal or no deal?"

Agreeing would mean two weeks in a row on Marva-watch. But Libby needed those scones, if she didn't want all her customers heading for Starbucks. "Deal," she said, in dismal resignation.

Julie grinned. "Great. See you in twenty minutes."

"Crap," Libby muttered, when her sister and nephew had reached the sidewalk and she knew Calvin wouldn't hear.

Julie took half an hour to get back, not twenty minutes, and in the meantime there was a run on iced coffee, so Libby nearly missed the "ding" of the timer on the oven. She rescued the scones in the nick of time and sold the last one just as Julie waltzed in, all pleased with herself.

"You're going, aren't you?" she asked, as soon as the customer and the scone were gone. "If Tate asks you out to dinner again, you'll say 'yes,' not 'maybe'?"

"Maybe," Libby said, annoyed. "And thanks a heap for sticking me with Marva for an extra week. I covered for you *last* month, remember, when you wanted to take your twelfth-grade drama class on that field trip to Dallas."

"They learned so much about Shakespeare," Julie said.

"And I came to understand the mysteries of matricide," Libby said, cleaning the spigots on the espresso machine with a paper towel. "Are you seriously planning to leave town so you can avoid Gordon and the new bride?"

"Yes," Julie answered. "According to his email, he sold his boat, or it sank or both and it went for salvage—I forget. That means good old Gordon is thinking of settling down, and I don't want him asking for joint custody or something, just because he's got a wife now."

"I understand where you're coming from, Julie," Libby said, after taking a few moments to prepare, "but you won't be able to hide from Gordon forever—if he really wants to be part of Calvin's life, he'll find a way. And he has a right to at least *see* the little guy once in a while."

"Gordon Pruett is the most irresponsible man on the planet," Julie reminded Libby, her eyes suspiciously bright and her voice shaking a little. "I can't turn Calvin over to him every other weekend, or for whole summers or for holidays. For one thing, there's the asthma."

A silence fell between them.

Libby hadn't witnessed one of Calvin's asthma attacks recently, but when they happened, they were terrifying. Once, when he was still in diapers, he'd all but stopped breathing. Libby's youngest sister, Paige, an RN, had jumped up and made sure he wasn't choking, then grabbed him from his high chair at the Thanksgiving dinner table at a neighbor's house, yelled for someone to call 911 and rushed to the shower, where she'd thrust the by-then-blue baby under an icy spray, drenching herself in the process, holding him there until his lungs were shocked into action.

Libby could still hear his affronted, frightened shrieks, see him soaked and struggling to get to Julie, who bundled him in a towel and held him close, once he'd gotten his breath again, whispering to him, singing softly, desperate to calm him down.

Paige had calmly turned on the hot water spigot in the shower then, and filled the bathroom with steam, and Julie had sat on the lid of the toilet, rocking a whimpering Calvin in her arms until the paramedics arrived.

The toddler had spent nearly a week in the pediatric ward of a San Antonio hospital, Julie at his bedside around the clock, and it had taken Paige months to win back his trust. He was simply too little to understand that she'd saved his life.

Now, he used an inhaler and Julie kept oxygen on hand, in their small cottage two blocks from the high school. Paige, living across the street from them in an old mansion converted to apartments, was on call 24/7 in case Calvin needed emergency intubation. Given that she usually worked four ten-hour shifts at a private clinic fifty miles from Blue River and the fire department EMTs were all volunteers, with little formal training, Paige had tried to show both Julie and Libby how to insert an oxygen tube, using a borrowed dummy.

While Libby supposed she could do it if Calvin's life were hanging in the balance, she was far from confident. It was the same with Julie.

In frustration, Paige had finally recruited one of Blue River's EMTs, a former Marine medic named Dennis Evans, and instructed her sisters to call him if Calvin had a serious asthma attack while she was too far away to help.

Julie kept Dennis's number on the front of her refrigerator, seven bright red, six-inch plastic digits with magnets on the back.

So far, Calvin's medications kept his condition under control, but Libby could certainly understand Julie's vigilance. Whenever he went through a bad spell, Julie didn't sleep, and dark circles formed under her eyes.

"So," Julie said now, returning to the main part of the shop after another batch of scones had been baked, and another rush of business had whisked the goodies out the door before they'd even cooled, "let's talk about Tate."

"Let's not," Libby replied. She'd been a codependent fool to even *think* about accepting a date with him, considering that he'd probably begun the process of forgetting all about her as soon as she'd been forced to leave the university and come home to help look after her ailing father. She'd taken what courses she could at Blue River Junior College, which was really just a satellite of another school in San Antonio and had since closed due to lack of funding, but she'd only been marking time, and she knew it.

"You really loved him, Lib," Julie said gently, taking Calvin's stool at the counter and studying Libby with thoughtful eyes.

"That's the whole point. I loved Tate McKettrick. He, on the other hand, loved a good time." Libby sighed. She hated self-pity, and she was teetering on the precipice of it just then. She tried to smile and partly succeeded. "I guess it made sense that he'd be attracted to someone like Cheryl. She's an attorney, and she was raised the way Tate and his brothers were—with every possible advantage. I didn't even finish college. Tate and I don't have a whole lot in common, when you think about it."

Julie frowned, bracing her elbows on the countertop, resting her chin in her palms. Her eyes took on a stormy, steel-blue color, edged in gray. "I really hope you're not saying you aren't good enough for Tate or anybody else, because I'm going to have to raise a fuss about it if you are."

Libby chuckled. "Julie Remington, making a scene," she joked. "Why, I can't even *imagine* such a thing."

Julie grinned, raised her beautiful hair off her neck with both hands to cool her neck, then let it fall again. "OK, so I might have been a bit of a drama queen in high school and college," she confessed. "You're just trying to distract me from the fact that I'm right. You think—you *actually think*—Tate threw you over for Cheryl because she fit into his world better than you would have."

Libby raised one eyebrow. "Isn't that what happened?"

"What *happened*," Julie argued, "is this—Cheryl seduced Tate. Oil wells and big Texas ranches can be aphrodisiacs, you know. Maybe she intended all along to get pregnant and live like a Ewing out there on the Silver Spur."

"Oh, come *on*," Libby retorted. "I might not admire the woman all that much, but it isn't fair to put all the blame on her, and you damn well know it, Jules. It isn't as if she used a date drug and had her way with Tate while he was unconscious. He could have stopped the whole thing if he'd wanted to—which he obviously didn't."

"That was a while ago, Lib," Julie said mildly, examining her manicure.

"All right, so he was young," Libby responded. "He was old enough to know better."

The front door of the shop swung open then, and Chief Brogan strolled in, sweating in his usually crisp tan uniform. He nodded to Julie, then swung his dark brown gaze to Libby.

"Do I smell scones?" he asked.

"Blueberry," Julie confirmed, smiling.

Brent Brogan, a fairly recent widower, was six feet tall with broad, powerful shoulders and a narrow waist. Tate had long ago dubbed him "Denzel," since he bore such a strong resemblance to the actor, back in Denzel Washington's younger years.

His gaze swung in Julie's direction, then back to Libby. "The usual," he said. "Please."

"Sure, Chief," Libby said, with nervous good cheer, and started the mocha with a triple shot of espresso he ordered every day at about the same time.

Brent approached the counter, braced his big hands against it, and watched Libby with unnerving thoroughness as she worked. "I would have sworn I saw that Impala of yours rolling down the alley last night," he said affably, "with the headlights out. Did you get the exhaust fixed yet?"

"That was my car you saw," Julie hastened to say.

It was a good thing Calvin wasn't around, because that was a whopper and he'd have been sure to point that out right away. Julie's car was a pink Cadillac that had been somebody's Mary Kay prize back in the mid-'80s. Even in a dark alley, it wouldn't be mistaken for an Impala, especially not by a trained observer like Brent Brogan.

Libby gave her sister a look. Sighed and rubbed her suddenly sweaty palms down her jean-covered thighs. "I had an appointment at the auto-repair shop," she told Brent, "but then a pipe blew in the kitchen and I had to call a plumber and, well, you know what plumbers cost."

Brent slanted a glance at Julie, who blushed that freckles-on-pink way only true redheads can, and once again turned his attention back to Libby. "So it *was* you?"

"Yes," Libby said, straightening her shoulders. "And if you give me a ticket, I won't be able to afford to have the repairs done for *another* month."

The timer bell chimed.

Julie rushed to take the latest batch of scones out of the oven.

"I'm going to give you one more warning, Libby," Brent said quietly, raising an index finger. "Count it. *One.* If I catch you driving that environmental disaster again, without a sticker proving it meets the legal standards, I am so going to throw the book at you. Is—that—understood?"

Libby set his drink on the counter with a thump. "Yes, sir," she said tightly. *"That is understood."* She raised her chin a notch. "How am I supposed to get the car to the shop if I can't drive it?"

Brent smiled. "I'd make an exception in that case, I guess."

Libby made up her mind to put the repair charges on the credit card she'd just paid off, though it would set her back.

Julie looked toward the street, smiled and consulted an imaginary watch. "Well, will you look at that," she said. "It's time to pick Calvin up at playschool."

The pit of Libby's stomach jittered. She followed her sister's gaze and saw Tate walking toward the door, looking beyond good in worn jeans, scuffed boots and a white T-shirt that showed off his biceps and tanned forearms.

Scanning the street, she saw no sign of his truck, the sleek luxury car he sometimes drove or his twin daughters.

Libby felt as though she'd been forced, scrambling for balance, onto a drooping piano wire stretched across Niagara Falls. It was barely noon—Tate had suggested *dinner,* hadn't he, not lunch?

Either way, she reflected, trying to calm her nerves with common sense, she'd said "Maybe," not "Yes."

Tate reached the door, opened it and walked in. His grin was as white as his shirt, and even from behind the register, Libby could see the comb ridges in his hair.

He greeted Brent with a half salute. "Denzel," he said.

Brent smiled. "Throw those blueberry scones into a bag for me," he said, though whether he was addressing Julie or Libby was unclear, because he was watching Tate. "I'd better buy them up before McKettrick beats me to the draw."

Tate was looking at Libby. His blue gaze smoldered that day, but she knew from experience that fire could turn to ice in a heartbeat.

"You had any more trouble with those rustlers?" Brent asked.

Libby ducked into the kitchen, nearly causing a sister-jam in the doorway because Julie had the same idea at the same time.

"Rustlers?" Libby asked, troubled.

"Not recently," Tate told his friend. Looking down into Libby's face, he added, "Rustling's a now-and-again kind of thing. Not as dangerous as it looks in the old movies."

Julie squirmed to get past Libby and leave to pick Calvin up at the community center.

"If you don't come straight back here," Libby warned her sister, momentarily distracted and keeping her voice low, "I'm only taking over with Marva for *half* of next week."

"Relax," Julie answered, turning back and grabbing a paper bag and tongs to fill the chief's scone order. "I'll bake all afternoon, and bring you a big batch of scones and doughnuts in the morning. My oven is better than this one, and I really do have to fetch Calvin."

Libby blocked Julie's way out of the kitchen and leaned in close. "What am I supposed to do if Brent leaves and Tate is still here?" she demanded.

Julie raised both eyebrows. "*Talk* to the man? Maybe offer him coffee—or a quickie in the storeroom?" She grinned, full of mischief. "That's about the only thing I miss about Gordon Pruett. Stand-up sex with a thirty-three percent chance of getting caught."

Libby blushed, but then she had to laugh. "I am *not* offering Tate McKettrick stand-up sex in the storeroom!" she said.

"Now, that's a damn pity," Tate said.

Libby whirled around, saw him standing in the doorway leading into the main part of the shop, arms folded, grin wicked, one muscular shoulder braced against the framework. Color suffused Libby's face, so hot it hurt.

Julie fled, giggling, with the bag of scones in one hand, forcing Tate to step aside, though he resumed his damnably sexy stance as soon as she'd passed.

"Well," he remarked, after giving a philosophical sigh, "I stopped by to repeat my offer to buy you dinner, since the girls are over at the vet's with Ambrose and Buford and therefore temporarily occupied, but if you want to have sex in a storeroom or anyplace else, Lib, I'm game."

"Ambrose and Buford?" Libby asked numbly.

"The dogs," Tate explained, his eyes twinkling. "They're getting checkups—'wellness exams,' they call them now—and shots."

"Oh," Libby said, at a loss.

"Could we get back to the subject of sex?" Tate teased.

"No," she said, half laughing. "We most certainly can't."

He straightened, walked toward her, in that ambling, easy way he had, cupped her face in his hands. She loved the warmth of his touch, the restrained strength, the roughness of work-calloused flesh.

His were the hands of a rancher.

"Dinner?" he asked.

"Are you going to kiss me?" she countered.

He smiled. "Depends on your answer."

"If I say 'no,' what happens?"

"You wouldn't do a darn fool thing like that, now would you?" he asked, in a honeyed drawl. Although his body shifted, his hands remained where they were. "Turn down a free meal, and a tour of a plastic castle? Miss out on a perfectly good chance to see how Ambrose and Buford are adjusting to ranch life?"

He meant to "buy" dinner at his place, then. The knowledge was both a relief and a whole new reason to panic.

"Will Audrey and Ava be there?"

"Yes."

"Garrett?"

"No. Sorry. He had to get back to Austin."

"Pressing political business?"

Tate chuckled. "Probably a hot date," he said. "Plus, he's afraid I'm going to kill him in his sleep for giving my kids a goddamn castle for their sixth birthday."

"Hmm," Libby mused.

"Well?" Tate prompted.

"I have a question," Libby said.

"What's that?"

"Why now? Why ask me out now, Tate—after all this time?"

He looked thoughtful, and a few moments passed before he answered, his voice quiet. "I guess it took me this long to work up my courage." He swallowed hard, met her gaze in a deliberate way. "Nobody would blame you if you told me to go straight to hell, Libby. Not after what I did."

She took that in. Finally, she said, "Okay."

"Is that an okay-yes, or an okay-go-take-a-flying-leap?"

Libby had to smile. "I guess it's an okay-one-dinner-is-no-big-deal," she answered. "We *are* still talking about dinner, right?"

Tate chuckled. God, he smelled good, like fresh air and newly cut grass distilled to their essences. And she'd missed bantering with him like this. "Yes, we're still talking about dinner."

"Then, yes," Libby said, feeling dizzy. After all, she'd promised Calvin she'd undo her lie if she got the chance, and here it was.

"Right answer," Tate murmured, and then he kissed her.

The world, perhaps even the whole universe, rocked wildly and dissolved, leaving Libby drifting in the aftermath, not standing in her shabby little coffee-shop kitchen.

Tate deepened the kiss, used his tongue. Oh, he was an expert tongue man, all right. Another thing she'd forgotten—or *tried* to forget.

Libby moaned a little, swayed on her feet.

Tate drew back. His hands dropped from her cheeks to her shoulders, steadying her.

"Pick you up at six?" It was more a statement than a question, but Libby didn't care. She was taking a terrible risk, and she didn't care about that, either.

"Six," she confirmed. "What shall I wear?"

He grinned. "The twins are dining in shorts, tank tops and pointed princess hats with glitter and tassels," he said. "Feel free to skip the hat."

"Guess that leaves shorts and a tank top," she said. "Which means you should pick me up at six-thirty, because I'm going to need to shave my legs."

Mentally, Libby slapped a hand over her mouth. She'd just given this hot man a mental picture of her running a razor along *hairy legs?*

"Here or at your place?" Tate asked, apparently unfazed by the visual.

"My place," Libby said. "I'd drive out on my own, but your friend the chief of police will arrest me if I so much as turn a wheel."

"Therein lies a tale," Tate said. "One I'd love to hear. Later."

"Later," Libby echoed, and then he was gone.

And she just stood there, long after he'd left her, the kiss still pulsing on her lips and rumbling through her like the seismic echoes of an earthquake.

CHAPTER FOUR

LIBBY CLOSED THE shop at five that day—no big sacrifice, since she'd only had one customer after lunch, a loan officer from First Cattleman's who'd left, disgruntled, without buying anything once he learned there were no more of Julie's scones to be had.

After cleaning up the various machines, stowing the day's modest take in her zippered deposit bag and finally locking up, she crossed the alley—trying not to hurry—and let a grateful Hildie out into the backyard.

The place seemed a little lonely without the formerly nameless dogs, but she'd see them that night, at Tate's. Given the way they'd thrown her under the proverbial bus when she'd dropped them off at the Silver Spur the night before, there was a good chance they'd ignore her completely.

"Now, you're being silly," she told herself, refreshing Hildie's water bowl at the sink, then rinsing out and refilling the food dish with kibble.

While Hildie gobbled down her meal, Libby showered, taking care to shave her legs, but instead of the prescribed shorts and tank top, she chose a pink sundress with spaghetti straps and smocking at the bodice. She painted her toenails to match, spritzed herself with cologne and dried her freshly shampooed, shoulder-length hair until it fluffed out around her face.

Libby owned exactly two cosmetic products—a tube of mascara and some lip gloss—and she applied both with a little more care than usual.

The phone rang at five minutes to six, and she was instantly certain that Tate had changed his mind and meant to rescind the invitation to have supper at the Silver Spur. The wave of disappointment that washed over her was out of all proportion to the situation.

But it wasn't Tate, as things turned out, calling with some lame excuse.

It was Gerbera Jackson, who cleaned for Marva three days a week, over at Poplar Bend.

"Libby? That you?"

"Hello, Gerbera," Libby responded.

"I know it isn't your week," Gerbera went on apologetically, "but I couldn't reach Miss Paige, or Miss Julie, either."

Gerbera, an old-fashioned Black woman, well into her sixties, still adhered to the mercifully outdated convention of addressing her white counterparts as "Miss."

"That's okay," Libby said, hiding her disappointment. A problem with Marva meant the evening at the Silver Spur was history, the great event that never happened. "What's up?"

"Well, it's your mama, of course," Gerbera said sadly.

Who else? Libby thought uncharitably.

"I'm worried about her," the softhearted woman continued. "I recorded her stories for her, just like always, since her favorites are on while she's out taking those longs walks of hers, but Miss Marva, she doesn't want to look at them tonight. Told me not to bother putting a chicken potpie into the oven for her before I left, too. That's one of her favorites, you know."

Libby closed her eyes briefly, breathed deeply and slowly. Marva's "stories" were soap operas, and she hadn't missed an episode of *As the World Turns,* or so she claimed, since 1972, when, recovering from a twisted ankle, she'd gotten hooked.

"Not good," Libby admitted. When Marva didn't want to watch her soaps or eat chicken potpie, she was depressed. And when Marva was depressed, bad things happened.

"She hasn't been herself since they eighty-sixed her from the bingo hall for lighting up a cigarette," Gerbera added.

Just then, a rap sounded at the front door. Tate had arrived, probably looking cowboy-sexy, and now Libby was going to have to tell him she couldn't go to the Silver Spur for supper.

"I hate to bother you," Gerbera said, and she sounded like she meant it, but she also sounded relieved. If she had a fault, it was caring too much about the various ladies she cleaned and cooked for, whether they were crotchety or sweet-tempered. Until her nephew, Brent Brogan, had moved back to Blue River, with his children, after his wife's death, Gerbera had managed Poplar Bend full-time, living in an apartment there.

She spent more time with her family now, cooking and mending and helping out wherever she could. Brent claimed her chicken-and-dumplings alone had put ten pounds on him.

"No bother," Libby said, brightening her voice and stretching the kitchen phone cord far enough to see Tate standing on the other side of the front door. She gestured for him to come in. "She's my mother."

Some mother Marva had been, though. She'd left her husband and small, bewildered children years before, with a lot of noise and drama, and suddenly returned more than two decades later, after what she described as a personal epiphany, to install herself at Poplar Bend and demand regular visits from her daughters.

She had, for some reason, decided it was time to bond.

Better late than never—that seemed to be the theory.

Marva had money, that much was clear, and she was used to giving orders, but any attempt to discuss her long and largely silent absence brought some offhanded response like, "That was then and this is now."

For all Libby and her sisters knew, Marva could have been living on another planet or in a parallel dimension all those years.

Libby wanted to love Marva; she truly did. But it was hard, remembering how heartbroken their dad had been at his wife's defection—she'd run away with a man who rode a motorcycle and earned a sketchy living as a tattoo artist.

Clearly, the tattoo man had been out of the picture for a long time.

For their father's sake, Libby, Julie and Paige took turns visiting and handling problems Marva herself had created. They fetched and carried and ran errands, but Marva wasn't grateful for anything. *I am your mother,* she'd told Libby, in one of her cranky moments, *and I am entitled to your respect.*

Respect, Libby had retorted hotly, unable to hold her tongue, *is not a right. It's something you have to earn.*

Tate let himself in, at Libby's signal, and Hildie started playing up to him as though he were some kind of cowboy messiah.

"Thanks, Gerbera," Libby said, realizing she'd missed a chunk of the conversation. "I'll head over there right away and make sure she's okay."

Gerbera apologized again, said goodbye and hung up.

Libby replaced the receiver on the hook in the kitchen and went back to greet her breathtakingly handsome guest.

"Problem?" Tate asked mildly. He filled Libby's small living room, made it feel crowded and, at the same time, utterly safe.

"My mother," Libby said. "I need to check on her."

"Okay," Tate replied. "Let's go check on her, then."

"You don't understand. It could take hours, if she's in one of her—moods."

Tate's shoulders moved in an easy shrug. "Only one way to find out," he said.

Libby couldn't let him throw away his evening just because her own was ruined. "You should just go home. Forget about supper." She swallowed. "About my joining you, I mean."

He was crouching by then, fussing over the adoring Hildie. She probably wanted to go home with him and be *his* dog. *Libby? That name seems vaguely familiar.*

"Nope," he said, straightening. "You and I and—what's this dog's name again?"

"Hildie," Libby answered, her throat tight.

"You and Hildie and I are having supper on the Silver Spur, just like we planned. I'll just call Esperanza and ask her to feed the girls early."

"But—"

Tate took in Libby's sundress, her strappy sandals, her semi-big hair. "You look better than fantastic," he said. Then he took Libby by the arm and squired her toward the front door, Hildie happily trotting alongside.

His truck was parked at the curb, and he hoisted Hildie into the backseat, then opened the passenger-side door for Libby. Helped her onto the running board, from which point she was able to come in for a landing on the leather seat with something at least *resembling* dignity.

"You don't have to do this," she said.

Tate didn't answer until he'd rounded the front of the truck and climbed behind the wheel. "I don't have to do anything but die and pay taxes," he replied, with a grin. "I'm here because I *want* to be here, Lib. No other reason."

Within five minutes, they were pulling into one of the parking lots at Poplar Bend, behind Building B. Marva lived off the central courtyard, and as they approached, she stepped out onto her small patio, smiling cheerfully. A glass of white wine in one hand, she wore white linen slacks and a matching shirt, tasteful sandals and earrings.

Libby stared at her.

"Well, *this* is a nice surprise," Marva said, her eyes gliding over Tate McKettrick briefly before shifting back to her daughter. "To what do I owe the pleasure?"

"Gerbera Jackson called me," Libby said, struggling to keep her tone even. "She was very concerned because you didn't want to watch your soap operas or eat supper."

Marva sighed charitably and shook her head. "I was just having a little blue spell, that's all," she said. She raised the wineglass, its contents shimmering in the late-afternoon light. "Care for a drink?"

Inwardly, Libby seethed. Gerbera was a sensible woman, and if she'd been concerned about Marva's behavior, then Marva had given her good reason for it.

Bottom line, Marva had decided she wanted a little attention. Instead of just saying so, she'd manipulated Gerbera into raising an unnecessary alarm.

"No, thanks," Tate said, nodding affably at Marva. "Is there anything you need, ma'am?"

Libby wanted to jab him with her elbow, but she couldn't, because Marva would see.

"Well," Marva said, almost purring, "there is that light in the kitchen. It's been burned out for weeks and I'm afraid I'll break my neck if I get up on a ladder and try to replace the bulb."

Tate rolled up his sleeves. "Glad to help," he said.

Libby's smile felt fixed; she could only hope it *looked* more genuine than it felt, quivering on her mouth.

Tate replaced the bulb in Marva's kitchen.

"It's good to have a man around the house," Marva said.

Libby all but rolled her eyes. *You had one,* she thought. *You had Dad. And he wasn't exciting enough for you.*

"I guess Libby and I ought to get going," Tate told Marva. "Esperanza will be holding supper for us."

Marva patted his arm, giving Libby a sly wink, probably in reference to Tate's well-developed biceps. "You young people run along and have a nice evening," she said, setting aside her now-empty wineglass to wave them out of the condo. "It's nice to know you're dating, Libby," she added, her tone sunny. "You and your sisters need to have more fun."

Libby's cheeks burned.

Tate took her by the elbow, nodded a good evening to Marva, and they were out of the condo, headed down the walk.

When they reached the truck, Tate lifted Libby bodily into the cab, paused to reach back and pet Hildie reassuringly before sprinting around to the driver's-side door, climbing in and taking the wheel again.

As soon as he turned the key in the ignition, the air-conditioning kicked in, cooling Libby's flesh, if not her temper.

She leaned back in the seat, then closed her eyes. Stopping by Marva's place had been no big deal, as it turned out, and Tate certainly hadn't minded changing the lightbulb.

But of course, those things weren't at the heart of the problem, anyway, were they?

All this emotional churning was about Marva's leaving, so many years ago.

It was about her and Julie and Paige, not to mention their dad, missing her so much.

Marva had departed with a lot of fanfare. Now that she was back, she expected to be treated like any normal mother.

Not.

"I guess your mom still gets under your hide," Tate commented quietly, once they were moving again.

Libby turned her head, looked at him. "Yes," she admitted. He knew the story—everyone around Blue River did. Several times, when they were younger, he'd held her while she cried over Marva.

Tate was thoughtful, and silent for a long time. "She's probably doing the best she can," he said, when they were past the town limits and rolling down the open road. "Like the rest of us."

Libby nodded. Marva's "best" wasn't all that good, as it happened, but she didn't want the subject of her mother to ruin the evening. She raised and lowered her shoulders, releasing tension, and focused on the scenery. "I guess so," she said.

The conversational lull that followed was peaceful, easy.

Hildie got things going again by suddenly popping her big head forward from the backseat and giving Tate an impromptu lick on the ear.

He laughed, and so did Libby.

"Do you ever think about getting another dog?" she asked, thinking of Crockett. That old hound had been Tate's constant companion. He'd even taken him to college with him.

"Got two," Tate reminded Libby, grinning.

"I mean, one of your own," Libby said.

Tate swallowed, shook his head. "I keep thinking I'll be ready," he replied, keeping his gaze fixed on the winding road ahead. "But it hasn't happened yet. Crockett and I, we were pretty tight."

Libby watched him, took in his strong profile and the proud way he held his head up high. It was a McKettrick thing, that quiet dignity.

"Your folks were such nice people," she told Tate.

He smiled. "Yeah," he agreed. "They were."

They'd passed mile after mile of grassy rangeland by then, dotted with cattle and horses, all of it part of the Silver Spur. Once, there had been oil wells, too, pumping night and day for fifty years or better, though Tate's father had shut them down years before.

A few rusty relics remained, hulking and rounded at the top; in the fading, purplish light of early evening, they reminded Libby of the dinosaurs that must have shaken the ground with their footsteps and dwarfed the primordial trees with their bulk.

"You're pretty far away," Tate said, as they turned in at the towering wrought-iron gates with the name *McKettrick* scrolled across them. Those gates had been standing open the night before; Libby, relieved not to have to stop, push the button on the intercom and identify herself to someone inside, had breezed right in. "What are you thinking about, Lib?"

She smiled. "Oil derricks and dinosaurs," she replied.

Tate pushed a button on his visor, and the gates swung wide, then whispered closed again as soon as they passed through. Hildie, quiet for most of the ride, began to get restless, pacing from one end of the backseat to the other.

Once again, Libby dared hope her dog wasn't planning to move in with Tate and forget all about her, the way Ambrose and Buford apparently had.

"Derricks and dinosaurs," Tate reflected.

"You might say there's a crude connection," Libby said.

Tate groaned at the bad pun, but then he laughed.

When they reached the ranch house, he drove around back instead of parking under the portico or in the garage, and Libby gasped with pleasure when she caught sight of the castle.

It was enchanting. Even magical.

"Wow," she said.

Tate shut off the truck, cast a rueful glance over the ornate structure and got out to help Hildie out of the backseat.

Set free, Hildie ran in circles, as excited as a pup, and when Ambrose and Buford dashed out of the castle and raced toward her, all former grudges were forgotten. She wag-tailed it over to meet them like they were long-lost friends.

The twins waved from separate windows in the castle, one at ground level and one in a turret.

"I've never seen anything like this," Libby said, shading her eyes from the presunset glare as she admired the oversized playhouse.

"Me, either," Tate said.

"Cometh thou in!" one of the little girls called from the tower.

Libby laughed. Tate shook his head and grinned.

Took Libby's hand just before he stooped to enter the castle, then pulled her in after him. The three dogs crowded in behind them, thick as thieves now that they weren't roommates anymore.

The inside was even more remarkable than the outside, with its fireplace and overhead beams and a stairway leading to the upper floor.

Libby wondered what Calvin would think of the place.

"It's so—big," she said slowly.

Ava nodded eagerly. "Dad says Audrey and I need to think about giving it to the community center, so other kids can play with it, too."

Libby glanced at Tate, saw that he was looking away.

"That's a very generous idea," she said, impressed.

"We haven't decided yet, though," Audrey put in, descending the stairs. "All Dad said was to *think* about it. He didn't say we actually had to *do* it."

Tate gestured toward the door. "I'm pretty sure supper is ready by now, ladies," he said. "Shall we?"

Audrey and Ava curtseyed grandly, spreading the sides of their cotton shorts like skirts.

"Yes, my lord," Ava said.

Tate laughed. *"Go,"* he said.

Both girls hurried out of the castle, the canine trio chasing after them, barking like dog-maniacs.

"'Yes, my lord'?" Libby teased, grinning, when the din subsided a little. "Now where would a pair of six-year-olds pick up an antiquated term like that?"

"Garrett probably taught them," Tate answered. "He likes to get under my skin any way he can."

Esperanza stood beside the patio table, laughing as she shooed the dogs out from underfoot and ordered the twins inside to wash their hands and faces.

Ambrose and Buford followed them, but Hildie paused, turned and scanned the yard, then trotted toward Libby with something like relief when she spotted her.

Touched, Libby bent to pat the dog's head.

Esperanza had outdone herself, preparing supper. There were tacos and enchiladas, seasoned rice and salad.

Libby enjoyed the food almost as much as the company, and she was sorry when the meal ended and Esperanza herded the twins into the house for their baths.

Overhead, the first stars popped out like diamonds studding a length of dark blue velvet, and the moon, a mere sliver of transparent light, looked as though it had come to rest on the roof of the barn.

Libby was totally content in those moments, with Tate at her side and Hildie lying at her feet, probably enjoying the warmth of the paving stones.

When Tate squeezed her hand, Libby squeezed back.

And then they drew apart.

Libby stood and began to gather and stack the dishes.

Tate got to his feet and helped.

Libby had forgotten how big the kitchen was, and as they stepped inside, she did her best not to stare as she and Tate loaded one of several dishwashers and cleaned up. The pool was visible on the other side of a thick glass wall, a brilliant turquoise, and looking at it, Libby couldn't help remembering the skinny-dipping episode.

She smiled. They'd been so innocent then, she and Tate.

So young.

And such passionate lovers.

Tate took her gently by the elbows and turned her to face him. Kissed her lightly on the forehead. "Thanks for saying 'yes' to tonight, Lib," he said. "It's good to have you back here."

Libby's throat tightened with sudden, searing emotion.

Tate cupped her chin his hand and tilted her face upward, looked into her eyes. "What?" he asked, very gently.

She shook her head.

He drew her close, held her tightly, his chin propped on the top of her head.

They were still standing there, minutes later, not a word having passed between them, when Esperanza returned, the front of her dress soaked, her lustrous, gray-streaked hair coming down from its pins. Barking and the laughter of little girls sounded in the distance.

"The dogs," Esperanza told Tate breathlessly, "they are in the bathtub, with the children."

Tate sighed in benign exasperation, then stepped away from Libby. "I'll be back in a few minutes," he said. As he passed Esperanza, he laid a hand on her shoulder, squeezed.

"These children," Esperanza fretted. "I am too old—"

Libby hurried over to help the other woman into a chair at the table. Brought her a glass of water.

"Are you all right?"

Esperanza hid her face in her hands, and her shoulders began to shake.

It took Libby a moment to realize the woman was laughing, not crying.

Relieved, Libby laughed, too.

Tears of mirth gleamed on Esperanza's smooth brown cheeks, and she used the hem of her apron to wipe them away.

Then, crossing herself, she said, "It is just like the old days, when the boys were young. Always in trouble, the three of them."

Tate returned, pausing in the doorway to take in the scene. Like most men, he was probably wary of female emotion unleashed.

Libby took in every inch of him.

Tate McKettrick, all grown up, was *still* trouble.

The kind it was impossible to resist.

CHAPTER FIVE

LIBBY WAS UP early the next morning, feeling rested even though she'd only had a few hours' sleep. After driving her home and walking her to her front door the night before, like the gentleman he could be but sometimes wasn't, Tate had kissed her again, and the effects of that tender, tentative touch of their mouths still tingled on her lips.

The sun was just peeking over the eastern horizon when she took Hildie for the first walk the poor dog had enjoyed since Ambrose and Buford had come to stay with them weeks before. It was good to get back into their old routine.

All up and down Libby's quiet, tree-lined street, lawn sprinklers turned, making that reassuring *chucka-chuck* sound, spraying diamonds over emerald-green grass. Hildie stopped for the occasional sniff at a fence post or a light pole or a patch of weeds—Julie, joint owner, along with Calvin, of a surprisingly active three-legged beagle named Harry, would have said the dog was reading her p-mail.

As Libby and Hildie passed Brent Brogan's house, a small split-level rancher with a flower-filled yard and a picket fence, Gerbera stepped out of the front door, bundled in a summery blue-print bathrobe, and hiked along the walk to get the newspaper.

Seeing Libby, Gerbera paused and grinned broadly. "Land sakes," she said, "I thought you'd given up on walking that old dog. Never see you go by here anymore."

Libby paused, holding Hildie's leash loosely. "I was fostering two puppies," she explained, "and walking the three of them at once was too much. I did manage to get the little buggers housebroken, though."

Gerbera cocked a thumb toward the white-shingled house behind her. "I've been after that nephew of mine to go on down to the shelter and get his kids a pet. Give them some responsibility and get them to unplug those earphones and wires from their heads once in a while. But Brent always says it would be him or me that wound up looking after any cat or dog we took in, once the kids lost interest."

"Well, if you manage to change his mind," Libby said, always ready to promote adoption when she knew a good home was a sure thing, "the kennels are usually full."

Gerbera got the rolled-up newspaper out of its box and tucked it under her arm. "You want to come in and have coffee? Nobody around but me. Kenda and V.J. are still sleeping, like kids do in the summertime, and Brent's been gone most of the night—that's why I stayed over."

Ironically, since she owned the Perk Up and java was her stock-in-trade, Libby drank very little coffee. It made her way too hyper. "We've got a ways to go to finish our walk," she said, with a nod toward the Lab. "Hildie and I both need all the exercise we can get. Another time?"

Gerbera smiled. "Sure enough," she agreed, before launching into a good-natured report. "Your mama called me last night and fussed at me something fierce for getting you all worked up, but I could tell she was pleased to get a visit from you and a good-lookin' McKettrick man."

Libby might have been annoyed with someone else, but Gerbera's intentions were always good. Hildie began to tug determinedly at the leash then, ready to go on, follow the route they always took, through several side streets, around the city park with its pretty gazebo-style bandstand, back home by way of the old movie house and the community center. "I think it was the good-lookin' McKettrick man that cheered her up, not me."

Something changed in Gerbera's face, something that went beyond the sparkle fading from her eyes and the way her mouth suddenly turned down a little at the corners. "Lordy," she said. "I swear, I get more forgetful every day!" She paused, drew in a breath. Her eyes were worried. "You don't *know*, do you? And how *would* you know?"

"Know what?" Libby asked, suddenly jittery, tightening her grip on Hildie's leash when the dog rounded the corner of the Brogans' fence ahead of her, pulling even harder now.

"Brent's been out there on the Silver Spur most of the night," Gerbera said slowly, "doing whatever he can to help. Libby, Pablo Ruiz is dead."

Libby gasped. Pablo was a friend, an institution in Blue River. He *couldn't* be dead. "What happened?" she managed to ask.

"There was an accident of some kind," Gerbera said, touching Libby's upper arm. "That's all I know."

An accident. Libby nodded, numbed by the news, thinking of Isabel, Pablo's wife, of Nico and Mercedes, their son and daughter, and the two nephews they'd brought to the United States, several years before, after Isabel's younger sister, Maria, had died of what turned out to be peritonitis.

Ricardo and Juan were teenagers now; honor students, well-mannered youths who stayed out of trouble; the kind of kids a community like Blue River was proud to call its own.

Nico, a close friend of Tate's, had once confided that when word of his aunt's death had reached them, he and Pablo had immediately set out for Mexico, expecting to find the boys living with neighbors in Maria's small village, or perhaps with their late father's family.

Instead, they'd been told that Ricardo and Juan had vanished, soon after Maria's death, and no one had seen them since.

There had been several more trips, Nico had said, each one a failure, before he and his father had finally tracked the children down to a nearby landfill. Both boys were filthy and half-starved, foraging for scraps of food, stealing and sleeping wherever they could find a safe place to lie down.

With a lot of help from Tate's cousin, Meg, a top executive with McKettrickCo at the time, Pablo had finally arranged for the boys to enter the country legally.

They had been almost feral in the beginning, those children, constantly afraid, stealing food, snarling and nipping when Pablo wrestled them into a tub and scrubbed them down on their first night in the United States. Eventually, Pablo and Isabel had won their trust, as well as their love.

What would happen to them now? What would happen to Isabel?

Libby's stomach did a slow, backward roll. "Oh, Gerbera," she whispered. "This is awful."

Gerbera nodded sadly. "I guess they look out for their own, though," she said. "Those McKettricks, I mean. And all the folks who work for them."

The reminder comforted Libby a little. It was true. Tate and his brothers would make sure Isabel and the boys lacked for nothing—that was the McKettrick way. And the long-term employees were like kin to each other.

Libby knew most of the dozen or so men who worked on the Spur year-round—everyone did. The married men lived with their wives and children in well-maintained trailers alongside one of the creeks, while the bachelors occupied a comfortable bunkhouse nearby. All of them got their mail and their groceries in Blue River, had their hair cut at the barber's or Valdeen's House of Beauty, came into the Perk Up on windy winter days for hot, strong coffee.

Gerbera shook her head, looking somber now. "I don't know what Isabel will do without that man. The kids, either. And now I wish I hadn't been the one to tell you, Libby. Brent specifically asked me not to 'broadcast' this until he was sure all the family had been informed."

Wanting to reassure her friend, Libby tried to smile. "Just about everybody in town owns a police scanner, so if Brent used his radio even once, the word's out." She spoke distractedly; half her mind had strayed to the Silver Spur; she couldn't help wondering how Tate and the children and Esperanza had taken the news. The other half was on Hildie, who was hunkered down and putting her full weight into the effort to drag her mistress back into motion.

"You'd better go on and I'd better get my old self ready for work," Gerbera said, noting the dog's antics with a sad smile.

Libby nodded, and she and Hildie were off again.

By the time they'd finished their walk almost an hour later, three different people had come to their front gates in bathrobes to ask if Libby had heard about Pablo Ruiz. They'd all gleaned the information from their police scanners, just as Libby had expected.

Nobody knew the exact cause; Chief Brogan had been closed-mouthed about it, when he'd called in the coroner. All they'd been able to gather was that there had been an accident on the ranch, a fatal one.

Most likely, the chief had made calls he didn't want half the county listening in on, over his cell phone.

Back home, Libby took a hasty shower—her breakfast was half a banana, since she didn't have much of an appetite—dressed in jeans and a sleeveless cotton top, bound her hair back in the usual no-fuss ponytail, and skipped the mascara and lip gloss.

While Hildie napped in a patch of sunlight in the kitchen, Libby let herself out the back door, crossed the yard and the alley, unlocked the rear entrance to the Perk Up and nearly jumped out of her skin when Calvin leaped out at her from behind a box of pop-on cup lids and yelled, "Boo!"

The fight-or-flight response stopped Libby in her tracks, one hand pressed to her pounding heart.

Julie peeked out of the kitchen, wearing an apron and holding a mixing bowl in the curve of one arm and a batter-coated spoon in the other. "For Pete's sake, Calvin," she scolded merrily, "how many times have I told you that you shouldn't scare the elderly?"

"You are just *too* funny," Libby said, directing the terse remark to her sister and a warm smile to her nephew.

Calvin had left his swim trunks and frog-floater at home that day, and he looked very handsome in his miniature chinos and short-sleeved plaid shirt. He was even wearing his good glasses, the ones with no adhesive tape spanning the bridge.

"Something big going on at playschool today?" Libby asked, setting her purse on a high shelf and reaching for an apron.

Calvin nodded eagerly. "We're getting a castle!" he crowed. "With turrets and everything!"

So, Libby thought, Tate's girls *had* decided to donate their birthday present to the community center. That was quick.

"You're getting a castle today?" she asked Calvin, wondering if Tate had intended to give away the massive toy all along; perhaps called to make the arrangements almost as soon as it arrived on the Silver Spur.

Calvin swelled out his chest. "No," he said. "Justin's mom is best friends with my teacher, Mrs. Oakland, and she told Justin's mom that it would take time and sweat and a lot of heavy equipment to move the thing."

Having seen the castle, Libby agreed. "Then why are you so dressed up?" she asked.

Calvin gave a long-suffering sigh. In his oft-expressed opinion, adults could be remarkably obtuse at times. "Because we're going to have a meeting at recess and elect a king," he said, very slowly, so his elderly aunt could follow. "I'm on the committee."

Libby and Julie exchanged looks. Julie smiled and shrugged as if to say, "That's what you get for asking a dumb question," but her eyes—pale violet that day because her T-shirt was purple— were solemn. She raised her eyebrows.

"Yes," Libby told Julie, an expert at sister-telepathy, "I heard."

"Heard what?" Calvin wanted to know, following as Libby headed for the front of the shop to fire up the various gadgets and switch the "Closed" sign to "Open."

"That you're campaigning to be king," Libby hedged. "Do you have your speech ready? Buttons and bumper stickers to pass out to the voters?"

"If nobody else is going to point out that kings are not elected officials," Julie said, still stirring the batter, "I will."

Calvin looked worried. "Buttons and bumper stickers?" he repeated.

Libby's heart melted. She bent to kiss the top of her nephew's blond head. "I was just teasing, big guy," she said. "And your mom is right. To my knowledge, there is not now and never has been one single king of Texas."

Calvin beamed. "Then I could be the first one!" he cried, delighted. Since he wasn't even in kindergarten yet and was already serving on committees, Libby figured he might just pull it off.

She smiled again, went to unlock the cash register and see if she had enough change on hand for the day.

"Calvin," Julie said, pointing, "sit down at that table in the corner, please, and watch for customers. If you see one approaching, let us know."

Calvin obeyed readily, and he sat up so straight and looked so vigilant that a whole new wave of tenderness washed over Libby.

Julie immediately maneuvered her toward the kitchen, where they could talk with some semblance of privacy.

"Gordon followed up his email with a phone call," she said, in a desperate whisper. "He's willing to take things slowly, but he *definitely* wants to get to know Calvin."

"Okay," Libby said. "What are you going to do?"

"Hide," Julie responded. "Calvin and Harry and I are going to hit the road. We'll be gone for as long as we have to—"

Libby held up both hands. "Julie! Are you *listening* to yourself? This is not something you can run away from. Besides, you have a house and a job and friends and—" she paused to clear her throat "—*family* in Blue River. Shouldn't you at least hear Gordon out?"

"Did Gordon hear *me* out when I told him I was expecting his baby?" Julie demanded, though she was careful to keep her voice down so Calvin wouldn't hear.

Libby knew there was no way to win this argument. Julie was just venting, anyway. "Did you hear about Pablo Ruiz?" Libby asked.

Julie's eyes widened. "No. What—?"

"He's dead, Jules. There was some kind of accident, yesterday or last night, on the Silver Spur—"

Julie gasped. "Not Pablo," she said, splaying the fingers of her right hand and pressing the palm to her heart.

Libby nodded sadly. "He was so proud of Mercedes," she whispered. Pablo and Isabel's only daughter would graduate from medical school in Boston in just a few weeks. She'd already been accepted into the internship program at Johns Hopkins; eventually, Mercedes wanted to become a surgeon.

Julie nodded, dashed at her wet eyes with the back of one floury hand, leaving white, sticky smudges on her cheek. "Do you remember how Pablo came and mowed our lawn every week, after Dad got too sick to leave the house?"

Libby did remember, of course, and she might have broken

down and cried herself, if Calvin hadn't yelled, at that precise moment, "I see one! I see a customer!"

Pablo's smiling face lingered in Libby's mind. She'd tried to pay him once, for taking care of the yard, and he'd refused with a shake of his head and a quiet, heavily accented, "Friends help friends. Mr. Remington, he helped our Mercedes with her schoolwork. Nico, too, when he was applying for scholarships. It is a privilege to do what little I can. "

"The scones!" Julie blurted out, suddenly remembering that they were done, and rushed to pull a baking sheet from the oven.

Despite an almost overwhelming sense of loss, there was work to be done. Libby straightened her shoulders and headed for the espresso machine again.

The customer Calvin had announced turned out to be Tate McKettrick, and he looked, as the old-timers liked to say, as if he'd been dragged backward through a knothole in the outhouse wall.

"I'm so sorry about Pablo," Libby said, wanting to go to him, take him in her arms, but uncertain of the reception she'd get if she did. The old sparks were definitely back, but she and Tate were older now and things were different. They had adult responsibilities—the shop for her, the children for Tate.

He was pale, he hadn't shaved—which only made him *more* attractive, in Libby's opinion—and his clothes, the same ones he'd worn the night before at supper, looked rumpled. What was he doing here, in the Perk Up, on the morning after he'd lost a dear friend and long-time employee?

He acknowledged her words of condolence with a nod. Shoved a hand through his hair. "It's either strong coffee," he said, "or a fifth of Jack Daniels. I figured the coffee would be a better choice."

"Sit down," Libby said, indicating the stools in front of the counter. "Where are the girls, Tate?"

He sat. Rested his forearms on the countertop. "With Esperanza. I haven't told them about Pablo yet—but of course they know something's going on..."

Calvin hurried over. "We're getting a *castle* at the community center, Mr. McKettrick," he announced exuberantly. "And I'm running for king."

"I heard about the castle," Tate said, with a wan smile. For a moment, his weary gaze connected with Libby's. "I didn't know there was going to be a special election, though."

"Only kids can vote," Calvin said importantly. "*Little* kids, who go to playschool. The big ones don't even know we're going to elect a king."

"Ah," Tate said, "a coup. I'm impressed."

"What's a koo?" Calvin asked.

Tate sighed.

"Never mind, Calvin," Libby interceded gently. "Go back to your table and watch for customers."

"Why?" He pointed to Tate. "We've already *got* one."

Tate chuckled at that, but it was a raw, broken sound, and hearing it made the backs of Libby's eyes burn.

"Calvin," she said evenly, but with affection, "I *said* never mind."

"Jeez," Calvin protested, flinging his arms out from his sides and then letting them fall back with a slight slapping sound. "People talk to me like I'm a *baby* or something, and I'm *four years old.*"

"Go figure," Tate said, with appropriate sympathy.

Libby set a cup of black coffee in front of Tate.

Calvin stalked back to his post to keep watch, clearly disgusted and probably still wondering what a coup was.

"That kid," Tate remarked, after taking an appreciative sip of the coffee, "is way too smart. Is he really only four—or is he forty, and short for his age?"

The way Tate said "kid," reflected Libby, was a 180 from the way Jubal Tabor did. Why was that?

"Tell me about it," Julie interjected before Libby could respond, as she came out of the kitchen and set a plate of fresh scones in front of Tate, along with a little bowl of butter pats in foil wrapping. She'd wiped the flour smears from her face at some point, and even with the pallor of shock replacing the usual pink in her cheeks, she was radiantly lovely. "Eat these, McKettrick. You look like hell warmed over. Twice."

"You always had a way with words, Jules," he replied. But, his big hands shaking almost but not quite imperceptibly, he opened two pats of butter, sliced a steaming scone in two, and smeared it on. "And with cooking."

Libby was seized by a sudden, fiercely irrational jealousy, gone as quickly as it came, fortunately. No matter how many new recipes she tried, how many chef shows and demonstrations she watched on satellite TV, taking notes and doing her best to follow instructions, when it came to cooking, she was doomed to be below average.

She was, she supposed, painfully ordinary.

Julie was the gypsy sister, with many and varied talents, of which baking was only one. She could sing, dance and act. Her scones were already drawing in customers, and if she ever made her float-away biscuits, folks would break down the door to get at them. She was great with kids—*all* kids, from her students to Calvin.

On top of all that, Julie had the kind of looks that made men stop and stare, even when they'd known her all their lives.

Paige, the baby of the family, was the smart one, the cool, competent one. And she was just as beautiful as Julie, though in a different way.

Libby bit her lower lip. As for her—well—she was just the *oldest*.

She was passably pretty, but she couldn't carry a tune, let alone perform in professional theater companies, singing and dancing in shows people paid money to see—spectacular productions of *Cats* and *Phantom of the Opera* and *Kiss Me, Kate,* as Julie had done periodically, during her college years.

She didn't shine in a life-and-death emergency, like Paige.

And why was she even thinking thoughts like this, when Pablo Ruiz, a man she'd liked and deeply respected, had just died—and long before his time, too?

"I don't see a single customer!" Calvin reported, his voice ringing across the shop.

"Keep looking," Julie counseled. "There's got to be one out there somewhere."

Libby was still watching Tate. Even wan and worn, with his dark beard growing in and his hair furrowed because he'd probably been raking his fingers through it all night, as all the ramifications of Pablo's death unfolded, he was a sight to stop her breath and make her heart skitter.

Here was *her* claim to fame, she thought gloomily.

She'd been dumped by Tate McKettrick.

For six months after the breakup, people had sent her cheery little cards and notes, most acting out of kindness, a few taking a passive-aggressive pleasure in her downfall. Her father had been diagnosed with pancreatic cancer by then—the dying by inches part would come later—but no one had mentioned her dad, in person or on paper. They'd written or said things like, "You'll find someone else when the time is right" and "It wasn't meant to be" and "What doesn't kill you makes you stronger."

Like hell. She'd been blindsided by Tate's betrayal. Fractured by it.

And here she was, letting him back in her life when she knew—*knew* what he could do to her.

While Libby was reconciling herself to reality, Julie collected her purse, jingled her car keys to attract Calvin's attention. "Time for playschool, buddy," she said. She squeezed Tate's shoulder as she passed him and promised Libby she'd be back in no time. If she needed scones for the midmorning rush—*if* she needed scones?— there were four dozen in the kitchen; Julie had baked them at home the night before, as promised.

As soon as Julie and Calvin had gone, Tate got off his stool, walked to the door, turned the "Open" sign to "Closed," and twisted the knob to engage the dead bolt.

Libby didn't utter a word of protest. She took the stool next to his, once he'd come back to the counter, and leaned his way a little so their upper arms just barely touched.

"Want to tell me what happened, cowboy?" she asked, very softly.

"Yeah," Tate said, pushing away his plate, now that he'd eaten the scones. He didn't meet her gaze, though. He just stared off into the void for a long time, saying nothing, though Libby saw his throat work a couple of times, while he struggled to control his emotions.

Libby simply waited.

"The dogs started raising hell, about half an hour after I went to bed," he told her, when he was ready. "They woke up Audrey and Ava, of course, since all four of them were bunking together. I went to see what was going on—I thought there was an intruder in the house or something, the way those mutts carried on. As soon as I opened the door to the girls' room, the pups shot past me, baying like bloodhounds picking up a strong scent. They ran down the stairs and straight to the kitchen—by the time I got there, they were hurling themselves at the back door like they'd bust it down to get out if they had to." He paused, drank the dregs of his coffee, but stopped Libby with a touch to her arm when she started to get up and go around the counter to get the pot and pour him a refill. After a long time, he continued. "Esperanza was awake by then, too, of course, and she kept the kids and the dogs inside while I went out to have a look around. I saw that the lights were on in the barn, and I'd turned them off after I checked on the horses an hour earlier, but I figured one of the ranch hands was out there, meaning to bunk in the hayloft. The younger ones do that sometimes, when they've had a fight with a wife or a girlfriend or gotten a little too drunk to go home."

He paused again then, swallowed hard, gazed bleak-eyed into that same invisible distance.

Once more, Libby bided her time. For Tate, not a talkative man, this wasn't just an accounting of what had taken place, it was a verbal epic, a virtual diatribe. Normally, he probably didn't say that much in half a day, never mind a few short minutes.

"I was pretty sure the dogs were just skittish because they're pups, and in a new place with new people," Tate went on presently. "They'd probably heard a rig drive in, I figured, and felt called upon to bark their damn fool heads off. I went outside, and I saw Pablo's company truck parked between the barn and that copse of oak trees."

Libby waited, seeing the scene Tate described as vividly as if she'd been there herself.

"It wasn't unusual for Pablo to turn up at the barn, even late at night—he didn't need much sleep and since he always had some project going on at his place, he stopped by often to borrow tools, equipment, things like that." Tate sighed. "I checked the barn, and Pablo wasn't inside, though all the horses were jumpy as hell, and, like I said, the lights were on. I headed for the truck, and I was nearly run down by a big paint stallion—that horse came out of nowhere.

"Pablo and I had talked about buying the stud if it went up for sale. We were going to turn him loose on the range, let him breed and see if any of the mares threw color—"

Libby touched Tate's arm, felt a shudder go through him. "Take your time," she said, very quietly.

"Pablo *had* bought that stallion," he went on, after swallowing a couple of times. "He picked him up from the buyer and brought him over, probably planning on leaving him in the holding pen until morning, when we could have the vet come and look the paint over before—"

Libby closed her eyes for a moment. By then, she'd guessed what was coming next.

Tate looked tormented. It seemed like a long time passed before he went on. "I found Pablo on the ground, behind the trailer, trampled to death."

Sorrow swelled in Libby's throat, aching there. Such accidents weren't uncommon, even among experienced men like Pablo Ruiz. Horses—especially stallions—were powerful animals, easily spooked and always unpredictable.

"I'm sorry, Tate," Libby said. "I'm so sorry."

He nodded, made a visible effort to center himself in the present moment.

The blue of his eyes deepened to the color of new denim and, very briefly, Libby pondered the mystery of why a loving God would give dark, thick lashes like that to a man instead of some deserving woman who would have appreciated them.

Like her, for instance.

Tate rose from the stool, stood so close to Libby that she could feel the heat of his skin, even through his clothes. She felt an irrational and almost overwhelming need to lead Tate to some private place, where the two of them could lie down, hold each other until things made sense again.

"How's Isabel?" Libby asked.

Tate had his truck keys out, but he hadn't moved toward the door. His concern for Pablo's widow was almost palpable. "She'll be all right in time, I guess," he said. "Esperanza checks on her every so often. Nico's been out of the country on business, but he'll be here as soon as he can."

Libby nodded.

Tate hesitated, then touched her face lightly with the backs of the fingers of his right hand. "Wish I could hold you," he said.

Talk about that old-time feelin'.

Libby choked up, and her eyes burned. "Probably not the best idea," she said, when she could manage the words. "You need to get some rest, and I have a business to run."

Tate dropped his hand to his side. "Yeah," he said. "I'd better get out of here. Esperanza's wonderful with the kids, but she can't say no to them. By now, they may have conscripted her and half the ranch hands to dig a moat around the castle."

Libby smiled slightly at the picture his words brought to mind, followed him to the door, and then outside, into the hot, dry sunshine beating down on the sidewalk and buckling the asphalt in the road.

"You'll call if you need anything?" she said, when Tate opened the door of his dusty truck to get behind the wheel.

He arched an eyebrow, and one corner of his mouth quirked upward, so briefly that Libby knew she might have imagined it. "You walked right into that one," he said. Then he leaned forward, kissed her briefly on the mouth, and got into his truck. "See you soon," he said.

See you soon.

"Come over and have supper with me tonight," she said, because she'd had to let go of Tate McKettrick one too many times in her life, and this time she couldn't. "Six o'clock," she hastened to add. "Bring the kids."

Idiot, Libby thought. *Why don't you just jump up onto the running board of that truck like some bimbo with hay in her hair and invite him to join you in an appearance on the* Jerry Springer *show?*

Maybe the episode could be called, "Women who chase after men who stomped on their hearts."

Tate flashed that legendary grin, the one folks claimed had been passed down through his family since the original patriarch, old Angus McKettrick, had broken his first heart back in the 1800s.

"Six o'clock," he confirmed. "We'll see about the kids."

Still ridiculously flustered, Libby finally registered that a number of her regular customers had gathered inside the Perk Up since she'd stepped outside with Tate, and they were peering out through the window as he drove away.

Embarrassed to be part of a spectacle, she hurried inside.

She could close up at five, she was thinking, hit the deli counter next door at Almsted's for cold chicken and potato salad and—whatever. She would improvise.

In the meantime, there were orders to fill.

What did kids like to eat? Libby wondered, her mind busy planning supper while her hands made lattes and frappes and iced mochas by rote. Hot dogs? Hamburgers?

The regulars had barely left when a tour bus full of senior citizens pulled up. They were on their way to San Antonio, Libby learned, to see the Alamo.

It was hectic, juggling all those orders, but Libby managed it, and stood waving in the doorway as the bus pulled away.

Long before Julie got back, sans King Calvin, the scones plus four bags of cookies hastily purchased at Almsted's were gone.

"What took you so long?" Libby asked, but she smiled a little as she waggled a handful of cash just plucked from the register.

"I had to walk Harry and put a load of towels in the washer," Julie answered, her eyes widening at the sight of all that loot. "What did you do, jimmy open an ATM?"

BONE-TIRED AND sick to his soul, but looking forward to seeing Libby again just the same, Tate made a point of passing Brent's office on the way out of town.

Beth Anne Spales, the dispatcher/secretary the chief had inherited from a long succession of predecessors, stood in the small parking lot, watering droopy pink flowers in terra-cotta pots. She wore a floppy sun hat and gardening gloves, and waved when she recognized Tate's truck.

His mind tripped back to last night.

He'd called Brent as soon as he'd found Pablo's body, then he'd concentrated on rounding up the agitated stallion, shutting it up in the corral. The chief had arrived quickly, as had the county coroner, whose regular job was running the Blue River Funeral Home.

The task of telling Isabel what had happened to Pablo fell to Tate.

He'd driven over to the house by the creek, unsurprised to find lights burning in the windows, late as it was. Isabel would have waited up for Pablo; by then, she'd know something was wrong.

Except for telling Garrett and Austin about the car accident that had taken their parents' lives, and telling Libby that he'd gotten another woman pregnant and meant to marry her, relaying to Isabel the news that Pablo was dead was probably the hardest thing Tate had ever had to do. Tiny, quiet, dignified Isabel had *yowled* when he told her, like an animal caught in the steel teeth of a trap.

Now, in the bright light of a new day, Tate pulled up to the only stoplight in town, which happened to be red and would be for a while, since the timing device had quit working on New Year's Eve of 1999, thus convincing the nervous types that Y2K, with cataclysmic results, was indeed upon them. He rested his forehead against the steering wheel while he waited, breathing slowly and deeply.

He felt sick.

Someone honked a horn behind him, and Tate sat up straight, frowning when he saw that the light was still red. Glancing in the rearview mirror, he spotted Brent, driving the squad car.

"Pull over," Brent instructed, through that damn bullhorn of his.

Tate cursed under his breath and maneuvered the truck into the bank parking lot to his right. Buzzed down his window.

"I don't know what my crime was," he said, as Brent approached the driver's side door, "but it sure as hell wasn't speeding."

Brent flashed him the Denzel grin, though he looked even worse than Tate felt. "You shouldn't be on the road in the condition you're in," the chief said. "You're wiped."

"You shouldn't, either," Tate replied.

Brent sighed. Tucked his thumbs into that honking service belt of his. His badge looked dull in the bright light of day. Resting one foot on Tate's running board, he took off his sunglasses and squinted at his friend, looking worried. "You doin' okay, here,

McKettrick?" he asked. "I know you were close to all the Ruizes, *especially* Pablo. You must be pretty broken up."

"I'll be all right," Tate said. *Eventually.*

"Isabel's in a big hurry to hold the funeral and move herself and those boys in with her sister, out in L.A.," Brent said. "Did she tell you that?"

"No," Tate answered. Thinking of the Ruiz house standing empty left him feeling as though he'd been punched in the gut. The place had been a second home to him and his brothers while they were growing up. Along with Nico, they'd fished and splashed in the cold water of the creek, stuffed themselves with apricots from Pablo's fruit trees, "camped out" in the Ruiz living room in sleeping bags. "No," he said again. "She didn't say anything about that. Seems like a pretty sudden decision."

Brent nodded. "It's her life," he said. "I just hope she's not being too hasty."

Tate agreed, and the two men parted ways.

Tate pondered Isabel's plans to move off the ranch as he drove toward home, navigating the familiar country roads by instinct. He nearly stopped off on the way to remind the woman that there was no hurry to clear out. He'd been planning on deeding the place over to Pablo anyhow, as soon as the old man retired.

In the end, though, Tate decided it was Isabel's own business if she wanted to live elsewhere. For all he knew, she'd hated living in the country all along, and here was her chance to live in a city.

When he pulled in next to the barn at home, Audrey and Ava and both dogs rushed him, were on him as soon as he stepped down out of the rig.

"Hey," he said.

"Can we ride our birthday ponies?" Audrey asked.

"Please?" Ava added.

Tate considered, decided a ride would be a good thing for everybody. He'd have to keep an eye on the pups, make sure they didn't try to weave back and forth between the horses' legs.

He'd planned on a few hours of shut-eye before going to supper at Libby's, but if they weren't out on the range too long, he and the kids, they could still make it.

"All right," he said, "saddle up."

The twins saddled their ponies with minimal help, having had lots of practice tacking up Bamboozle, while Tate threw a saddle on an old gelding named Bluejack.

Audrey and Ava were already outside, mounted on their matching "birthday" ponies, when Tate ducked his head to ride out through the barn door.

It was only then that he remembered the paint stallion, still in the holding pen at the back of the barn.

"Stay clear of the pen," he called to the girls. The steel fence surrounding the holding pen was twelve feet high, the poles set in concrete, and there wasn't more than six inches between the slats, though Ambrose or Buford might be able to dig their way under, he supposed. It didn't seem likely that they would.

Over the years, that pen had held bulls and many another stallion—some of them pretty determined critters. The steel surround had always held.

Still, *this* stallion was hell-born, a killer.

The huge animal tossed his head back and forth, snorted and pawed at the ground with his right front hoof. He looked ready to charge that fence, steel or no steel, concrete fittings or none.

A shudder ran down Tate's spine as he caught up to his daughters and rode on the side nearest the stallion.

"Is that the horse that stomped on Mr. Ruiz and crushed his heart?" Audrey asked, her blue eyes huge as she looked up at Tate. Her golden pony pranced fitfully beneath her, and no wonder—the poor little filly was a fifth the size of that stallion, if not less.

"That's the horse," Tate confirmed, his voice grating past his throat, fit to draw blood in the process. "Who told you Mr. Ruiz's heart was crushed?"

"I heard Esperanza telling somebody on the phone," Audrey said. "She didn't know I was listening."

"I see," Tate replied.

Ava looked back as they moved farther and farther from the pen and the pacing, whinnying stud, churning up clouds of dust.

"Why is he still on the Silver Spur," Ava asked reasonably, "if he hurt Mr. Ruiz?"

"Some of the ranch hands say he ought to be shot," Audrey observed worriedly. "Because he's a demon and won't ever be any different."

Tate knew, of course, about the talk going around the bunkhouse and the trailers along the creek, but he also knew Pablo wouldn't have wanted the horse destroyed. No, Pablo would have said the stud was wild and ought to be let out to run the range, siring foals and making a legend of himself.

The decision wasn't Tate's alone—the paint had killed a man, and the authorities would have a say in whether the animal lived or died. If the choice was his to make, Tate would have agreed with Pablo.

Some horses weren't meant to be tamed, just like some people.

"For now," Tate told his daughters solemnly, "here's all you need to know about that stud. Stay away from him, and keep your dogs away, too."

Ava looked back over one shoulder. "He doesn't look very happy," she said.

"I don't imagine he is," Tate agreed. "Do I have your word? You'll both stay as far from that stud as you can, no matter what?"

Both girls lifted their right hand, as though giving a oath.

"Unless we don't have any other choice, of course," Audrey said, after Tate had bent to open the wire-and-post gate so the three of them could ride through, headed for the range.

"Audrey," Tate said sternly, "I want your word—as a McKettrick."

Audrey rolled her eyes, then nodded.

Ava said, "You have my word."

Tate put the stallion from his mind then, rode with his girls and found that it cleared his head and his soul, just like always.

An hour later, back at the house, he dragged himself up to his bedroom, kicked off his boots and collapsed facedown on the bed, hoping to catch a little sleep before going back to town to have supper with Libby.

The twins joined him, and so did the dogs.

And just the same, he slept like a dead man.

CHAPTER SIX

DURING THE NEXT LULL, Libby locked up the shop for an hour and drove her car to the auto shop for the exhaust system repair, Julie following in her pink bomb to provide feminine moral support and a ride back.

Libby left the Impala with a mechanic and joined Julie in the Mary-Kay-mobile. She'd paid the cost in advance, using the profits from the coffee, scone and cookie sales she'd made to the people from the tour bus, but if the car needed extra work, especially something critical, she would have to use a credit card after all.

Julie reached over and patted her arm. "Don't worry," she said. "Gordon's check cleared this month. I can help you out if you need it."

"Thanks," Libby murmured, feeling like a charity case. "But doesn't that money go into Calvin's college account?"

"Most of the time," Julie said, checking all the mirrors before she backed out of her parking space. "It's no big deal, Lib. Pay me back when you can."

Relief coursed through Libby, but it didn't soothe all the places that ached. Things had seemed so wonderfully ordinary that morning when she'd taken Hildie out for her walk. Two kisses from Tate McKettrick the night before and she'd been walking on air.

The grass had been greener, the sky bluer.

Impossible things had begun to seem possible.

And then Gerbera had told her about Pablo Ruiz's death.

"Do you ever feel," she began, "as though no matter what you do, it's never going to be enough?"

Julie pulled right back into the parking space she'd just left, popped the elderly Cadillac into Park and shut off the engine. "Was that the voice of a depressed woman I just heard?" she asked. She spoke quietly, but at the same time she clearly meant to get a straight answer.

"I'm not exactly *depressed*," Libby said, thinking of Calvin getting out of playschool soon, and the shop closed for business and Hildie needing to be let out into the backyard for a little while. "*Overwhelmed* is more like it."

"Oh," Julie said. "Well, yeah, I know all about overwhelmed."

"I don't know how you do it," Libby said, with true admiration. "Raising Calvin alone, holding down a teaching job—"

"We all do what we have to," Julie replied when Libby fell silent, out of steam. "And I've wondered the same thing about you now and again, sister dear. You run the Perk Up by yourself most of the time, robbing Peter to pay Paul, and then there's Marva giving a grandstand performance every couple of weeks. Add on the way you always foster the overflow from the animal shelter and, hello, you make Wonder Woman look like an underachiever."

Libby blinked, surprised. "Wonder Woman?" she echoed, with an effort at a smile.

"You're too hard on yourself, Lib," Julie went on, after nodding once, with conviction. "No matter what comes at you, you just keep on trucking. I happen to admire that quality in a sister, or anybody else."

"Well," Libby responded, honestly puzzled, "what *else* can I do?"

Julie snapped her fingers. "See?" she said. "It doesn't even *occur* to you to quit. Do you think everybody's like that? My God, Lib, when Dad was sick, you were always there for him and for Paige and me, too. You were unstoppable, even after a body blow that would have dropped a lesser woman to her knees."

The body blow, of course, was Tate's defection to the Cheryl camp.

"That was pretty bad," Libby admitted, remembering. Bad?

She'd lost fifteen pounds and a lot of sleep, developing dark circles under her eyes. She'd dated a string of losers, too, ready to settle for Mr. Wrong if only to spite Tate, because there was only one Mr. Right and he was taken.

Fortunately, Julie and Paige had intervened, threatening to lock her up in a closet, bound with duct tape, so she wouldn't be able to ruin her life before she came to her senses. For good measure, they'd planned to spoon Ben & Jerry's into her until she regained every pound she'd lost and ten besides.

Julie leaned far enough to tap lightly on Libby's temple with an index finger and ask, "What's really going on in there?"

Back when he was healthy, their dad had done that whenever one of his daughters got too introspective, or came down with a case of what he called "the sullens."

"Tate's coming to dinner tonight, at my place," Libby said. "And that pretty much cinches it: it's time to book a suite at the Home for Stupid Women and learn the secret handshake."

Julie erupted with laughter. "Forget it," she said. "The waiting list is probably way too long."

Libby laughed, too—as she wiped away tears with the heel of one palm. "Just my luck," she said, sniffling. She straightened her shoulders, raised her chin. "We'd better get going. Calvin will be through soon."

Julie started up the car again, and they were on their way. "There's one bright spot in all this," she told Libby.

"Oh, yeah? What would that be?"

"You'll get to have sex."

"Sex?"

"You know," Julie said, with a sly grin. "That fun, sweaty, noisy, slippery thing men and women do together, usually but not always in a bed?"

"Tonight isn't about sex, it's about *dinner*," Libby said, turning red. "He's bringing the kids, the dogs and maybe even the housekeeper."

"You know damn well you're going to end up in bed with Tate McKettrick, sooner or later," Julie insisted. "And my money's on 'sooner.' Whenever the two of you are together, the air crackles."

"And you think I should just *go for it,* after all that happened?"

"That's exactly what I think. A lot of men aren't worth a second chance, but Jim and Sally McKettrick's boy? Definitely the one to bet on."

"The sisterly thing to say would be, 'Stay away from him. He hurt you once, and he'll hurt you again,'" Libby admonished.

"If that sister happened to be a cynic, maybe."

They reached the community center, and Julie parked the car. Calvin was on the playground, with a flock of other kids, engaged in a game of tag. Mrs. Oakland supervised, carrying a clipboard and wearing a whistle on a string around her neck.

"You're telling me you're not a cynic?" Libby countered. "You, the woman who's about to skip town to avoid a confrontation with her son's father?"

Julie sighed deeply, her hands tight on the steering wheel, watching Calvin with her heart in her eyes. "I'm not going anywhere," she said, very quietly. "Time to face the music." Then she turned to look at Libby. "And how was my plan 'cynical'?"

"Think about it," Libby said. "You didn't even consider the fact that Gordon might have turned over a new leaf, now that he's married and maybe even ready to settle down for real. You cared enough once to make a baby with him, but now you just assume he'll be nothing but trouble. If that isn't cynical, I don't know what is."

Julie smiled smugly. "Well, listen to you, Libby Remington," she said, as Calvin spotted them, spoke to Mrs. Oakland and, when the woman nodded her permission, ran toward the car. "Admitting it's possible for a man to *change*. Even one like, say, *Tate McKettrick*."

"Shut up," Libby said.

"No possible way," Julie retorted. "And watch how you talk to me, or I won't help you cook a gourmet dinner that will have a certain dark-haired cowboy begging for your hand in marriage."

Libby's eyes widened. "You'd do that? *Prepare a gourmet dinner just to make me look good?*"

Calvin reached the car and lugged open the back door to scramble onto the seat.

"Of course I would," Julie said, before turning to smile at Calvin and ask him how his day went.

"I'm ahead in the polls!" he exulted.

"That's it," Julie answered. "No more *Meet the Press* for you, buddy."

Libby laughed. "Here he is now," she quipped, looking over her shoulder at Calvin, who was busy buckling himself into his car seat. "The man who would be king."

"WHAT WOULD YOU say to a partnership?" Libby asked Julie, later that afternoon, the two of them practically lost in the wilderness of pots, pans and bowls that was Libby's kitchen. Instead of re-opening the shop, they'd raided Julie's cupboards and freezer for the makings of dinner, stopping at the supermarket for the few things she didn't already have.

"A partnership?" Julie echoed, dipping a spoon into a kettle of pesto sauce to do a taste test. "What kind of partnership?"

"At the Perk Up," Libby said, realizing too late what she was asking of her sister and wishing she hadn't brought the subject up at all. It wasn't as if the place were a runaway moneymaker—now that she had to compete with the famous franchise, she was oper-ating in the red, for the most part.

Calvin's laugh, accompanied by a lot of happy barking from Hildie, came through the screen door.

"Never mind," Libby backpedaled, embarrassed. "It was just a thought."

"How about sharing that thought with me?" Julie inquired. She'd changed into shorts and a pink top while they were at her place, and her eyes were a silvery gray.

"It seems silly now."

"I can do silly," Julie grinned. "In fact, it's a way of life. Keeps me sane. Talk to me, Lib."

"I was just thinking—well, your scones are so popular, and you're not working at the insurance agency this summer, so…"

"Oh," Julie said, getting it. She puffed out her cheeks, the way she always did when something surprised her and she needed to stall for a few seconds so she could think.

"I told you it was silly."

"We could sell lots of other things besides scones," Julie mused, as if Libby hadn't spoken. "Soup and sandwiches and salads. Change the name of the place, serve high tea—"

"What's wrong with the Perk Up?" Libby interrupted, thrown off. She'd done a lot of brainstorming to come up with that moniker.

"Well," Julie said, with kind forbearance, "it's not very original, now, is it?"

Libby sagged a little, around the shoulders. "I guess not," she admitted. Then, "Wait a second. You're actually considering my offer?"

"Of course I'd go back to teaching in the fall," Julie said. "That will mean cutting back to part-time here, doing the baking at night and on weekends. But, yes. I think the idea has merit."

"You do?"

Julie grinned, glanced at the stove clock. Wiped her hands on her apron before taking it off. "Yep," she said. "Calvin and I are out of here. My, how time flies when you're making pesto."

"You're going to *leave?*"

Julie widened her eyes and mugged a little. "Uh, *yeah,*" she said. "The salad is in the refrigerator. There are hot dogs, in case the kids don't like pasta. You do know how to heat hot dogs, don't you?" After Libby tossed her a look, she went on, undaunted. "All you have to do is boil the noodles and zap the pesto in the microwave and *voilà!* Pasta à la Julie."

"Stay," Libby pleaded.

Julie ignored her, walking to the back door and whistling through her teeth. "Yo, Calvin!" she called. "Time to boogie!"

"Julie—"

Julie turned, her arms folded. "You can do this, Lib," she said firmly. "Go change your clothes. And—hey—why don't you go wild and wear some lip gloss?"

AROUND FIVE O'CLOCK, showered, semi-rested and shaved, Tate studied his reflection in his bathroom mirror. "What the hell are you doing, McKettrick?" he asked himself, resting his hands on the countertop and leaning in.

There was no time to come up with an answer—a light rap

sounded at his door. "Are you decent?" Audrey called, from the other side.

Tate chuckled. Was he decent? Well, that depended on who you asked.

He adjusted the collar of his cotton shirt. He'd almost gone with a suit, one of the tailored numbers left over from his days with McKettrickCo, but in the end, he'd opted for his usual jeans and plain shirt. He didn't want to seem too eager, and besides, he'd be going to a good friend's funeral in a couple of days. One suit in a week was plenty.

"Who wants to know?" he teased.

"Audrey McKettrick, that's who!" his daughter yelled in reply.

"*And* Ava McKettrick!" cried the other daughter, not to be outdone.

"Come in," he said.

The door flew open and the twins and their dogs crowded through the gap.

"Uncle Garrett is on his way," Audrey reported.

"Uncle Austin, too," Ava added.

"I know," Tate answered, steering the pair and their faithful animal companions into the larger space that was his room. He sat down on the side of the bed to pull on his boots.

"Are they coming because they want to go to Mr. Ruiz's funeral?" Audrey asked.

"Yes," Tate said simply. He'd called them both, late the night before, to tell them what had happened. Pablo had been like a member of the family, and he'd really stepped up when their folks were killed. For a while, he'd functioned as a sort of surrogate father, and Isabel had mothered them as much as they'd allow.

Ava hiked herself up to perch on the bed beside him, and Audrey took the other side. "It's sad when somebody dies," Ava said solemnly.

"Yeah," Tate agreed. "It's real sad." Since the twins hadn't been born yet when their McKettrick grandparents passed away, he wondered what, if anything, they knew about death.

"Our goldfish died," Audrey confided. "Mom flushed them."

"Things like that happen," Tate said.

"They don't flush *people,* do they?" Ava asked, clearly concerned. "When they die, I mean?"

Tate wrapped an arm around both his girls, held them close for a moment. "No," he said gently. "They don't flush people."

"People are too *big* to flush, ninny," Audrey told her sister, leaning around Tate to look at Ava.

"No name calling," Tate ordered. Then he noticed that the girls were still in their playclothes. "Better clean up your acts," he said, "if you want to go to Libby's with me."

"Esperanza is cooking," Ava told him. "She says Mrs. Ruiz will need to have lots of food on hand, with so many people coming to visit."

"I imagine that's so," Tate said. "But what does it have to do with supper at Libby's?"

"We want to stay here and help Esperanza," Audrey replied.

"She keeps crying," Ava added. "I bet she's used a *million* tissues today."

"Plus," Audrey said, "Uncle Garrett and Uncle Austin will be here."

"Right," Tate acknowledged, giving the pair another simultaneous squeeze and clearing his throat before standing up. "It's possible, you know, that Esperanza might want to be alone for a while. And your uncles probably won't show up for hours yet."

"Esperanza needs us," Ava insisted, her eyes huge with a sorrow she felt but didn't understand, even though Tate had explained as best he could.

"We'll see," Tate said.

When they'd all trooped down to the kitchen, he saw that Esperanza was indeed cooking—with a vengeance. Fresh vegetables and stacks of her homemade tortillas, among other things, all but covered the center island, and lard smoked in a skillet on the stove.

Esperanza sniffled once, approached and straightened his shirt collar. "You look much better," she said.

He grinned. "Thanks," he replied, well aware of the girls crowding in behind him. "How about you, Esperanza? Are you doing all right?"

"When I am busy," she responded, "then I am also all right."

He nodded; he understood that particular tactic well.

"The girls," the housekeeper said. "You will let them stay?"

Tate raised one eyebrow. "If that's what you really want, sure."

Esperanza nodded. "It *is* what I really want," she confirmed.

Tate believed her. "All this food is for the Ruizes?" he asked, indicating the mountains of produce and other edibles. "They won't have room for all this—their house is pretty small."

Esperanza smiled moistly. "Isabel and her children will have much company," she said, "and anyway, Garrett and Austin are coming. They are always hungry when they've been away from home."

He leaned a little, placed a kiss on the top of Esperanza's head. "I won't be late," he said. As he passed the stove, he pushed the skillet back off the flames.

Ambrose and Buford would have gone along for the ride—they got hair all over the legs of his jeans letting him know they were more than willing—but he decided to leave them at home, since the girls were staying behind with Esperanza.

Before heading for the garage, he raided Esperanza's flower garden for a handful of pink daisies and a few sprigs of that white stuff florists always added to bouquets.

Instead of driving the truck, as he almost always did, he took his green Jaguar—the thing had been sitting in the garage for months, gathering dust. Maybe he'd blow out the carburetor on the last straight stretch before town.

And maybe not.

Brent Brogan—aka Denzel—was an equal-opportunity lawman. Best friends or not, he wouldn't hesitate to pull Tate over and write him a whopping ticket if he caught him speeding.

Especially in a Jag.

Tate thought of his daughters, and how they'd grow up with one parent—Cheryl—if he got killed being stupid on the empty road.

He stayed within the speed limit, all the way to Libby's place.

The flowers were starting to wilt, lying there on the passenger seat; he picked them up carefully, wishing he'd taken the time to stick them in a fruit jar full of water or something.

You're stalling, McKettrick, he told himself, sitting there in his too-fancy car in front of Libby's *not*-so-fancy house.

Libby appeared on the porch, wearing another sundress, this

one pale yellow. The light was just right, and he could see through the fabric. She'd be embarrassed if she knew, so he wouldn't tell her. Anyhow, he enjoyed the view.

"Where are Esperanza and the girls?" she called, taking a few steps forward and shielding her eyes from the sun with one hand.

"They're busy tonight," Tate answered. "I like your dress." *And what's under it.*

"Are those flowers?" she asked, and then blushed.

"I believe so," Tate joked, checking out the yard as he came through the gate. He didn't give a rat's ass about the overgrown lawn, but if he kept staring at Libby the way he had been, she might realize her dress was transparent and put on something else, thus ruining his whole night. "When was the last time somebody mowed the grass?"

"I keep meaning to get to it—"

Tate climbed the steps, bent his head to kiss her lightly on the mouth and handed over the flowers. "The lawn looks fine, and so do you," he murmured.

She laid a hand on his chest. "The neighbors might be watching," she whispered.

"Well, if they have that much free time," Tate replied, "one of them should have mowed your lawn by now."

Libby took his hand, pulled him inside.

"I'll just put these flowers in a vase and warm up the pesto sauce," she said, walking away.

His gaze fell to her delectable backside and got riveted there.

His groin tightened, and he wished he'd worn a hat so he'd have something to hold in front of his crotch until his hard-on went down.

Better yet, he thought, he could peel that see-through dress off over Libby's head, lay her down on a bed or ease her up against a wall and lick every golden inch of her and put the hard-on where it belonged.

This is not helping, said the voice of reason.

But Tate was well beyond reason by then.

And furthermore, he wasn't hungry. Not for pesto sauce, anyhow.

Light poured through the kitchen window as Libby stood at the sink, filling a vase from the faucet for the flowers. She might as well have been stark naked.

Hildie, her dog, gave him a sleepy look from the hooked rug in front of the refrigerator and then sighed and closed her eyes to get some more shut-eye.

Tate stepped behind a high-backed chair and pulled it in front of him. He just got harder, though, when Libby turned, smiling, and approached to set the flowers in the center of the table.

Her smile lost a little of its sparkle. She ducked her head a little, to look up into his face. "Is something wrong?"

Lots of things were wrong.

There was a damn plastic castle in his yard, and it might be weeks before he could get it moved to the community center.

Cheryl would be back in a few days, full of fresh poison, and she'd make a point of whisking Audrey and Ava back to town ASAP, because she knew it twisted his insides into a knot when they left the Silver Spur.

And Pablo Ruiz was dead.

He lowered his gaze, not trusting himself to speak, not wanting Libby to see what was in his eyes.

She rounded the table, pushed the chair aside, and put her arms around him.

Her eyes widened when she felt his erection, and fetching pink color bloomed in her cheeks. "Yikes," she said.

Tate chuckled. "'Yikes'?"

"I'd forgotten how—big you get. When you're—when—oh, God, why do I even *try* to talk?" Her face was on fire now.

So was his body.

He placed his hands on either side of her waist. "It's okay, Lib," he said, grinning in spite of all the sadness and hopeless need inside him. "We're both adults, here. And *big* isn't a word most men are offended by—not in that context, anyway."

Libby was wearing her hair down that night, instead of in a ponytail, and she swept it back off her shoulders—a gesture so inherently feminine that Tate's condition immediately got worse.

Or better.

Her eyes misted over. "What are we doing?" she asked, in a near whisper.

"Getting ready to make love?" Tate suggested hopefully.

"It scares me."

"Making love?"

"No," she said, slipping her arms around his neck and giving a little sigh as she let herself lean against him. "How much I want it. How much I want you."

He put his hands to her cheeks, eased her head back for the kiss he planned to give her. "Far be it from me," he murmured, as their breaths mingled, "to deny a lady what she wants."

Libby made a little moaning sound then, part need and part frustration, as he read it, and pulled back out of his arms before he could kiss her.

"Julie's wrong," she said, near tears. "I *am* stupid."

"Never," Tate said, and he meant it. Libby had every reason not to trust him, with her body or anything else, but she was one of the smartest and most resourceful people he knew. "I'm the stupid one, Lib. I had a chance to wake up every morning until the day I die with you beside me, and I blew it. If it's any comfort to you, I'll never stop regretting that."

He turned then, fully intending to leave her house and her life and stay gone.

"Wait," she said, just as he reached the doorway that led into the living room.

Tate stopped, but he didn't turn around.

Libby didn't speak again for so long that he thought she might have sneaked out the back door, leaving him standing there in the doorway like the fool he was.

"Tate." The way she said his name—it caught at his heart, and a few other vital organs, too. When they were together before, that tone had meant only one thing: that she wanted him.

He made himself turn back to her, even though every shred of good sense he possessed advised against it.

Libby was standing a few feet away, holding out one hand.

Confused, Tate just stood there, drinking in the sight of her and wishing he could thank whoever it was who'd skimped on the cloth for that dress. It might as well have been made of yellow cellophane.

She seemed shy, unaware of how beautiful she was. And very uncertain.

Tate felt as though he'd been underwater too long, and blood thundered in his ears. He was a man poised on the precipice of something big, something life-changing, and as much as he wanted Libby Remington, he was scared. They'd had great sex as kids. But they weren't kids anymore.

What if it was too soon?

What if it was too late?

What if it wasn't as good as before?

Good God, what if it was *better?*

Tate knew these renegade thoughts made no real sense, but he couldn't seem to rein them in.

Libby smiled, almost sadly. "Is something wrong, Tate?"

His boot soles might have been nailed to the floor, he stood so still.

Finally, he shook his head. Libby was the hometown-sweetheart type, the kind of woman a man was proud to take home to the folks, but she'd been a passionate lover, too.

He took a step toward her, closed his hand around hers. Pulled her against him, so that their torsos collided. And he kissed her. Gently at first, then, slowly and carefully, he turned up the heat.

Libby trembled—he knew she was torn between pulling away and giving herself to him then and there—and put her arms around his neck again.

Tate kissed her harder, cupped her perfect little rear end in his hands—he'd have sworn under oath that she was naked under that dress—and hoisted her up a little, her cue to wrap her legs around him.

She did.

Tate moaned, tore his mouth from hers, breathless. "Where?" he rasped.

"Right here, if you don't hurry," Libby replied, with a little laugh, a nervous mingling of desire and reticence, kissing him again.

Too preoccupied to see where he was going, Tate pushed open three different doors before he finally found her bedroom. Walking wasn't that easy, with a woman wound around him and their mouths welded together, but it was a challenge he meant to meet.

"Stop," Libby said with obvious reluctance, just as he was about to lower her sideways onto the bed, push the dress up around her waist and do what came naturally. "Tate, *stop*. Please."

He stopped.

She unclenched her legs and stood on her feet again, her face flushed, her conflict naked in her eyes.

"It's too soon," she told him miserably. "What if the time isn't right and we're not ready?"

Tate McKettrick was a Texas boy, raised right. If Libby didn't want to make love, that would be a disappointment, but of course he wasn't going to force the issue. Waiting would be hard, but Libby was worth it.

Anyhow, he hadn't brought condoms, and she probably wasn't on the pill. They'd been apart for a long time, and a lot had happened in between then and now.

Libby raised her hands to his face, and just that was almost his undoing. "Time," she said. "We need a little time first, that's all."

"How *much* time?" Tate rasped.

She laughed softly, but her eyes—her beautiful, expressive eyes—were awash in tears. "Enough to make sure we're not making a mistake," she said. "There's a lot to think about."

With a sigh, he sat down on the edge of Libby's bed, took her hand and pulled her onto his lap. Putting his arms around her, he rested his forehead against her right ear. "Did you wear that dress to torture me?" he asked, partly sighing the words, and partly grinding them out. His breath was still fast and shallow.

"What?" Was that surprise he heard in her tone, or mischief?

"Come on, Lib," Tate said. "I've seen toilet paper with more substance than that dress."

She laughed. "*Toilet paper?* Well, that's romantic, McKettrick."

He raised his eyes then, looked into hers, and the realization hit him like a whiskey barrel rolling downhill.

God help him, *he loved her*.

She sobered a little, still content, it appeared, to sit on his lap in a dress made out of spun nothing and stitched together with a short length of zilch. "You okay, cowboy?" she asked quietly.

"No," he said, because lying to Libby Remington had always been impossible, and that was still so. "Not really."

Libby ran the pad of one thumb over his mouth, lightly. "When was the last time somebody held you just because you needed holding, Tate McKettrick?" she asked.

The question made his throat cinch up tight and his eyes sting. Even if he'd had the voice to answer, he wouldn't have known what to say.

She slipped off his lap to sit beside him on the mattress, kicked away her sandals and then scooted to the middle, to lie down. And she waited, without a word.

Tate hesitated, but the pull of her was too strong. He took off his boots and stretched out beside her, confused by all the things she made him feel.

Libby had made it clear that she wasn't ready to make love, yet she took him in her arms and rested her forehead against his chest.

He was lost in the softness of her body, the scent of her hair and the silken feel of her skin, the solace she seemed to radiate from somewhere in the core of her being.

I love you, he wanted to say.

But it was too soon for that, too.

So he simply lay there and let Libby hold him. Just because.

CHAPTER SEVEN

THE SHIFT HAPPENED between one heartbeat and the next.

Lying there on her bed, facing Tate, Libby felt her heart soar and then plummet, as though she were riding some cosmic roller coaster. She'd loved this man since he was a boy and she was a little girl, barely older than Audrey and Ava were now.

Over the years, that love had changed, always finding its level. Like a river, it had sometimes overflowed its banks, and she'd been swept away by its force. After Cheryl arrived on the scene, it had gone underground, leaving only cracks and debris on the surface.

Now, the river was rising rapidly, springing up from some elemental and seemingly inexhaustible source of devotion, not only within Libby, but *beyond* her, bubbling and churning, swirling into violent eddies. This time, there would be no stopping it, no changing its course, no stemming the tide.

It would be what it was, and what it was becoming, and that was that.

Powerless before the enormity of it, Libby wept in stricken silence.

Tate must have felt her tears through his shirt, because he turned her gently onto her back, so he could look down into her face.

"What?" he asked, breathing the word, rather than saying it.

Libby shook her head. Even if she hadn't been afraid to tell him what she was feeling, she wouldn't have known how to put it into words. It was as though she'd died, and then been resurrected as a different woman, with a new soul.

Tate kissed her cheekbones, her eyelids. "Lib," he persisted, his voice husky. "What is it?"

A sob tore itself from her throat, raw and hurting, and, shaking her head again, she tried to roll onto her other side, turn her back to him. But he didn't allow it.

The former Libby, practical and wary, emotionally bruised and battered, had stopped him from making love to her for a lot of very good reasons.

The new one wanted him with an incomprehensible ferocity, an instinctual craving that would not be refused, delayed or modified.

Libby took Tate's hand, brought it to her mouth, and flicked at his palm with the tip of her tongue.

He made a low sound in his throat, but he never closed his eyes. He consumed her with them, drew her into that boundless blue, where all but her most primitive instincts faded away.

She moved his hand again, this time to cup her right breast, crooned when he used the side of one thumb to caress her nipple through the gossamer cloth of her dress and the thin silk bra beneath. Her back arched, of its own accord, and her heart thrummed so loudly that the sound of it seemed to fill the room, push at the walls.

Libby knew, in those moments, only one word—his name.

It came out of her, that name, on a long, low groan, and she struggled to get free of the dress, would have ripped it away as though it were burning, if Tate hadn't pulled the garment up and then off over her head.

She felt her bra go next, her bare breasts spilling free.

Tate closed his mouth over one aching nipple, then the other, and at the same time slipped his hand inside her panties to part her, tease her with gentle plucking motions of his fingers.

Libby cried out, flailing and whimpering, desperate to be naked, to be utterly vulnerable to him in every way. When the panties were gone, first dragged down over her thighs and knees and ankles so she could kick free of them, he parted her legs and, with the heel of his palm, made slow circles at her center until she was wet with the need of him.

To his credit, Tate tried to reason with her, his voice low and ragged, reminding her that only minutes before, she'd wanted to wait, take things slowly. But he couldn't have known about the river flowing within her, flowing *through* her from some other world, with all the force of an ocean surging behind it.

At some point, he must have realized there would be no turning back, because he knelt astraddle of her thighs, pulling his shirt out of his jeans, working the buttons, tossing the shirt aside.

When he leaned over to kiss her, Libby ran her hands over his chest, his shoulders, up and down his arms and his sides, frantic to touch him, to chart the once-familiar terrain of his body.

The kiss was devastating, a thorough taking in its own right, and Libby struggled to breathe when Tate broke away from her, nibbled his way down the length of her neck, suckled at one breast and then the other.

And still Libby spoke a language composed of a single word.

"Tate." She reveled in the sound of it. "Tate."

He moved down then, slid his hands under her, squeezing, hoisting her high off the bed. When he nuzzled through and took her into his mouth, she instantly splintered, shouting now, riding a ghost horse made of fire.

The long climax convulsed her, time and again, drove the breath from her lungs and melted her very bones, leaving her limp in its aftermath. She couldn't see or hear or speak—she could only feel.

And Tate wasn't through with her.

He draped her legs over his shoulders, squeezing her buttocks slightly as he continued to use his mouth on her, now nibbling, now sucking, now flicking at her with his tongue.

The next release was cataclysmic; and it, too, went on and on, something eternal.

Transported, Libby gave one continuous, straining moan as her body buckled and seized, rose and fell, quivered and went still.

Tate was relentless, feasting on her, summoning up every sensation she was capable of feeling.

She flung her head from side to side, pleaded and threatened and coaxed, all by uttering his name alone.

He sucked on her until she'd given him everything, and then he demanded even more.

Aware of him viscerally, in every fiber and cell, though he might have been an invisible lover for all she could see through the haze of near-desperate satisfaction that had settled over her after that last orgasm, she knew when he moved to take off his jeans.

She moaned and parted her legs for him when he covered her again, an act that took all the strength she had left.

"Libby," she heard him say, through the blissful void, "if you want me to stop, say so now, because once I'm inside you, I'm not going to pull out until it's over."

She managed only the slightest demur, still floating in a warm sea of sweet ambrosia. She wanted him inside her, deep, deep inside her, but not because she expected another climax. She'd come so many times, with so much intensity, that she was soft and moist and peaceful inside.

Until he took her in earnest, that is.

With the first powerful thrust, he opened a whole new well of need, a blazing lake of fire. Libby's eyes flew open, and she gasped in wanting and alarm.

He drove into her, nearly withdrew, drove again.

Libby went wild beneath him, digging her heels into the bed to thrust herself upward to meet him, stroke for stroke, clawing at his back and his shoulders and any part of him she could get hold of, calling to him, raging at him in her one-word litany.

They shattered simultaneously, Tate holding her high and driving into her with short, rapid thrusts. Through a storm of dazzling light, as her own body convulsed in helpless ecstasy, she saw him throw back his head, as majestic and powerful as a stallion claiming a mare. She saw the muscles straining in his neck and chest and felt the warmth of his seed spilling into her.

When it was over, he collapsed beside her with a hoarse exclamation, still spanning her with one arm and one leg.

Libby drifted, seemingly outside her body, and it was a long time before she settled back into herself. The landing was soft, featherlight—at first. But as her scattered wits began to find their way home, flapping their wings and roosting in her heart and her brain and the pit of her stomach, her very spirit began to ache.

What had she done?

What if she was pregnant?

What if she wasn't?

Tears gathered inside her, filled her, but she could not shed them, even though she yearned for the relief crying would bring.

Tate held her, brushing her forehead with his lips, murmuring to her that everything would be all right. She'd see, he promised. *Everything would be all right.*

For him, it would be. After all, he was a man.

He would get up, shower, get dressed and go back to his regular life—to his beautiful children and his sprawling ranch and all the rest of it.

The lovemaking hadn't changed him; he knew who he was, who he had always been and always would be: Tate McKettrick.

Libby, on the other hand, had been permanently altered by the experience they'd just shared, and she was going to have to get to know herself all over again.

The task seemed so daunting, so huge, so *impossible*, that she didn't know where to start.

She slept, awakened, slept again.

When she woke up the next time, Tate was gone.

His absence blew cold and bitter through her soul, like a winter wind.

Except for the aftershocks still rocking her sated body at regular intervals, she might have dreamed the whole thing.

Now came reality.

AUSTIN AND GARRETT were sitting at the kitchen table when Tate got home that night, a little after midnight.

Seeing his brothers, he immediately tucked in his shirt, something he'd forgotten to do before he left Libby's house. He felt heat rise in his neck and pulse along his jawline as Austin gave him that familiar, knowing once-over.

"Been with a woman," Austin said to Garrett. Except that he was thinner, and his brownish hair was in even worse need of barbering than usual, Austin resembled his old, pre-Buzzsaw self.

Physically, Tate knew, Austin had largely recovered.

But something deeper had been injured that day in the rodeo arena, and the jury was still out on whether or not he would come back from that.

"Yep," Garrett agreed sagely, shoving a hand through his dark blond hair. His fancy white politician's shirt was open to the middle of his chest, and, like Austin, he was nursing a glass of whiskey. Scotch on the rocks, unless Tate missed his guess. "He's definitely been with a woman."

Tate chose to skip the Scotch and have coffee instead. Since Esperanza had long since scrubbed out the pot and set it for the morning, he brewed a cup of instant, using the special spigot on the sink. "You can both shut up," he grumbled, "any old time now."

With all he'd felt making love to Libby Remington again, there was a lot of mental and emotional sorting to do. Dealing with his brothers was something he would have preferred to avoid, at least until morning.

Austin laughed, and something in the tone of that laugh brought home a previously unconsidered reality to Tate. His kid brother probably hadn't been in rehab all that long; more likely, he'd been shacked up someplace with a woman.

Maybe several.

"At least he didn't give *my* present to the twins to the community center," Austin told Garrett, more than slightly smug. No matter how much Tate protested, they both spoiled their only nieces extravagantly. Cheryl allowed it, but it galled Tate.

He didn't want Audrey and Ava growing up thinking they were entitled to everything they wanted.

Garrett scowled. "It's a perfectly good castle," he said, and belched unceremoniously.

Tate wondered how long the both of them had been swilling Scotch and swapping lies. "Maybe," he growled, "you two could stop talking about me as though I'm not even here."

"Would that be fun?" Austin asked Garrett. In Austin's world, everything had to be fun. He was the Western version of Peter Pan; Tate had long since given up the hope that his kid brother would ever grow up. He had more money than sense, and his looks—fatal to women—worked against him, in Tate's opinion.

Austin was used to coasting. Everything came too easily to him, and the effect on his character was less than impressive.

"No," Garrett said, after due and bleary consideration. "It would not be fun."

Tate took a jar of freeze-dried coffee from the cupboard and set it on the counter with more force than the enterprise really called for. "Some things never change," he said. "You're both as dumb as you ever were."

"Well, *he's* in a mood," Garrett remarked, and, after belching again, poured himself another double shot.

"God," Tate said, stirring coffee crystals into hot water and then approaching the table, "I hope you never get elected president. Two-and-a-quarter-plus centuries down the swirler. Everything Washington, Lincoln and FDR accomplished, gone."

Garrett belched again. "Now that was just plain low," he said.

"Downright mean-spirited," Austin agreed.

"You're both sloshed," Tate accused.

"Of course we're sloshed," Garrett said, his eyes suddenly haunted. "Pablo is dead. Jesus, stomped to death by a horse."

Austin looked away, but not before Tate saw that his eyes were wet. Ever quick to compose himself, Austin soon met Tate's gaze. "You found him?"

Tate nodded.

"Christ," Austin commiserated, shoving the bottle in Tate's direction. "Here. Put some of that in your chamomile tea, or whatever it is you're drinking."

"Austin?" Tate said quietly.

"Yeah?"

"Fuck off."

"So who's the woman?" Austin asked, typically unfazed. It had taken a murderous bull named Buzzsaw to get to him.

"Not Cheryl, I hope," Garrett said.

"Watch it," Tate warned, before lowering his voice to add, "She might be a bitch, but she's also the mother of my children."

"Her one redeeming virtue," Austin said.

Tate studied his youngest sibling carefully. Previously, he would have dodged a conversation with his brothers, but suddenly he was in another mode entirely. "Were you telling the truth, outside the operating room the day you were hurt, when you said you never slept with Cheryl? Because she claims it happened."

Austin raised his glass, already nearly empty again, in a mocking salute. "Nobody lies when they know they might be facing their Maker," he said. He downed what remained of his Scotch. Sputtered a little. His McKettrick-blue eyes were both looking in the same direction, but not for long if he kept drinking like that. "Besides, Tate, you're *my brother.* Much as I'd like to punch your lights out most of the time, I wouldn't do *that* even if the opportunity came my way—which, regrettably, it did."

An uncomfortable silence ensued.

More Scotch was poured.

"I'm not letting *that one* drop," Tate said.

Austin sighed, glanced in Garrett's direction.

Evidently, no help was forthcoming from the future president of the United States, who was already three sheets to the wind. If he ever made it to the White House, the tabloids would have no trouble at all digging up dirt on him.

Resigned and even a little regretful, Austin said, "I was in Vegas, for the finals. Cheryl showed up, told the desk clerk at the hotel that we were married. She must have shown him ID—her last name was McKettrick at the time, remember. Anyhow, when I got back to my room, after the ride and the buckle ceremony at South Point, Cheryl was waiting."

Tate and Garrett were both watching him, Tate with tight-jawed annoyance, Garrett with pity.

"And?" Tate prompted.

"And she was naked," Austin admitted.

"Good God," Garrett told his younger brother, "you *are* stupid, admitting a thing like that. Are you *trying* to get those perfect white teeth knocked out of your head?"

Austin flushed. "She was naked," he insisted.

"So you said," Tate observed.

"And crying," Austin added.

"Boo-hoo," Garrett said.

"God help America," Tate said, "if *you* ever get your name on the ballot."

"The press would make hash out of him," Austin remarked to Tate, cocking a thumb at Garrett, "before he ever got the nomination."

Garrett scowled, but said nothing. He could have bullshitted a lot of people, but his brothers weren't among them. They knew him too well.

"Cheryl was naked and crying in your hotel room *and*—?" Tate prompted, glaring at Austin.

"And," Austin said, with drunken dignity, "she said you didn't even ask for a divorce, you just told her you were filing for one. Did I mention she was in my bed?"

There had been more to Tate's decision to end the marriage, of course, but Cheryl, indignant that he'd refused to overlook her one-night stand with a prominent judge in Dallas and go on as if nothing had happened, wouldn't have included that part of the story.

Nor did Austin and Garrett need to know it.

"No," Tate said evenly. "You skipped that part, but you did say she was naked, so I guess it figures."

"She was in his bed," Garrett said, with portent. Where the hell had he been for the last minute or so?

"Thank you, Mr. President," Tate said. "And shut the fuck up, will you?"

"Listen to him," Garrett remarked to Austin. "I think I'll establish a national committee on casual profanity. Too many people swear. We need to get to the bottom of this, nip it in the bud, cut it off at the pass—"

"One more word," Tate told Garrett, "and I'm stuffing that whiskey bottle down your throat."

Garrett belched again.

Tate turned back to Austin. "Cheryl was in your bed," he reminded him.

"She was?" Austin said.

Tate reached across the table and got his kid brother by the shirt collar. "She was," Tate agreed. "And the next thing you did was—?"

Austin grinned. "Well, first, I wished you weren't my brother, and her husband, because mega-bitch that she is, Cheryl is one hot woman. I didn't ask her what she was after, because that was pretty obvious. She wanted to pay you back for divorcing her, in spades. I told her she needed therapy, and then I picked up my gear, walked out and slept on the couch in my buddy Steve Miller's suite."

"The buckle guy?" Garrett asked, evidently determined to be part of the conversation, even though he'd long since lost track of it.

"Yeah," Tate said tightly, "the *buckle guy.*"

Miller, a representative of the company responsible for designing and constructing the fancy silver belt buckles winning cowboys were awarded at various rodeos around the country, was familiar to all three of them.

"I think I'll go to bed now," Garrett announced.

"Hell of an idea," Tate agreed. "That will save me the trouble of kicking your ass."

Garrett got out of his chair and stumbled in the general direction of his part of the house. The place was Texas-big, which meant they each had their own private wing, and it was not only possible but common for them to live for months under the same roof and still keep pretty much to themselves.

"He's drunk," Austin confided drunkenly.

"Ya think?" Tate asked.

Suddenly, Austin was sober. His blue eyes were clear. "I didn't sleep with Cheryl," he said.

Tate gave a great sigh. "I believe you," he said. And it was true.

"Hallelujah," Austin said, with some bitterness.

"It wouldn't hurt you to hit the sack, either," Tate told him. "You're going to have one bitch of a hangover tomorrow, if there's any justice in this world."

Austin laughed. "Lucky for me there isn't," he said, and poured himself more Scotch. "You were with Libby Remington tonight, weren't you?"

"Officially none of your damn business," Tate proclaimed.

"Might as well admit it. Somebody turned you inside out tonight, big brother, and I'm betting it was Libby."

"Okay." Tate sighed, his energy flagging now that he and Austin had settled the Cheryl incident. "It was Libby."

Austin grinned. "You're a couple again? That's good."

Tate's jaw clamped, and he had to take a second or so to unstick the hinges. "It's not that simple," he said.

"Because—?"

"Because I sold her out," Tate rasped. Basically, he thought, he was no better than Cheryl. He hadn't been married to Libby when he'd gone swimming in the romantic equivalent of a shark tank, letting things go way too far with the wrong woman, but they'd had an understanding. She'd trusted him completely, and he'd betrayed that trust.

He'd wounded her on a deep level, and he wasn't naive enough to think that had changed, just because Libby had wanted sex. Libby had always enjoyed sex, and unless he missed his guess, she'd been doing without for quite a while.

On the other hand, maybe that was just wishful thinking.

She was a beautiful, desirable woman, and he wasn't the first—or the last—man to notice.

"Sounds to me," Austin observed dryly, after taking a few moments to mull over Tate's grudging admission that he had indeed been with Libby that night, "like all must be forgiven. Lib's nobody's fool—none of the Remington women are. If she took you into her bed, big brother, she's willing to forget the past, and that's a rare thing, especially for a woman."

The summer after he'd graduated from high school, Tate recalled, Austin had dated Libby's youngest sister, Paige. For a while there, things had been hot and heavy, if any part of the rumors flying around town had been true, but in the end, Paige had had the good sense to throw Austin over when she'd enrolled in nursing school that September and he'd gone right on risking his neck at the rodeo.

"At what point," Tate rasped, irritated, "did I say that Libby and I went to bed together?"

Austin chuckled. The sound, like the expression in his eyes and the set of his shoulders, was different somehow. His little brother had changed in ways Tate couldn't quite put his finger on.

"You didn't need to say it," Austin replied. "Your shirt was still half out of your pants when you came through the door a little while ago, your hair's furrowed from her fingers, and I'd bet money you've got a few claw marks under your clothes, too." He paused, obviously savoring Tate's silent but furious reaction to his blunt observations. "Even without all that, I'd know by the look in your eyes."

"You're wasted on rodeo," Tate all but growled. "You ought to be with the CIA or something."

Austin smiled. "Is all this going somewhere?" he asked. "You and Libby, I mean?"

Tate sighed. "Damn if I know," he said. "It could have been just one of those things."

"Or not," Austin said.

"While we're reading each other's minds," Tate ventured, "I see by my crystal ball that you haven't been in rehab most of these long months, as you led the rest of us to believe. Who is she and how serious is it?"

Austin wore a muted version of his old devil's grin while he decided whether he wanted to answer or not. "She's a waitress in San Antonio," he revealed, after considerable pause, "and it's over."

"You still think about Paige Remington every once in a while?" Tate knew he was pushing his luck, but that was a McKettrick family tradition, so long established that it was probably hereditary by now.

Austin looked away. "Yeah, sometimes," he admitted, and Tate thought they were getting somewhere, for a moment or two. As if. "When that happens, I wear garlic around my neck and nail the doors and windows shut at night."

Tate decided to let the subject drop. Shoved a hand through his hair, pushed back his chair. "Guess I'll look in on the kids and then turn in for the night. You'd better do the same, because with Pablo's funeral coming up in a few days and people coming from half a dozen states to pay their respects, things are bound to get wild around here."

Austin nodded, stood up, ready to head for his wing of the house. "What about the stud, Tate? Why's he still on the place, after he trampled Pablo like that?"

Tate thought of his little girls, asleep upstairs, and wouldn't let himself imagine the things that could happen if the devil-stallion ever got out of that pen. "The state vet took blood samples. He'll decide whether the stallion ought to be put down or not when the paperwork comes back."

Austin huffed out a breath. "You know what Dad would have done," he said. "Taken a rifle out there and dropped that horse in his tracks with a single bullet to the brain."

"Granddad, maybe," Tate answered, shaking his head. "But not

Dad. What happened to Pablo was an *accident,* Austin. Something spooked the stud, just as Pablo went to lead him down the ramp from the trailer and through the corral gate. Anyhow, you know Pablo wouldn't want him destroyed."

Austin reflected a few moments. "You know I hate to see any animal put down if there's a choice, Tate," he said, his eyes clear as he met his brother's gaze, "but sometimes it has to be done."

"I know that," Tate said, though maybe he sounded a little peevish.

Austin's grin flashed; mercurial changes were a way of life with him. "I could ride that paint," he said. "Settle him down a little."

"The hell you will," Tate snapped, because grin or no grin, he knew the chances were 80 percent or better that his brother wasn't kidding. "Buzzsaw damn near killed you, and now you want to give that crazy stud a shot at breaking your neck?"

"Good ole Buzzsaw," Austin replied. "If it's the last thing I ever do, I'll ride that son-of-a-bitch to the buzzer. I'll trail him from rodeo to rodeo if I have to, but I'll draw him and I'll ride him."

Tate went cold, through and through. "You can't be serious," he marveled. "You get on that bull again, and it *will* be the last thing you ever do."

"It's the principle of the thing," Austin said.

"Like hell it is," Tate argued, with more heat than he thought he had in him after all those go-rounds with Libby. "It's your dumb-ass McKettrick pride. You're a world champion, several times over, so there's nothing more to prove. Every cowboy gets thrown sooner or later, and Buzzsaw isn't the first bull to pitch you into the dirt, so why not let well enough alone?"

"There *is* something to prove," Austin countered quietly. "To myself."

Tate shook his head. "What? That you're certifiable?"

Austin looked Tate directly in the eyes. "I've never been scared of anything much in my life," he said. "But I'm scared of that bull. And that's something I can't live with, Tate. You know what Dad always said—if you get thrown from a horse, you'd better get right back on, because if you don't, the chances are good you never will."

Tate's gut clenched. He was the eldest; he'd always been the protector. Austin had just announced that he planned to commit suicide, and short of using some kind of unlawful imprisonment, Tate wouldn't be able to stop him.

Still, he couldn't let it drop. "Dad was talking about cow ponies, Austin," he reasoned, "not devil-bulls with blood in their eye."

Austin shrugged one shoulder. "Buzzsaw will be in the finals in Vegas this December, and so will I. There's got to be a showdown. And I'll draw him for my ride, because it's meant to be that way."

"Unless you don't enter," Tate said, chilled. "And you're a damn fool if you do."

"I've been called a lot worse," Austin answered. And then he turned and walked away from Tate, on his way to the stairs leading to his private living space on the second floor.

For a long time, Tate just stood there, his jawline tight, his fists bunched at his sides. At the moment, unlawful imprisonment looked like a viable option.

Then he shut out the lights and went upstairs.

Audrey and Ava were asleep in their beds, with one dog each curled up at their feet.

Quietly, he approached, straightening Audrey's covers and then Ava's, kissing each of them lightly on the forehead, so they wouldn't wake up.

Cheryl would be back in a few days, he thought, trying to re-sign himself to giving up his daughters again. Renewed by her time away from Blue River, she'd have rearmed herself, come up with new arguments for why the twins ought to compete in the Pixie Pageant. She'd work hard to wear him down; she probably knew the effort was destined for failure, but that would only in-spire her to get sneaky.

And Cheryl was real good at sneaky.

Audrey stirred in the midst of some dream, gave a soft sigh.

Her mother's daughter, she'd been working on him over the past few days, angling for his permission to enter the pageant, just as Ava had warned that she would. *Was* he just being bull-headed, refusing to sign, as Cheryl said?

Little-girl pageants offended him—he hated the costumes and the emphasis on looks—but surely they weren't *all* bad. Other-wise-sensible people—he did not include Cheryl in that category—

allowed their kids to participate. Seemed to view it as a confidence builder, like playing on a soccer team or something.

Sure, there were few winners and a lot of losers, but that was life, wasn't it?

On top of all that, this particular shindig was local, not a stop-over on the pageant circuit. They were holding it at the Blue River Country Club, a place as familiar to him as the post office or the feed store.

Maybe he'd been wrong, made the decision too quickly.

Audrey opened her eyes just then, smiled up at him. "Hi, Daddy," she said sleepily.

"Hello, sweetheart," he said, his voice coming out hoarse. This fathering business, he reflected, was not for cowards. You made one hard decision and there was another one coming along right behind it.

"Did you have fun at Libby's house?" his daughter asked, stretching.

Ava, in the next bed, slept on, dead to the world.

"Sure did," Tate told her.

"Esperanza cried all night," Audrey confided, worried. "I don't think she's ever going to stop."

Tate's throat tightened, aching right along with his heart. He could only shield his daughters from the hard realities, like death, for so long. "She'll probably do that for a while," he said quietly, leaning to kiss her forehead again. "But things will get better in time, you'll see."

Audrey nodded, yawned and closed her eyes. "'Night," she murmured.

Tate made as little noise as he could, leaving the room and closing the door behind him, assailed by the knowledge that while things *would* eventually get better, they might just get a whole lot worse first.

CHAPTER EIGHT

WHEN SATURDAY AFTERNOON rolled around, every business in town was closed for Pablo's funeral. Esperanza, Tate and both his brothers were among the first to arrive at the small Catholic church that would soon be bulging with mourners from every walk of life.

Since Cheryl had arrived home that morning, a day early and in a weirdly tractable state of mind, Tate had reluctantly allowed her to take the kids back to her place ahead of time. An open-casket funeral was no place for a couple of six-year-olds; they wouldn't understand about Pablo lying there in a box, still and waxy in the suit he'd bought to wear to his daughter's graduation from medical school.

A furious ache grabbed at Tate's heart as he walked slowly up the center aisle to pay his respects before the service got started. He and his brothers, along with one of Pablo's nephews and two of Isabel's, would be the pallbearers when it was time to carry the coffin outside to the hearse parked squarely in front of the churchyard gate.

There would be no graveside ceremony. Pablo had long ago arranged to be cremated, and despite church regulations he'd left written instructions with Isabel that he wanted his ashes spread on the Silver Spur, where he'd lived and worked and raised his children. When she'd shared that request with Tate, he'd called to make the arrangements.

Up close, Pablo fulfilled all the funereal clichés. He looked natural, as though he were merely sleeping, and his expression was strangely peaceful, but when Tate touched his friend's hand, he felt a chill so cold it burned like dry ice.

"We'll look after Isabel, Pablo," Tate said, in a ragged whisper. "We'll see that she and the kids have everything they need."

A hand landed on Tate's right shoulder, and he was startled, since he hadn't heard anyone approaching. He turned to see Brent standing behind him, Denzel-handsome in a freshly pressed uniform.

"This isn't your fault, old buddy," Brent said. His intuition was a force to be reckoned with; sometimes it seemed to Tate that his friend could read minds.

"If only I hadn't told Pablo I'd buy that stud if it went up for sale," Tate answered. Isabel had just arrived, a small, veiled figure, surrounded by sons and daughters and sisters and cousins and solicitous friends. "I should have been out there to help unload that horse. Would have been, if Pablo had just called to let me know he was bringing him in."

Brent dropped his hand to his side. "I've got some regrets myself," he said. "Sooner or later, you've got to let go of the if-onlys, Tate, because you'll go crazy if you don't."

Tate nodded; he was familiar with his friend's regrets, most of which centered around his young wife, who'd been shot in a scuffle on the concourse of an outdoor mall. He left Brent beside the casket and made his way to the front pew, where the Ruizes were settling in. Nico, the eldest son, lithe and dark and intense as a matador, put out his hand in greeting. Back when they were all kids, Nico had spent a lot of time at the main ranch house with Tate and his brothers, but over the years, they'd drifted apart.

"Thanks for being here, Tate," Nico said, swallowing hard to control his emotions.

Tate would have traveled from any part of the planet to say goodbye to Pablo Ruiz, and Nico knew that. Saying thanks was just a formality.

Tate nodded, too choked up to speak.

Isabel, already seated, her face nearly invisible behind the layers of black netting comprising her veil, put out her frail hands to

Tate, and he squeezed them with his own, felt her trembling. He nodded to Mercedes, who was weeping silently, and the younger boys, Juan and Ricardo. They were still in high school, Tate knew, and the luminous sorrow in their nearly black eyes tore at him.

How well he remembered the ache of that bleak and fathom-less loss of a parent—he still felt it sometimes, when he was rid-ing alone on the range, along trails he'd traveled so many times with his dad, or when he saw women around his mother's age, dressed up for church or some luncheon out at the country club. Sally McKettrick had dearly loved any occasion that gave her an excuse to wear a splashy hat, a pastel suit and high heels.

Some change in the atmosphere made Tate scan the pews as he left the Ruizes, intending to take his place alongside Esperanza and his brothers and brace himself to get through all that was to come.

His gaze settled on Libby—he hadn't seen her since the night they'd skipped supper to make love—and even in those grim cir-cumstances, she warmed something inside him. Her dress was navy blue and her hair swept away from her face, caught up in back with some kind of clip. Julie stood next to her, clad in dramatic black, and Paige was there, too, wearing a dark brown pantsuit, her short cap of glossy black hair catching colored light from the stained-glass windows.

Tate took a step toward the three sisters, his attention focused solely on Libby, but the aisle was already crowded, and he couldn't get through.

"Tate," he heard Esperanza whisper. "Here we are."

He looked to his right, saw the housekeeper sitting in a nearby pew, between Garrett and Austin, who appeared to be support-ing her with the pressure of their shoulders. Garrett studied the Remington women as they found places and sat down, but Aus-tin stared straight ahead, with determined disinterest, toward the altar and Pablo's gleaming casket.

Just before Tate joined the others in their pew, Libby's gaze found and connected with his. Nothing in her expression changed—he might have been a total stranger instead of the man who had so recently shared her bed—but an invisible cord seemed to stretch between them, drawing taut and then snapping back on Tate with an impact that made him blink.

He took a seat next to his family.

Other mourners crowded into the church, and it got so warm, even with the laboring air-conditioning system, that people began to sweat. The organist took her place and sonorous music joined with the oppressive heat, creating a humid stew of sound.

Tate longed to loosen his tie, but out of respect for Pablo and the Ruiz kin, he refrained.

Altar boys appeared, carrying lighted candles, followed by Father Rodriguez, a slight, trundling man who moved like one carrying an enormous weight on his narrow shoulders.

A pregnant woman toward the front fainted, and there was a brief flurry while she was revived with smelling salts and led out of the sanctuary by a side door. Esperanza, who had been weeping for days, sat dry-eyed now, all cried out except for the occasional sniffle. Although she had liked Pablo, as had everyone else for miles around, Tate knew the bulk of her grief was reserved for Isabel, left a widow with two children still at home.

Esperanza had lost a husband, too, before she left Mexico as a relatively young woman, but if she had kids of her own, she had never mentioned them to Tate. A woman of benevolent and unflagging faith, she believed both her own lost love and Pablo Ruiz were safe in heaven, and that those forced to go on alone were the ones to be pitied.

Although Tate wasn't sure there was such a place as heaven, he hoped so. Hoped his folks and Pablo and Crockett, his old dog, were all together somewhere, in some bright and painless place where there were horses to ride and plenty of green grass for their grazing.

Father Rodriguez conducted Mass in solemn Latin—no doubt Pablo, an old-fashioned Catholic, had wanted it that way—and then various people took their turns going up front to say a few words about Pablo. Tate was among them, as were Garrett and Austin. He was never able to remember, after that day, exactly what he'd said—only that he'd gotten through the brief speech without losing his composure.

It had been a close one, though.

After him, Libby rose, made her way to the microphone, and told the sweltering congregation, her voice trembling, how Pablo had come to the Remington house faithfully, every single week after her father got sick, how he'd mowed the lawn and weeded and raked the flower beds and fixed whatever needed repair, from the rain gutters to the washing machine. She honestly didn't know, she said, what they would have done without him.

The story stung Tate in some deep and tender place, one he'd never explored.

The townspeople had rallied to help the Remingtons in every possible way. Had *he* done anything?

His gut roiled with the guilt he'd never been able to shake.

Oh, yeah. He'd done something, all right. Far from home, overwhelmed by the demands of law school and, most of all, missing Libby, he'd gotten drunk at a party and wound up in bed with Cheryl. Gotten her pregnant, for good measure.

Tate lowered his head.

Garrett, sitting beside him, nudged him back to the here-and-now with a motion of one elbow.

Having completed her short eulogy, Libby returned to her pew and sat down, and someone else got up to speak.

The service ended after two full hours, and Tate, Garrett and Austin joined Pablo and Isabel's nephews up front.

The coffin's bright brass handles gleamed. The lid was lowered, and one of the Ruiz women cried out then, a piercing, anguished sound—and the organist began the recessional.

Red, yellow and blue light from the stained-glass windows played over the mounds of white flowers draped across the top of the casket as the six men carried it down the aisle, toward the dazzle of afternoon sunshine at the open doors.

The casket, surprisingly light, was loaded carefully into the back of the hearse. People streamed out of the church, milled in the yard and on the sidewalk, talking in quiet voices, some of them wiping their eyes with wadded handkerchiefs, others hugging, consoling each other. Some smiled through their tears, perhaps remembering how Pablo had loved to tell stupid jokes, or share the produce from his garden, or drop off a pan of Isabel's fine enchiladas when they were sick or out of a job or mourning the loss of a loved one.

Isabel, Nico and Mercedes and the boys accepted hugs and

handshakes and exhortations to call if they needed anything at all, and looked profoundly relieved when the funeral director steered them toward a waiting limousine. They were settled quickly inside, and then gone.

Tate looked around for Libby, the way a man might look for water when his throat was parched, found her standing under an oak tree, dappled in sun and shadow, Paige and Julie close by as always. They spoke quietly to friends, and though they bore little resemblance to each other, Tate knew it would have been clear even to a stranger that they were related. Something indefinable bound them together, made them a unit.

The heat was oppressive, but somehow, Libby looked cool as a mountain spring in that dark blue dress. Once in a while, her gaze strayed to Tate, only to bounce away again when their eyes met.

By tacit agreement—because that was the way things were done in places like Blue River, Texas—folks waited and foot-shuffled and fanned themselves with their simply printed programs, giving Isabel and her brood plenty of time to get home and get settled before they began stopping by with the ritual salads and spiral-cut hams and bakery goods. Personal condolences would be offered and graciously received, along with sympathy cards containing checks of varying size.

However much Isabel and the others might have preferred to be alone with each other and their memories of Pablo, the gathering at the modest house beside the winding creek was as important as the funeral. There would be a guestbook, and sooner or later, when she'd emerged from the haze of bereavement, Isabel would examine it, page by page, taking in the names of all those who'd cared.

With the throng still clogging the path between himself and Libby, Tate saw no way to get to her without shouldering his way through. So he shook hands with neighboring ranchers, kissed the cheeks of his mother's friends, and waited.

Finally, when he'd decided that enough time had passed, Father Rodriguez got into his dusty compact car to drive out to the Ruiz house, with Esperanza to keep him company on the way.

Maybe, Tate thought, he'd get a chance to talk to Libby over postfuneral coffee and a paper plate heaped with food he didn't want. On the other hand, she might have written their encounter off as a lapse of judgment and decided to steer clear from there on out.

Nobody would have blamed her for that, least of all Tate himself.

JULIE TOOK THE wheel of the pink Cadillac, while Libby claimed the passenger seat and Paige slipped into the back.

"For God's sake," Paige said distractedly, "turn on the air-conditioning. It's hot as hell's kitchen in here."

Julie complied, casting a brief glance in Libby's direction.

An understanding passed between them, no words necessary.

Paige, as upset over Pablo Ruiz's death as any of them, had spent most of the service trying not to look at Austin McKettrick and failing visibly.

Libby rolled down her window and fluttered the church bulletin under her chin. "Austin looks good," she commented, keeping her voice light, "for somebody who tangled with a bull not all that long ago."

"He's an idiot," Paige said, with a dismissive tone that didn't fool either of her sisters. They well remembered that, although Paige had been the one to end things with Austin, she'd grieved for months afterward.

Libby and Julie exchanged glances again, but Julie had to navigate the after-funeral traffic, so she quickly turned her attention back to the road.

"If only all idiots were that good-looking," Julie contributed. "How many guys have a whole calendar devoted just to pictures of them?"

"Shallow," Paige retorted, though she owned the calendar in question. "A Year of Austin," it was titled—she kept it pinned to the laundry room wall at her place, even though it was out of date, open to July and the image of her favorite cowboy riding a wild bull and wearing a stars-and-stripes shirt. "Austin McKettrick is *shallow*. And he'll never grow up."

"He looks pretty grown up to me," Libby observed, with a slight smile.

Julie made an eloquent little sound, part growl and part purr.

"Shut up," Paige said, peevish. "Do we have to go out to the

Ruizes' place? It will be jammed, and it's so hot. I'd rather go back to your house and keep Calvin and the dog company."

"Of *course* we have to go to the Ruizes'," Julie answered, in her big-sister voice, waving to people walking along the sidewalk. "How would it look if we didn't at least stop by? And it isn't as if Calvin and Harry are home alone. Mrs. Erskine is looking after them until we get back."

Paige sighed. She could be dramatic at times—especially when she knew she might come face-to-face with the man she'd dumped before starting nursing school. "I can't believe Pablo is gone," she said. "I just saw him at the post office a few days ago. He told me some silly knock-knock joke."

The caravan of cars and pickup trucks wound out of Blue River into the countryside; Libby imagined how it would look from high overhead—like a big metal snake.

She shifted in the seat, rolled her window back up when the AC finally kicked in. A sort of delicious unease stirred in her as she recalled making love with Tate—she both dreaded and anticipated seeing him again, up close and personal. Which meant she had no business remarking on Paige's reluctant fascination with Austin at the funeral.

"Why do things like this happen?" Libby asked, knowing there was no real answer.

"Good question," Julie said, with a little shudder. "What an awful way to die."

A silence fell, and a replay of their dad's lingering death flashed in Libby's mind. He'd been heavily sedated, in no physical pain to speak of, at least toward the end, but he'd suffered just the same, she'd seen that in his eyes. A proud man enduring the indignities of a failing body.

Her own eyes burned, though they were dry, and her throat tightened until it ached. Julie, who always seemed to know what she was thinking, reached over to pat her arm.

It wasn't far to the part of the Silver Spur where Pablo and Isabel had made their home for so many years, but the ride seemed interminable that day. Dust boiled up off the winding country roads, sometimes rendering the vehicles ahead all but invisible.

No more was said about Pablo's death, or about unfortunate

romantic attachments to certain men. Of the three of them, Julie was the only one unscathed by the legendary McKettrick charm, though, of course, she had demons of her own.

Gordon Pruett, Calvin's biological father, for instance.

Julie and Libby talked about the pros and cons of going into business together, turning the Perk Up into a café, but the conversation was dispirited, stopping and starting at odd times, when one or the other of them remembered why they were driving to the Silver Spur.

They were neither the first nor the last to arrive—there were cars and trucks everywhere, parked at strange angles at the edges of the Ruizes' expansive lawn. Julie found a place for the Cadillac, wedged it in and thrust out a sigh of resignation.

"Here goes," she said, shutting off the engine and shoving open her door.

The engine went through the usual sequence of clicks and clatters as it wound down.

Libby unsnapped her seat belt and climbed out, too, teetering a little because the ground was uneven and she wasn't accustomed to wearing high heels—she owned exactly one pair, relics of her high school prom—but Paige didn't move at all.

Bending her knees slightly, Libby rapped on the car window.

"I'm coming," Paige called testily, but she remained still.

The yard was crowded with people, most of them helping themselves to bottles of water jutting from metal tubs full of ice or food set out on long, portable tables tended by ladies from Isabel and Pablo's church.

Libby followed her sister's gaze and spotted Austin at the center of things, shaggy-haired but clean-shaven, and spruced up in a suit he probably wore as seldom as possible.

"Come on, Paige," she urged, growing impatient. She wanted to get on with it, so she could go home, peel off her sweaty clothes and the pantyhose that were chafing the insides of her thighs and take a long, cool shower, and the only way to get there was *through* the next stage of the ordeal. "Austin isn't going to bite you."

"That," Julie remarked, just loudly enough for Paige to hear her through the car window, "might be the problem."

Paige's pale, perfect complexion pulsed with pink. She thrust open the door and got out, glaring at Julie, who was characteristically unfazed. She linked arms with Paige, Libby taking the other side, and the three of them forged ahead.

They found Isabel first, and offered their condolences.

They signed the guestbook, and then joined the crowd on the lawn, accepting plates brimming with food they would only nibble at.

They would *circulate*, like the well-mannered Texas women they were, and make their escape at the customary signal from Libby. She was and always had been constitutionally incapable of standing in green grass without taking off her shoes; when she slipped them back on, everyone would say their farewells and converge on the car.

Libby couldn't have missed Tate, even if she'd tried. He towered over almost everyone else gathered in the Ruiz yard, his hair blue-black in the afternoon sunshine. Aware that he was making his way toward her, pausing to speak to this one and that one, Libby surrendered to the inevitable and waited, her shoes dangling by their narrow straps from her left index finger, her plate sagging in her right hand.

"Pretty good turnout," he said, when he reached her. Tate had never been good at small talk.

"Yes," Libby agreed simply, not inclined to make things easy for him.

Color flared up in his neck and under his jawline, then subsided. "About what happened—"

Libby raised both eyebrows, pretending confusion. As if she hadn't practically dragged the man to bed and then carried on like a she-wolf in heat while he did all the right things to her.

"Dammit, Libby," he muttered, onto the game, "knock off the deer-in-the-headlights routine. This is hard enough."

The phrase *hard enough* made an inappropriate giggle bubble into the back of her throat. She barely swallowed it in time.

"I assume," she said, with false ease, "you're referring to our having sex?"

"Will you keep your voice down?" Tate said, on a rush of breath.

"If I remember correctly," she continued, in an exaggerated

whisper, having already made certain no one was close enough to overhear, "we *did* have sex."

"I'm not denying that," Tate snapped.

"Why bring it up?" Libby asked mildly, knowing full well why he'd mentioned the tryst. He wanted to make sure she understood that the encounter had been meaningless, a fling. She mustn't expect anything more.

"Because," Tate said, leaning in close, his forehead nearly touching hers, "things have changed."

The statement took Libby by surprise, and when she widened her eyes and raised her brows this time, she wasn't pretending. "Changed?" she echoed stupidly.

Tate took her by the elbow, the one on the left, with the shoes dangling from the corresponding finger, and hustled her away from the gathering to stand in the small orchard, under one of Pablo's cherished apricot trees. She looked around, spotted Julie arguing quietly with Garrett, and Paige and Austin standing with their backs to each other, not a dozen feet apart, both of them stiff-spined.

Clearly, neither of her sisters would ride to her rescue.

"Tate, what…?"

"Stop it," Tate rasped. "*Something happened,* Libby, and I'm not going to pretend it didn't."

Another giggle, this one hysterical, tried to escape Libby, but she dropped her shoes and put her hand over her mouth to keep it in.

Tate let out his breath, and his broad shoulders sagged a little under the fine fabric of the tailored suit he was sweltering in. Once again, Libby imagined a cold shower, but this time Tate joined her in the fantasy, and the resulting surge of heat nearly melted her knees.

"I want another chance with you," he said, stunning her so thoroughly that he might as well have aimed a Taser gun at her and pulled the trigger. Shoving a hand through his hair, he sighed again. "I know I don't deserve it," he went on. "But I'm asking for another shot."

The plate fell from Libby's hand, potato salad and cold chicken and something made with green gelatin and sliced bananas plopping at their feet. Both of them ignored it.

"What?" Libby sputtered, amazed.

An expression of proud misery moved in Tate's strong face, was gone again in an instant. "A simple 'no' would do," he said. Maybe the misery had gone, but the famous McKettrick pride was still there.

"You—you mean, it wasn't—well—just one of those things?" Libby managed.

"'Just one of those things'?" His tone was almost scathing. "Maybe you have that kind of sex all the time, Lib, but *I don't.*"

This round, the giggle got past all her defenses. It was a shaky sound, a little raspy. "You think I have sex all the time?" she asked, only too aware that she was prattling and completely unable to help herself. Whenever sex and Tate McKettrick occupied the same conversation, or even the same thought, her IQ seemed to plummet. Incensed by this sudden realization, she raised both hands, palms out, and shoved them hard into Tate's chest. *"You think I have sex all the time?"*

Through the haze surrounding her, Libby sensed that heads were turning.

She caught a glimpse of Julie hurrying in their direction. Paige was probably on the way, too.

"Dammit, Libby," Tate almost barked, "this is a *wake.*"

Libby shoved him again, and then again. Enjoyed a brief mental movie in which he tumbled backward and landed on his fine McKettrick ass under Pablo's apricot trees.

Tate proved immovable, though, since he was so much bigger than she was. Just as Julie reached them, he grasped Libby's wrists to stay the blows.

"Look," he ground out, "that didn't come out right. I meant—"

Libby felt dazed, literally beside herself. Her heart pounded, and she was sure she was hyperventilating.

Julie stooped to snatch up Libby's shoes. "Time to go," she chimed.

Slowly, Tate released his hold on Libby. "I'm sorry," he said.

Libby stared at him, nearly blinded by tears. Didn't resist when Julie tugged her away, keeping to the edge of the crowd.

Paige caught up, double-stepping.

"What just happened here?" Julie asked moderately, when they were all in the car.

Before, the blast of cool hair from the vents on Julie's dashboard had been a blessed relief; now, it made Libby hug herself and shiver. Her lower lip wobbled, and she couldn't bring herself to look at her sister.

"I'm not sure," Libby said brokenly, but only after Julie had put the Cadillac into Reverse, stepped on the gas and negotiated a series of complicated maneuvers, involving a lot of backing up, inching forward and backing up again. "Things just—got out of hand."

"I'll say," Paige commented, from the backseat.

Fresh mortification washed over Libby. "Please tell me we weren't yelling."

"You weren't yelling," Julie said.

"Really? Or are you just saying that?"

Julie chuckled. "Honey, neither of you *had* to yell. The air crackled like it does before a good ole Texas lightning storm. From the looks of things, the two of you were either going to kill each other or make a baby on the spot."

Libby slid down in the seat, horrified. "Oh, my God," she moaned.

"McKettrick men," Paige offered calmly, "can turn a sane woman crazy."

Tate's words came back to Libby. *This is a wake.*

"Isabel will never forgive me," she said.

"Isabel," Julie soothed, in her practical way, "was inside the house by the time hostilities broke out, lying down with a cold cloth over her eyes. And don't look now, but sparks flying between you and the McKettricks' number one son aren't exactly breaking news around these parts."

Libby's embarrassment was now total. How would she face people after making such a scene? What had come over her?

She tried to retrace the conversation in her mind, to pinpoint exactly where she'd stepped on a land mine, but it was all a nonsensical jumble of he said/she said.

Except that Tate had basically accused her of being promiscuous.

Hadn't he?

"This is it," Libby decided aloud, as they bumped over the rutted dirt road leading back toward the highway. "I'm leaving town forever. I'll change my name, dye my hair—"

Paige unhooked her seat belt and poked her head between the front seats. "Don't be silly," she said. "Everybody makes a complete and utter fool of themselves now and then."

"Gee," Libby nearly snarled, "*that* was a comforting thing to say."

"If it's any consolation," Paige pressed on, undaunted, "Tate looked as if he wished the ground would open up and swallow him."

"It isn't," Libby replied.

"Let's not bicker," Julie interjected.

"We're *not* bickering," Paige bickered. "I was merely stating a fact. Playing the fool once in a while is only human."

"Paige?" Julie said sweetly.

"What?"

"Shut the hell up."

Paige sagged backward, fastened her seat belt back with a metallic snap, grumbling something under her breath.

"*You* never made a fool of yourself," Libby accused her youngest sister, her gaze colliding with Paige's in the rearview mirror. "Miss Perfect."

Paige rolled her eyes. "You've got a short memory," she shot back. "I tried to run Austin McKettrick over with a golf cart once, if you'll recall."

"Chased him right down Main Street," Julie reminisced fondly. "Good thing he was so quick on his feet."

"Shut up," Paige said.

"That was my line," Julie answered.

Libby began to laugh. Like the giggles she'd battled earlier, this laughter was more a release of tension than amusement. Still, it *had* been funny, watching Austin sprint down the white line, sometimes backward, laughing at Paige as she swerved behind him at lawn-mower speed.

Austin had finally taken refuge on the courthouse steps, gasping for breath, and Paige had plainly intended to drive right up after him. Fortunately, she'd commandeered a golf cart instead of an army tank—the front wheels bumped hard against the bottom stair and then the engine died. *Un*fortunately, she'd nearly been arrested and would probably have gone to jail for attempted assault if Austin hadn't refused to press charges.

"Okay," Libby admitted, turning to look back at Paige, "there was that one lapse. But I've never seen you lose your temper, before or since, which makes me wonder if you're an alien or something."

"Some of us," Julie remarked loftily, "have sense enough not to get involved with a McKettrick in the first place."

"Oh, for Pete's sake," Paige scoffed. "I saw you shaking your finger beneath Garrett's nose back there. If he wanted to get under your skin, he could—it's a gift. They all have it."

"Please," Julie said, gliding up to a Stop sign pocked with bulletholes, a common sight in that part of Texas, and signaling a left turn before swinging that big pink boat out onto the asphalt to head for town. "Me and *Garrett McKettrick?* The man is a *politician.* You know what I think of *that* species."

"He's also good-looking in the extreme," Libby pointed out.

"Not to mention McKettrick-rich," Paige added.

"He's a player," Julie went on. "God knows how many women he's stringing along."

Again, Libby's gaze connected with Paige's in the rearview mirror.

"Uh-oh," Paige said.

"I don't care about looks," Julie insisted. "*Or* money. Garrett McKettrick is definitely not my type."

"What *is* your type?" Libby asked, glad to be talking about something besides the debacle with Tate, back there in the Ruizes' orchard.

"I don't have one," Julie said. "I've resigned myself to being single. In fact, I *like* being single. Calvin and I are doing just fine on our own, thank you very much. The last thing we need is a man complicating our lives."

"What about sex?" Paige asked. "Don't you miss that?"

Libby began to feel overheated again. Why did *sex* have to come up in every conversation? She went months without think-

ing about the subject at all—much—and now it seemed to be in
her face every time she turned around. What was up with that?

"You don't have to be married," Julie reminded her sisters, "to
enjoy sex."

"No," Paige agreed, "but a *man* helps."

Libby's face flamed as her flesh prickled with remembered sen-
sations: Tate's mouth on her neck, on the insides of her elbows and
the backs of her knees, on her—well, *everywhere.*

"Don't tell me you're using a vibrator," Paige said, like it was a
crime or something. "You're still young, Julie. You need a man."

Julie's neck was bright red. "Who said anything about a vibrator?" she snapped. "And how do you know I'm not having a wild,
passionate affair? I do have *some* secrets from you two, after all."

"No, you don't," Paige replied smugly. "If you were seeing
someone, I'd know it, and so would everybody else in Blue River."

Here it comes. Libby bit down on her lower lip, closed her eyes.

But Paige was on a roll. "That's the problem with small towns,"
she went on mercilessly. "When somebody goes to bed with somebody else—" here, she paused for effect "—word gets around in
no time. Take Libby and Tate, for instance."

Libby winced.

"Libby," Julie said, sounding intrigued, as well as shocked,
"you didn't."

"Oh, yes, she did," Paige trilled, the triumphant little sister
avenging a multitude of childhood slights.

Libby covered her face with both hands and groaned.

"Is this true?" Julie asked slowly.

Libby would gladly have violated a lifetime of principles just
then and lied like a pro, but she knew both her sisters would see
right through it. They knew each other too well.

"Yes," she said, after a very long time. "Yes, I slept with Tate
McKettrick. Are you satisfied?"

"No," Julie said succinctly. "But I'll bet *you* were."

CHAPTER NINE

As far as Tate was concerned, the house was just too damn big.

He knew Garrett and Austin were around, but they were keeping to themselves, and with the kids back at Cheryl's place and Esperanza helping with the clean-up over at the Ruizes', Tate might as well have been alone on the planet.

Except, of course, for Ambrose and Buford.

Most likely missing the twins, the pups had found his best work boots next to the back door and systematically chewed them to pieces.

With a pang, he thought of Crockett. As a pup, his old dog had had a penchant for chewing boots, too. And Charlie, one of Crockett's many predecessors, had reduced a custom-made pair, Tate's dad's pride and joy, to shreds.

Tate recalled how scared he'd been. Another kid's father had shot a dog for a far lesser crime, and even though Jim McKettrick, a strict but fair father, had never raised a hand to any of his sons or their mother, Tate had been sure his beloved dog was facing immediate execution.

Eight years old at the time, he'd left home with Charlie, the two of them headed overland in the general direction of Oklahoma, going by the compass he'd gotten for Christmas. He was lugging the dog's plastic food bowl and a rolled-up sleeping bag and not much else, with no specific destination in mind.

His dad caught up to them on horseback about an hour into the journey, probably tipped off by one of the ranch hands. On a busy spread like the Silver Spur, it was hard for a kid to get away with much of anything since somebody was always watching, ready to run off at the mouth at the first opportunity.

"Where you headed?" Jim had asked, almost casually, pulling his well-worn hat down low over his eyes and shifting easily in the saddle. His big chestnut gelding snorted, peeved at being reined in when he'd rather be punching cattle.

Tears had welled up in Tate's eyes; all those years later, he could feel the burn of them, a sort of dry, scalding sensation. "Me and Charlie figured we ought to leave," he'd answered, dropping his head for a moment before meeting Jim's steady gaze. "Charlie went and chewed up your good boots—the ones Mom had made for your birthday, with our brand and the Alamo and the flag of the Republic on them."

Jim had taken off his hat then, run the sleeve of his sweat-stained chambray shirt across his face and leaned forward a little, resting one forearm on the saddle horn. "I see," he'd said quietly, before putting the hat back on. "And you reckoned that lighting out on your own was the best course of action?"

Tate had swallowed hard. Now, he was going to be in trouble for running away, he guessed, on top of Charlie taking a bullet in the head out behind the barn. Having no answer at hand, he'd simply looked up at his father and waited forlornly for the collapse of the known universe.

Jim had sighed, swung one leg over the gelding's neck, and jumped to the ground. Approaching Tate and the dog, he'd crouched to ruffle Charlie's mismatched ears, one a grayish-brown, one white. A stray who'd shown up at the ranch one day with his ribs showing and his multicolored coat full of burrs, Charlie wasn't much to look at, but except for boot-chewing, he pretty much behaved himself.

"Look at me, boy," Jim had said, his voice gentle.

Tate had met his father's fierce blue gaze. "You gonna shoot Charlie, Dad?" he'd asked.

"Now why in the devil would I do a thing like that?"

"That's what Ryan Williams's dad did when their dog wrecked the new carpet."

"Well, son," Jim had drawled reasonably, still sitting on his haunches, "I'm not Ryan Williams's dad, now am I? I'm yours."

Tate's heartbeat had quickened, and he'd almost flung himself into his father's arms before he remembered that he was eight years old and too big for that kind of stuff. "I guess I'm still in trouble, though?"

Jim had looked away, probably to hide a grin. "I guess you are," he'd answered presently. "Running away from home is a dangerous thing to do, Tate. Your mother is half frantic, calling all over the countryside looking for you."

"How about Charlie? Is he in any trouble?"

Jim had chuckled then. Stood up tall, with the sun behind him. "Charlie's in the clear. Dogs chew things up sometimes, because they don't know any better. You, on the other hand, don't have that excuse. You *do* know better. You're going to have to do extra chores for a month, and you can forget that school field trip to Six Flags next week, because you won't be going along."

Tate had merely nodded, too relieved that Charlie was going to be all right to care about staying behind when everybody else in the whole school went to Six Flags. He knew he'd care plenty when the time came, though.

His dad had laid a hand on his right shoulder. "Let's go on home now," he said, "before your mother calls in the FBI."

Tate had ridden back to the ranch house in front of Jim, clutching the dog bowl and the sleeping bag, Charlie trotting cheerfully alongside the horse.

Back in the present, Tate crouched the way his father had done that day. Ruffled one dog's ears, then the other's. "You're a pair to draw to," he said. "And this'll teach me to leave my boots by the back door when I come in from the range."

After that, he took the mutts outside.

They headed straight for the castle, sniffing the ground, probably trying to track Audrey and Ava.

Tate missed his daughters sorely as he watched their dogs searching for them. Even when he was a kid, broken homes were common, but he and his brothers had grown up under one roof, with parents who loved them and each other, and until the split with Cheryl, the concept had been foreign to him.

Now, he was all too familiar with it.

The dogs returned to him, tails wagging, taking their failure to scare up the twins in their stride. He wished he could accept the kids' absence as philosophically as the pups had.

When Garrett's black sports car zoomed backward out of the garage, Tate was so startled that he almost left his hide in a pool on the ground and stepped out of it like a pair of dirty jeans.

Seeing him, accurately reading the glower taking shape on his face like clouds gathering to dump a ground-pocking rain, Garrett winced. Rolled down his window.

"Sorry," he told Tate, with a sheepish grin.

Maybe if it hadn't been for Pablo's funeral and the way he'd blown things with Libby in the orchard and the kids being gone from home again, Tate would have held his temper. As things stood, though, his brother's careless mistake pushed him one step over the line.

Rounding the ridiculously expensive car, he slammed both fists down onto the shiny hood and glowered hard at Garrett through the bug-specked windshield.

"Hey!" Garrett protested, shoving open the driver's side door and piling out, face flushed, eyes flashing. "What the *hell*—"

Tate advanced on Garrett, seething. Gripped him by the front of his white dress shirt and hurled him back against the car. "Did you even glance in your rearview mirror before you shot out of that garage like a goddamm bullet?" he yelled. "What if one of the kids had been behind you, or one of these dogs?"

Garrett paled at the mention of possibilities he obviously hadn't considered.

Tate let his hands fall to his sides, stepped back out of his brother's space.

A few awkward beats of silence passed.

"You all right?" Garrett asked at last, his voice hoarse.

Tate looked away, didn't answer because anything he said would only make bad matters worse.

"Tate?" Garrett pressed, never one to leave well enough alone.

Tate met Garrett's gaze, held it steadily, still holding his tongue.

"Look," Garrett said, "I'll be more careful after this. It's been one hell of a day for all of us, and I guess I just wasn't thinking."

"You think this was a bad day?" Tate said, after grinding his back molars together for a second or so. "That wouldn't begin to cover it if you'd killed somebody just now."

Garrett surveyed him. "I said I was sorry, Tate," he replied evenly. "I said I wouldn't make the same mistake a second time. What more do you want—a strip of my ornery McKettrick hide?"

"I'll have a lot more than a *strip* of your hide if you ever do a damn fool thing like that again."

Garrett sighed and straightened his shoulders, and Tate could almost see the politician in him coming to the fore. Trouble was, Garrett *wasn't* a politician, he was a rancher, though it looked like he was going to be the last one to figure that out. "Can we start over, here? Before we wind up rolling around in the dirt the way we did when we were kids?"

Tate thrust out a breath. Allowed himself a semblance of a smile at the memory of all those barnyard brawls. Their mother had broken up more than one by spraying her three sons with a garden hose. Their dad's method had been more direct: he'd simply waded into the middle of the fray, got them by the scruff and sent them tumbling in three different directions.

"Okay," he said. "Let's start over."

Garrett grinned. Then he got into his car, drove it into the garage and backed out again, covering about an inch per hour.

Watching Tate, he raised both eyebrows as if to say, *Satisfied?*

"Where were you headed in such a hurry, anyhow?" Tate asked.

"The senator," Garrett said, the grin gone, "is having an emergency."

"The senator," Tate replied, "is *always* having an emergency. What is it now? Did the press catch him naked in a hot tub with three bimbos again?"

"That," Garrett replied, stiff with indignation, "is not what happened."

"Right," Tate scoffed. It was a wonder to him how Garrett's famously incompetent boss and so-called mentor kept getting re-elected to the U.S. Senate.

"You know what you are, Tate?" Garrett countered, scowling.

"You're a sore loser. You voted for the opposition, they lost by a landslide and now you're raking up muck. I'm surprised at you."

Tate gripped the edge of the open window and stooped a little to look directly into his brother's face. "Pull your head out of your ass, Garrett," he said. "*The senator,* as you so augustly refer to him, is a crook—and that's his *best* quality. When are you going to stop cleaning up his messes and set about making some kind of life for yourself?"

"A life like yours?" Garrett retorted, his eyes fairly crackling with blue fire. "Playing the gentleman cowboy while a bunch of ranch hands do the real work? Don't kid yourself, Tate. You might be all grown up on the outside, but inside, you're still the rich kid from the biggest ranch in four counties, feeling like you ought to apologize to folks who have to earn a living. When the kids are with Cheryl, you just mark time until they come back. Maybe that looks like a life to you, but I'd call it something else."

Physically, Tate didn't move. On the inside, though, he pulled back, stunned by Garrett's words—and the sickening knowledge that they were at least partly true.

"Oh, hell," Garrett said, sounding pained. "I didn't mean that—"

"Sure you did," Tate broke in gruffly. "And maybe I had it coming."

Garrett started to open the car door, waited pointedly until Tate got out of the way. "It wasn't your fault, what happened to Pablo," he said calmly, once he was on his feet again.

"Wasn't it?" Tate countered bitterly. "Pablo wasn't a young man. He shouldn't have been transporting that stallion on his own. *I'm* the one who thought it would be a good idea to breed ourselves some spotted ponies."

"And Pablo should have called you beforehand, let you know what was going on. You could have helped unload the horse, or arranged for someone else to make the delivery." Garrett paused, probably following the obvious mental trail, and frowned. "You might have been killed yourself, Tate."

Tate didn't reply. He was too busy imagining his girls with one parent—Cheryl. She'd have them in boarding school by puberty at the latest, and spend the bulk of her time trying to figure out how to get into their trust funds.

Garrett started to get back into the car. "I'd better get back to the capital," he said. "The senator has been under a lot of stress lately."

A sour taste filled Tate's mouth at the mention of the politician his brother revered so much, and he spat.

Garrett reddened. "His enemies are trying to discredit him," he said hotly. "The press dogs his every step and his older brother is dying of prostate cancer. Maybe you could cut the senator just a *little* slack."

"I'm sorry about his brother," Tate allowed. By his reckoning, the senator's other problems were his own doing.

Garrett glared. "The senator," he said, "is a truly great man."

Tate shook his head, resisted the need to spit again. "You've definitely got a blind spot where Morgan Cox is concerned, Garrett, whether you'll admit as much or not. What has to happen before you *get* it? You're climbing the ladder to success, all right, but it's up against the wrong wall."

"What you need," Garrett retorted furiously, after maybe thirty seconds of internal struggle, "is a woman. Maybe you'd have a better temperament than a grizzly with a bad toothache if you got laid. Why don't you go find yourself a lady again, and bang her, and get the burrs out from under your hide?"

Tate folded his arms. "I really hope," he said, "that that wasn't a reference to Libby Remington. Because if it was, I'm going to have to kick your ass from here to Houston and back."

A grin crooked up one corner of Garrett's mouth. The man, Tate reflected, was tired of living, egging him on like that. "Wait a second," Garrett said. "That little set-to the two of you had in the Ruizes' orchard this afternoon—"

"That was nothing," Tate said flatly, and without a hope in hell that Garrett would believe him.

"Damn," his brother went on, in the tone of the man enjoying a sudden revelation, "you could do a lot worse than Libby Remington. Come to think of it, you *did* do a lot worse than Libby Remington. Did I mention that I ran into Cheryl at a party in Austin the weekend before the twins' birthday?"

"No," Tate said. "Maybe you didn't mention it because you know I don't give a rat's ass what Cheryl does, as long as she takes good care of my kids when they're with her."

Garrett snapped his fingers. "Maybe that was it," he said, clearly delighted to be nettling Tate.

"In about another second," Tate replied, "I'm going to wipe up the ground with you, little brother."

Garrett removed his cuff links, rolled up his sleeves. "Bring it on," he said.

That was when the spray struck them, ice cold and shining like liquid crystal in the last light of a long, difficult day.

Both of them roared in surprised protest and whirled around to find Austin standing a few yards away, holding the garden hose and grinning like an idiot with a winning lottery ticket in his pocket.

"Peace, brothers," he said, and drenched them completely with another pass of the hose.

Water shot through the open window of Garrett's car and made a sound like fire on the fancy leather seats, then sluiced down the inside of the windshield.

Tate laughed out loud, but Garrett bellowed with rage and advanced on Austin, dripping wet, ready to fight.

Tate went after their kid brother, too, but for a different reason.

Water fights were something of a McKettrick tradition, and it had been way too long since the last one.

JULIE SEEMED A little troubled when she and Paige dropped Libby off in the alley behind the house they'd all grown up in.

"Are you sure you won't come home with us for supper?" she asked. "My special spaghetti casserole has been simmering in the slow cooker all day and Calvin would love to see you."

Libby, standing by her back gate with the straps of her high heels in one hand and her clutch purse tucked under the opposite arm, shook her head and smiled. "I'd love to see Calvin," she said sincerely, "but Hildie needs a walk, and I plan on getting to bed early tonight. The sooner I fall asleep, the sooner this day will be over."

Paige, out of the backseat and about to climb in up front, rose onto her tiptoes to peer at Libby over the roof of the car. "No hard feelings, Lib?" she asked hopefully.

Libby shook her head again. "No hard feelings," she replied.

"I could bring over some spaghetti casserole," Julie fretted.

"Leave it on the porch if you and Hildie are still out walking when I get here—"

Libby cut her off. "Julie," she said, *"I'm fine."*

Paige got into the passenger seat and shut the door.

Libby waved. *"Goodbye."*

Still, Julie waited until Libby had fished her keys out of her bag, unlocked the back door and stepped inside to greet an over-joyed Hildie.

Behind her, Libby heard the Cadillac drive off.

After receiving a royal welcome from her favorite canine, Libby opened the door again, and Hildie trundled out into the yard. By the time the dog returned, Libby had washed out and filled the usual bowls with kibble and water.

While Hildie ate and drank, Libby exchanged her dress for tan cotton shorts and a T-shirt. The hateful pantyhose went into the bathroom trash can, and she flung the shoes to the back of her closet. Short socks and a pair of sneakers completed the ensemble.

The walk was pleasant, restoring Libby a little, and by the time she and Hildie got home, she was getting hungry. Wishing she hadn't been quite so quick to turn down Julie's offer to drop off some of her famous spaghetti casserole, Libby was taking a mental inventory of the contents of her refrigerator as she stepped through the front gate, and didn't immediately notice the figure huddled on the porch steps.

Hildie gave a halfhearted little bark—she wasn't much of a guard dog—and Libby stopped in her tracks, fighting an urge to pretend she had the wrong house, turn around and flee.

"Marva?" she asked, instead.

Her mother wore a black and gold, zebra-striped caftan from her extensive collection of leisure garments, along with plenty of makeup. "It's about time you got home," Marva accused, making a petulant face. "I don't have a house key anymore, you know."

Libby considered the distance between the condominium complex and her place, and frowned. Marva often took long walks, but never without her prized athletic shoes, and tonight she was wearing metallic-gold flats with pointed toes. "How did you get here?" Libby asked.

Marva jutted out her chin, still angling for a welcome, evidently.

"I took a cab," she said. "It's not as if I could count on any of my *children* for a ride, after all."

Libby remembered to latch the gate, leaned down to unhook Hildie's leash. There was precisely one taxi in Blue River, and it was often up on blocks in the high weeds behind Chudley Wilkes's trailer-house, though he'd been known to fire it up when someone called, wanting a ride someplace and willing to pay the fare.

"Are you hungry?" Libby asked, sitting down beside her mother on the step. Up close, she could see that Marva's red lipstick had gone on crooked and was mostly chewed off. "I could make scrambled eggs—"

"The cabdriver was a hayseed," Marva went on, as though Libby hadn't spoken at all. "He claims he's related to John Wilkes Booth, on his mother's side. Booth's mother, not his."

"Chudley likes to spin a yarn, all right," Libby said. "Not many people call for a taxi in a town this size, so he has a lot of time to study the family tree. Over time, he's grafted on a few branches."

"Aren't you going to ask me in?" Marva asked. "I came all this way, and you just leave me sitting on the front porch like some beggar."

Libby figured there no use pointing out that she'd just offered to whip up some scrambled eggs and hadn't planned to serve them on the front porch. "Of course you can come in," she said, rising.

All this time, Hildie had been standing on the walk, head tilted to one side, studying Marva as though she had sprouted out of the ground only moments before.

"Whose dog is that?" Marva fussed, though she'd made Hildie's acquaintance at least once before. "I don't like dogs. It will have to stay outside." She made a go-away motion with the backs of her hands. "Scat! Go home."

"Hildie is my dog," Libby said carefully, a sick feeling congealing in the bottom of her stomach. "She *lives* here."

"Shoo," Marva said, paying no attention to Libby. Most of her conversations were one-sided; she did all the talking and none of the listening. "Go away."

Hildie hesitated, then backed up a few steps, confused.

"Mother," Libby said, annoyed, as well as alarmed, "*don't*. Please. You're scaring her."

But Marva had turned her head to stare at Libby. "Did you just call me 'Mother'?"

Libby wasn't sure how to answer. Years ago, before she'd packed a suitcase and left, Marva had hated being addressed by that term, or any of its more affectionate variations.

"It doesn't matter," she finally said. "Let's go in and I'll start the scrambled eggs." Then, more firmly, she called her dog. "Come on, Hildie."

Hildie hesitated, uncertain, then lumbered toward Libby, full of trust.

"I won't be in the same house with that horrible creature," Marva warned.

"Then you'll have to eat your supper out here," Libby replied, very quietly, "because Hildie is coming inside with me." *And, furthermore, she is not a "horrible creature."*

Marva began to cry, sniffling at first, then wailing. "You hate me! I'm all alone in the world!"

The truth was, Libby didn't hate Marva—she'd shut that part of herself down a long, long time ago—but she couldn't have said she loved her, either.

"Come inside," Libby urged gently. "I'll brew some tea. Would you like a nice cup of tea?"

Marva stepped over the threshold, stood in the small, modestly furnished living room, looking around. She didn't seem to notice when Hildie slunk in behind her and took refuge behind the couch.

"I lived here once," Marva said, as though she'd just recalled the fact.

"Yes," Libby confirmed, at once suspicious and sympathetic. "You lived here once."

And then you left. Even though Paige and Julie and I begged you not to go.

"Where did he die?" Marva asked. Her mascara had run, and her hair was starting to droop around her face, but the expression in her eyes was lucid. "Show me where he died."

Libby moved to stand where her father's rented hospital bed had been, during the last months of his life. "Here," she said. "Right here."

I was holding his hand. Paige and Julie were here, too. And the last word he said was your name.

"On the living-room floor?"

"In a hospital bed."

"Well, I'm not surprised. The man had no imagination."

Libby struggled to hold on to her temper. She'd lost it once already today, and she wasn't about to let it go again. Moments before, she'd considered the possibility that Marva was genuinely ill. Now, she suspected she was being played, manipulated—again. "Dying doesn't require much imagination," she remarked, with no inflection whatsoever. "A lot of courage, perhaps."

Dad raised us, provided for us, sacrificed for us. He loved us and we knew it. That's more than you ever did.

"Courage!" Marva huffed. "Will Remington was a small-town schoolteacher, content to plod along, living in this rattrap of a house and calling it home. Driving a secondhand car and buying day-old bread and clipping coupons out of the Wednesday paper. How much courage does that take?"

"A lot, I think," Libby said calmly. *He washed our hair. He told us bedtime stories and listened to our prayers before we went to sleep. Maybe it took some courage to hear his children asking God to send their mother home, night after night. Maybe, damn you, it took courage just to keep getting up in the morning.*

Marva whirled on her. "You do, do you?" she challenged hotly. "You think your father was such a hero? Well, let me tell you something, missy—Will was dead his whole life. *I'm* the one who did all the living!"

Hildie peered around the end of the couch and growled pitiably.

Libby left the room, trembling, and came as far as the inside doorway with her car keys in one hand. She jangled them at her mother. "It's time for you to go," she said.

Marva frowned. "What about the scrambled eggs?"

"I'm fresh out," Libby replied. "Of eggs, I mean."

"But I'm hungry!"

"Then we'll get you a hamburger on the way over. Let's go."

"This is a fine how-do-you-do," Marva ranted. "I come to visit my own daughter, in my own home, and I get the bum's rush!"

"This isn't your home," Libby said. *And I wish to God I wasn't your daughter.* "Things have changed. You moved out years ago."

Hildie whimpered. She wasn't used to stress.

"Please," Marva pleaded, with such pathos that, yet again, Libby wasn't sure if the woman was mentally ill or had simply changed her tactics. "Let me stay here. Just for tonight."

"Let's go," Libby said, hardening her heart a little against the inevitable guilt. What if Marva actually was sick? What if she was having a breakdown or something?

"I'm your mother," Marva reminded her.

Yes, God help me. You are. But I don't have to love you. I don't even have to like you.

"And I'm lonely," Marva persisted, when Libby didn't speak. "None of you girls are willing to make room in your lives for me."

Libby closed her eyes. *Don't go there,* she warned herself.

"Suppose I die? You'll be sorry you treated me this way when I die."

A year after you left, I started telling people you were dead. They all knew better, because they remembered you. They remembered the scandal. But they pretended to believe me, just to be kind.

"Dad loved you so much," Libby blurted out. Or was it the little girl she'd once been, not the woman she was, doing the talking? "He never stopped believing you'd come back."

"I couldn't take you with me," Marva said, true to form. Libby might not have spoken at all. "You were practically babies, the three of you. And we lived like gypsies, Lance and me." She paused, and a dreamy expression crossed her face, all the more disturbing because of her smeared makeup. "Like gypsies," she repeated softly.

Lance. Libby had never known Marva's lover's name.

Not that it mattered now.

She bit her lower lip, tried to think what to say or do, to get through to Marva, and jumped when a light knock sounded at the front door.

Hildie retreated behind the couch.

"Libby?" Paige let herself in, a small, lidded dish in her hands. "I brought you some of Julie's casserole—she insisted—" Seeing Marva, Paige's brown eyes widened. "Oh," she said.

"Yeah, oh," Libby confirmed. She could have hugged her little sister, she was so glad to see her. As a nurse, Paige would know if Marva needed medical help. "She's acting strangely," she added, gesturing toward their mother.

"Don't talk about me as though I weren't even here," Marva huffed.

The lid on Julie's dish rattled a little as Paige set it aside on the small table beside the door.

"I love casserole," Marva said, smiling happily.

Paige marched right over, confident as a prison matron taking charge of a new arrival, grasped their mother firmly by the arm and hustled her toward the door. "Some other time, maybe," she said cheerfully, casting a reassuring look at Libby. "Right now, Marva, you and I are going to take a little spin in my car."

"Thank you," Libby mouthed.

"You owe me," Paige said.

And just like that, the latest Marva episode was over.

For now, anyway.

Libby locked the front door, leaving the casserole dish right where it was, and turned to Hildie.

It took fifteen minutes to persuade the poor dog to come out from behind the couch.

THE WATER FIGHT turned out to be a dandy—even the dogs got involved. When it was over, Tate and Garrett and Austin all sat in the kitchen in their wet clothes, drinking beer and talking about the old days.

It was generally agreed that when it came to dousing people with a hose, their mother was still the all-around champ. She'd had an advantage, of course—raised Southern, none of them would have considered wresting the thing out of her hands and soaking her in retribution, the way they would have done with each other.

Sober and a little chilled, Tate was about to head upstairs to take a hot shower and hit the sack, the dogs set to follow on his heels, when his cell phone rang.

He picked it up off the table, checked the digital panel to see who was calling and flipped it open. "Cheryl? Are the kids all right?"

"Yes," Cheryl said. "They're fine. Sound asleep."

Tate glanced at the clock; it was after eleven. "And you're calling me at this hour because—?"

"Don't be mean," she purred.

Good God. Was she *drunk?* What if the house caught fire, or one of the kids got sick?

"Cheryl, are you all right?"

Austin scraped back his chair and rose from the kitchen table, shaking his head. Garrett gave Tate a pitying look and headed for his own part of the house. Evidently, he'd forgotten the senator's "emergency," whatever it was.

"No," Cheryl burst out, sobbing all of the sudden. It still amazed Tate, the way she could change emotional gears so quickly. "I'm *not* all right. I'm divorced. I'm an attractive, educated woman, in the prime of my life, stuck in Blue River, Texas, for the next twelve years—"

"Have you been drinking?"

"Would you care if I had been?"

"Hell, yes, I'd care," Tate snapped. "You're alone with my children."

"I'm perfectly sober, and they're *my* children, too."

Tate drew in a long, deep breath, released it slowly. This was no time to needle her. "Yes," he said, in what he hoped was a reassuring tone of voice. "They're your children, too."

Cheryl was quiet for a few moments, so quiet that Tate began to wonder if she'd hung up. "We could try again, Tate," she said tremulously. "You and me. We could try again, make it work this time."

Tate closed his eyes. If she wasn't drunk, she must have snorted something. The subject of reconciliation had come up before, usually after she and some boyfriend had had a falling-out and gone their separate ways.

"No, Cheryl," he said, when he figured he could trust himself to speak. "You don't really want that, and neither do I."

"Because of Libby Remington," she said, with a trace of bitterness. "That's why you won't try to save our marriage. Did you think I wouldn't hear about you and Libby, Tate?"

Save their marriage? They'd been divorced for five years.

"We're not going to talk about Libby," Tate replied, silently commending himself for not reminding her that this marriage she

wanted to save had long since died an acrimonious—and permanent—death. "Not tonight, anyway."

"I hate this town." Three-sixties were common with Cheryl
when she was upset. There was no telling where she'd try to take
the conversation next.

"The solution is simple, Cheryl," Tate reasoned. "Let Audrey
and Ava live with me. You'd be free to do whatever you wanted,
then. You could live anyplace, practice law again."

"You'd like that, wouldn't you?" The question, though softly
put, was a loaded one, and Tate proceeded accordingly.

He was already on his feet, heedless of his damp clothes, rum-
maging for his truck keys. Austin lingered, leaning against one
of the counters, sipping reheated coffee and not even bothering
to pretend he wasn't eavesdropping. The dogs waited patiently to
go upstairs, wagging their tails.

"I'll take care of the mutts," Austin said, between swallows
of coffee.

Cheryl's rant continued, rising in volume and making less and
less sense.

Tate nodded his thanks to his brother and stepped into the garage.

"Are you *listening*, Tate McKettrick?" Cheryl demanded.

"I'm listening," Tate said, climbing into his truck and pushing
the button to open the garage door behind him. It rolled up silently,
an electronic wonder. "Keep talking."

She started crying again. "It would have been so perfect!"

"What would have been perfect?" Tate asked, backing out into
the moonlit Texas night, stars splattered from one horizon to the
other.

"Our life together," Cheryl said, after a small, choked sob.

"How do you figure that?" There was a limit to Tate's ability
to play games, and he'd almost reached it.

"We could have had it all, if only—"

Tate frowned, turning the truck around, pointing it toward town.
"If only what?"

"If only you hadn't been in love with Libby Remington the
whole time," Cheryl said. "She came between us, from the very
beginning. You never got over her."

"That's crazy, Cheryl," he said, racing down the driveway to the main road.

She went off on another tangent, something about her lonely childhood, and how money didn't buy happiness, and she'd *always* wanted a real family of her own.

You could have fooled me, Tate thought.

But he listened, and when she ran down, he got her talking again.

Long minutes later, he braked in front of Cheryl's house, bolted from the truck, leaving the door open and the engine running, and strode to the front door.

"Let me in," he said, into his cell phone.

"Let you in? Where are you?"

Tate shoved his free hand through his hair and let out his breath. "On your porch," he said. "Open the damn door, Cheryl. *Now.*"

CHAPTER TEN

CHERYL SWUNG HER front door open slowly, and Tate, just snapping his cell phone shut on their disturbing conversation, which had spanned the distance between the ranch and her house in town, was stunned. He'd expected to find his ex-wife an emotional train wreck, given the way she'd whined and fussed. Instead, her skin glowed with what looked like arousal, her makeup was perfect, her dark hair wound neatly into a single, glossy braid reaching nearly to her waist. And in her eyes, Tate saw a guarded glint of triumph.

"Come in," she said, her voice throaty and all Texased-up with heat and honey, a neat trick since she didn't have a drop of Southern blood in her.

And the keyword was *trick*.

Tate stood stiffly on the doormat. If he allowed his gaze to drop, even slightly, he knew he'd get the full impact of what she was wearing—a sexy nightgown that revealed a lot more than it covered up and barely breezed past her thighs. She held a glass of white wine in one hand.

"Want some?" she asked, ever the mistress of the double entendre, and took a sip.

"This was a *setup?*" The question was rhetorical, of course, and the situation wasn't all that surprising, but Tate seethed with indignation just the same. She'd cast her line into the water using the kids as the bait—something she often accused *him* of doing—knowing he'd have no choice but to take the hook.

In that moment, Tate's dislike for his former wife deepened to outright contempt.

Cheryl retreated a step, an oddly graceful move, almost dance-like, and then he couldn't help taking her in. He waited for a visceral response—though mad as a cornered rattler, he was as well-supplied with testosterone as any other man—and was a little surprised when it didn't come.

"A setup?" Cheryl replied softly, her lower lip jutting out in a pout. "I wouldn't exactly put it *that* way."

Tate swayed slightly on his feet, caught in a swift, spinning backwash of fury, averted his eyes and shoved a hand through his hair. "I need to see the kids," he said, on a long, raspy breath. "Then I'm leaving."

Even without looking directly at Cheryl, he knew when her face crumbled. He also knew the reaction didn't stem from the heartbreak of unrequited love. Cheryl had never loved him, any more than he'd loved her. They'd simply collided, at an unfortunate intersection of their two lives, both of them distracted by unrelated concerns, and two innocent and very precious children had been the result.

She stepped back again, gesturing with her left hand, still holding the wine, slopping some onto the spotless white carpet as she did so. "They're asleep. They won't even know you're here," she said wearily. "But suit yourself. You always do."

Tate turned sideways to pass her, headed straight for the stairs. The words *You always do* lodged between his shoulder blades like a knife, but he shook them off out of habit. All he wanted to do right then was gather his girls up, one in each arm, and carry them out of there, take them *home,* where they belonged. Audrey and Ava were McKettricks—they needed to grow up on the land.

Cheryl, however dysfunctional, was neither drunk nor high. Pissed off as he was, Tate had realized that the moment she'd opened the door. Under the terms of their custody agreement, this was Cheryl's week with the twins, and he couldn't rightly intervene.

At the same time, he wasn't about to leave that house without making sure Audrey and Ava were okay. If there were consequences, so be it.

He was halfway up the staircase when his daughters appeared at the top, barefoot and sleepy-eyed, wearing their matching pink pajamas, the ones with the teddy bears printed on the fabric. They huddled close to each other, their small shoulders touching.

Even as babies, they'd done that. They'd only begun to thrive, in fact, when some perceptive pediatric nurse had cornered their doctor and persuaded him to let them share an incubator.

Tate's heart did a slow, backward tumble at the memory.

The idea had made sense to him then, and it made sense to him now. Audrey and Ava had been together in Cheryl's womb, aware of each other on some level, possibly since conception. Born too early, each had still needed the proximity of the other.

"What's wrong, Daddy?" asked Audrey, always quick to read his expression and generally the first to speak her mind.

Tate turned his head to look back over one shoulder at Cheryl. By some devious magic, she'd donned a rumpled robe made of that bumpy cloth—he could never remember what it was called—pale lavender and worn thin in places. She was projecting Mommy vibes so effectively that, for one moment, he thought he must have imagined the sexy nightgown she'd had on when she'd answered the door, the glass of wine in her hand.

"Want some?"

It was the gotcha look in Cheryl's green eyes that convinced Tate he was still sane, though that probably wasn't the reaction she'd been going for. This whole thing was some kind of game to her; she got a weird satisfaction out of jacking him around, and when she felt thwarted, the next attempt was bound to be a real son-of-a-bitch.

"Daddy?" Ava prompted, clasping Audrey's hand tightly now, leaning into her sister a little more. "Is everything okay?"

Tate put Cheryl out of his mind, focused all his attention on his children. *We have to stop this,* he thought. *Somehow, Cheryl and I have got to call a truce.*

"Everything's fine," he said, with a lightness he hoped was convincing. "I was in town, so I came by to tuck you in and say good-night, that's all."

Both girls looked relieved.

"Did you bring Ambrose and Buford?" Audrey asked.

Tate shook his head. "No, sweetie," he answered. "They were headed off to bunk in with your uncle Austin when I left the house."

Behind him, Cheryl cleared her throat, an eloquent little sound. Tate made no attempt to decode it.

"I'd be happy to tuck both of you in," she told her daughters, her tone sunny. "Unless you'd really rather have your daddy kiss you good-night than me."

Tate closed his eyes, sickened. *Unless you'd really rather have your daddy kiss you goodnight than me.* With Cheryl, everything was a contest, a case of either/or—even the love of their children.

"Why can't you *both* kiss us good-night?" Ava asked, her voice fragile.

Tate gazed up at his daughters, full of love and despair and tremendous guilt. They were tearing these children apart, he and Cheryl, and whether he wanted to believe it or not, he was equally responsible.

It had to stop—no matter what.

"One at a time, though," Audrey said. "Because you always fight when you're in the same room."

God in heaven, Tate thought.

"Daddy first," Ava said.

"Certainly," Cheryl chimed, and Tate knew by her voice that she'd turned away. "Why consider *my* feelings? I'm only your mother."

"Cheryl," Tate ground out, not daring to face his ex-wife. "Don't. *Please,* don't."

Cheryl said nothing, but he could feel her bristling somewhere behind him, a little off to the side, a porcupine about to throw quills in every direction.

By deliberate effort, Tate unfroze his muscles and climbed the stairs, forcing a smile. Reaching the top, he herded the little girls, now giggling, in the direction of the large, pink and frilly room they shared.

He tucked them back into their matching canopy beds.

He kissed their foreheads.

He told them he loved them.

And he waited, perched on the cushioned seat set beneath the bay windows overlooking the street, until, at long last, they slept.

Tate dreaded going downstairs again, because it might mean another run-in with Cheryl. He wasn't sure how much self-restraint he had left, and while he'd never struck a woman in his life and didn't intend to start now, words could be used as effectively as fists, and the ones crowding the back of his throat in those moments were as hard and cold as steel.

Fortunately, there was no sign of Cheryl, although as soon as he'd stepped over the threshold onto the porch, he heard the dead bolt engage behind him with a resolute thump. She must have been lurking just inside the living room.

He started down the walk, wasn't even half surprised when Brent Brogan's cruiser pulled in behind his truck. While he'd been saying good-night to Audrey and Ava, waiting for them to drift off into peaceful, little-girl dreams, Cheryl had been summoning the police.

Another segment in the continuing drama.

Suppressing a sigh, Tate opened the gate in the picket fence and stepped through it, onto the sidewalk. "Evenin'," he said, with a half salute, when Brent rolled down his driver's side window to look him up and down. "Slow night, Chief?"

Brogan shook his head. "Not according to the former Mrs. McKettrick," he said, with a nod toward the house. "What are you doing here, Tate? It's pretty late, in case you haven't figured that out already."

Tate stayed where he was, shoved his thumbs into the waistband of his jeans, which were still a little damp from the water fight with Garrett and Austin, hours before. He found that strangely comforting. "She called you," he said flatly.

"She called me," Brent confirmed. "Cheryl said she felt threatened."

Tate gave a raspy chuckle. Thrust the splayed fingers of his right hand through his hair. "Did she? Well, Denzel, that's bullshit and you know it. About forty-five minutes ago, she called *me*, too, and I'd have sworn she was either high or drunk, going by the things she said and the way she sounded. I got here as fast as I could, because, as you may recall, my *kids* live here when they're not on the ranch."

Brent shut off the cruiser's engine, pushed open the door, got out to stand facing Tate there beside the quiet street. He was wearing civilian clothes, instead of his uniform, which meant he was off duty. "I've got to knock on that door, see Ms. Darbrey with my own eyes, and hear her say she's all right," he said. And when Tate started to speak, Brogan held up a hand to silence him. "It's procedure. She's a citizen, she called in a complaint, and whatever my personal opinion of the lady might be, it's my job to follow through."

Tate understood, though it rubbed him a little raw in places that, even for professional reasons, Brent couldn't take him at his word. After all, they'd been buddies since second grade, when his friend's dad, Jock Brogan, had come to work on the Silver Spur as a wrangler and all-around handyman, glad to have a steady paycheck and a trailer to live in. Jock's seven-year-old son had arrived by bus a week later, right on time for the first day of school, sweating in the suit and bow tie he'd worn to his mother's funeral a month before, as it turned out, and scared shitless.

It had taken some time, but eventually Brent, a city boy, had loosened up a little, gotten used to ranch life, and asked Tate to teach him "something about horses." Within a couple of months, the new kid was riding like a pro, keeping up with Tate and Garrett, Austin and Nico Ruiz as easily as if he'd been born in the saddle. Being in the same class at school, and with a lot of common interests, Tate and Brent had formed a special bond.

They'd competed in junior rodeos together.

Played on the same baseball and basketball teams in their teens.

On the day they graduated from high school, Brent announced that he was joining the Air Force instead of going on to the university with Tate, the way they'd always planned. Jock Brogan had scrimped and done without and worked overtime to save enough to cover the better part of his son's college expenses, Brent said, and he wasn't going to take a dime of that money. He'd always wanted to be a cop, he'd reminded Tate, and the military was willing to provide all the training he needed and pay him wages in the bargain.

He could be an asset to his dad from then on, instead of a liability.

Standing there in the night, waiting for Brent to satisfy himself that Cheryl was still in one piece, the words Garrett had thrown in his face earlier that night came back to Tate.

—inside, you're still the rich kid from the biggest ranch in four counties, feeling like you ought to apologize to folks who have to earn a living—

Tate tipped his head back, looked up at the blanket of stars spilling lavishly across the Texas sky. *Was* he "still that rich kid," always wishing he could make up somehow for having more, just by virtue of being born a McKettrick, than so many other people did?

People like Brent Brogan.

People like Libby.

Did he want a second chance with her because what she made him feel was real love—or was he just feeling guilty because she'd had a tough road from early childhood on, while he'd coasted blithely through life until a truck crossed the median one night and crashed into his parents' car, leaving both of them fatally injured?

Brent returned, slapped him companionably on the back. "Uh-oh," he joked. "You're looking introspective. And that's almost *always* a bad sign, old buddy."

Tate sighed. Managed a grin. He did have a tendency to think too damn much, there was no denying that.

"Did you find my ex-wife tied up in a closet? Swathed in duct tape?" he asked.

Brent grinned. "No."

"Damn the luck," Tate said.

"Let's get a cup of coffee," Brent suggested.

"Look, it's been one hell of a day and—" Tate began, but the protest fell away, half-finished. There was no reason to hurry home—the kids weren't there, and Austin, while not the most dependable person on earth, could be trusted to take care of two sleeping dogs.

"Don't I *know* it's been one hell of a day," Brent agreed wearily. "I was at the funeral, remember, and the wake, too. Had a long talk with Nico, in fact, once the leftovers had been stuffed into

Isabel's fridge and most everybody else had gone home. Follow me to my place, and I'll brew up some java and tell you about it."

"If I don't get some sleep," Tate said, with a shake of his head, "I won't be good for much of anything tomorrow, so I'll pass on the java this time."

"All right," Brent replied, opening the door of the cruiser, key-ring in hand. When he hesitated, Tate knew his friend had more to say. "I spoke to Isabel Ruiz," Brogan went on. "She's going to L.A., all right, moving in with her sister."

The decision seemed hasty, but in the final analysis, it wasn't his business what Isabel did. So Tate merely nodded, opened the door of his truck and climbed in. It hurt to imagine that sturdy but humble house, buzzing with life and laughter for as long as he could remember, standing empty, with just the whisper of the creek or a passing wind to break the silence.

Pablo was gone for good; that was something he had to come to terms with in much the same way he'd had to accept the loss of his mom and dad. Things changed, that was the one thing a man could count on, and folks came and went, and you never knew when the last thing you'd said to them, or failed to say, might really be the last chance you were ever going to get, one way or the other.

On the lonely drive back to the ranch, through a sultry summer night, Tate missed his old dog even more than usual. It would have been a fine thing to have Crockett riding shotgun, as he'd done before, a sympathetic listener with his ears perked up and his eyes warm with canine devotion.

Had Crockett been there, Tate would have told him how worried he was about Audrey and Ava, and the way they were growing up, bouncing back and forth between two different houses. He'd have said what a hard thing it was knowing Pablo had died so sense-lessly, hard, too, wondering if he could have prevented what happened somehow, and if his friend had suffered or had had time to be afraid before the end came.

He might even have said that he loved Libby, not in the fevered, grasping way of a boy, as he had before, but hard and strong and steady, in the way of a man, but he'd rather do without her for the rest of his days than risk hurting her again.

Tate might have said a lot of things to Crockett that night, but all that actually came out of his mouth was a quiet, "I sure do miss you, old dog."

BY THE NEXT DAY, Libby was entirely recovered from her mother's unexpected visit the night before, and *mostly* over making such an idiot of herself out at the Ruizes' place after Pablo's funeral.

She rarely did anything impulsive—she couldn't afford the luxury—but that bright summer morning, after she and Hildie had taken their walk, Libby decided not to open the Perk Up for business at the usual time.

Today, she just felt like playing hooky.

So she scribbled a message on a piece of yellow-lined paper, crossed the alley and let herself into the shop by the back way, passed through the kitchen into the main area and taped the sign to the glass in the front door.

CLOSED FOR REPAIRS, the notice read. BACK BY NOON. PROBABLY.

The "repairs" Libby needed to make weren't the kind that required wrenches and screwdrivers, and while she fully intended to be serving coffee and smoothies and scones, if Julie had baked any, by midday, she wasn't sure that would happen. That was why she'd added the "probably"—to give herself an out if the need should arise.

Back home, Libby switched her shorts and tank top for her best jeans and a sleeveless blue cotton blouse, then put on a pair of comfortable sandals. Brushed her hair, leaving it loose instead of binding it back in the usual ponytail, and applied some lip gloss.

Hildie, munching kibble in the kitchen when her mistress jingled the car keys in invitation, looked up, cocked both ears as she considered her options and promptly went back to eating her breakfast.

Libby smiled at that. "I'll be back soon," she promised, stroking the dog's broad back with one hand before heading out the door.

Standing on the back porch, she looked around her yard and wished she hadn't let the shrubs and flower beds get so out of hand. She'd never been much of a gardener, mostly because she'd never had the time, but now she felt a new and strangely keen longing to get her hands dirty, to weed and water and plant things just to watch them grow.

First, of course, she'd have to prepare the ground, and that would be a big job, one that might take weeks. By the time she'd finished, folks around Blue River would probably be fertilizing and tilling their garden plots under, to lie fallow until spring, when the nursery section down at the feed store would be awash in starter plants and brightly colored seed packets.

Before getting into her car and backing it into the alley, she looked under dusty tarps in the detached garage until she found her dad's old push-mower. The blades were probably dull; maybe later, she'd heft the ancient apparatus into the trunk of the Impala and take it out to Chudley Wilkes for sharpening. When he wasn't running his one-taxi empire, Chudley fixed things.

Just *thinking* about mowing the lawn empowered Libby a little, though she supposed she'd be whistling a different tune once she'd made a few swipes through the high grass. As kids, she and Julie and Paige had taken turns doing yard chores, and she remembered the blisters, the muscle aches and all the rest.

They'd begged their dad to invest in a gas-powered mower, but he'd said hard work and exercise were good for the character. Of course, he hadn't been able to afford fancy equipment, especially with three young daughters to raise.

With a pang, Libby paused to pat the dusty handle. Indeed, hard work and exercise *were* good for the character—and she'd get a sense of accomplishment, the incomparable scent of fresh-cut grass and a tighter backside out of the deal.

Chudley's place was in the opposite direction from where she was headed, and stopping there would delay the opening of her coffee shop by at least an hour, but Libby popped open the Impala's trunk and hoisted the mower inside anyway. It was heavier than it looked, that machine, and the handles stuck out, so the trunk wouldn't close again.

She'd just have to alter her plans slightly, Libby concluded, after standing there in the alley biting her lower lip for a few moments. She'd drop the mower off at Chudley's first, then go on about her business. If Wilkes happened to be going through one of his ambitious phases—these were famously rare—the machine might be ready to cut grass later in the day.

Libby got behind the wheel, cranked up the engine and jostled off down the alley, wincing every time she hit a bump, causing the lid of the trunk to slam down on the shaft of the mower.

The Wilkes's home, two trailers welded together sometime in the fifties and surrounded by what seemed like acres of rusted-out cars, treadless tires and miscellaneous parts of God-knew-what, had been an eyesore for so long that folks around Blue River had long since stopped getting up petitions to force Chudley and his wife, Minnie, to clean the place up.

Libby pulled into the gravel driveway and waited a few moments before pushing open her car door, since Chudley had been known to keep mean guard dogs and once, reportedly, even an ostrich that might have killed the UPS man if Minnie hadn't rushed outside and driven it off with a broom handle.

Outsiders might have scoffed at that tale, thinking the odds were in the big bird's favor. Anybody who thought that had never met Minnie Wilkes.

She stepped out onto the sagging porch, wiping her hands on a faded apron and squinting, probably trying to place the green Impala. Six feet tall, with shoulders like a linebacker's, Minnie was a formidable sight, even pushing eighty, as she must have been.

Libby got out of the car. Smiled and waved. "It's me, Mrs. Wilkes," she called. "Libby Remington."

A blinding smile broke across Minnie's face. In her youth, the story went, she'd been quite a looker. Nobody'd ever been able to work out what caused her to throw in her lot with a little bantyrooster like Chudley. "Will's girl? Well, now, you've turned out just fine, haven't you? You still smitten with Jim and Sally McKettrick's oldest boy?"

Libby felt a little pinch inside her heart. Was *smitten* the word? "I see him around town," she said, approaching the gate, with its rusted hinges and weathered wooden latch, then hesitating. "Is that ostrich still around?"

Minnie's laugh boomed out over the seemingly endless expanse of junk. "Now there's a yarn that got right out of hand," she said, still standing on the porch. "Started out with one cussed old rooster, too stringy for the stewpot. Stubby—that was the rooster—went after the UPS man, right enough. But by the time that driver got through spreadin' the story around Blue River and half the county, I'll be darned if poor old Stub wasn't seven feet tall and a whole different kind of bird."

Libby smiled, started to open the gate.

Minnie stopped her. "You just stay right there, honey. We got another rooster pecking around here somewheres, and he might come at you, spurs out and screechin' like a banshee, if he don't happen to like your looks or somethin'."

Libby shaded her eyes and waited for her heartbeat to slow down, so her words wouldn't come out sounding shaky. "I was hoping Chudley could sharpen my lawn-mower blades," she said.

"He'll do it," Minnie said, with a decisive nod. "He's out on a taxi run just now, takin' Mrs. Beale home from the supermarket— she bought more than she could carry in that little pushcart of hers again—but he ought to be back soon. *One Life to Live* is fixin' to come on any minute now, and Chud never misses it."

Libby went around to the back of the car to unload the mower. Minnie, who had a light step for such a big woman, appeared beside her, elbowed her aside and lifted the all-metal machine from the trunk as easily as if it were a child's toy, made of plastic.

"I'd invite you in for a neighborly chat," Minnie said, holding the mower off the ground with one hand, the way she might have held a rake or a hoe. "But Miss Priss had her kittens on the couch yesterday, and she ain't ready to move them just yet. What with Chudley's magazines and such, there's no other place to sit."

Libby smiled. "Thank you just the same," she said. "But I'd have had to say 'no' anyway, because I've got so much to do today."

Minnie, bless her, looked relieved. She was known as much for her pride as for her bad housekeeping, and Libby had always liked her. Wouldn't have hurt her feelings or embarrassed her for anything.

"I'll see that Chudley brings this here piece of machinery by your place later on," Minnie said. "Good as new."

Libby opened the car door, reached for her purse.

"Keep your money," Minnie huffed, already trundling back through the gate, taking the mower along with her. "I meant to send over one of my sugar pies when your daddy was sick, and I never got around to it. Always felt bad about that—Will Remington was a fine man—but if it ain't one thing around here, it's another. Anyhow, Chudley will fix this mower right and proper, and I'll feel a sight better about not buildin' that sugar pie."

Libby's eyes burned. She knew the Wilkeses could have used even the small amount of money Chudley probably charged for sharpening the blades of a push lawn mower, but she wouldn't have discounted Minnie's belated but heartfelt condolence gift on any account. It would have been kinder to slap the woman across the face.

"Thank you, Mrs. Wilkes," she said.

Minnie plunked the mower down next to the porch steps, which dipped visibly under her considerable weight. Her thick hair, dyed an unlikely shade of auburn and bobby-pinned into a messy knot on top of her head, bobbed a little when she spoke, as it might tumble down around her shoulders. "You're a woman grown now," she said, with firm good grace. "Old enough to call me Minnie, if it suits you."

"Minnie," Libby repeated. It *did* make her feel more like a mature adult, addressing an older woman of slight acquaintance by her given name.

By the time she added a "Goodbye" Minnie had already disappeared back inside the conjoined trailers. After all these years, the seam still showed, a brownish, welded ribbon wrapping the structure like a gift and stopping directly above the front door.

Libby got back into her car, backed slowly into the turnaround and pointed the Impala back down the driveway toward the county road.

There, she stopped and looked both ways. On the left was an old porcelain toilet, red flowers—possibly geraniums—billowing from the bowl, riotous with well-being.

She smiled.

And to think people considered this place a blight upon the landscape.

CHAPTER ELEVEN

A WEEK HAD passed since Pablo Ruiz's funeral, and during that time, Tate McKettrick hadn't called once. Maybe, Libby thought, watching as a rare and badly needed rain pelted the road out in front of the Perk Up, her dad had been right, in years past, when he used to moralize that there wasn't much point in buying the cow when you could get the milk for free.

Libby sighed. A few days ago, she'd bitten the bullet and called Doc Pollack to ask for a prescription for birth control pills, which she'd filled at Wal-Mart, her cheeks burning with mortification. She knew every single person in Blue River, and they knew her, and it was just her luck that Ellie Newton, her high school nemesis, happened to be clerking in the pharmacy that day.

A brief scenario unfolded on the screen of Libby's mind, in which Ellie switched on a microphone and announced to the whole store that, in case they hadn't heard, Libby Remington was catting around with Tate McKettrick again. And after he'd made a fool of her in front of the whole county, too, throwing her over for that fancy woman he'd met in Austin.

Yes, folks, the imaginary version of Ellie Newton proclaimed in triumph, she had the proof right here, a little packet of pills.

While none of that *actually* happened, Libby would have sworn she'd seen just the tiniest spark of smug judgment in Ellie's eyes as she rang up the purchase.

Ellie's husband, Joe, worked on the Silver Spur as a ranch hand, Libby reflected; alone in the Perk Up with all the chores caught up, she had way too much time for introspection. Suppose Ellie had driven straight out there to the nice single-wide trailer she and Joe shared and told Joe that Libby was on birth control pills? *Further* suppose, Libby thought, gnawing on her lower lip, that Joe, hearing this news, went straight to his boss, none other than Tate McKettrick, and told *him?*

Tate would think she was hot to trot, jumping right on the pill when they'd been to bed exactly once.

And maybe she *was* hot to trot. With Tate, anyway.

Libby pressed the fingertips of both hands to her temples. What was the big deal here? This wasn't 1872. Consenting adults *had sex,* preferably responsible sex, all the time. And it wasn't as if she planned to keep the pills a secret from Tate—she just wanted to be the one to tell him, that was all.

It didn't help that business was slow.

A lot of Libby's regular customers had gone on vacation— good Lord, did they travel in a *herd,* or something? Every year, it seemed they all left at once.

No tour buses passing through town en route to the Alamo or Six Flags or some art or music fest in Austin stopped at Libby's place.

Even her sisters weren't around much—Paige was working double shifts at the clinic, and Julie had been helping out at Calvin's playschool, since the venerable Mrs. Oakland was recovering from an impacted wisdom tooth.

The McKettrick twins' castle was due to be delivered soon— volunteer fathers had dug and poured a cement foundation for it, along with a well for a very shallow fishpond nearby. Unless Mrs. Oakland's swelling went down soon, Julie would be in charge of the dedication ceremony.

All by her lonesome in the Perk Up, Libby wished the place had a jukebox, so she could have dropped some coins into the slot and played a sad song.

Instead, she checked the clock—4:37 p.m.—and made an executive decision; she'd close up early. Go home and let Hildie out for a run in the backyard.

Chudley had returned her lawn mower, sharpened and rust-free and ready to go, the day before. If the rain let up soon enough, she'd cut the grass.

If it didn't, she'd clean out some of the flower beds. Maybe it was too late in the season to plant, but just pulling the weeds would be an improvement.

After locking up, Libby crossed the alley and let herself into her yard through the back gate. The dust-scented rain had slackened to a drizzle, and a cool breeze dissipated some of the humidity.

While Hildie was outside, Libby changed into shorts, a sleeveless sweatshirt and flip-flops. She poured kibble in the dog's empty bowl, refilled her water dish and pushed open the screen door.

Hildie crunched happily away while Libby went outside, set her hands on her hips, and looked up at the gray sky. Texas had been in the grip of a drought for more than a decade, so any kind of precipitation was welcome, but her spirits dipped a little lower just the same.

The only sure remedy for the blues, at least in Libby's experience, was physical work—if it brought out a sweat and left her with achy muscles, so much the better. She hauled the mower out of the garage, considered the fact that it was made almost entirely of steel and put it back.

Work therapy was one thing. *Shock* therapy, courtesy of a lightning bolt, was another.

Hildie, finished with her supper, then scratched politely at the screen door from the inside.

Libby smiled, mounted the porch steps and let the dog out.

She was on her knees, pulling up weeds, when Hildie, lying under her favorite tree, out of the misty rain, rose to her haunches and gave an uncertain woof, more greeting than challenge.

Something tickled Libby's nose, so she ran a gloved hand across her face before turning around, expecting to see Julie, or Paige or even Marva.

But it was Tate who stood watching her, a slight smile curving his mouth upward at one side. "Hey," he said.

Libby swallowed. *If I filled a prescription for birth control pills, it's my own business,* she thought. "Hey," she replied, feeling stupid.

Tate hadn't *mentioned* her prescription, had he? Most likely, Ellie hadn't told Joe and therefore Joe couldn't have told Tate. Ellie had been a mean gossip in high school, it was true, but that was years ago and besides, she'd found religion—and Joe—since then.

"I tried to call," he said, when the silence stretched. "But you didn't pick up."

Libby hadn't thought to check her voice mail when she came home from the Perk Up—she didn't get that many calls. Paige and Julie usually just stopped by when they wanted to talk to her.

"What can I do for you?" she asked, her face heated.

Tate, wearing comfortable jeans, a T-shirt and old boots, crossed the grass and crouched beside her. "Well," he drawled, "you can *relax*, for a start."

Libby fought an insane urge to weep, and that used up any energy she might have employed in talking. Anyway, she was too afraid she'd say something even stupider than *What can I do for you?*

Gently, Tate used the backs of his fingers to wipe a smudge of dirt from Libby's cheek. "I've missed you, Lib," he said. "A lot."

She swallowed.

One of his powerful shoulders moved in a partial shrug. That ghost-of-a-grin touched down on his mouth again, and she noticed that his eyelashes were spiky from the moisture in the air. "The last time we were together," he reminded her, "things didn't go all that well."

Libby stood up, telling herself it was because her knees were starting to cramp, and dusted her hands off against the damp fabric of her shorts.

Tate stood, too. His dark hair curled a little in the light rain.

It was all Libby could do not to bury her fingers in that hair. The thought made her flesh tingle, all over.

She raised her chin a notch, remembering the minor spectacle the two of them had made, out there in Pablo's orchard after the funeral.

"I'll apologize if you will," she said.

Tate laughed. "Deal," he said. Then he sobered, and the blue of his eyes seemed to intensify. "I'm sorry."

Libby's breath caught, just looking into those eyes. "Me, too."

If black holes were that color, she thought, the entire universe would have been sucked into oblivion long ago.

"Maybe I could make it up to you with dinner," Tate said.

Libby blinked, pulled herself back from the blue precipice. Looked down at her muddy shorts and T-shirt. "I'd have to change clothes first," she heard some foolish woman say.

Tate grinned. "I was thinking of steaks at my place," he told her. The grin rose to dance, mischievous, in his eyes. "We suspended the dress code years ago. In fact, we never really had one, unless you count Mom's stubborn refusal to allow barn boots any farther than the back porch."

"I can't go like this," Libby said, still serious. "I'm all muddy and—and sweaty."

Tate chuckled. "All right," he said, "if you're going to insist, may I suggest that yellow dress? The one you wore the other night?"

Libby's cheeks burned again. Right. The yellow dress he'd said he could see through—the one she'd been so eager to get out of, after making such a big, damn deal about how it was too soon to make love.

And now she had a packet of birth control pills in her medicine cabinet.

Libby pretended she hadn't heard his suggestion and started for the house.

He chuckled.

Hildie, the traitor, hung back so she could walk with Tate.

While Tate waited in the kitchen with the dog, Libby headed for the bathroom. A glance at herself in the mirror over the sink made her shake her head.

A streak of good Texas garden dirt ran the length of her right cheek, and her hair, caught up in the customary ponytail, would frizz like crazy when she turned it loose.

She started the shower running, adjusting the faucets until she got just the right temperature—tepid, with the merest hint of a chill. She used a lot of conditioner after shampooing, hoping her hair wouldn't do its fright-wig thing.

Finished with her shower in record time, Libby dried off, pulled on her faded pink cotton robe, and collected clean jeans, fresh underwear, and a long-sleeved black and white T-shirt from her room.

Although she felt strangely rushed, she took the time to blow-dry her hair and even applied some mascara, though she skipped the lip gloss.

Just because she had birth control pills in her medicine cabinet didn't mean she wanted to go sending "Seduce me" messages to Tate McKettrick by making her mouth all shiny and inviting.

Of course, if Tate hadn't been in the picture, she wouldn't have called Doc Pollack and then endured Ellie Newton's studied indifference to get the prescription in the first place.

Gripping the edges of the sink, Libby looked at her steam-blurred image in the mirror.

"You're *asking* for trouble, Libby Remington," she told herself.

Then she opened the bathroom door and stepped into the hallway.

Mustn't keep trouble waiting.

TATE LOADED HILDIE INTO the backseat of his truck, but although he'd opened the front passenger-side door for Libby, he stood back instead of helping her aboard, just so he could watch that sweet little ass in action, under the perfectly fitted jeans, as she made the climb.

Hot damn. A silent groan reverberated through him.

"Are the girls at the ranch?" Libby asked, once she was settled and he was behind the wheel. Hildie leaned between the seats and licked Tate's right ear just as he turned the key in the ignition.

He laughed, not at the question but at the dog, and immediately drew a confused glance from Libby.

"No," he said, as Hildie rested her muzzle on his shoulder and gave a contented little sigh. If only *all* females were so docile. "Audrey and Ava are in New York with their mother for a couple of days. Cheryl's folks moved into an assisted-living place in Connecticut a few months back, and she's putting their apartment on the market."

Libby offered no comment, only a nod. She shifted uncomfortably in the seat—and Tate figured she'd probably been counting on having the kids around as a sort of buffer.

Esperanza, Garrett and Austin were all at the main house, as it happened, but Tate wasn't taking Libby to the mansion. Where they were going, it would be just the two of them—and the old dog drooling on his shirt as he drove toward the outskirts of town.

"Are we going to talk?" Tate asked, when they'd traveled several miles in silence.

She smiled softly. "Do we need to?"

Damn. He wanted to pull over to the side of the road, right then and there, take Libby Remington into his arms and kiss her senseless.

"Probably," he said hoarsely.

"About—?"

"Things," Tate said, thrown by the scent of her, the warmth of her, the softness he could sense from three feet away, no touching necessary. Highly desirable, but not necessary.

"Things like—?"

"Like where we're headed, you and I," Tate said.

Libby's smile was faint and a little saucy. "I assumed, since you're behind the wheel, that you had our destination all figured out."

"That isn't what I mean," Tate said, mildly irritated, "and you know it."

"Where are we going, Tate?" Libby asked, with exaggerated patience, of the smart-ass variety. There was an undercurrent of excitement there, too, unless he missed his guess.

"On one level," Tate replied, "I'd say we're on our way to a soft spot in some tall grass." Out of the corner of his eye, he saw her blush, and took some satisfaction in that. "On another level—the long-range one—everything depends on you, Libby."

Libby turned in her seat, her eyes flashing a little. He could see her nipples jutting against the inside of her blouse, so he figured she was up for the proposed tumble in the grass.

All right by him.

"Now, why would everything depend on me?" she asked, her eyes wide.

Tate didn't give her an answer until he'd brought the truck to a stop at the edge of the yard that had been Pablo and Isabel's for so long.

"You're the one with all the forgiving to do, Lib," he said, gripping the steering wheel and staring straight ahead through the windshield. The lumber and other building supplies he'd been buying and hauling out from town all week waited, moist from the drizzling rain.

Libby turned slightly in the seat, gently eased Hildie back, off his shoulder. "Tate McKettrick," she said, "look at me."

He did. A big lump rose in his throat. He wanted her physically, but there was so much more to it than that.

"If you're talking about that fling with Cheryl," Libby told him, "I forgave you for that a long time ago."

Tate raised his hand to her cheek, brushed it lightly with the backs of his knuckles. "Maybe you believe that," he said, "but I'm not sure I do."

Her eyes widened again, and patches of pale pink pulsed in her cheeks, then faded. "If you could go back in time," she asked, after several long moments, "what would you change, Tate? Can you even imagine a world without your children in it?"

Tate unhooked Libby's seat belt, laid his hands on either side of her face so she wouldn't look away before she heard him out. "No," he said gruffly, "but if I had the kind of power we're talking about here, *you and I* would have conceived the twins. They'd be ours, together."

She turned her head, and her lips moved, light as the flick of a moth's wings, against his palm.

Fire shot up Tate's arm, set his heart ablaze, spread to his groin and hit a flash point. He barely contained the groan that rose from somewhere in the very center of his being.

Libby met his gaze again. Held it. "Do you know what would have made it impossible to forgive you, Tate? If you'd denied those little girls, or bought your way out of the situation somehow—a lot of men in your position would have done that—but you took all the fallout. You did right by your children, and I'm pretty sure you *tried* to do right by Cheryl—"

In the back, Hildie whimpered, wanting out.

Tate shut off the engine, but made no move to get out of the truck and lower Hildie to the ground. "What about *you,* Lib?" he asked miserably. "I sure as hell didn't do right by you, now did I?"

She reached across, touched his arm. "I'm a big girl now," she said. "I'm over it."

"Over it enough to trust me?"

She thought for a moment, then nodded. "Until you give me reason not to," she said.

Hildie began to carry on in earnest.

Tate got out of the truck, opened the back door and two-armed the chubby old dog out of the vehicle and onto the ground.

Libby got out, too, and stood at the edge of the Ruizes' lawn, looking toward the house. Tate watched as she shook her head in response to some private thought.

"I guess you heard," he ventured, after a while, "that Isabel decided to take the boys and go live with her sister." He was distracted, still thinking about how she'd said she'd trust him until he gave her a reason to stop.

Libby Remington was an amazing woman.

Libby turned her head to look at him again, nodded. "She didn't waste much time getting out of here," she observed, and there was a deliberately noncommittal note in her voice that diverted some of Tate's attention from the riot she'd caused in his senses.

He hooked his thumbs into the waistband of his jeans and tilted his head to one side. Hildie squatted a few feet away, then came back to stand between him and Libby, tail wagging, tongue lolling, eyes hopeful that a good time would be had by all, dogs included.

"I told Isabel she was welcome to stay here on the Spur for as long as she wanted," Tate said quietly, "but she decided to leave right away. Nico said she saw Pablo everywhere she looked, and that was too painful."

Libby considered that, nodded. Hildie went off, found a short, crooked stick in the grass, brought it to Libby, and dropped it at her feet.

With a smile, Libby bent, picked up the stick and tossed it a little way.

Hildie trundled awkwardly after it. Brought it back.

"Why the impromptu dinner invitation, Tate?" Libby asked mildly. "And what's with all the lumber and shingles and bags of cement?"

Tate bent, picked up Hildie's stick, and threw it a little farther than Libby had. While the dog searched through the wild grass that grew beyond the edge of the lawn, Tate held out a hand to Libby.

"Come on," he said. "I'll explain while I show you around."

Libby hesitated, then took his hand. Hildie had found the stick, clasping it between her teeth, but she seemed to be done playing fetch for the time being.

Tate took care not to crush Libby's fingers as he led her up the front steps and into the house. The sexual charge that had arced between them on the drive out of town had gone underground, though Tate knew it would reassert itself sooner rather than later.

He watched Libby as she looked around, waited for the dog to waddle in, then quietly shut the door.

Over the few days since Isabel and Pablo's relatively few possessions had been loaded into a rented truck and hauled away, Tate had removed the old flooring and knocked out several walls. Sheets of drywall waited to be nailed in place once the new framing was in.

Libby's expression was curious and a little pensive when she looked at him. "I still don't understand," she said. "All this—?"

Tate put a hand to the small of her back and steered her toward the kitchen. It was the only room in the house he hadn't torn apart—yet.

"I'm planning on living here, Libby," he said, and his heart beat a little faster, because her reaction to that news was vitally important to him. "Maybe not for good—but for a while."

"Why?" she asked reasonably, folding her arms. The last light of day flowed in through the window behind her, and to Tate, she looked almost luminous, like a figure in stained glass.

"I'm not sure I can explain," he answered, reaching out to flip a switch so the single bulb dangling from the middle of the ceiling illuminated the kitchen. "I want to see what it's like to live in a regular-size house. Drive to a job every day. Actually work for a living."

Libby smiled faintly at that. She *did* live in a "regular-size house," and she certainly made her own way in the world. "I wouldn't know about commuting," she quipped, "but working for a living is overrated, in my opinion."

Tate shoved a hand through his hair, more nervous than he'd expected to be. He'd planned this evening carefully, right down to the steaks marinating in the refrigerator and the coals heating in the portable barbecue grill out back and the good red wine tucked away in one of the cupboards. It had made so much sense during those night hours spent prying up carpeting and stripping walls to the insulation and framework.

Libby came to him, laid her palms to his chest.

The gesture was probably meant to be comforting, but she might as well have hit him with a couple of defibulator paddles, given the effect her touch had on him.

"Tate?" Libby urged.

He sighed. He'd meant to ask Libby to move in with him, come and live in that modest house by the bend in the creek as soon as the remodeling was done; but now he realized what a half-assed, harebrained idea it was. Libby wasn't ready for that kind of constant intimacy, and he wasn't, either.

The twins barely knew Libby, and of course the reverse was true, as well. He would make any sacrifice for his children, but he couldn't expect Libby to feel the same way.

"Give me a minute," he finally said, his voice hoarse, "to pull my foot out of my mouth."

She moved closer, frowning, then slipped her arms loosely around his waist. "What are you talking about?" she asked.

A reasonable question, Tate thought. "I wish I knew," he said.

Libby rested her head against his chest for a few moments, as though she were listening to his heartbeat, and the smell of her hair made him feel light-headed—it was as though all the oxygen had suddenly been sucked out of the room.

Finally, she looked up at him, and her eyes were at once tender and curious. "You're serious about living here, aren't you?" she asked.

Tate nodded. Maybe she'd hate the idea—that would be a problem for sure. And maybe she wouldn't give a damn—which would be even worse.

"And for some reason," Libby went on, "my opinion matters to you."

"Yes," he ground out. "For some reason, it does."

"Why?" Libby seemed completely, honestly puzzled.

"Because—" Again, Tate's neck burned. "Well, because it *would* matter to some women—they'd think I was crazy, moving out of a place like the ranch house, into this one…"

Libby brought her chin up a notch and set her hands on her hips. "Would it matter to you, if I thought you were crazy?"

"No," he answered, after some thought. "If you *didn't* think that, I'd figure you hadn't been paying much attention."

She laughed, stood on tiptoe to kiss the cleft in his chin. Then she looked around. "Alone at last," she said. "Do you want me as much as I want you, Tate?"

"Yeah," he replied, "and I've got the hard-on to prove it."

"So I've noticed," Libby crooned, grinding into him again. This time, there was no mistaking things—the move was deliberate.

"You might want to watch it," Tate warned, his hands making their own way to where they wanted to be—cupping Libby's ass and lifting her closer so he could do a little grinding of his own. "This time, I'm prepared. I have condoms."

Libby moaned, her eyes half-closed, her head back. A fetching wash of pink played over her cheekbones.

When Libby was fifteen and Tate was seventeen, he'd taken her virginity in the backseat of his dad's car, and she'd looked just the way she did now—flushed, eager, unafraid.

"I'm prepared, too," she said, so softly that Tate barely heard her.

His knees weak, Tate dropped into one of the four folding chairs he'd bought to go with the card table, his temporary dining suite. Standing Libby between his knees, he unsnapped her jeans, undid the zipper, pulled them down, waited for her to protest.

She didn't.

In fact, she kicked off her shoes and shed her jeans, right there in the kitchen. She was wearing ice-blue panties, trimmed in lace.

He nipped at her through the moist crotch, and she groaned, entwining her fingers in his hair.

"What do you mean, you're prepared?" he murmured, hooking his thumbs under the elastic waistband.

"I'm—I'm on the p-pill—" she gasped.

Had the table been sturdier, Tate would have laid Libby down on it and eaten her thoroughly, but he knew the thing wouldn't support even her slight weight. So he lowered her panties and plied her with gentle motions of his fingers until she was good and wet.

Then he opened his jeans and eased her down slowly, onto his shaft, giving her a little at a time.

She wanted to ride him, and hard—that was evident in the way she moved, or tried to move.

Tate grasped her hips and stopped her. "Easy," he murmured. "Slow and easy, Lib."

She made a strangled sound, her eyes sultry, but she let him set the pace. Let him strip off her lightweight T-shirt and open her bra, so her perfect breasts were there for the taking.

Tate enjoyed them at his leisure until Libby made another sound—this one exasperated—and drew him into a kiss so hot that he nearly lost control and came right then and there.

"Do it," she gasped, when the kiss finally ended, "damn you, Tate McKettrick, *do it!*"

He chuckled, a raspy sound, and took her in earnest then, raising and lowering her, fast and then faster, deep and then deeper.

The release was cataclysmic, blinding Tate, rending a long, hoarse shout from him, like that of a dying man. Through it, he heard Libby, calling his name over and over again.

And then they were both still.

Slowly, the world reassembled itself around them.

"*Damn,* woman," Tate growled. "That was good."

Libby giggled. "Yeah," she said, moving to disengage herself. "Is there a working shower in this place?"

Tate stopped her from rising off him by tightening his grasp on her hips. He was getting hard again, and she was in for another ride.

"No," he said, raising her and then lowering her again, until she'd taken all of him, until she gasped. "No shower."

"*Tate—*"

He bent his head, tongued her right nipple until she groaned and arched her back, offering him full access. "Ummm?" he asked, his mouth full of her then.

"I—oh, God—I'm already coming—I—"

Tate slid his hands up, supporting her with his palms so she could lean back, give herself up to the orgasm.

He watched, fighting his own release, as Libby arched away from him, golden-fleshed, nipples hard and moist from his mouth, her hair falling free, her beautiful body buckling and seizing with pleasure.

When she cried out his name, and a long, sweet shudder of full surrender went through her, Tate couldn't hold back anymore. He let himself go, with a raspy shout, and she rocked on him until he'd given her everything he had to give.

"I'm not sure I can survive a whole lot of that," she admitted, a long time later, when they'd helped each other, bumbling and fumbling, back into at least some of their clothes.

"We need to spend more time together," Tate said. "Get in some practice."

Libby sighed contentedly. "And we'd—*practice* a lot?"

Tate grinned. "Maybe not on the kitchen floor, though. I was sort of planning on buying a bed, but, yeah, there would be a lot of rowdy sex."

Libby made a comical move that might have meant her underpants were wedged in where they shouldn't be. "I like rowdy sex," she said.

He laughed. Padded over to the fridge for the steaks. "So I've noticed," he responded.

Suddenly, she looked sad, and some of the glow was gone. "What if sex is all we have together, Tate? All we've *ever* really had."

Tate, halfway to the back door with the package of steaks in one hand by then, turned to look at her. "Then I'd say we were pretty damn lucky," he responded. "But there's more, and you know it."

"Not that I'm angling to get married," she blurted out. Then she blushed miserably and groaned. "But nobody said anything about marriage, did they?"

"You're not ready for that," Tate told her, setting the meat on the counter and going back to stand facing her, "and neither am I. I've got things to prove to you, Libby."

She blinked. "Like what?"

"Well, first of all, you need to be sure you can trust me. For a lifetime."

"What if I told you I trust you now?" Another pause. "Although you're perfectly right—we're not ready to get married. I hope I didn't seem—well—*pushy*."

He grinned. "Never that," he said.

The steaks turned out perfectly.

They went on to the main ranch house and took a shower together in his en suite bathroom and made love again.

They slept, arms and legs entangled after hours of lovemaking, in his bed.

He should have known it had all been too easy.

CHAPTER TWELVE

A PHONE SHRILLED in the night, jarring Libby, in lurching stages, out of a rest so profound that no shred or tatter of a dream could have reached her. She opened her eyes, blinking, to utter darkness, and knew only that she wasn't in her own bed—the mattress, the bedding, the angles were all wrong.

"Tate McKettrick," Tate said, his voice gravelly with sleep and the beginnings of alarm.

Libby sat up, drawing her knees to her chest and wrapping her arms around her shins.

"Calm down, Cheryl," Tate went on. "I can't understand you—"

Libby closed her eyes a nanosecond before she heard the click of a lamp switch. Light flared against her lids, a fiery orange-red. She looked at Tate, blinking.

He sat up. "Take a breath," he said, shifting the phone from his right ear to his left, so he could close his fingers around Libby's hand and squeeze once. He threw back the covers, got out of bed, began pulling opening drawers, dressing—jeans, a T-shirt, socks and boots.

"Okay," he said. "Okay."

Libby's heart thrummed. A call at that hour—3:17 a.m. by the digital clock on Tate's night table—could not be good.

Tate was listening again; the glance he tossed in Libby's direction bounced away without connecting.

For the briefest moment, she felt dismissed, invisible.

"Put her on, Cheryl," Tate said. A long pause. "Cheryl? I said *put Ava on the phone.*"

Libby scrambled off the bed, nearly fell because she was so entangled in the top sheet. Her clothes were on the far side of the room, and she tripped twice, hurrying to get to them.

"Yes, Ava," Tate said, "it's Dad. What's the problem, Shortstop? I thought you were excited about visiting New York."

Libby could hear the timbre of the child's voice, if not the words. Ava was practically hysterical.

She forgot about getting into her clothes and went back to the bed, carefully managing the train of bedsheet in the process, plunking down on the end of the mattress and watching Tate as he paced, listening, nodding.

"You'll be home in a few days, honey," he told his daughter gently, when there was a break in the conversation.

Tate sat down beside Libby, slipped his arm around her waist. She felt a little less like an outsider.

"Ava?" Tate waited. "I love you. I'll be right here when you get back. You can ride your ponies, and we'll go fishing in the creek—"

More hysteria on the other end of the line.

Tate sighed, and his shoulders sagged a little. "Let me talk to your mother."

Again, Libby wanted to flee. She didn't know exactly what she was hearing, but she was sure she shouldn't be hearing it.

Tate's entire bearing seemed to change when his ex-wife came back on the phone. "Yes," he said. "Yes—sometime tomorrow. I'll let you know. And, Cheryl? Don't call in twenty minutes and say you've changed your mind. We're not going to pretend this didn't happen."

Libby lowered her head, waited.

Finally, Tate snapped his phone shut.

For a long time, he just sat there beside Libby, looking down at the floor.

Libby shifted, ran a hand down his back. "Anything I can do to help, cowboy?" she asked quietly. She didn't want to interfere, but she couldn't just sit there, either.

"I have to head for New York," he said. "First thing in the morning."

Libby nodded. Waited. If Tate wanted to explain, he would. If he didn't, that was okay, too.

Tate shoved a hand through his hair. His eyes were bluer than usual, and bleak, even as he tried to smile. "This is what my life is like, Lib," he said, very quietly. "I have an ex-wife and two kids and executive control over a ranch the size of some counties. There's always some kind of crisis, and a lot of them seem to happen in the middle of the night."

Libby drew the sheet more closely around her. "Audrey and Ava—they're okay?"

Tate held her against his side, rested his chin on top of her head. She felt his nod. "I didn't get the whole story," he said, "but the gist of it seems to be that getting her parents' apartment ready to put on the market is more work than Cheryl expected it to be, and the girls aren't making it any easier because they're fussy and homesick. Apparently, Ava had a pretty bad dream tonight—Cheryl showed the twins around the school she went to and asked them how they'd like to go there when they start first grade in the fall, and that must have freaked Ava out." He paused, sighed. "According to our divorce agreement, neither Cheryl nor I can reside anywhere but Blue River, Texas, without forfeiting custody to the other— but knowing my ex-wife, I'd say she figures I might give ground if I thought the girls really wanted to grow up somewhere else."

"Cheryl wants to live in New York?"

"Who knows?" Tate asked, letting go of Libby, standing. "I've never been able to figure out what Cheryl wants. I'm not sure *she* knows, actually."

Libby watched as he took a leather carry-on bag from the enormous closet, threw in a change of clothes and some shaving gear. "So you're going to bring the twins back home?"

He turned, looked at her. "Yeah," he said. Sadness moved in his eyes. "Ava wants to be in Blue River, anyway. I'm not so sure about Audrey. She might choose to stay on and come back with Cheryl, after the apartment's ready to be sold."

Libby stood, still draped in the top sheet, and crossed the room to pick up her clothes. While she didn't know Tate's daughters very well, she *had* figured out that Audrey was the bolder of the two. Ava, with her glasses and hearing aid, while just as bright as her sister, was shy.

"Lib—would you like to come along? To New York, I mean?"

Libby hadn't expected that question. She'd just assumed Tate would want to travel fast and light—get to the city, collect his children, bring them back to Texas.

Excuses rushed through her mind. She had the Perk Up to run, there was Hildie to consider—and what about mowing the lawn and cleaning out the flower beds?

What she actually *said* was, "It could be pretty confusing for the twins—my just showing up like that." She dressed slowly, not looking at Tate. "They're not used to seeing us together, after all."

Tate sighed. "Point taken," he said. "But if we're going to keep seeing each other, they need to start getting used to our being together, Lib."

She was wearing all her clothes by then, but she still felt naked, stripped to the soul. "Maybe it's a little soon to spring that on them," she ventured. "Our spending time together, I mean."

He left off packing then, crossed the room, took her gently by the shoulders. "When I've finished the house," he said, "I plan on asking you to come and live with me. You might as well know that." Curving his fingers under her chin, he lifted her face so he could look directly into her eyes. "As for sex—I'll be granting no quarter, Libby. Whether we're sharing a house and a bed or not, I promise you, I'll seduce you every chance I get, any way I can, any*place* I can."

Libby blushed so hard it hurt. Tate knew what she liked, in and out of bed. He knew all the right words to say, all the secret, special places where she loved to be caressed, nibbled, teased.

But, then, Libby knew a few things herself.

Two could play that game.

"You'd better be real quick to make the first move, cowboy," she said, unfastening his jeans, pushing her hand inside, loving the way he groaned, the way he swelled when she closed her fingers around him. "Or you might just find *yourself* being seduced."

Tate swallowed hard. "Libby—"

"No quarter, Tate," she said, working him, enjoying the way he responded. "No prisoners. If I want you, I'll have you. On the spot."

A powerful shudder moved through him, even as he gave a strangled laugh, perhaps at her audacity.

"In fact," Libby murmured, "I'm pretty sure I want you right now."

"Libby—"

"Right—here—"

He moaned aloud as Libby proceeded to prove her point.

TATE CAUGHT AN early flight out of Austin, and the landing at La-Guardia went without a hitch. Since he'd only brought a carry-on—he didn't plan on staying even overnight—he didn't have to wait with the crowds around the luggage carousels.

The cab line was long, as usual, but it moved quickly.

The drive into the city passed almost unnoticed—Tate's mind was back in Texas, for most of the ride, with Libby.

When the taxi stopped in front of Cheryl's parents' building, though, he made the necessary mental shift—time to think about the business at hand.

He paid the cabdriver and turned, bracing himself.

The doorman stood under a green-and-white awning, eyeing him warily.

"My name's Tate McKettrick," Tate said. "I'm here to see Ms. Darbrey."

The older man smiled fondly at the mention of Cheryl. "I'll buzz her," he said, stepping inside and pressing one of a series of brass buttons gleaming on a panel behind his desk.

Tate waited outside, taking in the sounds and sights of a great city just gearing up for a new day. He was a rancher—body, mind and spirit—but he liked New York, liked the energy and buzz of the place.

The doorman returned, holding the door open. "Go right up, Mr. McKettrick," he said. "Apartment 17B."

Tate merely nodded and, gripping the handle of his carry-on, passed the doorman and headed for the elevator.

Outside 17B, minutes later, Tate stopped to prepare himself for whatever he might have to deal with. Since he'd been announced, there wasn't much point in knocking or ringing the doorbell.

On the other side of the door, a sequence of sliding chains and turning bolts began. Then the door opened, and Ava, still wearing pajamas, launched herself into his arms.

Audrey was there, too, but she stood back a little way, and Tate felt dread pinch his heart as he studied her small face.

He kissed Ava's cheek as he closed the door, gathered Audrey against his side.

Cheryl appeared in the arched doorway leading into the gracious living room, with its gas fireplace, built-in bookcases, and high, ornately molded ceilings. She looked coolly elegant in white slacks—the tails of her red silk shirt were tied at her midriff, revealing a flat, tanned stomach, and her hair was plaited into a single braid.

"Come in," she said. "Breakfast is almost ready."

"Are we going home today?" Ava wanted to know. "Are we going back to Texas?"

Cheryl's face tightened a little, but her smile remained in place. Nobody would have guessed, to look at her, that she'd called Tate in the middle of the night complaining that the twins in general and Ava in particular were about to drive her out onto the nearest ledge.

"We're going home today," Tate confirmed quietly, setting Ava on her feet.

Then, to Cheryl, he said, "Is there coffee?"

She nodded. "You haven't shaved," she remarked, and her cat-green eyes narrowed a little. Wheels were turning behind that alabaster-smooth forehead. "Late night, maybe?"

"I was in a hurry," he said, galled that he'd explained even that much.

They were in the living room now, and he looked around. No moving boxes, he noted. No clutter, either. Gone were her father's teetering stacks of reference books, notes and file folders bulging with clippings.

Cheryl's parents had fallen on hard times—mostly of their own making—long before she and Tate were married, but they *had* managed to hold on to the apartment, mainly by mortgaging it repeatedly.

By the time the twins were born, the place had gone into fore-closure and Cheryl was making noises about bringing Mom and Dad to live with her and Tate, in Blue River.

Tate, unable to get cell reception, had promptly called his law-yer from a hospital pay phone and instructed him to buy the Park Avenue place outright and put the deed in Cheryl's name.

Her folks had gone on living there until just a few months ago, when she'd finally made the decision to move them into an as-sisted-living place. He was picking up the tab for that, too, since they couldn't afford it on their own.

"I want to go home today," Ava said firmly.

Audrey made a face. "You're such a baby."

"Hush," Tate said.

In the kitchen, which was as spacious as the living room and also showed no evidence that anybody had been packing for a move, Cheryl set out four mismatched antique plates on the round table. The piece, Tate decided, was probably supposed to look an-tique and French—"distressed," his ex-wife termed it—meaning it had been falsely aged with things like sandpaper and rusty bi-cycle chain, swung hard.

He could identify.

In a classic *you-big-dumb-cowboy* moment, Tate realized that Cheryl had never had any intention of selling the apartment. She'd probably spent the girls' weeks with him right here, getting set-tled. Making new friends, or reconnecting with old ones, circu-lating her résumé.

"Mommy got a job offer," Audrey said, confirming his thoughts.

"Audrey Rose," Cheryl said, "*hush.* I wanted to tell your daddy about that myself."

Tate's blood seemed to buzz in his veins; the feeling was a combination of pissed off and thank God. Calmly, he washed his hands at the kitchen sink, sat down in the chair his ex-wife indi-cated. Although his glance sliced to Cheryl, he held his tongue and kept his face expressionless.

Avoiding his gaze, Cheryl served him hot, strong coffee, while the girls had orange juice. Bagels and smoked salmon, cream cheese and capers followed, and fresh strawberries finished off the meal.

"Go and get dressed, both of you," Cheryl told the kids when they'd obviously eaten all they intended to, for the time being at least.

They balked a little, especially Ava, who seemed reluctant to let Tate out of her sight for fear he'd vanish, but the pair finally hurried off to put on their clothes.

"It's a long commute between here and Blue River," Tate commented quietly.

Cheryl sighed, and her cup rattled in its saucer when she reached for it. "I could be there every other weekend," she said, avoiding his gaze. When she finally looked at him, though, he saw a different woman behind those green eyes, a woman he'd probably never known in the first place.

"The job—it's a good one, Tate."

"I'm happy for you," he said, without sarcasm.

"Don't ruin this for me," she whispered. *"Please."*

"I'm not out to ruin anything for you, Cheryl," Tate told her reasonably, and in all truth. "But we have a custody agreement, and I'm not willing to change it."

Tears brimmed in Cheryl's eyes. "Ava wants to live with you, on the Silver Spur. I thought Audrey could—"

Tate leaned forward in his chair, careful to keep his voice down. "You thought Audrey could *what?*" he asked.

"Stay here, with me," Cheryl said. "Just during the week. Tate, Audrey loves New York, just like I do. It would be so good for her—"

"You want to split them up?"

Cheryl's shoulders moved in a semblance of a shrug, but there was nothing nonchalant in her expression. She looked miserable. "I know it's not an ideal situation," she said. Then she bit down on her lower lip, and when she spoke again, her voice had dropped to a desperate whisper. "I can't stay in Blue River until our daughters are eighteen, Tate. I just can't. I'll lose my mind if I try!"

Tate felt sorry for Cheryl in that moment—she was a beautiful woman, with a law degree and a lot of ambition. She wasn't cut out for the kind of life she'd been living in Blue River; she needed a career. She needed the throb and hurry of a city around her, subway trains rumbling under her feet, traffic lights changing, horns honking 24/7.

"I understand that," he said, and he did. "But, as I said, we have an agreement, Cheryl. It would be wrong—*worse* than wrong—to separate the twins, have them grow up apart."

Cheryl put her hands over her face and began to cry.

Tate loved Libby Remington—the time he'd just spent with her had left him more convinced of that than ever—but as bitter as his and Cheryl's marriage and divorce had been, he didn't like seeing her hurting the way she was.

"I'm going home later today," he told his ex-wife quietly, even gently, "and I'm taking Audrey and Ava with me. If you really want to practice law again though, here in New York or anywhere else, you ought to do it."

She lowered her hands. Her eyes were wet, puffy and a little red around edges. "Do you mean that?"

In the near distance, Tate heard his daughters approaching, engaged in some little-girl exchange that was part giggle and part squabble.

"Yes," he said. "I mean it."

"You wouldn't hold it against me—think I was a bad mother—if I stayed here?"

Born and raised in the country, among old-fashioned folks, a mother willingly living apart from her children was a foreign thing to Tate. Times were changing, though—maybe not for the better—and Cheryl had worked hard to earn that law degree. Barely gotten to use it.

"I think," he replied carefully, "that what you do with your life is your own business."

Audrey and Ava burst into the kitchen, wearing jeans and short-sleeved cotton blouses with little red and white checks.

"All packed to go back to Blue River?" Tate asked.

Ava nodded.

Audrey looked less certain. That gave him a pang.

"I need to talk to your mom alone for a few more minutes," he said. "Ava, maybe you could help your sister get her things together."

Audrey glanced at Cheryl, then turned and followed Ava out of the room again.

Cheryl shifted in her chair, cupped her hands around her coffee mug, as though to warm them. "I know I was supposed to sell this apartment, Tate, but—"

"Let's worry about that later," Tate said, when her words fell away. "This is a big decision, Cheryl. It might be the right one, and it might be one you'll come to regret someday. Possibly, it's both those things, life being what it is."

She swallowed, nodded. "What will you tell them?" she asked, her voice small. "When you take Audrey and Ava back to Texas, what will you tell them?" She glanced anxiously at the doorway, then her gaze swung back to Tate's face and clung. "It isn't that I don't love the kids."

"I know you love them," Tate said gruffly, and he *did* know. Like most people, Cheryl was probably doing the best she could. The insight made him feel incredibly sad. "I won't try to convince them otherwise, I promise."

"Thank you, Tate."

He pushed back his chair, meaning to stand, but Cheryl stayed him by touching his arm.

"Have another cup of coffee," she said. "There's no big rush, is there?"

Tate sighed. He liked New York well enough, but the walls of that apartment seemed to be creeping in on him, an inch or two at a time. "How are your folks doing at the assisted-living place?" he asked, while Cheryl hurried to the counter for the coffeepot.

Cheryl looked sad as she refilled his cup, then her own. It felt strange, her pouring coffee for him. "Not so well," she said, setting the pot on the table and sinking into a chair. "Every time I call or visit, they beg to come back here. When begging doesn't work, they start accusing me of things, like *stealing* their home out from under them—"

Tate guessed it was a tough row to hoe, having aging parents, but from his point of view, it sure beat not having any at all. "That might pass, once they get used to the new place," he said. "And if it doesn't, well, you know they don't really mean any of those things."

Cheryl sniffled, nodded.

A silence descended on that kitchen. They'd never had much to say to each other, unless they were talking about the girls.

Half an hour later, Tate was in a cab with both his daughters, headed for LaGuardia. Ava fairly bounced on the seat, she was so happy to be going home, but Audrey was—subdued, he guessed he'd call it.

"You like the Big Apple, Shortstop?" he asked her, squeezing her small hand.

She looked up at him, nodded. "Mommy was going to let me audition for TV commercials," she said wistfully. "And take singing and dancing lessons, too."

"I see," Tate said seriously, because to his daughter, these *were* serious matters.

"She thought you might let us live in New York with her for a while," Audrey added. "So you'd have more time to get reacquainted with Libby."

An acid sting shot through Tate's stomach. "I do like spending time with Libby," he confirmed evenly. "But I'd miss you way too much if you lived here."

Audrey's remarkably blue eyes widened slightly. "Then you still want us around? Wouldn't we be underfoot?"

Tate turned in Audrey's direction, tightened his arm around Ava's shoulders at the same time. "Of course I want you around," he said. "And you can get underfoot all you want."

Audrey smiled. "Okay," she said, and with a little sigh, she rested the side of her head against his chest.

"She still wants to be in the Pixie Pageant," Ava said righteously, folding her arms. "You don't even know when you're being *played,* Dad."

Tate hugged Ava closer. "I'm smarter than I look," he told her, and kissed the top of her head. Then he squeezed Audrey again. "Is that true, monkey? You really want to take on this Pixie thing?"

Audrey nodded. "I just want to *try,* Daddy. I'll be okay if I don't win."

Sometimes the maturity of a six-year-old could take a man by surprise.

"Tell you what," Tate said, when he'd mulled the insight over for a few moments. "When we get home, I'll look into this pageant deal and see if it's something we can both live with. Sound fair to you?"

The little girl beamed. "Sounds fair to me," she said, putting up her right hand for Tate's high-five.

ONCE THEY'D CHECKED IN, gone through security and boarded a plane bound for Austin, where Tate's truck would be waiting in the airport parking garage, the twins, seated side by side across the aisle from him, flipped the pages of the catalogs and airline magazines like a pair of vertically challenged adults.

They were only six.

And they would be grown women long before he was ready for that to happen.

The girls each had a suitcase, so they had to wait in baggage claim for a while, but soon enough they were in the truck and on their way to the ranch.

Ambrose and Buford were waiting when they arrived, barking their fool heads off and jumping as if they'd swallowed a bucket of those Mexican beans, but they stayed well clear of the truck—which meant that, between the two of them, they might have a lick of sense.

There was a big, blank spot in the yard where that ridiculous castle had stood, but if Audrey and Ava noticed at all, they didn't react. They were too glad to see the pups again.

The feeling was certainly mutual.

Tate grinned and shook his head as he watched his daughters, in their expensive playclothes, kneeling in the grass to accept canine adoration in the form of face-licking and happy yips and impromptu wrestling matches on the ground.

Esperanza came out onto the patio, wearing yet another apron from her vast collection, waving.

Audrey and Ava and the dogs scrambled toward her, all but tumbling over each other, and as he watched, Tate's throat thickened and his eyes burned.

He belonged on that land, and so did his children.

After all, they were McKettricks.

CHAPTER THIRTEEN

LIBBY WAS MOWING her lawn, sweat-soaked and bug-bitten, even after the streetlights had come on, determined to finish the job come hell or high water. Hildie sat on the front porch, head tilted to one side, ears perked, watching her mistress with pitying curiosity.

A light rain began, a mist at first, then a sprinkle, cooling Libby's overheated flesh and at the same time causing her to grit her teeth. *Here's the high water,* she thought, *so hell can't be far behind.*

She stopped at the edge of the flower bed below the front porch, turned the mower grimly in the opposite direction, and saw Tate McKettrick pull up to the curb in his big truck.

The rain made his dark hair curl at the ends and dampened his white shirt.

At once embarrassed to be caught looking like the proverbial drowned rat and delighted to see Tate, no matter what, Libby froze.

Tate opened the gate, came through, shut it again.

Hildie gave a welcoming woof and started down the porch steps, but Libby neither moved nor spoke. The rain came in fat droplets now, spiking her eyelashes and blurring her vision.

Tate bent to ruffle Hildie's ears in greeting, then straightened to face Libby. He pried the handle of the push-mower from her fingers and leaned in to land a kiss on her right temple.

Damn, but he smelled good.

"Hey," he said.

Libby waited, her heart pounding, full of both delicious relief because he'd come back from New York and potential misery because he might have brought his ex-wife home with him.

Nobody knew it better than Libby did: This man would do *anything* for his kids, including marry a woman he'd never claimed to love. He'd done that once already, and she had no doubt whatsoever that he'd do it again, if he thought it was best for Audrey and Ava.

Tate smoothed Libby's soggy bangs back off her forehead, his touch light and, at the same time, electric. "You do realize," he began, in that easy and oh-so-familiar drawl of his, "that lightning could strike at any time?"

Libby stared up at him, baffled. As far as she was concerned, lightning had *already* struck, way back in second grade, when she'd suddenly looked at Tate McKettrick, that pesky ranch kid with all the freckles and the lock of dark hair forever falling into his blue eyes, in a startling new—and *old*—way. Barely seven at the time, Libby wouldn't have been able to articulate the feeling then, except to say it was like remembering—without the actual memories.

Heck, she wasn't sure she could articulate it *now*, and she was all grown up. Love? Lust? Some combination of the two?

Who knew?

All grown up into a pesky ranch *man*, sans the freckles but still with an impish glint in his too-blue-to-be-legal eyes, Tate chuckled and steered Libby up the porch steps, Hildie following.

Libby stood just out of the rain, watching as Tate went back down the steps, easily hoisted the heavy push-mower off the ground, carried it onto the porch and set it in a corner, where it would stay dry.

She finally found her voice. "Did you bring the twins home?"

Tate nodded, opened the screen door, laid his hand on the small of her back and gently pushed her into the lighted living room.

"They're sound asleep in their own beds, and Esperanza is looking after them," he said, his eyes traveling the length of her, from her sturdy hiking boots to her jean shorts to the blouse with the tie front. He frowned as he closed the door behind him. "What's with the all-weather yardwork?" he asked. "You didn't hear the thunder? See the flashes of lightning? On top of all that, it's *dark*."

Libby had been jumpy all day—and some of the night, too. She'd been so busy over the last five years, looking after her dad, starting the Perk Up, and now helping out with Marva, too. Her life had been hectic, yes, but now it seemed things happened at warp speed; one moment, she was in bed with Tate, the next, she was trying to mow the lawn in the rain.

"I guess I just have too much energy," she said. *I'm going crazy, and it's your fault. For so long I could pretend you didn't exist, that we didn't have a history. Now I can't pretend anymore, because you won't let me.*

Tate folded his arms, and she saw a muscle bunch in his jaw, then relax again. "You need to warm up, Lib; your lips are blue and your teeth are chattering a little. Take a hot shower, and while you're doing that, I'll warm up some milk for you."

Warm milk? Not what she would have expected from a confirmed cowboy like Tate. And she got the clear impression that he wasn't planning to strip out of his own rain-dampened clothes and join her in the shower, either.

This was both a disappointment and a relief.

Libby swallowed, just to keep from sighing. She hated warm milk unless it was liberally disguised with chocolate.

"Okay," she said, and her voice sounded tinny in her ears, as though she were one of those old-fashioned talking dolls, and someone had just pulled the string in her belly.

Resigned, she headed for the bathroom.

Fifteen minutes later, Libby joined Tate in the kitchen; by then she was wearing cotton pajamas, her unsexiest robe, and furry slippers from the back of her closet. As hot and muggy as that Texas night was, she felt oddly chilled.

Tate sat at the table, ruminating as he sipped instant coffee from a mug, but he rose to his feet when he spotted Libby, the chair scraping back behind him as he stood. "Sit down," he said.

His serious tone, on top of all that thinking, worried Libby. *Had* Tate and Cheryl reconnected somehow, while he was in New York, as she had secretly feared they would? Decided to give their marriage another try, if only for the children's sake?

"Why are you here?" she asked, crumpling a little on the inside.

Tate drew back a chair for her, waited in silence until she sat. Then he poured hot milk for her, added a dollop of brandy from a dusty bottle stored on the shelf above the broom closet, brought it to the table.

"We need to talk," he said.

Libby's heart began to thrum. *Here it comes,* she thought, *the part where he says he still has feelings for Cheryl, or the kids need him 24/7 or we're just plain moving too fast and need to take a breather...*

"Okay," she replied hoarsely, glad he couldn't see her hands knotted together in her lap because the tabletop was in the way. Then she squared her shoulders, raised her chin, looked him right in the eye, and waited.

"Drink the milk," Tate said. "It has to be hot to work."

Libby unknotted her hands, picked up the cup, took a sip.

It wasn't half bad—but it wasn't half *good,* either.

She made a face.

Tate grinned, reached across to smooth away her milk mustache with the pad of one thumb.

Libby set the cup down, felt some of the tension drain from her muscles.

Tate's expression changed; he leaned slightly forward, his dark brows lowered but not quite coming together. "What do you know about this Pixie thing?" he asked gravely.

Libby blinked, mystified. And almost dizzy with relief, because he hadn't said he and Cheryl were getting back together.

"'Pixie thing'?" she echoed.

Was he asking if she believed in fairies, little people?

Tate looked deep into her eyes and a grin broke over his face. "Sorry," he said. "I guess I should have laid a little groundwork before I threw that question at you. I'm talking about the Pixie Pageant. It's some kind of shindig they're holding at the country club, for charity. Like a beauty contest, but for little girls."

"Oh," Libby said, vaguely remembering a piece she'd skimmed in the *Blue River Clarion,* the town's weekly newspaper, "*that* Pixie Pageant."

Tate's jaw tightened. "Audrey is real set on signing up for the thing," he said.

Libby smiled. "What about Ava?"

"Ava thinks it's silly and wants no part of it. I happen to agree. But, like I said, Audrey is determined."

"A determined McKettrick," Libby mused, grinning. "Just *imagine* it."

Tate gave a wan grin at that, relaxed a little. "I've been dead set against this—Audrey joining up with this Pixie outfit, I mean—from the first. There are so many ways she could get hurt—"

Libby chuckled, took another sip of the milk-brandy mixture, and set her cup down. "As opposed to some *safe* activity, like rodeo?" she teased. Tate, Garrett and Austin had all been involved in the sport from earliest childhood.

Tate sighed, shoved a hand through his hair, leaving moist ridges where his fingers passed. "I get your point," he said, and sighed again. A pause followed, long and somehow comfortable. Tate finally ended it with, "What do you think I should do? Let Audrey sign up for this thing, or stand my ground?"

"I think," Libby said carefully, "that this is a conversation you should probably have with Cheryl, not me."

"I know what Cheryl thinks. I want to know what you think, Libby."

Her heart beat a little faster. She drew a fast, deep breath and huffed it out. "Why?" she asked.

"I need an unbiased opinion."

"Did you ask Esperanza?"

"Yes, as a matter of fact," Tate answered. "I did. And she's biased."

"For or against?"

"For," Tate admitted. "She thinks the whole thing is harmless and if Audrey gives it a try, she'll lose interest. Get it out of her system."

"Makes sense," Libby said, still careful. This was dangerous ground; Cheryl was the twins' mother, Esperanza had been the family housekeeper forever. But *she,* Libby, was what to them? Their father's girlfriend?

Not even that.

She was someone he slept with when they weren't around.

"Come on, Lib," Tate urged.

"What makes you so sure *I'm* unbiased?" Libby asked, more than a little hurt, now that she thought about it. The term merely meant "impartial," she knew that, but it sounded so indifferent in this context—she might have been someone stopped by a survey taker, on the way out of a supermarket, for heaven's sake. *Did she prefer laundry detergent with or without bleach?*

Tears scalded her eyes.

"I'm overreacting," she said. "I'm sorry."

Tate looked as though he wanted to touch her, rise from his chair and pull her into his arms, or tug her onto his lap.

But he did none of those things.

He cleared his throat. Looked away from Libby, then looked back. "Tell me something," he said.

Something tensed in the pit of Libby's stomach. "What?"

"If we get together, you and I," Tate ventured quietly, "you'll be around the kids a lot. Does that bother you?"

"*Bother* me?"

"If they hadn't been conceived—"

Adrenaline stung through Libby's system. "You're *not* suggesting that I blame *those precious children* for *our* breakup?"

"It would bother some women," Tate said, sounding a little defensive and a lot relieved.

"I'm not one of those women," Libby told him, her voice tight. While it was true that she didn't know Audrey and Ava very well, she had always loved them, albeit from afar, because they were Tate's.

"Good," Tate said. "Now, how about giving me an opinion on the Pixie Pageant?"

She laughed. "You never give up, do you?"

"Never," he answered, but he wasn't laughing, or even smiling.

Libby was quiet for a while, thinking. Finally, she said, "Okay, here's my opinion—you should check the pageant out, talk to the people putting it on, find out exactly what's involved. If it's something you can live with, let Audrey compete if she still wants to."

Tate sighed. "What if I miss something?" he asked.

Libby smiled uncertainly. "Miss something?"

"I'm a man, Lib. I don't know squat about this Pixie thing. They'll probably need tutus and stuff—"

Libby pictured Tate shopping for tutus and put a hand over her mouth to keep from laughing. Then, seeing that he was truly concerned, she sobered. "Can't Cheryl take care of that kind of thing?"

"Cheryl," Tate said, "is staying in New York for the time being. Right now, she plans on coming back here every other weekend, to be with the kids, but I don't suppose that will last long."

Libby stared at him. "Cheryl is staying in New York," she repeated stupidly.

"I didn't mention that before?"

"You didn't mention that before."

"Oh." Tate pushed back his chair, stood. "Well, she is. Will you help me, Lib? With the Pixie Pageant, I mean?"

Libby stood up, went to him, rested against his chest. "Yes," she said. "I'll help you."

He grinned down at her, sunshine bursting through a bank of dark clouds. "Do you have any idea how sexy you look in those pajamas and that worn-out bathrobe?"

Libby made the time-out sign, straightening the fingers of her left hand and pressing them into the palm of her right.

"What?" Tate asked, sounding innocent, though the twinkle in his eyes was anything *but* innocent.

"No sex," Libby was surprised to hear herself say. "Not tonight, anyway. I'm still recovering from last time."

"Recovering?" Tate asked, pretending to be hurt. The twinkle remained, though.

"Yes, *recovering,*" Libby said, blushing. "It's not just sex when we're together, Tate. Not for me."

He raised a questioning eyebrow, looked intrigued.

Ran his hands down her back and cupped her bottom.

"Lib?" Tate prompted, when she didn't say anything else.

She caught her breath, found her voice, lost it again.

Sex wasn't just sex to Libby, not with Tate McKettrick. But how the hell was she supposed to explain that, without coming right out and saying that she still loved him? That, like a fool, she'd never *stopped* loving him, even while he was another woman's husband?

Even after his and Cheryl's divorce, Libby had been careful to stay away from Tate. She managed pretty well, too, until the day of the twins' birthday, when he'd walked into the Perk Up and the earth had shifted on its axis.

No, for Libby, sex with this one man was cosmic. It was a personal apocalypse, followed by the formation of new universes.

The one thing it would never be was *just sex*.

Libby didn't even have names for the things she felt when she and Tate were joined physically, and for hours or even days afterward.

"It's getting late," she said, avoiding Tate's eyes because she knew she'd get sucked into them like an unwary planetoid passing too near to a black hole if she let him catch her gaze just at that moment. "Maybe you should go."

He held her close again. She breathed in the scent of him, knew she would be powerless if he made the slightest move to seduce her.

"You're okay?" he asked, his voice hoarse, his breath moving through her hair like the faintest breeze. He propped his chin on top of her head, a sigh moving through his chest.

"I'm okay," she confirmed.

He moved back, curved a finger under her chin, and lifted. "Lib?"

She looked up at him.

Don't kiss me.

I'll die if you don't kiss me.

God help me, I've lost my mind.

"Everything's going to be okay," he told her.

She nodded. Tears threatened again, but she managed to hold them back.

He kissed her forehead.

And then he drew back, no longer holding her.

He bent to ruffle Hildie's ears in farewell.

Then he left.

Libby poured the remains of her milk—now cold—down the sink. She listened to Tate's retreating footsteps, fighting the urge to run after him, call him back, beg him to spend the night. She heard the front door open, close again. Then, distantly, the sound of his truck starting up.

Only then did she walk through the living room to lock up.

She switched off the lamps, went back to the kitchen, let Hildie out into the yard one last time.

Once the dog was inside again, Libby retreated to the bathroom, where she brushed her teeth and shed the robe, hanging it from the peg on the back of the door.

"What a pathetic life I lead," she said, looking at the robe, limp from so many washings, the once-vibrant color faded, the seams coming open in places.

Hildie, standing beside her, gave a concerned whimper, turned and padded into Libby's room.

The two of them settled down for the night, Libby expecting to toss and turn all night, sleepless, burning for the touch of Tate's lips and hands, the warm strength of his arms around her, the sound of his heart beating as she lay with her head on his chest.

Instead, sweet oblivion ambushed her.

She awakened to one of those washed-clean mornings that so often follow a rainstorm, sunlight streaming through her bedroom window.

DAWN HADN'T BROKEN when Tate got out of bed, but a pinkish-apricot light rimmed the hills to the east. He hauled on jeans, a T-shirt, socks and boots. He'd shower and change and have breakfast later, when the range work was done.

He looked in on his girls in their room, found them sleeping soundly, each with a plump yellow dog curled up at her feet. His heart swelled at the sight, but he was afraid to let himself get too happy.

Things were still delicate with Libby.

And Cheryl could change her mind about New York, the apartment, all of it, at any time—come back to the house in Blue River and start up the whole split-custody merry-go-round all over again.

The thought made his stomach burn.

Quietly, Tate closed the door to his daughters' room and made his way along the hallway, toward the back stairs leading down into the kitchen.

The aroma of brewing coffee rose to meet him halfway.

He smiled.

Esperanza was up, then. Maybe he'd have to reconsider his decision not to take time for breakfast, since she might not let him out of the house until he'd eaten something.

Tate paused when he stepped into the brightly lit kitchen.

Garrett stood at the stove, wearing jeans, boots and a long-sleeved work shirt, frying eggs. "Mornin'," he said affably.

Tate blinked, figuring he was seeing things.

Even when he was on the ranch, which wasn't all that often, Garrett never got up before sunrise, and he sure as *hell* never cooked.

"You're dead and I'm seeing your ghost," Tate said, only half kidding.

Garrett chuckled. There was something rueful in his eyes, something Tate knew he wouldn't share. "Nope," he replied. "It's me, Garrett McKettrick. Live and in person."

Tate fetched a mug from one of the cupboards, filled it from the still-chortling coffeemaker on the counter, watched his younger brother warily as he sipped. "What are you doing here?"

"I live here," Garrett said. "Remember?"

"Vaguely," Tate replied. "To be more specific, what are you doing *in the kitchen, at this hour, cooking,* for God's sake?"

"I'm hungry," Garrett answered quietly. "And if you never went to bed in the first place, it doesn't count as getting up early, does it?"

"Oh," Tate said. His brain was still cranking up, unsticking itself from sleep.

"Have some eggs," Garrett said, looking Tate over, noting his get-up. "Planning on playing cowboy today?"

Tate felt his neck and the underside of his jaw turn hot, recalling Garrett's earlier jibe about feeling guilty over the money and the land, making a show of working for a living. He took a plate from the long, slatted shelf and shoveled a couple of eggs—"cackleberries," their grandfather had called them—onto it.

They both sat down at the big table in the center of that massive room, and Tate took his time responding to Garrett.

"Yeah," he finally ground out. "I'm planning on 'playing cowboy' today." He let his gaze roll over Garrett's old shirt once, making his point. "Where did you get that rag? From wherever Esperanza stashes the cleaning supplies?"

Garrett chuckled, glancing down at his clothes. "Found them in the back of my closet," he said. "On the floor."

"Okay," Tate said, "I'll bite. What's with the getup?"

Garrett sighed. Possibly practicing his political skills, he didn't exactly answer the question. "The lights were on in the bunkhouse and all the trailers along the creek when I came home a little while ago," he explained, before a brief shadow of sadness fell over his face. He needed a shave, Tate noticed, and there were dark circles under his eyes. "Except the Ruizes', of course. That was dark."

Tate dealt with his own flash of sorrow in silence. He knew Garrett had more to say, so he just waited for him to go on.

"I knew the men were up and around, getting ready for a long day herding cattle or riding fence lines," Garrett eventually continued. "I decided to put on the gear, saddle up and see if I still have it in me—a day of real work."

Tate felt a surge of something—respect, pride? Brotherly love?

He didn't explore the emotion. "These eggs aren't half bad," he said.

"Well," Garrett answered, "don't get used to it. I don't cook, as a general rule."

Tate chuckled, though it was a dry, raspy sound, pushed back from the table, carried his plate to the sink, rinsed it and set it in the dishwasher. Leaned against the counter and folded his arms, watching as Garrett finished his meal and stood.

"Everything all right?" Tate asked, very quietly.

"Everything's *fine,* big brother," Garrett replied. He was lying, of course. From the time he was knee-high to a garden gnome, Garrett hadn't been able to lie and look Tate in the eye at the same time.

Now, he looked everywhere *but* into Tate's face.

"Let's go," Tate said, after a few moments, making for the door.

Just then, Austin came down his personal stairway, clad in work clothes himself, though his shirt was only half-buttoned and crooked at that, and he had a pretty bad case of bed-head. Wearing one boot and carrying the other, he hopped around at the bottom of the steps until he got into the second boot.

"Is there any grub left?" he asked.

"You're too late," Garrett told him.

"Shit," Austin said, finger-combing his hair. "Story of my life."

"Cry me a river," Tate said, with a grin and a roll of his eyes, pulling open the back door.

The predawn breeze felt like the kiss of heaven as it touched him.

He thought about Libby, sleeping warm and soft and deliciously curvy in her bed in town. Since about the last thing he needed right then was a hard-on, he shifted his mind to the day ahead, and the plans he'd made for it.

He strode toward the barn, Garrett and Austin arguing affably behind him, glanced back once to see Austin tucking his shirt into his jeans, none too neatly. It was like the old days, when they were boys, and their dad roused them out of their beds at the crack to do chores, not only in the summer but year-round. The Silver Spur was their ranch, too, Jim McKettrick had often said, and they had to learn how to look after it.

So they fed horses and herded cattle from one pasture to another.

They shoveled out stalls and drove tractors and milked cows and fed chickens.

The chickens and the dairy cows were long gone now, like the big vegetable garden. The quarter-acre plot had been his mother's province; she and Esperanza had spent hours out there, weeding and watering, hoeing and raking. Tate and his brothers had done their share, too, though usually under duress, grumbling that fussing with a lot of tomatoes and green beans and sweet corn was women's work.

"You eat, don't you?" Sally McKettrick had challenged, more than once, shaking a finger under one of their noses. "You eat, you weed, bucko. That's the way the real world works."

Reaching the barn door, Tate smiled to himself, albeit sadly. Most of the bounty from that garden had gone to the ranch hands and their families and to the little food bank in town. And what he wouldn't give to be sweating under a summer sun again, with his mom just a few rows over, working like a field hand and enjoying every minute of it.

He switched on the overhead lights.

The good, earthy scents of horse and grass-hay and manure

stirred as the animals moved in their stalls, nickering and shifting, snorting as they awakened.

Tending the horses wasn't new to Tate—he'd taken the job over from a couple of the ranch hands when he and Cheryl split and she moved into the house in town—though he rarely got to the barn this early in the day.

The work went quickly, divided between the three of them.

Austin turned his childhood mount, Bamboozle, out with the other, larger horses, since the little gelding was used to them and they were used to him, but Audrey's and Ava's golden ponies had to be kept in a special corral, for their own safety.

In the meantime, Tate saddled Stranger, the aging gelding, a strawberry roan, that had belonged to his father. Garrett chose Windwalker, a long-legged bay, while Austin tacked up a sorrel called Ambush.

In his heyday, Ambush had been a rodeo bronc, and he could still buck like the devil when he took the notion.

Austin, being Austin, probably hoped today was the day.

Tate grinned at the thought, shook his head.

His little brother was stone crazy, but you had to love him. Most of the time.

The paint stallion kicked and squealed in his holding pen, scenting the other horses, wanting to be turned loose.

"What are you planning on doing with that stud?" Garrett asked, as the three of them rode away from the barn, toward the range.

"Brent said we might have to put him down," Tate answered. He hated the idea, knew Pablo would have hated it, too, but there had been a death—and that meant the authorities had a say in the matter.

"And you're just going to go along with whatever he says?" Austin wanted to know.

Tate bristled. "The law's the law," he said. "I'd rather not shoot that horse, but I might not have a choice."

"You could just let him go," Garrett suggested. "Say he got out on his own somehow."

"And lie to Brent?" Tate asked. "Not only the chief of police, but my best friend?"

Garrett went quiet.

Austin didn't seem to have anything more to say, either.

So they rode on, the purple range slowly greening up ahead of them.

The herd bawled and raised dust in the dawn as cowboys converged from all directions, some coming from the bunkhouse, which had its own rustic but sturdy stables, and from the various trailers along the creek. Some of the men were on horseback, while others drove pickups with the Silver Spur brand painted on the doors.

Tate and his brothers fell in with the others as easily as if they had never been away from the work, driving cattle between different sections of land to conserve the sweet grass, rippling like waves under a rising wind.

Resting the roan, Stranger, at the creek's edge, Tate nodded as Harley Bates rode up alongside him. Harley had ridden for the McKettrick brand almost as long as Pablo had, though Tate didn't know him as well. Married when he signed on, Bates lived in one of the coveted trailers, although his wife had long since boarded a bus out of town, never to be seen again.

"It ain't the same without ole Pablo," Harley said, resettling his hat, which, like the rest of his gear, had seen better days.

"No," Tate agreed.

Bates shifted in his saddle, and the odor of unwashed flesh wafted Tate's way. "I see you've been fixing up that house by the bend in the creek."

A beat passed before Tate figured out what the man was talking about. He nodded again. "So I have," he said.

"Guess it'll go to the new foreman," Bates speculated. All the men were probably wondering who would replace Pablo Ruiz, and they'd either put Bates up to finding out, or he'd come up with the idea on his own, maybe hoping for a raise in pay and more spacious quarters than the one-bedroom single-wide he bunked in now.

"Yep," Tate answered, standing in the stirrups to stretch his legs a little before turning to meet the other man's gaze. "You're looking at the new foreman," he said. "For the time being, anyway. I'll be moving into the Ruiz place myself, as soon as the renovations are finished."

Whatever Harley Bates had expected to hear, it wasn't that.

His small eyes popped a little, and his jaws worked as though he were chewing on a mouthful of gristle. "*You're* the new foreman?"

Tate nodded. He couldn't blame the other man for being surprised, even skeptical. After all, the foreman did real work, especially on a spread the size of the Silver Spur. Although Tate could ride and brand and drive post holes with the best of them, he couldn't claim that he'd filled his dad's boots.

And that was why he'd decided to take on the job. If he was going to run the Silver Spur, he had to get serious about it. He had to learn all there was to know about every aspect of running the ranch.

Although it stung, he knew Garrett had been at least partly right, accusing him of playing at being a rancher.

Bates took off his hat, slammed it once against his thigh, and slapped it on again with such force that it bent the tops of his ears.

Tate suppressed a sigh. "Tell the men there'll be a meeting tonight," he said. "Six o'clock, at the new place."

"You mean, the Ruiz place?" Bates all but snarled.

"I mean, the new place," Tate answered evenly. "Six o'clock. I'll provide the chicken and the beer."

Bates scowled, nodded once, wheeled his horse around and rode away.

CHAPTER FOURTEEN

TATE APPEARED AT the Perk Up at four-thirty that afternoon, with his daughters and their dogs, though Buford and Ambrose waited in the truck.

Julie stayed in the kitchen, but Calvin stood at Libby's side, watching as Audrey and Ava bounced into the shop. They were wearing jean shorts and matching cotton blouses, blue and white checked.

"It was nice of you to give us your castle," Calvin said, very solemnly. "Thanks." Although he had yet to be elected king, he apparently considered himself a spokesperson for the community.

And by *us,* of course, Calvin meant the town of Blue River— the wonder toy was now installed on the lawn at the community center, and according to Julie, so many kids wanted to play in and around the thing that parents had been recruited to supervise. A few people even wanted to sell tickets.

Audrey and Ava looked at each other, then up at Tate, then at Calvin.

"You're welcome," Ava said, with great formality. She was definitely the more serious twin, Libby noted, though no less confident than her sister.

"Daddy made us do it," Audrey added forthrightly. "But we still have our ponies."

"You have *ponies?*" Calvin said, with wonder in his voice. Then, again, as though such a thing were almost beyond the outer reaches of credibility, *"You have ponies?"*

Audrey nodded at him. "Three, if you count Uncle Austin's. His horse is Bamboozle, but we call him Boozle for short, and he's really old, and we haven't named our ponies yet—they're twins, like we are, or at least they *look* like twins. They're not, really, but they're the same age and the same color and—" She paused, though not for very long, to haul in a breath. "Are you a friend of Libby's?"

Tate and Libby exchanged amused glances.

"She's my aunt," Calvin replied, with a note of pride that warmed Libby's heart.

Audrey smiled at him. "Maybe you can come out to our place sometime, and ride Boozle. He's old, like I said. Uncle Austin got him when he was ten. Uncle Austin was ten, I mean, not the pony."

"How come you weren't at our birthday party?" Ava asked. "We know you from daycare at the community center. Your name is Calvin."

Calvin was unfazed. "I don't think I was invited," he said reasonably.

"Oh," Ava said.

"How old are you?" Audrey wanted to know.

"Four," Calvin admitted, squaring his little shoulders.

"Well, that's probably why," Ava said matter-of-factly. "You're practically a baby."

"I am *not* a baby!" Calvin asserted indignantly.

Libby rested a hand on his shoulder.

"You talk like a grown-up," Audrey allowed, and after surveying Calvin thoughtfully for a moment or so, she graciously conferred her approval. "He's right, Ava. He's not a baby."

"Guess not," Ava agreed, with the barest hint of reluctance.

Calvin was clearly mollified. Grinning toothily and adjusting his glasses yet again with the poke of one slightly grubby finger, he said, "It was probably a real girly party, anyhow. Lots of pink stuff."

Tate chuckled, subtly steering the girls toward the stools at the short counter. Libby had noticed, and appreciated, the way he'd paid careful attention to the exchange between the three children but hadn't intervened.

"Of course it was girly," Ava said, looking back at Calvin over one shoulder. "We're *girls.*"

"Orange smoothies all around?" Libby piped up, figuring it was time to change the subject.

"Yes, please," Ava said, speaking like a miniature adult.

"Please," Audrey echoed, scrambling up onto a stool.

"Me, too, Aunt Libby," Calvin chirped, getting into the spirit of the thing. "But I want strawberry, please."

Julie stuck her head out of the kitchen. Nothing wrong with her hearing, Libby thought, with an inward smile. It was probably a mother thing.

"No way, José," Julie told Calvin. "You'll spoil your supper."

"It's not even five o'clock yet," Calvin complained.

"Grandma's coming over for meat loaf," Julie reminded him, "and she likes to eat early, so she can get back to her condo in time to watch her TV shows. We're picking her up in a little while, and we have to run a few errands first."

Calvin sighed his weight-of-the-world sigh. It rarely worked with Julie, and this instance was no exception, but with Calvin, hope sprang eternal.

"You'd be welcome to come out to the Silver Spur sometime soon and ride Bamboozle," Tate told the little boy quietly, his gaze shifting to Julie's face. "If it's all right with your mom, that is."

Julie smiled. She liked Calvin to have new experiences, and riding horses on the McKettrick ranch certainly qualified. As kids, Julie, Paige and Libby had been to lots of parties on the Silver Spur, but those days seemed long ago and far away.

In fact, Libby hadn't been on a horse since before she and Tate broke up over Cheryl.

"That would be nice," Julie told Tate. "Thank you."

He nodded. He looked ridiculously good in his dark blue T-shirt and battered jeans, and the shadow of a beard growing in only added to the testosterone-rich effect. "My pleasure," he drawled.

The timbre of his voice found a place inside Libby and tingled there.

She shook off the sensation and finished brewing up the orange smoothies, setting them in front of Audrey and Ava and smiling.

"There you go," she said.

They smiled back at her.

Several moments of silence passed.

"Audrey needs a tutu," Ava announced, without preamble, after poking a straw into her smoothie and slurping some up. She rolled her lovely blue eyes at Libby and giggled. "She's pixilated."

Tate took the third stool, next to the cash register. Rested his muscular forearms on the countertop and intertwined his fingers loosely. He had an easy way about him, as if it were no trouble to wait around.

Not every man was that patient, Libby thought.

"Pixilated?" she asked, to get her mind off Tate's patience and his muscular forearms and his five-o'clock shadow.

She was only partly successful.

"Ava's talking about the Pixie Pageant," Tate said easily.

Libby liked the way he could just sit there, not needing to fiddle with something to keep his fingers busy. There was a great *quietness* in Tate McKettrick, a safety and serenity that reached beyond the boundaries of his skin, big enough to take in his daughters, the old dog, Crockett, his family and the whole of the Silver Spur Ranch.

And maybe her, too.

Libby met his eyes, an effort because she felt shaken now, as though something profound had just happened between her and Tate. Which was silly, because the situation couldn't have been more ordinary, nor could the conversation.

"I guess things checked out okay, then? The Pixie Pageant is a go?"

Tate nodded, looking beleaguered but mildly amused. *Females,* his manner seemed to say: *Sometimes there's no figuring them out.*

"Yeah," he said. "It checked out, and it's a go. A lot depends on your definition of *okay,* though."

She smiled, resisting an impulse to pat Tate's shoulder, and poured him a cup of coffee. "On the house," she said.

Libby realized she'd lost track of her sister and her nephew, shifted her focus.

"Julie?"

Julie, it turned out, was ready to leave; she'd gathered her belongings and her son and was standing almost at Libby's elbow, a knowing and slightly bemused smile resting prettily on her mouth.

Of course Libby knew what was going through her sister's mind; Julie and Paige could stop worrying about their big sister if Libby and Tate got back together.

"See you tomorrow?" Libby asked, wishing Julie would stay just a little longer.

"Sure," Julie replied hastily, barely looking back. "Tomorrow."

"Bring scones," Libby called after her.

Julie laughed, gave a comical half salute and left the shop. The bell jingled over the door, and Calvin looked back, one hand smudging the glass, his eyes full of yearning.

The sight gave Libby a pang. She knew the feeling: on the outside, looking in. It grieved her to see the knowledge in Calvin—he was so young, and she loved him so much.

"We just came from the country club," Tate told Libby, when Julie and Calvin had left, and she'd snapped out of the ache over her nephew's little-boy loneliness. He watched with an expression of mystified fondness as his daughters giggled over their drinks. "The pageant is a one-day thing. As far as I can tell, it's no big deal."

"You have to have a talent to win," Ava interjected.

Audrey elbowed her. "I *have* a talent," she said.

"Oh, yeah?" Ava countered. "*What* talent?"

"That's enough," Tate said, though he seemed as still and as calm as ever. "Both of you."

"I *do too* have a talent," Audrey insisted, as though he hadn't spoken. What were these two going to be like as *teenagers?* "I can sing. Mom says so."

Tate tried again. "Girls," he said.

"If you call that singing," Ava said, with a little shrug and a flip of her ebony hair. "I think you sound awful. Anyhow, you know how Mom is about this pageant thing. Her eyes get all funny when she talks about it."

Although the reference to Cheryl made her mildly uncomfortable, Tate's expression made Libby want to smile. But since that might have undermined his parental authority, she didn't.

For all his calm, he was obviously at a loss, too. What to do?

The answer, Libby could have told him, was nothing at all. This was simply the way sisters related—twins or not. She and Paige and Julie still bickered, but it didn't mean they didn't love each other. There was nothing Libby wouldn't have done for Paige and Julie, and she knew the reverse was true, as well.

Libby opened her mouth to make a stab at explaining, realized she didn't have the words, and closed it again.

"One more word," Tate told the children, "and nobody rides horseback, swims in the pool, goes to the library or plays a video game for a whole month."

Two sets of cornflower blue eyes widened.

"Okay," Ava breathed, looking and sounding put-upon. She adjusted her glasses, though not by shoving them upward at the bridge of her nose, the way Calvin did.

"That's a word," Audrey pointed out triumphantly. "*Okay* is a word!"

"You just said a *whole bunch* of words!" Ava cried.

"Let's go pick up the fried chicken and beer," Tate said, shoving off his stool to stand, and the girls scrambled off their stools, too, orange smoothies in hand.

He paid for the drinks.

"Daddy's having a cowboy meeting at the house where Mr. and Mrs. Ruiz used to live," Ava said to Libby, her tone and expression serious. "He's going to tell them where the bear shit in the buckwheat."

Tate flushed, the color throbbing in his neck and then pulsing briefly above his jawline and darkening his ears a little. *"Ava."*

"That's what you told Uncle Austin," the little girl retorted. "I *heard* you."

"Esperanza's going to take care of us while Daddy's at the cowboy meeting," Audrey explained, rapid-fire. "Because cowboys cuss and we shouldn't be around to hear things like that. So we get to have tacos for supper and make popcorn and spend the whole night in Esperanza's suite and watch as many movies as we want to, even if it's a hundred!"

"Wow," Libby said, very seriously, widening her eyes a little for emphasis, "a hundred movies?"

"More like one movie, a hundred times," Tate said dryly.

Libby laughed.

Ava spoke up again. "I don't see why it takes a whole meeting just to tell people where a bear—"

Tate cupped a hand around the child's mouth. "Maybe I could stop by your place later, so we could talk about the tutu and stuff?" he said, his eyes practically pleading with Libby to agree.

The image of Tate McKettrick shopping for a tutu was beyond funny. She could hold back another burst of laughter, but not the twinkle she knew was sparkling in her eyes as she enjoyed the mind-picture.

"What time does the buckwheat meeting get over?" Libby asked sweetly, resting her hands on her hips and heartily enjoying Tate's obvious discomfort. At the same time, it touched her heart, the way he cared so much about being a good father, getting things right.

Even to the extent of shopping for tutus, when it came to that.

Her throat ached. Her dad had been the same way.

She missed him so much.

"Eight o'clock, maybe," Tate said, looking hopeful. "Is that too late?"

"Not for me," Libby answered, "but *you* look a little tired, cowboy."

He flashed her a grin, maybe to prove he wasn't all *that* tired.

The twins were at the shop door by then, still squabbling.

Tate bent his head, spoke quietly into Libby's ear. "I'll save you some chicken and beer," he said. "Meet me at the new place later, and bring the dog if you want to."

"Maybe," Libby said firmly, unsettled now. "Last time—"

The patented McKettrick grin came again, even more dazzling than before. "Yes," Tate said. "I remember."

Libby was wavering, and she didn't want him to know that.

She all but pushed Tate to the door, and that made the girls laugh.

"Later?" he asked. His voice was a sexy rumble.

"Don't count on it," Libby said, but she was rattled and planning on showing up at his place for sure and they both knew it.

Tate smiled and left, shepherding his daughters across the street, hoisting them into the backseat of the truck, assisting with buckles and belts affixed to safety seats while gently fending off a pair of overjoyed pups.

Libby watched, resting her forehead against the glass in the front door of the Perk Up.

When she sensed that Tate was about to turn in her direction, she pulled back quickly and turned the "Open" sign to "Closed."

She locked the door.

Shut down all the machines and cleaned them.

Tucked the day's profits into a deposit bag, and the bag into her purse. Although the Perk Up had been doing a lot better financially since Julie had started baking scones and other goodies, Libby had been giving most of the money to her sister.

Which meant she was still just breaking even, most days.

At home, she let Hildie out into the backyard, as usual, and went back inside when she heard the phone ringing.

"Have you seen Marva?" Julie blurted anxiously.

"No," Libby said. "Isn't she at the condo?"

"No, she's not at the condo!" Julie almost screamed. "Libby, she stole my car!"

Libby sagged against the counter. "Oh, my God, Julie, Calvin wasn't—?"

"Calvin wasn't in the car, thank heaven," Julie answered, only moderately less hysterical than before.

Libby echoed that sentiment, letting out her breath, then asked, "Have you called Chief Brogan?"

Julie was beside herself. "Are you kidding? Call the cops on my own mother? Libby, I can't do that!"

"Calm down," Libby said firmly. "Julie, *calm down.* Take a slow, deep breath."

"But my car—my mother—oh, my *God*—"

"I'll be right over," Libby said. "If I see Marva along the way, I'll do my best to flag her down."

The words were disturbingly prophetic, as it turned out.

Libby had no more than uttered them when she heard an odd noise, looked through the window over the sink, and saw Julie's pink Cadillac speeding down the alley, bouncing over the ruts, tailpipe dragging and throwing off blue and orange sparks.

It all happened quickly, and yet Libby took in the scene in vivid and minute detail.

Marva was at the wheel, the windows rolled down. She was smoking a long brown cigarette jutting from a holder and singing along with the Grateful Dead at the top of her lungs.

"I don't believe this!" Libby gasped into the phone, one hand pressed to her heart. "I just saw her go by!"

"Try to catch her," Julie pleaded. "Go! Now!"

"Oh, right," Libby said, feeling pretty frantic herself, now. "Maybe I could sprint to the corner and just leap onto the hood and pound on the windshield with my fists. Julie, I know you're upset, but will you get real?"

"Libby, you've got to *do* something!"

"I'll go after her, but she's driving so fast the wheels are barely touching the ground. Get here as quickly as you can, and call Paige, too."

"Get *where* as quickly as I can?"

"To wherever I am, of course." With that, Libby hung up with a bang, raced out the back door and down the steps, passing Hildie, who had settled herself comfortably in her favorite shady spot under the big tree.

"Stay!" Libby told the dog.

Hildie hadn't shown any signs of moving so much as a muscle, but a person couldn't be too careful.

"Marva!" Libby yelled, running for the alley.

Dust roiled, but there was no sign of the Caddie.

"Marva," Libby repeated, this time as a plea.

She was about to go back inside the house, since she'd forgotten the keys to the Impala and it wouldn't be much use giving chase on foot when she heard the crash.

It was deafening, so loud it seemed to shake the earth and the fillings in Libby's teeth.

Glass tinkled.

A horn tooted and then honked steadily, a long, terrifying drone.

A cloud of dust billowed far above the roof of Libby's shop, and except for the horn everything was silent, for one quivering moment.

And then the roof of the Perk Up collapsed.

Libby stood staring, unable to move.

A siren blared somewhere.

"Oh, no," Libby whispered. *"Oh, no."*

Running full out, Libby dashed through the narrow space between Almsted's Grocery and her coffee shop. More dust and plaster showered down on her.

The horn continued to blow.

Libby finally reached the sidewalk, and there was the pink
Cadillac—or part of it, at least—taillights still shining bright red,
half buried under the rubble of the Perk Up.

A crowd, probably driven from Almsted's by prudence, clustered on the sidewalk.

Brent had already arrived; his cruiser was parked at the curb,
lights flashing dizzily, siren shrieking fit to wake all the corpses
in the Blue River Cemetery. Along with several passersby and
members of the volunteer fire department, the chief dug franti-
cally through fallen timbers and old drywall and shards of glass
with his bare hands.

Where she got the strength, Libby did not know. But somehow she pushed through until she was shoulder to shoulder with
Brent, and dug hard.

The roof of the car appeared, and the driver's-side window. Un-
broken, thank God. The windshield had held, too.

"Marva?" Libby whispered.

Marva turned and looked at her dreamily, both hands still resting on the steering wheel. Except for a small cut above her right
eyebrow, she seemed to be all right, but there was no way of knowing that until she'd been examined by a doctor, of course.

Marva rolled down the car window. "Oops," she said.

"Is she drunk?" Chief Brogan demanded of Libby. He was
sweating, like everybody except Marva, who looked cool as could
be.

"I doubt it," Libby said, as wave after wave of residual shock
washed over her. She had to grip the edge of the open window to
steady herself. "Are you all right, Marva?" she asked, in someone else's voice.

Marva nodded. "I'm fine," she said calmly.

The Perk Up was a complete shambles, but Marva was alive and, it appeared, unhurt. For the moment, nothing else really mattered. It would be a short moment.

"I forgot how to stop," Marva said, amazed. "I can't believe I forgot how to stop."

"Does anything hurt anywhere?" Brent asked.

Marva shook her head. Her gaze meandered slowly from Libby's face to Brent's. "Am I under arrest?" she asked. "I'm stone sober, you know. And I didn't actually *steal* this car, either. It belongs to my daughter, and I'm sure Julie will vouch for everything I say."

Libby, dizzy, put a hand to her own forehead.

"Let's not worry about the legal implications right this minute, ma'am," Brent answered, very politely. "For now, we're just going to concentrate on making sure you're all right."

"I demand a lawyer," Marva said.

"You don't need a lawyer," Libby said.

"She might," Brent countered, in a whisper.

"Winston," Marva said, tilting her head back and closing her eyes, "will kill me."

"Winston?" Libby asked, puzzled.

"My husband," Marva answered, without opening her eyes. "Winston Alexander Vandergant the Third."

Libby blinked. "Your—?"

"Husband." Marva sighed.

"Would you mind spelling that?" Brent asked, taking a little notebook from his shirt pocket and clicking a pen with his thumb.

Marva calmly spelled out the entire name.

Brent wrote it down.

"You have a husband?" Libby echoed.

"Call him," Marva told Brent. "He'll straighten out this whole situation. Winston is just a whiz when it comes to problem solving."

Brent merely nodded.

Two EMTs politely elbowed Libby and Brent aside so they could remove Marva from the car.

Libby was standing on the sidewalk when Paige roared up to the curb in her subcompact car, Julie in the passenger seat.

By then, the paramedics had put a neck brace on Marva and

placed her carefully on a stretcher. She was loaded into the ambulance; according to protocol, she would be examined at the Blue River Clinic, and if her injuries were serious, transported from there to a trauma center.

Julie, standing on the littered sidewalk, assessed Marva, the collapsed roof of the Perk Up and her nearly buried car. *"What happened?"*

"I think that's obvious," Paige said dryly, but she ran over and climbed into the ambulance just as the doors were about to be closed, scrambling inside to take Marva's hand. The vehicle raced away.

Libby ran home, retrieved the keys to her Impala from the kitchen, backed the car out of the garage, and stopped for a still-stunned Julie in front of what was left of the Perk Up.

They headed for the clinic.

"Where's Calvin?" Libby asked, as she navigated the familiar streets. By then, her brain was clearing; she was starting to think in practical terms again.

"With Marva's neighbor, Mrs. Kingston," Julie answered.

Libby nodded, reassured. Mrs. Kingston, unlike their mother, was quite sane. A responsible human being.

"She could have killed herself," Julie fretted. "Marva, I mean."

"Right," Libby agreed tensely. "And a lot of other people, too."

Her mind raced. Julie's Cadillac might be salvageable, but the Perk Up was a total loss. What was she going to do now? How was she going to earn a living?

She'd barely been getting by as it was.

Ashamed of worrying about herself when Marva might be lapsing into a coma in the back of the ambulance at that very moment—she doubted it, but anything was possible—Libby blinked a couple of times and bit down hard on her lower lip. "Julie, how did Marva manage to swipe your car?"

Julie closed her eyes tightly, hugged herself. "I left the keys in the ignition. I was talking to that nice Mrs. Kingston, Marva's neighbor—she has the loveliest climbing roses and I wanted to know how often she pruned and fertilized because I'm thinking of putting in a garden next spring myself and—"

Libby broke into the nervous flow of her sister's conversation.

"Do you know how lucky we are that Calvin wasn't in the car? Or behind it, or *in front* of it—"

"Do *you* have to remind me of what *could* have happened?" Julie snapped. "It seems to me that what *did* happen is bad enough!"

"I'm sorry," Libby said, to keep the peace.

Julie reached over, squeezed her hand. "Me, too," she said. "I shouldn't have snapped at you."

Less than a minute later, they reached the clinic, a small brick building on the eastern edge of town. Thanks to the generous support of the McKettricks and other oil-and-cattle-rich families in that part of Texas, the facility was well-staffed, with four different doctors working in rotation, several nurses, a full office staff and assorted technicians.

The equipment was state-of-the-art, and there were two spacious four-bed wards for overnight patients.

Paige was waiting in the parking lot looking fidgety, when Libby and Julie wheeled in.

The three of them hurried past the parked ambulance, its rear door still standing open. Brent's cruiser stood beside it, empty.

The receptionist explained that Dr. Burt was examining Marva, and they might as well sit down because it would be a while.

Paige led the way into the small waiting room, plunked some coins into a vending machine, and watched as a cup dropped down a chute and began to fill with steaming coffee.

"She has a husband," Libby said, apropos of nothing. "Marva, I mean."

"A husband?" her sisters chorused.

"Winston Alexander Vandergort the Third, or something like that."

"Who?" Julie asked.

"That's all I know," Libby insisted, defensive.

Julie began to pace. "A husband," she muttered.

"Do you both have insurance?" Paige asked, ever practical, her gaze traveling between Libby and Julie.

"Yes," Julie said. "But that Cadillac was a classic. Irreplaceable."

"So was my business," Libby said. "Irreplaceable, I mean."

"Let's not panic here," Paige said.

"That's easy for you to say," Libby said.

"Yeah," Julie agreed.

"Everything will work out," Paige insisted.

Again, easy for *her* to say. She had a good job, with benefits, and she definitely didn't live from paycheck to paycheck, either. *Her* car hadn't been wrecked. *Her* coffee shop hadn't been reduced to a pile of broken boards and bits of plaster.

"We'll *manage*," Paige said, putting one arm around Libby's shoulders and one around Julie's and squeezing. "I promise."

"We?" Libby challenged.

"We," Paige confirmed. "I have savings. I can help—"

"I won't take your money," Libby said.

"Neither will I," Julie agreed.

Brent came out of one of the exam rooms and approached them.

"Well," he said, "we won't be charging your mother with driving under the influence, anyway. Which is not to say her sanity isn't in question."

"But is she going to be all right?" Julie asked anxiously, staring up at Brent.

"She seems to be," Brent replied patiently. "The doctor wants to run a CT scan and take some X-rays. Could be a long wait."

Julie glanced down at her watch. "Calvin is probably worried," she said, pale with anxiety.

"Let's pick him up and bring him here," Paige suggested. She looked up at Brent. "Would you mind giving us a ride back to my car, Chief? I left it at the Perk Up to ride in the ambulance with Marva."

"Sure thing," Brent replied, cocking a thumb toward the cruiser. "Hop in."

Julie nodded, then shook her head. Gave a despairing little giggle at her own contradictory response. "I mean, I don't have a car seat now—"

"I do," Paige reminded Julie. She'd purchased the seat at a garage sale two summers before, because she and Calvin spent a lot of time together when her schedule clicked with Julie's. "I'm beginning to think you're in worse shape than Marva is. Are you all right?"

"My car is buried under tons of rubble," Julie answered, almost snappishly. "Why wouldn't I be all right?"

They both climbed into the backseat of Brent's cruiser, still bickering.

Yep, Libby thought sadly, Julie's car was under tons of rubble. And that rubble had once been her business. Her livelihood.

Not that it had ever been all that lively.

Paige got out of the cruiser, came back to Libby and brought her cell phone out of her purse, handing it over. "Just in case," she explained.

Libby stared down at the device. It was a moment before she remembered Brent was still there.

Looking up at him, she calmly asked for Tate's cell number.

Brent gave it to her, and Libby nodded her thanks and keyed in the digits as she walked around the corner of the clinic to stand in the side parking lot, out of earshot.

She watched as the cruiser pulled out onto the highway, then looked up, surprised to see that the moon was already visible, even though the sun hadn't fully set. The sky blazed crimson and lavender and apricot.

He answered after two rings. "Tate McKettrick," he said, a puzzled note in his voice.

Of course, Libby realized, Paige's number would have come up in the caller ID panel, since she was calling on her sister's phone.

Libby leaned back against the brick face of the Blue River Clinic, suddenly exhausted. "It's me," she said. "Libby."

"Lib? Are you all right?"

She had to swallow a throatful of tears before answering. "I'm okay," she said, and then it all came tumbling out, in a crazy rush. "But Marva—my mother—drove my sister's Cadillac through the front of the Perk Up, so we're all down here at the clinic so I can't make it to your place for leftover chicken and beer—and I don't suppose it even matters that much but I—"

"Libby," Tate said, firmly but with kindness. "Honey, take a breath."

Honey.

Libby fell silent. Honey. What an ordinary, beautiful word.

"Was anybody hurt?" Tate asked. His voice was level.

Libby's chest ached and her eyes burned and she still didn't trust herself to stand up straight, even though the bricks comprising the clinic's outer wall were digging right through her blouse into the flesh of her back. "Marva's being examined right now," she said.

"I'll be there as soon as I can," Tate said.

"Tate, no, I—I'm fine, really."

"I'm on my way."

"But—"

He hung up.

Slowly, Libby closed Paige's phone.

She hadn't expected Tate to drop everything and come to her—had she? If not, why had she called him in the first place, going to the trouble to borrow a phone and ask Brent Brogan for the number?

Damn. She didn't want to wind up like Marva, needy and manipulative.

Doing numbers on people.

Her eyes stung.

The automatic doors swung open, and one of the nurses stepped out, looked around. Seeing Libby, the woman smiled.

She was fortyish, and Libby remembered her vaguely from the Perk Up. Yes. Double mocha with extra espresso and chocolate shavings.

"Your mother would like to see you," she said. "And maybe a doctor should have a look at those scratches on your hands."

Libby nodded, then shook her head. "I'm okay," she said. "I just need to wash up." Dropping Paige's phone into her purse, she followed the nurse into the clinic, through the lobby and back to one of the exam rooms.

Going straight to the sink, Libby washed her hands, saw that the scratches weren't deep.

Marva was alone, lying on a gurney. She wore a hospital gown, and a plain white blanket covered her legs.

She was so still that, for one terrible moment, Libby thought her mother was dead.

"Marva?"

Marva turned her head, smiled. Stretched out a hand to Libby. "I don't know what came over me," Marva confided, her voice croaky and miserable. "Suddenly, I just *had* to drive again, and there was Julie's car—"

"Shh," Libby said. "We can talk about it later, when we're sure you're all right."

Tears filled Marva's eyes, rolled over her temples into her mussed-up hair. "I'm sorry, Libby," she said. "I'm so sorry."

Libby just stood there, with no idea how to respond, willing herself not to cry.

Marva gazed up at her, squeezed her hand once, and let go.

There was, it seemed, nothing more to say.

CHAPTER FIFTEEN

TATE MUST HAVE had the pedal to the metal all the way in from the ranch, because he was waiting in the lobby when Libby left Marva's exam room. Just seeing him was like a deep draught of cold well water after a long spell of thirst.

Libby walked into his arms. He embraced her loosely, and she rested her forehead against the hard wall of his chest.

"She's sorry," Libby told him, her voice muffled. "My mother is *sorry.*"

Tate rocked her slightly, from side to side. "It's okay, Lib," he murmured. "Everything will be okay."

Why did people keep *saying* that? Everything would be okay for Paige, with her top-notch nursing skills and high-paying job. Everything would be okay for Julie, too, because she had Calvin and a career she loved. And everything would *certainly* be okay for Tate and all the other McKettricks, if only because they *were* McKettricks.

Libby loved her sisters and was proud of their accomplishments.

But she was tired of false reassurances.

Her shop was gone.

She had virtually no savings.

And jobs weren't exactly plentiful in Blue River.

There had been lower points in her life, of course—when Marva left, so long ago, when her dad died, when, with no warning at all, she'd lost Tate.

The pain of that most recent and totally unexpected loss seared through her, as fresh as if it had just happened. Libby knotted her fists and pushed pack from Tate.

He paled slightly, under his rancher's tan. "I drove by the shop on my way here," he told her, his voice gravelly. "Libby, I can help—"

"Stop," Libby said. Realizing her hands were still bunched against Tate's chest—she could feel the strong, steady *thud-thud-thud* of his heart—she splayed her fingers for a moment, drawing in the substance of him like a breath of the soul. And then she let both hands fall to her sides. "Don't say what I think you're about to say, Tate. I can't take money from you."

Julie and Paige had returned, along with Calvin; Libby was aware of them, on the periphery of the haze that seemed to surround her and Tate.

"Libby," he said. "Listen to me. Please."

She shook her head. Stepped back a little farther.

Both Paige and Julie had worked their way through college with the aid of scholarships and loans. They'd made something of themselves.

Paige saved lives.

Julie shaped young minds.

What had *she* done? Started a doomed coffee shop—one that had barely brought in survival wages even in the best of times— right there in the old hometown.

She'd loved one man her whole life—Tate McKettrick—and he'd betrayed her. While she'd forgiven Tate, she knew she'd never forgive *herself* if the same thing happened all over again.

Tate's hands still rested lightly on her shoulders.

He couldn't have known what she was thinking—that maybe it was time for her to leave Blue River, leave Texas. Go someplace entirely new, where she might be able to get some perspective. Come up with some goals.

No, he couldn't have known, but he looked as though he did.

The truth? Libby Remington had had only one goal, one dream, ever, and it was hopelessly old-fashioned. Politically incorrect to the nth degree.

All Libby had ever wanted was to marry Tate, love him and be loved in return, to bear and raise his children. To get old with him, and have flocks of grandbabies.

It would all be easier, she supposed, if Tate weren't rich—if he really were just a foreman on a big ranch, a hired hand with a steady paycheck, a simple three-bedroom house beside a creek and a good truck to drive. Instead, he was a multi-*multi*-millionaire, with his choice of beautiful women—supermodels, movie stars and professional women of all sorts. Doctors. Lawyers. Indian chiefs.

What did he want with her?

Sex?

Their lovemaking had been transcendental for Libby, but Tate was a man—to him, sex was sex. He probably took it where he could get it—and God knew, she had no compunction about giving it to him.

"Is Marva all right?" Julie asked, hovering a few feet away and wringing her hands.

Libby saw herself and Tate through Julie's eyes, standing almost toe-to-toe, as though he'd been comforting her in the aftermath of bad news.

"We haven't heard anything yet, Jules," Libby said, hugging her sister.

Julie hugged her back, sniffled.

Libby's eyes roamed, stopped on her nephew. Calvin was on the other side of the lobby, admiring the colorful fish in the clinic's fish tank. Paige stood beside the little boy, but she was watching her sisters and Tate, not the bright, flashing population of the large saltwater tank.

"Look, Aunt Paige," Calvin crowed, pointing a chubby finger at one of the fish and almost certainly leaving a smudge on the glass. "That one is transparent—I can see his guts!" He bent closer, and even though his back was to Libby, she knew when he adjusted his glasses. "And *that* one has a red line inside it, like a thermometer."

The mood lightened a little.

Julie stepped back out of Libby's embrace, and her gaze moved between Libby and Tate. She smiled slightly, turned and joined Calvin next to the fish tank.

Paige approached Libby. "May I have my cell phone back, please?" she asked. "It might be a long night, and I think the time has come to order pizza."

"Pizza!" Calvin whooped, overjoyed.

In spite of the stress and frustration and a host of other emotions, Libby laughed. She dug through her purse, found Paige's phone and handed it to her sister.

"Just tell me what kind of pizza you want," Tate said. "I'll go pick it up."

Calvin materialized immediately. It was almost as if he'd teleported himself from the fish tank across the lobby to where they stood. "Are you going to the Pizza Shack, Mr. McKettrick? Can I go with you? Where are your kids? Do you have any boys, or just girls?"

Tate crouched, so he could look Calvin straight in the eye. "Your mom and your aunts are kind of worried right now," he said seriously. "I think they need a man around, so maybe you ought to stay here."

Calvin's glasses had wriggled down his freckled nose, and he replaced them with the usual thrust of his right index finger. He threw his shoulders back a little, and raised his chin. "They're all pretty good at taking care of themselves," he told Tate. "And you didn't answer my other questions."

Tate's mouth quirked up at one corner. "My daughters— Audrey and Ava—are at home. And, no, I don't have any boys." As he stood up again, he caught Libby's gaze. "Yet," he added quietly.

She felt the usual achy heat, and rose above it as best she could.

The man was an addiction, and she was thoroughly hooked.

Ready to leave town to get away from him one moment, charmed out of her socks the next.

As if getting charmed out of her *socks* was any part of the problem.

"I have the regulation car seats in my truck," Tate told Julie. "And we wouldn't be gone long."

"*Please,* Mom," Calvin pleaded. "I need a male role model. I spend way too much time around women. Mrs. Oakland said so."

Julie flushed to her ears. "Mrs. Oakland said that, did she?"

"Maybe it was Justin's mom," Calvin faltered.

"You're sure he wouldn't be any trouble?" Julie asked Tate.

"I'm sure," Tate said. This time, he didn't look at Libby. She might have vaporized, for all the notice he seemed to take of her.

"I'll call in the order," Paige put in, cell phone in hand. "The usual?" she asked her sisters.

Libby merely nodded, wanting Tate McKettrick out of her space so she could think straight, but Julie, the thoughtful one, had the good manners to ask if he'd prefer something other than thick-crust Hawaiian with extra cheese.

He said he'd already eaten.

"Do I get to go or not, Mom?" Calvin demanded.

"Go," Julie relented, and though she was smiling, Libby glimpsed pain in her sister's eyes.

Calvin let out a yippee that made the receptionist look up from her desk behind the glass window and smile.

The little boy fairly skipped out of the clinic, but he stayed close to Tate, as if to prove to anyone concerned that he meant to behave himself and follow all the rules.

Paige finished placing the pizza order, closed her phone, and dropped it into her purse. "You really ought to grab that one," she said, nodding in Tate's direction and simultaneously elbowing Libby lightly in the ribs. "He's obviously a good father."

Before Libby had to reply, Dr. Burt Renton appeared, a weary smile creasing his familiar face. The physician, a widower with no children, had been born and raised in Blue River, and returned home as soon as his training was finished to open an office on Main Street. After thirty years in practice, he'd tried to retire, but all that idleness, as he called it, "wasn't good for my character." He'd been working part time at the clinic since it had opened for business nearly a decade before.

Julie, Paige and Libby all hurried toward him, stood in a tight little semicircle at the edge of his personal space, waiting.

"I ran a CT scan, the usual blood tests and took X-rays," Dr. Burt told them kindly. "Your mother is shaken up, but with a few days of rest and some pampering, she'll be fine."

Libby backed up a step. Maybe it was the word *pampering*.

Julie and Paige looked at her curiously.

Julie was the first to get the message. Her face softened, and Libby could have hugged her for the understanding in her eyes.

"Marva can stay with Calvin and me," Julie volunteered.

Guilt nudged Libby back into the half circle of sisters. She was the firstborn, and, as such, she had certain responsibilities. Marva was, for all her shortcomings, *her* mother, too.

She opened her mouth to say she'd look after Marva for as long as necessary, but the words wouldn't come out.

"I'd like Marva to stay here overnight," Dr. Burt was saying, "just to be on the safe side. That way, the nurses can keep an eye on her."

"Tell them to hide their car keys," Paige quipped, but she was watching Libby, still curious, maybe even a little worried.

Dr. Burt chuckled at that, but his eyes were solemn. "She feels very bad about that. Says she doesn't know what came over her."

In her mind, Libby saw her mother's tear-filled eyes again, heard her voice.

I'm so sorry.

"No one was hurt," Julie said. "That's the important thing."

"You can look in on Marva if you'd like. She's been sedated, though, so she'll probably drift off to sleep pretty soon." Dr. Burt pointed toward the corridor on the right, where the two large in-patient rooms were. "She has Unit B all to herself."

Julie and Paige started for the corridor immediately.

Libby remained where she was.

"I saw her earlier," she said when Dr. Burt glanced at her.

A few minutes later, Tate and Calvin returned with several huge pizza boxes and, with Libby's help, arranged the feast on the low-slung coffee table in the small waiting room. Calvin had scored a stack of paper napkins six inches high.

The child's face was luminous with delight. "Tate said we could get cold drinks out of the vending machine here," he said importantly. "And I get to ride horses on the Silver Spur whenever I want and go fishing in the creek as long as my mom approves and there's at least one grown-up with me."

"Wow," Libby said softly, ruffling her nephew's sweaty hair.

Over the pile of pizza boxes, her gaze connected with Tate's.

"That's a lot of food," she said.

Calvin jumped right in with an answer. "Tate said the people who work here might want to eat, too," he said, before helping himself to a slice, breaking off a long strand of cheese with a karate chop.

Tate grinned, watching him.

"Tate used to have a dog named Crockett," Calvin went on, with his mouth partially full. "Crockett rode with him everywhere—they were buddies."

Libby's throat tightened. "Crockett was a good dog," she said, remembering.

She heard Julie and Paige approaching the waiting room, talking in low, hurried voices.

Tate didn't look at Libby; his gaze had turned toward the doorway, and he stood as her sisters entered.

"I *thought* I smelled pizza!" Julie said, leaning down to give her son a quick squeeze.

"Do you think Grandma would like some?" Calvin asked. His face was smeared with tomato sauce by then, and what was probably a piece of pineapple had gotten stuck in his hair.

"She's asleep," Paige told her nephew brightly.

Julie and Paige used a bottle of hand sanitizer from Julie's purse, helped themselves to napkins and pizza, and began to eat.

Tate didn't touch the food, and neither did Libby, until Paige finally plopped a slice onto a napkin and forced it into her hands.

Tate got up and left the room to let the staff know there was pizza aplenty and they were welcome to join the party. The invitation brought a fairly steady stream of hungry people in scrubs, but Tate didn't come back.

Having eaten all she could get down—a little less than half of the portion Paige had given her—Libby excused herself and left the waiting room.

She could see Tate through the plate glass door at the front of the clinic, talking on his cell phone. His expression was serious, he was pacing and he kept thrusting a hand through his hair.

Libby hurried away, headed for the restroom, not wanting him to see her and think she'd been looking for him. Even though that was exactly what she'd been doing.

Once she'd washed her hands, stinging mildly now, from the scratches she'd gotten digging Marva out, splashed her face with cold water and grinned humorlessly into the mirror, to make sure there was no pizza detritus stuck between her teeth, she straightened her spine and marched back to the lobby.

Now that Marva had been examined and was resting comfortably, according to Dr. Burt, there was no point in sticking around. She'd go home, attend to the ever-patient Hildie, and then she'd switch on the TV set and stare mindlessly at the screen until she couldn't keep her eyes open anymore.

She could start thinking about the rest of her life tomorrow—or the day after that.

Or she could just pack a bag, gas up the Impala, load Hildie and her kibble and bowls into the backseat and strike out for parts unknown.

Yes, sir, she could go out there and *accomplish something.*

What that something would be, she had no idea.

Which was why she didn't want to think just yet.

"I guess I'll go on home now," she announced to her sisters and nephew and a couple of X-ray technicians, from the doorway of the waiting room. "Hildie will be waiting for me."

"Sure," Julie said uncertainly, leaning a little, to look past Libby. "Did Tate leave? I didn't get a chance to repay him for the pizza, or even say thank you."

Libby shrugged one shoulder. "He was outside a little while ago," she answered as casually as she could. "Talking to someone on his cell phone. Maybe something came up out at the ranch."

"Marva will be at our place after she's released," Julie told Libby. "In case you want to stop by and see her or anything."

Libby merely nodded, promising nothing.

She wanted to get away from the clinic.

She wanted this day to be over.

She waved a farewell to her family and the X-ray guys, turned and ran directly into Tate.

He steadied her by gripping her upper arms. If he hadn't, she would have fallen.

Libby pulled free, went around him.

He followed her through the automatic door and outside without speaking, or touching her.

It was dark and sultry, and the sky was splattered from horizon to horizon with enormous stars. Like the sunset earlier, the sight made Libby's breath catch.

Texas.

It was fine and dandy to think about starting over someplace far away.

But could she *really* call anywhere else "home"? Would she even be able to breathe properly outside the Lone Star State?

"Come home with me, Libby," Tate said, somehow steering her away from her car and toward his truck without laying a hand on her.

"Tate, I have a dog to feed and walk, and you have children—"

"We'll pick Hildie up on our way out of town. Along with your toothbrush and whatever else you figure you need to get you through till morning." He cleared his throat. "The twins are okay. They're with Esperanza."

Libby stopped, looked up at him. "Look, I know I agreed to come out to the Ruiz—to *your* place for chicken and beer, but—" She spread her arms wide, let her hands slap against her sides.

A slight and damnably sexy grin tugged at his mouth, was gone again. "But?" he prompted, his right hand resting lightly on the small of her back, ready to turn her gently, the way he'd turn a mare if she started off in the wrong direction.

"But what?" she challenged.

Tate chuckled. "I was waiting for an excuse. And you're going to have to do better than that poor old dog. She'd love a road trip to anywhere, and you know it."

She should have told him right then.

Speaking of road trips…she could have said, *I'm thinking of leaving Blue River for a while. You might say I have to find myself. No, that's too corny. Nobody worries about finding themselves anymore. Which just goes to show how out of touch I am, when it comes to the world outside central Texas.*

Libby choked up again. "Tate, what do you *want?*"

"Not what you think I want," he told her, opening the driver's-side door of the Impala so she could get in. "Not *just* that, anyhow."

Libby didn't know which was making her crazier, the conversation she was carrying on with Tate, or the one in her own head. "Good night," she said. "And thank you for the pizza."

She reached into her purse, closed her fingers around her keys, took a couple of stabs at the ignition before she managed to start the engine.

"You're not getting rid of me that easily," Tate said affably, before closing her door and turning to walk away.

Libby watched him climb into his truck, blinked when his headlights came on, bright. He dimmed them, but she was still dazzled.

Almost a minute passed before Libby could see well enough to drive. Tate drove to the parking lot exit, but waited until she pulled in behind him.

She followed *him* to *her* house.

What was wrong with this picture?

Libby parked in the garage, off the alley, careful not to look toward the late, great Perk Up Coffee Shop. Wondered if Julie's car had been pulled from the rubble yet, and whether or not the vehicle could be salvaged.

Tate parked in front of the house.

By the time Libby had unlocked the back door and nearly been run over as Hildie shot from the house like a popcorn kernel from hot oil, Tate was there and ready to follow her up the porch steps and into the kitchen.

"You know," Libby said to Tate, leaving the door open for Hildie but wishing she could slam it for the sake of emphasis, "some people would consider this stalking. Your walking in here like this, I mean."

"If you want me to leave," Tate replied reasonably, "all you have to do is ask." He opened her refrigerator, scanned the contents, sighed with what might have been resignation, helped himself to a soda, popped the top and raised the can briefly, as though toasting her.

Libby opened her mouth, closed it again.

Tate drank deeply of the soda, swallowed audibly. At least he didn't belch.

"That Calvin," he said, "is one cute kid. And a fair hand to have along on a pizza run."

Libby couldn't help softening, thinking of her nephew and how glad he'd been to spend some time in Tate's company. "He's so smart, it's scary," she said.

Hildie, having completed her tour of the yard, scratched at the screen door. Libby opened it to let her in, filled her kibble dish and freshened her water.

"Calvin wants to get to know his dad," Tate said.

The statement fell between them like a flaming meteor.

Libby stood utterly still. Even though she'd encouraged Julie to work out some kind of visitation agreement with Gordon Pruett, she understood her sister's reluctance. Gordon might be a good man—or he might be a jerk.

Julie would be taking a big chance by letting Gordon into her life and Calvin's, but if he chose to force the issue legally, she wouldn't have a choice

"Calvin said that?" Libby nearly whispered, after a heartbeat or two.

Tate nodded. "Is this a problem?"

"It could be," Libby said simply. She wasn't comfortable discussing Julie's private business, and Tate seemed to know that, didn't press.

Libby shut and locked the back door. Hildie stood looking back and forth between Tate and her mistress instead of curling up on her dog bed, as she normally would have done.

"You have to promise we won't have sex," Libby blurted out. Tate was like some big, hard, human magnet, standing there in her kitchen. She felt the pull of him in every cell in her body—any second now, she'd go *splat,* like a bug on a windshield.

Tate indulged in a rather obvious struggle to hold back a grin, and one of his eyebrows rose into an ironic arch. "Forever?" he asked. "Or just for tonight?"

"Just for tonight," Libby said. "Forever seems unreasonable."

He chuckled. "Forever," he said, "is downright *impossible.* But I won't make love to you tonight, Lib. I promise you that much." He paused. "Not even if you tear my clothes off in an insane fit of unbridled desire."

"Don't hold your breath waiting for *that* to happen, cowboy," she said, with a lofty sniff.

Please God, don't let me tear off his clothes in an insane fit of unbridled desire.

"If I have to promise," Tate said, "so do you."

"Oh, for Pete's sake," Libby said. "All right."

With that, she went into her bathroom and got her hairbrush and her packet of birth control pills. There was no need to take pajamas along, because she intended to sleep in her clothes.

If she slept at all.

They went to the main ranch house, instead of Tate's "new" place by the creek, and except for a single light burning under the portico, the massive structure was completely dark.

Libby panicked a little. "Tate, Audrey and Ava—"

"It's a big house," Tate said. "And besides, we're not going to have sex anyway, so I don't see the problem."

"I don't want to confuse them," Libby said.

"Neither do I," Tate answered, and another grin twitched at his mouth.

"You don't think it will be confusing when they wake up tomorrow morning and I'm in their house?"

"I think they need to get used to seeing you around," Tate said quietly.

Libby didn't dare go there. It was late, she'd been through a lot that day, and if she wasn't careful, she might say something she'd regret.

For the rest of eternity.

Tate pulled up to one of the garage doors, pushed a button on his visor, and drove in.

Once he'd parked and shut off the truck, he turned to Libby.

She looked neither left nor right. She *certainly* wasn't going to look in Tate's direction.

"Lib," Tate said, pulling the keys from the ignition, "don't look so worried. All I want to do is take care of you."

All I want to do is take care of you.

Libby could barely remember what it was like to be "taken care of" by anyone. Before her dad had gotten sick—long before—she'd felt safe, as though somebody always had her back.

But since then? Not so much.

She straightened her spine, found she still couldn't look directly at Tate.

He opened the door, rounded the truck, set Hildie gently on the cement floor, opened Libby's door and unbuckled her seat belt.

"Come on," he said.

He took her by the hand, led her through the darkened house, up the stairs, into his room. Hildie followed.

There, Tate stripped Libby bare, pulled one of his T-shirts over her head, and tucked her under the covers of his bed.

Then he lay down on top of those same covers, pulled her into his arms, and held her, his embrace strong and sure, until she slept.

CHAPTER SIXTEEN

LIBBY AWOKE WITH a start, sunlight burning through her lids.

She opened her eyes, found herself almost nose to nose with one of the twins—Ava, she realized. The child was wearing glasses.

"Good morning," Ava said, grinning.

Oh, dear God. She was in Tate McKettrick's bed—*with* Tate McKettrick.

And here was his six-year-old daughter.

Libby blinked, glanced wildly around, having no idea what to say or do, and saw that Tate was still sleeping. He was wearing all his clothes, boots included, and lying on top of the covers, though one leg and one arm sprawled across Libby's body.

"Good morning," Libby whispered back to Ava, embarrassed but trying hard to behave in a normal way.

Whatever that might be, in these circumstances.

Tate stretched, his powerful body lengthening as he rolled away from her. He yawned lustily and opened his eyes.

"Hey," he said to Ava, resting a hand on Libby's shoulder, as if to console or reassure her. Or maybe because he knew she wanted to bolt.

"Hey, Daddy," Ava replied, still showing no overt signs of trauma at finding a woman in bed with her father. "Esperanza said to tell you breakfast is ready and Uncle Austin already fed the horses and did the chores and stuff."

Tate groaned, but it was a comfortable sound, good-natured. "So much for setting a good example as the new foreman," he said.

"That's all you're worried about?" Libby whispered.

He grinned down at her. "If you don't make a big deal out of this," he said casually, and there was a subtle singsong note to his tone, "nobody else will, either."

He was right, of course.

The child didn't seem curious, let alone traumatized, but making a fuss might change the easy flow of things.

New concerns assailed Libby. She put a hand over her mouth. How could the man wake up with *good breath?* He had—but she probably hadn't.

"Go and tell Esperanza we'll be right down," Tate told Ava. His voice was easy, as if he and Libby shared a bed *every* night. "Take Hildie with you—I imagine she'd like to go outside and then have a little of Ambrose and Buford's dog food."

Ava nodded importantly. "Come on, Hildie," she said, with cheerful authority. "Let's go."

Hildie got up, gave Libby one questioning glance, and then followed the little girl out of the master bedroom.

Libby tried to get out of bed the moment the door closed behind Ava and Hildie, but Tate pressed her back down with one hand splayed in the middle of her stomach and deliberately kissed her on the mouth.

Thoroughly.

Libby finally turned her face away, even though she'd liked the kiss.

"If you don't let me up," she said, "you're going to be sorry."

Tate chuckled at that—the threat was clearly an empty one—but he let Libby get up.

She found her way to the bathroom, which was roughly the size of her kitchen and living room combined, used the facilities, and rummaged through cupboards and drawers under the long marble countertop until she found a new toothbrush, still in its package.

She was standing at one of the antique brass sinks, scrubbing her teeth, when Tate ambled in, calm as you please, shedding clothes as he walked. The long mirror over the counter reflected his every move in exquisite detail.

He was completely, wickedly, *deliciously* naked by the time he reached the shower. In all that time, he hadn't so much as glanced in Libby's direction.

She, on the other hand, couldn't help staring.

From behind the glass door of the room-size shower, Tate grinned at her.

Libby tore her gaze away, flushing to the roots of her hair.

Stomped out of the bathroom and searched until she found her clothes, neatly folded and stacked on the seat of a sumptuous leather chair facing the cold fireplace.

Libby hauled them on, with the exception of her underpants; she wadded those into a ball and stuffed them into her purse.

Libby probably would have sneaked out of the house, sprinted down to the main road and *hitchhiked* into town, except that she couldn't abandon Hildie, not even knowing the dog was perfectly safe.

Besides, Ava had already seen her. In bed with Tate.

By now, the little girl had surely told her twin and Esperanza—and that was the *optimistic* count. Ava had mentioned Austin, saying he'd done the barn chores, so he might have heard, as well. And if Garrett happened to be around, he probably knew, too.

Dressed, but having no real idea what to do next, Libby plunked down on the edge of the bed. At least Tate had kept his word.

He'd slept on top of the covers, in all his clothes.

She'd been underneath them the whole night, clad in one of his T-shirts.

They hadn't made love. Libby figured she should have been happier about that than she was.

Because the shower was still running, indicating that she could expect a few more moments of privacy before Tate returned, she pressed the T-shirt to her face, drew in his scent. It seemed to seep into her cells and settle there, that lusciously distinctive smell, destined to remain a part of her forever, like her DNA.

Damn.

Just yesterday, at the clinic, despite a lot of misgivings, Libby had basically made up her mind to leave Blue River, start over somewhere else, make something of herself.

Like what? she wondered now.

Nothing occurred to her.

The sound of running water fell away into silence.

A minute or so later, Tate strolled out of the bathroom, barefoot, wearing button-front jeans and not much else. His hair was wet, though he'd towel-dried it and, from the looks of the ridges, he'd run his fingers through several times.

Could it be that he was as nervous as she was?

Surely not.

He crooked a grin at Libby. "Hungry?" he asked.

"I just want to go home," Libby said, blushing. Looking down at the floor.

What would she do at home?

Dig more weeds?

Cut more grass?

Get down on her knees on the sidewalk in front of her erstwhile shop and paw through the rubble looking for—what? A stray dream? A few tattered hopes?

"No problem," Tate said, his voice was quiet and so gentle that it made her want to cry. "If you want to go home, I'll take you there."

Libby didn't know what to say after that. Since Tate hadn't given her an argument, as she'd expected, she was stuck for a response.

The house in town was home—her dad had died there. She and her sisters had grown up under that roof, within those walls—but Julie and Paige had moved on.

She'd gotten stuck, somehow.

Tate disappeared into the massive walk-in closet, returning with one arm thrust into the sleeve of a light blue shirt, the other about to go in. His muscular chest was fully visible, lightly sprinkled with dark hair and tanned by occasional exposure to the sun.

He tossed Libby a pair of jeans and a yellow ruffled blouse; both garments were vaguely familiar.

Libby caught them, a funny little skitter dancing in her heart, let them rest in her lap, her head lowered. "Are these Cheryl's things?" she asked, thick-throated.

"No," Tate said gently. "They're yours."

Libby's gaze shot to his face. Her throat tightened even more, and her cheeks blazed. *Of course,* Tate wouldn't give her his ex-wife's clothes to wear. What had she been thinking?

"You left them here once, a long time ago, when my folks were away," he reminded her, a grin resting on his mouth and twinkling in his eyes. He probably knew what was going through her mind, or pretty close to it, anyhow. "Esperanza was visiting her cousin, and Garrett and Austin were both gone, too, on the rodeo circuit. We spent the whole weekend pretending we were married—remember?"

Libby felt a bittersweet pang of mingled nostalgia and sorrow. Back then, marrying Tate McKettrick had seemed like a sure thing. They'd nearly eloped several times in their late teens and Libby sometimes wished they'd gone through with the plan.

Sometimes, and only until she came to her senses.

She and Tate had been so young. She'd had to drop out of college and come back to Blue River to take care of her dad after he got sick. Tate might have given up school, too, and eventually come to resent Libby and the demands she made on his time.

And Audrey and Ava wouldn't have been born.

Inconceivable.

The silence seemed to have weight.

"You don't really think I can still get into these jeans," Libby joked, to break the spell.

Tate laughed. "Can I stay and watch you try?"

Libby giggled, waved him away. "Get out," she said.

He smiled, buttoning his shirt to the middle of his breastbone. "I was headed downstairs for coffee anyhow," he said. "Bring you some?"

She shook her head, stroking the yellow blouse. She'd loved the thing, saved her allowance and babysitting money to buy it. Felt so sexy with all those sun-colored ruffles floating around her. "No thanks," she said. "Maybe some tea?"

"You got it," Tate said.

With that, he left the huge room, closing the double doors behind him.

LIBBY HASTENED INTO THE bathroom, shut the door and wriggled into the jeans. They were a little tight, but they zipped up, and the blouse looked as good as it ever had.

Libby's raised spirits drooped a bit, though, as she considered the prospect of going downstairs and facing Esperanza and the twins.

She made up the bed, which was barely mussed, a stall tactic for sure.

Tate returned just as she was fluffing the pillows. Sipping from one cup, he carried a second. "The coast is clear," he said. "Audrey and Ava are out in the barn, with all three dogs and the ponies. Esperanza is with them, supervising."

Libby accepted the fragrant tea with a nod of thanks, took a sip, and felt better instantly. "Have they come up with names yet?" she asked. "For the horses, I mean."

"I don't think so." Tate grinned, touching Libby's hair lightly. His voice was low and throaty and he smelled so...clean. "It's a big decision."

"Maybe you could drive Hildie and me home, while they're busy?"

Not that she wanted to go.

Tate sighed. "Lib, they already know you're here."

She lowered her head, breathing in the steam rising off her tea.

Tate curved a finger under her chin and looked into her eyes. "Relax," he said. "We talked about this. Audrey and Ava need to get used to seeing you around."

"*You* talked about it," Libby said. "*I* didn't venture an opinion. Tate, they're children. And I'm not their mother. Letting them 'get used' to changes and their finding me in their father's bed first thing in the morning are not the same thing."

"You don't believe in total immersion?" Tate teased.

"Don't be a smart-ass," Libby countered.

"Sorry," he responded, after a long sip from his coffee. "I probably can't deliver on that one—not long term, anyhow."

"Be serious," she whispered angrily. "We're talking about your *children,* here."

Tate leaned in, touched his forehead to hers. "I'm aware of that," he whispered back, with exaggeration. "Lighten up a little, Libby. It's not as if Ava came in here and found us swinging naked from the curtain rods and yelling, 'Yahoo.' Yes, you were in my bed, but I was on top of the covers, wearing all my clothes." He backed up a little. Waggled his eyebrows. "Which, by the way, was a noble sacrifice on my part, and if ever there was a fine opportunity for a quickie, it's right now."

Libby laughed, in spite of herself. Gave him an affectionate push with her free hand, carefully balancing her tea in the other. "You really are impossible," she said.

"You'd forgotten that? That I'm impossible?" Tate asked. "I'm hurt."

"I should go home now."

"Why?"

"You know why."

"No, Libby. I don't know why. It's not as if you have to open the shop."

Her shoulders dropped a little. Of course she hadn't forgotten what Marva had done to the Perk Up, but she *had* managed to keep the full reality at a bearable distance.

Until now.

"Thanks," she said, terse now. It was a defense, not against Tate, but against a part of herself—the hoochy-mama part, born to boogie. She turned away, cup in hand, headed for the door.

Tate caught hold of her arm. "Let's take a breath here, Lib," he said. "Stay and have some breakfast. I'll saddle up some horses and we'll ride. I've already called the clinic, and your mother is doing fine. She wants to stay another day, in fact. Sounds to me like she's enjoying the attention."

"You talked to my mother?"

"No," Tate said. "To one of the nurses. I called her when I was downstairs."

Libby let out her breath, and Tate set his coffee aside, and her tea, and took a light hold on her shoulders.

"How long has it been since you've been on the back of a horse?" Tate asked, his chin resting on top of her head. "You used to love it, remember?"

A tremor went through Libby. *I used to love so many things. And suddenly, they weren't part of my life anymore. You weren't part of my life anymore.*

"Scared?" Tate asked, without moving.

She saw no point in denying it; he obviously knew. She nodded, swallowed.

"Of me?"

"No," Libby said, letting herself be held, just as she had during the night. It felt so good. She'd never feared Tate, but she *was* afraid of what he could make her feel, and what she might be willing to risk because of that. "Of course not."

"Then, what?"

She shook her head, unable to answer.

Tate kissed the crown of her head. Sighed.

"You can call Julie and Paige," he said, after a long time. "Give them my cell number. If they need to reach you for any reason, they'll be able to do that."

"I don't know...."

Once again, he lifted her chin. "Just for once, never mind what you think you *should* do. Concentrate on what you *want* to do. Do you even know what that is anymore, Libby?"

She swallowed, her throat suddenly full of tears, shoved back her bangs with one hand. "Of course I know what I want—"

"Okay. What?"

You and me, together for good. Kids and dogs and horses and a garden...

But there was another part of her, with other dreams.

She'd never seen the Eiffel Tower, or the Great Wall of China, that other Libby. And she wanted to.

Libby looked away from his face, looked back. Some of the anxiety she'd felt drained away, but another kind of charge sizzled in its place. "I want to go riding with you and your little girls," she admitted. "But what I *should* want—"

Tate interrupted, grinning and shaking his head. "Let's go downstairs and have breakfast," he said. "After that, we'll ride."

Libby considered that. "But my mother—my sisters—"

"Are all grown women," Tate said, taking her hand. "They don't need you with them to survive the day, Lib." He gave her a little pull. "Let's go."

She let him lead her downstairs.

To her relief, the big kitchen was empty.

Breakfast awaited in various chafing dishes, the kind Libby normally saw in buffet restaurants. There were blueberry pancakes, scrambled eggs, bacon and sausage to choose from, along with yogurt cups arranged in a bowl of ice.

Libby surveyed it in amazement.

"All this is for us and two six-year-olds?" she asked.

"And some of the guys from the bunkhouse," Tate said, handing her a plate before taking one of his own.

Libby felt her eyes go round. "You mean, a whole bunch of *cowboys* might come walking in here at any moment?" she asked, horrified. If that happened, the news that Libby Remington had spent the night in the main house on the Silver Spur—*again*—would circulate from the feed store to the post office to the Amble On Inn, where the old-timers hung out because "A man could still get a good beer for cheap."

"Maybe," Tate said. "Why does it matter?"

"You know damn well *why it matters!*"

Grinning, Tate took a step back and raised both his hands, palms out. "Okay, I know why it matters," he admitted. "You don't want the whole town of Blue River to hear that you showed up at breakfast."

Libby raised her chin a notch. "That's right."

"You can't possibly be that naive." He leaned in, whispered close to her ear, and even the warmth of his *breath* turned her on, for pity's sake. "We're old news, Libby. Everybody knows we're getting it on."

"'Getting it on'?" Libby jabbed two sausage links and plopped them onto her plate, moved on to the scrambled eggs. "Is that what you call it?"

Tate grinned down at her, speared four pancakes along with bacon and sausage. "What would *you* call it?" he countered, so obviously enjoying her heated discomfort that she wanted to spear him with a fork.

Libby decided to ignore the question, since she didn't want to say *making love*—that might sound sappy—and the f-word was out, too, because it was ugly. She turned her back on him, marched to the table with her plate and sat down.

Tate swung a leg over the back of a chair and sat across from her, setting his full plate down with a *plunk*. A mischievous—make that evil—grin danced at the corners of his mouth and sparked in his too-blue eyes.

"For somebody who could probably set the record for multiple orgasms," he observed, "you are pretty old-fashioned."

Libby blushed. "I consider that *your* fault," she said, poking at her eggs.

"Your orgasms are *my* fault?" He speared a sausage link and bit off the end, took his time chewing and swallowing.

"Well," Libby said, "I don't have them *by myself*."

He laughed. "It's okay, Libby," he told her. "I don't mind taking the credit."

"You mean the blame."

"No. I mean the credit."

Color flared in Libby's cheeks. "Could we just eat?"

"See how testy you are? If you'd just let me have you against a wall before we came downstairs this morning, you'd be mellow right now, instead of wound up tight like an old pocket watch with the stem turned one too many times."

"Tate," Libby said, leaning toward him a little. "Shut up."

He sighed. "I'm just saying."

Fortunately, the back door opened just then, and Audrey and Ava bounded in, faces alight, with three dogs and a housekeeper in their wake.

"Can we go fishing in the creek?" Audrey asked.

"Not on your own," Tate answered.

"That spotted horse is trying to kick his way out of the pen," Ava added, looking worried. "He can't get out, can he?"

"He can't get out, honey," Tate assured his daughter.

Ava turned to Libby, her blue eyes serious behind smudged lenses. "That's the horse," she whispered, "that stepped on Mr. Ruiz and made him die."

Libby felt a maternal urge to gather the child in her arms and hug her. She glanced at Tate, wondering why a dangerous animal like the stallion was still on the place.

She quickly dismissed the concern. Tate was a rancher, descended from generations of ranchers; he certainly knew horses. He would do what needed to be done, when it needed to be done.

Tate calmly finished eating, stood, his gaze connecting with

Libby's as he rose. "So how about that horseback ride?" he asked, and though his tone was easy, she knew by the expression in his eyes that her answer was important to him.

Audrey and Ava immediately began to jump up and down, eager to go along.

Ambrose, Buford and Hildie all barked, caught up in the excitement.

And Esperanza smiled serenely to herself.

The children—and the dogs—would have been too disappointed if she'd said "No." Or, at least, that was what Libby told herself.

In fact, Tate had been right earlier, reminding her how she'd once loved riding horses.

"Okay," she said. "But I need to call Julie and Paige first."

Mayhem broke out—dogs barking, little girls cheering and clapping.

Shaking her head benevolently, Esperanza picked up a laundry basket and started up one of the three sets of stairs that intersected on the far side of the McKettricks' kitchen.

"We can saddle our *own* ponies!" Ava cried jubilantly.

"Go and do it, then," Tate told the kids. "And take the dogs with you."

The big house seemed to let out its breath when it was just Tate and Libby again, alone in the room. He stood behind her, handed his cell phone past her right shoulder before moving away.

Libby dialed Julie's home number first, since it was still fairly early.

"Hello?" Julie answered sleepily, as Tate went out the back door.

"It's me, Libby," Libby whispered. It was silly to whisper, she decided, since she had the kitchen to herself, but whisper she did.

Julie sounded a lot more awake when she answered. "Are you with Tate?"

"Yes," Libby replied, since the only alternative was to lie. "We're—we're going horseback riding today, so Tate suggested that I give you his cell number, just in case you or Paige need to reach me for any reason—"

Julie giggled. "Wonderful," she said.

Libby bristled. "What do you mean, 'Wonderful'?" she snapped. "You do realize, don't you, that little elves didn't stop by and rebuild the Perk Up while we were sleeping, or bring the Pink Bomb back to its former glory?"

There was a pause.

Libby used it to rinse off her plate and stick it into the nearest dishwasher.

"This probably isn't a good time to tell you," Julie finally said, "that the tow-truck guy says the Cadillac can be repaired. It's going to take some major bodywork and a paint job, but the car is still structurally sound."

"Now why," Libby nearly snarled, "would this be a bad time to tell me anything?"

Hearing herself, she sucked in a hissy breath and squeezed her eyes shut for a moment. Exhaled.

"Let me try that again," she said, measuring out the words.

Julie gave a nervous laugh. "Libby, every—"

"Don't you dare say everything will be all right!"

At just that moment, Tate stuck his head inside the back door, assumed an expression of mock terror, ducked out as though he expected some missile to come hurtling his way and then stepped over the threshold.

"Horses are ready to ride," he said, just as Julie was speaking.

"Okay," Libby's sister said, very gently, "I won't say that. But it will be. You wait and see."

"Call me when the next disaster hits," Libby said, and she wasn't kidding. She held Tate's phone away with both hands and squinted at it, trying to find his phone number.

Standing close to her now, he fed it into her ear, digit by digit, while Libby repeated each new number to Julie. She felt silly, the whole time.

Everyone had a cell phone these days.

Except for her.

Why was that?

It wasn't just the money, although that was a factor in everything she did. Except for Paige and Julie, who were always either dropping by or calling her on either the shop phone or the one at home, she'd had no one to call or be called by.

Now she felt ridiculously behind-the-times.

Tate's hand rested on her shoulder, sending bolts of soft fire through her.

"Libby?" Julie prompted. "Are you still there?"

Libby nodded, swallowed, said, "Yes," in a frog-voice.

Tate's fingers began to work the taut muscles where her shoulders and neck met. She rolled her head, barely bit back a groan of pure pleasure.

For her, those particular muscles and the soles of her feet were erogenous zones. Thank God he wasn't massaging her feet—she might have reached a climax.

"I'm here," she said, croaking again and several beats late. "D-did you get the number?"

"Yes," Julie answered, and Libby could just see her smiling. "Are you all right?"

"Of course I'm all right!"

"Now, don't get your panties in a wad," Julie counseled. Then, wickedly, she added, "If you're wearing any, that is."

"Julie Remington, you have a dirty mind!"

"No," Julie said, "I'm just trying to think positively."

"Funny. Ha-ha, Julie, you are *so funny.*"

"I'll call, or Paige will, if anything important happens," Julie went on, sounding so pleased with herself that Libby's back molars clamped together.

"Thanks," Libby said once she'd released her jaw, and shut the phone with a bang. Turned and fairly shoved it at Tate.

"You *really* need that quickie," he whispered.

She punched him.

But her heart wasn't in it.

TATE RODE STRANGER, the roan gelding, while Libby was mounted on a gentle—and equally aged—mare named Buttons. The twins followed on their golden, nameless ponies, with Ambrose and Buford frolicking alongside. Hildie brought up the rear, moving slowly, and Tate was keeping an eye on the old dog, same as Libby was.

The sun was hot and high, the sky a brassy blue that ached in the heart, as well as the eyes. Grass rippled and flowed around them like light on water, and clusters of cattle grazed here and there, while horses, some of them almost as wild as the stallion penned up back at the barn, lowered their heads for creek water.

Tate stood in the stirrups, stretching his legs, keeping an eye on his daughters bouncing happily along on their birthday ponies, a few dozen yards ahead of him and Libby, the dogs keeping up easily.

When Libby reined in, it was a moment before he noticed. Buttons wanted to keep up with the other horses, and kept turning around and around in a tight circle, tossing her head, resisting Libby's efforts to bring her to a full stop.

Half in the saddle and half out, Libby had one foot in a stirrup and no place to put the other one. Back a ways, Hildie sat in the high grass, panting hard, tongue lolling.

Tate rode back, got Libby's horse by the bridle strap, spoke firmly to the animal. It settled down right away.

The Ruiz place was close—less than a mile from the main house, traveling overland, as they were—and before setting out, Libby and Tate had agreed that Hildie could surely make it that far, since she and Libby took a long walk almost every day.

For whatever reason, Hildie obviously didn't plan on going another step.

Libby had shifted back into the saddle with an ease that did Tate proud, though he could not have said why.

When he was sure Buttons would behave, he got down off Stranger and walked back to Hildie, crouching when he reached her.

"Is she all right?" Libby called, anxious.

Up ahead, the girls had stopped to wait, turned their ponies around.

Tate and the dog were eye to eye. "Hey, girl," he said gently. "You get tired of walking?"

Hildie licked his right cheek and favored him with a dog smile. Her tongue, long and pink, hung out of the side of her mouth.

"You better ride with me for a ways," Tate said, easing the animal to her feet, making sure she could stand. Her flanks quivered, but then she steadied, and he checked her paws for thorns or stones, the way he would have done with a horse.

Libby had ridden back to him by then, Stranger following, reins dragging along the ground.

"Is Hildie hurt?" Libby asked, sounding so worried that Tate looked up at her and felt his heart rush into his throat.

I love you, Libby, he wanted to say. *Trust me with your heart, the way you trust me with your dog.*

"Just tired, I think," he said. "A little overheated, too, maybe."

With that, Tate lifted the dog in both arms, careful to support her back, and managed to remount the gelding without dropping Hildie. The trick wasn't quite so easy to pull off as it had been when he was a kid, forever sharing a horse's back with one family dog or another.

Libby moved in close enough that their horses' sides touched, and her smile lodged somewhere deep in Tate's soul, a place beyond all reach until that day, and that woman.

"Thanks," she said. Her blue eyes shone with light.

Tate centered himself and Hildie, scooting farther back in the saddle so she wouldn't be jabbed by the horn and then reaching around to take hold of the reins again. "If I'd known all it would take for you to look at me like that was to ride double with your dog, Hildie and I would have been working the range together long before this."

Libby smiled tentatively, then made a dismissive motion with one hand.

The girls waited until Libby and Tate caught up.

"Did Hildie get tired?" Ava asked.

"She's not hurt, is she?" Audrey wanted to know.

Tate's pride in his daughters was a swelling in his chest some of the time, a pinch in the wall of his heart or a catch in his breath—it varied. That day, it was a scalding sensation behind his eyes.

"No, Hildie's not hurt," he said, for Libby's benefit, as well as the children's. "She just needed a little help, that's all."

Audrey and Ava nodded sagely.

The Ruiz place—*his place*—was just ahead, gleaming in the curved embrace of the creek. The grass was green, and the round-topped oaks threw great patches of shade onto the ground.

Tate rode down to the creek and then right into the shallow part, making the girls shriek with delight.

Stranger bent his big head and drank, up to all four ankles in crystal-clear water, and Tate dismounted, set Hildie down gently on smooth pebbles that glittered like jewels.

Hildie shivered, gave a happy woof and drank thirstily before bounding up the creek bank like a pup, apparently refreshed and ready for adventure.

Tate slogged after the dog, pretending he was wetter than he was, and Hildie waited until he was within range to shake herself off with vigor, flinging water all over him.

Libby's laughter, and that of his little girls, rang in the pure light of that summer morning, weaving together, ribbons of sound.

CHAPTER SEVENTEEN

VARIOUS CONTRACTORS' TRUCKS and vans encircled the former Ruiz house—painters, electricians, plumbers, drywallers and roofers plied their trades, swarming in and out. The ring of hammers and the shrill, devouring roar of power saws sliced the air, thick with summer heat.

Libby wondered how she could have failed to notice all that noise and activity. She'd been entirely transported, watching Tate ride his horse into the creek, balancing Hildie in his strong arms. Watching as he'd set the dog down in the water and grinned that one-of-a-kind patented grin of his as she drank—while, for the amusement of his small daughters, he'd pretended to be stunned and outraged when Hildie shook herself off and drenched him in the process.

The muscles on the insides of Libby's thighs throbbed from even that short time in the saddle as she climbed down, pausing a moment on shaky legs, the balls of her feet tingling. She left the mare to graze with Tate's horse and the two ponies.

"Looks like you've given up on landing a spot on the DIY Network," Libby teased, nodding toward the house, wanting to touch Tate where sweat and creek water dampened the fabric of his shirt. *Lord knows, you've got the looks for TV, though. I can see you with a tool belt slung low around your hips, like an Old*

West gunslinger's gear, and breaking the hearts of female home-improvement enthusiasts everywhere.

Tate's moist hair curled slightly around his ears and at the back of his neck. His smile was white, perfect and absolutely lethal, and the shadows of the leaves over their heads darkened his eyes, lightened them again.

"Yep," he drawled, with a shrug of shoulders made strong and broad first by heredity, and then by loading and unloading bales of hay and sacks of feed, by shoveling out stalls and carrying sweet old dogs who couldn't or wouldn't walk another step. "I admit it. I ran a white flag up the pole and sent for reinforcements. At the rate I was going, I figured the kids and I would be moving in here next year sometime, or the year after that. I want us to be living under this roof before Audrey and Ava start school in the fall."

"Can we go fishing, Daddy?" Ava asked, tugging at his sleeve. "Those poles you bought us are on the back porch, right?"

"Right," Tate said. "Dig the worms first."

The girls rushed off to do his bidding, and Ambrose and Buford followed, leaping and bounding through the grass. Hildie, bless her heart, was content to lie down in the shady grass under a nearby tree, keeping Libby in sight and staying clear of the grazing horses.

"Why?" Libby asked quietly.

"Why?" Tate echoed, eyes dancing. "Why should the kids dig worms before they go fishing?"

Libby smiled and shook her head. "Why do you want to live in this house when you have a perfectly good mega-mansion?"

Tate shoved a hand through his hair, turned to watch as his daughters knelt in the middle of the large garden plot, between rows of cabbage, an old coffee can nearby, the pair of them digging for earthworms with their bare hands.

They'd be ring-in-the-bathtub filthy when they got back to the ranch house—the way little kids should be. When he and his brothers were small, their mother used to joke about hosing them down in the yard before letting them set foot on her clean floors.

He smiled at the recollection.

The pups, never far away from the twins, day or night, sniffed curiously at the ground, tails wagging, and Ambrose lifted his leg against a cornstalk.

"My reason for wanting to live here hasn't changed since we talked about it before," Tate answered, at some length.

Libby tilted her head to one side. Her expression was friendly, but skeptical, too. "You claim you want to see how 'regular' people live," she said. "I'm not convinced, Tate. Even if you moved into a tent, or a crate under a viaduct, you still wouldn't be an ordinary guy. You'd be a McKettrick."

"There's so much pride attached to that," Tate said, still watching his daughters and their dogs in the near distance. They were sun-splashed, and their chatter rang in the weighted air like the distant toll of country church bells. "Being a McKettrick, I mean. These days, it mostly means having money." He turned to face Libby, and because the light changed, she couldn't read his eyes. "Once, it meant something more, Lib. Something better."

She waited, listening with her heart, as well as with her ears.

"When Clay McKettrick took over the original hundred acres that became this ranch," he said huskily, "Blue River was a wide spot on a dusty cattle trail, and nobody had a clue there was oil here. Probably wouldn't have cared much if they *had* known—cars being few and far between, especially four hundred miles up the backside of no place." Tate paused, as if remembering. As if he'd been there, back in the early twentieth century. The McKettricks tended to know all about their kin, living and dead—it was just the way they were. "Clay started with the help of the woman he loved and the strength in his back. Part of the Arizona bunch—old Angus was his grandfather and Clay was the youngest of Jeb and Chloe's brood—he could have stayed right there on the Triple M and nobody would have thought the worse of him for it. But he wanted to do something on his own, and he did, Libby. He did."

Libby debated for a moment before moving closer to him. There were too many people around for any display of affection, so standing a little nearer and letting her upper arm touch his under the dappling shadows of the oak leaves overhead had to do.

"There are those who start things," she said, quietly, "and those who carry them on. Clay founded this ranch, and generations of McKettricks kept it going, made it grow. You're part of that, Tate—so are your brothers. How is that a bad thing?"

Tate watched the sparkling creek water, most likely pondering what she'd said, though he didn't reply.

Libby turned her eyes toward the garden—some of it had already been tilled under, and a lot of the produce had already been removed, probably given away. Ava and Audrey were high-stepping toward them, the partially rusted coffee can in hand, no doubt with worms squirming in the bottom. Ambrose and Buford kept pace, and the old house was a beehive of activity.

"Tate?" Libby prompted gently. "What's wrong with the other house? What do you hope to prove by moving into this one?"

He looked at her sharply, but then everything seemed to ease. His jaw and shoulders relaxed visibly. "There's nothing wrong with the main ranch house," he said quietly. "It has a long history. The memories are mostly happy ones. But it's *big*, Libby. Even when the kids are there, well, it's as if we were all staying in a hotel or something—on vacation all the time, and never just hanging out around home."

Libby nodded. She did understand.

Tate went on, his eyes fond and solemn as he watched his daughters, who'd stopped to argue over which one of them was going to carry the can of worms. His mouth crooked up in a semblance of a grin as they pulled it one way and then the other.

"Maybe we'll stay here for good," Tate went on, "and maybe we won't. But my daughters will at least have a sense of how normal people live."

"Would you ever leave the ranch, Tate?" Libby asked; for her, it was a bold question. "Would you ever leave and not come back?"

He looked at her closely then. "Nope," he said, with certainty. "I'm Texas born and bred. It's as if this dirt and this sky and these people are in my cells, Lib. What about you?"

Libby raised her shoulders, lowered them again. Sighed. "Sometimes I wonder who I'd be, away from here."

Tate squinted, as though to see her better, and he would surely have pursued the subject except that one of the twins let out a shrill shriek before he could say anything.

Shaking his head, Tate strode in their direction to settle the dispute over the worms.

"Hold it!" he said, holding up both hands.

Libby smiled, reminded of her dad. He'd been the peacemaker, the one who mediated little-girl arguments over whose barrette was whose, whose turn it was to bring in the newspaper or wash the dishes or weed the garden or sweep the kitchen floor.

Her dad had never raised his voice, as far back as she could re-member. He'd certainly never lifted a hand to any one of them in anger, though he'd wiped away a great many tears and treated a million skinned elbows and scraped knees.

Who *was* Libby Remington, really?

Her father's daughter, and Marva's.

Julie and Paige's big sister, and Calvin's aunt.

Hildie's mistress, and a friend of animals everywhere.

The owner of the Perk Up Coffee Shop, now passed on into the realm of legend.

And most certainly the naive girl Tate McKettrick had dumped for somebody else.

She was over that last part—being dumped, anyway—she'd grown safely into a woman, and if there was one thing she'd learned in the process, it was that life was rarely easy, rarely sim-ple, and often painful.

And it was worth all of that, to be here, now, doing nothing on a sunny summer day.

Libby watched as Tate dropped to his haunches, facing his daughters, after taking the can and peering inside.

Libby couldn't hear his words, but she saw the white flash of his grin, and knew he was working that McKettrick magic of his. She could imagine him saying what fine specimens those worms were, that he'd never seen better ones, that they were sure to catch the biggest trout in the creek.

The little girls listened with such earnest trust in their faces that Libby's eyes smarted. With a surreptitious swipe of one hand, she wiped them away, gave a delicate sniffle.

Straightening, Tate kept the rusty worm can, caught Libby's eye and winked, then gestured toward the house and said something more to the children. They raced around back, giggling again, the yellow dogs trotting behind them, baying like hounds on the hunt.

On his way back to where Libby stood, Tate stopped to speak

with the plumber, and then the man loading a battered wooden tool chest, the old-fashioned kind, into the back of his van.

Libby knew all the men, of course, knew their wives and their children, their mothers and fathers, and in some cases, their grandparents, too. She realized, standing there, how silly it was to think she could have hidden her relationship with Tate, even briefly.

As he said, everybody knew they were "getting it on."

He came toward her now, grinning and carrying the worm can.

As she watched him moving nearer and nearer, Libby's heart swelled and then somersaulted in her chest, a big, slow and graceful motion, like that of some sea creature frolicking in deep waters.

Bold as you please, Tate leaned in and kissed her. It wasn't just a peck, either. There was tongue involved.

She gasped, breathless and unsteady on her feet, when he drew back. "Trout for supper," he said.

"I beg your pardon?" Libby asked, confused.

Tate held up the worm can. "Audrey and Ava are fetching the fishing poles even as we speak," he said. "Here's the agenda: we catch a few trout. The guys knock off early, gather up their gear and leave. There's a fish fry. We all stuff ourselves and I catch the horses and saddle them up again, and we all ride back to the main house. The dogs and the kids are exhausted—bound to sleep like rocks. Esperanza cleans them up and puts them to bed. I tend to the horses. Then you and I take a shower together—this time I remember to lock the bedroom door—and I make love to you until all the kinks are worked out of that perfect little body of yours."

Libby's knees went weak. "All the—?"

"Kinks," Tate finished for her. "It might take some doing," he added seriously.

She thought about it.

A sweet, hot shiver of anticipation went through her.

Then she grinned, rose onto her tiptoes and kissed the cleft in his chin. "Sounds good to me," she said.

TATE WAS HAPPIER than he'd been in a long time; it almost scared him.

Needing something physical to do, at least until his emotions settled down a little, he spoke to the contractors, asked them to take the rest of the day off.

Then he unsaddled the horses, took off their bridles, too.

They'd stay close, he knew, because the grass was sweet and plentiful, the creek was nearby and the trees provided shade.

After that, Tate just allowed himself to marvel at what a lucky bastard he really was, and forget the oil shares and the money. His kids were healthy, and they were *here,* with him, with Libby.

Sunlight gilded his baby girls like full-body halos. Their voices, their laughter, their concern for worms and fishes, as well as dogs and horses—all those things roosted in Tate's heart, flapped their wings and settled in to stay.

The land, the trees, the sky seemed to go on forever.

And in the center of all this magic was Libby, as sturdy and practical and down-home as a sunflower, sprung up in some unlikely place, but at the same time, as dazzling as crystals glittering on fresh snow.

She helped Audrey and Ava to bait their hooks and cast their lines into the creek—and made sure they didn't snag each other in the process. She laughed a lot, and they liked being close to her, leaning into her sides when she wrapped an arm around each of them and squeezed.

"You know how to *fish?*" Audrey had marveled at the beginning, obviously surprised. Her eyes glowed as she looked up at Libby, and so did Ava's. She seemed to fascinate them.

She certainly fascinated *him,* though in a different way.

As simply as Libby lived, as ordinary as she seemed to think she was, there was a sense of mystery about her, of depths and heights, an interior landscape, a planet, maybe even a *universe,* waiting to be explored.

That was Libby.

"You bet I know how to fish," she had beamed, answering Audrey's question. "My dad used to take my sisters and me camping whenever he could, and if we wanted trout or bass for supper, we had to catch it."

The afternoon progressed, slowed down with the heat. Tate and Libby wound up sitting side by side on the creek bank, their knees drawn up and their heels dug in and each of them with their arms around one of the twins, showing them when to let out the line, when to reel it in.

In the end, there was no fish fry, though.

They threw back everything they caught.

The kids wanted mac-and-cheese, anyway. The boxed kind was Tate's culinary specialty; when he felt like swanking it up, he added wieners.

He'd give Esperanza the night off, he decided—maybe she'd like to go to the movies or visit a friend.

By the time the mosquitoes were out and drilling for blood, Audrey and Ava were finally starting to run down. Hunger made them cranky, and they began to bicker.

"Seems like they've had all the fun they can stand," Tate told Libby.

She nodded, grinned up at him. Her eyes looked dreamy; the quiet afternoon had been good for her.

If Tate had his way, the night would be even better.

For a while, it looked as though that was actually going to happen.

Once the kids had stowed their fishing poles, everyone checked out the progress the contractors had made on the house. The twins' room was coming together, and so was the bathroom they would share. The kitchen and the master bedroom both had a ways to go.

Tate decided he might get back into the home-improvement groove after all. Delegate some of his duties as foreman—not that he was real clear yet on what those duties actually were.

He wished he'd spent more time riding with Pablo now, both on horseback and in the company truck. And not just because of the things he might have learned.

The man's absence was still a persistent ache in Tate's middle, a wind that sometimes abated and sometimes howled.

He saddled his horse and Libby's, checked to see that the girls had gotten their cinches tight enough and wouldn't be rolling off their ponies' backs onto the ground.

Not that they'd have far to go, he thought, with a smile.

The ponies were about the size of a large dog.

Once Libby was on Buttons's back and squared away, Tate handed Hildie up into her arms, made sure she had a good grip.

That dog looked as easy in the saddle as if she played polo on weekends.

Letting the kids get a head start, Tate took his time swinging up into the saddle and turning Stranger in the direction of the main house.

Sometimes I wonder who I'd be, away from here.

Libby's remark had snagged in his mind, beneath all the sunshine and the fishing and the easy enjoyment of a sunny day.

If she thought he was going to let *that* one go, she should have damn well known better.

"So," Tate began, as they rode slowly onto the range again, the big house towering in the distance, like the castle it was. "Who do you think you'd be, Lib, away from Blue River?"

She nestled her chin onto the top of Hildie's head, her arms stretched around the dog's ample body, holding on to the saddle horn for balance and letting the reins rest loosely across the mare's neck.

After a long time, she replied sadly, "I don't know. Maybe someone who's accomplished things."

Tate nudged his horse a bit closer to Libby's, not to crowd her, but in case holding the dog got to be too much for her. He raised an eyebrow and shifted his gaze to the space between Stranger's ears, though he was still watching Lib out of the corner of one eye.

"Like what?" he asked, very carefully.

If Libby truly believed she had something to prove, well, as far as Tate was concerned, that was cause for concern. Especially if she thought she had to leave Blue River to do it.

She sighed. She shook her head.

Gently, he took Hildie from her.

Their horses moved apart again.

Hildie tilted her head back to lick the underside of Tate's chin.

He chuckled. The girls were too far ahead, almost to the fence, the pups weaving around them.

Tate gave a shrill whistle to get Audrey and Ava's attention, signaled them to wait for him and Libby.

"Will you do me a favor, Lib?" he asked, when she didn't say anything. "Before you decide to take off for parts unknown, so you can 'accomplish' things, will you give us a chance? You and me, I mean?"

Tears glistened in her eyes when she looked at him. "What kind of chance?"

"You know what kind of chance."

"What if it doesn't work?"

"What if it does?"

Libby bit down on her lower lip and looked away. "It didn't before."

"That was before. We weren't living in the same town. And that was a long time ago, Lib."

She met his eyes, with a visible effort. "Isn't that what we're doing now, Tate?" she asked quietly. "Giving things a chance?"

"I want to sleep with you every night, Libby. I want to shower with you and eat breakfast with you and do a whole lot of other things with you." He paused, looked back over his shoulder. "The house isn't finished, but it's livable. I'll rustle up some furniture, and we'll move in. You, me and the kids and the dogs."

She was quiet for a long time. So long that Tate started to get nervous.

"You're suggesting that we *live* together?" Libby finally asked. "In the same house with your children?"

The scandalized note in her voice made Tate chuckle. "Hello? The parents of half the kids in their kindergarten class 'cohabitate.'"

"There's cohabitation," Libby said, "and there's *shacking up.*"

"You know, for someone as sexually responsive as you are, Lib, you can really be prudish."

Her cheeks glowed with pink splotches. "You're not concerned that Audrey and Ava will be—confused?"

Tate huffed out a sigh. "No," he said. "Did Ava seem 'confused' this morning, when she found us in bed together? For better or worse, it's a different world, Libby." He watched her for a long moment, trying to gauge her reactions. They had almost caught up with the girls, so he lowered his voice. "If it really bothers you, though—*living in sin,* I mean—we could go ahead and get married."

"Married?"

"Well, wouldn't that be better than 'shacking up,' as you put it?"

"What about—" She stopped, swallowed so hard that Tate felt the dry ache in his own throat. "What about love?"

"Love isn't our problem," Tate replied quietly. "*Trust* is our problem."

Libby didn't affirm that assertion, but she didn't deny it, either. So he still had a fighting chance.

For now, though, the conversation was over.

Deftly, Ava reached, without dismounting, to work the gate latch.

In the distance, the stud kicked and squealed like he'd tear that pen apart, rail by rail and bolt by bolt. The sound of that animal's rage sent a shiver tripping down Tate's spine.

As soon as he'd ridden through the gate, Tate got down from the saddle, set Hildie on the ground and strode toward the pen, leaving Stranger to go into the barn on his own.

"Shut that gate," he called over one shoulder, "and go on into the barn."

Through the gaps between the steel rails, Tate saw the stallion bunch its hind quarters, put its head down and send both its back legs slamming into the pen's gate with enough force to shake the ground.

The gate held.

Tate swore under his breath. Fumbled for his cell phone and called Brent Brogan's direct line.

"Hey, Tate," Brent said, affably distracted, like he was doing paperwork or something. "Everything okay out there on the Ponderosa?"

Tate answered with a question of his own. "You heard a decision on what Animal Control wants to do with this stud?" he asked. "Because he's in a foul mood—fixing to kick his way out of the pen and kill somebody else."

Brent sighed. "I'll make a few calls," he said, "and get back to you."

"Thanks," Tate said. Call waiting clicked in his ear. "Later." Then, after pressing the appropriate button, "Tate McKettrick."

"It's Julie Remington, Tate. I need to speak with Libby."

So much, Tate thought, for loving the "kinks" out of Libby's delectable little body later on, when they would have been alone. He grabbed hold of the pen gate with his free hand and gave the thing a hard shake, making sure the stud hadn't sprung it.

"Sure," he said glumly. "Hold on a second."

Libby had gone into the barn, along with the twins, and when Tate reached the doorway, she and Audrey and Ava were all in separate stalls, unsaddling their horses and getting ready to brush them down. Stranger stood in the breezeway, waiting his turn, although Libby must have removed his saddle and blanket and bridle.

The old horse ambled toward Tate, nudged him good-naturedly in the chest.

Leaving Buttons's stall, Libby was smiling, dusting her hands together.

Job well done.

"For you." Tate held the cell out to her, and she took it.

"Julie," he added, opening the door to Stranger's stall and stepping aside so the animal could precede him.

Libby nodded, looking mildly troubled, and headed for the open door at the end of the breezeway.

Tate closed the stall door and began brushing down his horse.

"I'M *NOT* KIDDING," Julie said. "Marva is leaving. For good. The movers will come in a few days and clear out her apartment."

Libby rounded the corner of the barn, keeping to the shade, and gazed at the stallion in its big metal cage. The creature had quieted, but its flanks and sides were lathered as though it had run for miles and miles. It stood with its head hung low, its sides expanding, drawing in, expanding, drawing in again.

She thought about Pablo; how startled and afraid he must have been when he fell under the stallion's hooves. The pain, though probably brief, would have been horrendous.

"Julie, what do you want me to say?" Libby asked, backing away from the stallion now, resisting a strange and probably suicidal desire to reach between those steel slats and try to comfort it somehow. Speak softly and stroke its sweat-drenched neck. "If Marva wants to leave, she can leave. Hitting the road is her forte, after all, isn't it?"

"Nobody's denying that she left us, Lib," Julie said so quietly and so gently that Libby was ashamed of herself. "We were little girls. We needed her. She abandoned us and she abandoned Dad. But—"

"But?" Libby snapped.

On some level, she was still that terrified, heartbroken and *furious* kid who wanted her mother.

"Look," Julie went on, when Libby was silent for a long time, "she wants to see all three of us, tonight. At her place. She says it's important."

Libby wanted to scream, though of course she didn't. That would have alarmed the kids, and Hildie, who had followed her out of the barn and sat looking up at her now, pink tongue lolling.

"Why does it have to be tonight?"

"Because she's flying out of Austin tomorrow," Julie said. "Libby, I know you have issues with Marva—valid ones. We all do. But the woman *is* our mother, and I think we can do this much for her."

Libby's head began to throb. She dug into her right temple with three fingers and rubbed.

Returning to town meant she couldn't pretend the Perk Up was still standing.

It probably meant no sex with Tate.

And she'd been looking forward to that, to getting naked in the shower with him. To soaring outside herself.

Love isn't our problem, he'd said. *Trust is our problem.*

Did that mean he still loved her?

Dammit, she wanted to know. She *needed* to know.

"Just come," Julie said. "Please, Lib. Six-thirty, Marva's place."

Libby looked at her wrist, realized she wasn't wearing her watch, and asked, "What time is it now?"

"A little after five," Julie answered. "You're with Tate, aren't you?"

"Not for long, it would seem," Libby lamented. *We were starting to get somewhere, Tate and I.*

"I'm sure he'll understand."

"Of course he will. *I'm* the one having a hard time understanding."

"Well, *that* was certainly cryptic," Julie remarked. Then, barely missing a beat, "You'll be at Marva's, then?"

Libby nodded, glummer than glum. "Yes." She looked up, and Tate was standing maybe a dozen yards away, waiting, looking pensive.

And so deliciously hunky.

"See you at six-thirty," Julie said.

"See you," Libby answered, and closed the phone.

Walking up to Tate, she handed the device back to him.

"I have to go back to town," she said. "It seems my mother is leaving Blue River again—her work here is done now that my business is in ruins—and she wants to say goodbye. Tonight."

Tate sighed, took Libby's shoulders in his hands. "You're okay with this? Her leaving, I mean?"

"It's not as though she's been an integral part of my life, Tate." Libby spoke without bitterness; she was simply stating a fact she'd accepted long ago. Mostly.

He drew her close, as she'd hoped he would do, and held her, resting his chin on the top of her head. "Let me make sure Esperanza can look after the kids tonight, and then I'll drive you to town."

She nodded, wanting to cling to him, forcing herself not to clutch at the fabric of his shirt. "I don't want to go."

"Then don't."

"I *have* to, Tate."

She felt the motion of his jaw; knew he was smiling even before he held her a little way from his chest so he could look down into her face.

"This was a good day," he said.

"It was a good day," Libby agreed.

But the best part was over.

Fifteen minutes later, they were in Tate's truck, headed for Blue River. Hildie rode in the rear seat, but she wasn't any happier about leaving the Silver Spur than Libby was, evidently. The dog sat backward, looking out the window over the truckbed, and every few moments, she gave a small whimper.

Libby wanted to reassure Hildie that they'd be back, but she was strangely hesitant to make such a promise.

At home, she took a quick shower and put on a simple cotton sundress. She tracked Tate to the kitchen, where he was leaning calmly against the counter, arms folded, watching Hildie gobble up her kibble. He'd refilled her water dish, too, and even brought in the newspaper and the mail.

Libby, her hair still damp from the shower steam, searched for her car keys until she finally found them—hanging on their hook near the back door, where they were supposed to be.

"It always throws me," she admitted to Tate, "when things are where they're supposed to be."

He chuckled at that.

"You don't have to stay," she said, hoping he would.

Which was crazy, because he had children at home. He had a ranch, livestock. Responsibilities. It was just plain wrong to expect him to sit here in this house until she got back from Marva's at whatever time, in whatever emotional condition, just because she might need someone to talk to later on.

He crossed the room, opened her refrigerator, shook his head. The pickings were slim; she had to admit that.

"What do you live on?" he asked, and from the tone of his voice, he was only half kidding. "You have three green olives, a box of baking soda, and I don't even want to think about the expiration date on that cheese. It's not supposed to be blue-green at the corners, is it?"

Libby laughed. "I depend heavily on canned goods," she said.

"Yuck," Tate said.

The wall phone rang.

Libby grabbed the receiver, hoping for a reprieve. In a fraction of an instant, she came up with the perfect scenario: Julie was calling to say that Marva was still leaving, soon and for good, but tonight's visit had been postponed—better yet, canceled altogether.

"Good, you're home," Julie said. "Can you pick me up? Paige is still at work, so she's going to be a few minutes late, and—"

"Sure," Libby broke in, deflated. So much for perfect scenarios. "I'll swing by and get you. But chill out a little. This isn't a rocket launch, Julie. There's no second-by-second countdown."

Incredibly, Julie burst into tears. "Maybe you don't want to know *where the hell* our mother has been all these years," she blurted out, in a very unJulie-like way, "but I do! *By God,* that woman isn't going *anywhere* until she gives me *some* kind of explanation!"

"Julie," Libby said gently, her gaze connecting with Tate's, "where's Calvin?"

Julie sniffled inelegantly. "He's spending the night with Justin."

"All right. That's good. I'll be over in a few minutes."

Goodbyes were said, and both sisters hung up.

Tate jingled his keys at Libby. "Hildie and I are going out to pick up something decent for dinner," he said. "We'll be here waiting when you get back."

"It might be late," she warned.

He approached, kissed her lightly. "We'll be here," he repeated. "Hildie and me."

She nodded, too choked up, all of a sudden, to say more.

Since the Impala was parked in her garage, off the alley, Libby couldn't avoid getting a glimpse of the caved-in roof and tumbled-down walls of the Perk Up.

It wasn't enough that Marva had abandoned them all way back when, she reflected bitterly.

Six months ago, with no warning at all, she'd returned to Blue River, rented the condo, furnished it and begun trying to "make up for lost time" and get to know her daughters.

But an invasion of their lives wasn't enough for Marva. Oh, no. She had to destroy the one thing Libby had to show for her attempts to jerry-rig some kind of career for herself. She had to reduce the Perk Up to scrap metal and firewood.

Libby climbed into the Impala, started the engine, calmly backed into the alley, remembering those early days after Marva's sudden reentry into her and her sisters' lives.

She'd seemed genuinely baffled, Marva had, when they resisted her overtures—the phone calls, the unannounced visits, the gifts.

Julie had been the first to give ground.

She wanted Calvin to know his grandmother, she'd said.

Paige, to Libby's initial surprise, had fallen under the spell of Marva next. Of course, Paige was the baby; she'd still been wearing footed pajamas and sucking her thumb when their mother bailed.

She'd cried the longest and the hardest. Climbed into Libby's or Julie's bed at night, dragging her tattered "blankie" and whispering, "Do you know where Mommy is? When will she be back? Tomorrow? Will Mommy come home tomorrow?"

Remembering, still the big sister, Libby ached with the same helpless fury she'd felt back then.

Julie was waiting by her front gate when Libby pulled up, the diamond-paned windows of her pretty cottage alight behind her. Flowers climbed trellises, tumbled, riotous, over fences, and the fierce dazzle of the setting sun glowed around it all.

"I can't believe she's just going to take off again," Julie said, instead of hello.

"Believe it," Libby said grimly.

CHAPTER EIGHTEEN

AFTER A SHORT SPEECH, Marva produced three envelopes from her handbag and, with a flourish, presented one to each of her daughters.

To Libby, it seemed that the floor of the condo's living room pitched from side to side, like a swimming raft bobbing on choppy water. She squeezed the bridge of her nose between her thumb and forefinger, trying hard to stem the headache beating behind her eyes like a second heart.

The tick of the mantel clock was hypnotic—steady as a metronome—and it didn't help that Marva kept pacing back and forth in front of the cold fireplace, arms folded, the hem of her wildly colorful silk caftan billowing at her heels.

Julie, seated in the wingback chair, was the first to open her envelope, the first to speak. Staring down at the check inside, she whispered, "This is—this is *a lot* of money."

Paige, perched on the edge of a chintz-covered ottoman, couldn't seem to speak at all. She pressed one hand to the base of her throat, shaking, her eyes squeezed shut.

Libby didn't move so much as a muscle. She was too stunned.

Marva stopped pacing and stood still, sweeping Libby, Julie and Paige up in a single cheerfully magnanimous glance.

"Paige? Libby? Don't either of you have anything to say?" their mother demanded, her voice a touch too high.

Paige opened her eyes, swayed slightly. "Holy crap," she said.

Libby straightened her spine. The headache receded slightly, and the floor leveled itself out and stayed still. "Please, Marva," she said, in a near whisper, "sit down. You're making me dizzy."

Marva plunked down next to Libby, on the couch. Took one of Libby's hands between both her own, as though the two of them were as close as any mother and daughter, ever. "I added a little something to your share, dear," she said, in a whisper no one could have helped overhearing, even if they'd been in the next room. "Because I crashed into your little coffee shop and everything."

And everything.

Did I mention that Dad kept asking for you, right up until the day he couldn't talk anymore, because the hospice nurse and Doc Burt put him on a ventilator, and there was a tube in his throat, and even then he asked with his eyes?

That until the middle of first grade, Paige thought every ring of the doorbell, every car stopping out front, meant you were home?

Oh, yeah, and Julie saw you everywhere, for years—in the grocery store, in other cars at stoplights, on the River Walk in San Antonio.

Me, I just wanted to talk to you. I was so pathetic, I would have settled for a few more phone calls. Letters or postcards.

Hell, I'd have settled for smoke signals.

And everything, indeed.

"I can't accept your money," Libby said stiffly, after finding her voice and pulling free of Marva's grasp.

Julie glared at Libby from across the small room, fanning her flushed face with her check. "Lib," she said, "this is *no time* to let your pride do the talking."

Marva fluttered a hand, the gesture taking them all in. "It isn't *my* money, anyway," she said, in merry dismissal. "It's *yours*. I had a sizable insurance policy on your father's life—he and I took it out together, soon after you were born, Libby—and when he died, I collected. Winston—my present husband—is very good with money, and he invested the proceeds and—" She beamed, flinging her hands out wide. "*Voilà!* You are women of means!"

Women of means, Libby thought. Bile scalded the back of her throat.

"How—?" Paige paused, started again. "How could you leave us like that? We were *little kids,* Marva."

"I've never claimed to be perfect," Marva said, mildly indignant. The brilliant smile was gone.

A short, bristly silence followed. "I should have listened to Winston," Marva continued presently, frowning thoughtfully into the middle distance. "I thought if I came back to Blue River, well, we'd all get to know each other and bygones would be bygones. After all, we're all grown-ups, aren't we?" She sighed, causing her shoulders to rise and fall in an ebullient shrug. "Winston said you wouldn't react well, and he was right. I miss him terribly, and frankly I'm tired of being the only one around here who even *tries* to build a relationship. I want to get on with my life. I want to go home."

Home, Marva had explained earlier, before the ceremonious presentation of the envelopes, was a condominium overlooking a beach in Costa Rica. Winston was a retired proctologist and, apparently, a very indulgent husband—as well as a financial whiz.

Since responding to the things Marva had said would have amounted to crossing a conversational minefield, none of the sisters said anything.

The evening was, for all practical intents and purposes, over.

Libby left her envelope, still unopened, on Marva's coffee table.

She said goodbye, travel safely, and other things she couldn't quite recall later, when she looked back on the experience.

She had almost reached the Impala when Julie caught up to her, shoved the envelope at her. Her name was neatly inscribed on the front, in flowing cursive.

"Don't be an idiot," she said. "Marva destroyed your business. And, anyway, Dad would have wanted you to have this money. He probably kept up the premiums the whole time Marva was away. *Take it.*"

Libby swallowed, snatched the envelope out of Julie's hand, shoved it into her purse as Paige joined them, shivering a little, hugging herself, even though the night was warm.

"I wouldn't make any investments or impulse purchases if I were you," Libby told both her sisters, as she opened her car door to get in and drive away. "Not before these checks clear the bank, anyway."

With that, she got into the Impala and started the engine.

"Are you coming with me?" Libby asked Julie, who was staring at her as though she'd turned into a total stranger.

"I'll go with Paige," Julie said, recovering enough to offer a thin smile. "She's a little shaken up."

Aren't we all? Libby thought wearily.

When she got back to the house, Tate was waiting for her, just as he'd promised he would be. He'd been to the store, too—supper was grilled chicken breast from the deli at the supermarket, along with potato salad and biscuits. Almsted's, which had abutted Libby's building, was closed until inspectors could determine whether or not there had been structural damage.

Hildie, resting contentedly in her usual place in front of the stove, rolled her eyes open in greeting, then closed them again. She'd had a big day, out there on the Silver Spur.

They all had.

Once Libby had washed her hands, dried them and sunk into the chair Tate held for her at the table, the day caught up with her, too. With an impact.

She was exhausted.

"So?" Tate asked, sitting down across from Libby. "Are you going to tell me what the big summons was all about?"

"Yes," Libby said, helping herself to a piece of chicken and some potato salad. "She's going back to her husband, Winston, the retired proctologist, in Costa Rica."

"I see," Tate said.

They ate in silence for a while.

"There's money," Libby said. "Sort of."

Tate raised an eyebrow. "Sort of?" he echoed. "How can there 'sort of' be money?"

Libby got up, rummaged through her purse for the envelope, handed it to Tate.

"See for yourself. There should be a check inside. I'm not getting excited until it clears the bank."

Tate chuckled at that, started to set the envelope aside, still sealed.

Libby's heart climbed into her throat. "Open it," she said, almost in a whisper. "Please?"

"It's yours, Lib. You should be the one to open it."

Libby shook her head. "I can't."

"Okay," Tate said. Slowly, probably giving her time to change her mind, he inserted the blade of a butter knife under the flap and slit the crease, pulled the check out without looking at it.

Libby closed her eyes. Waited.

"Tell me," she said.

Tate gave a long, low whistle of exclamation.

When he read off the amount, she gasped.

He handed it across the table. "Looks legitimate to me," he said quietly.

Libby briefly examined the check, groped for the envelope and shoved it back inside. Then she put the envelope on top of the fridge, under the cookie jar.

Out of sight, out of mind.

As if.

"I suppose it's too soon to ask if you have plans?" Tate ventured, when they'd both finished eating.

"Plans?" Libby echoed. He seemed to have withdrawn from her somehow, pulled ever so slightly back into a space she couldn't quite reach—but maybe she was imagining that.

Tate stood, began clearing the table, putting things in the fridge, scraping bones and other scraps into the trash bin. "Yeah," he said gently. "You could do a lot with that kind of money, Libby. You need to think about this." He sighed. "Without me distracting you."

"Distracting me?" She felt the floor tremble beneath her.

"Libby, you have some new options now, that's all I'm saying. You need to explore them."

To think *she'd* been hung up on Tate's earlier statement that he planned on asking her to move in with him, once the house was ready. She'd pretty much decided she'd say "yes," when and if the time came, but now—now Tate was talking about thinking and options and explorations.

For Libby, the money hadn't changed anything, really.

But maybe it had, for Tate. Maybe he'd liked her better when she was running a failing business, living on a shoestring. Or maybe he'd just felt sorry for her—poor Libby—and now that she was a "woman of means," as Marva had put it, he could cut her loose, with no strain on his noble McKettrick conscience.

Dammit, was the man looking for an out?

She loved Tate.

She loved his daughters, too—that hadn't taken long. Two minutes, maybe.

Yes, there had been dreams. She'd wanted to travel a little, perhaps take some courses online, buy a decent car...

But all those were things she could have done without leaving Blue River, or at least without leaving Tate.

"I'm not even sure the check is good," Libby reiterated, after letting out a long breath. If Tate was having second thoughts, looking for an exit, she could deal with that. She could survive it—just as she had before. "Marva could be delusional—or even some kind of con artist, for all I know."

Tate leaned back against the counter, watching her. Sadness illuminated his eyes. "But if it is good?"

"I don't know, Tate. Do I have to decide tonight?"

He crossed the room, leaned down, kissed the top of her head, lightly, in a way that said, See you later. "No," he said hoarsely. "All you need to do tonight is get some sleep. We can talk tomorrow or—whenever."

Whenever? Libby thought. Her disappointment was out of all proportion to the situation. *Whenever?*

"Lock up behind me," Tate said.

He bent, patted Hildie on the head and started toward the front of the house.

Just like that, he was leaving.

Going back to the ranch—alone.

Libby waited until Tate was down the front steps, through the gate, on the sidewalk—until he'd actually driven away in his big-ass redneck truck—before she engaged the dead bolt on the front door and stormed back to the kitchen. Shot that dead bolt, too.

Hildie hoisted herself up off the floor, yawning.

Libby shut off the kitchen lights and led the way down the hall toward her bedroom. By then, she was absolutely certain she'd been dumped again.

Slam, bam, thank you, ma'am.

"Never trust a man," she told the dog.

Hildie plopped down on the rug at the foot of Libby's bed, while Libby peeled off her clothes and flung them away. Shimmied into an oversized T-shirt and hauled back the covers on her bed.

"He's probably got you snowed," Libby said, heading for the bathroom, where she washed her face and brushed her teeth. On her return, she resumed the one-sided conversation. "All that McKettrick charm. 'You're too tired to walk? Poor old dog. Here. Let me carry you, on my horse—'"

Hildie sighed, dog-tired.

Libby climbed into bed. Switched out the lamp.

A tear trickled down over her right temple, tickling.

"What exactly did Tate do to make me so angry, you ask? As anyone would. He *left*. As soon as a challenge comes up—*poof!*— Tate McKettrick is out of here." She paused, pulled up a corner of the top sheet to dry her cheeks. "The thing is, Hildie," she finished, staring up at the darkened ceiling, "I'm in love with the man. What do you say to that?"

Hildie, of course, said nothing at all.

Somehow, against all odds, Libby slept.

HE HADN'T SEEN—or spoken to—Libby in four days.

Cheryl called on Friday morning—early, even taking the time difference between Texas and New York into account.

Tate, sleepless since leaving Libby's house the night of the meeting with her mother, had just started the coffee brewing. Having glanced at the caller ID panel, his usual greeting was gruffer than usual.

"Tate McKettrick. What do you want, Cheryl?"

"My," Cheryl said. "Aren't we testy?"

Tate drew in a breath, let it out slowly. "You don't know the half of it," he said.

"How are my babies?" The chirpy note in Cheryl's voice made him instantly suspicious. He hated it when she wheedled, and that chirp was the equivalent of a fire alarm.

"Audrey and Ava are fine," he said evenly. "Looking forward to seeing you tonight. A whole weekend with Mommy. Audrey wants to show you the routine she's been practicing for the Pixie Pageant. What time does your plane get in?"

Cheryl was silent for a few moments. "You're letting Audrey enter the Pixie Pageant?"

"Yeah," Tate said. "I might have been wrong, saying 'no' out of hand the way I did. She's giving it a shot."

"*You,* Tate McKettrick, were *wrong* about something?"

"I can think of several," Tate answered. A pause, during which he restrained himself from listing those things he'd been wrong about. It would surprise Cheryl to know she wasn't number one on that list—that slot went to screwing up what he'd had with Libby in the first place. "Can we cut to the chase now, Cheryl? You didn't call to shoot the breeze. It's not even four o'clock out here—the girls are sleeping."

A short, stormy silence, during which he could feel the bad mojo building. "Dammit, Tate," she finally burst out, "you *know* why I called, and you're *deliberately* making it all as difficult as possible!"

Since there was some truth in her accusation—he *had* known why she was calling—Tate decided to chill out a little. "Okay," he said. "I'll stop making things difficult for you. Go ahead and say it."

She sighed, and her voice sounded moist; either she was crying, or she wanted him to think she was. "It's the job—I'm new—low man on the totem pole—"

Tate suppressed a sigh. His knuckles tightened around the cell phone. God knew, he didn't give a rat's ass if Cheryl *ever* came back to Blue River, but the girls did. They were only six, and they loved and missed their mother.

"I'd suggest that Audrey and Ava come here," Cheryl went into her bravely-carrying-on routine. "But there wouldn't be much point in that, when I'll be at the office all weekend."

"No," Tate said. "There wouldn't be much point in that."

"I'll come *next* weekend," she promised, rallying. "And bring presents." A pause. "Will you tell them that? That I'll come next weekend and bring presents?"

"No," Tate replied. "They need to hear it from you."

Cheryl sounded pained. *"Why?"*

"Because this is between you and the kids."

He heard her draw in an angry breath. "You *love* making me look bad, don't you?"

Tate closed his eyes, held back the obvious retort.

"All right." He nearly growled the words. "I'll explain—this time. But you still need to call Audrey and Ava yourself, Cheryl. They're your daughters. They miss you, and they'll want to hear your voice."

"I'll call," Cheryl said, after a long time.

"Yeah," Tate said, and hung up without a goodbye.

Right about then, Austin meandered down his private stairway, wearing nothing but a pair of black boxers. Scars from two different rotator-cuff surgeries laced his right shoulder, front and back.

He ruffed up his already mussed hair and gave an expansive yawn.

"Tell me you stayed out all night," he drawled, "because nobody in his right mind gets up this early, even on a freakin' ranch."

Tate chuckled, but the sound was rueful. "*You're* up," he pointed out.

Austin all but staggered to the counter, took a mug from the cupboard and poured coffee into it, even though the stuff was still percolating in the fancy steel-and-steam apparatus Garrett had donated to the cause when their mother's old electric pot finally conked out.

"Hell, yes, I'm up," Austin grumbled. "The bad vibes were practically bouncing off the walls."

Tate shook his head, exasperated. "Cheryl isn't coming home for the weekend," he said. "I knew things would come to that eventually, but I thought it would take a while. The girls are going to be let down, Austin. Big-time."

"Are they?" Austin asked, after rubbing his eyes. "If they're missing anybody, I'd say it's Libby." He took a cautious sip of coffee, made a face at the taste. He'd been doing that for as long as Tate could remember.

"Why do you drink coffee if you don't like it?" he snapped.

Austin chuckled. "Is your tail in a twist or what?" he countered, clearly amused. "And what the hell are you talking about?"

"The way you grimace."

"I grimace?"

"Yeah. When you drink coffee."

Austin laughed, shook his head again. "It's just something I do," he said. "Who cares why?"

Tate sighed. "You're right. Who the hell cares why?"

"This is about Libby—this weird mood you're in."

"What makes you say that?"

Austin lifted his cup in a half-assed toast. "I'm psychic. I might just set up my own toll-free number and start telling fortunes. Here's yours for free—If you don't get a handle on things with Libby Remington, once and for all, you're going to wind up as one of those crusty, grizzled old sons-of-bitches who grouse about everything from taxes to the breakfast special at the Denny's three towns over, train their dogs to bite and post No Trespassing signs on every other fence post."

Tate couldn't help a wan grin. "That was colorful," he said.

"What's the problem between you and Libby?"

"What if I said it was none of your business?"

"I'd keep right on asking," Austin said, smiling over the rim of his cup.

Tate sighed. "She came into some money."

"And that's bad?"

"I suppose not. It gives her a lot of options, Austin. She could leave, start herself a whole new, Tate-free life someplace else."

"And you'd rather she didn't have any choice but to stay here with you?"

For all the chewing and mulling he'd done, Tate hadn't thought of that. "No," he said hoarsely. "I just want her to stay. To *want* to stay."

"And she doesn't?"

"I don't know—I don't think *she* knows, either. Libby is deciding what she wants. I'm trying to give her enough space to do that."

"Space is good," Austin agreed. "But too much of it might make Libby think you just don't give a damn, one way or another. Talk to her, Tate. Tell her what you feel, and what you want. *Then* say you'll give her space to think things over."

"You might be the next Dear Abby."

Austin laughed. "I applied," he joked. "Too much bull on my résumé."

"Hilarious," Tate said.

"Yeah," Austin said. "I'm a one-man tailgate party. Bring your own six-pack."

"Speaking of bulls," Tate said. "You've given up on the idea of tracking Buzzsaw down and riding him, haven't you?"

Austin shook his head, set his coffee mug aside with a thunk. "Nope," he said. "I know the stock supplier who owns him. Buzzsaw and me, we have a date with destiny."

Tate's gut tightened. "Let this go, Austin," he said quietly. "That bull almost killed you before. Why give him a second chance?"

Austin's eyes were grave. "You know why."

"All you have to do is turn your back. All you have to do is walk away."

But Austin shook his head again, and Tate knew that particular conversation was over.

MARVA LEFT TOWN, on schedule.

A day later, a moving van pulled up in front of her condominium, and her furniture and other household goods were removed.

Just like that, she was gone.

Again.

Libby, Julie and Paige drove all the way to Austin in Paige's car, just to deposit the checks Marva had given them. That way, they had each other for moral support, and it would be considerably less embarrassing than walking into First Cattleman's Bank in Blue River and finding out there was no money, carefully invested by a fiscally minded, retired proctologist.

The checks were good.

They plunked down on a bench in front of the bank, the three of them in a row, stunned.

"We're rich," Julie said.

"Not rich," Paige clarified. "Comfortable."

"I'm a teacher," Julie countered. "You're a registered nurse with state-of-the-art skills. Maybe this kind of money says 'comfortable' to you, but it says 'rich' to me."

Libby laughed. "Hot damn," she said.

She could go anywhere, do practically anything.

She had choices.

"What are you going to do with your share?" Julie asked, probably relieved that Libby hadn't torn the check into little pieces and tossed them into the breeze.

"Buy a new car," Libby said.

"That's all you want?"

"It's not all I want," Libby answered, smiling to herself. *And sometimes you have to go after what you want, and have confidence that you'll get it.*

The clarity was sudden, and it was glorious.

"Let's get lunch," she said. "I have things to do at home."

"Don't we all?" Paige agreed.

They had salads at a sunny sidewalk café.

Libby bought a cell phone and, between Paige and the salesman, figured out how to operate it.

And then they drove back to Blue River.

"You look like a woman with a purpose," Paige said, dropping Libby off at the back gate.

Inside the house, Hildie began to bark a relieved welcome.

Libby merely nodded; she knew her mysterious smile and wandering attention had been driving her curious sisters nuts all morning.

Waggling the fancy phone, which was probably capable of polishing the lenses of satellites deep in outer space, she smiled and unlatched the gate with her free hand.

"Call you later," she said.

Paige honked her horn in farewell and drove away.

Libby hurried up the walk and unlocked the back door.

Hildie spilled out gleefully, greeted her with a yip and squatted next to the flower bed.

While the dog enjoyed a few minutes of fresh air, Libby changed out of her go-to-the-bank-in-Austin dress and sandals and pulled on comfy jeans, a short-sleeved black T-shirt and tennis shoes. She brushed her hair and pulled it back from her face.

She put on lip gloss.

"Come on," she said to Hildie, grabbing up her purse and the new cell phone and the keys to the ratty old Impala. "We're on a mission."

During the drive, Libby rehearsed what she'd say when she reached her destination.

I love you, Tate McKettrick.

Let's give "us" a chance.

Now that we're all grown up, let's make it work.

She'd done a lot of thinking in the days since Tate had left her to consider her options. She'd realized he hadn't so much dumped her as assumed she was going to dump him. But she wasn't, and she trusted that he'd respond to her rehearsal speech just the way she wanted him to.

She stopped at the small house first; there were signs that Tate had been there, pounding nails and splashing paint onto the walls, but he wasn't around at the moment.

Libby called Hildie back from the creek where she'd been exploring, and they moved on to the main place.

There were trucks everywhere, parked at odd angles, but Libby didn't see anyone, either by the barn or in the spacious yard.

She was standing there, beside the Impala, trying to decide whether to knock on the kitchen door or check out the barn, when she heard the small, shrill scream.

Libby's heart actually seized in her chest.

For one terrible moment, she couldn't move.

Couldn't speak.

The scream came again, smaller now, more terrified.

And it was followed by the sound of the stallion trying to kick his way out of the pen again.

Libby broke into a run. "Tate!" she yelled. "Somebody—anybody—*help!*"

She rounded the corner of the barn.

The stallion was kicking in all directions now, raising dust, a whirling dervish.

And through that choking dust, Libby saw one of the twins—Ava, she thought—wriggle under the lowest rail and right into the stud pen.

Jesus, Libby prayed, *Jesus, Jesus, Jesus...*

She slammed against the side of the pen, grabbing the rails with both hands to steady herself.

Ava huddled within inches of the stallion's flying hooves, sheltering one of the pups with her little body.

Raising her eyes, the child spotted Libby.

Libby flopped to her belly in the dirt, but she clearly wasn't going to fit under that fence. She bolted back to her feet and started up the side, hand over hand, rail to rail.

"Tate!" she screamed, once more, as she reached the top.

And then she was over, landing in a two-footed crouch in the churned up dust and dried manure, Ava within reach.

The stallion froze, quivering all over, sizing her up.

Libby knew the respite was only temporary.

She could barely see for the dust, and her eyes scalded. Her heart pounded, and her throat felt scraped raw.

Moving slowly, she got Ava by one skinny upper arm, pulled.

Ava held on to the puppy.

The stallion snorted, laid back his ears.

A bad sign, Libby thought, strangely calm even though her body was stressed to the max. A very bad sign.

She pressed Ava and the pup behind her, against the rails. Pinned them with her back, spread her arms to shield them as best she could.

"Easy," she told the stallion, hardly recognizing her own voice. Her nose itched. She thought she might throw up. But she didn't dare move her arms. "Nobody wants to hurt you."

"Hold on, Lib." The voice was Tate's. He was just behind her. Thank God he was there.

Thank God.

"Daddy," Ava whimpered. "I know I gave my word as a Mc-Kettrick, but Ambrose dug a hole under the stud-pen fence and got inside and I—"

"Hush," Tate said, very gently.

He started up the rails, making the same climb Libby had.

Libby became aware that Austin was there, too, fiddling with the padlock on the pen's door. A rifle rested easily in the crook of one of his arms as he worked.

Everything seemed to be happening in slow motion.

The stallion began to get agitated again, tossing his head, snorting. Pawing at the dirt with one front hoof, then the other.

Tate was over the fence, in front of Libby.

Shielding her and Ava and the little dog, he spoke to the stallion. His words were quiet, and their meaning innocuous—it was the tone of his voice, the energy Tate projected, a sort of calming authority, that made the difference.

The pen gate slowly creaked open.

The stallion turned his huge head in that direction, then back to Tate.

The danger was by no means past.

The pen was small, the stallion still riled. Sweat glistened on his hide, and his eyes rolled, all whites except for tiny slits of dark along the upper lids.

Libby let her forehead rest against the back of Tate's right shoulder.

Behind her, Ava and the puppy squirmed.

Austin moved away from the pen gate, wide-open now, and cocked the rifle.

Dear God, was he going to shoot the horse?

She must have wondered aloud, because Tate answered her. "Only if the stallion turns on us, Lib," he said.

Libby closed her eyes, clutched at Ava and the pup, holding them in a sort of backward hug, and waiting—waiting for the stallion to make up his mind.

Had Pablo's heart pounded like this?

Or had death come too swiftly for fear to take hold?

"Come on, now, horse," Austin said mildly, backing farther out of the path of freedom. "You come on now."

The stud took one step toward the gate, then another.

Quivered again, from behind his ears, laid sideways now, all the way to his flanks and down his haunches.

Then, with breath-stopping suddenness, the enormous and terrifyingly beautiful beast kicked out his hind legs, high and hard, missing Tate by inches.

And bolted and ran.

Cowboys stayed clear, though one rider opened a series of corral gates, clearing the way to the range beyond, the hills beyond that.

Tate finally let out his breath, turned around to look into Libby's eyes.

Ava set Ambrose on the ground, and he promptly fled.

"Daddy," she whispered, as Tate hooked an arm around her, lifted her and held her tightly against his side. She buried her face in his neck, sobbing.

Tate's gaze was riveted to Libby's.

"I love you," she said. "Maybe this isn't the right time to say so, but I do. I have choices. I can go away or I can stay here, and this is where I want to be. I really, truly, forever *love you,* Tate McKettrick."

The white flash of his grin made a dazzling contrast to his unshaven face and the stud-pen dust embedded in his skin and lightening his hair.

"I'll be damned," he said, throwing back his head, giving a whoop of joyous laughter.

"Hardly romantic," Libby said, pretending to be indignant.

"I'm saving the romantic stuff for when we're by ourselves," he answered.

Austin handed off the rifle to another cowboy and took Ava from Tate. She clung for a moment, then attached herself to her uncle.

"Where is Audrey?" Libby asked.

"Rehearsing for the Pixie Pageant," Tate answered, taking her hand.

Hildie was still shut up in the Impala, crazy to get out.

Tate opened the door for her, and promptly hoisted her into the backseat of his truck. He did the same with Libby.

"What about Ava?"

"She'll be fine with Austin and Esperanza," Tate answered, getting behind the wheel and starting up the big engine.

They drove to the other house.

Not a contractor in sight.

Tate lifted Hildie to the ground, and she immediately settled under a shade tree, the picture of canine contentment.

Progress had been made on the inside of the house—the kitchen was coming together, boasting granite countertops, glass-fronted cupboards and travertine tile floors.

There was still no furniture, but the shower in the master bath was working fine, and a sizable blow-up mattress stood in the center of the largest bedroom.

Tate opened the etched-glass shower door, reached in to turn the brass spigots.

Water shot, like a hard rain, from the matching showerhead, which looked as though it was roughly the same diameter as a manhole cover.

When Tate was satisfied with the temperature of the water, he tugged Libby closer, hooked a finger in the neckline of her T-shirt.

"I love you, Libby," he said gruffly. "I mean to spend the rest of my life proving that to you but, for now, it'll have to be sex."

"Oh, no," Libby joked, kicking off her shoes, unfastening her jeans, wriggling out of them.

Tate laughed, pulled her close.

They began to kiss.

And undress each other.

And the water from the big brass showerhead poured down over both of them, washing away the worst of the dust.

Washing away, it seemed, the mistakes and the heartbreaks and the disappointments of the past.

The foreplay was brief; they were both too desperate for contact to drag things out. Tate teased Libby to the absolute verge of a climax, then took her against the slick wall of the shower, the first thrust as hard and deep as the last.

Long minutes later, they both erupted, mouths locked together, tongues sparring, shouts of release ricocheting from one to the other.

They sank to the floor of the shower when it was over, leaning into each other for support.

"Will you marry me, Libby?" Tate asked, both of them kneeling under the fall of water. "Please?"

She nodded, traced his jaw with the tip of one finger, tasted his mouth. "Yes," she said. "I want a big wedding, on New Year's Eve." She nibbled at his lower lip. "In the meantime, though," she said, caressing him intimately, loving the way he groaned—and grew—in response, "let's keep working on sex until we get really, really good at it."

Tate gasped. "We're—pretty—good at it now."

Libby kissed him. "Practice makes perfect," she said.

September...

"YOU LOOK LIKE a princess in that sparkly blue dress," Ava said, a mite wistfully, as she and Libby made their way backstage at the Pixie Pageant, just a few steps behind Tate.

Libby smiled, squeezed the little girl against her side. "Thank you, sweetheart," she said. "You're not unlike royalty yourself, as it happens."

Up ahead, she saw Tate lean down to catch Audrey up in his arms. Libby's heart clenched with love as he straightened, this man she would marry on New Year's Eve.

They caught up, Libby and Ava; the four of them were together.

After tearful explanations over the phone, Cheryl had sent an impressive bouquet from New York; she was working on a big case and hadn't been able to get home for the pageant.

She and Libby emailed each other fairly regularly, always about the girls. Libby took a lot of pictures, uploaded them and sent them to Cheryl.

"I lost," Audrey announced cheerfully, as Tate set her back on her feet.

"Nobody wins all the time," Ava said consolingly.

Audrey shrugged. "It was fun," she said, "but I'm ready to move on."

Libby and Tate exchanged smiles at that.

"Could we get pizza?" Audrey asked her dad.

"Yep," Tate said. "We can get pizza."

They stopped on the way home, picked up the steamy, fragrant boxes—Hawaiian with extra cheese. Back at the house, Hildie, Ambrose and Buford greeted them with a lot of barking and jumping around.

The meal was happy cacophony, around their kitchen table. Audrey was still wearing her tutu, leotard and full stage makeup.

"So," Ava asked her twin, with real interest, "what are you going to do next, now that you're not into beauty pageants anymore?"

Audrey gave the question due consideration, even though it

was clear to Libby that she'd already made up her mind. "Rodeo," she said.

"Rodeo?" Ava echoed.

Tate put down his second slice of pizza and opened his mouth to speak.

Libby laid a hand on his arm.

"Barrel racing, I think," Audrey went on.

"I want to do that, too!" Ava decided.

"Mom won't like it," Audrey warned. "Not unless we get to be rodeo queens."

Libby hid a smile behind a paper napkin.

"Barrel racing," Tate repeated, after clearing his throat.

"We'll need lessons," Ava said, ever practical.

Tate caught Libby's eye. *Help,* his expression said.

"You'll be fantastic," Libby told the girls. "You're McKettricks—rodeo is in your blood."

Tate gave her a *This isn't helping* look.

"Can we call Mom and tell her we're going to be barrel racers?" Audrey asked excitedly.

"Yeah, can we?" Ava chimed in.

"Go," Tate said.

They raced to the cordless phone on the kitchen counter, and Ava got there first.

"Don't you dare dial Mom's number," Audrey cried, "until I have the phone from Dad and Libby's bedroom!"

"Thanks for jumping right in there and taking my side," Tate told Libby, a wry grin tilting his mouth up on one side. But he took her hand, moved the big diamond in her engagement ring back and forth with the pad of his thumb a couple of times, and then kissed her palm, sending fire shooting through her.

"Don't do that," Libby whispered.

An impish twinkle lit Tate's wonderfully blue eyes. Where he'd been kissing, he flicked his tongue.

Libby groaned.

He laughed, tugged her onto his lap. Nibbled at her earring.

"You look hot in that dress," he murmured.

"Like a princess, I'm told," Libby said.

"You'll look even hotter when I get you out of it, of course."

She blushed. "Tate."

He slipped a finger under her low neckline, inside her bra, found her nipple. Grinned. "Do we have to wait until New Year's to get married?" he asked, his voice a low rumble, his gaze fixed on her mouth.

Libby removed his hand, afraid the girls would come back. "Yes," she said. "We have to wait until New Year's. Why?"

"Because I want to make a baby with you."

He kissed her, long and deep.

She forgot they were in the kitchen.

"You'll want to get it right, naturally," she whispered.

"Absolutely," he responded. "And that means we need to keep right on practicing."

They kissed until the twins burst into the room again.

"Mom says we *cannot, under any circumstances,* take up barrel racing!" Audrey announced.

"Does she, now?" Tate asked. He didn't move Libby off his lap, or even stop kissing her, really.

Ava heaved a big sigh. "Come on, Audrey. Let's go watch TV."

"Yeah," Audrey agreed.

"They're practicing again," Ava said.

Audrey nodded. "And that's so boring," she replied.

They vanished into the living room.

"Boring?" Libby asked, against Tate's mouth. "I don't *think* so."

* * * * *

McKettricks Of Texas: Garrett

Dear Reader,

Welcome back to Blue River, Texas—home of the McKettricks!

Garrett is the second brother, and the second book, in this trilogy about modern-day McKettrick men. These three Texas-bred brothers—Tate, Garrett and Austin—meet their matches in the Remington sisters. Political troubleshooter Garrett and drama teacher Julie are as different as two people can be, but opposites have a way of attracting!

These stories give me a chance to bring together some of my favorite things: Western settings, cowboys and ranches, romance... Not to mention kids and animals!

Speaking of animals, I want to make my usual plug for them. My cats, dogs and horses have always been an important part of my life, and I'm sure the same is true for you. Let's make sure every pet is a wanted pet; spay and neuter—and encourage others to be equally responsible. Animals bring so much love into our world, and we owe them the best care we can give them in return.

Please visit my website, lindalaelmiller.com, for information on upcoming books, contests, my (almost) daily blog and more. And please feel free to leave your own comments!

Now, saddle up, and let's head out to Blue River, where the sky is endless and the land seems to go on forever. The people in this friendly town invite you to join them for a visit...

With love,

For Jeremy Hargis
with love

CHAPTER ONE

GARRETT MCKETTRICK WANTED a horse under him—a fleet cow pony like the ones bred to work the herds on the Silver Spur Ranch. But for now, anyway, the Porsche would have to do.

Because of the hour—it was a little after 3:00 a.m.—Garrett had that particular stretch of Texas highway all to himself. The moon and stars cast silvery shadows through the open sunroof and shimmered on the rolled-up sleeves of his white dress shirt, while a country oldie, with lots of twang, pounded from the sound system. Everything in him—from the nuclei of his cells outward—vibrated to the beat.

He'd left the tuxedo jacket, the cummerbund, the tie, the fancy cuff links, back in Austin—right along with one or two of his most cherished illusions.

The party was definitely over—for him, anyhow.

He should have seen it coming—or at least listened to people who *did* see it coming, specifically his brothers, Tate and Austin. They'd done their best to warn him.

Senator Morgan Cox, they'd said, in so many words and in their different ways, wasn't what he seemed.

Against his will, Garrett's mind looped back a few hours, and even as he sped along that straight, dark ribbon of road, another part of him relived the shock in excruciating detail.

Cox had always presented himself as a family man, in public

and private. A corner of each of his hand-carved antique desks in both the Austin and Washington offices supported a small forest of framed photos—himself and Nan on their wedding day, himself and Nan and the first crop of kids, himself and Nan and *more* kids, some of whom were adopted and had special needs. Altogether, there were nine Cox offspring.

The dogs—several generations of golden retrievers, all rescued, of course—were pictured as well.

That night, with no warning at all, Garrett's longtime boss and mentor had arrived at an important fundraiser, held in a glittering hotel ballroom, but not with Nan on his arm—elegant, articulate, wholesome Nan, with her own pedigree as a former Texas governor's daughter. Oh, no. This powerful U.S. senator, a war hero, a man with what many people considered a straight shot at the White House, had instead escorted a classic bimbo, later identified as a twenty-two-year-old pole dancer who went by the unlikely name of Mandy Chante.

Before God, his amazed supporters, the press and, worst of all, Nan, the senator proceeded to announce that he and Mandy were soul mates. Kindred spirits. They'd been lovers in a dozen other lifetimes, he rhapsodized. In short, Cox explained from the microphone on the dais—his lover hovering earnestly beside him in a long, form-fitting dress rippling with ice-blue sequins, which gave her the look of a mermaid with feet—he hoped everyone would understand.

He had to follow his heart.

If only the senator's *heart* were the organ he was following, Garrett lamented silently.

One of those freeze-frame silences followed, vast and uncomfortable, turning the whole assembly into a garden of stone statues while several hundred people tried to process what they'd just heard Cox say.

Who *was* this guy, they were probably asking themselves, and what had he done with the Morgan Cox they all knew? Where, Garrett himself wondered, was the man who had given that stirring eulogy at the double funeral after Jim and Sally McKettrick, his folks, were killed a decade before?

The mass paralysis following Morgan's proclamation lasted only a few seconds, and Garrett was quick to shake it off. Automatically, he scanned the room for Nan Cox—his late mother's college roommate—and found her standing near the grand piano, alone.

Most likely, Nan, a veteran political wife, had been in transit between one conversational cluster and another when her husband dropped the bombshell. She was still smiling, in fact, and the effect was eerie, even surreal.

Like the true lady she was, however, Nan immediately drew herself up, made her way through friends and strangers, enemies and intimate confidants to step up to Garrett's side, link her arm with his and whisper, "Get him out of here, Garrett. Get Morgan out of here *now*, before this gets any worse."

Garrett glanced at the senator, who ignored his wife of more than three decades, the mother of his children, the flesh-and-blood, hurting woman he had just humiliated in a very public way, to gaze lovingly into the upturned face of his mistress. The mermaid's plump, glistening lower lip jutted out in a pout.

Cox patted the young woman's hand reassuringly then, acting as though *she*, not Nan, might have been traumatized.

The cameras came out, amateur and professional; a blinding dazzle surrounded the happy couple. Within a couple of minutes, some of that attention would surely shift to Nan.

"I'm getting *you* away first," Garrett told Nan, using his right arm to lock her against his side and starting for the nearest way out. As the senator's aide, Garrett had a lot of experience at running interference, and he always scoped out every exit in every venue in advance, just in case. Even the familiar ones, like that hotel, which happened to be the senator's favorite.

Nan didn't argue—not then, anyway. She kept up with Garrett, offered no protest when he hustled her through a corridor crowded with carts and waitstaff, then into a service elevator.

Garrett flipped open his cell phone and speed-dialed a number as they descended, Nan leaning against the elevator wall now, looking down at her feet, stricken to silence. Her beautifully coiffed silver hair gleamed in the fluorescent light.

The senator's personal driver, Troy, answered on the first ring, his tone cheerful. "Garrett? What's up, man?"

"Bring the car around to the back of the hotel," Garrett said. "And hurry."

Nan looked up, met Garrett's gaze. She was pale, and her eyes looked haunted, but the smile resting on her mouth was real, if slight. "You're probably scaring poor Troy to death," she scolded, putting a hand out for the cell phone.

Garrett handed it over just as they reached the ground floor, and Nan spoke efficiently into the mouthpiece.

"Troy? This is Mrs. Cox. Just so you know, there's no fire, and nobody's been shot or had a heart attack. But it probably *is* a good idea for me to leave the building, so be a dear and pick me up behind the hotel." A pause. "Oh, you are? Perfect. I'll explain in the car. Meanwhile, here's Garrett again."

With that, she handed the phone back to Garrett.

When he put it to his ear, he heard Troy suck in a nervous breath. "I'm outside the kitchen door, buddy," he said. "I'll take Mrs. Cox home and come straight back, in case you need some help."

"Excellent idea," Garrett said, as the elevator doors opened into the institution-sized kitchen.

The senator's wife smiled and nodded to a bevy of surprised kitchen workers as she and Garrett headed for the outside door.

True to his word, Troy was waiting in back, the rear passenger-side door of the sedan already open for Mrs. Cox.

He and Garrett exchanged glances as Nan slipped into the backseat, but neither of them spoke.

Troy closed her door, but she immediately lowered the window.

"My husband needs your help," she told Garrett quietly but firmly. "This is no time to judge him—there will be enough of that in the media."

"Yes, ma'am," Garrett answered.

Troy climbed behind the wheel again, and Garrett was already heading back through the kitchen door when they pulled away.

He strode to the service elevator, pushed the button and waited until it lumbered down from some upper floor.

When the doors slid open, there were the senator and the bimbo.

The senator blinked when he saw Garrett. He looked older somehow, and he was wearing his glasses. "*There* you are," he said. "I was wondering where you'd gotten to, young McKettrick. Nan, too. Have you seen my wife?"

Nan's remark, spoken only a minute or two before, echoed in Garrett's mind.

My husband needs your help.

And juxtaposed to that, the senator's oddly solicitous, *Have you seen my wife?*

Garrett made an attempt at a smile, but it felt like a grimace instead. He narrowed his eyes slightly, shot a glance at the mermaid and then faced the senator again. "Mrs. Cox is on her way home, sir," he said.

"I imagine she was upset," Cox replied, looking both regretful and detached.

"She's a lady, sir," Garrett answered evenly. "And she's behaving like one."

Cox gave a fond chuckle and nodded. "First, last and always, Nan is a lady," he agreed.

Beside him, the mermaid seethed, clinging a little more tightly to the senator's arm and glaring at Garrett.

Garrett glared right back. This woman, he decided, was no mermaid, and no lady, either. She was a barracuda.

"It would seem I haven't chosen the best time to break our news to the world, my dear," the senator said, patting his beloved's bejeweled and manicured hand in the same devoted way he'd done upstairs. "I probably should have told Nan in private."

Ya think? Garrett asked silently.

"You work for Senator Cox," said the barracuda, turning to Garrett, "*not* his wife. Why did you just go off and leave us—him—*stranded* like that? The reporters—"

Garrett folded his arms and waited.

"It was awful!" blurted the barracuda.

What had the woman expected? Champagne all around? Congratulatory kisses and handshakes? A romantic waltz with the senator while the orchestra played "Moon River"?

"Luckily," the senator told Garrett affably, as though there had been no outburst from the sequined contingent, "I remembered how often you and I had discussed security measures, and Mandy and I were able to slip away and find the nearest service elevator."

The corridor seemed to be closing in on Garrett. He undid his string tie and opened the top three buttons of his shirt. "Mandy?" he asked.

The senator laughed warmly. "Mandy Chante," he said, "meet Garrett McKettrick, my right-hand man."

"Mandy Chante," Garrett repeated, with no inflection at all.

Mandy's eyes blazed. "What are we supposed to do now?" she demanded.

"I guess that depends on the senator's wishes," Garrett said mildly. "Will you be going home to the ranch tonight, sir, or staying in town?"

Or maybe I could just drop you off at the nearest E.R. for psychiatric evaluation.

"I'm sure Nan will be at the condo," the senator mused. "Our showing up there could be awkward."

Awkward. Yes, indeed, Senator, that would be awkward.

Garrett cleared his throat. "Could I speak to you alone for a moment, sir?" he asked.

Mandy, with one arm already resting in the crook of the senator's elbow, intertwined the fingers of both hands to get a double grip. "Pooky and I have no secrets from each other," she said.

Pooky?

Garrett's stomach did a slow roll.

"Now, now, dear," Cox told Mandy, gently freeing himself from her physical hold, at least. "Garrett means well, and you mustn't feel threatened." Addressing Garrett next, the older man added, "This is not a good time for a discussion. I'd rather not leave Mandy standing alone in this corridor."

"Sir—"

"Tomorrow, Garrett," the senator said. "You and I will discuss this tomorrow, in my office."

Garrett merely nodded, clamping his back teeth together.

"It's weird down here," Mandy complained, looking around. "Weird and spooky. Couldn't we get a suite or something?"

"That's a fine idea," Cox replied ebulliently. There was more hand-patting, and then the senator turned to face Garrett again. "You'll take care of that for us, won't you, Garrett? Book a suite upstairs, I mean? Under your own name, of course, and not mine."

"Sure," Garrett answered wearily, thinking of Nan and the many kids and the faithful golden retrievers. Pointing out to his employer that nobody would be fooled by the suite-booking gambit would probably be futile.

"Good," the senator said, satisfied.

"Do we have to wait here while he gets us a room, Pooky?" Mandy whined. "I don't like this place. It's like a cellar or something."

Cox smiled at her, and his tone was soothing. "The press will be watching the lobby for us," he said reasonably. "And we won't have to wait long, because Garrett will be quick. Won't you, Garrett?"

Bile scalded the back of Garrett's throat. "I'll be quick," he answered.

That was when he started wanting the horse under him. He wanted to hear hooves pounding over hard ground and breathe the clean, uncomplicated air of home.

Duty first.

He went upstairs, arranged for comfortable quarters at the reception desk, and called the senator's personal cell phone when he had a room number to give him.

"Here's Troy, back again," the senator said on the other end of the call, sounding pleased. "I'm sure he wouldn't mind escorting us up there. If you'd just get us some ice before you leave, Garrett—"

Garrett closed his eyes, refrained from pointing out that he wasn't a bellman, or a room service waiter. "Yes, sir," he said.

Fifteen minutes later, he and Troy descended together, in yet another service elevator. For a black man, Troy looked pale.

"Is he *serious*?" Troy asked.

Garrett sighed deeply, looking up and watching the digital numbers over the doors as they plunged. His tie was dangling; he tugged it loose from his shirt collar and stuffed it into the pocket of his tuxedo jacket. "It would seem so," he said.

"Mrs. Cox says the senator is having a mental breakdown, and we all have to stick by him," Troy said glumly, shaking his head. "She's sure he'll come to his senses and everything will be fine."

"Right," Garrett said, grimly distracted. He'd sprint around to the side parking lot once he and Troy were outside, climb into his

Porsche, and head for home. In two hours, he could be back on the Silver Spur.

They were standing in the alley again when Troy asked, "Why do I get the feeling that this comes as a surprise to you?"

The question threw Garrett, at least momentarily, and he didn't answer.

Troy thumbed the fob on his key ring, and the sedan started up. "Get in, and I'll give you a lift to your car," he told Garrett, with a sigh.

Garrett got into the sedan. "You knew about Mandy and the senator?" he asked.

Troy shook his head again and gave a raspy chuckle. "Hell, Garrett," he said, "I drive the man's car. He's been seeing her for months."

Garrett closed his eyes. Tate had accused him once of having his head up his ass, as far as the senator's true nature was concerned. And he'd defended Morgan Cox, been ready to fight his own brother to defend the bastard's honor.

"What about Nan? Did she know, too?" Remembering the expression on her face earlier, in the ballroom, Garrett didn't think so.

"Maybe," Troy said. "She didn't hear it from me, though."

He drew the sedan to a stop behind Garrett's Porsche. News vans were pulling out on the other end of the lot, along with a stream of ordinary cars.

Film clips and sound bites were probably already running on the local channels.

Turn out the lights, Garrett thought dismally. The party's over.

The senator not only wouldn't be getting the presidential nomination, he'd be lucky if he wasn't forced to resign before he'd finished his current term in office.

All of which left Garrett himself up Shit's Creek, without a paddle.

He got out of the sedan and said good-night to Troy.

After his friend had driven away, Garrett climbed into the Porsche.

He made a brief stop at his town house, swapping the formal duds for jeans, a Western shirt and old boots. Once he'd changed, he could breathe a little better.

Returning to the kitchen, he turned on the countertop TV, flipping between the networks, watching in despair as one station after another showed Senator Cox and Mandy slipping out of the ballroom, arm in arm.

Deciding he'd seen enough, Garrett turned off the set.

NOW, NEARLY TWO hours later, only about a mile outside of Blue River, Garrett sped on toward home, the word *fool* drumming in his brain. He was stone sober, though a part of him wished he were otherwise, when the dazzle of red and blue lights splashed across his rearview mirror.

Garrett swore under his breath, downshifted—Fifth to Fourth to Third to Second, finally rolling to a stop at the side of the road. There, without shutting off the ignition, he waited.

He buzzed down the passenger-side window just as Brent Brogan, chief of police, was about to rap on the glass with his knuckles.

"Are out of your freakin' *mind*?" his brother's best friend demanded, bending to peer through the opening. Brogan's badge caught a flash of moonlight. "I clocked you at almost one-twenty back there!"

Garrett tensed his hands on the steering wheel, relaxed them without releasing his hold. "Sorry," he said, gazing straight ahead, through the bug-splattered windshield, instead of meeting Brogan's gaze. Tate had dubbed the chief "Denzel," since he resembled the actor's younger self, and used the nickname freely, especially when the moment called for a little lightening up—but Garrett wasn't on such easy terms with Brent Brogan as his brother was.

"You're sorry?" Brogan asked, in a mocking drawl. "Well, that's another matter, then. Garrett McKettrick is *sorry.* That just makes all the difference in the world, and pardon me for pulling you over before you killed yourself or somebody else."

Garrett thrust out a sigh. "Write the ticket," he said.

"I ought to arrest you," Brogan said, and he sounded like he was musing on the possibility, giving it real consideration. "That's what I ought to do. Throw your ass in jail."

"Fine," Garrett said, resigned. "Throw me in jail."

Brent opened the passenger door and folded himself into the

seat, keeping his right leg outside the car. He was a big man, taller than Garrett and broader through the shoulders, and that made the quarters feel a mite too close. "There's no elbow room in this rig," Brogan remarked. "Why don't you get yourself a truck?"

Garrett gave a harsh guffaw, with no humor in it. Shoved his right hand through his hair and waited, too stubborn to answer.

It was the chief's turn to sigh. "Look, Garrett," he said, "I know you—you're not drinking and you're not high. Of all the people I might have pulled over tonight, shooting along this road like a bullet headed for the bull's-eye, you've got more reason to know better than most."

The old ache rose inside Garrett, lodged in his throat.

He closed his eyes, trying to block the images, but he couldn't. He heard the screech of tires grabbing at asphalt, the grinding crash of metal careening into metal, even the ludicrously musical splintering of glass. He hadn't been there the night his mom and dad were killed in a horrendous collision with an out-of-control semi, but the sounds and the pictures in his mind were so vivid, he might as well have been.

For the millionth time since the accident, a full decade in the past now, Garrett tried to come to terms with the loss of his parents. For the millionth time, it didn't happen.

What would he have given to have them both waiting at the ranch house, just like in the old days?

Just about anything.

"You fixing to tell me what's the matter?" Brogan asked, when a long time had passed. "I'm on duty until eight o'clock tomorrow morning, when Deputy Osburt relieves me. I can sit here and wait till hell freezes over *and* till the cows come home, if that's what I have to do."

Garrett assessed the situation. Dawn was hours away. The September darkness was weighted with heat, and with Brogan holding the Porsche's door open like that, the air-conditioning system was of negligible value. He tightened his fingers around the steering wheel again, hard enough to make his knuckles ache.

"I had a bad day, that's all," he said. *And a worse night.*

Brogan laid a hand on his shoulder. "You headed for the Silver Spur?"

Garrett nodded, swallowed. He could feel the pull of home, deep inside; he was drawn to it.

"I'm going to follow you as far as the main gate," Brogan said, after more pondering. "Make sure you get home in one piece."

Garrett looked at him. "Thanks," he said, without much inflection.

Brogan got out of the Porsche, shut the door, bent to look through the open window again. "Meantime, keep your foot light on the pedal," he warned. "About the last thing on this earth I want to do right now is roust your big brother from his bed and break the news that you just wrapped yourself around a telephone pole."

Tate was only a year older than he was, Garrett reflected, and they were about the same height and weight. So why did "big" have to preface "brother"? He was pretty sure nobody referred to him as *Austin's* "big brother," though he had a year on the youngest member of the family, along with a couple of inches and a good twenty pounds.

Garrett waited until Brogan was back in his cruiser before pulling back out onto the highway. The town of Blue River slept just up ahead; the streetlights tripped on, one by one, as he passed beneath them.

At this time of night, even the bars were closed.

As Garrett drove, with his one-man police escort trailing behind him, he thought about Tate, probably spooned up with his pretty fiancée, Libby Remington, in the modest house by the bend in the creek, and felt a brief but bitter stab of envy.

They were happy, those two. So crazy in love that the air around them seemed to buzz with pheromones. Tate and Libby were planning the mother of all weddings for New Year's Eve, following that up with a honeymoon cruise in the Greek Islands. The sooner they could give Tate's six-year-old twin daughters, Audrey and Ava, a baby brother or sister, they figured, the better.

Garrett calculated he'd be an uncle again about nine months and five minutes after the wedding ceremony was over.

The thought made him smile, in spite of everything.

The countryside slipped by.

At the main gates opening onto the Silver Spur, Brogan flashed his headlights once, turned the cruiser back toward town and drove off.

Pushing a button on his dashboard, Garrett watched as the tall iron gates, emblazoned with the name *McKettrick*, swung open to admit him.

Home, he reflected, as he drove through and up the long driveway leading toward the house. The place where they have to take you in.

HOW DID ANYBODY manage to sleep in this huge place? Julie Remington wondered, as she flipped on the lights in the daunting kitchen of the main ranch house on the Silver Spur Ranch. She and her four-going-on-five-year-old son, Calvin, along with their beagle, Harry, had been staying in the first-floor guest suite for nearly a week because there were termites at their rented cottage in town and the whole structure was under a tent.

Taking her private stash of herbal tea bags from a cupboard, along with a mug one of her high school drama students had given her for Christmas the year before, Julie set about brewing herself a cup of chamomile tea.

Coffee would probably have made more sense, she thought, pumping hot water from the special spigot by the largest of several sinks, since it would be morning soon, but she still had hopes of catching a few winks before the day began in earnest.

She had just turned, cup in hand, planning to head back to bed, when the door leading into the garage suddenly opened.

Julie nearly spilled the tea down the front of her ratty purple quilted bathrobe, she was so startled.

Garrett McKettrick paused just over the threshold, and she knew by the pensive look in his eyes that he was wondering what she was doing in his kitchen.

She was unprepared for the grin breaking over his handsome face, dispelling the strain she'd glimpsed there only a moment before.

"Hey," he said, shutting the door behind him, tossing a set of keys onto a granite countertop.

"Hey," Julie said back, wondering if he'd remembered her yet.

She crossed the room, put out her free hand for him to shake. "Julie Remington," she reminded him.

He laughed. "I *know* who you are," he replied. "We grew up together, remember? Not to mention a more recent encounter at Pablo Ruiz's funeral."

A trained actress, Julie was playing the part of a woman who didn't feel self-conscious standing in someone else's kitchen in the middle of the night, drinking tea and wearing an old bathrobe. Or *trying* to play the part, anyhow.

It was proving difficult to carry off. Especially after she blew her next line. "I just thought—with all the people you must know—"

All the women you must know...

Garrett's eyes were that legendary shade of McKettrick blue, a combination of summer sky, new denim and cornflower, and solemn as they regarded her.

Julie's heart took up a thrumming rhythm. "I suppose you're wondering what I'm doing here," she prattled on.

What was *wrong* with her? It wasn't as if she'd been caught breaking and entering, after all. Tate had practically insisted that she and Calvin move into the mansion, instead of taking a motel room or making some other arrangement, while the cottage was being pumped full of noxious chemicals.

One corner of Garrett's mouth tilted up in a grin, and he walked over to the first of a row of built-in refrigerators, pulled open the door and assessed the contents.

"Actually," he said, without turning around, "I wasn't wondering that at all."

Julie, who was not easily rattled, blushed. "Oh."

He plundered the refrigerator for a while.

"Well," Julie said, too brightly, "good night, then."

Holding a storage container full of Julie's special chicken lasagna, left over from supper, Garrett faced her, shouldering the refrigerator door shut in the same motion. "Or good morning," he said, "depending on your viewpoint."

"It's barely four," Julie remarked.

Garrett stuck the container into the microwave, pushed a few buttons.

"Don't!" Julie cried, rushing past him to rescue the dish. "This kind of plastic melts if you nuke it—"

He arched an eyebrow. "I'll be damned," he said. Then, while Julie busied herself transferring the contents of the container onto a microwave-safe plate, he added, "Are your eyes really lavender, or am I seeing things?"

The question flustered Julie. "It's the bathrobe," she said, as the microwave whirred away, heating up the lasagna.

"The bathrobe?" Garrett asked, sounding confused. He was standing in Julie's space; she knew that even though she couldn't bring herself to look directly at him again, which was stupid, because just as he'd said, Blue River was home to both of them. They'd gone to the same schools and the same church growing up. And with their siblings engaged, they were practically family.

Julie, who never blushed, blushed again, and so hard that her cheeks burned. She was really losing it, she decided.

"My—my eyes are actually hazel," she said, "and they take on the color of whatever I'm wearing. And since the bathrobe is purple—"

As soon as the words were out of her mouth, Julie bit down on her lower lip. Why couldn't she just *shut up*?

Mercifully, Garrett didn't comment. He just stood there at the counter, waiting for the microwave to finish warming up the left-over lasagna.

"Mom?" Calvin padded into the kitchen, blinking owlishly behind the lenses of his glasses. He wore cotton pajamas and his feet were bare. "Is it time to get up? It's still dark outside, isn't it?"

Julie felt the usual rush of motherly love, and an undercurrent of fear as well. Recently, Calvin's biological father had been making overtures about "reconnecting" with their son and, although he'd paid child support all along, Gordon Pruett was a total stranger to the boy.

"Go back to bed, sweetheart," she said gently. "You don't have to get up yet."

The dog, Harry, appeared at Calvin's side. The adopted beagle was surprisingly nimble, although he'd been born one leg short of the requisite four.

Calvin's attention shifted to Garrett, who was just sitting down at the table, the plate of lasagna in front of him.

"Hello," Calvin said.

Harry began to wag his tail, though Julie figured the dog was at least as interested in the Italian casserole as he was in Garrett, if not more so.

"Hey," Garrett responded.

"You're Audrey and Ava's uncle, aren't you?" Calvin asked. "The one who gave them a real castle for their birthday?"

Garrett chuckled. Jabbed a fork into the food. "Yep, that's me."

"It's at the community center now," Calvin said, drawing a little closer, not to his mother, but to Garrett. "The castle, I mean."

"Probably a good place for it," Garrett said. "You want some of this pasta stuff? It's pretty good."

Unaccountably, Julie bristled. *Pasta stuff? Pretty good?* It was an original recipe, and she'd won a prize for it at the state fair the year before.

Calvin reached the table, hauled back a chair and scrambled into it. With a jab of his right index finger, he pushed his glasses back up his nose. His blond hair stuck out in myriad directions, and his expression was so earnest as he studied Garrett that Julie's heart ached a little. "No, thanks," the little boy said solemnly. "We had it for supper and, anyway, Mom makes it all the time."

Garrett looked up at Julie, smiled slightly and turned his full attention back to Calvin. "Your mom's a good cook," he said.

Harry advanced and brushed up against Garrett, leaving white beagle hairs all over the leg of his jeans. Garrett chuckled and greeted Harry with a pat on the head and a quiet "Hey, dog."

"Calvin," Julie interceded, "we should get back to bed and leave Mr. McKettrick to enjoy his...breakfast."

Garrett's eyes, though weary, seemed to dance when he looked up at Julie. "'Mr. McKettrick'?" he echoed. His gaze swung back to Calvin. "Do you call my brother Tate 'Mr. McKettrick'?" he asked.

Calvin shook his head. "I call him Tate. He's going to marry my aunt Libby on New Year's Eve, and he'll be my uncle after that."

A nod from Garrett. "I guess he will. I will be, too, sort of. So maybe you ought to call me Garrett."

The child beamed. "I'm Calvin," he said, "and this is my dog, Harry."

And he put out his little hand, much as Julie had done earlier.

They shook on the introduction, man and boy.

"Mighty glad to meet the both of you," Garrett said.

CHAPTER TWO

THE COMBINATION OF a fiercely blue autumn sky, oak leaves turning to bright yellow in the trees edging the sun-dappled creek and
the heart-piercing love she felt for her little boy made Julie ache
over the bittersweet perfection of the present moment.

She turned the pink Cadillac onto the winding dirt road leading to the old Ruiz house, where Tate and Libby and Tate's twin
daughters were living, and glanced into the rearview mirror.

Calvin sat stoically in his car seat in back, staring out the window.

Since Julie had to be at work at Blue River High School a full
hour before Calvin's kindergarten class began, she'd been dropping him off at Libby's on her way to town over the week they'd
been staying on the Silver Spur. He adored his aunt, and Tate, and
Tate's girls, Audrey and Ava, who were two years older than Calvin and thus, in his opinion, sophisticated women of the world.
Today, though, he was just too quiet.

"Everything okay, buddy?" Julie asked, tooting the Caddie's
horn in greeting as her sister Libby appeared on the front porch of
the house she and Tate were renovating and started down the steps.

"I guess we'll have to move back to town when the bugs are
gone from our cottage and they take down the tent," he said. "We
won't get to live in the country anymore."

"That was always the plan," Julie reminded her son gently.

"That we'd go back to the cottage when it's safe." Recently, she'd considered offering to buy the small but charming house she'd been renting from month to month since Calvin was a baby and making it their permanent home. Thanks to a windfall, she had the means, but this morning the idea lacked its usual appeal.

Calvin suffered from intermittent asthma attacks, though he hadn't had an incident for a long time. Suppose some vestige of the toxins used to eliminate termites lingered after the tenting process was finished, and damaged his health—or her own—in some insidious way?

While Julie was trying to shake off *that* semiparanoid idea, Libby started across the grassy lawn toward the car, grinning and waving one hand in welcome. She wore jeans and a navy blue sweatshirt and white sneakers, and she'd clipped her shiny light brown hair up on top of her head.

A year older than Julie, Libby had always been strikingly pretty, but since she and Tate McKettrick, her one-time high school sweetheart, had rediscovered each other just that summer, she'd been downright beautiful. Libby glowed, incandescent with love and from being thoroughly loved in return.

Julie pushed the button to lower the back window on the other side of the car, smiling with genuine affection for her sister even as she felt a brief but poignant stab of stark jealousy.

What would it be like to be loved—no, cherished—by a full-grown, committed man like Tate? It was an experience Julie had long-since given up on, for herself, anyway. She was independent and capable, and of course she had no desire to be otherwise, but it would have been nice, once in a while, not to have to be strong every minute of every day and night, not to blaze *all* the trails and fight *all* the dragons.

Libby gave Julie a glance before she leaned through the back window to plant a smacking welcome kiss on Calvin's forehead.

"Good morning, Aunt Libby," she coached cheerfully, when Calvin didn't speak to her to right away.

"'Good morning, Aunt Libby,'" Calvin repeated, with a reluctant giggle.

"He's a little moody this morning," Julie said.

"I'm *not* moody," Calvin argued, climbing out of the car to stand beside Libby on the gravel driveway, then reaching inside for his backpack. "I just want to live on a ranch, that's all. I want to have my very own horse, like Audrey and Ava do. Is that too much to ask?"

Julie sighed. "Well, *yeah*, Calvin, it kind of *is* too much to ask."

Calvin didn't say anything more; he merely shook his head and, lugging his backpack, headed off toward the house, his small shoulders stooped.

"What was that all about?" Libby asked, moving around to Julie's side of the car and bending to look in at her.

Julie genuinely didn't have time for a long discussion, but she had always confided in Libby, and now it was virtually automatic, especially when she was upset.

"Maybe I shouldn't have let you and Tate talk me into staying on the Silver Spur," she fretted. "It's only been a week, but Calvin's already too used to living like a McKettrick—riding horses, swimming in that indoor pool, watching movies in a *media room*, for heaven's sake. I can't give him that kind of life, Libby. I'm not even sure I'd want to if I could. What if he's getting spoiled?"

Libby raised an eyebrow. "Take a breath, Jules," she said. "You're dramatizing a little, don't you think? Calvin is a good kid, and it would take a lot more than a week or two of high living at the ranch to spoil him. Both of you are under extra stress—Calvin just started kindergarten, and you're back to teaching full-time, with your house under a tent because of termites—and then there's the whole Gordon thing..." Libby stopped talking, reached through the window to squeeze Julie's shoulder. "The point is— things will even out pretty soon. Just give it time."

Julie worked up a smile, tapped at the face of her watch with one index finger. *Easy for you to say*, she thought, but what she said out loud was, "Gotta go."

Libby nodded and stepped away from the car, raised a hand in farewell. She seemed reluctant to let Julie go, and a worried expression flickered in her blue eyes as she watched her back up, turn around and drive off.

Libby had done her little-girl best to stand in after their mother had abandoned the family years before. She'd given up finishing college and arguably a lot more besides when their dad, Will Remington, was diagnosed with pancreatic cancer. Libby had moved back to Blue River, started the Perk Up Coffee Shop—now reduced to a vacant lot across the alley from the house they'd all grown up in—and looked after their father as his illness progressed.

Of course, Julie had helped with his care as much as possible and so had Paige, but just the same, most of the hard stuff had fallen to Libby. Sure, she was the eldest, but the age difference was minor—they'd been born one right after the other, three children in three years. The truth was, Libby had been willing to make sacrifices Julie and Paige couldn't have managed at the time.

Julie bit down on her lower lip as the town limits came into view, and she began reducing her speed. Their mother, Marva, had reappeared in Blue River months ago, moved into an apartment, and tried, in her own way, to establish some kind of relationship with her daughters. The results had been less than fabulous.

At first, Libby, Julie and Paige had resisted the woman's every overture, but even after deserting them when they were small, breaking their hearts and their father's as well, Marva was blithely convinced that a fresh start was just a matter of letting bygones be bygones.

In time, Julie and Paige had both warmed up to Marva somewhat, Libby less so.

The Cadillac bumped over potholes in the gravel parking lot behind Blue River High. The long, low-slung stucco building had grown up on the site of an old Spanish mission, though only a small part of the original structure remained, serving as a center courtyard. Classrooms, a small cafeteria and a gymnasium had been added over the decades, and during an oil boom in the mid-1930s, Clay McKettrick II, known as JR in that time-honored Southern way of denoting "juniors," had financed the construction of the auditorium, with its two hundred plush theater seats, fine stage and rococo molding around the painted ceiling.

Erected on school property, the auditorium belonged to the entire community. Various civic organizations held their meetings and other events there, and several different denominations had used it as a church on Sunday mornings, while their own buildings were under construction or being renovated.

The auditorium, cool and shadowy and smelling faintly of mildew, had always been a place of almost magical solace for Julie, especially in high school, when she'd had leading roles in so many plays.

Although she'd performed with several professional road companies later on, Julie had never wanted to be an actress and live in glamorous places like New York or Los Angeles. All along, she'd planned on—and worked at—getting her teaching certificate, returning to Blue River and keeping the theater going.

There was no room in the budget for a drama department— the high school theater group supported itself by putting on two productions a year, one of them a musical, and charging modest admission. Like her now-retired predecessor, Miss Idetta Scrobbins, Julie earned her paycheck by teaching English classes—the drama club and the plays they put on were a labor of love.

Julie was thinking about the next project—three one-act plays written by some of her best students—as she hurried down the center aisle and through the doorway to the left of the stage, where she'd transformed an unused supply closet into a sort of hideaway. Officially, her office was her classroom, but it was here that she met with students and came up with some of her best ideas.

Hastily, she tossed her brown-bag lunch into the small refrigerator sitting on top of a file cabinet, kicked off her flat shoes and pulled on the low-heeled pumps she kept stashed in a desk drawer. She flipped on her computer—it was old and took forever to boot up—locked up her purse and raced out of the hideout, back up the aisle and out into the September sunshine.

She was five minutes late for the staff meeting, and Principal Dulles would not be pleased.

Everyone else was already there when Julie dashed into the school library and dropped into a utilitarian folding chair at one of the three long tables where students read and did homework. The library doubled as a study hall throughout the school day.

Up front, the red-faced principal puffed out his cheeks, turning a stub of chalk end over end in one hand, and cleared his throat. Julie's best friend at work, Helen Marcus, gave her a light poke with her elbow and whispered, "Don't worry, you didn't miss anything."

Julie smiled at that, looked around at the half dozen other teachers who were her colleagues. She knew that Dulles, a middle-aged man from far away, made no secret of his opinion that Blue River, Texas, hardly offered more in the way of cultural stimulation than a prairie-dog town would have. He considered her a flake because of her colorful clothing and her penchant for putting on and directing plays.

For all of that, Arthur was a good person.

Like Julie, most of the other members of the staff had been born and raised there. They'd come home to teach after college because they knew Blue River needed them; high pay and job perks weren't a factor, of course. To them, odd breed that they were, the community's kids mattered most.

Dulles cleared his throat, glaring at Julie, who smiled placidly back at him.

"As some of you already know," he began, "the McKettrick Foundation has generously agreed to match whatever funds we can raise on our own to buy new computers and special software for our library. Our share, however, amounts to a considerable sum."

The McKettricks were community-minded; they'd always been quick to lend a hand wherever one was needed, but the foundation's longstanding policy, except in emergencies, was to involve the whole town in raising funds as well. At the name *McKettrick*, Julie felt an odd quickening of some kind, at once disturbing and delicious, thinking back to her encounter with Garrett in the ranch-house kitchen.

The others shifted in their seats, checked their watches and glanced up at the wall clock. Students were beginning to arrive; the ringing slam of locker doors and the lilting hum of their conversation sounded from the wide hallway just outside the library.

Julie waited attentively, sensing that Arthur's speech was mainly directed at her, but unable to imagine why that should be so.

No one spoke.

Arthur seemed reluctant, but he finally went on. He looked straight at Julie, confirming her suspicions. "It's a pity the drama club is staging those three one-act plays for the fall production, instead of doing a musical."

The light went on in Julie's mind. Since the plays were original, and written by high school seniors, turnout at the showcase would probably be limited to proud parents and close friends. The box-office proceeds would therefore be minimal. But the musicals, for which Blue River High was well known, drew audiences from as far away as Austin and San Antonio, and brought in thousands of dollars.

The take from last spring's production of *South Pacific* had been plenty to provide new uniforms for the marching band *and* the football team, with enough left over to fund two hefty scholarships when graduation rolled around.

Arthur continued to stare at Julie, most likely hoping she would save him the embarrassment of strong-arming her by *offering* to postpone or cancel the student showcase to produce a musical instead. Although her first instinct was always to jump right in like some female superhero and offer to take care of everything, today she didn't.

They'd committed, she and Arthur and the school board, to staging *Kiss Me Kate* for this year's spring production—casting and rehearsals would begin after Christmas vacation, with the usual three performances slated for mid-May.

She had enough on her plate already, between Calvin and her job.

The silence grew uncomfortable.

Arthur Dulles finally cleared his throat eloquently. "I'm sure I don't need to remind any of you how important it is, in this day and age, for our students to be computer-savvy."

Still, no one spoke.

"Julie?" Arthur prodded, at last.

"We're doing *Kiss Me Kate* next spring," Julie reminded him.

"Yes," Arthur agreed, sounding weary, "but perhaps we could produce the musical *now*, instead of next spring. That way it would be easy to match the McKettricks' contribution, since our musicals are always so popular."

Our musicals, Julie thought. As if it would be *Arthur* who held tryouts every night for a week, and then two months of rehearsals, weekends included. Arthur who dealt with heartbroken teenage girls who hadn't landed the part of their dreams—not to mention their mothers. Arthur who struggled to round up enough teenage *boys* to balance out the chorus and play the leads.

No, it would be Julie who did all those things.

Julie alone.

"Gosh, Arthur," she said, smiling her team-player smile, "that would be hard to pull off. The showcase will be ready to stage within a month. We'd be lucky to get the musical going by Christmas."

Bob Riza, who coached football, basketball and baseball in their respective seasons, in addition to teaching math, flung a sympathetic glance in Julie's direction and finally spoke up. "Maybe the foundation would be willing to cut us a check for the full amount," he said. "Forget the matching requirement, just this once."

"I don't think that's fair," Julie said.

Arthur folded his arms, still watching her. "I agree," he said. "The McKettricks have been more than generous. Three years ago, you'll all remember, when the creeks overflowed and we had all that flood damage and our insurance only covered the basics, the foundation underwrote a new floor for the gymnasium, in full, and replaced the hundreds of books ruined here and in the public library."

Julie nodded. "Here's the thing, Arthur," she said. "The showcase won't bring in a lot of money, that's true. But it's important—the kids involved are trying to get into very good colleges, and there's a lot of competition. Having their plays produced will make them stand out a little."

Arthur nodded, listening sympathetically, but Julie knew he'd already made up his mind.

"I'm afraid the showcase will have to be moved to spring," he said. "The sooner the musical is under way, the better."

Julie knew she'd lost. So why did she keep fighting? "Spring will be too late for these kids," she said, straightening her spine, hiking up her chin. "The application deadlines are—"

Arthur shook his head, cutting her off. "I'm sorry, Julie," he said.

Julie swallowed. Lowered her eyes.

It wasn't that she didn't appreciate Arthur's position. She knew how important those new computers were—while most of the students had ready access to the internet at home, a significant number of kids depended on the computers at the public library and here at the high school. Technology was changing the world at an almost frightening pace, and Blue River High had to keep up.

Still, she was already spending more time at school than was probably good for Calvin. Launching this project would mean her little boy practically *lived* with Libby and Paige, and while Calvin adored his aunts, *she* was his mother. Her son's happiness and well-being were her responsibility; she couldn't and wouldn't foist him off and farm him out any more than she was doing now.

The first period bell shrilled then, earsplittingly loud, it seemed to Julie. She was due in her tenth-grade English class.

Riza and the others rose from their chairs, clearly anxious to head for their own classrooms.

Julie remained where she was, facing Arthur Dulles. She felt a little like an animal caught in the headlight beams of an oncoming truck, unable to move in any direction.

He smiled. Arthur was not unkind, merely beleaguered. He served as principal of the town's elementary and middle schools as well as Blue River High, and his wife, Dot, was just finishing up a round of chemotherapy.

"It would be a shame if we had to turn down the funding for all that state-of-the-art equipment," Arthur said forthrightly, standing directly in front of Julie now, "wouldn't it?"

Julie suppressed a deep sigh. Her sister was engaged to Tate McKettrick; in his view, that meant Julie was practically a McKettrick herself. Maybe Arthur expected her to hit up the town's most important family for an even fatter check.

"Couldn't we try some other kind of fundraiser?" she asked. "Get the parents to help out, maybe put on some bake sales and a few car washes?"

"You know," Arthur said quietly, walking her to the door, pulling it open so she could precede him into the hallway, "our most dedicated parents are *already* doing all they can, volunteering as crossing guards and lunchroom helpers and the like. I know you depend on several women to sew costumes for the musical every year. The vast majority, I needn't tell you, only seem to show up when they want to complain about Susie's math grades or Johnny playing second string on the football team." He straightened his tie. "It isn't like it used to be."

"How's Dot feeling?" she asked gently. Arthur's wife was a hometown girl, and everybody liked her.

Arthur's worries showed in his eyes. "She has good days and bad days," he said.

Julie bit her lower lip. Nodded. So this was it, she thought. The showcase was out, the musical was in. And somehow she would have to make it all work.

"Thank you," Arthur replied, distracted again. Once more, he sighed. "I'll need dates for the production as soon as possible," he said. "Nelva Jean can make up fliers stressing that we're going to need more parental help than usual."

Nelva Jean was the school secretary, a force of nature in her own right, and she'd been eligible for retirement even when Julie and her sisters attended Blue River High. But aged miracle though she was, Nelva Jean couldn't work magic.

Julie and Arthur went their separate ways then, Julie's mind tumbling through various unworkable options as she hurried toward her classroom, her thoughts partly on the three playwrights and their own hopes for the showcase.

She'd met with the trio of young authors all summer long, reading and rereading the scripts for their one-act plays, suggesting revisions, helping to polish the pieces until they shone. They'd worked hard, and were counting on the production to buttress their college credentials.

Julie entered her classroom, took her place up front. She had no choice but to put the dilemma out of her mind for the time being.

Class flew by.

"Ms. Remington?" a shy voice asked, when first period was over and most of the students had left.

Julie, who'd been erasing the blackboard, turned to see Rachel Strivens, one of her three young playwrights, standing nearby. Rachel's dad was often out of work, though he did odd jobs wherever he could find them to put food on the table, and her mother had died in some sort of accident before the teenager and her father and her two younger brothers rolled into Blue River in a beat-up old truck in the middle of the last school year. They'd taken up residence in a rickety trailer, adjoining the junkyard run by Chudley Wilkes and his wife, Minnie, and had kept mostly to themselves ever since.

Rachel's intelligence, not to mention her affinity for the written word, had been apparent to Julie almost immediately. Over the summer, Rachel had spent her days at the Blue River Public Library, little brothers in tow, or at the community center, composing her play on one of the computers available there.

The other kids seemed to like Rachel, though she didn't have a lot of time for friends. She was definitely not like the others, buying her clothes at the thrift store and doing without things many of her contemporaries took for granted, like designer jeans, fancy cell phones and MP3 players, but at least she was spared the bullying that sometimes plagued the poor and the different. Julie knew that because she'd taken the time to make sure.

"Yes, Rachel?" she finally replied.

Rachel, though too thin, had elegant bone structure, wide-set brown eyes and a generous mouth. Her waist-length hair, braided into a single plait, was as black as a country night before the new moon, and always clean. "Could—could I talk with you later?"

Julie felt a tingle of alarm. "Is something wrong?"

Rachel tried hard to smile. Second period would begin soon, and students were beginning to drift into the room. "Later?" the girl said. "Please?"

Julie nodded, still thinking about Rachel as she prepared to teach another English class. Probably because she'd had to move around a lot with her dad, rambling from town to town and school to school, Rachel's grades had been a little on the sketchy side when she'd started at Blue River High. The one-act play she'd written—tellingly titled *Trailer Park*—was brilliant.

Rachel was brilliant.

But she was also the kind of kid who tended to fall through the cracks unless someone actively championed her and stood up for her.

And Julie was determined to be that someone.

Somehow.

A PHONE WAS RINGING. Insistent, jarring him awake.

With a groan, Garrett dragged the comforter up over his head, but the sound continued.

Cell phone?

Landline?

He couldn't tell. Didn't give a damn.

"Shut up," he pleaded, burrowing down deeper in bed, his voice muffled by the covers.

The phone stopped after twelve rings, then immediately started up again.

Real Life coalesced in Garrett's sleep-fuddled brain. Memories of the night before began to surface.

He recalled the senator's announcement.

Saw Nan Cox in his mind's eye, slipping out by way of the hotel kitchen.

He recollected Brent Brogan providing him with a police escort as far as the ranch gate.

And after all that, Julie Remington, a little boy and a three-legged beagle appearing in the kitchen.

Knowing he wouldn't be able to sleep after Julie had taken her young son and their dog back to bed in the first-floor guest suite—the spacious accommodations next to the maid's rooms, where the housekeeper, Esperanza, stayed—Garrett had gone to the barn, saddled a horse, and spent what remained of the night and the first part of the morning riding.

Finally, when smoke curled from the bunkhouse chimney and lights came on in the trailers along the creek-side, Garrett had returned home, put up his horse, retired to his private quarters to strip, shower and fall facedown into bed.

The ringing reminded him that he still had a job.

"Shit," he murmured, sitting up and scrambling for the bedside phone. "Hello?"

A dial tone buzzed in his ear, and the ringing went on.

His cell phone, then.

He grabbed for his jeans, abandoned earlier on the floor next to the bed, and rummaged through a couple of pockets before he found the cell.

"Garrett McKettrick," he mumbled, after snapping it open.

"It's about time you picked up the phone," Nan Cox answered. She sounded pretty chipper, considering that her husband had stood up at the previous evening's fund-raiser and essentially told the world that he and Mandy Chante were meant to be together. "I'm at the office, and you're not. You're not at your condo, either, because I sent Troy over to check. Where *are* you, Garrett?"

He sat up in bed, self-conscious because he was talking to his employer's wife, one of his late mother's closest friends, naked. Of course, Nan couldn't see him, but still.

"I'm on the Silver Spur," he said, grabbing his watch off the bedside table and squinting at it.

Seeing the time—past noon—he swore again.

"The senator needs you. The press has him and the little pole dancer cornered in their hotel suite."

Garrett tossed the comforter aside, sat up, retrieved his jeans from the floor and pulled them on, standing up to work the zipper and the snap. "I can understand why you think this might be my problem," he replied, imagining Morgan and Mandy hiding out from reporters in the spacious room he'd rented for them the night before, "but I'm not sure I get why it would be *yours.* Some women would be angry. They'd be talking to divorce lawyers."

"Morgan," Nan said quietly, and with conviction, "is not himself. He's ill. We still have five children at home. I'm not about to turn my back on him now."

"Mrs. Cox—"

"Nan," she broke in. "Your mother and I were like sisters."

"Nan," Garrett corrected himself, his tone grave. "Surely you understand that your husband's career can't be saved. He won't get the presidential nomination. In fact, he will probably be asked to relinquish his seat in the Senate."

"I don't give a damn about his career," Nan said fiercely, and Garrett knew she was fighting back tears. "I just want Morgan back. I want him examined by his doctor. He's not in his right mind, Garrett. He needs my help. He needs *our* help."

Although the senator was probably going through some kind of delayed midlife crisis, Garrett wasn't convinced that his boss was out of his mind. Morgan Cox wouldn't be the first politician to throw over his wife, family and career in some fit of eroticized egotism, nor, unfortunately, would he be the last.

"Look," Garrett said quietly, "I've given this whole situation some thought, and from where I stand, resignation is looking pretty good."

"Morgan's?"

"Mine," Garrett replied, after unclamping his jaw.

"You would *resign*?" Nan asked, sounding only slightly more horrified than stunned. "Morgan has been your *mentor*, Garrett. He's shown you the ropes, introduced you to all the right people in Washington, prepared the way for you to run for office when the time comes…"

Her voice fell away.

Garrett thrust out a sigh. *Would* he resign?

He wasn't sure. All he knew for certain right then was that he needed more of what his dad would have called range time—hours and hours on the back of a horse—in order to figure out what to do next.

In the meanwhile, though, Morgan and the barracuda were pinned down in a hotel suite in Austin, two hours away. The senator was obviously a loose cannon, and if he got desperate enough, he might make things even worse with some off-the-wall statement meant to appease the reporters lying in wait for him in the corridor.

"Garrett?" Nan prompted, when he didn't speak.

"I'm here," he said.

"You've got to do something."

Like what? Garrett wondered. But it wasn't the sort of thing you said to Nan Cox, especially not when she was in her take-on-the-world mode. "I'll call his cell," he told her.

"Good," Nan said, and hung up hard.

Garrett winced slightly, then speed-dialed his boss.

"McKettrick?" Cox snapped. "Is that you?"

"Yes," Garrett said.

"Where *the hell* are you?"

Garrett let the question pass. The senator wasn't asking for his actual whereabouts, after all. He was letting Garrett know he was pissed.

"You haven't spoken to the press, have you?" Garrett asked.

"No," Cox said. "But they're all over the hotel—in the hallway outside our suite, and probably downstairs in the lobby—"

"Probably," Garrett agreed quietly. "First thing, Senator. It is *very* important that you don't issue any statements or answer any questions before we have a chance to make plans. None at all. I'll get back to Austin as soon as I can, but in the meantime, you've got to stay put and speak to no one." A pause. "Do you understand me, Senator?"

Cox's temper flared. "What do you mean, you'll get back to Austin as soon as you can? Dammit, Garrett, where are you?"

This time, Garrett figured, the man really wanted to know. Of course, that didn't mean he had to be told.

"That doesn't matter," Garrett replied, his tone measured.

"If I didn't need your help so badly," the senator shot back, "I'd fire you right now!"

If it hadn't been for Nan and the kids and the golden retrievers—hell, if it hadn't been for the people of Texas, who'd elected this man to the U.S. Senate three times—Garrett would have told Morgan Cox what he could do with the job.

"Sit tight," he replied instead. "I'll call off the dogs and send Troy to pick you up. You're still going to need to lie low for a while, though."

"I want *you* here, Garrett," Cox all but exploded. "*You're* my right-hand man—Troy is just a driver." Another pause followed, and then, "You're on that damn ranch, aren't you? You're two hours from Austin!"

Garrett had recently bought a small airplane, a Cessna he kept in the ramshackle hangar out on the ranch's private airstrip. He'd fire it up and fly back to the city.

"I'll be there right away," Garrett said.

"Is there a next step?" Cox asked, mellowing out a little.

"Yes. I'm calling a press conference for this afternoon, Senator. You might want to be thinking about what you're going to tell your constituents."

"I'll tell them the same thing I told the group last night," Cox blustered, "that I've fallen in love."

Garrett couldn't make himself answer that time.

"Are you still there?" Cox asked.

"Yes, sir," Garrett replied, his voice gruff with the effort. "I'm still here."

But damned if I know why.

HELEN MARCUS DUCKED into Julie's office just as she was pulling a sandwich from her uneaten brown-bag lunch. Having spent her lunch hour grading compositions, she was ravenous.

At last, a chance to eat.

"Big news," Helen chimed, rolling the TV set Julie used to play videos and DVDs for the drama club into the tiny office and switching it on. Helen was Julie's age, dark-haired, plump and happily married, and the two of them had grown up together. "There *is* a God!"

Puzzled, and with a headache beginning at the base of her skull, Julie frowned. "What are you talking—?"

Before she could finish the question, though, Garrett Mc-Kettrick's handsome face filled the screen. Commanding in a blue cotton shirt, without a coat or a tie, he sat behind a cluster of padded microphones, earnestly addressing a room full of reporters.

"That sum-bitch Morgan Cox is finally going to resign," Helen crowed. "I feel it in my bones!"

While Julie shared Helen's low opinion of the senator—she actually mistrusted *all* politicians—she couldn't help being struck by the expression in Garrett's eyes. The one he probably thought he was hiding.

Whatever the front he was putting on for the press, Garrett was stunned. Maybe even demoralized.

Julie watched and listened as the man she'd encountered in the ranch-house kitchen early that morning fielded questions— the senator, apparently, had elected to remain in the background.

Helen had been wrong about the resignation. Senator Cox was not prepared to step down, but he needed some "personal time" with his family, according to Garrett. Colleagues would cover for him in the meantime.

"So where's the pole dancer?" Helen demanded.

"Pole dancer?" Julie echoed.

Garrett, the senator and the reporters faded to black, and Helen switched off the TV. "The *pole dancer*," she repeated. "Some blonde the senator picked up in a seedy girlie club. He wants to marry her—I saw it on the eleven o'clock news last night and again this morning." The math teacher rolled her eyes. "It's *true love*. He and the bimbette have been together in other lives. And there's our own Garrett McKettrick, defending the man." A sad shake of the head. "Jim and Sally raised those three boys of theirs right. Garrett ought to know better than to throw in with a crook like that."

Just then, Rachel Strivens appeared in the doorway of Julie's office. "I'm sorry," she said quickly, seeing that Julie wasn't alone, and started to leave.

"Wait," Julie said.

Helen had already turned off the TV set and unplugged it, rolling it back out into the hallway on its noisy cart. If Helen had planned on staying to talk, she'd clearly changed her mind.

Blushing a little, Rachel slipped reluctantly into the room.

"Rachel," Julie said quietly, "sit down, please."

Rachel sat.

"What is it?" Julie finally asked, though of course she knew. She'd announced the suspension of plans to produce the showcase—it was only temporary, she'd insisted, she'd think of something—in all her English classes that day.

Rachel looked up, her brown eyes glistening with tears. "I just wanted to let you know that it's okay, about the showcase probably not happening and everything," she said. The girl made a visible effort to gather herself up, straightening her shoulders, raising her chin. "I can't do any extracurricular activities anyway—Dad says I need to start working after school, so I can help out with the bills. His friend Dennis manages the bowling alley, and with the fall leagues starting up, they can use some extra people."

Julie took a moment to absorb all the implications of that.

Rachel hadn't said she wanted to save for college, or buy clothes or a car or a laptop, like most teenagers in search of employment. She'd said she had to "help out with the bills."

She wasn't planning to *go* to college.

"I understand," Julie said, at some length, wishing she didn't.

Rachel bit her lower lip, threw her long braid back over one shoulder. "Dad tries," she said, her voice barely audible. "Everything is so hard, without my mom around anymore."

Julie nodded, holding back tears. In five years, in ten years, in twenty, Rachel might still be working at the bowling alley—if she had a job at all. Julie had seen the phenomenon half a dozen times. "I'm sure that's true," she said.

Rachel was on her feet. Ready to go.

Julie leaned forward in her chair. "Have you actually been hired, Rachel, or is the job at the bowling alley just a possibility?"

Rachel stood on the threshold, poised to flee, but clearly wanting to stay. "It's pretty definite," she answered. "I just have to say yes, and it's mine."

Things like this happened, Julie reminded herself. The world was an imperfect place.

Kids tabled their dreams, thinking they'd get back to them later.

Except that they so rarely did, in Julie's experience. One thing led to another. They met somebody and got married. Then there were children and rent to pay and car loans.

Rachel was so bright and talented, and she was standing at an important crossroads. In one direction lay a fine education and every hope of success. In the other...

The prospects made Julie want to cover her face with her hands.

After Rachel had gone, she sat very still for a long time, wondering what she could do to help.

Only one course of action came to mind, and that was probably a long shot.

She would speak to Rachel's father.

CHAPTER THREE

TATE WAS WAITING at the airstrip in his truck when Garrett landed the Cessna around five that afternoon.

Garrett taxied to a stop outside the ramshackle hangar that had once housed his dad's plane and shut off the engines. The blur of the props slowed until the paddles were visible.

He climbed down, shut the door behind him and walked toward his brother.

They met midway between the Cessna and Tate's truck.

Obviously, Tate had heard about the scandal in Austin by then, and Garrett figured he was there to say, "I told you so."

Instead, Tate reached out, rested a hand on Garrett's shoulder. "You okay?"

Garrett didn't know what to say then. Flying back from the capital, he'd rehearsed another scenario entirely—and that one hadn't involved the sympathy and concern he saw in his brother's eyes.

He nodded, though he couldn't resist qualifying that with "I've been better."

Tate let his hand fall back to his side. Folded his arms. "I caught the press conference on TV," he said. "Cox isn't planning to resign?"

Garrett sighed, shoved a hand through his hair. "He will," he said sadly. "Right now, he's still trying to convince himself that the hullabaloo will blow over and everything will get back to normal."

"How's Nan taking all this?"

"She's holding up okay," Garrett said. "As far as I can tell, anyway."

Tate took that in. His expression was thoughtful. "Now what?" he asked, after a few moments had passed. "For you, I mean?"

"I catch my breath and look for another job," Garrett replied.

"You quit?" Tate asked, sounding surprised. If there was one thing a McKettrick didn't do, it was desert a sinking ship. Unless, of course, that ship had been commandeered by one of the rats.

Garrett grinned wanly. Spread his hands at his sides. "I was fired," he said.

Now there, he thought, was a first. In living memory, he knew of no McKettrick who had ever been fired from a job. On the other hand, most of them worked for themselves, and that had been the case for generations.

The look on Tate's face would have been satisfying, under any other circumstances. *"What?"*

Garrett chuckled. Okay, so his brother's surprise *was* sort of satisfying, circumstances notwithstanding. It made up for Garrett's skinned pride, at least a little. "The senator and I had words," he said. "He wanted to go on as if nothing had happened. I told him that wouldn't work—he needed to fess up, stand by his wife and his kids, if he wanted to come out of this with any credibility at all, never mind holding on to his seat in the Senate. I agreed to handle the press conference because Nan practically begged me, but when it was over, the senator informed me that my services were no longer needed." Still enjoying Tate's bewilderment, Garrett started toward the Cessna he'd just climbed out of, intending to roll it into the hangar. He stopped, looked back over one shoulder. "You wouldn't be in the market for a ranch hand, would you?"

Tate smiled, but there was a tinge of sadness to it. "Permanent or temporary?"

"Temporary," Garrett said, after a moment of recovery. "I still want to work in government. And I've already had a couple of offers."

Tate's disappointment was visible in his face, though he was a good sport about it. "Okay," he said. "How long is 'temporary'?"

Garrett wasn't sure how to answer that. He needed time—thinking time. Horse time. "As long as it takes," he offered.

Tate put out a hand so they could shake on the agreement, nebulous as it was. "Fair enough," he said.

Garrett nodded, watched as Tate turned to walk away, open the door of his truck and step up on the running board to climb behind the wheel.

"See you in the morning," Tate called.

Garrett grinned, feeling strangely hopeful, as if he were on the brink of something he'd been born to do.

But that was crazy, of course.

He was a born politician. He belonged in Austin, if not Washington. He wanted to be a mover and a shaker, part of the solution. Working on the Silver Spur was only a stopgap measure, just as he'd told Tate.

"What time?" he called back, standing next to the Cessna.

Tate's grin flashed. "We've got five hundred head of cattle to move tomorrow," he said. "We're starting at dawn, so be saddled up and ready to ride."

Garrett didn't let his own grin falter, though on the inside he groaned. He nodded, waved and turned away.

IF RON STRIVENS, Rachel's father, carried a cell phone, the number wasn't on record in the school office, and since Strivens did odd jobs, he didn't work in the same place every day, like most of her students' parents. In the end, Julie drove to the trailer he rented just across the dirt road from Chudley and Minnie Wilkes's junkyard, and found him there, chopping firewood in the twilight.

Seeing Julie, the tall, rangy man lodged the blade of his ax in the chopping block and started toward her.

Julie sized him up as he approached. He wore old jeans, beat-up work boots and a plaid flannel shirt, unbuttoned to reveal a faded T-shirt beneath. His reddish-brown hair was too long and thinning above his forehead, and the expression in his eyes was one of weary resignation.

"I'm Julie Remington," Julie told him, after rolling down the car window. "Rachel is in my English class."

Strivens nodded, keeping his distance. Behind him loomed the battered trailer. Smoke curled from a rusty stovepipe, gray against a darkening sky, and Julie thought she saw Rachel's face appear briefly at one of the windows.

"What can I do for you, Ms. Remington?" he asked, shyly polite.

Julie felt her throat tighten. Money had certainly been in short supply while she was growing up, and the family home was nothing fancy, but she and her sisters had never done without anything they really needed.

"I was hoping we could talk about Rachel," she said.

Strivens glanced back toward the trailer. The metal was rusting, and even curling away from the frame in places, and the chimney rose from the roof of a ramshackle add-on, more like a lean-to than a room. "I'd ask you in," he told her, "but the kids are about to have their supper, and I don't think the soup will stretch far enough to feed another person."

Julie ached for Rachel, for her brothers, for all of them. "I'm in sort of a hurry anyway," she said, and that was true. She still had to pick Calvin up at Libby and Tate's place, and then there would be supper and his bath and a bedtime story. "Rachel tells me she's taking on an after-school job."

Strivens reddened a little, nodded once, abruptly. He'd been stooping to look in at Julie through the window, but now he took a couple of steps back and straightened. "I'm right sorry she has to do that," he said, "but the fact is, we're having a hard time making ends meet around here. The boys are always needing something, and there's rent and food and all the rest."

Julie's heart sank. What had she expected—that Rachel's father would say it was all a big misunderstanding and what had he been thinking, asking a mere child to help support the family?

"Rachel is a very special young woman, Mr. Strivens. She's definitely college material. Her grades aren't terrific, though, and she's going to have even less time to study once she's working."

Pain flashed in his eyes, temper climbed, red, up his neck to pulse in the stubble covering his cheeks and chin. "You think I don't know that, Miss Remington? You think I wouldn't like for my daughter, for *all three* of my kids, to have a nice place to live and clothes that didn't come from somebody's ragbag and a chance to go on to college?"

"I didn't mean—"

Strivens glanced toward the trailer again. Softened slightly. "I know," he said, sounding so tired and sad that the backs of Julie's eyes scalded. "I know your intentions are good. We've come on some hard times, my family and me, but we're still—" he choked up, swallowed and went on "—we're still a family. We'll get by somehow, but only if we all do our part."

Avoiding Strivens's eyes, Julie opened the little memo book with its miniature pencil looped through the top and scrawled her cell and school numbers onto a page, then handed it out the window. "If there's anything I can do to help," she said, "please call me."

Strivens took the piece of paper, stared down at it for a long moment, then turned away from Julie, shoving it into his coat pocket as he did so. Prying the ax out of the chopping block, he silently went back to work.

Half an hour later, when Julie pulled into one of the bays of the McKettricks' multicar garage, it was already dark. The door had barely rolled down behind her before Calvin was scrambling out of his car seat to dash inside the house.

It would have been impossible not to note the contrasts between the mansion on the Silver Spur and the single-wide trailer where Rachel lived with her father and brothers.

Feeling twice her real age, Julie got out, reached into the backseat for her purse and the quilted tote bag she used as a briefcase. Harry, the beagle, could be heard barking a joyous welcome inside the house, and that made her smile.

The kitchen was warm and brightly lit, and fragrant with something savory Esperanza was making for supper.

Hungry and tired, Julie felt a rush of gratitude, smiling her thanks at the other woman as she stepped around Calvin and the dog to carry her things into the guest quarters in back.

After getting out of her skirt and sweater and putting on jeans and a long-sleeved royal-blue T-shirt, Julie washed her face and hands in the guest bath and returned to the kitchen to help Esperanza.

"How many places shall I set?" Julie asked, pausing in front of a set of glass-fronted cupboards. The number varied—sometimes, it was just Esperanza, Calvin and herself, but Tate and Libby and the twins often joined them for supper, even on weeknights, and it wasn't uncommon for a couple of ranch hands to share in the meal as well.

Esperanza turned from the stove, where she was stirring red sauce in a giant copper skillet. "Four of us tonight," she answered. "Garrett's back, you know."

Julie smiled. "Yes," she said, knowing how Esperanza loved it when any of her "boys" were around to cook for, fuss over and generally spoil.

Calvin, meanwhile, continued to wrestle with Harry.

"Go wash up," Julie told her son. "And don't leave your coat and your backpack lying around, either."

Calvin gave her a long-suffering look, sighed and got to his feet. He and Harry disappeared into the guest quarters.

Julie had just finished setting the table when she felt the prickle of a thrill at her nape and turned to see Garrett standing in the kitchen. He looked more like a cowboy than a politician, Julie thought, wearing jeans and old boots and a cotton shirt the color of his eyes.

Grinning, he rolled up his sleeves, revealing a pair of muscular forearms.

"Well," he said, in that soft, slow drawl of his, "howdy all over again."

Julie, oddly stricken, blinked. "Howdy," she croaked, froglike.

Esperanza, about to set a platter of enchiladas on the table, chuckled.

"Where is el niño?" she asked, looking around for Calvin.

"I'll get him," Julie said, too quickly, dashing out of the room.

When she got back, Calvin in tow, Esperanza was at the table, in her usual place, while Garrett stood leaning against one of the counters, evidently waiting.

Only when Julie was seated, Calvin on the bench beside her, did Garrett pull back the chair at the head of the table and sit.

Everybody bowed their heads, and Esperanza offered thanks.

Calvin had probably been peeking at Garrett through his eyelashes throughout the brief prayer, though Julie could only speculate. Grace seemed particularly appropriate that night.

The Strivens family was having soup. And not enough of it, apparently.

"Aunt Libby had the news on when Audrey and Ava and I got home from school today," Calvin told Garrett. "I saw you on TV!"

Garrett grinned at that, though Julie caught the briefest glimpse of weariness in his eyes. "All in a day's work," he replied easily.

Esperanza gave him a sympathetic glance.

"Tate says the senator ought to be lynched," Calvin went on cheerfully, his chin and one cheek already smudged with enchilada sauce.

Julie handed him a paper napkin, watched as he bunched it into a wad, dabbed at his face and wiped away only part of the sauce.

Garrett's grin slipped a little, Julie thought, and a glance at Esperanza revealed the other woman's quiet concern.

"Is that right?" Garrett responded, very slowly. "Tate said that?"

Calvin nodded, thrilled to be carrying tales. "He didn't know I heard what he said," the little boy explained, "but when Aunt Libby poked him with her elbow, he almost choked on his coffee." A pause. "That was funny."

Garrett chuckled. "I suppose it was," he agreed.

"What's 'lynched'?" Calvin persisted, gazing up at Julie. "Aunt Libby wouldn't tell me when I asked her. She said I'd have to ask you, Mom."

Thanks a lot, sis, Julie thought wryly. "Never mind," she said. "We're eating."

"Is it something yucky, then?"

"Yes."

"Will it give me bad dreams?"

"Maybe," Julie said.

Again, Garrett chuckled. "How old are you, buddy?" he asked, watching the child.

"Almost five," Calvin answered, proudly. "That's how come they finally let me into kindergarten. Because I'm almost five."

Garrett gave a low, exclamatory whistle. "I'd have sworn you were fifty-two," he said, "and short for your age."

Calvin laughed, delighted by the joke—and the masculine attention.

Julie felt a pang, barely resisted an urge to ruffle her son's hair in a fit of unrestrained affection. He would have been embarrassed, she thought, and the pang struck again, deeper this time.

Eventually Calvin finished eating, and excused himself to feed Harry and then take him outside. Julie knew he'd ask about lynching again, but she hoped she could put him off until morning.

Esperanza began clearing the table, and waved Julie away when she moved to help.

Calvin and the dog came back inside.

"Time for your bath, big guy," Julie said.

For once, Calvin didn't argue. Maybe he wanted to look good in front of Garrett McKettrick; she couldn't be sure.

Once the boy and his dog had vanished into the guest suite, and Esperanza had served the coffee, started the dishwasher and gone as well, Julie was alone with Garrett.

The realization was deliciously unsettling.

She cleared her throat diplomatically, but when she opened her mouth, intending to make some kind of pitch concerning the foundation's funding the new computers in full, not a sound came out.

Garrett watched her, amusement flickering in his eyes. He could have thrown her a lifeline, tossed out some conversational tidbit to get things started, but he didn't. He simply waited for her to make another attempt.

That was when Calvin reappeared, tugging at Julie's shirtsleeve and startling her half out of her skin. "Do I *have* to take a bath tonight? I had one *last* night and I hardly even got dirty today."

Garrett's smile set Julie back on her figurative heels.

Flustered, she turned to her son. "Yes, Calvin," she said firmly, "you *do* have to take your bath."

"But Esperanza and I were going to watch TV," Calvin protested, his usual sunny-sky nature clouding over. "Our favorite show is on, and somebody's sure to get voted off and sent home."

Julie turned back to Garrett. "Excuse me," she said, rising.

Garrett merely nodded.

She took Calvin to their bathroom, where Esperanza was filling the tub. The older woman smiled at Julie—she'd already gotten out the little boy's pajamas, and they were neatly folded and waiting on the lid of the clothes hamper.

Bless the woman, she went out of her way to be helpful.

Julie felt yet another rush of gratitude.

Harry sat on a hooked rug in the middle of the bathroom, panting and watching the proceedings.

"I'll make sure young Mr. Calvin is bathed and in his pajamas in time to watch our program," Esperanza said. Then she made a shooing motion with the backs of her fingers. "You go back to the kitchen."

Was Esperanza playing matchmaker?

Julie made a little snorting sound as she left the bathroom. Herself and *Garrett McKettrick*?

Fat chance.

The man was a *politician*, for cripes' sake.

Anyway, he had probably lit out for his part of the house by then, either because he'd already forgotten their encounter or because he'd guessed that she was about to ask for something— with all the pride-swallowing that would entail—and wanted to avoid her.

Garrett was still at the table, though, drinking coffee and frowning at the newspaper spread out in front of him. He'd recently topped off his cup—the brew steamed at his right elbow—and when he looked up, Julie saw that he was wearing wire-rimmed glasses.

For some reason, that struck her in a tender place.

Seeing her, he stood.

"I guess you must have heard about Senator Cox," Garrett said, with a nod toward the paper, his voice deep and solemn and very quiet.

Julie nodded. "I'm sorry," she told Garrett, and then she felt foolish. "If that's the appropriate sentiment, I mean," she stumbled on. "Being sorry, that is."

She closed her eyes, sighed and squeezed the bridge of her nose.

When she looked at Garrett again, he smiled, took off his glasses and folded down the stems, tucked them into the pocket of his shirt.

His eyes were the heart-bruising blue of a September sky.

His expression, unreadable.

"Did I read you wrong, or did you want to speak to me about something earlier, before the interruption?"

Oh, but there was a slight edge to his tone—or was she imagining that?

Totally confused, Julie raised her chin a notch. "Sit down," she said. "Please."

"Not until you do," Garrett said, grinning again.

Julie smiled, plunked herself down on the bench and waited until Garrett was back in his chair.

She was instantly nervous.

Her heart thrummed away at twice its normal rate, and she knew it wasn't just because she meant to look a gift horse in the mouth, so to speak.

"The foundation—your family's, I mean—has very generously promised to match any money the school district can raise to buy new computers and software for use in the library at Blue River High and—"

A sudden blush surged up Julie's neck and cut off her words. What was the matter with her? Why was she so self-conscious?

This just wasn't like her.

"And?" Garrett finally prompted, putting his glasses back on.

"We appreciate the gift," Julie managed lamely.

"You're welcome," Garrett said, puzzled now.

Damn her pride.

And for all she knew, Garrett wasn't even directly involved with the McKettrick family's foundation. Hadn't she read once that his cousin, Meg McKettrick O'Ballivan, who lived in Arizona with her famous country-singer husband, handled such things? She would have to do some research before she broached the subject again, could have kicked herself for not thinking of that sooner.

Garrett waited, and though he wasn't smiling, something danced in his eyes. He was enjoying this.

In the end, though, Julie outwaited him.

Presently, with a tap of one index finger to the front page of the newspaper, he asked, "As a voter, what's your take on the senator's future in politics?"

"I'm probably not the right person to ask," she said moderately, remembering their somewhat heated exchange after a mutual friend's funeral a few months before. It had been fairly brief, but they *had* gotten into a lively discussion of one of the major issues of the day.

"Why would you say that?" Garrett asked, sounding genuinely curious.

"I voted against the senator in the last election," she admitted. Her cheeks burned, not with chagrin but with lingering conviction. "And the one before that."

"I see," Garrett said, and his mouth quirked again, at the same corner as before.

"Why?"

Julie straightened. "Because I liked his opponent better."

"That's the only reason?"

Julie's shoulders rose and fell with the force of her sigh. "All right, no. No, it isn't. I never liked Morgan Cox very much, never trusted him. There's something…well, *sneaky*…about him."

"Something 'sneaky'?" Garrett challenged, a wry twist to his mouth, sitting back in his chair, watching her. He slid the newspaper in her direction, somehow directing her gaze to the photo spread—every shot showed Senator Cox with smiling children, or golden retrievers, or an adoring and much-admired *Mrs.* Cox or some combination thereof.

Julie hesitated, choosing her words carefully. "The whole thing seemed too perfect," she finally replied. "Almost as though he'd *hired* people to *pose* as his all-American family. And then there was that hot-tub incident. It was downplayed in the media, strangely enough, but it happened. I remember it clearly."

Garrett gave a hoarse chuckle at that. He didn't sound amused, though. "Ah, yes," he said, far away now. "That."

"That," Julie agreed. "Senator Morgan Cox in a hot tub with three half-naked women, none of whom were his wife. It was a family reunion, he claimed, and they were all just a happy group of cousins. As if any idiot would believe a story like that."

Something changed in Garrett's face. "I can think of at least one idiot who believed it," he said quietly.

Julie wished she'd kept her opinions to herself, but it was a little late for that. "What happens now?" she asked, and this time her tone was gentle.

"I can't speak for Senator Cox," Garrett said, after a long time, "but I'll be staying on here for a while."

A strangely celebratory tingle moved through Julie at this news.

Not that she cared whether Garrett McKettrick was around or not.

"Well, good night," she said.

"Good night," Garrett replied.

Julie turned around too fast, bumped into the cabinet behind her, and gasped with pain.

Garrett caught hold of her arm, turned her to face him.

One wrong move on either of their parts, Julie reasoned wildly, and their torsos would be touching.

"Are you all right?" Garrett asked. His hands rested lightly on her shoulders now.

Their faces were only inches apart.

It would be so easy to kiss.

No, Julie thought. *No, I am* not *all right.*

"Julie?" Garrett prompted.

"I'm fine," she lied, easing backward, out of his grasp.

Julie turned around carefully that time, and walked, with dignity, out of the kitchen, managing not to crash into anything in the process.

Tomorrow, she told herself, *is another day.*

CHAPTER FOUR

DAWN ARRIVED LONG before Garrett was ready for it, and so did his brother. When he stumbled out the back door of the ranch house, after a brief shower, there was Tate, already waiting in front of the barn. He'd saddled old Stranger, their dad's roan, for himself, and a black gelding named Dark Moon for Garrett.

After flashing Garrett a grin, Tate swung up onto Stranger's back and took an easy hold on the reins.

"I'd kill for coffee," Garrett said, hauling himself onto Dark Moon, shifting around to get comfortable. He'd forgotten how hard a saddle could be, especially when the rider was less than thirty minutes from a warm, soft bed.

"It won't come to that," Tate assured him, still grinning. "But I know the feeling." He turned, pulled a medium-sized Thermos bottle from one of his saddlebags and tossed it to Garrett. "Made it myself."

Garrett chuckled. "I might have some just the same," he said, unscrewing the cup-lid and then the plug. He poured a swig and sipped. "Not bad," he allowed. "You wouldn't happen to have a plate of bacon and eggs in the other side of those saddlebags, would you?"

Tate chuckled and shook his head. "Sorry," he said. "We'd best get moving. Most of the crew is already on the range, ready to work."

Garrett resealed the coffee jug, rode close to hand it back to Tate, watched as his brother stowed it away again.

He hadn't had nearly enough java to jump-start his brain, but he supposed for the time being it would have to do.

Tate led the way through a series of corral gates, and by then the darkness was shot through with the first flimsy rays of sunshine. They crossed the landscape side by side, their horses at a gallop, and Garrett was surprised at how good he felt. How...right.

"You heard anything from our little brother lately?" Tate asked, slowing the roan as they neared the temporary camp, where a small bonfire burned. Cowboys and horses milled all around, raising up dust, and the cattle bawled out there in the thinning gloom as if they were plain dying of sorrow.

"No," Garrett answered. God knew, he had troubles of his own, but he worried about Austin. Their kid brother had taken his time growing up, and then he'd nearly been killed riding a bull at a rodeo over in New Mexico. Coming that close to death would have made some people a mite more cautious, but the effect on Austin had been just the opposite. He was wilder than ever.

Tate reined in a little more, and so did Garrett. "I figure if we don't get some word of him soon, we'll have to go out looking for the damn fool."

Garrett nodded, stood in the stirrups to stretch his legs. He'd be sore for the next few days, he supposed, but riding wasn't a thing a man forgot how to do. His muscles would take a little time to remember, that was all. "I'll do some checking," he said.

"I'd appreciate it," Tate answered.

A couple of the cowboys hailed them from up ahead, and the din and the dirt clouds increased with every stride their horses took toward the herd.

"Garrett?"

Garrett turned to his brother. "Are you going to jaw at me all day, Tate?" he joked. Of the three McKettrick brothers, Tate was normally the one least likely to run off at the mouth.

Tate grinned. "No," he said. "But I've got one more thing to say." He paused, adjusted the angle of his hat, pulling the brim down low over his forehead. "It's good to have you back."

With that, Tate nudged Stranger's flanks with his boot heels, and the horse bounded ahead, leaving Garrett to catch up.

And since Garrett was out of practice when it came to cowboying, he was pretty much catching up all morning long.

WITH A FEW minutes to go before she had to be at school, Julie followed an impulse and drove by the cottage she'd been renting since her return to Blue River, when Calvin was just a baby. The exterminator's giant tent still billowed around it like a big, putty-colored blob.

Watching the thing undulate from within, Julie didn't immediately notice Suzanne Hillbrand, of Hillbrand Real Estate. Her Mercedes was parked nearby.

Wearing high heels, a pencil skirt and very big hair, Suzanne was examining the spiffy new For Sale sign out by the curb.

The shock of seeing that sign struck Julie like a slap across the face. She cranked the Caddie into Park and got out, slamming the door hard behind her.

"Well," Suzanne trilled, beaming, "*hello*, Julie Remington!"

Suzanne's outgoing personality wasn't an affectation designed to sell properties; she'd always been that way. Even in kindergarten. The big hair only went back as far as high school, though.

"Hello, Suzanne," Julie responded, not smiling. She indicated the sign with a motion of one hand. "Are you sure this isn't a mistake?"

"Why, *of course* I'm sure, darlin'!" Suzanne replied, with exhausting ebullience, shading her perfectly made-up eyes with one perfectly manicured hand. "It isn't as if there's a real estate boom on here in Blue River, after all. I've got this cottage and the old Arnette farm on the books, and that's it."

The flash of adrenaline-fueled annoyance that had propelled Julie from behind the wheel of her Cadillac dissipated in an instant. She bit down on her lower lip.

"I take it Louise didn't tell you she was putting the place on the market?" Suzanne asked quietly.

"She might have tried," Julie admitted, picturing her very efficient and quite elderly landlady. "I'm not sure she has my cell number, and I keep forgetting to check my voice mail."

Suzanne's smile came back full force. "We all know you and Libby and Paige came into some money a while back," she said. "Things like that get around, of course. Well, here's the perfect investment for you. Your very own cottage. Think how easy it would be. You wouldn't even have to pack up and move!"

In spite of herself, Julie smiled. She'd always liked Suzanne, and the woman's enthusiasm was catching. Plus, she'd often dreamed of buying the cottage—back when she didn't have the means, especially.

"What's the asking price?"

Suzanne named a figure that would nearly wipe out Julie's considerable nest egg.

So much for enthusiasm.

"No way," Julie said, backing up a step.

Suzanne stayed happy. "Louise is firm on the price," she said. "I told her she wouldn't get that much, considering the state the market's in right now, but she's not about to budge. The place is paid for, and she doesn't need the money. All that works in your favor, of course, because you'll probably have all kinds of time before it actually sells—to find somewhere else to live, I mean."

All kinds of time to find somewhere else to live.

Oh, right.

There weren't a lot of housing options in towns the size of Blue River.

Let's see. She could move in with Paige, who was in the process of renovating the small house they'd all grown up in, rent by the week at the seedy Amble On Inn on the edge of town, or make an offer on the Arnette farm, which was almost as much of an eyesore as the Wilkeses' junkyard.

A fixer-upper, Suzanne would call it.

In Julie's opinion, the only hope of making that old dump look better was a bulldozer.

For the time being, she'd have to stay on at the Silver Spur.

Darn.

Remembering the time, Julie checked her watch and turned to head back to her car. Calvin was in another mood, and she'd had to cajole him into getting out of bed, eating his breakfast, finding his backpack.

By the time she'd dropped him off at Libby's, so he could ride to school with the twins, Julie had been working on a mood of her own.

"You think about making an offer, now!" Suzanne called after her.

Julie waved, got back into her car and headed for Blue River High.

Okay, so the day was definitely going in the downhill direction, she thought, as she pulled into the teachers' lot and spotted a shiny blue SUV over in visitors' parking. Things could still turn around, if she just looked on the bright side, counted her blessings.

She had a wonderful, healthy son.

She had a job she loved, even if it was a bummer sometimes.

And, yeah, someone might come along and buy the cottage right out from under her and Calvin, but given the economic slowdown, selling would probably take a while. In the meantime, she and her little boy had a roof over their heads, and for the first time in Julie's life, thanks to a fluke, she had money in the bank.

A person didn't have to look far to see that a lot of other people weren't so fortunate. The Strivens family, for instance.

Julie parked the Cadillac, grabbed her tote bag and her lunch, and got out.

While she was locking up, she saw the driver's-side door of the strange blue SUV swing open.

Gordon Pruett got out.

She barely recognized him, with his short haircut, chinos and polo shirt. A commercial fisherman by trade, Calvin's father had always been a raggedy-jeans-and-muscle-shirt kind of guy.

Julie's stomach seemed to take a bungee jump as she watched the man she'd once loved—or *believed* she loved—strolling toward her as though they both had all the time in the world.

Like Calvin's, Gordon's eyes were a piercing ice-blue, and both father and son had light blond hair that paled to near silver in bright sunshine.

"Hello, Julie," Gordon said. He was tanned, and a diamond stud sparkled in the lobe of his right ear, making him look something like a pirate.

"Gordon," Julie managed, aware that she hadn't moved since

spotting him moments before. "What are you doing here? Why didn't you call?"

"I did call," Gordon answered mildly, keeping his distance, squinting a little in the dazzle of a fall morning. "I've emailed, too. Multiple times, in fact. You've been putting me off for a couple of months now, Jules, so I figured we'd better talk in person."

Julie sighed. Her throat felt dry and raw, and her knees were wobbly, insubstantial. "Calvin isn't ready to see you," she said.

"If that's true," Gordon responded, "I'm more than willing to wait until he is ready. But are you sure our son is the reluctant one, Julie? Or is it you?"

Tears of frustration and worry burned in her eyes. She blinked them away, at the same time squaring her shoulders and stiffening her spine. "Calvin is barely five years old," she replied, "and you're a stranger to him."

"I'm his father."

Julie closed her eyes for a moment, drew a deep, deep breath, and released it slowly. "Yes," she said. "You're his father—biologically. But you didn't want to be part of Calvin's life or mine, remember? You said you weren't ready."

Gordon might have flinched; his reaction was so well-controlled as to be nearly invisible. Still, there *had* been a reaction. "I regret that," he said. "But I've taken care of Calvin, haven't I? Kept up the child support payments? Let you raise him the way you wanted to?"

Julie's throat thickened. She swallowed. Gordon wasn't a monster, she reminded herself silently. Just a flesh-and-blood man, with plenty of good qualities and plenty of faults.

"I have classes to teach," she said at last.

"Buy you lunch?"

The first-period bell rang.

Julie said nothing; she was torn.

"I could meet you somewhere, or pick up some food and bring it here," Gordon offered.

Already hurrying away, Julie finally nodded her agreement. "The Silver Dollar Saloon makes a decent sandwich," she called back. "It's on Main Street. I'll meet you there at eleven-thirty."

Gordon smiled for the first time since the encounter had begun, nodded his head and returned to the SUV.

Julie normally threw herself into her English classes, losing all track of time, but that day she simply couldn't concentrate. When lunchtime came, she grabbed her purse and fled to the parking lot, drove as fast as the speed limit allowed to the Silver Dollar.

Gordon's SUV was parked in the gravel out front; she pulled the battered Caddie up beside his vehicle, shaking her head as she looked over at his ride. Although he'd made a good living as a fisherman, Gordon had never cared much about money, not when she knew him, anyway. Instead of working another job during the off-season and saving up to buy a bigger boat, or a starter house, or—say—an engagement ring, as some of his friends would have done, Gordon had partied through every nickel he earned. By the time he went back to sea, he was not only broke, but in debt to his father and several uncles besides.

The SUV looked fairly new.

His clothes, while nothing fancy, were good.

Obviously, Gordon had grown up—at least a little—since the last time Julie had seen him.

Now, reflecting on these things, she steeled herself as she walked up to the door of the Silver Dollar, started a little when it opened before she got hold of the handle.

Gordon stood just over the threshold, in the sawdust and peanut shells that covered the floor, acting for all the world like a gentleman.

Maybe he truly *had* changed. For Calvin's sake, she hoped so.

She swept past him, waited for her eyes to adjust to the change of light.

The click of pool balls, the steady twang from the jukebox, the aroma of hot grease wafting from the grill—it was all familiar.

The Silver Dollar was doing a brisk business for a weekday, and folks nodded at Julie in greeting as she let Gordon steer her toward the back, where he'd scored one of the booths.

He waited until she was seated before sliding into the seat across from hers.

"You're as beautiful as ever," he said. "It's good to see you again, Julie."

The waitress appeared, handed Julie a menu. "The special is a grilled chicken sandwich, extra for cheese."

"I'll have that, please," Julie said. "Without the cheese. Unsweetened iced tea, too, with lemon."

Gordon asked for a double-deluxe cheeseburger with curly fries and a side of coleslaw, plus a cola.

"Fishing must be hungry business these days," Julie commented, to get the conversation going.

"I'm not fishing anymore," Gordon answered. "I'm in construction."

"I see," Julie said, though of course she *didn't*, not really.

"How is Calvin?" Gordon asked.

"Except for his asthma, and he hasn't had any problems with that for a while, he's healthy and happy. He has a dog, a beagle named Harry, and he's been learning to ride horseback out on the Silver Spur."

"I can't believe he's in kindergarten," Gordon said.

Their drinks came, and neither of them spoke until the waitress had gone.

"Believe it," Julie said. "Calvin can already read and do simple math, and he would have skipped kindergarten and gone directly into first grade if I hadn't refused to let him do that."

Gordon watched her pensively, stirring his tall, icy cola with his straw. "I'm not here to make trouble, Julie," he said.

"I didn't say you were," Julie pointed out.

He grinned. "No," he agreed, "you didn't. But you're not happy to see me, are you?"

"No," Julie admitted glumly.

Gordon chuckled at that. "Okay," he said. "That's fair. I appreciate the honesty."

The food came, and Gordon took the time to salt and pepper his burger, line up the little wells of ketchup for dunking fries.

Julie cut her sandwich in half to make it more manageable and surprised herself by eating a few bites.

"I think I told you about Dixie," Gordon began. "My wife?"

"You told me," Julie said. "Are you still living in Louisiana?"

Gordon shook his head. "Dallas," he said. "That's Dixie's hometown. Lots of construction going on, so I've been working steady."

"That's good," Julie said carefully.

She had lived with this man.

Made love with him, borne his child.

Even back then, in the throes of passion, she'd known so little about Gordon Pruett. Never met his parents and very few of his friends. She wondered, then and now, if he'd been trying to keep her a secret for some reason.

"Dixie's dad owns the construction company," Gordon explained, with no trace of apology or defensiveness. "We have a nice home in a good neighborhood and—"

"You can't have Calvin," Julie broke in, frightened again. Still. "I'm all he knows, and I won't just send him off to live with total strangers, Gordon."

Gordon raised both hands in a bid for peace. "Julie," he said, leaning toward her a little, his voice slow and earnest, "let's be clear from the beginning. I have no intention—*zero*—of going after full custody, or even *shared* custody. I'll continue to make the child-support payments. But I want to get to know Calvin, and have him get to know me."

Julie eased up a little. Although her appetite was gone, she made herself eat a little more, so her blood sugar wouldn't plunge in the middle of the afternoon.

"And how would you go about this? Getting acquainted with Calvin, I mean?"

Gordon smiled, and Julie was reassured by the kind twinkle in his eyes. "Very slowly and carefully at first," he replied. "Maybe we'd just go out for pizza in the beginning, or play some miniature golf. Of course, you'd be included in any outings Dixie and I planned for Calvin—we wouldn't expect you to be comfortable with any other kind of arrangement, at least in the beginning."

Julie's relief must have shown clearly in her face, because Gordon reached across the table, took her hand in a gentle grip and gave it a fleeting squeeze.

"Except for spending the night with one or the other of my sisters, Libby or Paige, Calvin's never been away from home," she said tentatively. "His asthma doesn't flare up very often, but when it does and it's bad, he's terrified. Usually the inhaler works, but sometimes he needs a ventilator."

Gordon's Calvin-blue eyes were solemn. Looking across the table at this man, this familiar stranger, Julie slipped into a time warp for just a fraction of an instant and saw her little boy, all grown up.

"Dixie's an RN," he said. "She knows all about medical equipment and medicines and the like. And she *loves* kids. In fact, we're expecting one of our own next April."

Julie felt a too-familiar ache on Calvin's behalf.

Gordon was excited about the baby he and Dixie were expecting. He was ready to be a father. Where had all this maturity been when *Calvin* was born?

On the other hand, shouldn't she just be grateful that Gordon wanted a relationship with his son at all? As absentee fathers went, he was surely one of the better ones.

"How long will you be in town?" she asked, after taking a long sip of iced tea to wet her nerve-parched throat.

"We've got to be back in Dallas by the day after tomorrow," Gordon answered. "I was hoping you and Calvin could have supper with Dixie and me tonight. The café at the Amble On Inn isn't much, but they serve a decent meal."

Julie would have liked a little more time to prepare Calvin for his first real meeting with his dad and stepmom, but since she'd sort of forced Gordon's hand by dodging his calls and emails for more than a month, the opportunity was clearly lost.

Gordon had been patient, even kind, but he was nobody's fool. If he and Julie couldn't work out a visitation schedule they'd both be able to live with, he would almost certainly take things to the next level and hire an attorney.

"Okay," Julie said, checking her watch again. Her lunch period was almost over, and after eleventh-grade English literature, she was meeting with Arthur Dulles and several school board members in his office. He was determined to make her set aside the three one-act plays she'd intended to showcase and put on a big, splashy musical instead, because those made more money. And he was rolling out the major cannons. "What time?"

"Let's meet at the café at six, if that works for you," Gordon said.

Julie nodded, pulling her wallet from her purse when the check arrived. Gordon picked it up and waved away her offer to at least pay the tip.

He stood.

She stood.

He said thank you.

She said he was welcome.

He walked her back to her car and waited until she was inside before turning to head for his SUV.

Julie immediately got out her cell phone headset and speed-dialed Paige. "Are you busy?" Julie asked, steering with one hand as she pulled out onto the main road.

Paige, a highly skilled surgical nurse, worked in a private clinic an hour from Blue River, and her schedule was a bugger. She put in four twelve-hour days every week, and spent most of the other three sleeping off her exhaustion and overseeing the changes she was making in the house.

"Me, busy?" she joked. "Let's see. Just as I was getting off work last night, search and rescue airlifted an accident victim in from some farm in the next county. Kid chopped off his left arm trying to sculpt a bear out of an oak stump with a chain saw—but we're the best. Dr. Kerrigan sewed it right back on. I guess that constitutes 'busy.'"

Julie felt slightly queasy. "Thanks for sharing," she said. "If you don't have time to talk, just say so."

"I have time to listen," Paige said. "What's going on, Jules?"

"The cottage is up for sale," Julie answered. "I've been renting that house from Louise Smithfield for five years, and she didn't even bother to tell me she was putting it on the market."

"So we change the renovation plans for the house," Paige said easily. "We'll make it a duplex. You and Calvin can live on one side, and I'll live on the other."

Julie's palm was damp where she was clasping the phone.

"But you didn't call to tell me about the cottage, did you?" Paige prompted.

"It's Gordon," Julie said shakily. "He's in town. He finally just... showed up. Calvin and I are having dinner with him and his wife. *Tonight.*"

"Julie?"

"What?"

"Take a breath. This is a *good* thing, sis."

"So why do I feel terrified?"

"Because you've probably been going over worst-case scenarios ever since you got that first email from Gordon."

Ah, yes, the worst-case scenarios.

Julie knew them all.

Gordon snatches Calvin and whisks him off to Mexico or some other third-world country, and Julie never sees her child again.

Gordon has a secret addiction—alcohol, gambling, drugs— maybe all those and more. Calvin is not only in danger when he visits his father, he's more prone to engage in said addictions himself.

Gordon is a perfectly good father, and Calvin loves him so much that he doesn't want to live even part-time with his mom anymore.

And those were the *cheerier* ones.

"All right, I admit it," Julie all but whimpered. "I'm scared to death."

"I know," Paige said, gentling down a little. "Listen, Jules, you're the best mother in the universe," she went on softly. "But be that as it may, Calvin still needs a father."

Julie had reached the school by then, and she maneuvered into her parking spot. "You're right."

Paige laughed. "Of course I am." A pause. "Did Libby mention our getting together, the three of us, on Saturday? She wants to start shopping for her wedding dress."

The thought of Libby and her happiness made Julie feel better instantly. "We talked about it a little this morning, when I dropped Calvin off at her and Tate's house."

"Do you not think it just a little strange that they want to live there instead of the mansion?"

"It's not strange, Paige. I'm sure the small house is cozier, better suited to family life. Anyway, you know Tate's never been much for high living, and neither has Libby."

"You're staying in the main house," Paige pressed. "What's it like?"

"You've been in the ranch house, Paige. At least as far as Austin's bedroom, not to put too fine a point on things."

"Ha," Paige said. "So funny. It was dark, we were young, and I wasn't exactly thinking about architectural detail."

"I don't suppose you were," Julie drawled back. "Gotta get back to work now. Thanks for listening."

"Keep me in the loop," Paige chimed in reply.

Goodbyes were said, and the call ended.

Julie dropped her phone into her tote bag and wove her way through a river of teenagers flowing along the hallway.

Their energy exhilarated Julie, made her smile. Parents and administrators could wear her down, but the kids themselves always energized her. Many nights, after a theater group rehearsal or a performance, she was high for hours, too excited to sleep.

The afternoon sped by.

The meeting with Arthur Dulles and two school board members went exactly as Julie had expected it to—the showcase was out, unless she wanted to stage the three one-act plays in addition to the musical.

That would be impossible, of course.

Which was exactly why she was going to do it.

CHAPTER FIVE

CALVIN.

On a midnight-black horse.

As Julie drove into the yard at Tate and Libby's place late that afternoon, the sight of her child made her heart catch. Calvin looked not just happy, but transported, perched in that saddle with Garrett McKettrick behind him.

The reins rested easily in Garrett's leather-gloved hand, and his hat threw his face into shadow, but Julie felt his eyes on her as she stopped the Cadillac, shut off the motor and got out.

Man, boy and horse.

The image, Julie thought, with a sort of exhilarated terror, would remain in her mind forever, etched in sunlight, with the creek dancing behind and the sky a shade of lavender-blue that scalded her eyes.

"Look, Mom, I'm riding a horse!" Calvin crowed.

Her boy, her baby, was safe within the steely circle of Garrett's arms, she could see that plainly. And yet Julie's heart scrambled up into the back of her throat and flailed there as she thought of all the terrible things that *could* have happened.

A snake might have spooked the horse, causing him to be thrown. Badly hurt, or even killed.

Or something—some dirt mote or bit of pollen—could have brought on one of Calvin's rare but horrifying asthma attacks.

Did he have his inhaler handy, or was it still stashed in the bottom of his backpack, as usual?

She looked around, saw Tate on another horse nearby, Audrey riding in front of him, Ava holding on from behind. Libby smiled from over by the clothesline, where she was unpegging white sheets and dropping them into a basket.

Julie stared at her sister, amazed, angry, admiring. Libby's happy grin seemed to dim a little around the edges as she left the basket behind in the grass, billowing with what looked like captured clouds, and came toward her.

"Mom!" Calvin yelled again, evidently thinking Julie hadn't noticed him. "Look! *I'm riding a horse!*"

Julie's smile felt brittle on her face, and slippery, barely holding on to her mouth. *Be reasonable*, she told herself. *No need to panic.*

"Isn't that—wonderful," she said.

Libby was at her side by then. "He's all right," she said, very quietly, and with big-sister firmness. "Garrett wouldn't let anything happen to Calvin, and Tate and I were right here all the time."

Julie swallowed, watched as Garrett took off his hat, plunked it down on Calvin's head. The little boy's face disappeared inside the crown, and his muffled laugh of delight was sweet anguish to Julie.

Her Calvin.

It hurt to love so much.

"I guess this ride's over, pardner," Garrett told Calvin, reclaiming the hat and settling it back on his own head. All the while, the man's eyes never left Julie's face, and even caught up in a tangle of conflicting emotions, she would have given a lot to know what Garrett McKettrick was thinking just then.

Keeping one arm around Calvin's middle, Garrett swung his right leg over the horse's neck and jumped easily to the ground. Set Calvin on his feet.

Giggling, the little boy staggered slightly and whooped, "Whoa!"

Garrett was still watching Julie.

She marched toward him, gave another rigid smile and reached down to grab Calvin's hand.

"We have dinner plans," she said, and while she was looking back at Garrett, she was actually *speaking* to Calvin.

Wasn't she?

Calvin looked up at her. The sun lit his hair, and he shielded his eyes with one grubby little hand. "But Tate's going to barbecue," he protested. "Hot dogs and hamburgers and *everything.*"

"Another time," Julie said.

Calvin jerked his hand free of hers, and she felt stung, somewhere down deep. "But I want to stay here!"

Garrett took off his hat again, held it in one hand as he crouched next to Calvin. "A cowboy always speaks respectfully to a lady," he told the boy, "especially when that lady is his mama."

Calvin's lower lip jutted out. "She's just mad because I got on a horse without permission," he said. He turned to Julie again, his round little face and baby-blue eyes full of rebellion. "Aunt Libby *said* I could ride with Garrett! And she's the boss of me when you're not here!"

Inwardly, Julie sighed. Outwardly, she kept her cool. "We can talk about this in the car, Calvin," she said evenly. "Get your backpack, please. Right now."

Furious, Calvin pounded off toward the house to retrieve his belongings.

Garrett rose back to his full height. For a moment, it seemed he was about to say something, but in the end he just turned, stuck a foot in the stirrup and mounted again. He rode up alongside Tate, and one of the twins—Audrey, Julie thought—leaped from her dad's horse to her uncle's.

Garrett and Tate turned their horses and rode down the gently sloping creek-bank to let the animals drink.

Which meant Julie and Libby were alone for the moment, with Calvin still inside the house.

"If you didn't want Calvin to ride," Libby said mildly, "you should have told me."

Julie realized she'd been holding her last breath and let it out in a whoosh. "I'm sorry," she said. "I was just—startled."

Libby raised one eyebrow, watching Julie closely. "Startled?"

Julie bit her lower lip. "Gordon is in town," she said, very quietly, watching as Calvin stormed out of the house again, his backpack bump-dragging behind him. "Calvin and I are having dinner with him and the wife."

"Tonight?" Libby asked.

Julie nodded brusquely. "Yes. How do I prepare Calvin for this? What do I say, Libby? 'After five years, your father has finally decided he wants to meet you'?"

Libby put an arm around her, gave her a squeeze. "So *that's* why you were so peevish and unreasonable."

"I was *not* peevish and—"

"Yes, you were," Libby interrupted, smiling. "It's okay, Jules. I know you get stressed out about Calvin sometimes. I understand."

Libby *did* understand, and the knowledge was so soothing to Julie that she finally began to relax.

"I was having fun!" Calvin declared, standing a few feet away now, and glaring up at Julie. "Until *you* came along, anyway!"

"Calvin Remington," Julie said, "that's quite enough. Get in the car."

"Goodbye, Aunt Libby," he said, with all due drama. "If I don't see you again, because my *mother* is mad at you for letting me *have fun*, and she sends me away to *military school*, I'll get in touch as soon as I'm eighteen!"

Julie held on to her stern face—Calvin's behavior was *not* acceptable—but there was a giggle dancing inside her all the same. Just like the one she saw twinkling in her sister's eyes.

Libby waggled her fingers at Julie. "See you tomorrow?" she asked.

"See you tomorrow," Julie confirmed, with a sigh.

"IS THAT HIM?" Calvin whispered, a little over an hour later, when Julie led him into the Amble On Inn's small café. Gordon rose from a table over by the jukebox as they entered, while the lovely blonde woman accompanying him remained seated. "Is that my dad?"

"Yes," Julie said. After giving Calvin a lecture for acting like a brat at Libby and Tate's house, she'd explained about their dinner plans. He'd been unusually quiet since then, hadn't even protested when she'd made him shower and change clothes. "That's him."

It all seemed surreal.

How many times, over the short course of Calvin's life, had she hoped Gordon would change his mind, take a real interest in their son, be a father to him?

An old saying came to mind: *Be careful what you wish for....*

Gordon had crossed the room, and now he stood facing them. His gaze connected briefly with Julie's—he mouthed the word "thanks"—and then dropped to Calvin.

"Hey, buddy," Gordon said, putting out a hand.

Calvin studied his father's hand for a few moments, his expression solemn and wary, but finally, he reached out.

They shook hands. "Hey," Calvin replied, looking the stranger up and down.

Julie gave his back a reassuring pat. Silent-speak for *Everything's going to be okay.*

"Anybody hungry?" Gordon asked, gesturing toward the table, where the blonde waited, smiling nervously. She was dressed in a pale rose cotton skirt with a ruffled top to match, and her hair fell past her shoulders in a sumptuous tumble of spun gold. Her skin and teeth were perfect.

"We were *supposed* to have barbecue at Aunt Libby's," Calvin said gravely, though he allowed Gordon to steer him toward the blonde and the table.

The evening to come, Julie knew, would be pivotal, changing all their lives forever, even if it went well. If, on the other hand, things went badly...

Julie reined in her imagination.

"Hush, Calvin," she said, looking around. The scarred café tables, the patched-vinyl chair seats and backs, the crisply pressed gingham curtains—all of it was familiar, and therefore comforting.

"I'm Dixie," Gordon's wife said, as he pulled back a chair for Julie.

"Julie," she responded—warmly, she hoped—once she was seated. Calvin took the chair beside hers, and Gordon sat with his wife, the two of them beaming at Calvin, drinking him in with their eyes.

A sort of haze descended, at least for Julie. Later, she would remember that Gordon had been wearing a blue-and-white-striped shirt, and that Dixie had ordered a chef's salad with Thousand Island dressing on the side, and that nothing of staggering importance had been said, but she would not be able to recall what she'd eaten, or what Calvin had, either.

After dessert—there *had* been dessert, because Calvin had a smudge of something chocolate on the clean shirt he'd put on after his bath, back at the ranch house—Dixie produced a digital camera from the depths of her enormous cloth handbag and took what seemed like dozens of pictures—Calvin by himself, Calvin posing with a crouching, grinning Gordon.

Telephone numbers were swapped, and Dixie promised to email copies of the photographs as soon as she and Gordon got home.

Calvin, though polite, seemed detached, too.

After the goodbyes were said in the parking lot, and he was safely buckled into his car seat in the back of the Cadillac, Julie slipped behind the wheel and waited a beat before speaking.

"So," she said, as Dixie and Gordon went by in their big blue SUV, Gordon flashing the headlights to bright once, in cheery farewell. "That's your dad. What do you think?"

Calvin was quiet.

"Calvin?" Julie finally prompted, adjusting the rearview mirror until her son's face was visible.

At some length, Calvin huffed out a sigh. "I thought it would be different, having a dad," he said. "I thought *he* would be different."

"What do you mean?" Julie asked carefully, making no move to start up the car, though she *had* pressed the lock button as soon as she and Calvin were both inside.

"I was hoping he'd turn out to be a cowboy," Calvin admitted. "Like Tate and Garrett and Austin."

"Oh," Julie said, at a loss.

"But he's a builder guy instead," Calvin mused.

"That's good, isn't it? Building things?"

"I guess," Calvin allowed, sounding way too world-weary for a five-year-old. "I bet he gets to wear a hard hat and a tool belt and cool stuff like that, but I kind of liked it better when I could still wonder, you know?"

She *did* know. Calvin's IQ was off the charts. Young as he was, he'd probably constructed a pretty imaginative Fantasy Father in that busy little head of his. Now, he was going to have to get to know the real one, and he was bright enough to see the challenges ahead.

"Yeah," she said, very gently. She hadn't hooked up her seat belt yet, and turned sideways so she could look back at Calvin instead of watching him in the rearview. "Is something else bothering you, big guy?"

Calvin took a long time answering. "Do I have to visit my dad someplace far away, like Audrey and Ava visit their mom in New York sometimes?"

Julie's heart slipped a notch. "Not unless that's what you want," she said, when she'd injected a smile into her voice. "And you don't have to decide for a long time."

"Good," Calvin said, and the note of relief in his voice brought tears to Julie's eyes—again.

She turned once more, facing forward now, waited a few breaths, hooked on her seat belt and started the car.

"I thought I wanted a dad," Calvin confided, when they were on the main road and headed out of town. "Now, I'm not so sure. I think maybe having Tate and Garrett and Austin for uncles might be good enough."

Julie swallowed. "Well," she said, with manufactured brightness, "like I said, you don't have to decide right away." The Welcome to Blue River sign fell behind them, and it seemed to her that the night was subtly darker, the stars a little closer to the earth.

"How come you got so mad about me riding the horse?" Calvin asked, when they were well out of town, almost to the tilted mailbox marking the turnoff to Libby and Tate's little house. "I wasn't all by myself, you know. I wouldn't have gotten hurt, because Garrett was right there, behind me."

"Tell you what," Julie offered, after taking another long breath. "I'll say sorry for reacting without thinking first and getting all overprotective when I saw you on that horse, if you'll say sorry for the rude tone."

Calvin considered the deal.

"Okay," he said, at long last.

"Okay," Julie agreed.

By the time they arrived at the ranch house, Calvin was sound asleep.

He'd had a very big day for such a little guy.

Garrett happened to be in the garage when Julie pulled in. He was standing on the front bumper of an old red pickup truck, the hood raised, doing something to the works inside.

Seeing Julie, he gave a grin that stopped just short of his eyes, got down off the bumper with the same grace as he'd descended from the horse in Tate's yard earlier, and reached for a rag to wipe his hands clean.

Julie looked him over, and didn't see so much as a smidgeon of grease. When her gaze came back to his face, and she realized he'd been watching her scan him from head to foot, she blushed.

"Need some help?" he asked, when she opened the back door of the car, about to hoist Calvin out of his safety seat.

The child was nodding, half awake, half deeply asleep.

He was heavy, and Julie suddenly felt the weight of all the things she carried, visible and invisible, as she moved out of Garrett's way. Allowed him to unbuckle Calvin and lift him into his arms.

Calvin yawned, laid his head on Garrett's shoulder and went back to sleep.

The sight of this man carrying her son struck Julie in a tender place, and she wondered why that hadn't happened when she'd seen Calvin and Gordon together earlier, at the restaurant.

Julie shut the car door and followed Garrett into the kitchen, across that wide space and into the hallway leading to the guest suite she and Calvin had been occupying since the exterminators had tented the cottage.

The apartment was comfortable, though small. It boasted two bedrooms, a full bath and a little sitting room with a working fireplace and large, soft armchairs upholstered in a floral pattern made chicly shabby by age.

Harry lay curled up on a rug in front of the cold hearth, and looked up with a big dog yawn as they entered.

"You're quite a guard dog, Harry," Julie told the animal wryly.

Garrett chuckled at that, paused to look back at her.

"To your right," Julie said, in answer to the unspoken question.

He nodded, carried Calvin into the tiny bedroom.

Julie switched on the lamp on the pinewood dresser, rather than the overhead, and watched as Garrett put Calvin down carefully on the bed and stepped away, then out of the room.

Calvin stirred, blinking, his glasses askew.

Julie, now seated on the edge of his bed, set the specs aside and kissed the little boy's forehead.

"Do I have to wash and brush my teeth?" he asked.

"Yes," Julie told him. She got it then—Calvin had almost surely been pretending to be asleep all along, so Garrett would carry him. "And you have to put on your pajamas, too."

"What about my prayers?" Calvin negotiated, as Julie shifted to tug off his little tennis shoes. "Do I have to say them?"

"That's between you and God," Julie replied.

She stood, went to the dresser, took a set of yellow cotton PJ's from the top drawer, handed them to him.

Calvin was on his feet by then, resigned to washing up and brushing his teeth.

Julie waited, smiling to herself.

She heard the toilet flush, then water running in the sink.

When Calvin returned, Julie was sitting on the side of his bed and Harry was snugged in down by the footboard. Remarkably agile on his three legs, the dog had jumped up unassisted, just as he did every night.

Julie rose, and Calvin climbed into bed, staring soberly up at Julie while she tucked him in. She was oddly aware of Garrett nearby, either in the sitting room of the suite or beyond, in the big kitchen.

"I love you," she said.

Calvin grinned. "I love you more," he countered. It was a game they played, the two of them.

"I love you all the way to the moon and back," Julie replied.

"I love you twice that much."

"I love you *ten times* more," Julie batted back.

"I love you all the numbers in the world," Calvin finished triumphantly.

Julie laughed, accepting defeat gracefully. She could have thrown infinity at him, but he would merely have doubled it.

Her heart was full when she kissed Calvin once more, for good measure. She barely kept herself from hauling him into her arms and holding him tight, tight, tight.

Of course, that would have worried him.

"Can I ride on Dark Moon again tomorrow?" he asked as switched off the lamp. "If Tate is there, or Garrett?"

Julie debated silently for a few moments, then gave a suitably noncommittal answer. "Let me talk the idea over with your aunt Libby first," she said. "Maybe it would be better if you rode one of the twins' ponies instead of a big one. The ponies are more your size."

Calvin's smile, though tentative, was worth everything to Julie. "I wish I could have my own pony," he said, in an awed whisper. "My very own pony, black and white. I'd name him something cool, like Old Paint."

"Even if he wasn't old?" Julie teased. She knew she shouldn't have played along with the pony fantasy—not even for a few moments—since it wasn't one she could fulfill, but she didn't have the heart to throw cold water on the idea.

Calvin beamed. "He could be *Young* Paint, then, I guess," he said. Without his glasses he looked even younger than he was, and more vulnerable, too.

Again, Julie wanted to gather her baby into her arms and clutch him close to her. Again, for the sake of Calvin's dignity, she resisted the urge.

He yawned big and closed his eyes. Made a little crooning sound as he settled into his pillow, into his little-boy dreams.

Julie rose and went to the doorway, lingered on the threshold, listening as his breathing slowed and deepened.

He was asleep within moments.

And Garrett was still in the sitting room.

"Got a minute?" he asked.

Julie longed for a bath, a soft nightgown and eight full hours of sleep, but nodded.

"Sit down," Garrett said.

She took one of the shabby-chic chairs, and he took the other.

The chairs faced each other, and their knees, his and hers, almost touched.

"About today," Garrett began.

Julie put up a hand. "I overreacted," she said. "To the horse, I mean. I just—I don't know—a lot of things happened earlier, and I guess I just panicked—"

Garrett grinned. "You're the boy's mother," he added, when she fell silent. "If you don't want him riding horseback, that's certainly your prerogative."

Julie nodded, then shook her head, then blushed. What was it about being in this man's presence that made her feel so rattled and so confused, so off balance? No one else affected her that way—no one ever had. Not even Gordon, when they were together.

"Libby and Paige are always telling me I'm too protective of Calvin," she said. "And they're right. He has asthma, but it's not as if he's fragile or anything. I don't want him to grow up frightened of all the things that scare *me*."

"What scares you, Julie?" Garrett asked, resting one booted foot on the opposite knee and settling back in the big armchair. He was so wholly, uncompromisingly male, so at home in his own skin, that Julie began to feel warm again.

"The uncertainty, I guess," she answered, after giving the question some thought. "What if he gets hurt? What if he gets sick? What if—?" Julie stopped herself, shook her head. "You see what I mean."

Garrett nodded. "Libby looks out for Calvin when you're not around," he told her. "So does Tate."

"I know," she said.

Garrett leaned forward a little. Lamplight played in his longish dark blond hair. "Are you afraid of horses, Julie?"

She stiffened. "Afraid?"

"Afraid for yourself, I mean."

She shook her head. "I used to ride a lot," she said. "When I was younger."

That wicked, McKettrick-patented grin flashed. "But now that you're old and decrepit, you don't?"

She laughed. "It's been a while," she admitted, sobering.

"There's a bright moon out," he said. "How about a ride?"

The prospect, out-of-the-blue, off-the-wall *crazy* as it was, had more appeal than Julie would have expected it to. "Calvin's in bed," she said. "I can't just go off…"

"Esperanza's still up," Garrett said easily, when Julie ran out of steam in the middle of her sentence. "I heard her TV when we came in earlier. She could sit with Calvin for a while."

Julie shook her head. "I wouldn't want to impose."

Garrett was already on his feet, headed for the door. He seemed to have no doubt at all that the family housekeeper would agree to serve as an impromptu babysitter.

In the doorway, he stopped and looked back at Julie. "You'll want to switch that getup for jeans and a warm shirt, a jacket and boots," he said.

"But I—"

But Garrett had already left the room.

Within twenty minutes, Esperanza had settled herself on the sitting room couch, knitting and smiling while she watched TV, the sound muted.

Julie was wearing jeans, boots, a thick shirt and a denim jacket.

How did this happen? she asked herself, as she followed Garrett across the kitchen, out the back door, across the broad, grassy yard toward the barn. *How did I get here?*

The moon and stars were so bright that night, she could have read by them. Small print, no less.

"Is this even safe?" she asked. "Going riding? What if the horses can't see?"

Garrett glanced back at her. "Does everything you do have to be safe?" he countered.

"I'm the single mother of a very young child," she retorted, mildly defensive. "So, *yes*, everything I do has to be safe. As safe as I can make it, anyway."

"I'll put you on the tamest horse we have," Garrett replied, waiting until she caught up, fell into step next to him. "We'll stay on soft ground—not that Ladybug would ever throw you—and it's like daylight out here."

Julie said nothing. She didn't look at Garrett, didn't want him to see in her face that for all her misgivings, she was excited by the adventure. Maybe even a little thrilled.

"Unless, of course," Garrett went on, stepping in front of her just before they reached the entrance to the barn, blocking her way, causing her to look up at him in surprise, "it's not the horse you're afraid of."

Julie thrust out her chin, rested her hands on her hips, elbows sticking out. "If you're implying that I'm afraid of *you*, Garrett McKettrick—"

"No," he agreed, curving a finger under her chin and lifting, "but you might be a little scared of *yourself.*"

She gave a huffy burst of laughter, though the truth was that she *was* scared. "Oh, right," she said, having no choice but to tough it out. "I'm *terrified.* I might be overcome by your masculine charms, lose control, throw myself at you. It could happen at any moment!"

Garrett laughed again, and for one lovely, dreadful skittering beat of her heart, she thought he was going to kiss her.

Instead, he took her hand and led her into the barn.

Various motion-sensor lights came on as they entered, but mostly the stalls were dark.

Julie sat on a bale of hay, trying to think of a way to get out of going riding in the dark without sounding chicken, wanting, at the same time, more than practically anything, *ever*, this ride, on this night, with this man.

Garrett whistled under his breath as he led two horses out into the wide sawdust-covered aisle between the long rows of stalls and saddled them.

And Julie wondered why she wasn't behaving like a sane woman, a teacher and a mother, soaking in a nice bath, or sipping a cup of herbal tea, or a glass of white wine, before climbing into bed.

"Ready?" Garrett asked, startling her a little.

She stood. "Ready," she said.

They led the horses out into a star-silvered night, and Julie mounted without waiting for Garrett. She hadn't ridden in years—not since high school, when she'd sometimes visited the McKettrick ranch with Libby. Even then, her sister and Tate had been in love, though they would have a lot of rivers to cross before they found their way back to each other.

Garrett climbed onto his own horse, and although she couldn't be sure, Julie would have sworn he winced a little as he lowered himself into the saddle.

A smile touched down on Julie's mouth, immediately flew away again. Of *course*, she thought, Garrett had been wearing a suit to work for years. Sitting at desks. Yes, he was a McKettrick through and through, and riding was in his blood, but she wasn't the only one likely to be sore in the morning.

He bent from the saddle to work the latch on a gate, rode through and waited for Julie before shutting it again behind her.

They followed the shining ribbon of creek winding along the lower end of the range, and the lights of staff trailers and Tate and Libby's house gleamed distantly through the trees.

The peace was all-encompassing, and there was no need for words.

Julie drank it all in, the country quiet, the cloppity-clop of the horses' hooves, the babbling murmur of the creek, the sighs and whispers of the wind. The cattle were quiet, some lying down, dark lumps in the moonlight, others still grazing. Once in a while, one of them gave a low, mournful call.

She tilted her head back, breathed in not only fresh, cool air, but the very light of the stars and the moon, or so it seemed to her. She hadn't done anything this impulsive since—well, since she couldn't remember when. She was a single mother, a teacher. She loved her son, she worked and struggled and...she survived.

Moonlit horseback rides with a true cowboy, born and bred, were not part of her everyday experience.

When she and Garrett started back toward the ranch house after half an hour or so, Julie was sorry to see the odyssey end. As tired as she was, as emotionally wrung out from the evening with Gordon and Dixie, the ride left her feeling restored.

She would be ready for whatever came next.

CHAPTER SIX

JULIE STOOD FACING the big bulletin board in the high school cafeteria late the next afternoon, tacking up the printed notice announcing that tryouts for *Kiss Me Kate* would begin on Monday afternoon of the following week, as soon as the day's classes were over.

"So it's official, huh?" the girl asked, trying to smile. "The showcase is out and the musical is in?"

Julie had been inside all day, and she needed some fresh air. She felt frustrated and out of sorts—none of which was Rachel's problem. "I was thinking we could do a single performance of each of the plays—no props, no extras of any kind—and record them. Send digital copies—"

Rachel colored up so quickly that Julie fell silent.

The worst was true, then. Rachel had already given up on going to college.

"My little brothers need me," she said, at once shy and fierce. "They're having a really hard time without Mom, and Dad tries, but it isn't the same."

The last bell of the day shrilled, signaling dismissal.

Julie waited for it to stop, but even when it had, the din was joyously horrendous—kids poured out of classrooms, locker doors squealed open and slammed shut again, exuberant plans were shouted, and most likely texted, from one end of the school's main corridor to the other.

Julie had always loved the sounds and the energy of kids. Her dad had often said, with a look of tired contentment in his eyes, that he'd been born to teach and Julie had never doubted he was right.

In that way, she was like Will Remington—teaching was her gift. She loved children, related to them, thrilled to the excitement some of them radiated when she finally got through, and they grasped some concept that had eluded them before.

Of course there were always others who, for one reason or another, couldn't be reached. She didn't want Rachel to be one of those kids.

But what could she say? In Rachel's place, she might have done the same thing. And it was sobering to think that, in some ways, Libby *had* been in a position similar to this young girl's.

Libby hadn't joined the school band or acted in plays or tried out for cheerleader. She'd come straight home every day, after her last class, to mother Julie and Paige.

Something buzzed, jolting Julie out of her reflections.

Rachel took a cheap cell phone from the pocket of her hooded sweatshirt and peered at the screen. The phone looked like a pay-as-you-go model, the kind sold in convenience stores, along with tacky cigarette lighters, energy boosters in little bottles and candy bars in faded wrappers.

Julie wasn't really surprised to see the cell, of course. Kids with virtually nothing else had phones. It was a sign of the times.

"Dad sent me a text," Rachel explained, though Julie hadn't asked. "He wants me to go over to the elementary school and take the bus home with my brothers before I head over to the bowling alley for work."

Julie nodded. "I could give you a ride," she offered, wondering how Rachel planned to get back to the bowling alley after she took the boys home and if there would be anyone to look after them after she left.

But Rachel shook her head. "That's okay," she said.

Still, she didn't move to walk away.

"Was there something else, Rachel?" Julie finally asked.

"I just—I just wanted to say thank you, Ms. Remington. For

picking my play to be in the showcase and everything. It really meant a lot to me." Sorrow shone in the girl's wide, luminous eyes, and a kind of determined bravery. "Guess I'd better get moving, or I might miss the elementary school bus." With that, Rachel was gone, hurrying through the crowds of departing kids, disappearing from view.

Julie was still pensive, half an hour later, when she stopped by Libby and Tate's to pick up Calvin.

He was down at the creek-side, with the twins and Libby, all of them wielding fishing poles.

Julie parked the pink bomb and got out, cheered by the sight.

"Have you caught anything yet?" she called, from the top of the bank, her arms folded against a chilly wind. It was bonfire weather, leaf-burning, blue-skied, hot-soup-simmering-on-the stove weather.

"Not one single fish," Libby called back, grinning. She wore jeans, a heavy sweatshirt, sneakers and a ponytail. Briefly, guiltily, Julie envied her sister, soon to be married to a man who loved her. "Guess it's beans and wieners for supper tonight!"

Julie laughed, because envy or no envy, she loved both her sisters. And she was happy for Libby, happy for Tate, happy for Audrey and Ava, the six-year-old twins who needed the stability their father and future stepmother provided.

Calvin seemed set apart from them all somehow, and Julie felt an ache of sadness as he reeled in his fishing line and turned to trudge up the bank behind Libby and the twins.

"Hi, Mom," he said, without particular enthusiasm.

Julie laid a hand on his head, ruffled his hair. "Hey," she said back.

"You might as well stay for supper," Libby said quietly, slipping an arm around Julie's waist and steering her toward the little house. She gave Julie a mischievous grin and a sisterly squeeze. "I'm not *really* serving beans and wieners," she said. "We're having stew, and it's been simmering in the Crock-Pot all day. It smells like heaven."

"*You* cooked?" Julie teased.

Libby laughed, sent the three kids around back to put the fishing poles away on the covered porch and take off their muddy shoes. "Now that I don't have the Perk Up to run, I'm developing all sorts of new skills."

Julie's insides warmed at the twinkle in her sister's eyes—and the aroma of savory stew, as they stepped into the living room. Until their mother, Marva, had driven Julie's Cadillac through the front wall and brought the whole place down, timber-and-brick, Libby had been the harried owner of a coffee shop on Main Street.

Three dogs—Libby's aging Lab, Hildie, and the twins' matching mutts, Ambrose and Buford—barked a greeting.

Libby shushed them, while Julie looked around at the living room, admiring the renovations anew, even though she'd seen the project unfolding all along. A row of floor-to-ceiling windows overlooked the creek and the towering oak trees in one direction, and the old orchard in the other. A fire crackled on the hearth of the natural stone fireplace, and the screen of Libby's new computer ran a perpetual slide show of photos she'd taken herself—Tate, the girls, Calvin, the breathtaking scenery that surrounded them on all sides.

"How's the online degree coming along?" Julie asked, as the dogs deserted them, en masse, for the kitchen, where the kids were entering from the back porch.

Libby looked back at her, shrugged. "It's coming," she said. "I've mostly been looking at pictures of other people's weddings online." She dropped into a cushy armchair, legs dangling over one side, looking more like a teenager than a woman about to be married. "Sit," she added.

Julie sat. The kids and the dogs were making a commotion in the kitchen, but it didn't seem to bother Libby, so Julie didn't worry, either.

"Are we still on for the shopping trip on Saturday?" Libby asked.

"Why wouldn't we be?" Julie countered. The snap in her voice surprised her as much as it did Libby.

Julie frowned.

Libby waited a few beats. "What's bothering you, Jules? Did dinner with Gordon and the missus go badly?"

Julie sighed. Shook her head. "It was…okay," she said. "I'm

still worried about how this whole thing is going to be for Calvin, but for right now, anyway, I think I can feel my way through."

"Then, what?" Libby inquired gently. She wasn't pushy, but she wasn't going to be put off, either. "The cottage being under a tent? The job?"

Again, Julie sighed. "Arthur Dulles and the school board have spoken," she said. "I'd planned on showcasing the one-act plays—I told you about them—but a musical always brings in more money, so it's scratch the showcase and stage the umpteenth amateur production of a Broadway staple."

Libby smiled, looking a little puzzled. "I've never known you to balk at an excuse to sing and dance," she said. "Even vicariously, by directing instead of actually treading the boards."

Julie laughed, feeling better already, but the bittersweet sensation, like sadness but *not* sadness, lingered. "*Kiss Me Kate* will be lots of fun," she admitted. "But I was counting on the showcase to help those three kids get into college."

Libby raised an eyebrow. "Won't they get in anyway? They're all smart."

"Tim and Becky will," Julie nodded, thinking of the two young playwrights whose plays she'd planned to produce, along with Rachel's. Both of them were from middle-class families, and they had scholarships and loans in place. "I'm not so sure about Rachel."

Libby simply waited, so at ease sprawled in that chair.

Julie told her sister what little she knew about the girl's circumstances.

"You're afraid she won't go to college because her dad and her brothers need her?" Libby recapped, when Julie had finished. Julie nodded.

Calvin, the twins and the three dogs all straggled in from the kitchen.

"Can we watch TV?" one of the twins asked. Both girls were beautiful, with their father's McKettrick-blue eyes. They wore mismatched jeans, boots, plaid flannel shirts and long, ebony-dark braids. They were alike—and at the same time, different.

"No, Audrey," Libby replied cheerfully.

"Not even if it's something educational?" the other twin asked, while Calvin looked on earnestly, his glasses a little crooked. He was still wearing his coat, though he'd left his shoes on the back porch, that being the house rule whenever the kids had been down by the creek or out in the garden, and was therefore padding about in his stocking feet.

Julie ached with mother-love, just looking at him. He was so beautiful—and he would be a little boy for such a short time.

For a moment, she wanted to stop every clock in the world, stop the universe itself. *Wait, wait. My baby is growing up too fast....*

She shook off the fanciful thoughts, gestured for Calvin to come to her.

He did, dragging his feet only a little along the way, and she un-zipped his two-toned nylon coat. Pushed it back off his shoulders.

"We're staying for supper," she told him.

Calvin's face lit up instantly, and Julie felt another rush of help-less love for her boy.

"Yippee!" he yelled.

The dogs barked again, the twins echoed Calvin's shouts and Libby and Julie merely waited for the hoopla to subside.

The swooping roar of an airplane engine distracted everybody.

"I bet that's Uncle Garrett!" Ava yelled, dashing to the front door, wrenching it open and rushing outside, soon followed by the dogs and her sister and Calvin, still in his stocking feet.

Libby and Julie brought up the rear, Julie scooping Calvin off the ground with a laugh and a squeeze, all of them with their faces turned skyward.

Julie's heart lifted off like a rocket from a launcher, as she stood watching. The small plane flew low, tracing the crooked path of the creek for a few hundred yards, then circled back, tipped a wing twice and finally banked to zoom away over the range.

"It *is* Uncle Garrett!" Audrey whooped, beaming.

"I bet Dad's with him!" Ava agreed.

Libby laughed and held both girls against her sides for a mo-ment, bending to kiss each of them on top of the head once be-fore letting them go.

"We'd better get the table set," Libby told the kids. "There are at least two hungry McKettrick men headed our way."

The next few minutes were happy chaos—more dog-barking, more kid-laughter, a lot of washing of hands and faces, along with the clinking of silverware and the colorful everyday dishes Libby loved to mix and match.

When Tate came in, some minutes later, Libby and the twins flew at him, and he laughed and somehow managed to enfold them all. Garrett was right behind him, taking off his hat as he crossed the threshold, the gesture so old-fashioned that it almost made him seem shy.

Garrett's too-blue gaze caught on Julie as he hung his hat on a peg by the door, shrugged out of his faded denim jacket and hung that up, too. When he shifted his attention from her to Calvin, she felt it again—that same sensation of leaving the ground that she'd experienced earlier, while watching the airplane.

"Hey, buddy," he said. And then, with no hesitation at all, Garrett swept Calvin up, as he might have done with a boy of his own, and added, "How's my horseback ridin' partner?"

Calvin beamed, all but transported. "Pretty good," he said. Then, breathlessly, "Was that you and Tate in the airplane?"

Garrett nodded. "Sure enough was," he said. "Didn't you see us waving at you?"

"Yep," Calvin said, delighted. "I saw the wings tip, like you were saying hello. Will you take me flying with you sometime?"

Garrett's grin didn't falter, but his gaze moved from Calvin to Julie. "That's up to your mother," he said quietly.

Calvin seemed to deflate. "Oh," he said, dejected.

Garrett bounced him once before setting the child back on his feet. "Hello, Julie," he said, watching her.

Hello, Julie. It was a perfectly ordinary greeting, nothing more.

And yet, for just the length of a heartbeat, the floor—the earth itself—seemed to shift beneath Julie's feet.

It was all too easy, during that momentary interlude, to flash on another warm, bright kitchen, in some unknown house, homey like this one, with Garrett pulling *her* into his arms, just the way Tate was doing with Libby, and kissing her soundly. It was all too easy to imagine a *lot* of things.

She blushed.

"Can I go flying with Garrett, Mom?" Calvin demanded, breaking the spell.

"Someday," Julie said. Her son was standing right in front of her, tugging at the sleeve of her teacherly—make that *dowdy*—cardigan sweater. With it, she wore a long tweed skirt and a prim blouse. And just then, her gaze still locked with Garrett's, she had to shake off the odd sensation that she'd mistakenly put on someone else's clothes that morning—the garments of a much older person.

Garrett smiled.

She blushed harder.

"Someday?" Calvin protested.

"Someday," Julie repeated.

Tate lifted the lid off the Crock-Pot and drew in an appreciative breath, while the kids, including Calvin, scrambled into chairs at the big table in the center of the kitchen. Libby bent to take a baking sheet from the oven—*biscuits?*—and Tate gave his future wife a subtle pat on her blue-jeaned bottom.

Julie smiled at that, aware of Garrett still standing near enough to touch, near enough that she could feel the heat and the hard strength of that cowboy body of his.

"Hey," Libby said, making a face at Tate. "Cut it out, bucko."

Tate laughed.

"You made biscuits?" Julie marveled.

"There is no end to my talents," Libby replied.

"You can say that again," Tate told her, in a low growl, grinning the whole time.

"Little pitchers," Libby reminded him, singsong, indicating the kids with an eloquent nod of her head.

But the kids were oblivious, Audrey and Ava scrapping over who got to sit by Garrett, Calvin wistful behind the lenses of his glasses, which were steamed up after Libby passed the basket full of biscuits under his nose.

Julie sat down, and so did Libby, but Garrett and Tate remained on their feet until after they were settled. Garrett winked at the twins, and they each moved one seat over, as if by tacit agreement, leaving a space open next to Calvin.

Garrett dropped into the seat.

Grace was offered, and then everyone dove in, ravenous.

Julie prided herself on her cooking—it had always been *her* area of expertise—but Libby's stew and biscuits were wonderful, and she seemed so proud of the accomplishment that Julie was touched.

Overall, confusion reigned—there was a lot of laughter—and Calvin drank his milk without the usual complaints. He hated the stuff, rarely missed an opportunity to remind Julie that no other species on the planet drank milk after they were weaned *except* humans.

Five going on fifty-two, that was Calvin. Just as Garrett had recently remarked.

But tonight the little boy sported a milk-mustache and listened wide-eyed as Garrett and Tate talked about flying high over the Silver Spur, and how it was a handy way of knowing which part of the herd was where.

They'd seen part of a remote fence down, too, which explained some missing cattle, though there had been no sign of the cattle themselves. At first light, they meant to head out there in Tate's truck, a crew following, and have a closer look.

"Rustlers?" Libby asked. She'd been about to take a bite of stew, but she lowered the spoon back to her bowl then, looking worried.

"Maybe," Tate said, clearly unconcerned.

Garrett flung a look across the table at his brother, then turned to favor Libby and all three kids with an easy sweep of a smile, heavy on the McKettrick charm. "Fences," he said, "have been known to fall down on their own, with no help at all from rustlers. Sometimes cattle trample them, too."

Libby didn't look reassured, and Julie was with her on that one. Rustlers were still a problem on far-flung ranches like the Silver Spur. They herded other people's cattle into the backs of waiting semis now, under cover of darkness, instead of driving the creatures overland on horseback, as in the movies, but they were still criminals, and at least some of them still carried guns, too.

Julie and Libby exchanged glances.

The conversation turned to airplanes again. Back in college, Garrett had worked summers for a crop-dusting outfit. That was how he'd learned to fly. Calvin listened, spellbound, as Garrett and Tate swapped memories of some pretty wild adventures—including taking their dad's plane up once, when he'd gone to Houston on business, and nearly plowing that restored World War II bomber into the side of a mountain when the throttle got stuck.

Garrett had managed to pull out of the dive in time and make a safe landing, but word of the exploit must have gotten back to Jim McKettrick, though he never mentioned it, because a week later, he'd sold the plane.

"You think he missed it?" Tate asked Garrett thoughtfully, settling back in his chair. He'd made a respectable dent in the stew, and consumed a few biscuits, too. "The bomber, I mean?"

Garrett chuckled. "Maybe," he answered, "but you know how Mom hated it when he went up in that thing. I like to think things were a little more peaceful here on the home front, when it was gone."

For a few moments after that, both men were quiet, probably remembering their parents, missing them. Jim and Sally McKettrick, Julie recalled sadly, had been killed in a car crash a decade before.

After the meal was over, Garrett and Tate cleared the table and loaded the dishwasher, while the kids got underfoot trying to help.

Libby smiled and shook her head at the sight, her face so full of love that, yet again, Julie's throat tightened.

Not for the first time, it struck Julie how reckless, how truly dangerous it was, to love with one's whole heart.

But what else could a person do?

Seeing that Calvin was finally starting to run down, Julie told him to gather up his things, they both said their thank-yous and Garrett grabbed his coat and hat from the pegs and came outside with them, into the deepening chill of an autumn twilight.

"Catch a ride back to the ranch house with you?" Garrett asked. Seeing him standing there in his cowboy getup, Julie could almost forget that he was really a politician, more at home in an expensive suit, making deals behind closed doors.

Sharing hot tubs with any number of half-naked women who were most definitely not his cousins.

Julie shook off the image; she was being downright silly.

And, anyway, Garrett wasn't married. He could cavort with all the women he wanted to, half-naked or otherwise.

"Sure," she answered finally, holding Calvin's backpack while he scrambled into his seat in the back. "We'd be glad to give you a lift."

Calvin was being so good. He normally made a fuss whenever

they left Libby and Tate's place—it was as if he wanted to live there, instead of with her.

Grateful for small favors, Julie made sure he was properly fastened in before sliding behind the wheel.

"This is quite a car," Garrett said, settled in on the passenger side of the pink Cadillac.

"It's a classic," Julie said fondly. She'd always loved the pink bomb, but lately she'd been thinking of trading it in for something smaller and more fuel-efficient. "It burns a lot of gas, though."

"It's a dinosaur," Calvin contributed, from the peanut gallery. "Some woman won it, about a hundred years ago, for selling a lot of face cream and stuff."

Garrett chuckled at that.

Julie caught Calvin's eye in the rearview mirror and made a face at him.

Calvin was revved up again. "My grandma drove this car right through the front of Aunt Libby's coffee shop, and all that happened was it got a few dents and scratches."

"I heard about that," Garrett said. His voice was a low rumble of amusement, and Julie realized she was aware of him in a holographic sort of way—every cell in her body seemed to contain the whole.

Julie concentrated on driving. *Back up. Turn around. Point the headlights down the driveway, toward the main road. Don't go too fast. Don't go too slow.*

"This car is built like a tank," Calvin went on. "That's what Aunt Libby says."

Garrett smiled, adjusted his hat. "Is that right?" he asked conversationally, and Julie felt his gaze touch her in the relative darkness as they bumped over an old cattle guard.

The moon was out, as it had been the night before, when she and Garrett had gone riding. When they reached the mansion, Julie used the remote control Esperanza had given her to open the garage door.

Julie couldn't help flashing back on the previous evening, when she and Calvin had come back here after having supper in town with Gordon and Dixie, and Calvin had pretended to be asleep so Garrett would carry him inside.

The way fathers had always carried sleeping children into houses, generation upon generation.

That night, however, Calvin was mobile, clearly still trying to make a good impression on Garrett. Harry greeted them at the garage door, wagging hard and whimpering a little, and Garrett took the dog outside.

Calvin submitted to his nightly bath without significant fuss.

He brushed his teeth, took off his glasses and crawled into bed, hands clasped together, lips moving and eyes closed in silent prayer.

Julie bent and kissed his forehead. "I love you a lot, big guy," she told him.

"I love you, too, Mom," Calvin whispered, his eyes open wide now. "But I really think you should give me permission to go up in Garrett's airplane with him."

Harry came in and leaped up onto the foot of Calvin's bed to settle in for the night.

"You really think that, do you?" Julie grinned.

"Yes," Calvin said, blinking. Looking into the pale, innocent blue of her son's eyes, she caught a momentary glimpse of forever—her heart embraced his children and their children's children.

Because she was so moved, Julie's response came out sounding a little croaky. "Why?" she asked, genuinely curious. Calvin had always talked a lot about horses—he loved race cars and roller coasters, too, though he'd never had a direct experience with either—but he'd never shown any particular interest in airplanes.

Of course, he was young.

He still had a lot to discover.

Calvin's small shoulders moved beneath the cotton top of his pajamas as he executed a nonchalant shrug. "It sounds pretty exciting. Being able to wave at people from the sky and stuff."

Julie nodded in agreement. "A lot of things are exciting," she said, "but that doesn't mean we need to rush out and do them."

"Is that like when I used to say I crossed the road without permission because my friend Justin did, and you asked me if Justin jumped off a bridge, would I do it, too?"

She smiled. "Sort of," she said. "My point is, you've got lots of time. You can do all the things you really want to do—eventually."

"But not now?" he sounded monumentally disappointed.

"Some now," Julie conceded, smoothing back his hair. "Some, later."

"Like that?" Calvin pressed. "Like what?"

"Riding horses," Julie heard herself say. "As long as Tate or Libby—" she paused, swallowed, because this was hard for her, as much as she trusted her sister and future brother-in-law "—or Garrett is around. No trying to ride by yourself or with just the twins around. I need your word on that, Calvin."

Calvin looked thrilled. "Will you tell them it's okay for me to ride even if you're not there?" he wanted to know. "Because Aunt Libby thought it was okay, because it's always been okay before, and then you saw me on the big black horse with Garrett and you got upset—"

Julie pressed a finger to Calvin's mouth. "Shhh," she said. "I'll tell them."

"Good!" Calvin said, burrowing down into his covers and his pillow and squinching his eyes shut tight, the way he did on Christmas Eve, because Julie had told him Santa wouldn't come until he was asleep.

Julie doubted that he still believed, but he was willing to pretend for a little while longer, and so was she.

She kissed him again, patted Harry good-night and stood.

Tired as she was, Julie knew she wouldn't be able to sleep yet; her mind was racing. After peeking into the kitchen to make sure Garrett wasn't there, reading the newspaper or something, she went back to her room, changed into her swimsuit, a black one-piece, clipped her hair up on top of her head, grabbed a towel and headed for the indoor swimming pool.

What she needed, she decided, was a little exercise.

Her body wasn't particularly sore from the horseback ride the night before, but her *mind* could use some unkinking, that was for sure.

After crossing the kitchen, Julie stood on the tiled edge of the magnificent pool and looked up.

The retractable roof was shut, but the light of the stars and moon shimmered through the glass panels arching two stories overhead, and danced on the dark water at her feet. She and Calvin had used the pool several times during their short stay, and it was usually lit from beneath, from a dozen different angles, but she didn't know where the switches were and saw no point in searching for them.

Julie dropped her towel onto a chaise longue and stepped into the pool at the shallow end. The water was perfect, not too cool, and not too warm, either, and she felt pure joy as she plunged forward and swam vertical laps back and forth, back and forth.

The flood of multicolored light rose up around her suddenly; it was as though she were inside a giant prism. She stopped, blinking, in the grip of the strange magic she'd begun to sense earlier, when she'd said good-night to Calvin.

"Oops," Garrett said. "Sorry."

Julie turned, saw that he was standing on the side nearest the kitchen, barefoot, tousle-haired, and wearing a terrycloth robe.

"You scared me," she said, without recrimination. And then she laughed, treading water in the middle of that gigantic pool, with all those shafts of colored light rising up around her.

He grinned. "Sorry," he said again.

Julie's gaze dropped. Was he wearing swimming trunks under that bathrobe?

Surely he was.

Wasn't he?

Before Julie could decide one way or the other, Garrett shed the robe, revealing a pair of trunks. He dove into the water and surfaced about a foot in front of her, droplets flying as he gave his head a shake. His eyelashes were spiky with moisture, and his mouth curved into a mischievous smile.

Julie's heart, still pounding from the start he'd given her by switching on the underwater light show, began to slow down a little, find its normal beat.

And then she laughed again, because Garrett did a couple of slow somersaults in the water, as deft as a seal, before surfacing again, this time closer. Close enough to make her breath catch, in fact.

Was he showing off?

No, she decided. Garrett was *reveling*, celebrating his own agility and the water itself.

And there was something so elemental, so sexy about that, that Julie felt a fierce grab of desire, unlike anything any other man had ever aroused in her, in a place so deep inside her that it went beyond the physical.

That was when she knew she was in big, *big* trouble.

CHAPTER SEVEN

AS FAR AS Garrett was concerned, kissing Julie Remington was as inevitable as drawing in his next breath. There, in the middle of the pool, he cupped his hands on either side of her face, bent his head and touched his lips to hers—lightly at first, in case she wanted to pull back—and then more deeply when she gave a soft moan and slipped her arms around his neck.

Garrett had kissed a lot of women in his time—he'd enjoyed all those kisses, even thrilled to some of them, but this one, *this one*, seemed to clutch at something deep inside him and hold on, squeezing the breath out of him.

When he finally came up for air, it was out of pure desperation, because his lungs demanded oxygen. He had an odd sense of settling back into himself after being catapulted to somewhere else, and when he opened his eyes and saw Julie staring back at him, looking as baffled as he felt, he laughed.

Julie eased back a little way, although she wasn't out of reach. Pink splotches glowed on her cheeks, and her wonderful chameleon eyes shifted between blue and violet as they drew color from the water.

Garrett longed to pull her close again, kiss her again, hell, do a *lot more* than kiss her. But he didn't move. She was as rattled as he was—all five of his known senses told him that, and a few besides. If he came on too strong, he'd scare her away, maybe for good.

"What just happened here?" Julie asked, her toned arms moving gracefully as she went on treading water.

Garrett couldn't hold back a grin. He was too damn happy. "I think you kissed me," he said, though he knew her question had been rhetorical.

He was rewarded by a widening of her eyes and an indrawn breath. "I beg your pardon, Garrett McKettrick," she said. "*You* kissed *me.*"

"So I did," he replied easily. "Now that we agree on what 'just happened' here, let's figure out what comes next."

"*Nothing* comes next," Julie said, turning and gliding toward the side of the pool. Gripping the tiled edge with one hand, she looked back at him.

Her spirally copper hair was coming down from the clip on the top of her head, but she didn't seem to notice, and that was fine with Garrett. In the shifting, watery light, she looked like the goddess of ice and fire. There was only one thing he wanted to do more than look at her, and that was touch her, all over, inside and out.

Whoa, he thought. *Go easy, cowboy.*

Julie moved toward the ladder, probably intending to climb out of the pool and flee.

"Wait," Garrett heard himself say. The voice, though his own, was strange to him, hoarse.

She'd reached the ladder, gripped one of the rungs. Looking back at him over one delectable and faintly freckled shoulder, she bit her lower lip, as though pondering some inner dilemma.

"If you say nothing happens next, Julie," Garrett told her, keeping his distance, "then that's the way it will be. You don't have to run away."

She gave a little burst of laughter, part indignation and part relief, and let go of the ladder, moved away from the side of the pool, though she remained well out of Garrett's reach. Her hair escaped the clip and she raised both arms to attend to the problem, causing her perfect breasts to jut forward.

"Who says I was running away?" she asked.

The kiss had made Garrett hard; the lift of Julie's breasts sent scorching heat pounding through him, rendering him speechless. In a vain effort to cool off, he ducked under the water, considered staying down there long enough to drown himself, and then surfaced again.

When he did, Julie had secured her hair in the squeeze clip, though tendrils spiraled down around her cheeks, her shoulders, the side of her neck.

Garrett wanted to trace the length of that lovely neck with his lips, the tip of his tongue, find her earlobe and nibble at it, make her moan.

He didn't move, though. The water did little to cool his blood; in fact, he half expected the contents of that pool to come to a slow simmer around him.

"So," he said, "are you seeing anybody?"

Are you seeing anybody? Talk about hokey. Why didn't he just put on a bad toupee, one of those two-tone jobs maybe, hang a slug of gold chains around his neck, and ask what her sign was?

She smiled. "No," she said, after considering the question for a long moment. That was it, just "no," and then she left him to dangle.

Garrett might as well have been a kid again, he felt so awkward. Where, he wondered, was the mover and shaker, the bring-it-on guy, the smooth operator who could handle anything?

Someplace else, evidently.

Nobody here but a beautiful woman and a country boy making a damn fool out of himself, he thought.

Being a McKettrick meant never knowing when to quit, a trait that could be a blessing or a curse, depending on the situation. Garrett kept talking, when he might have been better off shutting up. "Maybe—we could—well—do something?"

Julie chortled at that—the sound was warm and throaty, made him imagine waking up next to her, deeply rested after a night of frenetic sex, followed by hours of exhausted sleep. She turned, moved to the ladder and climbed up it. Water sluiced off her in iridescent sheets, and her backside swayed slightly. Things ground together inside Garrett, an achy shift in a place where he hadn't known there *was* a place, up to now.

Sitting on the edge of the pool, Julie reached for a towel, wrapped it around her shoulders, idly moved her feet in the water. She was shivering a little.

"What kind of 'something' do you have in mind, Garrett?" she asked, in her own good time.

She knew, of course, that she was getting to him. And she was enjoying it.

The single mother, devoted to her son.

The teacher, dedicated to her students and her work.

It amazed him that she was the same person as the offbeat girl he'd known in high school.

Julie Remington was all those things, and a lot more besides. There was mischief in her, and fire, and the rare, lasting mystery that just keeps on unfolding, indefinitely. A man could spend a lifetime, he realized with a jolt, maybe longer, just uncovering all the layers of who she was, what she wanted, what she had to give.

The prospect enticed him and, at the same time, scared the hell out of him. At no time in his life, in no situation, had he ever felt out of his depth.

He did now.

"Garrett?" she prompted, raising one eyebrow slightly.

"I was thinking maybe we could go out to dinner," he said, and was surprised by his own ability to speak coherently. Inside, all was chaos—collisions, things sparking off each other and igniting. "Maybe to a movie."

"Dinner," she repeated, still swinging her legs back and forth. "Where?"

Except for the café at the Amble On Inn, the Silver Dollar Saloon, a snack bar in the bowling alley and a few fast-food places, Blue River didn't have much to offer in the way of restaurants. "Paris?" he asked.

Julie smiled. She probably thought he was kidding.

The weird thing was, he wasn't.

He was thinking "private jet." Sex in swanky hotel rooms with views of the Seine, room service champagne, more sex.

"Be serious," she said.

"How about Austin, then?" Garrett persisted, though he made up his mind, then and there, that he would take Julie Remington to Paris, sooner rather than later. "Or maybe San Antonio?"

While he waited for her answer, Garrett let himself imagine what it would be like to pleasure this woman. The thought of her buckling against his mouth or under his hips in the last frantic throes of an orgasm turned his hard-on from problematic to out-and-out painful.

Something sparked in Julie's eyes, putting Garrett in mind of a tigress, living fierce and free in some jungle. He knew in one dizzying flash of insight—or perhaps it was pure animal *instinct*—that here was a woman capable of throwing her whole self into the fire, of abandoning inhibition, of giving in completely to her own responses and those of the man lucky enough to be making love to her.

If it hadn't been for the little guy, Calvin, snoozing away in his room in the guest quarters, Garrett figured he would simply have gotten out of the pool, whisked the tempting Ms. Remington up into his arms and carried her upstairs, Rhett Butler-style. He'd have had her in the shower first, after peeling away that clinging wet bathing suit and shedding the swim trunks.

But Calvin was a reality.

"It would probably be easier," she mused, "if I just cooked dinner for you." She bit her lower lip. "Us. You and me and Calvin, I mean—"

She was as nervous as he was. Garrett found that reassuring. *You and me and Calvin...*

Garrett shook off the momentary daze he'd slipped into, thinking about Julie naked in his private shower, warm and slick and, unless he missed his guess, hyperorgasmic.

"Wouldn't you rather go to a restaurant?" he asked. The passing moments, it seemed to Garrett, were marked by the beat of his own heart.

The atmosphere was humid, almost sultry, and the play of lights, having gone through a programmed sequence, slowed and then stopped, throwing the pool and the area surrounding it into something akin to twilight.

"Julie?" he said, low, because she'd been silent for so long, pondering.

She slipped forward, eased back into the water, waited by the side. Either she couldn't speak or she'd chosen not to—Garrett could guess which one.

He went to her, but slowly. Ever so slowly.

"Kiss me again," she murmured, when he was facing her.

He pressed his mouth to hers, all but pinning her body against the smooth-tiled wall of the pool. Everything in him ached to have her—*here, now*—but even then, lost in that second, deeper kiss, he was careful.

No sudden moves, he thought.

When the kiss ended, leaving both of them breathless, Garrett kept the hard angles of his frame close against Julie's curvy softness, but without pressure. He said her name again, nibbled at the side of her neck, tasted her earlobe, the way he'd wanted to do earlier, delighted in the little moan she uttered.

"Garrett," she whispered. He felt her palms flatten against his chest, but she didn't push. "It's too soon—we have to stop, and I don't think—I don't think I can do that if you don't help me out a little here."

He drew back far enough to leave a space between them, probably no thicker than the fabric of her swimsuit. His breath was ragged, and he gripped the pool's edge on either side of Julie, not to trap her, but to keep himself from sinking.

"Okay," he rasped out. "Okay."

She planted a wet kiss in the cleft of his chin, then ducked under his left arm, grabbed hold of the ladder again and climbed out of the pool.

He couldn't bear to watch her this time. That trim waist, that perfect backside—dammit, there was a limit to what one man could take without going crazy.

"Good night, Garrett" he heard her say.

Garrett closed his eyes, rested his forehead against the tile, held on to the pool's edge with both hands. A verbal response was more than he could manage—he merely nodded once, and listened as she hurried away.

After a long time, he returned to his own part of the house, stood in the long living room, with its row of floor-to-ceiling windows, looking out over the darkened range. Although he hadn't been around a lot since going to work for the senator right after law school, it wasn't because the quarters lacked creature comforts.

He turned, taking in the huge natural rock fireplace, the full-sized kitchen beyond the dining area. There were two bedrooms, each with its own bath, in addition to the master suite. The apartment covered nearly five thousand square feet, and it had two exits of its own, one leading to the garage on the lower level, one to a set of stone stairs ending in the yard.

After their folks' death, Garrett recalled grimly, one of them—Austin or Tate or himself, he didn't know—had suggested dividing the big house into sections.

The idea had seemed like a good one at the time, Garrett thought now, with a rueful smile. The kind of thing young men tend to come up with, he supposed, when they've just lost their folks and feel a need to dig their roots in deeper and hold on to their piece of ground.

Garrett had draped a towel around his waist before leaving poolside, but he was dripping on the slate-tile floors. He made his way into the master bath, opened the shower door and stepped inside.

The space boasted a stone bench and fully a dozen different sprayers that could be angled to suit.

If Julie had been there, he might have done some fancy sprayer-arranging, but since it was just him—dammit—he used only the big round one, overhead. He took off the swim trunks and let them hit the shower floor with a soggy plop, and switched on the water.

He soaped and rinsed, but shaving seemed like a waste of time, since he'd have to do it again in the morning.

Scrubbed, smelling of soap and shampoo, Garrett snatched a towel, dried himself rigorously and walked out of the bathroom with the towel hooked around his waist.

He was hungry.

He meandered into his kitchen—since he rarely bothered to stock the shelves or the refrigerator, preferring to cadge meals from Esperanza when he was on the ranch—and checked out the supply situation.

It amounted to meager—or a little less than that.

The fridge was empty except for half a loaf of blue-crusted bread and an egg carton with an expiration date that made Garrett hesitant to lift the lid.

He chucked both items into a garbage bag, nose wrinkled, and headed for the inside staircase, planning to dispose of it in one of the trash bins outside the garage.

Realizing he was naked except for the towel, he paused at the top of the stairs, garbage bag in hand, debating the wisdom of going down there in what practically constituted the altogether.

Running into Julie would be one thing—he took a few moments to savor the fantasy—but meeting up with Calvin or Esperanza would be another. With a sigh, Garrett set the bag down, returned to his bedroom and pulled on a pair of jeans.

Then he took the garbage downstairs and outside, where the chill bit into his bare chest and the soles of his feet, so that he did a hopping little dance back into the kitchen.

He washed his hands at the nearest sink, checked the multiple refrigerators for leftovers, and wound up munching on cold cereal because nothing else appealed to him.

He was just sticking his empty bowl into a dishwasher when the dog padded out on his three legs, wagging his tail.

Garrett acknowledged the animal with a smile, was about to head back upstairs, where he *might* get some sleep, when Harry pressed his beagle-snout to the crack between the outside door and the frame.

He glanced toward the guest quarters, half expecting—hell, *hoping*—that Julie would be there.

Only she wasn't.

The dog gave a benign little whimper.

Garrett sighed. "It's *cold* out there," he protested.

The dog whimpered again.

He bent, checked the tags on the mutt's collar. "Listen, *Harry*," he said, drawing on his negotiation skills, "maybe you wouldn't mind doing your thing on some newspaper, just this once—"

Harry gave an urgent whine, raised one of his front paws to scratch at the door—he had two legs in front and one in back— and he teetered a little, trying to stay balanced.

"Oh, *all right*," Garrett said, steeling himself for a second bare-foot, naked-chested venture into the night air.

He waited, shivering, while the dog took care of business.

"I THINK GARRETT asked me out," Julie confided in Libby, bright and early the next morning, when she stopped by with Calvin. She didn't say it, of course, until her little boy had joined Audrey and

Ava, who were playing in the leaves beneath the oak trees on the other side of the yard.

Libby chuckled. "What do you mean, you *think* Garrett asked you out?" she replied. "Either he did or he didn't."

Julie bit back the admission that he'd kissed her, too. Twice. There wasn't much she didn't tell her sisters, but she had yet to make sense of what had happened in the pool the night before.

And something *had* happened.

"He mentioned dinner in Austin or San Antonio," Julie said.

Libby raised one eyebrow, her eyes twinkling. "And you said…?"

Julie's face burned. "And I said maybe I should cook instead," she murmured.

Libby folded her arms; it was chilly that morning. Tate's truck wasn't in its usual place in the driveway; he must have gotten an early start, as Garrett had. Watching through one of the kitchen windows at the main ranch house, Julie had seen him drive off before the coffee had finished perking.

"It's not like you to blush over a man," Libby pointed out, grinning and giving her a light jab with one elbow. Her eyes rounded with a sudden and delighted realization. "You're *interested* in Garrett—sexually, I mean."

"Libby!" Julie protested, pained.

Libby laughed. Shook her head. "This is *so* not you. This reticence thing, that is. Of the three of us, you've always been the bold one, the adventurous one—and now the idea of making dinner for a man has you turning red?"

"Okay, so I'm *interested*," Julie blurted. With a slight motion of her head, she indicated Calvin, happily plunging in and out of the gloriously colored leaf piles across the yard. "I can't just have a fling with Garrett McKettrick—I have to think about my son."

"As if there's any danger that you *won't* think about Calvin," Libby said gently. "You're a great mother, Jules. The little guy knows you love him, knows you'd go to the wall for him."

"It was just a kiss—okay *two kisses*—but Libby, the things Garrett made me feel…"

Her voice fell away.

Libby smiled, gave her a brief, tight hug. "I know all about what a man can make a woman feel, Jules," she said. "A *McKettrick* man, anyway."

Julie gnawed at her lower lip for a moment, watching Calvin and the twins and the happy dogs, frolicking in rustling mounds of orange and yellow and crimson leaves, scattering them in all directions. "Garrett and I live under the same roof," she reminded Libby. "Things could get really awkward, really fast."

Libby's blue eyes were alight with love as she watched the kids and the dogs. "So much for the two hours I spent raking the yard yesterday afternoon," she said good-naturedly. Then she turned and looked directly at Julie again. "Is this my frankly sensual sister speaking? The one who lamented, not all that long ago, the lack of hot stand-up sex in her life?"

She was going to be late for work if she didn't hurry.

Hedging, Julie got into the Cadillac and turned the key in the ignition until it made a grinding sound. Then she gunned the engine a couple of times before responding to what Libby had said. "I'm going to lose my mind if I think about stand-up sex, hot or otherwise, so don't remind me, okay?"

"I think stand-up sex is *always* hot," Libby speculated mischievously.

Julie couldn't help laughing, and that expelled some of the tension that had been building up inside her since the night before.

Temporarily, anyway.

"And of course you speak from experience," Julie teased, making Libby laugh. "You lucky woman."

With that, she shifted the Caddie into Reverse, tooted the horn in farewell and waved to Libby and to the kids jumping in the leaf piles under the oak trees.

Calvin was too busy having a good time to wave back.

HAVING APPROPRIATED AUSTIN'S battered old red pickup from the garage at home, since the Porsche wasn't suitable for the kind of day he was bound to have, Garrett pulled up behind Tate's blue Silverado, parked across the road from the downed fence line the two of them had spotted from the airplane the day before, late in the afternoon.

A pair of horses grazed nearby, while Tate and two of the ranch hands crouched, examining something in the dirt.

The sinking sensation in Garrett's gut told him it was nothing good, even before he got there and saw the tread marks sunk into the soft dirt on the shoulder. They'd been left by a big rig, those tracks, not a car or a pickup.

The dirt around the fallen fence was churned up, pocked with the impressions of a few hundred hooves.

Seeing Garrett approach, Tate straightened, stood.

"Well," he said grimly, "it's official."

"Rustlers," Garrett confirmed, with a nod. "Any idea how many cattle we're missing?"

Tate sighed. "Henson and Bates are running a quick tally right now," he answered, gesturing toward two distant men on horseback. "Offhand, though, I'd say fifty to a hundred head."

Since even a semi wouldn't hold that many cattle, the thieves must have made several trips, maybe even over a period of days. The Silver Spur rambled on for miles in all four directions, like a giant patchwork quilt spread over a lumpy mattress, and while there were great, grassy expanses of open range, there were also stands of oaks and other deciduous trees hiding shallow canyons and old wagon trails and even a dry riverbed.

A crew arrived to repair the fence, began setting the posts back in their holes and packing dirt and rocks in around them. Once that was done, they'd secure them with cement and then string new wire.

Tate put a call through to Brent Brogan on his cell phone, walking toward his truck as he explained the situation to the lawman and gesturing for Garrett to come along.

When the call ended, Tate had the driver's-side door open and one foot up on the running board. "Let's take that plane of yours up again, have another look around. Maybe we missed something last time."

Garrett nodded. "Meet you at the hangar," he said, turning and sprinting back to Austin's pickup.

Twenty minutes later, they were in the sky.

Tate's voice came through Garrett's headphones, sounding tinny and a lot farther away than one seat over. "Let's make a pass over the oil field," he said.

Garrett nodded and banked the plane to the right, began a gradual decline, and swung in low over the rusty derricks and the two long Quonset huts where equipment had been stored in the old days.

The shacks built to house the workers were gone now, just bits of foundation jutting out of the grass here and there. Once, though, there had been *homes* on this piece of land—nothing fancy, but clean and sturdy and warm in winter. Folks had laughed and fought and loved and raised kids, made a community for themselves— there had even been a church and a one-room schoolhouse, way back when.

During the Great Depression, when so many men and women were desperate for work, the oil had just kept on coming, and the shantytown had been a haven for several dozen workers and their families; back at the main ranch house, there were boxes of old pictures of the place and the people.

It gave Garrett a hollowed-out feeling, thinking how there could be so much life and energy in a place, and then—nothing.

They made a wide loop and then passed over the area again.

Not so much as a blade of grass moved down there; the broken foundations, the Quonset huts, the time-frozen derricks...the place was as still as any ghost town.

Just the same, Garrett felt uneasy, and when he glanced at Tate, he saw that his brother was frowning, too.

"Can you land this thing down there?" Tate asked.

"I can land anywhere," Garrett answered.

The wheels bumped and jostled over the hard-packed dirt when they touched down a couple of minutes later, rolling to a stop a few dozen yards from one of the huts.

"This," Tate said, indicating the larger of the two Quonset huts with a nod of his head, "would be a damn good place to hide a semi between raids on the herd."

Garrett braked, shut down the engine, pulled off his earphones. He'd never run from trouble in his life, and there was no sign of any that he could see, but he knew something was off, just the same. Maybe it was because he hadn't gotten much sleep, thanks to Julie Remington and all the fantasies she'd inspired.

"It can't hurt to look around," he said, his voice gruff.

The two brothers climbed out of the plane, walked toward the tail, in order to avoid the still-spinning blades on the wings.

Here there were no tracks to indicate the comings and goings of any kind of rig, big or otherwise. The padlocks securing the roll-up doors on the Quonsets were not only fastened, but rusted shut, and the panes in the windows remained intact.

So why were the little hairs on his nape standing straight up like a dog's hackles? Garrett wondered. He glanced at Tate, saw his brother wipe off a corner of one of the windows to look inside.

Garrett turned, scanning the immediate area.

He saw old derricks, tumbleweeds and not much else.

And it gave him the creeps.

"See anything?" he asked, when Tate stepped back, dusting his hands together.

Tate shook his head. "Just cobwebs and a lot of dust," he answered.

"Is it just me," Garrett pressed, "or is there something about this place that doesn't feel right?"

Tate's teeth flashed as he grinned. "You spooked?" he asked.

"No," Garrett said, too quickly. As kids, they'd explored this area on horseback, he and Tate and Austin. The dry bed of an ancient river cut through the land just beyond a nearby rise, and there were a number of caves around, too, though most of them had probably fallen in a long time ago. "*Hell*, no, I'm not spooked."

Tate chuckled, slapped Garrett on the back. "Remember when you and Austin and I used to camp out here sometimes, with Brent Brogan and Nico Ruiz?"

Garrett nodded, relaxed a little. "We liked to scare the hell out of each other with yarns about ghosts and guys with hooks for hands," he said. "That one time, when you were twelve and I was eleven and Austin was ten, we told our baby brother we were going to sneak back home as soon as he dropped off to sleep, and he was so worried about being left alone in camp that he didn't shut his eyes for the rest of the night and kept us awake, too, saying one of our names every five minutes."

Tate grinned. "We had to do all the usual chores the next day. Damn, I was too tired to spit. Served us right, I guess."

Garrett laughed. "You and I and Brent and Nico did chores," he corrected. "Austin got to go to the cattle auction with Dad, if I recall it correctly."

Tate seemed to enjoy the recollection as much as Garrett did, though neither of them had thought the experience was funny back then. Remembering, he chuckled and shook his head.

"That little runt must have snitched on us," Garrett said, referring to Austin. "How else could Dad have known we gave him a hard time?"

Tate slapped him on the shoulder. "After all these years," he jibed, though not unkindly, "you still haven't realized that we just *thought* we were all by ourselves out here? Dad and Pablo Ruiz took turns bedding down within a hundred yards so they could keep an eye on us."

Garrett *hadn't* known, and he figured Tate hadn't, either, at least not until after the fact, because they'd talked about practically everything in the relative anonymity of country-dark nights, staring up at that endless expanse of stars. Neither their dad nor Pablo had ever let on that they'd overheard.

He smiled, but at the same time his throat went so tight that his voice came out sounding raw, as if it had been scraped off his vocal chords. "I miss Dad," he said. "Mom, too."

Tate nodded, tightened his fingers on Garrett's shoulder for a few moments, then let go. "We were damn lucky to have them as long as we did," he said hoarsely.

Garrett, having left his hat in Austin's pickup, shoved a hand through his sweaty hair and looked away, struggling to compose himself. "I thought Morgan Cox was like Dad," he said, unable to meet Tate's gaze. Contempt for the senator and for his own judgment roiled up inside Garrett. "It galls me that I believed it, even for a minute."

"Maybe you *needed* to believe it for a while," Tate said quietly.

By tacit agreement, they walked toward the riverbed and the caves they'd loved to explore as kids. They'd found arrowheads there, some of them ancient, along with colorful bits of crockery from the shantytown years. In those days, according to their mother, things like oatmeal and flour and tea and laundry soap had been sold with premiums inside—cups and saucers and sugar bowls and the like.

Boys being boys, they would have discarded the shards of old dishes—the arrowheads were a lot more interesting—but Esperanza liked to glue the prettiest china pieces to plant pots and table-tops, so they'd lugged them home to her in plastic grocery sacks.

The riverbed had been dry for a thousand years, if not longer, but if he closed his eyes and concentrated, Garrett could almost hear it flowing by, almost smell the water. He bent, picked up a stick and flung it hard, the way he would have done alongside any of the creeks crisscrossing the ranch.

At some point, long, long ago, the river had changed course. It ran on the other side of the clustered oaks now, through the canyon it had carved into the land over centuries.

Tate watched him, squinting a little against the sun.

"I'd swear I remember when that river ran through here," Garrett said.

Tate, probably guessing that something else was on Garrett's mind, simply waited. He'd always been the quiet type, Tate had, but since he and Libby had reconnected a few months before and gotten engaged to be married, his thoughts seemed to run deeper.

Or he was just more willing to share them.

"Maybe you can tell me," Garrett said, "how I could have grown up around Blue River, gone through school with Julie Remington, from kindergarten to graduation from high school, and never noticed that she's beautiful."

Tate chuckled. They walked one dusty bank of the river, though Garrett couldn't have said what they were looking for, beyond some sign of trespassers.

"So you're taken with Julie, are you," he said. It was a comment, not a question.

"I didn't say I was *taken* with her, Tate," Garrett pointed out, instantly on the defensive. "I said she was beautiful."

"She's that, all right," Tate agreed. Again, without ever voicing the decision, they were headed somewhere in particular—back to the plane.

Without intending to, Garrett asked, "Is Calvin's father in the picture?"

Tate sighed, rubbed his chin with one hand. Like Garrett, he had a stubble coming in, though Tate's was dark, like his hair, while Garrett's was golden. "According to Libby, the guy—Gordon Pruett is his name—hasn't shown much interest in Calvin until recently. He paid child support and remembered birthdays, so I guess you could say he was trying, but he definitely kept his distance."

Picturing Calvin, squinting up at him through the smeared lenses of those very serious glasses of his, Garrett ached. How could a man father a child and then just ignore him, except for writing a check once a month and sending birthday gifts?

"Until lately," Garrett said.

"Pruett wasn't around," Tate nodded. "Until lately. Now, I guess he's decided he wants to be part of Calvin's life, and Julie's pretty concerned, according to Libby."

"Why the change?" Garrett asked. They'd reached the plane and the glare off the metal sides made him pull his sunglasses from the pocket of his work shirt and put them on.

"I guess because he got married," Tate said. "Pruett, I mean. Now, all of a sudden, he's a family man."

Garrett felt a combination of things, none of which he wanted to examine too closely right at that moment. "How's Calvin taking all this?"

Tate raised and lowered one shoulder in a nearly imperceptible shrug. "He's like any little kid," he said. "He wants a dad."

"This Pruett—he's all right?"

Tate opened the door on his side of the plane, climbed in. "As far as I know," he replied. "Libby stands up for him. And she's a pretty good judge of character."

Garrett laughed. "Oh, yeah? She's marrying *you*, isn't she?" he joked, rounding the plane to hoist himself back into the pilot's seat. "Just how good a judge of character can she be?"

Tate grinned. "You've got a point," he said.

"You're one lucky bastard," Garrett told him. "You know that, don't you?"

Tate nodded. "Sure do," he answered.

CHAPTER EIGHT

WHEN JULIE AND CALVIN arrived at the McKettrick house that evening, Garrett was in the kitchen again, chatting up Esperanza while she put the finishing touches on one of her simple but wonderful suppers. Tonight it happened to be fried chicken, mashed potatoes with gravy and steamed corn.

Harry scrambled up off a rug in front of the crackling fire on the hearth to greet Calvin with face licks and tail wagging and a low, eager whine that meant he wanted to go outside.

Calvin gave Esperanza and Garrett a jaunty wave, then took Harry into the backyard. Julie, thrown by Garrett's presence for no reason she could identify, nodded to him, smiled at Esperanza and sped off into the part of the house she and Calvin shared.

Her heart was pounding, as if she'd had some sort of close call, and she felt the sting of a blush in her cheeks. Chiding herself for being silly, she dumped her purse and tote bag—briefcase, got out of her cloth coat and headed for "her" room.

The master bedroom in the guest suite was twice the size of the one she slept in at the cottage. There were cushioned window seats under the bay windows, and an unimpeded view of rangeland and foothills unfurled from there.

If she'd had the *time* to sit and dream, Julie silently lamented, she'd have chosen that spot for the purpose.

Alas, she seemed to have less and less free time these days, and more and more responsibilities. With the high school musical to cast, rehearse and stage—a task she usually undertook when she had the momentum of spring fever working for her—with her rental house officially on the market and Gordon Pruett dead set on being part of Calvin's life—

Well, it would be easy to feel overwhelmed.

Since that wasn't an option, either, she sucked in a deep breath, blew it out, and murmured one of her favorite, if most irreverent, mantras.

Shit happens.

After kicking off her low-heeled pumps and shedding the tailored gray pantsuit she'd worn to work that day, Julie hastened into worn jeans and a blue-and-white-striped T-shirt with long sleeves.

She had never been shy, but that dreary autumn afternoon, the temptation to hide out in the guest quarters required some overcoming on her part.

It didn't help, knowing she was acting like an adolescent. But the moment she'd stepped into the house and locked gazes with Garrett McKettrick a couple of minutes before, every cell in her body had begun to buzz with awareness. Although the vibrations were beginning to slow—she splashed cold water on her face at the bathroom sink to help the process along a little—the second they were in the same room together again, she knew she'd feel as though she'd stuck a finger into some cosmic light socket.

Julie had worn her hair up that day, pinned into a thick bun at the back of her head, and now, standing in front of the bathroom mirror, she let it tumble down around her shoulders.

Instantly, she regretted the action.

Wearing her hair down when she wasn't working was normal for Julie, but that afternoon, it seemed to say, *Come hither*.

She didn't want Garrett to think she was a red-hot mama with almost as many erogenous zones as she had freckles. Of course she *was*, or at least had been, but—that was *beside the point*.

Julie drew in another breath, gathered her hair back into a ponytail, grabbed a rubber band to secure it.

There, she thought. *You don't look the least bit sexy.*

She didn't look the least bit like herself, either. So she removed the rubber band, finger-fluffed her hair, and turned purposefully away from the mirror to march right back out into the main kitchen.

Since when had she based her hairstyles on a *man's* opinion—for or against? She'd left that kind of stuff behind at the end of junior high, hadn't she?

Upon reaching the kitchen, she saw that Calvin and Harry were back from the yard—Calvin's cheeks were pink from the cold and the lenses of his glasses were fogged up. He'd apparently gotten his jacket zipper stuck, because Garrett was crouched in front of him, trying to work the tab.

Both of them were laughing, and the sound snagged in Julie's heart, a sweet pain, too quickly gone.

Esperanza smiled at Julie, but Garrett and Calvin hadn't noticed her.

"Stick 'em up, Pilgrim," Garrett told the child, when the zipper remained immovable.

Calvin laughed again and flung both his hands up in the air, and Garrett lifted the partially zipped jacket off over the child's head, jostling his glasses in the process.

Calvin took off his specs, wiped them with the tail of his shirt and stuck them back on his face. Julie knew he'd seen her, but all his attention, it seemed, was reserved for Garrett.

Garrett, giving Julie a sidelong look, handed her the jacket and then scooped Calvin up, tickling as he lifted him high.

Calvin's laughter rang like bells on a clear summer day.

Harry barked in delight.

Esperanza chuckled and shook her head, her eyes misted over.

And Julie just stood there, watching, stricken with some combination of joy and sorrow, wonder and caution.

Catching something in her expression, Garrett carefully set Calvin back on his feet, ruffled his hair.

"He shouldn't get overexcited," Julie explained, as though Calvin weren't there, or didn't comprehend the English language. Even as she said the words, she regretted them, but they came out automatically. "He has asthma."

Calvin spared her a single glance, wounded and angry, and then turned away, ruffling Harry's ears and asking loudly if the dog was ready to have some supper.

Julie let out her breath, and her shoulders drooped, and the hem of Calvin's jacket brushed the floor. "Too bad real life doesn't have a Rewind button," she told Garrett miserably.

Garrett, cowboy-handsome in clean boots, newish jeans and a fresh-smelling, long-sleeved Western shirt, quirked up one corner of his mouth, underscoring the grin that was already twinkling in his impossibly blue eyes.

"Supper's ready," he said, relieving her of Calvin's jacket, setting it aside, and steering her toward the table, one hand resting lightly against the small of her back.

The gesture was subtle—barely a touch of his fingers—and at the same time, utterly masculine. Julie loved the way it felt.

Calvin, having filled Harry's kibble bowl and given him fresh water as well, disappeared, without being told, to wash his hands.

He returned holding them up as evidence that he'd followed the rules, well-scrubbed and a little damp.

He'd even slicked a wet comb through his hair.

"You look very handsome," Julie told her son sincerely.

Calvin favored her with a forgiving smile. "Thanks," he said, straightening his glasses before climbing onto the chair beside his. Then, after making sure both Esperanza and Garrett were paying attention, he wriggled his right front tooth.

"Sthee?" he lisped. "It's going to come out."

"Calvin," Julie corrected gently. "Not at the table."

After that, everyone bowed their heads and Esperanza offered a brief prayer of thanksgiving.

"Esperanza," Garrett said, having made sure the chicken platter went around the table before helping himself to two large pieces, "I haven't even tasted this food yet, but I can already tell you've outdone yourself. Again."

The older woman beamed, enjoying the praise. "Shush," she said, pleased.

A distant grinding sound alerted them to the rising of one of the garage doors.

Harry, just finishing his kibble, perked up his ears and gave an uncertain bark.

As guard dogs went, Harry was a wuss, but he liked to go through the motions.

A couple of beats passed, during which no one spoke, and then the door between the kitchen and the garage swung open and Austin stepped over the threshold.

The youngest of the McKettrick brothers, Austin was just as good-looking as Tate or Garrett, and famous on the rodeo circuit. Even when he was being friendly, it seemed to Julie, who didn't know him all that well, there was a go-to-hell look in his eyes.

"Well," Garrett said easily, settling back in his chair to survey his brother, "you look like five miles of bad road, but welcome home anyhow."

"Let me get you a plate!" Esperanza told Austin, already on her feet.

Austin stopped her with a tired gesture of one hand. "I had a burger outside of San Antonio," he said. He took off his hat, which looked as though it had fallen into a chute at the rodeo and been stomped on, and hung it on a peg.

His light brown hair was shaggy, curling above the collar of his denim jacket, and his boots were nothing fancy. That night, he looked more like a drifter hoping for a berth in the bunkhouse than a McKettrick son and heir.

Austin grinned at Calvin, then the dog. His McKettrick-blue eyes were weary when he looked at Julie, but he smiled. "Hello, Julie," he said. "Good to see you."

She smiled back and nodded. "Hi, Austin."

Esperanza was all aflutter, even though she'd sunk back into her chair at Austin's wave. "You'll be hungry later," she insisted.

"When that happens, I'll come down here looking for grub," Austin teased.

What was it about him that made Julie's throat tighten, and tears burn behind her eyes? She stole a glance at Garrett and saw that he was frowning a little as he studied his brother.

"In the meantime," Austin said, opening one of the refrigerator doors and pulling out a long-necked bottle of beer, "I just want to take a hot shower and crash in my own bed."

Nobody responded to that.

Austin nodded a farewell, taking them all in, and headed up one of the three sets of stairs rising from the kitchen to the second floor.

Esperanza sat stiffly, staring down at her food.

Garrett wasn't eating, either, and Julie, hungry as she was, didn't pick up her fork.

Only Calvin, gnawing happily on a drumstick, seemed to have an appetite.

Austin's footsteps echoed overhead.

Garrett pushed back his chair, exchanged glances with Esperanza and muttered, "Excuse me."

Rising, he left the table and then the room, taking the same stairs Austin had used moments earlier.

"Do you think you can fix my zipper?" Calvin asked. "Because I'm going to need that jacket tomorrow to go to the horse sale with Tate and Audrey and Ava, while you and Aunt Libby and Aunt Paige are in Austin shopping for Aunt Libby's wedding dress."

Julie blinked, refocused her attention on her son and even picked up her fork to resume her supper. "I can fix the zipper," she assured him. "But it's time you had a new coat, anyway. Maybe I'll pick one up at the mall."

A protest took shape in Calvin's earnest little face. "Not without me," he said, and then swallowed. "You might get something geeky-looking."

Julie chuckled, and Esperanza smiled, too.

"Gee, buddy," Julie said, mussing up Calvin's hair with one hand, "thanks for the vote of confidence. When was the last time I bought you something 'geeky-looking'?"

Calvin straightened his spine. "At Christmas," he replied. "You gave me that sweater with that lame duck on the front."

Julie defended herself. "That was Santa."

Calvin blew through both lips and then said, "Puleeeeze, Mom."

So he had been humoring her—he didn't believe in Santa anymore. And he was only five. She'd hoped for one more believing Christmas, just one more, but apparently it wasn't to be.

The backs of Julie's eyes stung again, the way they had when she'd looked at Austin a few minutes earlier, but she managed a smile.

"Finish your supper," she said. "We'll figure out the new-jacket thing later."

By the time Garrett returned, Julie and Esperanza had cleared the table, except for his plate and utensils, and Calvin was happily splashing away in the bathtub in the guest quarters, with Julie checking on him every few minutes.

Returning from one of these runs, she paused to look at him for a moment, wondering what to say, if anything, before she gave up and began helping Esperanza load the dishwasher.

With a sigh, Garrett sat down.

"I could heat that food up for you," Esperanza offered, watching him.

He smiled, but he looked tired. "I could heat it up for myself," he said. "But there's no need."

"Is Austin all right?" Esperanza asked, in the tone of a woman who has held back a question as long as she was able.

Garrett didn't answer right away. When he did speak, his voice was low and slightly rough. "Probably not," he said. "I tried to get him to talk, and he told me to leave him the hell alone, so that's what I plan on doing. For tonight, anyhow."

Esperanza lifted worried eyes toward the ceiling. She murmured something, probably a prayer, and shook her head.

"He'll be fine in a few days, Esperanza," Garrett said quietly.

Esperanza opened her mouth, closed it again.

"I'll finish cleaning up," Julie told her, very gently. "You've been working all day."

"So have you," Esperanza pointed out, cheering up a little, reaching back to untie her apron. With a sigh, she added, "But I think I'll take you up on your kind offer, Julie. Put up my feet and read for a while before bed. There's nothing decent on TV."

Julie took the apron from Esperanza's hand, nodded.

After the housekeeper had gone, Garrett got up from the table and put his plate into the microwave, pushed a few buttons.

Meanwhile, Julie wiped down counters, rinsed out the sponge, washed her hands and applied lotion. The air trembled with that now-familiar tension, and she stole several glances at Garrett, trying to figure out if he was feeling it, too.

The microwave timer dinged, and he took out his plate, returned to the table, sat down to eat. Sighed before picking up his fork.

From the looks of things, he'd forgotten Julie was even in the room.

She suppressed a sigh and started for the doorway. It was time to get Calvin out of the tub, into his pajamas, oversee the tooth-brushing ritual.

"Julie?"

Garrett's voice stopped her on the threshold of the corridor leading to the guest quarters and to Esperanza's living area. She straightened her spine, waited for him to go on, but didn't turn around or speak.

"Would you mind coming back here after you tend to Calvin?" he asked quietly. "Just to keep me company for a little while?"

There was nothing needy in his tone, and nothing demanding, either. Garrett was making a simple request.

She turned her head, felt an actual impact when their two gazes met. If she hadn't figured out instantly that something was happening when he kissed her the night before in the pool, she'd have known it then.

"Okay," she replied, in a smaller voice than she'd used in a long time.

Since the next day was Saturday, and Calvin was looking forward to spending the time with Tate and the twins, he was unusually tractable about brushing and flossing, being tucked in and kissed and saying his prayers. Libby, Paige and Julie would be away for hours, visiting a whole series of bridal shops in search of Libby's wedding dress.

Harry jumped up onto the bed and curled up at Calvin's blanketed feet, starting to snore practically the moment he'd settled in.

Calvin squeezed his eyes tightly shut, determined to sleep. The sooner he fell asleep, he probably reasoned, the sooner it would be morning.

Julie chuckled and kissed his forehead. "You're trying too hard," she whispered.

Calvin's eyes popped open, wide and faintly dazed because he wasn't wearing his glasses. "It's *never* going to be morning!" he fretted.

Julie smoothed his hair lightly, remembering when she was little, looking forward to something, counting the days till it finally came—Christmas, or a birthday, or the last day of school, or the *first* day of school.

Back then, she and her sisters had wanted to speed time up.

Usually, their dad would smile wistfully and tell them not to wish their lives away.

"It *will* be morning," Julie reminded her eager son.

"When?" he asked fitfully.

She leaned down, kissed his forehead just once more. *"When it's morning,"* she answered. "Happy trails and sweet dreams, cowboy."

Calvin huffed out a sigh, but he grinned at her before turning onto his side, snuggling down into his pillow and his covers and squeezing his eyes closed again. "'Night, Mom."

Julie lingered in the doorway, savoring this child, this fleeting place in time. It was all too easy, she reminded herself, to get caught up in causes and concerns and plans for the future and forget what truly mattered—loving and being loved, in the present moment.

She closed the door softly, took her time returning to the kitchen.

Garrett was putting his plate, glass and utensils in the dishwasher when she arrived, and she noticed that he'd set out a bottle of red wine and two glasses.

Catching her looking at them, he chuckled, turned to face her, leaning back against the counter and folding his arms. His dark blond hair looked especially shaggy, and his beard was coming in, bristly and golden. His blue eyes twinkled with a certain benevolent mischief.

"It's okay, Julie," he told her, in a tone he might have used to reassure a skittish mare, indicating the wine with a slight inclination of his head. "I'm not out to seduce you."

An unspoken *yet* hovered between them.

"A glass of wine would be nice," she said, struggling to find her equilibrium.

"Good," Garrett said. He picked up the wine in one hand and caught the stems of the glasses together in the other, then led the way onto the indoor patio on the near side of the pool.

The lighting was soft, the water was a great sparkling rectangle of turquoise, and the retractable roof was open to the silvery dance of a zillion stars spread across the night sky.

Garrett chose one of several tables, set down the things he was carrying, and drew back a chair for Julie to sit.

She hesitated—it was here, after all, in this very swimming pool where she'd felt a degree of desire she'd never even imagined to be possible—and the equation was obvious. Sexy man plus starlight plus wine and privacy equaled extreme vulnerability on her part.

Sex was one thing—it would be beyond good with Garrett, no doubt about that—but emotional entanglement was another. Easy manner, cowboy getup and horseback riding aside, he was a man with serious political aspirations—everybody in Blue River knew his association with Senator Cox was an apprenticeship of sorts, a way of learning the ropes.

And the fact of Garrett's association with a man Julie had always considered a scoundrel sent up all kinds of red flags in her mind. If Garrett had respected Cox enough to work for him from the time he finished law school and passed the bar, which he had, until their recent break in the midst of the pole-dancer scandal, what did that say about Garrett's judgments and values?

Once she took a chair, Julie just sat there, feeling like a lump.

Garrett gave a small, rueful smile, wry at the edges, and poured wine into her glass, then his own.

"We need to talk," she blurted, and immediately felt like four kinds of fool.

Garrett sat back comfortably in his chair—hell, he was damnably comfortable in his skin—and waited indulgently for her to go on.

She reached for her wineglass, nearly spilled it and set it down again, without taking so much as a sip.

Garrett smiled again, though his eyes were solemn. And still he waited. Wine by the pool under a universe full of shimmering stars had been *his* idea, but now that she'd opened her big mouth and clearly regretted it, he wasn't going to let her off the hook.

She cleared her throat, picked up her glass again, and sloshed back a gulp that nearly choked her.

Garrett didn't say one word, but a hint, a shadow, of amusement lingered on his mouth, and his eyes never left her steadily reddening face.

Julie took a second sip of wine, this time slowly, stalling in the hopes that her composure would return.

It did, sort of.

"What happened last night," she said, nodding toward the pool, "our kissing each other and everything…"

She ran out of steam.

Garrett chuckled, sipped his wine. Set his glass down and took his sweet time picking up the conversational ball. "At least you're willing to admit it was mutual," he said. "Last night, you seemed bound and determined to put all the blame on me."

Julie's cheeks pulsed with heat. She knotted her fingers together in her lap. "I'm not denying there's a certain *attraction*," she ventured, and then had to stop and clear her throat, which was mortifying.

Garrett gave an almost imperceptible nod of agreement. Or encouragement. Or *something*. But he went right on letting her dangle.

"Feel free to jump in and contribute to this exchange at any time," Julie said, annoyed.

That made him laugh. It wasn't just a chuckle—oh, no. Garrett McKettrick threw back his head and gave a husky shout of amusement.

Turnabout, Julie decided, was fair play. *She* waited now.

He watched her for a long time, and his regard felt, she thought, like a caress. Which was just ridiculous, in her opinion, because he wasn't touching her.

Thank *God*, he wasn't touching her.

"It seems reasonable to assume," he said, after a long time, "that you and I might wind up in bed together one of these days— or nights—since there's a *certain attraction* here. You've probably guessed that the whole idea works for me, on every possible level, but it has to work for you, too, Julie—because if it doesn't, it can't happen at all."

Julie hadn't been involved with a lot of men, but she wasn't naive, either. Garrett's blunt honesty was new, in her admittedly limited experience, and she didn't know quite what to make of it.

Did he actually *mean* what he said?

Would he *really* back off if she told him this wasn't the right time in her life for a—well—a fling?

Garrett picked up the bottle, leaned, topped off her glass. "What?" he prompted, watching her face, raising one eyebrow.

"We're very different," Julie said.

He grinned. "In all the right places," he replied.

"That isn't what I mean and you know it." She steadied herself with another sip of wine. It was a very nice wine, she thought. A shiraz, maybe, or a merlot. Even without peering at the label— which she refused to do—she knew the full-bodied red was way out of her price range.

And Garrett McKettrick, her pragmatic side pointed up, was out of her league. Not because he was better—of course he wasn't— but because he traveled in different circles, normally. Very sophisticated ones. Not that Julie couldn't fit in, if she made the effort, but that was the problem. She didn't want to change.

She liked her life a lot—teaching English in a small high school, despite all the attendant problems, and running the drama club.

She loved her sisters.

Most of all, she loved Calvin, and she wanted to raise him in the little town of Blue River, where she'd grown up herself.

Garrett smiled, evidently enjoying her frustration. "Talk to me," he said.

"You're not working for Senator Cox anymore?" she asked, back in blurting mode.

Dammit, she thought. She was intelligent. She was certainly competent. Why did her IQ make a swan dive whenever she spoke to or even looked at this man?

"No, that's over," he replied.

"What about your career?"

"What about it?"

Her temper flared in the way Libby and Paige swore made her hair crackle. "Surely your *career* isn't over," she said. "We didn't run in the same crowd in school—you were a popular rodeo jock and I was artsy and a little weird—but—"

Again, one of his eyebrows rose. "A *little* weird?" he teased. "You wore white lipstick all through junior year."

Taken by surprise, Julie spoke without thinking. "You noticed that? The white lipstick phase?"

Garrett laughed. "It was hard to miss, especially since you dressed like Morticia Addams most of the time."

"I did *not* dress like Morticia Addams!" Julie protested, laughing too. "I just wore a lot of black, that's all. I was making an existential statement."

He rolled his marvelous eyes. "Whatever."

The muscles linking Julie's shoulders to her neck let go in a sudden burst of relaxation; the swiftness of it made her feel lightheaded.

This was *some* wine.

She finally looped back to where she'd left off—Garrett's career. "My point is, even in high school you were interested in politics. You wanted to serve in the U.S. Senate, if not be president. Has all that changed?"

Garrett stopped smiling. Turned his wineglass slowly on the tabletop, by the stem. Then he looked straight into her eyes. "The truth is, I'm not really sure," he said. "Why do you ask?"

Why *was* she asking?

Because she needed to know his long-term plans, if she was going to get involved with Garrett, even on a temporary basis.

To a man, a fling was a fling, and when it was over, it was over. But Julie knew that if she shared her body with this particular man, there was a good chance her heart would jump ship, too.

Julie was a risk taker by nature, or, at least, she *had* been, until Calvin was born. Now, she was more careful, because if her heart got broken, Calvin's surely would, too. And she had to stay strong to be the kind of mother to him that her own had never been to her or to her sisters.

It would make a lot more sense to simply walk away, right now, before things got any more out of hand.

Except that she was a normal woman, not yet thirty, with healthy desires and needs that made her body ache with a singular loneliness sometimes—okay, *often*—in the depths of the night.

"I have a son," Julie said, very quietly and at considerable length. "What I do affects him. We're between homes, Calvin and I, and he just met his father for the first time since he was a baby. I don't want to confuse him. He looks up to Tate, and now you, and like any little boy, he's impressed by airplanes and all the rest—"

She was rambling.

Tears sprang to Julie's eyes at that moment, and she was completely unprepared for them.

Garrett reached over, took her hand and pulled her easily onto his lap.

"Hey," he said. "Everything's going to be okay."

"That," Julie sniffled, making no move to get back to her own chair, "is easy for *you* to say. For you, everything *will* be okay, because you're a man, and a *McKettrick* man, at that."

Garrett cupped her cheeks in his hands, let the pad of his right thumb brush lightly over her mouth.

"Don't you dare kiss me," Julie said, thinking she'd die if he didn't do exactly that.

"I can wait," he told her, his voice a sleepy, rumbling drawl. "Because sooner or later, Julie Remington, I mean to kiss you all over, and I'm only *starting* with your mouth."

A hot shiver went through her.

It was going to be one of those achy nights, and there wasn't a damn thing she could do about it.

Garrett traced the edges of her mouth with his thumb again. "Did you mean it when you offered to cook for me?" he asked, his voice slow and low. His face was so close to hers that she could feel the warmth of his breath against her lips.

She nodded. There was no sense in denying it. When Julie offered to cook for a man, it was a big deal. "Yes," she said.

"Tomorrow night?" he prompted. "My place?"

Julie swallowed hard. On the inside, she felt like a pinball machine on *tilt*. "I'm going shopping with my sisters tomorrow," she said. "For Libby's wedding gown."

"I see," Garrett said, barely breathing the words. "And you won't be in the mood to—cook—after a long day on the town?"

"I have to consider Calvin," she reminded him.

"Calvin likes spending the night over at Tate and Libby's place, doesn't he? With the twins?"

Julie was almost hypnotized. She knew what was happening— she was being seduced—and she was going along with it. She was letting Garrett lead her, however circuitous the route, right to his bed.

"Your place?" she asked. She knew he had a condo or a house or something in Austin.

He raised his chin, looked briefly toward the ceiling. "Upstairs," he said.

Julie had been curious about Garrett's private quarters. Now she was going to get the tour.

Sort of.

"No strings," she warned. "On either side."

Garrett tipped his head a little to the right, nibbled briefly at the side of her neck. "No strings," he agreed.

Julie nearly cried out, the pleasure of his mouth on her skin was so intense. "We're both adults here," she said, breathlessly.

Who was she reminding—Garrett or herself?

"Consenting adults," Garrett said.

Julie got shakily to her feet. The irony was, she would have fallen back into Garrett's lap if he hadn't steadied her by taking a firm grip on her hips.

When he bent forward and nipped at her, very lightly, where the legs of her jeans met, she couldn't hold back a groan of desire so keen that it spiked through her like a bolt of lightning.

He chuckled. "I thought so," he mused, almost under his breath.

Julie regained her senses—mostly—and stepped away from him. She still tingled where he'd put his mouth to her, ached to give herself up to him then and there.

She didn't, of course.

She still had some dignity, *some* self-control.

But not much.

CHAPTER NINE

It was an achy night.

Julie barely slept, and when she arrived at Libby and Tate's place the next morning, with an excited Calvin in tow, Paige was there ahead of her. Bright-eyed and dressed for marathon shopping in jeans, running shoes and a long-sleeved red T-shirt, Paige looked even younger than her twenty-eight years.

Happy chaos reigned in the small kitchen—dogs barked, the twins squabbled and Tate gave a shrill whistle to get everybody's attention.

The dogs and the kids went silent, stricken with what appeared to be awed admiration. After all, not everybody could whistle like that.

It was impressive.

Tate was impressive.

"Breakfast!" Tate announced, as a follow-up to the whistle, setting a platter piled high with pancakes in the center of the table, alongside a dish of scrambled eggs and a plate of crisp bacon.

Since Calvin's jacket zipper was still stuck, he threw the whole shebang off over his head, disappeared into the nearest bathroom to wash his hands and scrambled to join in the meal as soon as he got back to the kitchen. The way he dug into that food, Julie thought with rueful affection, a casual observer would think he was being starved at home.

Libby, dressed in dark slacks and a long-sleeved white blouse, looked pretty spiffy compared to her sisters; like Paige, Julie had elected to go casual, wearing jeans, comfortable shoes and a lightweight sweatshirt.

Libby and Tate exchanged a light kiss, in the midst of all that breakfast hubbub, and there was something so sizzly-sweet in the way they looked together that Julie's throat went tight and her eyes stung.

Paige gave her a light elbow bump. "Libby is getting married," she said. "Can you believe it?"

"*I* can believe it," Tate said, when another, longer kiss ended, smiling down into Libby's happy eyes. "And it's none too damn soon, either."

Paige was driving that day—her car was a four-door and easy on gas.

There was a flurry of departure—goodbyes, reiteration of plans and assigned chores for the day—and then the Remington sisters were outside, ready to roll.

When Libby climbed into the back of Paige's late-model compact, Julie shrugged and took the front passenger seat, feeling a lot more awake and ready for the day now that the three of them were setting off on their own.

Paige slid behind the wheel, started the engine and reached to switch off the radio when country music blared into the car.

"You're growing your hair out," Julie observed, with some surprise, noticing that Paige's dark, glossy cap of hair was getting longer.

"It's been too long since you two have seen each other," Libby remarked, from the back, "if you're just now noticing that Paige changed her hair, Jules."

Paige backed up the car, turned it around and started down the bumpy dirt driveway toward the main road. "It has definitely been too long," she agreed. "We need to do this more often. Get together, I mean, just the three of us."

Julie wondered at Paige's words, though they sounded lighthearted. As different as they were from each other, the bond between the sisters had always been tight. Since Libby and Tate had fallen in love, though, things weren't the same.

They had always been busy with their separate lives, but they'd spent more time together before.

Briefly adjusting the rearview mirror for a quick look, Julie saw Libby's eyes looking back at her.

"Are you feeling neglected, little sister?" Libby asked, addressing Paige. Her voice was gentle—as the firstborn, she'd looked after Julie and Paige, especially after their mother, Marva, deserted the family when they were small.

Before Paige could answer—she'd surely been about to say yes—they met Garrett, driving Austin's red truck, about halfway down the long driveway.

Julie, unnerved, would have preferred just to wave as they passed, but Paige stopped her car and rolled down the window, prompting Garrett to stop, too.

Julie stared straight ahead while they exchanged pleasantries.

Just the night before, she'd let this man kiss her—heck, she'd kissed him *back*—and they'd made plans to have sex and supper, though possibly not in that order—and the night before *that*, they'd gone horseback riding in the moonlight.

Considering all that, Julie couldn't bring herself to even look at Garrett, let alone make small talk. What would she say, after all?

She imagined the conversational possibilities.

I don't usually plan sex—it's always been an impulse thing with me.

How could I have known you all these years, Garrett Mc-Kettrick, and never noticed how hot you are?

I'm worried—you might have the power to break my heart.

All discards, of course.

Soon, mercifully, Paige and Julie had finished the informal country-road chat with Garrett, and they were off again.

Julie snuck a glance at the rearview, watching as Garrett barreled on up the driveway, a plume of dust churning behind the old truck.

"Phew," Paige said, "when I first saw that red truck—"

"You thought it was Austin," Libby finished for her. "You two have been out of high school for ten years now. The breakup, spectacular as it was, is water under the bridge. Don't you think it's about time you stopped avoiding each other? Especially now that you're going to be family?"

Remembering Austin's mood the night before, when he'd shown up during supper, Julie felt her spirits dampen a little. Something was definitely wrong there, and it made her sad.

"Family," Paige scoffed. "Austin will be part of *your* family, Lib, not mine."

"Meaning if Austin is going to be at our place for, say, Thanksgiving dinner, you'll stay away?" Libby asked, sounding hurt.

Paige and Julie exchanged glances.

And then Paige softened a little, braking for the stop sign at the bottom of the hill and signaling a left turn, toward town. Their favorite mall, outside of Austin, was nearly two hours away, but they'd agreed to stop for breakfast at a roadhouse between Blue River and San Antonio.

"I promise to be civil to Austin McKettrick if I can't avoid him," Paige said, raising one hand as if to swear an oath. "Fair enough?"

"Fair enough," Libby replied, though Julie knew she was still troubled. Then, after an eloquent sigh, Libby added, "You know, Paige, you need to mellow out."

"*I* need to mellow out?" Paige repeated, with a giggle. "Easy for you to say, Lib—*you're* getting regular sex."

Julie scooted a little further down in her seat, hoping the subject would change before she felt compelled to blurt out to her sisters, with whom she shared pretty much everything, that she had decided to go to bed with Garrett McKettrick.

"It's not just *regular* sex," Libby said, amused. "It's extremely good sex."

Julie, who usually would have jumped on the topic with more aplomb than either Libby or Paige, remained silent. Miserably silent.

"What's the matter with you?" Libby finally demanded, poking her in the shoulder from behind.

"Nothing," Julie lied. "Nothing whatsoever is the matter with me."

"We're talking about sex and you haven't said anything outrageous," Paige told her. "Who are you and what have you done with our sister, Julie?"

Finally, Julie laughed. She couldn't help it. Nor could she hide the note of despair underlying her amusement. A tear streaked down her cheek, and she wiped it away with the back of one hand—though not quickly enough to keep Paige from seeing.

Paige pulled the car to the side of the road and flipped on the safety blinkers.

"All right, spill it," she told Julie.

With her brown eyes and dark hair, Paige looked the most like their father. The resemblance gave her an odd authority, at least some of the time.

"What's going on?" Libby demanded, unhooking her seat belt and scooting forward to shove her head between the seats and study Julie.

Julie sniffled. "I'm going to sleep with, of all people, Garrett McKettrick," she burst out. "And I don't even have the excuse of not knowing any better!"

Libby began to laugh.

Paige beamed. "Wow," she said. "You and *Garrett*?"

"There is no 'Garrett and me,'" Julie countered quickly. "This is only about sex."

"I can't believe I'm hearing this," Libby said. "'This is only about sex'?"

"Hot damn," Paige said, clearly delighted. Then she repeated, more slowly that the first time, *"You and Garrett."*

"Maybe we can have a double wedding!" Libby chimed in, thrilled.

"No double wedding," Julie was quick to say. "Garrett and I aren't like you and Tate. This isn't a love match—it's pure lust. We don't have the same goals, or even the same values, unless I miss my guess."

"Garrett's a hunk and you could really use a man in your life," Paige put in, careful to keep her eyes mostly on the road, though she did sneak a few glances in Julie's direction. "Goals can be adapted, and let's face it, the McKettricks are known for being straight shooters, so there shouldn't be any problem with values."

"He's a politician," Julie reminded her sisters.

"Think of how great this would be for Calvin," lobbied Paige.

"Garrett is a politician," Julie repeated.

"You make it sound like he has a case of leprosy," Libby said.

"That might be an improvement," Julie insisted. "Garrett is aligned with Senator Cox, and Senator Cox, in case you haven't been watching the news, has the morals of an alley rat."

"But you're planning to *sleep* with the man," Paige said, in a let-me-get-this-straight tone of voice. "Despite an obviously low opinion of his political affiliation?"

"His *former* political affiliation," Libby put in. "Garrett doesn't work for Morgan Cox anymore."

"We've admitted there's an attraction, that's all," Julie tossed into the verbal jumble, making her tone lofty. "Since we're both consenting adults, we've decided to go to bed together. It's just that simple."

"Straight to bed?" Paige teased, shutting off the blinkers and easing carefully onto the road again. "Without passing go and collecting two hundred dollars?"

Julie rolled her eyes at the reference to the board game they'd played throughout their childhood. Paige had always been the one to buy up all the little green houses and red hotels, erecting them on the most expensive properties, too. A shark, winding up with piles of pastel-colored money at the end of every session.

She'd been downright ruthless when it came to collecting the rent.

"I'm cooking dinner for him first," Julie said.

"Well," Libby said, drawing out the word and waving both hands for emphasis, "*that's* different, then. You're going to cook a gourmet meal for Garrett and *then* fall into bed with him. Where, pray tell, is Calvin going to be during this—this *escapade*?"

Julie turned in the seat and found herself almost eye to eye with Libby. Libby's words had been inflammatory, but now Julie saw that her sister's baby blues were twinkling with mischief.

"I hope," Julie answered, "that Calvin will be at your place, spending the night."

"That's it?" Paige marveled, sounding thrilled. "Take Calvin to a babysitter, cook a meal and hit the sheets? That's your plan?"

"I'm not a babysitter," Libby said, miffed. "I'm Calvin's aunt."

"That's the plan," Julie admitted.

"I like it," Paige said, with enthusiasm.

They all laughed then.

The topic of conversation turned to breakfast, and the day ahead—which bridal shops and upscale department stores ranked highest on Libby's list, what color their bridesmaids' dresses should be.

Audrey and Ava would be junior bridesmaids, and Calvin was the official ring bearer.

During breakfast at the roadhouse, they talked about the cottage Julie had been renting being put on the market, and the whole tenting-for-termites experience, and Paige, an RN, confided that she'd been offered a job at Blue River's clinic. It paid less than she was making now, but the benefits were good and the hours were shorter, and she wouldn't have to commute fifty miles every day, and that was worth something, wasn't it?

Libby and Julie agreed that it was.

They visited two different malls and three bridal shops before they found The Dress.

It was a cloud of gossamer silk, that dress, with a fitted bodice and lovely full sleeves and tiny ivory pearls and pinpoint rhinestones setting it alight, as though it had been fashioned from some long-ago snowfall. The veil seemed to be made of air and candlelight.

Libby stood frozen on the sidewalk in front of the small Austin boutique when she spotted it in the window, a fairy-tale gown, more fantasy than fabric.

Trying it on only magnified the magical effect.

Of course, there would be alternations—the dress was too big through the waist and too small in the bodice—but the sight of Libby swathed in all that soft glory brought tears to Julie's eyes, and to Paige's.

They stared at their sister in wonder, outside the dressing room, marveling. Libby seemed translucent; like a human pearl, she glowed with soft, creamy brilliance.

Happiness looked good on Libby, and so did that marvelous dress.

The exquisite gown, the saleswoman explained, was vintage, on consignment from the costume department of a movie studio. As far as she knew, no one had ever actually worn it in a film, but

Julie pictured Loretta Young wearing it, and then Vivien Leigh, and neither of them could compare to Libby.

Paige snapped a photo with her cell phone, planning to zap it off to Tate, but Libby absolutely forbade that. The dress had to be a surprise, she maintained—her groom was not to see her in that gown until their wedding, scheduled for New Year's Eve.

The save-the-date cards had already gone out, and the caterers had been hired.

The honeymoon had been planned, the flowers selected and ordered.

Except for finding Libby's dream dress, which had involved a lot of research, both online and in magazines—and those Julie, Paige, Audrey and Ava would wear—everything was done.

"That's a silly superstition," Paige protested, but Libby was adamant.

"It's bad luck," Libby insisted.

Paige merely shook her head.

Julie smiled at Libby, so happy for her sister that she thought she might burst. "You're going to be the most beautiful bride *ever*," she said.

The antique dress rustled as Libby hugged her.

Libby paid for the dress, and she and the store owner set up an appointment for the first of several fittings.

Next, the three sisters had lunch in a favorite Mexican restaurant.

"You don't really believe in bad luck, do you?" Paige pressed, over guacamole and chips. "That's just an old wives' tale, you know—that something terrible will happen if Tate sees you wearing the dress before you walk down the aisle."

Libby considered the question, shrugged slightly. "I'm not taking any chances," she said.

"Good idea," Julie said, smiling across the table at Libby. "Better safe than sorry."

Paige gave a small snort of laughter. "Since when have you lived by *that* motto?" she asked, turning to look at Julie, who sat beside her in the restaurant booth.

"Since Calvin," Julie answered.

The mood shifted.

"When is the big supper-and-sex date?" Paige asked, her dark eyes tender now, and luminous with affection.

"Garrett suggested tonight," Julie said, squirming a little.

Libby's eyes rounded.

"Yes!" Paige said, punching the air with one fist.

"I didn't say I agreed," Julie pointed out reasonably.

The waitress came and they took their orders—the three of them would share a plate of nachos, heavy on the goop.

"I'm bringing Calvin home with me tonight," Paige decided. "We'll take in a movie, the big guy and me, and go out for pizza. I've been working so much—this is the first weekend off I've had in months."

"I thought Calvin was going to stay with Tate and the girls and me," Libby said.

"I haven't said yes," Julie reiterated.

"But you're going to," Paige reasoned. "It's written all over you. You're hot to trot. Ready to tango."

"Stop," Julie pleaded, blushing.

Paige and Libby both giggled.

"What are you planning to cook?" Paige asked.

"What will you wear?" Libby wanted to know.

Since both of them had spoken at once, Julie took a moment to untangle their words.

"It's more about what she's *not* going to wear," Paige observed, in the gap.

"I thought I'd cook something very simple," Julie said, her cheeks burning now. "And I will be fully dressed, thank you very much."

"That's only important if you're frying something," Libby said. "Otherwise, cooking naked can be—"

Both Julie and Paige stared at her, grinning.

Now it was Libby who blushed.

The nachos arrived, and the waitress refilled their ice tea glasses.

Libby started picking off hot peppers and setting them aside.

The food was delicious, fattening and delightfully messy to eat. The three of them clowned around a little, Paige karate-chopping a long strand of cheese stretched between the plate and the loaded chip she raised to her mouth.

Libby accidentally got a slice of hot pepper and drank from all three of their water glasses in turn.

Julie laughed and shook her head. She loved spicy food—the hotter, the better. "Wimp," she said, with love.

"Food," Libby sputtered, after filling her mouth with ice and sluicing it around before chewing and swallowing, "should not be painful."

After lunch, they returned to one of the bridal shops they'd visited earlier, to take a second look at a bridesmaid's dress that had caught Libby's eye.

It was way too ruffly, and tied in a big bow at the back.

What was it, Julie wondered, that drew otherwise sensible brides to dresses seemingly designed to please Little Bo Peep?

"It comes in a lot of colors," Libby mused, studying the tag.

"You're my sister, and I love you," Paige told her. "I'll do anything for you, Lib. Dance barefoot over hot coals. Donate a kidney. Throw myself in front of a train. *Anything* but wear that god-awful dress."

Libby looked so discouraged that Julie slid an arm around her older sister and gave her a quick squeeze. Naturally, the wedding meant a lot to Libby, and she must have been feeling pressure to tie up all the loose ends.

"You found the perfect wedding gown," Julie reminded Libby. "That's progress."

Paige nodded in agreement. "The right bridesmaids' dresses are out there somewhere," she put in, "and we'll find them."

"Just not today, probably," Julie added gently.

Libby smiled and nodded, and her whole face seemed to light up. "Let's go," she said.

They stopped at a supersize discount store on the way back to Blue River—Libby wanted a big bag of dog food, Paige planned to pick up some toiletries and Julie was in the market for a play jacket for Calvin.

"Is this geeky-looking?" she asked, holding up a blue and beige coat, when Paige wheeled her cart up alongside Julie's.

"Everything looks good on Calvin," Paige replied. Then, after a beat, "So what's on the menu for the romantic rendezvous with Garrett?" She leaned in a little way, lowered her voice. "Besides you, I mean."

Julie swatted at her. Of course, on some level, she'd been rifling through her mental recipe collection since the night before, considering one dish, then deciding against it and moving on to another.

Her specialty was lasagna, but that took hours to prepare, and she didn't have that kind of time. Besides, Garrett had already eaten her lasagna, albeit as leftovers.

"Why did I agree to make dinner for him?" she whispered to Paige. "I could at least have given myself some time!"

Paige grinned. "Come on, relax. You're a great cook—everything you make is delicious."

"Help," Julie pleaded miserably.

Libby showed up then, with a huge bag of kibble filling up her cart. "Are you two about finished with your shopping?"

Paige rammed Julie's cart with her own, though gently. "Our sister is on the horns of a dilemma," she said, turning to Libby. "She promised Garrett a dinner, and she can't decide what to serve."

"Meatballs," Libby said helpfully. "You make the *best* meatballs."

"Too messy," Julie said, imagining herself up to her elbows in a mixture of ground beef, spices, onions, bread crumbs and raw eggs.

"Fried chicken?" Paige suggested. "Most men love fried chicken."

"Esperanza made that last night," Julie replied.

"The man's not thinking about food, anyway," Paige said. "Why don't you just buy a frozen entrée and nuke it in the microwave?"

Julie made a face and pushed between Paige's cart and Libby's, rolling on into the aisle, and headed for the grocery section. At that moment, she almost wished she hadn't told her sisters *anything* about her plans for the evening.

Paige and Libby trailed after her, whispering and giggling between themselves the way they would have done back in high school.

Cowboys liked steak, didn't they? Julie wondered, reaching the meat counter and peering at the selection of beef.

For all she knew about Garrett McKettrick, she realized, he could be a vegetarian.

That didn't seem likely, given that the McKettricks were cattle ranchers and had been for more than a hundred years, but still.

"Your chicken spaghetti," Libby said, selecting a package of poultry and tucking it into a plastic bag, "is bound to be a hit." She dropped the works in Julie's cart, taking care that it didn't land on Calvin's new jacket.

Julie's gratitude was all out of proportion to the favor Libby had done her. She felt teary and overly sentimental. Why hadn't *she* thought of chicken spaghetti on her own? She'd won prizes for the stuff, and she knew all the other ingredients she'd need were in Esperanza's pantry back at the ranch.

"What?" Paige asked, plucking a tissue from the little package she carried in her purse and handing it to Julie.

Julie dabbed at her eyes, sniffled, shoved the crumpled tissue into her jeans pocket. "This is crazy," she said.

"Come on," Libby said, pulling at the front of Julie's cart while pushing her own forward at the same time. "If we hurry, we can beat the weekend traffic."

"What's crazy?" Paige asked, squeaky-wheeling it alongside Julie as they all moved toward the checkout counters at the front of the store.

Julie made a face. "My plans for the evening," she said primly, aware of other people, all of them strangers, crowding in around them. Possibly listening.

Paige's eyes twinkled. She'd probably considered responding with something like, *Your plans? Oh, yes, I forgot. You're going to sleep with Garrett McKettrick.* Fortunately, she didn't.

They were in the parking lot, stuffing their purchases into the trunk of Paige's car, when Libby spoke up.

"You were crying in there," she said to Julie, her tone matter-of-fact.

"Definitely hormonal," Paige commented.

"What if you're ovulating?" Libby wanted to know. "You could get pregnant."

"Will you lower your voice?" Julie demanded, annoyed. "And while you're at it, give me credit for the sense God gave a goose."

They all got into the car, spent a few noisy moments juggling their purses and fastening their seat belts.

"What if you get pregnant?" Paige insisted.

"I'm not going to get pregnant," Julie snapped.

"That's what you said when you and Gordon hooked up," Libby reminded her. "And, presto!" She snapped the fingers of both hands. "Heeeeeere's Calvin!"

"Will you stop?" Julie begged.

"Are you on the Pill?" Paige asked, ever the nurse. She was busy navigating the crowded parking lot, working her way toward one of several exits.

"No," Julie said, after a few moments of internal struggle.

"Some other form of birth control?" Libby pressed, popping her head between the seats again.

"Don't you think this conversation is getting a little personal?" Julie countered. "Even for sisters?"

"We're just trying to help," Libby said.

Julie closed her eyes, drew in a deep breath, and let it out again. "Unlike some people I could name," she said evenly, "I happen to know exactly where I am in my cycle at all times. And, anyway, I've decided to call the whole thing off. I don't know what I was thinking, agreeing to such a thing."

"Do I still get to keep Calvin for the rest of the weekend?" Paige asked.

"Yes," Julie said. "And if he thinks the coat I bought him is 'geeky,' I'm going to tell him *you* picked it out."

After a few more minutes of sisterly banter, the Remington women were all talked out. They lapsed into a comfortable silence, and Paige tuned the radio to an easy-listening station.

There was still a little light when they reached the outskirts of Blue River, and the cottage was just two streets over, so Julie automatically glanced in that direction, expecting to see the giant exterminator's tent looming against the darkening sky.

It was gone.

"Drive by the cottage," Julie said, turning to Paige. If the tent had been taken down, she and Calvin could move back in, at least until the place was sold.

Paige signaled and they left the main highway.

Sure enough, the tent had been deflated, but not removed. It bulged and rippled all around the little house, like a garment on top of an open heat vent.

Julie had barely taken that in when Paige nudged her. "Look," she said, pointing.

It was then that Julie spotted the real estate sign. Suzanne Hillbrand had scored—there was a big, red Sold sticker plastered across the other information.

"Sold," Julie whispered, her heart sinking. She guessed she hadn't really believed it would come to this.

"They can't just kick you out," Paige said quickly, and a little angrily as well. "You have a lease. Your landlady has to serve adequate notice."

"I thought it would take a while to sell the cottage," Julie said, as though her sister hadn't spoken. "You know, with the market the way it is and everything. And I *don't* have a lease—it's month to month."

Libby reached forward from the backseat to place one hand on Julie's shoulder and squeeze lightly. "Were you planning on making an offer yourself?" she asked, very quietly.

Julie sniffled, shook her head no. She felt bruised and somehow bereft.

For all intents and purposes, she and Calvin were homeless.

They couldn't stay on the Silver Spur forever, and the house she and Libby and Paige had grown up in was under renovation.

By tacit agreement, they headed for the ranch.

At Tate and Libby's, they were greeted by a crowd of eager children and yipping dogs. Audrey and Ava flung themselves at Libby, wrapping their arms around her waist, making her laugh.

Calvin, Julie noticed, hung back a little, keeping to the fringe of things. It made her heart hurt.

"Don't get mad, okay?" he said, when Julie approached her small son and drew him close for a hug, there in the yard.

"Okay," Julie said cautiously, looking him over more closely now, in the light spilling from Libby and Tate's front porch, and the tall, wide windows on either side of the door.

No casts. No stitches. No bandages, blisters or burns.

Calvin's chin wobbled as he looked up at Julie. "I was down at the creek by myself," he blurted, "and I fell in."

Julie's heart nearly stopped. The creek wasn't particularly deep, nor did the water move especially fast, but it had been cold all day.

Automatically, she checked his forehead for a fever, but his temperature was normal. His clothes, though wrinkled, were dry.

"Garrett was here and he waded in and got me," Calvin hastened on. "I had to take a warm shower and wear one of Tate's shirts until my clothes came out of the dryer. *And* I had a time-out."

Tate appeared, shooing kids, dogs and women toward the house. There was no sign of Garrett.

Tate hung back, once everybody was inside, and Julie paused, too, both of them standing just inside the threshold. He shut the door and spoke quietly.

"I'm sorry, Julie," he said. "The kids were playing soccer in the yard, after we got back from the stock sale this afternoon, and, well, Calvin chased the ball right into the creek."

Julie sighed. Obviously, Tate expected her to be angry with him. Instead, she stood on tiptoe and kissed his cheek.

"Calvin's okay," she reminded her future brother-in-law, the man who had already brought her sister so much happiness. "That's what's important."

Tate nodded, looking relieved. Beyond, in the kitchen, Libby and Paige and all three of the kids seemed to be talking at once.

"Did she find the dress?" he asked. Often, when Tate spoke of Libby, a note of hoarse reverence came into his voice. It happened then, too.

Julie smiled. "Yes, and it's fabulous," she answered.

Tate's grin was as swift and as lethal as Garrett's, though it didn't have the same effect on Julie as Garrett's did. "*Libby's* fabulous," he said.

"No argument there," Julie replied.

Paige appeared in the doorway from the kitchen. "It's okay for Calvin to come home with me, right?" she asked. Calvin was pressed up against his aunt's side by then, clinging to her and gazing hopefully at his mother.

Calvin loved to spend time with either or both of his aunts, but he and Paige had a special bond.

Julie folded her arms, frowned a little and tapped one foot. "I don't know," she said, pausing to run her teeth over her lower lip. "There *was* that whole creek incident, requiring a time-out."

Paige ruffled Calvin's hair and made a face at Julie.

"Oh, all right," Julie relented, as though making a great concession.

By then, she'd decided to tell Garrett she'd changed her mind about everything but making supper.

Julie loved cooking, and she was good at it.

For tonight, Garrett McKettrick would just have to be satisfied with food.

CHAPTER TEN

AUSTIN, CLAD ONLY in faded black sweatpants and a shit-eatin' grin, turned from the refrigerator in the main kitchen to give Garrett an idle once-over. After a low whistle of exclamation, he plucked a can of beer from a shelf and shut the door, popped the top on the beer and raised it in a mocking toast.

"Dressed like that, big brother," Austin drawled, "you're either announcing your candidacy for something, or fixing to charm some woman into the sack."

Considering that he'd gone to some trouble to strike a casual tone, Garrett was not pleased by this observation—particularly since it struck so close to the bone. After he'd gotten back from Tate's place an hour or so before, he'd showered, dressed in moderately new jeans, a long-sleeved Western shirt open at the throat, with the sleeves rolled up to his elbows, and donned a pair of decent boots.

He glared at Austin's beer, then at Austin.

"If anybody around here is a candidate for anything," he replied, "it's you. You've been elected the resident lunatic by a landslide."

Austin, suffering from a bad case of bed-head—on him, even that looked good, dammit—gave a companionable belch and took a long swallow from the brew. "So it's the woman, then," he said. "Julie Remington, I presume?"

No comment, Garrett thought.

"How about making yourself scarce?" he said aloud.

Austin mugged like he was wounded to the quick and pretended to pull a blade from his chest. He was scarred where a whole team of surgeons had put him back together after a bad turn with a mean bull on the rodeo circuit earlier that year, but that probably appealed to women, rather than putting them off.

"Well," he said now, "*that* ain't neighborly."

"We're not neighbors," Garrett pointed out, casting an anxious glance toward the door leading in from the garage. "We're brothers. Get lost—and spare me the hillbilly grammar while you're at it."

Instead of obliging, Austin padded over to the huge table in the middle of the room, drew back a chair and sat down. "I know it's inconvenient at the moment," he said, "but I *live* here."

Even looking like he did—he might have been sleeping on the floor of somebody's tackroom closet for a week—Austin had a way about him, especially with women. It would be just like him to wangle an invitation out of Julie to join them for supper, and then hang around for the rest of the night, knowing damn well he was getting in the way.

Garrett resisted an urge to shove a hand through his hair. He'd just combed it after his shower, gotten rid of the crease left by his hat. He'd spent the day helping the fence crew drive postholes and string wire, except for a stop at Tate's place on the way back home.

He smiled, recalling that. Maybe all wasn't lost, after all.

He'd fished Calvin out of the creek, though the kid had never been in any serious danger of drowning, and that might have earned him a few points with Julie.

"Okay," Garrett said, almost sighing the word. "What's it going to cost me to get you the hell out of here for the rest of the night?"

Austin's eyes twinkled with a faint reflection of the old mischief, then hardened slightly. "You've been kowtowing to Morgan Cox for too long, brother," he said. "Not everybody has a price, whatever your boss may have led you to believe."

Garrett's back molars ground together. He stood beside the table, gripping the edge, and did his best to loom. Not that Austin was intimidated, the little bastard—he was cocky as a rooster.

"Maybe I'll pretend you didn't say that," Garrett said slowly and evenly. "The fact is, right about now I'd just as soon drown you in the pool as anything else."

Austin chuckled, but the sound was raspy and there was no amusement in it. He shook his head once, and then leaned back to drain the beer can. That done, he stood up so fast that his chair nearly tipped over. He caught it before turning toward Garrett.

"Bring it on," he challenged. His blue eyes flashed with temper, and with pain.

"Some other time," Garrett replied quietly. Something was sure as hell eating his kid brother alive, but whatever it was, Austin wasn't ready to talk about it.

Austin raised an eyebrow. "Scared?"

In the near distance, one of the garage doors rolled up.

"You know I'm not," Garrett said. "I happen to have other plans, that's all, and they don't include getting into a pissing match with you, little brother."

Some of the granite drained out of Austin's eyes and his jawline; he looked almost like his old self again.

Almost, but not quite.

He slapped Garrett on the shoulder and headed for one of the stairways, and by the time Julie stepped into the kitchen, carrying one plastic grocery bag and her purse, Austin was gone.

"Where's Harry?" she asked, looking around the kitchen.

It took Garrett a moment to realize she was referring to the dog.

He smiled, crossed the room and took the bag from her hand. "He's taken to hanging out in front of my fireplace," he explained. "I hope that's all right with you."

"I wouldn't have thought he could manage the stairs," Julie said, her tone fretful and her gaze straying up the steps.

"I carried him," Garrett said. And just then, the three-legged beagle appeared on the landing above, making a happy whining sound down deep in his throat and wagging his tail and both hips.

Julie seemed strained and pretty tired, but a smile transformed her face. "You carried him?" she asked, as though she wasn't sure she'd heard him correctly.

"Yeah," Garrett admitted, puzzled. The dog was about to start down the stairs, a decision that could prove disastrous, considering the critter's anatomical limitations, so he said, "Hold it right there" and bounded up there to head Harry off.

He caught the mutt in the curve of one arm, hoisted.

Julie stood at the bottom of the stairs, looking up at them, that soft smile still gracing her face. For a moment, it seemed to Garrett that she glowed like a stained-glass Madonna in a church window. The sight of her made his breath catch and then swell in his throat.

"I hear you saved Calvin in the face of certain survival," she quipped, the smile turning to a grin. "Thanks for that, Garrett."

He chuckled. "You're welcome," he answered, frozen where he was, at the top of the stairs, with a dog under his arm and a grocery sack dangling from his other hand. His voice came out sounding hoarse. "Come on up," he said. "Whatever's in this bag, we'll cook it together."

She hesitated, set her purse aside on a countertop and mounted the stairs, looking down at her feet as she climbed. It was only when she'd reached the landing that Garrett saw the heat burning in her cheeks.

She was still wearing her coat, and the rich autumn-brown color of the cloth turned her changeable eyes to a smoky shade of amber. "About what we were planning—for after supper, I mean—"

Garrett set Harry down, and the dog greeted Julie with a few jabs of his nose to her shins, then turned and trotted off toward the double doors opening into Garrett's living area.

Garrett shifted the grub-sack to his other hand and pressed his palm lightly into the small of Julie's back, steering her toward the well-lit privacy of his living room. He meant the gesture to reassure her, and she did seem to relax a little. At the same time, he felt energy zipping through her like electricity through a wire.

"Wow," she said, after crossing the threshold.

A fire crackled on the hearth, and the tall windows overlooking the range seemed speckled with stars. Lamps burned here and there, switched to "dim," giving the room a welcoming glow.

Garrett grinned at her, but proceeded to the kitchen, where he looked into the bag, saw that it contained a package of boneless, skinless chicken breasts, and tossed the works into the refrigerator.

He'd opened a good shiraz earlier, to let it "breathe," though he was secretly skeptical about the respiratory capacity of wine, no matter how fancy its label.

He slid two wineglasses from the built-in rack under one row of cupboards, holding them by their stems, and set them on the counter as Julie slid out of her coat and draped it over the back of one of the barstools at the counter.

Garrett washed his hands at the sink, remembering that he'd been holding the dog, dried them on a dish towel, and gave Julie a questioning look as he reached for the wine bottle.

She nodded, met his eyes as he handed her a glass and then clinked his own against it, very lightly.

"To a friendly supper," he said huskily, wanting to put her at ease, "between two friends."

Julie looked relieved, but a little disconcerted, too, as she nodded and then sipped. Closing her eyes, she said, "Ummm," and things ground inside Garrett, like rusted gears freshly oiled and just starting to turn again.

If it hadn't felt so damn good, he reflected, it would have hurt like hell.

"Are we friends, Garrett?" she asked.

"I hope so," he answered.

As if that settled something, Julie set the wineglass down, washed her hands and opened the fridge door to retrieve the bag. "Let's cook," she said. "I'm starved."

Right on cue, Garrett pulled a baking sheet lined with stuffed mushrooms from the oven. They'd been warming there for a while, thanks to Esperanza, but they weren't shriveled, and they smelled fine.

Julie's eyes widened. "You cook?"

If only he could have lied and taken the credit. Alas, Garrett came from a long line of compulsive truth-tellers. "I know how to fry eggs," he confessed. "Esperanza keeps a stash of frozen finger foods on hand at all times. Her theory is, You never know when a dinner party might break out."

Julie laughed at that. Reached for one of the mushrooms and lifted it to her mouth, taking a delicate sniff before she bit into it.

"Ummmm," she said again, just the way she had before, when she first tasted the wine. She *breathed* the sound, and there was something so sensual about it that Garrett's brain turned to vapor inside his skull and then seemed to dissipate like mist under a hot sun.

In that moment, the sophisticated Garrett McKettrick, former top aide to a U.S. senator, forgot everything he'd ever known about women, except for one thing: He loved them.

Loved the way they looked, the way they smelled, the way they felt.

Or maybe it was just this particular one he loved.

He was still standing there, dumbstruck by the implications, when Julie opened those marvelous, magical eyes, looked straight into his, and suddenly popped a mushroom into his mouth.

It was an ordinary gesture, entirely innocent.

And it struck Garrett with all the wallop of a punch.

It was only by superhuman effort that he refrained from taking the wineglass out of her hand, pressing her body against the wall or the refrigerator door, with the full length of his own, and kissing her like she'd never been kissed before.

Even by him.

"Whoa," he ground out, amazed that it was so hard to rein himself in.

Julie gave a breathy little giggle and fluttered a hand in front of her face like a fan. "Phew," she said. "Esperanza must have stuffed those mushrooms with jalapeños."

Garrett laughed as some new and startled kind of joy welled up inside him and broke free. His heart pounded and his breath came shallow and raspy.

He loved Julie Remington.

No, he instantly corrected himself. He couldn't *possibly* be in love with her—it was too soon.

And he was in transition.

"We'd better cook," he said, desperate to distract her.

And equally desperate *not* to.

Julie giggled again and put her wineglass on the counter, then slid both arms around his neck. He felt her breasts, soft against the hard wall of his chest. "Oh," she said, "I think we're *already* cooking."

Garrett, like his brothers, like his father and his grandfather and a whole slew of greats, had been raised to be a gentleman.

Cursing his upbringing, he took a very light grip on Julie's wrists and brought her arms down from around his neck. He held on to her hands, though. Squeezed them.

"Food first," he said, and the rumble in his voice reminded him of the pre-earthquake sound of tectonic plates shifting far underground.

Julie's cheeks glowed and something flashed brief and bright in her eyes. But then she swallowed visibly and nodded.

"Food first," she agreed.

THE WHOLE TIME she and Garrett were assembling that batch of chicken spaghetti, Julie was torn between equally strong impulses to run in the other direction, as fast as she could, and fling herself at him again.

Not that putting her arms around Garrett's neck really qualified as *flinging herself at him*, she thought. On the other hand, what *else* could she call it?

She couldn't blame it on the wine. Two sips weren't enough to make her brazen.

No, it hadn't been the wine.

She'd raised that stupid stuffed mushroom to his mouth—what had possessed her to do such a forward thing she would never know—and he'd taken it from her. Moreover, he'd sucked lightly at her fingers as she withdrew.

That was the moment it happened. The moment she lost her mind.

They worked reasonably well together, Julie thought, taking occasional and very slow sips from her wineglass, and chatted like the old friends they most definitely were not while she slipped the casserole into the preheated oven and set the timer, after musing over the dials and buttons a little.

While the main course baked, Garrett threw together a very decent salad, and Julie watched, munching on another stuffed mushroom.

"And you said all you could do was fry eggs," she said.

Garrett winked. "Oh, I can do *lots* of things besides fry eggs," he told her.

The kitchen was big, though not as enormous as the one downstairs, and wired for sound. When an old Patsy Cline ballad melted in through the speakers, like some shimmering liquid, nearly visible, Garrett turned the volume up and the lights down and pulled Julie into his arms, waltzing her around the perimeters of the island in the center of the room.

If he'd kissed her then, she would have been lost. But he didn't. He simply danced with her.

Until the song ended and she was dizzy, and her breathing was all messed up.

Silently, Julie reminded herself that Garrett was only passing through—even this legendary ranch wasn't big enough to accommodate his ambitions. He wanted to play on the world stage, and when he left, she couldn't—and wouldn't—go with him.

Still, she'd been alone for so long.

And Garrett had roused things in her that no other man had even stirred.

Her body—every cell of it—was suddenly asserting itself, making demands, crying out for things her mind would have called foolish. And among those things was the simple solace of being held by a man.

Just held.

In a last-ditch effort to resist, to override flood-tide passion with common sense, Julie did the opposite of what her entire physicality craved: She pulled out of Garrett's arms, turned from him, and stood leaning against the counter opposite the door, her head down, gasping for breath.

And her body wept.

Garrett moved to stand behind her, rested his hands on her shoulders, barely touching her, but touching her just the same. Touching her in a way that caused her very essence to gather within her and then surge, like some sparkling force summoned by a wizard, into the rein-roughened palms of his hands.

The sensation was so deliciously compelling, so utterly unnerving, that Julie sagged, suddenly boneless, and might have collapsed if Garrett hadn't held her upright, turned her in his arms, held her against his chest.

She was trembling.

"Shhh," he murmured. It was what she needed—*holding*—and somehow he knew that.

Garrett curved a finger under Julie's chin and lifted, so she was looking into his eyes.

Without a word, he kissed her.

There was undeniable wanting in that kiss, but it was exquisitely controlled. It made promises, that sweet pressure of his mouth on hers, but demanded nothing in return.

I'm losing my mind, Julie thought, feeling swept away.

Garrett stretched—she realized he was switching off the oven—and then swung her easily up into his arms.

"If you say 'stop,'" he told her, "if you even *think* 'stop,' I will."

She nodded to let him know she understood, and rested her face in the curve where his neck and shoulder met, loving the smell of his skin, the warmth and substance and strength of him.

He carried her into a darkened room, and she knew by the fresh-air, Garrett-scent of the place that this was where he slept.

She felt dazed, needy, incredibly safe.

Garrett stood her beside the shadow of a bed. "Where's Calvin?" he asked.

Julie swallowed, scrounged around in the depths of herself until she found her voice. "With Paige," she answered. "For the weekend."

He began peeling away her clothes, and the touch of his hands seemed reverent, rather than forceful. "Good," he said, and the word vibrated down the length of her neck, because he spoke it into the hollow beneath her right ear. "That's good."

She didn't have to be strong, Julie thought, bedazzled.

For once, for a little while, she didn't have to be strong.

Garrett was strong enough for both of them.

Garment by garment, Garrett bared Julie, then himself. He took a condom from the nightstand.

"Just hold me," she whispered, as they sank together into rumpled sheets, fragrant with detergent and sunshine and Garrett.

He stretched out beside her on the bed, drew her close, so that their bodies fit together.

But he did not kiss or caress her.

Not then.

Honoring his tacit promise, Garrett simply *held* Julie in the strong, warm circle of his arms. He propped his chin on top of her head, and she took comfort in the steady meter of his breathing. He said nothing. Asked for nothing.

Gave everything.

Julie lay there, in Garrett's easy embrace, and felt no shame, no sorrow and no need of anything more than what she had, in that precise moment.

After a long time, she spoke his name, whispered it, like a plea.

And he understood, and eased on top of her, bracing himself on his elbows and forearms.

"Are you sure, Julie?" he asked.

She bit her lower lip, nodded.

From Julie's perspective, there was no need for foreplay. Her surrender to Garrett was a gift, and not a fulfillment of any desire she possessed. She eased her thighs apart, lifted her hips just slightly, delighting in the groan the motion elicited from him.

"I'm sure," she told him.

He eased inside her.

Julie cried out, not in pain, but in celebration—the friction, the fit, was perfect. It sent her spinning away from herself, in a glittering spiral of light and heat, and the sounds she made were expressions of awe and delight.

He was so big.

So strong.

So hard.

Julie gave herself up to the most primitive aspects of her own femininity, let herself be lost in Garrett.

He entwined his fingers with hers, pressed her hands into the pillow on either side of her head and pumped hard with his hips.

Julie kept pace, meeting him stroke for stroke, thrust for thrust.

The climb was a sacred quest, every new level intensified the pleasure.

Their bodies flirted, then danced, then slammed into each other, fierce in their need for union, for the deepest kind of contact, for satisfaction.

When the climax came, it was simultaneous. Garrett tensed on top of Julie, with a guttural shout, a warrior's cry of conquest and triumph. Julie, in turn, flung herself upward to meet him, to take him deep inside her, to clench around him and wring from him everything he had to give to her, and then still more.

That first, apocalyptic release was followed by a series of progressively smaller ones, soul-wrenching and utterly involuntary.

When it was over, a long, long time had passed, and Garrett and Julie lay still, exhausted.

Julie was glad of the darkness, because suddenly her eyes were awash in tears—not of sorrow and certainly not of regret, but of wonderment and awe. When had she last felt those things, soared like that?

Never, that was when.

The thought jolted Julie; she sneaked up a hand to dry her cheek. And she began to rationalize.

She'd responded in the soul-shattering way she had because it had been so long since she'd had sex, that was all.

It wasn't Garrett, she insisted to herself. Any reasonably skilled man could have satisfied her just as thoroughly as he had.

Probably.

Garrett lay sprawled beside her, where he'd fallen, one leg draped across her thighs. When he moved to switch on the lamp, his upper arm brushed against the side of her face, and he felt the moisture on her skin.

He looked solemn as he gazed down at her. "Are you—? Did I—?"

She smiled, touched his beard-bristled cheek, ran the pad of her thumb over that sensuous mouth of his. And she shook her head. "I'm all right, Garrett," she said.

He leaned over her, kissed her right cheekbone, and then her left. "Stay there," he told her.

He got off the bed, and Julie heard a rustling sound. Though she couldn't bring herself to look at him, she knew he was pulling on his jeans.

As soon as he'd left the room, Julie got up and scrambled for the master bathroom.

When Garrett returned, though, she was back in bed, wearing her shirt and her jeans, the covers pulled up to her chin in a way that was, once she had time to think about it, pretty ridiculous.

Garrett, carrying a plate piled with Esperanza's stuffed mushrooms, chuckled when he saw her. Then he maneuvered until he was sitting beside Julie, his back to the pillows fluffed between him and the headboard, and offered her a morsel.

She hesitated, feeling self-conscious, and then her stomach rumbled.

Garrett laughed, touching the mushroom to her mouth.

Julie took it. Chewed for a long time, finally swallowed.

"I turned the oven back on," Garrett said. "How long do you think it will take for the spaghetti to finish cooking?"

Now it was Julie who laughed, though more with relief than because anything was funny. She didn't know what she'd expected from Garrett—regret? Dismissal, or even contempt?

It hadn't been a perfectly ordinary question about dinner, that was for sure.

"Maybe fifteen minutes," she said, feeling incredibly awkward, fully clothed and hiding everything but her head under the covers.

Garrett smiled, tossed a mushroom into his mouth and offered Julie another one. When she shook her head, he set the plate aside on the bedside table.

Then he slid an arm under Julie's back and eased her against his side.

His chest was bare, lightly dusted with hair the color of brown sugar.

Julie wanted to place her palm in the center of his taut belly, spread her fingers wide, but she refrained. Contented herself with resting her head on his shoulder.

"So why were you crying?" he asked, very quietly and after a long time.

Julie sighed. "Because it was so good," she admitted.

He chuckled, a low and entirely masculine sound that struck some tender places hidden away in Julie's heart. Whatever else he might be—an expert at spin, Blue River, Texas's, favorite son—Garrett was a cowboy, too.

The real deal, born and bred on the Silver Spur Ranch.

Raised to be all man and yet capable of a degree of tenderness, at least while making love, that made Julie marvel just to recall it.

She was glad when the timer dinged out in the kitchen, because she was just about to cry again. Instead, she leaped out of bed as eagerly as if supper came around once a month instead of every day.

Garrett stayed behind in his room long enough to pull a T-shirt on over his head. It was plain, with a hole in one side seam, but clean.

They ate sitting cross-legged on the floor in front of Garrett's fireplace, Harry snoozing nearby and opening one eye every now and then, probably hoping for a scrap.

"Damn," Garrett said, with an appreciative grin. "You can cook."

Julie's cheeks ached with heat as she stared down at her plate. "Thanks."

A companionable silence ensued. Garrett picked up his wineglass, which he'd set on the coffee table earlier, and took a sip, but Julie was off the sauce, at least for the evening.

Why was it so easy to fall into this man's bed, and so hard to talk to him afterward?

"Hey," he said, when he'd taken both their plates to the kitchen and returned to sit on the rug again, facing her. "Are you ever going to look at me?"

Julie blinked, made herself meet Garrett's eyes. She was acting silly, she knew that, but she couldn't seem to figure out how to stop.

"You're a woman," Garrett said, holding her gaze, the firelight flickering over the strong angles of his face, the powerful set of his shoulders, "and I'm a man. What just happened between us—happened. And that's okay, Julie. It's a lot *better* than okay, in fact."

"I don't usually—" She paused, miserably embarrassed. Where was the old, confident, sensual Julie? "I mean, you must think—"

Garrett cupped his hand under her chin, and her skin tingled where the tips of his fingers touched. "I *think*," he told her firmly, though his voice was gruff, "that you are one hell of a woman, and *I'm* one lucky son of a gun to be spending an evening with you."

An evening. He was lucky to spend *an evening* with her.

Well, what had she expected?

A lifetime commitment, an avowal of undying love?

After one roll in the hay?

"It *was* good," she admitted, wondering when she'd be able to shake off the strange shyness possessing her now.

"Ya think?" Garrett teased, raising one eyebrow slightly.

Julie laughed, and just like that, the tension was broken, the shyness gone. Still, a part of her wanted to ask, *Now what?*

More sex?

More wine?

More chicken spaghetti?

Was this a fling, or an affair, or just a one-night stand?

And what was the difference between a fling and an affair?

Julie sighed and pressed her fingers to her temples. And she blurted it right out.

"Now what?"

Garrett scooted forward, so their knees touched. Then their foreheads.

"Now," he ventured, "we take a shower together and make love again?"

"You can't possibly be serious," Julie said.

Garrett tugged her T-shirt up until her breasts were uncovered. She'd forgotten to put her bra back on.

"Hot damn," he said, admiring her for a long, delicious moment before he ducked his head and took her nipple into his mouth. He suckled until she moaned, then turned and thoroughly attended to her other breast before meeting her eyes again. "Still think I'm not serious?" he asked, lifting the T-shirt off over her head and arms and tossing it away. "If you need more convincing, I'll be happy to oblige."

She felt beautiful, powerful, even slightly dangerous, like some nomadic princess about to enjoy a captive lover, sitting there on Garrett's floor, with their knees and shins touching, and her naked breasts bathed in the dancing light of his fire.

Mischief widened her eyes and made her smile saucy. "You know," she said, "I'm just not sure—I think I *might* actually need some convincing."

He laughed and eased her backward onto the floor, then luxuriated in her breasts, kissing them, caressing them, weighing them in his hands. "Then maybe," he said, after making a slow circle around each of her nipples with the tip of his tongue, "I'd better have you again, right here and right now, while I've got you on your back."

"That was such a sexist thing to say," she gasped.

He was kissing her belly, working the snap on her jeans, and then the zipper. "You're not on your back?" he teased, his voice sleepy and slow.

"You know what I mean," Julie whimpered, as he slid down her jeans. She'd forgotten her panties, too, she realized, not just her bra.

"Ummmm," he murmured.

And then he made Julie call out his name, not once, not twice, but half a dozen times before he finally took her.

CHAPTER ELEVEN

JULIE LAY PERFECTLY STILL, her eyes closed, reorienting herself. It was a slow process, grasping at wispy fragments of consciousness, trying to fit them into some sensible pattern.

She wasn't in her usual bed—which wasn't her usual bed, either, to be perfectly accurate—the directions and the angles were all wrong.

And then it all fell into place, and Julie sucked in a sharp breath.

Oh, God. She'd had sex with Garrett McKettrick—crazy, sweaty, unbridled, *consequences?—what consequences?—*sex.

Now, the proverbial chickens had come home to roost. It was time to pay the piper, face the music.

Welcome to the dreaded Morning After.

The mattress shifted. "Open your eyes," Garrett drawled. He smelled of soap and aftershave, and his breath was minty.

Julie was fairly certain hers wasn't.

He knew she was awake—there was no point in trying to fake it so he'd go away and leave her alone long enough to get her act together.

Not that she had any idea how to go about doing that, at the present moment, at least.

"Julie?"

She opened her eyes. Wide.

Garrett was so close that their noses were almost touching.

"Mornin'," he said, one corner of his mouth crooking upward in a teasing grin.

"Mmmm," Julie said, with a nod, clasping one hand over her mouth. "Breath," she explained, through her fingers.

Garrett chuckled, shook his head once, and placed a brief, smacking kiss on her forehead before rolling off the bed and landing on his feet with that grace peculiar to people who've spent a lot of time on horses, cowboys in particular.

He was wearing jeans and nothing else.

Tossing her a blue cotton bathrobe, heretofore draped over the back of a leather-upholstered wingback chair, he said, "Coffee's almost ready."

The moment he left the room, Julie pulled the robe under the covers, wriggled herself into it, and even tied the belt before throwing back the blankets to rise.

Given that the horse was already out of the barn, she thought ruefully, it was a little late to be closing the barn door.

Garrett's bathroom was large, and there was travertine tile everywhere—on the walls and the floor and the long counter with two bronze sinks set into it. The matching faucets, beautifully cast, were shaped like horses' heads, and although Julie quickly found a new toothbrush and toothpaste in a drawer, it took her a while to figure out how to turn on the water.

Once she'd accomplished that, she scrubbed her teeth with a fury.

A sound startled her—a masculine rap of knuckles on wood.

Julie went to the door, opened it an inch and peeked out.

Garrett was standing there, holding a neat stack of folded clothing. Jeans. A lightweight gray sweatshirt. Socks and even underwear.

Julie recognized the garments—vaguely—as her own things.

He chuckled, noting her reluctance to open up.

This was, after all, *his* bathroom. And it wasn't as if she had anything he hadn't already seen. She was behaving like an idiot, and she couldn't seem to help it.

"Don't you want to get dressed?" he asked.

Julie flushed, nodded, opened the door just far enough to reach out and grab her clothing. Where had he gotten these things?

Garrett must have seen the question in her face, because he answered it.

"I told Esperanza you needed something to wear," he said, "and she fetched this stuff from the laundry room."

Julie's eyes widened. "You *told* Esperanza…?"

"Oops?" Garrett inquired. There was a distinct twinkle in his eyes.

Julie made a growling sound of frustration, and he laughed, and she shut the door in his face and turned the lock for good measure.

"I was kidding," Garrett called through the closed door. "I found your gear in a basket in the laundry room. Esperanza's not around—she always goes to church on Sundays."

Julie rested her forehead against the panel, smiling a little. "Okay," she replied, after letting out a long breath. "Thanks."

But she didn't unlock the door.

She used Garrett's fancy shower—the one they'd shared the night before—between making love on the living room floor and making love *again* in bed.

Julie's knees weakened a little as she took off the borrowed robe, stepped into the shower, adjusted the spigots. She tried not to think of the things she and Garrett had done in that steamy cubicle, but of course that would have been impossible.

She washed quickly, trying not to get her hair wet, used a monogrammed bath sheet to dry off, and hastily pulled on the clean clothes Garrett had rustled up for her.

She finger-combed her hair—fortunately, it hadn't frizzed overmuch—tidied up the bathroom and unlocked the door.

Julie found Garrett in the kitchen, scrambling eggs on the stovetop set into the island.

He was wearing a blue chambray shirt and boots now, along with the jeans.

"You look like a man about to swing up into the saddle and strike out for other parts," Julie remarked, willing herself not to blush again.

And she didn't.

Two thick slabs of bread popped out of the toaster, and Garrett slid the skillet of eggs off the burner before deftly buttering the slices.

Harry, Julie noted, was eating kibble out of a bowl in a corner.

Fresh clothes for her, dog food for the beagle. Garrett, it seemed, had thought of everything.

"Tate called a little while ago," he said, in belated answer, plopping the eggs and the toast onto two plates and carrying them to the breakfast bar. "We've been having some trouble with rustlers lately and he wants to make a few passes over some of the canyons in my plane—see if we can spot anything."

A little niggle of dread curled in Julie's stomach, like smoke.

We've been having some trouble with rustlers lately...

Rustlers were criminals.

Criminals tended to be dangerous.

And although Tate and Garrett probably thought they were invincible, since they were rock-ribbed McKettricks, they could be hurt, like anyone else.

"Shouldn't the police handle things like this?" she asked, in a cracked-china voice.

Garrett, perched on the stool next to Julie's, sat with his fork suspended in one hand, watching her as though she represented a dozen delightful curiosities to be puzzled out, one by one. "Tate's been keeping Brent Brogan up to speed," he said, his tone as thoughtful as his expression. "Brent's just one man, though, and the Silver Spur is our worry—Tate's and Austin's and mine—not his."

Julie's jaw tightened. She relaxed her face by force of will. "This isn't the Old West, Garrett," she reasoned. "You and your brothers don't have to stand against these—these cattle thieves, all by yourselves."

There it was again, that registered-weapon of a grin. Garrett narrowed his true-blue eyes slightly as he studied her. "Why, ma'am," he joked, heavy on the Texas twang and the schlock, "are you frettin' your pretty little head over a ring-tailed polecat like me?"

She laughed, though reluctantly, and moved one hand a little, as if to swat at him. "Stop it," she said. "This is serious. What if someone gets hurt?"

Something tender moved in his eyes. "It happens," he said quietly. Maybe, like Julie, he was thinking of Pablo Ruiz, the longtime ranch foreman and a close friend of the McKettricks. Pablo, a good man and a much beloved member of the community, had been *killed* a few months before, trying to unload a half-wild stallion from a horse trailer.

"Yes," Julie agreed, "it happens."

I don't want it to happen to Libby's future bridegroom, the man she loves, body, mind and soul.

I don't want it to happen to you, Garrett McKettrick.

The silence stretched between them, drawn taut, about to spring back on itself.

"We'll be careful," Garrett said.

Julie pushed her plate away—the eggs weren't bad, but she'd lost her appetite—and looked down at her hands, knotted together in her lap. Yes, she'd spent the night with Garrett, and to say they'd been intimate would have been the understatement of the century.

But the reality was, she had no claim on Garrett, no say in how he ran his life. If he wanted to put himself in danger, to play hero instead of calling in the authorities to deal with the rustlers, there wasn't a damn thing she could do about it.

She didn't have to like it, though.

And she couldn't seem to shut up.

"Just remember," she said, tearing up a little, "that Tate has children. Audrey and Ava need him. And my sister, *my sister*, loves that man with everything she has and everything she is. If anything happened to him—"

"I haven't forgotten the twins, Julie. They're my nieces and I love them." Garrett's eyes were solemn, his hand strong when he laid it over Julie's. Only when his fingers squeezed hers did she realize she'd been shaking. "I know what Tate means to Libby," he went on, his voice husky, "and what she means to him. Trust me when I tell you that I'll watch his back."

And who will watch yours? Julie wanted to ask, but she didn't, because she couldn't get the words out and, anyway, she already knew what his answer would be. Garrett and his brothers would watch out for *each other*, the way brothers—and sisters—did.

Suppose it wasn't enough?

Seeing that Julie was finished eating, Garrett collected their plates and silverware and carried them to the sink.

Harry, having scarfed up his morning kibble, nudged Julie's

ankle with his muzzle and whimpered to let her know he needed to go outside.

Mundane as the task was, Julie was glad to have something to occupy her. She slid off the high barstool and sighed. "Come on, dog," she said. "Let's go."

"He might have some trouble with the stairs," Garrett said, his voice unusually deep, as though he'd just had a testosterone rush. With that, he leaned down, whisked Harry up into his arms and headed for an outside door.

Before stepping through it, Garrett took an old jeans jacket from a peg on the wall and handed it to Julie.

"Put this on," he said. "It's probably chilly out there."

Julie shrugged into the coat, at once comforted and unsettled because Garrett's scent rose from the denim.

There was a small landing, then a set of stone steps leading down to a cozy, grassy yard, walled in with stucco. Julie followed Garrett down onto the private lawn, folded her arms against the cold while Harry sniffed around, looking for a place to relieve himself.

"I didn't know this was here," Julie remarked, because the silence made her antsy. "It's almost like a secret garden."

Garrett's side-tilted grin reappeared. "Yeah," he agreed, "except for the—er—*garden*."

Harry was taking his sweet time finding just the right place to lift his leg.

Smiling, Julie stood in the center of the yard and turned in a slow circle, closing her eyes to dream of roses and peonies and all manner of other colorful plants and bushes.

A white wrought-iron bench would be lovely, too, and perhaps a small fountain, and a birdfeeder or two.

Suddenly dizzy, Julie stopped turning and opened her eyes and was startled to find Garrett standing so close to her that she could feel the hard man-heat emanating from his flesh.

Her breath caught.

Garrett chuckled hoarsely and set his hands on her hips, holding her in a way that brought back a flood of steamy memories from the night before.

"I won't be gone long, Julie," he said, his mouth very close to hers, his warm breath dancing on her skin, "just an hour or two."

He kissed her then, so gently that some new and unnamed emotion surged up within her, rendering speech impossible.

"I have to make lesson plans," she blurted out, the moment their mouths parted. "And call my landlady. Get Calvin ready for a new week—"

Garrett had not released his grasp on her. She could feel the press of his thumbs on her hipbones, the spread of his fingers over her buttocks, even through the relatively heavy fabric of her jeans. Her whole body remembered their lovemaking then, in a visceral rush of echoed sensation, and she gasped slightly and felt heat thrumming in her face again.

Garrett smiled, as though he'd read all of that and more in her expression, and maybe he had.

It was a disconcerting thought.

"Make your lesson plans and call your landlady while I'm gone," he told her. "Because I've got a few plans of my own for when I get back."

Garrett hadn't exactly issued a command, Julie reasoned, but he wasn't making a request, either.

"Like what?" she asked, because she couldn't just let him get away with a thing like that. Whatever that thing was.

If there even *was* a thing.

Again, that slow and patently lethal cowboy grin. "You really want me to tell you? Right here and now?"

"No," she said quickly.

Yes, protested everything besides her voice.

Just then, Harry made it known that his errand had been completed. He was ready to go back in the house and lose his dogself in the depths of a nap, preferably near a warm, crackling fire.

All was well in Harryworld.

With a chuckle, Garrett bent to ruffle the dog's ears. "This way, buddy," he said. But instead of heading back up the stairs, he led Julie and the dog out of the hidden yard by a side gate.

There was the barn, the concrete driveway leading to the multicar garage, the acres of grass.

Garrett walked up to the back door, turned the knob and opened it.

Harry rushed into the otherwise empty kitchen, found his water dish in its usual place and started lapping like crazy.

Garrett waited patiently until Julie, oddly shaken, feeling as though she'd just traveled between two worlds instead of two parts of the same huge house, remembered she was wearing his jacket and took it off.

She handed it over.

"I'll be back in a while," Garrett said, shrugging into the garment.

Thinking of the rustlers again, Julie felt an almost overwhelming need to get him to stay, whether by coaxing or cajoling or even coercion. She bit down hard on her lower lip to keep from nagging.

"I might not be around," Julie said casually, although she was feeling anything *but* casual.

She'd made a terrible mistake, sleeping with Garrett McKettrick.

She'd lowered her defenses, and he had breached them.

And now he was inside, possibly to stay.

If he hadn't been standing right there, looking directly into her face, Julie might have covered said face with both hands and wailed in frustration and chagrin.

Garrett merely arched an eyebrow, waited for her to go on.

"I'll probably go to town," she said. "Stop by the cottage and see if the place is habitable, now that the exterminators are finished."

He chuckled, gave her a light kiss. "It's too late to run away now, Julie," he said. "We're in too deep for that."

Julie opened her mouth to protest, realized she didn't have a leg to stand on, so to speak, and closed it again. And again, heat pulsed in her cheeks.

At least he'd said *we're* in too deep.

"It was only sex," Julie felt compelled to argue. After all, that was the rationale she'd used to justify the indulgence to herself.

"'Only'?" he teased in response. "Not a word I would use to describe what happened between us."

Julie didn't trust herself to reply—the likelihood that she'd put her foot in her mouth was entirely too high.

Garrett turned and headed for the door to the garage then, and

Harry gave a little whine of sorrow at his going. Julie barely stifled a mournful whimper of her own.

"Hush," she said to Harry, her voice husky. "You mustn't get attached."

Standing there in the vast McKettrick kitchen, Julie closed her eyes and swayed against a sudden rush of sadness.

Harry *was* attached to Garrett.

So was she.

And so, most worrisome of all, was Calvin.

She had to step back, move out of the ranch house, do whatever was necessary to put some distance between herself and Garrett.

Resolute, Julie found her address book, unplugged her cell phone from its charger and punched in her landlady's number.

Julie and Calvin's rental had been Louise Smithfield's "honeymoon cottage," until Mr. Smithfield's death twenty years before.

Unable to stay where there were so many memories, Louise hadn't been prepared to let the place go, either. She'd decided, she'd told Julie, to visit a cousin in Austin for a while, get some perspective before she made any big decisions.

One thing led to another, of course, and Louise made new friends in Austin, found a job she liked and eventually bought a condo there.

The honeymoon cottage became a rental, and Louise was content to let it pay off its own mortgage. Julie, the latest in a long line of tenants, had loved the place, allowed her heart to feel at home there.

"Hello?" Louise croaked, in her rickety old-lady voice, startling Julie out of her reverie. "Who is this? If you're a telemarketer, I'm on that list and you'd better not call me again."

"Mrs. Smithfield?" Julie interrupted, with a timorous smile, "I'm not selling anything. It's me, Julie Remington."

Mrs. Smithfield was quiet.

"Your tenant?" Julie prompted.

"I know who you are," Mrs. Smithfield said crisply, but not unkindly. "I'm sorry, Julie. You've been a marvel, taking such good care of the cottage, always paying your rent on time. I'm not getting any younger, though, and it's time for me to liquidate some of my assets."

Julie's throat ached. She *had* been happy at the cottage. "When does the sale close?" she asked.

Louise sighed. "The buyers are paying cash," she replied. "The transaction can be completed as soon as—as soon as you've moved your things out, dear." A pause, slightly breathless, belied what she said next. "Not that there's any hurry."

Julie closed her eyes for a moment, dazed by the prospect of packing all her and Calvin's belongings and leaving the cottage for good.

Where would they go?

She supposed she could put the furniture and the pots and pans and all of their other stuff into storage, wedge into Paige's apartment on a temporary basis, start watching the classified ads for that rarest of Blue River phenomena, a house or apartment whose lease was coming up and whose tenants were leaving.

Or she could stay right there on the Silver Spur, continue to go to bed with Garrett McKettrick whenever Calvin wasn't around, and risk breaking not just her own heart, but her little boy's, too.

The dog whimpered and scratched at the door Garrett had passed through minutes before.

"Julie?" Mrs. Smithfield said, sounding concerned. "Are you still there?"

"Yes, Mrs. Smithfield," Julie answered. "I'm still here. The cottage is definitely sold, then?"

"Yes," the landlady replied, sounding both relieved and defensive. "Frankly, I was a little surprised that *you* didn't make an offer, Julie."

There was no point in saying that the asking price had been too high; after all, someone had met or even exceeded it. Someone who could pay cash, no less.

"If the sale falls through for any reason," Julie responded gently, "I hope you or Suzanne will get in touch with me."

Louise promised to do that, and Julie promised to be out of the cottage by the first of the month, a date barely two weeks in the future.

She did not need this, she thought, hanging up after a cordial goodbye. Not on top of the musical she had to stage at school, her disappointment over shoving the showcase of one-act plays to a back burner and Gordon Pruett suddenly deciding he wanted to play a role in Calvin's life after all.

Among other things.

Julie's gaze rose briefly to the ceiling.

What is it with you, Remington? she asked herself. *Your life wasn't complicated enough, without adding Garrett McKettrick to the mix?*

Julie shook the thought off. She hadn't been fibbing when she told Garrett she had things to fill her time that day besides going back to bed with him.

The thought of which made her nipples harden, her knees weaken and her insides melt.

"Enough," she told herself and Harry, who sat at her feet now, head tilted to one side, ears perked up.

Resolutely, Julie marched into the quarters she and Calvin shared. She was a whirlwind, dusting and vacuuming, putting fresh sheets on the beds, clean towels on the rack in the bathroom.

All too soon, the rooms were spotless.

How long had Garrett been gone? she wondered, checking her watch. If he got back before she'd either picked Calvin up at Paige's place in town, or Paige had brought him home, well, it didn't take a rocket scientist to predict what would happen.

Before she knew what hit her, she'd be on her back in Garrett's bed, bare-ass naked, boinking away.

She felt herself go moist with longing.

"Get a grip," she said.

Harry, who had followed her from room to room during the brief cleaning frenzy, wagged his tail and watched her with interest. Clearly, he was expecting something to happen.

"Come on," Julie told him, taking his leash from the top drawer of the small antique bureau in the hallway between her bedroom and Calvin's and clipping it to his collar. "We're going on a reconnaissance mission."

As soon as he saw the leash, Harry was beside himself with joy.

It did not take much to please Harry.

Julie grabbed a casual jacket before leaving the house—her regular coat, along with yesterday's clothes, was still upstairs in

Garrett's hideaway, she remembered with more burning of the face—and tracked down her purse.

By the time she had installed Harry in the backseat of her Cadillac and raised the garage door using the remote Tate had given her when she moved in, Julie almost felt like some sort of crook fleeing the scene of a crime.

Once out and pointed in the right direction, she ferreted through her purse for her cell phone headset, put it on and speed-dialed Paige's number before heading down the driveway.

She got her sister's voice mail.

"It's Julie. I'm on the way over to the cottage to start getting ready to move, and I'll probably be there for a while, so maybe you can drop Calvin off there and save yourself a trip out to the ranch. Call me when you get this. 'Bye."

The phone rang just as she reached the main gates, which, fortunately, were standing open.

"Paige?" she said, instead of hello.

"Libby," her other sister replied, with a smile in her voice. "Listen, I'm making a big potato salad, and Tate took a *bunch* of steaks out of the freezer before he went to meet Garrett at the airstrip, so it just makes sense to throw a big barbecue, don't you think?"

Julie chuckled, carefully looking both ways before pulling onto the main road. "What else can you do," she joked, "*besides* throw a big barbecue?"

"My thoughts exactly," Libby said, with a laugh.

She sounded so happy, Libby did.

What would it be like to be that happy?

"You'll be here, then?" Libby prodded, when Julie didn't speak again right away.

"Sure," she said. Most likely, Garrett would be invited, and that might be a little awkward, but Calvin would be around, too, and Paige, and the rest of the crowd. She would have buffers. "What time, and what should I bring?"

"Six-thirty," Libby answered, "and just bring yourself."

Julie smiled. "Have you spoken to Paige? She didn't answer her cell phone."

"She's here," Libby said, "with Calvin. Her phone is probably in the bottom of her bag, and the kids are playing a video game and making so much noise nobody heard it ring. Why don't you swing by?"

Julie considered the offer. As short as her time apart from Calvin had been, she missed him. Still, with less than two weeks to go before she had to have everything out of the cottage, she needed to do some serious planning and maybe even pack some boxes.

"I have some things to do at my place," she explained. "Even though the exterminator's tent is down, I'm not sure what the air quality is like inside, and with Calvin's asthma—"

"Enough said," Libby interrupted gently. "Calvin is right here, and he's fine. Join us when you can."

"Thanks, Lib," Julie said, genuinely grateful. "I'll be there later on."

"Jules?"

Julie, about to end the call, hesitated. "What?"

"Are you okay? You sound sort of—I don't know—*distracted.*"

No worries, Julie imagined herself explaining. *It's just that I spent most of the night twisting the sheets with Garrett McKettrick, and now I'm wondering what the hell I was thinking.*

"I'm fine," she said instead. But she couldn't resist adding, "This rustling thing. How serious is that, do you know?"

"To a rancher," Libby replied, "rustling is *always* serious. According to Tate, they've lost as many as a hundred cattle, by the latest estimate, and since the critters are currently going for around a thousand dollars a head, that's a lot of money."

"You're not worried?"

"About the cattle?" Libby countered.

"About Tate and Garrett going after the rustlers instead of sending the law," Julie clarified, somewhat impatiently. Libby knew damn well what she meant.

Libby was quiet for a few moments, interpreting Julie's words and her tone and drawing conclusions. "So I guess it's safe to assume the big date went off okay?" she finally asked.

She wasn't about to dish with her sister. Not while she was driving, anyway. And certainly not when there was even the remotest chance that Calvin might overhear. "It was—okay," she said.

"Just 'okay'?"

Julie sighed. "Not now, Lib," she said.

"But later?" Libby persisted. "You'll tell us—Paige and me—all about it later?"

"Not *all* about it," Julie said.

Libby laughed. "My imagination is already filling in the blanks," she said.

"*Goodbye*, Libby," Julie said. The Cadillac was rolling along at a pretty good clip, and the town limits would be coming up pretty soon. She needed both hands and all her attention to drive.

"See you soon," Libby practically sang, and the call ended.

When Julie reached the cottage, she saw that the tent had been taken away. The little house looked forlorn, standing there, with a Sold sign in the front yard and no sign of light or life at any of the windows.

Julie pulled into the gravel driveway—there was no garage—and shut off the car. She sat for a few moments, just staring at the tidy brick building she and Calvin had moved into while he was still a baby.

Calvin had never lived in any other house.

Even Harry, realizing where they were, began scrabbling at the inside of the car door behind Julie, eager to run through the grass again, or dig up one of the many bones he'd stashed in various places around the yard.

Feeling overly emotional, Julie got out of the car, opened the door for Harry and pulled the keys from the ignition.

The lock on the front door proved stubborn—nothing new there—and Julie drew a deep breath of fresh air before turning the knob and pulling.

A strong chemical smell struck her immediately, and she was glad she hadn't brought Calvin with her. He hadn't had a serious asthma attack in a long time, but she never knew what would set one off.

She left the front door standing open to air the place out a little and stepped inside. Harry was busy exploring the yard—the grass needed mowing.

The small living room was dusty, and there were ashes on the hearth from the first fire of the season. She and Calvin had roasted marshmallows over the flames that night after supper, Julie recalled fondly, and made some preliminary plans for Calvin's Halloween costume.

He wanted to dress up as Albert Einstein.

Julie smiled sadly and ran one hand over the afghan draped over the back of her couch. Paige had crocheted the coverlet, choosing yarn in the lush autumn shades Julie loved, during what Paige called her Earth Mother phase.

The desk over by the windows was empty—Julie had taken her PC with her when she and Calvin went to stay on the Silver Spur—and the sight made her feel strangely forlorn.

Sure, it was an inconvenience, having to move, a big one. But it was hardly a tragedy, now was it?

So why was she so emotional?

It was no great leap to identify the reason: Garrett. The way he'd made love to her had touched her on so many levels.

She couldn't help taking the whole thing seriously, she thought, and wasn't now a fine time to think of that?

Garrett, of course, would suffer no pangs of guilt or regret over the night just past, and the things it might have set in motion. He was a man, and used to getting what he wanted, when he wanted it.

He would get bored soon, and go back to his life in the fast lane, and that would be the end of it.

For Julie, the parting wouldn't be so easy.

Sometime between that first kiss and breakfast this morning, she'd fallen in love with Garrett McKettrick.

And she was under no illusion whatsoever that she'd be falling *out* of love with him anytime soon.

CHAPTER TWELVE

TATE AND GARRETT covered most of the Silver Spur in Garrett's plane that morning, and they found more downed fences, the carcasses of half a dozen cattle near a remote watering hole and no sign whatsoever of the rustlers.

At least, nothing visible from the air.

"Son of a bitch," Tate rasped, leaning in his seat as if straining for a closer look at the dead animals. "Put this thing on the ground."

That section of the ranch, nestled against the foothills as it was, happened to be especially rugged, pocked with gullies and gorges, and honeycombed with waist-deep ruts.

Garrett eyed the area dubiously. Shook his head. "Now that would be one stupid thing to do," he said. "We'd better go back to the barn and trailer a couple of horses. I wouldn't be averse to bringing along a rifle or two, either."

"Now how many times have you told me you could land an airplane anywhere?"

"My aim in this instance," Garrett said, "is to land the plane *and* live through it."

Tate scowled at him, impatient with the delay, though he didn't argue the point any further.

They returned to the airstrip, landed and headed for the main place in Tate's dusty Silverado, leaving Austin's rattletrap truck where it was, parked alongside the hangar. A plume of good Texas dirt billowed out behind them as they raced over country roads, both of them silent, occupied with their own thoughts.

Garrett was thinking of Julie, and how he'd promised her he'd keep Tate safe, for Libby's and the twins' sakes, and it took him a while to realize he was grinding his back molars together fit to split his jawbones.

Except for a rotating skeleton crew of three or four men, none of the ranch hands worked on Sundays, but that day, it seemed that everybody on the payroll had gathered around the smallest of several corrals adjoining the barn. Cowboys crowded the fence rails and looked on from the haymow, high overhead.

"If I didn't know better," Garrett remarked, as Tate slammed on the truck's brakes, "I'd swear there was a rodeo going on, right here on the Silver Spur."

Tate frowned and climbed out of the Silverado, leaving the driver's-side door ajar in his haste to find out what was going on. For the moment, the dead cattle out there on the range must have slipped his mind.

As it turned out, there *was* a rodeo going on.

Of the one-man variety.

Garrett didn't figure Tate was really any more surprised than he was. He slipped his sunglasses down a little way and peered over the rims, watching as Austin leaped from the top rail of the inoculation chute on the far side of the corral and straight onto the bare back of a bronc Garrett didn't recognize.

The stallion was magnificent, for all that there were burrs tangled in his mane and tail and old battle scars marking his flanks and breast and front legs. Garrett wondered if the wild horse had been caught on their own rangeland or purchased for breeding purposes.

Tate spat a curse, then started up the slats of the fence as if he meant to go right on over and haul Austin down off the back of that horse in front of God and everybody else.

Garrett caught Tate by the back of his denim jacket and pulled him back. "Let him ride," he said quietly, relieved that most of the men were too busy watching Austin and the bronc to notice Tate's attempt to intervene. "Let him ride."

The bronc stood quiver-flanked inside that chute, with his four legs straddled out as wide as the limited space allowed. His ears crooked forward and its head was down.

Austin sat that horse with the same idiotic confidence he'd shown riding Buzzsaw, the bull that had nearly killed him in front of a packed rodeo arena and a TV audience numbering in the hundreds of thousands.

"Turn him loose," Austin said clearly, after calmly resettling his battered, sweat-stained hat.

One of the men swung the chute gate open, and Garrett held his breath as the animal stood there, evidently deciding on a course of action.

When he'd made up his mind, he sprang out into the corral, pitched forward to kick out both hind legs and splinter the gate behind him with that one powerful thrust.

Delighted, Austin let out a celebratory whoop and nudged the bronc with the heels of both boots.

Watching, Tate shook his head. "I'll be goddamned," he muttered, measuring out the words. "Is he *trying* to kill himself?"

Garrett, standing next to Tate there by the corral fence, slapped him on the shoulder, but he never took his eyes off Austin. One thing you had to say for the crazy little bastard—he could ride damn near anything.

That stallion went up and he went down. He went sideways, and then he spun like a tornado. When that didn't unseat his rider, he switched directions, the motion sharp as the hard crack of a whip.

Austin stayed on him, covered in dirt, waving his hat and grinning as if he had half the sense of a fence post.

The bronc finally bucked himself out and stood with his chest heaving in the middle of the corral.

Casual as could be, Austin swung a leg over that critter's neck and leaped to the ground, landing on his feet with the grace of a cat.

Wearing that infamous shit-eatin' grin of his, he approached the fence, the whites of his eyes in stark contrast to the dusty grime masking his face.

The crew kept its collective distance, probably because Tate was throwing pissed-off-boss-man vibes fit to singe the bristles from a hog. "Easy," Garrett told Tate. "Take it easy. He's all right."

Tate glared at Austin, ignoring Garrett altogether. His knuckles were white where he gripped the fence rail, as if he wanted to vault over it, grab their kid brother by the throat and throttle him right on the spot.

But it was Austin who came over the fence, standing there, cocky as a rooster, with his dust-caked hair stuck to his neck with sweat and that fuck-you look in his eyes.

"Where the hell is my truck?" he demanded.

Garrett suppressed a chuckle, but Tate looked mad enough to bite the ends off carpet tacks and spit them clear to the far side of the creek.

He moved to grip Austin by the front of his shirt, but stopped just short of follow-through. His fingers flexed and unflexed, but he didn't make fists.

"Your truck?" The way those words tore themselves from Tate's throat, it was a wonder they didn't take the hide with them. "You just rode a horse you don't know anything about, and you're worried about your *goddamn truck?*"

Austin's eyes shot blue fire. After that ride, the adrenaline was still surging through his system, and he was spoiling for a fight.

Obviously, Tate was inclined to oblige.

The stallion, meanwhile, trotted back and forth in the corral, nickering and tossing his head, raising up five acres of dust in the process. He wanted a piece of somebody, that bronc, that was for sure.

Garrett, not usually the peacemaker, stepped between his brothers.

"I took your truck," he told Austin. "Screw your damn truck. We've got trouble, plenty to go around. We sure as hell don't need trouble with each other on top of it."

Austin swallowed hard. His gaze darted past Garrett's face to sear into Tate's flesh like a hot branding iron, then swung back, reluctant. Resigned.

"What kind of trouble?" Austin asked slowly, grudgingly.

"Dead cattle trouble," Tate said tersely. "More downed fences, too."

"We spotted the carcasses from the plane a little while ago," Garrett added.

"Shit," Austin said, with conviction, shoving a hand through his hair. "Why are we just standing here, if we've lost livestock?"

Tate thrust out a sigh and tilted his head back for a moment.

Garrett gripped Austin's shoulder with one hand and Tate's with the other, just in case they were to change their minds about the tacit truce and spring at each other all of a sudden. He'd sure as hell seen it happen before.

"I'll get the rifles while you two saddle the horses," Garrett said.

Tate nodded grimly and spoke to the cowboys standing silently at the bulging periphery of his McKettrick temper. As Garrett turned to head into the house, he heard Tate give Austin a brief explanation of the carnage they'd seen on the range.

SOMETHING IN THE weight of the atmosphere inside the kitchen told him Julie wasn't anywhere around, though Esperanza was back from church, sporting an apron and fixing to shove a couple of chickens into the oven for Sunday dinner.

While Garrett was relieved not to be gathering guns and ammo while Julie was there to raise questions, let alone an objection, he felt oddly bereft at her absence, too. It was a cold thing, missing her, and it blew through him like a bitter wind.

Esperanza hadn't spoken, but as he passed through the kitchen on his way to the nearest of several gun-safes around the place, the housekeeper slammed the oven door shut with a force no prudent man would ignore.

Grinning to himself, Garrett walked into the study that had been his father's, his grandfather's, his great-and great-great-grandfather's. There, he uncovered the safe not-so-subtly hidden behind a bookcase on hinges and spun the dial to the first digit of the combination.

He opened the heavy steel door, colorfully emblazoned with the name McKettrick Cattle Company, and reached inside, bringing out one rifle, then another, then a third.

Garrett took out a box of shells, too, and then set the rifles aside long enough to close and lock the safe. When he turned around, he nearly jumped out of his hide, because Esperanza was standing so close behind him he might have trampled her, and he hadn't even heard her come into the room.

He bit back a swear word and took a firmer hold on the rifles.

Esperanza's dark eyes followed his every move. "What are you doing?" she asked, folding her arms.

"It's just a precaution, taking the rifles along," Garrett said, starting around her. "Nothing to worry about."

"Nothing to worry about?" Esperanza argued, staying right on his heels as he strode out of the room. "It was bad enough that Austin had to risk his fool neck out there in the corral, riding that wild horse. Now the three of you are up to something that calls for *guns?*"

Lying to Esperanza would do no good. She'd been with the family since before Tate was born, and she knew the McKettrick brothers too well to be deceived by bullshit denials.

"There are some cattle down," Garrett explained, slowing his words but not his pace. "It could be bad water or some kind of poison weed that got them—we only saw the carcasses from the air—but since some more fence lines have been cut in that area, it's a safe bet that somebody shot them."

For a hefty woman, Esperanza was quick on her feet. She got ahead of him somehow as he started across the kitchen, and blocked his way. "I don't see a badge pinned to your shirt, Garrett McKettrick," she said. "Have any of you lunkheads troubled yourselves to call Brent Brogan and report this?"

"Brogan knows about the rustling," Garrett said, shuffling the three rifles and then going around her, which took some doing because she'd set her feet and dug in her heels. "It's not as if we're playing posse here, Esperanza. Most likely, whoever cut those fences and slaughtered a half dozen of our cattle for what seems like no reason but pure meanness is long gone. Just the same, if Tate and Austin and I have to defend ourselves, or each other, we'd prefer to be ready."

"Wait, Garrett," Esperanza said, very quietly. "Don't take the law into your own hands. Let Chief Brogan handle this. He can bring in the state police, if need be, but you've got no business heading out there with guns."

He hesitated, opened the outside door. "I'm sorry," he said, and he meant it. Esperanza was a lot more than an employee; she was a member of the family, and her intentions were good.

She wanted to protect Jim and Sally McKettrick's boys—that was all.

"Be careful," she said. Her dark eyes were luminous with sorrow. "You just be careful, and make sure your brothers are, too."

He nodded. Stepped out onto the side porch, started down the steps.

One of the trailers had been hitched to Tate's truck, and Austin and another man were loading saddled horses inside.

Tate came out of the barn, saw Garrett with the rifles and walked toward him, his expression grim.

"Esperanza," Garrett said, "is not real happy with any of us right about now."

Tate gave up a spare grin. "I don't suppose she is," he agreed.

They stored the rifles and the ammunition in the backseat of the Silverado, since there were no gun racks.

Tate got behind the wheel when Austin called that the horses had all been loaded, and Garrett grabbed the shotgun seat. That left the back for Austin.

Moments later, they were rolling down the long driveway. Just before they reached the main gates, Tate took a left turn onto a narrow utility road that wound along the front of the property and then forked out onto the range in three directions.

"What the hell were you doing back there?" Tate bit out, after steaming in silence for a while.

Garrett gave his brother a sidelong glance but said nothing. Tate wasn't talking to him, after all, but to Austin.

"Back where?" Austin asked, baiting him. He knew damn well what Tate wanted to know, unless Garrett missed his guess, and that was why he'd ridden a bucking bronc, and a wild one fresh off the range in the bargain. It hadn't been that long since Austin had undergone extensive emergency surgery—his survival had by no means been a sure thing—and even after his release from the hospital, he'd spent several months in physical therapy.

Sure, he was Texas tough, and he was only twenty-eight, so he had youth going for him, but he was a long way from his old self, too.

"If you want to die," Tate rasped furiously, "why don't you just say so, straight out?"

Austin spat a curse. "Why don't *you* stop being such a grandma?" he retorted. "Maybe nobody's ever mentioned it to you, but there are times when you carry this big-brother bullshit too damn far, Tate."

Tate checked the side mirror, taking his half of the road out of the middle, since the trailer was wide and heavy with good horse-flesh. He made a visible effort to calm down. "There isn't a damn thing you need to prove," he said evenly.

Even without looking back at him, Garrett knew Austin was still plenty riled.

"Is that what you think I was doing, Tate?" Austin snapped. "Trying to *prove* something?"

"Weren't you?" Tate challenged. The question probably would have been less inflammatory if he'd yelled it, instead speaking softly, in a tone he might have used to calm a skittish horse or a frightened dog.

Garrett sighed inwardly, but he didn't say anything. Too much had been said already.

Austin swore and shifted around in the backseat like he wanted to bust out of there or something. "I don't need to prove anything to *you*," he answered, after drawing and huffing out a few audible breaths.

Something had gotten under his hide, no doubt about it. But Garrett figured there was more going on here than Austin's need to show the world—and himself—that even though that bull had torn him up good and put him in the hospital for a long time, he was back. He still had it.

Instinct said that wasn't all.

Garrett had tried to find out the whole truth, but Austin wasn't in the mood to confide in anybody. Ten to one, though, their kid brother's mood had more to do with some woman than Buzzsaw, the bull.

"Can we work this out later?" Garrett asked.

"Out behind the barn, maybe?" Austin interjected.

Then he laughed, a ragged sound, like nothing was funny, and Tate gave up a gruff chuckle with about the same degree of good humor. And the tension inside that truck cab tightened like a screw.

"So, Garrett," Austin said, after a few beats, his tone deceptively affable, even hearty, "I hear the senator shit-canned your career right along with his own."

Garrett stiffened, adjusted his sunglasses.

Tate gave a little snort.

"Where'd you hear that?" Garrett asked, with a mildness that probably didn't fool either of his brothers.

"Hell," Austin replied, "it's all over the internet. The word on the web is that you've had a lot of job offers already, and turned them down."

One of the ranch pickups was coming toward them along the private road; the driver pulled to the side to make room for Tate's truck and the horse trailer, tooted the horn and waved as they passed.

Tate tapped the Silverado's horn once, in response.

"Is that true?" he asked, glancing Garrett's way.

"Is what true?" Garrett countered.

"That you've had job offers," Tate said, with an exaggerated effort at patience.

Garrett shrugged. "I've had a few calls," he said. "Nothing I was interested in."

"You're needed here," Tate said carefully, downshifting as they came to a wide cattle guard set into the road. The wheels of the truck and then the trailer it was pulling bumped over the wooden grate as they crossed it.

"You've gotten by just fine without me, up to now," Garrett pointed out. Then he jutted a thumb over one shoulder to indicate Austin. "And Billy the Kid here is even more dispensable than I am."

"Gee," Austin said, "thanks."

Tate's shoulders strained beneath his shirt and denim jacket. "I'm serious," he said. "It's a lot of responsibility, running this place, especially now that Pablo Ruiz is gone. I've got two kids and I'm about to get married. Libby and I want to get a baby started ASAP. And what I'm getting at here is this—you two each own a third of the Silver Spur, just like I do—and you're drawing dividends for it—but you're not carrying your fair share of the load."

Garrett was surprised, though upon reflection he could see Tate's point.

"You hard up for money, Tate?" Austin joked, possibly as clueless as he sounded, but more likely just obnoxious. "If you are, I'll be glad to help you out with a few bucks."

Tate eased the truck to a stop alongside the road, mindful of the trailer and the horses riding inside it. They were probably two miles from the place where they'd seen the dead cattle and the breached fence lines, but that was as close as they could get in a rig. It was time to unload the horses, mount up and ride in.

Shoving his door open, Tate got out of the truck and stood waiting for Austin.

Austin climbed out, too.

They faced each other on that dirt road, Tate and Austin, like a pair of gunslingers about to draw.

The air was crackling again.

Garrett rounded the front of the truck at a sprint, but he was too late.

Tate had grabbed Austin by the front of his shirt and slammed him hard against the door of the pickup.

Austin bounced off it and lunged into Tate's middle with his head down.

Garrett dove between them and caught somebody's fist hard under his right eye.

He staggered, seeing stars. He was going to have a shiner, at the very least.

"Shit!" he yelled, furious, pressing the back of his hand to his cheekbone. It came away bloody.

"Sorry," Austin said.

Tate's hoarse chuckle turned to a guffaw.

Austin laughed, too.

"I'm glad you two think this is funny!" Garrett yelled. So much for keeping the peace. If his eye hadn't been swelling shut already, he'd have gone after both of them at once and settled for trouncing whichever one he got hold of first.

"I think it's freakin' *hilarious*," Austin said, and then hooted again.

Garrett glared at him.

Tate grinned, flashing those movie-cowboy teeth of his, and slapped Garrett on the shoulder just a mite too hard. "Hope there aren't any press conferences on your schedule, Mr. President," he said. "There isn't enough pancake makeup on the planet to cover up the black eye you're going to have about five minutes from now. You definitely aren't ready for prime time."

"It was such a pretty face, too," Austin observed, in a voice an octave higher than his real one.

"Shut up," Garrett growled. The whole right side of his head ached.

Tate merely chuckled and shook his head.

Several ranch trucks pulled in behind them, and Austin started back to help unload the horses.

"When I figure out which one of you hit me," Garrett vowed to his brothers, reaching into the truck for the rifles, "I'm going to kick his ass from here to the Panhandle and back again."

Austin chuckled and walked away.

Tate grinned and followed.

Within a couple of minutes, they were all on horseback, with loaded rifles in the scabbards affixed to their saddles, as were the men who'd come along to help.

While the state of Garrett's face drew a few glances, nobody was stupid enough to make a comment.

They rode uphill, single file, nine men in all, putting Garrett in mind of an old-time posse heading out to round up outlaws.

Normally, he would have smiled at the picture that took shape in his brain, but between the punch he'd taken, Tate's complaint about running the ranch without help and the dead cattle waiting up ahead, Garrett wasn't feeling especially cheerful.

It took half an hour or so to reach the first dead cow; shot through the neck, the animal had bled out on the ground. Flies swarmed, blue-black and buzzing.

There were five more cattle just ahead, killed the same way.

Tate was the first to dismount. He crouched beside one of the carcasses, seemingly heedless of the flies, and touched the critter's blood-crusted side with his right hand. Something about the motion—gentleness, maybe—tightened Garrett's throat.

"What kind of sick son of a bitch shoots an animal and leaves it to rot?" Austin ranted, taking in the scene.

Garrett shook his head, having no other response to offer at the moment, and swung down from the saddle. The ranch hands rode on, looking at the other slaughtered cattle and keeping their thoughts to themselves, as cowboys usually do.

He looked around, but the ground was hard and dry, and if there had been any tracks—a man's, a horse's or those of an off-road vehicle of some kind—the wind had already brushed them away.

Garrett leaned down to pick up a spent shell, showed it to Tate and Austin, then dropped it into his jacket pocket.

Tate rose from the crouch next to the cow. Austin remained on his horse, silhouetted against a dry, blue sky.

Austin adjusted his hat, surveyed the far distance and then looked down at his brothers with eyes the same color as the sky behind him. "Now what?" he asked.

Tate walked back to his horse, stuck a foot into the stirrup and remounted. "We do the next logical thing," he answered wearily.

"Which is?" Garrett asked, returning to the saddle himself. The skin around his eye throbbed, and he wondered what Julie would think when she saw he'd been hurt.

Maybe, he thought, mildly cheered up, he was in line for a little feminine sympathy.

Yes, sir, he could do with some of that.

"It wouldn't be right to leave these animals to be picked apart by buzzards and coyotes," Tate answered grimly. "We'll burn the carcasses and then ride the fence lines, see if we can pick up some kind of trail."

Once again, Austin fiddled with his hat, as he always did when something stuck in his craw and there was no other way to react. "Cattle thieving is one thing," he said, gazing off into the distance, "and killing for the hell of it is another. Whoever did this is carrying a mean grudge."

Garrett nodded in grim agreement. Now and then, especially when times were hard, somebody killed and butchered a McKettrick cow, but it was generally to feed his family.

That was understandable, at least.

This was wanton slaughter.

He felt a lot of things, sitting there in the saddle, with the stench of shed blood filling his nostrils and making his gut churn with the need to do something about it.

It didn't seem possible that, not so many hours ago, he'd been in bed with Julie Remington. She'd driven him outside of himself, Julie had, and as many women as he'd been with in his life, he couldn't recall ever feeling the things she'd made him feel, even once.

They rode on, past the other fallen cattle.

There were signs of horses on the other side of the downed fence line, and more spent cartridges scattered on the ground.

Bile scalded the back of Garrett's throat. Who hated Tate—or all the McKettricks—enough to massacre living creatures for the sport of it?

He scanned the other men, the ones who'd loaded horses of their own back at the main place, followed in trucks, come along to help if they could. As a kid, Garrett had known everybody who worked on the Silver Spur, but now that he'd been away so much, a lot of them were strangers.

In fact, Charlie Bates was the only one he knew. A crabby old bachelor, Bates had lived on the ranch for years, and he'd always been a hard worker.

Tate spoke to Bates, and the other man nodded and sent two riders off on some errand. They returned with gas cans and shovels fetched from the trucks down on the road.

Tate took one of the shovels and turned up a shovelful of dirt all around one of the cattle, making it known what he wanted done.

Once these precautions had been taken, the carcasses were doused in gas and burned.

The smoke burned the eyes, and the smell of singed hide and charred beef-flesh damn near turned Garrett into a vegetarian on the spot. For a while, he thought, he'd stick to chicken and fish—assuming he could bring himself to eat at all.

He ached, watching those flames.

He helped to quell them with shovelfuls of dirt, when the time came to do that.

Two men stayed behind to make sure there were no flare-ups; the rest rode back down to the dirt track below.

On the way out, they'd argued, Garrett and Tate and Austin.

On the way back, nobody said one word.

Not one.

At home, Austin and Bates and a few of the other men unloaded the horses from the trailer and led them to the barn. Tate backed the trailer into the equipment shed, and then unhitched it, while Garrett returned to the house with the rifles.

This time, Esperanza wasn't alone in the kitchen.

Calvin was there, perched on a barstool at the long counter, with a plate of cookies and a glass of milk in front of him. At the sight of the guns, the kid looked wide-eyed.

Garrett gave the boy a friendly nod and kept walking.

In the study, he locked the rifles up again, along with the box of ammunition he'd shoved into his jacket pocket earlier.

When he got back to the kitchen, Esperanza was basting the roasting chickens, and the scent of them made Garrett's stomach rumble with hunger.

Pausing by the stove, he lifted the lid off a pot and looked inside, pleased to see potatoes, peeled and salted and ready to boil up and mash.

"Yes," he muttered.

Esperanza looked at him over one shoulder as she closed the higher of two wall ovens. She was clearly still in a peckish mood; Garrett half expected her to tell him he needn't let his mouth get to watering over her crispy-skinned chicken, thick gravy and mashed potatoes, because he wasn't sitting down to any meal *she'd* fixed.

"Is your mom around?" Garrett asked Calvin, who was watching him with an expression akin to fascination.

Garrett had forgotten the shiner either Tate or Austin had given him out there on the road. From the look on Calvin's face, it was a dandy.

And it explained some of Esperanza's annoyance, too.

Calvin shook his head. "She's at the cottage, packing up our stuff. What happened to your eye?"

"I ran into something," Garrett hedged, his gaze snagging on Esperanza's and then breaking away. He opened one of the refrigerators and pulled out a bottle of beer.

"Want a cookie?" Calvin asked, pushing the plate toward him.

"Ought to go great with beer," Garrett grinned, taking the stool next to Calvin's and accepting the offer by helping himself to a couple of oatmeal-raisin cookies. He munched a while before speaking again. "How come your mom is packing up all your stuff?" he asked.

Calvin leaned in a little, squinting up at Garrett's shiner with the sort of interest little boys usually reserved for dead bugs and dried-up snakeskins. "We have to move," he answered. "You didn't really run into something, did you? You got in a *fight*."

Esperanza glared at Garrett over the top of Calvin's blond head. Her expression said he was setting a poor example for the boy.

"It wasn't a fight," Garrett told Calvin. "Not exactly, anyhow. Where are you moving to?"

Calvin's small shoulders stooped a little then, and he ducked his head. "Don't know," he mumbled. "Aunt Paige didn't tell me that."

Garrett frowned, confused.

"She thought Mom was here," Calvin explained. "Aunt Paige did, I mean. That's why she brought me to the Silver Spur. When Mom called her on her cell phone and told her she was at the cottage instead, Aunt Paige asked Esperanza to watch me for a while, so she could go help Mom."

"I see," Garrett said, though he was still pretty much in the dark.

Calvin sighed. "I wish we could live here," he said in a small voice, after a long time had passed. "I wish Mom and Harry and me could stay on the Silver Spur forever."

The earnest way the kid spoke wrenched at something deep inside Garrett.

Maybe because he was starting to wish the same thing.

CHAPTER THIRTEEN

EXCEPT FOR THE marshal's office, which was a minor tourist attraction, the fire station was the oldest public building in Blue River. The engine itself dated back to 1957, but it still ran, and so did the old-fashioned, hand-cranked siren.

Harry howled when the alarm sounded the first long, tinny wail, and Paige and Julie, busy in Julie's kitchen, both stopped wrapping dishes in newspaper to press their hands to their ears.

The siren droned to silence, then wound up again.

Harry did his beagle-best to drown it out, singing along.

Paige rushed for the back door, that being the nearest exit, and Julie followed, after leaning down to give Harry a brief and reassuring pat on the head and instructing him, in vain, to hush up.

By tradition, the intended warning could be anything from a lost child to a full-scale invasion by space aliens.

The smell of smoke was sharp in the air, but Julie couldn't tell where it was coming from until she and Paige ran around to the front yard.

A black, roiling cloud of the stuff loomed against the afternoon sky.

Fire, Julie thought, strangely slow-witted. Then, of *course* it was fire.

She gave in to a moment of pure panic before pulling herself together to focus on her first and highest priority—Calvin.

Her son, she reminded herself, as if by rote, was on the ranch. Paige had taken him there before returning to town to help Julie get ready for her imminent move. The smoke, to her relief, was rising in the opposite direction from the Silver Spur.

The siren revved up once more, and Harry bayed in concert.

Around town, other dogs had joined in, a yip here, a yelp there. The bell on the fire engine clamored in the near distance, a resonant clang in the heat-weighted, acrid air.

The volunteers, rallied by the emergency siren, were on the job then, already racing down Main Street. The old truck rarely saw action, except each year on the Friday after Thanksgiving, when it carried the Lions Club Santa to the tree-lighting ceremony in the park.

Paige, shading her eyes with one hand, assessed the growing plume.

"What do you suppose is burning?" Julie asked. She was good at a lot of things, but reading smoke signals wasn't among them.

Mercifully, the siren had finally gone silent, having alerted everybody in the county that there was Some Kind of Trouble, and so had Harry and the canine chorus.

"Probably, it's Chudley and Minnie Wilkes's place, or somewhere pretty near it," Paige answered, looking worried.

Cars and pickup trucks raced by, two streets over on the main drag.

Paige dashed into the cottage, summoned Harry to follow, shut him inside and came out jingling her car keys at Julie. "The dog will be fine," she said. "Let's go!"

Julie nodded, feeling slightly sick as she scrambled into Paige's car on the passenger side and snapped on her seat belt. Chudley and Minnie lived in a pair of single-wide trailers, welded together, just a few miles outside of town.

The Wilkeses' home was surrounded by several acres of rusted-out wrecks, most of them up on blocks, but it was the mountain of old tires that worried Julie now. If all that rubber caught fire, it might literally burn for *weeks*, and the greasy smoke would be a respiratory hazard for just about everybody.

Especially Calvin, with his asthma.

Practically everybody in the county was headed for that fire, or so it seemed—more than a few were gawkers, like Paige and Julie, with no real business showing up at all—but many wanted to help put out the flames and contain the blaze before it spread. Or simply be on hand to do whatever might need doing.

Wildfire was always a danger in dry country—it could race overland for miles, in all directions, if it got out of hand, gobbling up people, livestock and property, anything in its path.

Up ahead, Brent Brogan and his two deputies were running what amounted to a roadblock, letting only certain vehicles through.

Julie peered through the windshield of Paige's car, watching as the chief of police lifted a megaphone to his mouth.

"Folks," his voice boomed out, full of good-natured authority, "we just can't have all these rigs clogging up the road now. There's an ambulance on its way over from the clinic right this minute, and you don't want to hold it up, do you?"

Paige, a registered nurse with a lot of experience in emergency medicine, nosed her car right up to the front, tooting her horn.

Chief Brogan looked furious, until he recognized Paige. Immediately after that, he gestured for her to proceed.

Paige rolled down her window as they pulled up beside the frazzled lawman.

"It's that trailer Chudley rents whenever he can find a sucker," Brent said, bending to look inside the car. His fine-featured brown face glistened with sweat. "Everybody's out, but the girl and the little boys are pretty shaken up. For my money, all three of those kids are in shock."

Paige nodded and drove on, while Julie sat rigid on the seat, Brent's words echoing in her mind.

The girl—the little boys—all three of those kids are in shock.

It finally penetrated. Rachel Strivens and her brothers—they were the kids Brent had been talking about. They lived, with their father, in a house trailer rented from Chudley Wilkes.

"Oh, my God," Julie said. "Rachel—she's in one of my English classes—"

The fire engine was parked broadside, its bulky hose bulging with water, helmeted volunteers all around.

Paige got out of the car and ran forward, and Julie was right behind her.

The flames were out, though smoke churned through the roof of the trailer, having burned part of it away. The structure had been reduced to a blackened ruin, with strips of charred metal curling from it like oddly placed antennae. Hometown firemen, ranchers and farmers and store owners and insurance agents, among others, were everywhere, wielding axes and shovels, and there seemed to be no air left for breathing.

Julie's eyes burned as though acid had splashed into them, and so did her lungs and her throat, and she was so frightened for Rachel and her brothers that her heart began to pound in painful thuds.

She and Paige spotted the three children at the same moment, sitting huddled together on the ground under a tree on the far side of the property. Norvel Collier, a retired pharmacist who looked like he might need medical attention at any moment himself, kept thrusting an oxygen mask at them, and getting no takers.

"Norvel," Paige greeted the old man, with a businesslike nod.

Norvel nodded back. "Hello, Paige," he said, blinking at her, his eyes reddened from the smoke.

"You'd best let me take over there," Paige told him. "You go rustle up some more oxygen for me, why don't you? And a few blankets, maybe?"

Norvel didn't protest. He nodded, and Julie helped him to his feet. She received a grateful, faltering smile for her effort.

"Much obliged," he said.

"What can I do to help?" Julie asked Paige.

Paige had already persuaded the smaller of the two boys to let her place the oxygen mask over his nose and mouth. "Stay out of the way," Paige answered, her tone brisk but not unkind.

Rachel sat slumped, with one arm around each of her brothers, her clothes sooty and her hair singed. She locked gazes with Julie, but said nothing.

Despite Paige's instructions, Julie knelt to pull Rachel into a brief hug.

"Everything will be all right," she told the child. "I promise."

And then she got to her feet again, and stepped back out of the way.

The ambulance was making its way through the traffic on the

gravel road, its siren giving short, uncertain bleats, like a confused sheep separated from the flock and calling out to be found.

"My kids!" a man's voice yelled, full of anguish. *"Where are
my kids?"*

An instant later, Ron Strivens came into view, having torn his
way through the crowd of firemen and able-bodied locals. He
looked around wildly, spotted Rachel and the boys, and hurried
toward his children.

Dropping to his knees, but not touching any of them, Strivens
focused on the oxygen mask covering his youngest son's face.
The glance he threw at Paige, who was overseeing the process
and lightly stroking the boy's hair in an effort to keep him calm,
was nothing short of frantic.

The man's skin was gray with fear, his lips pressed into a tight
blue line.

"They'll be fine," Paige assured him, with the firm, in-control
confidence Julie and Libby had always admired in their younger
sister. Even before she'd gone through nursing school, graduating
at the top of her class, Paige had been the type to keep her head in
any kind of emergency.

Nothing and no one had ever caused her to lose her composure.

No one except Austin McKettrick, that is.

"How did it start?" Strivens croaked, sparing a glance for what
remained of the mobile home but mainly concerned, naturally,
with the well-being of his family.

Rachel started to answer, but before she got a word out, her little brother pulled the oxygen mask from his face long enough to
say, "It wasn't Rachel's fault, Dad—"

Gently, Paige shook her head and replaced the mask.

The older of the two boys took up where the younger one had
left off. "Rachel brought half a pizza home from the bowling alley
when she got off work," he explained eagerly, his face as filthy as
his sister's, his voice high and rapid. "She said we could have some,
soon as she heated it up in the oven. But she wanted to change her
clothes first, and that always means she's going to take forever.
Me and Colley didn't want to wait, because we was *real* hungry,
but the pilot light was out in the oven, so I lit it and—"

Once again, Colley pulled off the mask. He shouted, "Boom!" before Paige got it back in place.

Tears welled up in Rachel's eyes, already red and irritated from the smoke. "The place went up so fast," she told her father. "All I could think of was getting Max and Colley out of there—"

"You did good," Ron Strivens told her, reaching out to squeeze her shoulder.

By then, the paramedics had arrived.

Paige spoke to them briefly and went to stand with her upper arm pressing against Julie's. All their lives, the Remington sisters had communicated silent strength to each other in just that way.

The EMTs crouched to examine Rachel and the boys, and it was decided that while all three children were probably going to be fine, it couldn't hurt to take them on over to the clinic and let one of the doctors have a look to make sure.

"Where are we going to live, now that the trailer's gone?" Colley asked his father, who had hoisted the younger boy into his arms to carry him to the ambulance.

A paramedic trotted behind, holding the oxygen tank.

Julie didn't hear Ron Strivens's reply, but her gaze connected with Paige's.

It was a good question. Where *was* the family going to live?

Julie knew well, of course, how hard it was to find housing in and around Blue River. Except for the town's one apartment complex, which was always full to capacity, there simply weren't any rentals.

Paige merely spread her hands.

Chudley Wilkes appeared in the junker-choked field, driving an ancient tractor with a high metal seat, Minnie riding on one running board, her heavy cloud of gray hair billowing in the sooty breeze. They made for a colorful sight, Chudley and Minnie on that tractor.

About to head for Paige's car, Julie stopped to watch their approach, as did her sister.

Chudley's grizzled old face was hidden in shadow, since he was wearing a billed cap, but his neck seemed to bulge above the collar of his grungy shirt, the veins engorged, the flesh a frightening mottle of purple and red.

"Lord," Paige breathed, "that old fool is going to have a stroke right here if he doesn't calm down." She went back to the car and returned quickly with a blood-pressure cuff and a stethoscope.

Chief Brogan, who was a hands-on sort of cop, walked over to meet Chudley, and because Paige followed him, so did Julie.

"Chudley Wilkes," Paige said, as soon as he'd shut off the tractor motor and it had clunked and clattered and popped to silence, "have you been taking your blood-pressure medicine?"

"Never mind my blood pressure!" Chudley yelled in response. "I'm ruined! I'm bankrupted! Why, there ain't nothin' left of my trailer but the axles!"

Shaking her head, Minnie got down off the running board to examine the wreckage. "You ain't ruined, you damn fool," she said. Then, addressing Chief Brogan and the rest of them, she added, "Pay him no mind. He's just tightfisted, that's all. Why, he could bail out a middlin'-sized *country* with the money he's got stashed."

"Now, you hush up, Chudley Wilkes," Paige ordered, taking Minnie's place on the running board and wrapping the blood-pressure cuff around Chudley's tattooed upper arm with dispatch. She listened through the stethoscope and watched the digital meter while the inflated band slowly deflated.

"Just what I thought," Paige clucked, turning to Brent. "You'd better get Chudley to the doctor right away, Chief. He's in real danger of blowing a gasket."

Chudley grayed under his crimson flush and the grime that was probably as much a part of his skin as the pigment by this late date. He moved to fire up the tractor again.

"Minnie," he called to his wife, "get back on here, right now! We got to get me to the clinic!"

Minnie started toward the tractor, but Brent stopped her. "I'll drive you in the squad car," he said.

Chudley looked the chief over suspiciously, and Julie could just imagine what he was thinking. Never mind that Brent had been part of the community since he was a little boy—his dad had worked for Jim McKettrick out on the Silver Spur—never mind that he'd served bravely in the military and done a creditable job as the chief of police.

Perceptive, Brent sighed. "Come on, Chudley," he said.

Chudley looked down at Minnie, who waited in silence. "You got your purse with you?" he demanded.

"You see any *purse* in my hand, Chudley Wilkes? My purse is up there to the house, where I left it when you dragged me away from my Sunday afternoon TV movie to watch this here old trailer go up in smoke!"

"Well, we've got to get it, then," Chudley insisted, though he did allow Brent and one of the volunteer firemen to help him down off the high seat of that tractor. "I'll be needin' my Medicare card, and it's in your wallet, Minnie, and your wallet is *in your purse!*"

"You been into it for beer money, that's how you know what's in my *wallet*, you mangy old hoot owl!" Minnie retorted, bristling.

Julie began to fear for Minnie's blood pressure, as well as Chudley's.

"Let's just head on over to the clinic," Brent interjected reasonably. "Folks know you in Blue River, Chudley. You can give them your Medicare number later."

"That trailer had a good ten years left in it," Chudley complained, though he allowed Brent to steer him toward the squad car. The fire was out by then, and the volunteers were stowing the hoses and putting away shovels and picks.

The structure was a total loss, that was plain to see.

"Nobody got hurt," Brent told him. "That's what's important here."

Chudley shook his head as he stooped to plunk himself down in the passenger seat of the police car. Brent stood by patiently, holding open the door.

"That's easy for you to say," Chudley growled in response. "You didn't lose a perfectly good trailer."

Once again, Brent sighed, loudly this time, and with a visible motion of his broad shoulders. "Now, Chudley, you know damn well," Julie heard him tell the old man, "that trailer ought to have been condemned years ago."

Minnie had tarried there by the tractor, frowning as though she might be debating whether she wanted to accompany her husband to the clinic or not. When she made a move in that direction, though, Brent quickly opened the back door.

She had long since resigned herself to life with Chudley Wilkes—everyone in Blue River knew that.

Julie, watching the scene, started when she felt Paige's elbow nudge her lightly in the side. "Ready to call it a day?" she asked.

"Oh, yeah," Julie said.

Paige drove her back to the cottage, so Julie could fetch Harry and lock up. She wanted to see Calvin, hold him in her arms, ruffle his hair and kiss the top of his head.

Of course, she'd have to disguise her affection as a tickle attack—as young as he was, Calvin was already reticent about getting hugs and kisses.

"Thanks for letting Calvin visit over the weekend," Julie told her sister, when Paige pulled up in front of the converted Victorian mansion where she rented an apartment. Conveniently, Paige's place was right across the street from Julie's cottage. "He always has such a good time with you."

Paige nodded, but there was something vague about her smile, and her eyes were watchful. "We didn't talk about it while we were packing dishes," she said, "but that doesn't mean I don't want to hear all about last night's big date."

Julie blushed. Looked away. Made herself look back. "It was—a date," she replied.

"It was more than a date," Paige insisted good-naturedly. "But we can talk about it tomorrow, after the school day is over, while we're packing up your kitchen."

Julie shook her head. "The tryouts start at three-fifteen—for the musical, I mean. I'll be busy at school until at least seven o'clock."

"What about Calvin?" Paige asked, pulling her purse and the blood pressure gizmo from the backseat of her car.

"He'll be with Libby and Tate," Julie said, feeling unaccountably guilty.

Paige nodded. The impish light in her dark eyes had faded, though, and her expression was pensive. "This unexpected move—I know it's stressful—" She stopped and made another start. "What I mean is, there's a lot going on, what with Gordon turning up out of nowhere and your having to stage a musical at school now instead of in the spring, when you'd planned, and then Libby's wedding—"

Julie chuckled, rounded the back of the car and gave her sister a hug. "I'm really, truly all right, so don't be a fussbudget."

Paige smiled, and her eyes glistened with moisture. "'Fussbudget,'" she repeated. "I haven't heard that word in years. Not since before Grammy died."

After their mother had abandoned the family, their paternal grandmother had done her best to fill in the emotional gaps, but Grammy's health had already been failing, and she simply hadn't had the energy to deal with young children for any length of time.

Julie felt a pang of loss, remembering Grammy, a sweet, well-meaning woman, fragile as a bird. She'd kept her little house down the street from theirs impeccably tidy, Elisabeth Remington had, and baked cookies for them whenever she was feeling well enough.

"Maybe *I'm* the one who should be asking if something is wrong," Julie said, resting her hands on Paige's shoulders. "What's up, Paige?"

Paige looked away, looked back. Bit her lower lip.

"Tell me," Julie said firmly.

"I thought it was such a good idea to change jobs," Paige confessed. "I'm so tired of commuting. The renovations on the house are coming along well—we could all move in there, Julie, you and Calvin and me—even though we'd have to rough it for a while—"

Julie, taller than her sister, bent her knees to look more directly into Paige's face. "Wait," she said. "Hold it. Let's get back to how you *thought* it was a good idea to work at the clinic here in town instead of driving fifty miles each way, but now—what? You don't think that anymore?"

"But now Austin McKettrick is back," Paige said. She tried for another smile, but it was spoiled by the bleak expression in her eyes.

"Oh," Julie said.

"Yeah," Paige agreed ruefully. *"Oh."*

"I didn't realize you knew Austin was home."

Across the street, inside the cottage, Harry began to bark his come-and-get-me bark.

"Word gets around," Paige said.

Julie nodded. "But it's more than that, right?"

Paige sighed. "I seem to have radar, as far as Austin's concerned. If he gets within fifty miles of me, I can feel it."

"You still care about him, then?" Julie asked, miserable on her sister's behalf.

Austin was charming and he was handsome and he was sexy as hell. He was also a wild man, a renegade. He was all wrong for practical Paige, the nurse, the devoted aunt and sister, the career woman who secretly yearned for a home and a family.

Oh, yes, Austin was all wrong for Paige.

As wrong as *Garrett* was for *her.*

Julie closed her eyes for a moment. Drew a deep breath.

"No," Paige said, "I *don't* still care for Austin. It's just that—well—I don't particularly want to run into him in the supermarket and at the dry cleaner's—"

A corner of Julie's mouth kicked up in a grin. "I doubt if Austin does much of the grocery shopping or hangs around the cleaner's a lot, Paige."

Pain moved in Paige's exquisitely beautiful face. "With Libby marrying Tate, and now you getting involved with Garrett—Austin and I are bound to be thrown together more often than either of us wants. Julie, *what* am I going to do?"

Julie's face heated, and a protest rose in her throat, but she was more concerned about her sister's feelings than setting Paige straight by pointing out that she most definitely *was not* "involved" with Garrett.

She was just—well—*having sex* with him.

"It's true that things could get awkward," she said moderately, "now that Libby and Tate are getting married, but Austin doesn't spend all that much time on the Silver Spur, let alone in Blue River, does he?"

Paige took a half step back. Tugged the strap of her purse up over one shoulder and tucked the blood pressure gear under one elbow. She was already in retreat, Julie knew, though she was trying to be subtle about it. "You're right," she said, too quickly. "I don't know why I'm so worried about bumping into Austin. The man wants to avoid me as much as *I* want to avoid *him.*"

Julie wasn't so sure about that. She also wasn't fool enough to say so. Harry was barking, and she needed to go home to Calvin, prepare herself to get through the week to come.

"Call me," she told Paige, in parting.

Half an hour later, she and Harry arrived in the driveway of the main ranch house on the Silver Spur.

Calvin waved at her from his high perch on Garrett's shoulders as they came through the open doorway of the barn.

Harry, beside himself with joy, demanded to be released from the car, and by the time Julie had gotten out herself, opened the rear door and lifted the beagle to the ground, Calvin and Garrett were standing next to her.

"We've been feeding the horses!" Calvin crowed.

Julie's first impulse, whenever Calvin was around any animal other than Harry or Tate and Libby's three dogs, was to worry that the dander might trigger an asthma or allergy attack in her son. Seeing the delight on Calvin's somewhat grubby face, she caught the knee-jerk protest before it could leave her mouth.

Feeling oddly shy, in light of the deliciously scandalous things she and Garrett had done together the night before, Julie managed to avoid the man's gaze, for the moment, at least.

"You were?" she smiled. "You were feeding horses? Calvin Remington, I am *impressed.*"

The happiness in the child's small, earnest face was sweet to see, but it also sent tiny cracks splintering through Julie's heart. Calvin *was* thrilled that he'd helped with grown-up chores, but simply being in Garrett's presence mattered more.

It was natural, she supposed, for a little boy, especially one raised without a father, to look up to a man like Garrett McKettrick.

But what if Calvin was growing attached to him?

Garrett reached up, removed his hat and set it on Calvin's head with unerring accuracy. Julie felt Garrett's gaze on her face and made herself meet it.

She saw a pensive expression in his eyes, along with gentle humor and a kind of—well—patience, a willingness to wait, that moved her in a way she wouldn't have anticipated. His face was badly bruised, as if he'd been in a fight, and Julie instinctively skirted the topic. She would ask about it later.

Harry, a dog wanting his boy, bounded around them, yipping cheerfully.

Garrett grinned and set Calvin on the ground. Still wearing Garrett's hat, Calvin giggled as Harry leaped up to lick his face and sent the both of them tumbling in the grass.

Julie's sinuses burned, and she had to blink a couple of times.

Garrett rested a hand lightly against the small of her back, urging her toward the house.

"I have to put the car away," she said.

"I'll do that later," Garrett responded.

A noise coming from the direction of the service road down by the gates made all of them turn to look.

A flatbed truck came into view, pulling half of a double-wide mobile home.

Julie watched it for a few moments, putting two and two together in her stress-and-sex-addled brain, and turned her eyes back to Garrett. The motion was quick and sure, like the needle of a compass swinging toward true north.

"Brent called," Garrett explained, sounding almost shy. "He said there was a fire in town, and it left a family with no place to live."

Before Julie could respond, Calvin tugged at the sleeve of her coat, thus commanding her attention. "Esperanza roasted two whole chickens for supper," he said. "And that's a lot of food, so Libby and Tate and Audrey and Ava are coming over to eat with us."

The way her child said the word *us* made Julie's throat go tight again.

Inside, the big kitchen was warm and glowing with welcoming light, and the atmosphere was savory with the aroma of Esperanza's roast chickens. A poignant sense of gratitude struck Julie in that moment, but it was bittersweet.

Was she getting too comfortable in this temporary place? With this very temporary man?

Suddenly aware that her clothes and hair must smell like smoke, Julie excused herself to take a quick shower and change her clothes.

When she returned from the guest apartment, perhaps twenty minutes later, Libby and Tate had arrived with the twins, and Austin, looking spiffy in clean jeans and a pale blue T-shirt, was setting the table for a crowd.

Julie took a moment to savor the scene, a happy family—or a *mostly* happy one, anyway—gathered to share a meal on a chilly fall evening. If Paige had been there, she thought, it would have been perfect.

A smile twitched at the corner of her mouth, lightening her mood. Well, maybe not perfect, she thought.

Could any space contain *both* Austin McKettrick *and* Paige Remington without bursting into flames?

Garrett bumped her lightly from behind, stopping just short of wrapping his arms around her waist—or that was the feeling she had, anyway. Maybe it was her imagination.

Or some serious wishful thinking.

"What?" he asked, after shifting to stand beside her.

Calvin was still wearing Garrett's hat, making sure Audrey and Ava noticed it.

Don't, Julie pleaded silently, watching her son. *Don't care too much.*

"Nothing," she lied. She couldn't have explained what she was feeling to GarrettMcKettrickit was all so complicated, she didn't understand it herself.

Libby and Tate were helping the twins out of their coats, taking off their own.

Libby turned her head, caught Julie's eye.

Julie watched as her sister's glance moved to Garrett, no doubt noticing how close the two of them were.

A smile twitched at Libby's mouth, and she widened her eyes at Julie, as if to say, *Well, now...what have we here?*

Self-consciously, Julie moved away from Garrett just a bit.

He chuckled at that, and shook his head.

Esperanza oversaw all this, but when it was time to sit down and eat, she pleaded a full schedule of must-see TV, took a plate and left the kitchen for her own sitting room.

Julie couldn't help noticing that Calvin, who usually sat beside her, had squeezed in between Garrett and Austin at the other side of the table. Thankfully, Austin had casually relieved him of the oversize hat, setting it aside on a nearby breakfront.

The fire at the Strivenses' place was the first topic of conversation.

"It's just lucky one of the staff trailers was empty," Libby said. Tate was next to her, and she paused to give him a look that said he'd not only hung the sun and the moon, but the stars, too.

Watching Libby, Tate looked wonderstruck, as though he couldn't believe his good fortune in being loved by such a woman.

Julie, seeing all this, made herself look away, not because she was envious, exactly, but because suddenly she yearned—oh, yes, *yearned*—to find what Libby and Tate had together. And in looking away, she immediately snagged gazes with Garrett.

It was a struggle, breaking free.

The air almost crackled between them.

And for just a little while, Julie allowed herself to pretend it would last.

CHAPTER FOURTEEN

"ARE WE GOING to pretend last night didn't happen?" Garrett asked.

Julie, startled half to death, stopped on the threshold of her small sitting room, one hand pressed to her heart. She'd just tucked Calvin into bed and listened to his prayers.

"You scared me," Julie said, although that was probably obvious.

Garrett sat, relaxed, on the sofa, with Harry snuggled right beside him. The dog's muzzle rested on Garrett's thigh and, barely acknowledging Julie's arrival, the animal casually rolled his luminous brown eyes in her direction but otherwise didn't move a muscle.

Not exactly protective.

"Sorry," Garrett said, but the grin quirking at the corner of his mouth belied the sincerity of his apology.

Julie didn't retreat, but she didn't move forward, either. She just stood there, and this was not at all like the self she knew, and that was irritating to the nth degree. Of all the men who might have breached her defenses, why did it have to be this one?

"Julie?" Garrett prompted, stroking Harry's ears, evidently willing to wait as long as necessary for an answer to his question.

"It might be better if we *did* pretend that last night didn't happen," she said.

Garrett studied her in silence for a long moment. Then he shook his head. "I don't believe that," he decided aloud, "and I don't think you do, either."

Julie bit down on her lower lip, wedged her hands, backward, into the hip pockets of her jeans, and rocked back, ever so slightly, on the heels of her sneakers.

"Come here," Garrett said, patting the Harry-free side of him on the sofa.

She hesitated. Pulled a hand free of its pocket to cock a thumb over one shoulder, indicating that Calvin was just down the hallway. The little dickens hadn't had time to fall asleep, and if he'd heard Garrett's voice, caught even the timbre of it, he was surely listening in.

"Calvin," Julie mouthed.

Garrett chuckled and shook his head again. "I wasn't planning on saying—or doing—anything ungentlemanly," he said.

"You *did* mention last night," she pointed out.

"So did you," Garrett reasoned, sitting there looking all cowboy-hunky, with his boots and his jeans and his Western shirt open at the throat. "Just now."

Julie narrowed her eyes, rested her hands on her hips. Harry had rolled onto his back for a tummy rub. Traitorous dog. Next, he'd be living upstairs with Garrett and riding around with him in trucks.

"Just remember," she said, "that Harry is *my* dog."

"Don't kid yourself," Garrett replied, still amused. His eyes seemed to drink her in in big guzzling gulps. "He's *Calvin's* dog, through and through." He glanced fondly down at Harry, who lay surrendered, all three legs in the air. "He's also something of a hedonist, it would seem."

Julie did not join Garrett on the sofa—that would have been giving too much ground, tantamount to sprawling on her back, like Harry, in hopes of a tummy rub.

Or something.

She did perch on the arm of a nearby chair, though. She folded her arms and tried to look as though the man hadn't turned her entire universe on its ear with one night of lovemaking.

"So the decision is…?" Garrett said, after watching her a little longer.

"There's supposed to be a decision?" she countered, stalling.

Garrett sighed. After easing Harry aside, he got up off the couch, walked to the archway leading into the small corridor, no doubt to make sure Calvin wasn't crouched just outside the glow of the hallway nightlight, eavesdropping.

Returning—the coast must have been clear—Garrett stood in front of Julie.

He gripped her shoulders, very gently, and raised her to her feet.

And then, slowly, and with a thoroughness that proved he meant business, Garrett McKettrick kissed her.

Julie practically swooned. There were now two categories of kissing in her personal lexicon—being kissed by Garrett Mc-Kettrick and being kissed by any *other* man in the world.

The first had totally ruined the second, for all time.

Julie had tears in her eyes when it ended. "You'll just go away," she blurted out in an anguished whisper, and instantly regretted the outburst.

Garrett curved his fingers under her chin. "I always come back," he said, his voice husky, his gaze tender on her face. "And you might like some of the places I go. Did you ever consider that?"

What was he saying? What did *And you might like some of the places I go* actually mean?

"I have a son," she said, taking a tremendous risk with her pride. He'd know she'd interpreted his remark as an invitation of sorts, or at least a suggestion that she might be traveling with him in the future—and that was way more than she was ready to acknowledge. "I have a job and two sisters." Julie's gaze dropped to Harry, still on the couch, though now curled contentedly into a furball. "I'm pretty sure I still have a dog. In other words, I'm not a jet-setter like you, or the people you know, Garrett. I'm a hometown kind of gal."

He frowned, apparently puzzled. A fraction of a second later, though, she saw his wondrous, dark-denim eyes widen with some realization he might or might not be willing to share. "I see," he said.

"I'm not sure you do," Julie replied, without meaning to say anything at all.

Her dad would have said her tongue was hinged at both ends, the way she kept blathering on. Why couldn't she just shut up?

The recollection of her gentle, often sad father brought the faintest hint of a smile to Julie's mouth.

Garrett merely raised one eyebrow, waiting for her to go on.

"You and I come from different worlds, Garrett," she told him finally.

He actually had the nerve to roll his eyes. "That is so corny," he said. "'You and I come from different worlds'? Have you been watching soap operas or something?"

Garrett was mocking her, Julie decided, and she should have been angry—or at least indignant. Instead, this ridiculous and completely unfounded happiness burgeoned inside her, and she almost laughed.

Now, the new-jeans eyes were twinkling. It was disconcerting how quickly he read her, Julie thought—and how well.

"You know what I mean," she insisted, determined to salvage something of the perfectly reasonable argument she was trying to make. "There are some pretty obvious contrasts between us, after all."

"Umm-hmm," Garrett agreed. He was about to kiss her again; she could feel his breath, a pleasant tickle on her mouth. "Viva la contrasts, baby."

Julie pressed her palms to his chest then, meaning to push him away, or at least hold him at a little distance. Instead, though, her hands slid, as if of their own accord, to join at the back of his neck.

The second kiss left her swaying.

Garrett's hands rested, strong and sure, on either side of her waist. Then he gave a long, comically beleaguered sigh. "Good night, Julie," he said, the words blowing past her ear like the softest of summer breezes.

He walked away then, and as soon as he turned his back, Julie rested one hand on the back of the armchair, just to steady herself, afraid she was going to hyperventilate.

Harry, still on the couch, lifted his head, thumped at the cushions a few times with his tail, and jumped, with remarkable grace, to the floor.

The dog hesitated, watching her with something like sympathy, then toddled off down the hall, headed for Calvin's room.

Julie followed, quietly opening the door, careful not to let the light from the hallway fall on her little boy's face.

Harry trotted in and bounded up onto the mattress on his own, settling into a sighing heap at Calvin's feet.

Julie blew a kiss to her sleeping son, slipped out of the room and softly closed the door.

"YOU'RE LIVING WITH this guy?" Gordon asked the next morning, his voice grating at Julie through her headset. She'd just dropped Calvin off at Libby and Tate's, and she had a full day of teaching ahead, to be followed by the first round of tryouts for the musical.

You're living with this guy?

The question was so off the wall that Julie was thrown by it.

That particular reaction was short-lived. "What did you just ask me?" she retorted.

Gordon sighed. "Look, as lousy as my track record is, I *am* Calvin's father," he said. "I'm concerned about his...environment, that's all."

Julie actually trembled, and for a moment she thought the cheap plastic housing of her cell phone might actually crack, she was squeezing it so tightly. She pulled over to the side of that country road, for her own sake and that of other drivers, put the car in Park, flipped on the blinkers.

With a conscious effort, she loosened her grip on the phone and lightened up on the pressure against her skull.

"His *'environment'*?"

"You know what I'm talking about," Gordon said, but with less certainty than before.

"No, Gordon," Julie countered, "I do *not* know what you're talking about." She did, actually, but she wasn't going to make this easy.

Gordon had been the one to initiate the call.

And he'd made her sound like some kind of tramp, shacking up with this guy or that one and leaving Calvin to manage on his own.

Another sigh came then, gusty and long-suffering. "Maybe I could have been more diplomatic," he ventured.

"Think so?"

Gordon sounded suitably remorseful. Even sad. But Julie knew from experience how quickly his mood could change. "I never knew how to talk to you, Julie. That was our main problem."

In her opinion, their "main problem" had been Gordon's complete inability to commit himself to either her or their son. Fortunately for Dixie and the new baby, due in April, he had evidently changed.

Tension stretched between them, almost palpable.

The invisible rubber band finally snapped.

Just as Julie had expected, Gordon retrenched. "Are you or are you not living with a man you're not married to?" he demanded.

So much for his concern about being more diplomatic.

"I'm not *living with* Garrett McKettrick," Julie said, "not that it would be any of your damn business if I was. I hardly feel any compunction to account to you for my behavior, Gordon."

"You're right," Gordon allowed, after a few beats. "What you do in your—romantic life—isn't my concern. It's just that Calvin told me—"

"When did you speak with Calvin?" Julie broke in.

She glanced into the rearview mirror and saw an old red pickup pull up behind her. It was the same truck Garrett had been driving on Saturday, when she and Libby and Paige were heading out to shop for Libby's wedding dress.

Great, she thought.

"I gave Calvin my cell number the other night, when we all had supper together," Gordon said. "He's called me a couple of times since then."

This was news to Julie. Calvin hadn't mentioned calling his father.

What did it mean—if anything?

She watched as the driver's-side door of the red truck swung open.

Julie's breath caught. "Listen, I'm due at work. Maybe we could talk later?"

"All right," Gordon said. "When would be a good time?"

"Later—I'll call you later. Sometime—"

Gordon clicked off, after making a disgruntled man-sound in her ear.

Julie felt a little jolt when she turned her head and saw Austin standing beside her car, instead of Garrett. It was both a disappointment, she decided fitfully, and a relief.

She rolled the window down.

Austin bent, grinning at her. "You having car trouble or something?" he asked.

"No," Julie said, embarrassed. "I was just—talking on my cell phone and—"

The man's smile was wickedly boyish, Julie thought, detached from Austin's charms in a way she couldn't seem to manage with Garrett. No wonder Paige wanted to steer clear of her old flame—when it came to this guy, the needle on the cute-o-meter was bobbing into the red zone, and there was a distinct danger of spontaneous combustion.

For Paige, anyway.

Austin tugged genially at his hat brim, every inch the cowboy. "I'll be on my way, then," he said, "if you're sure you're all right, that is."

Julie nodded to indicate that she was fine. "Thanks for stopping," she said.

Austin grinned and sprinted back to the truck.

Julie straightened her shoulders, drew in and released a few deep breaths, and drove on.

At school, the halls were jammed.

Even though phone calls, texts and emails had probably been flying back and forth among them all weekend, the kids were eager to discuss the latest calamity—the fire at the Strivenses place—face-to-face.

Julie wove her way through the crowd, catching a snatch of conversation here and there.

...the McKettricks gave them a trailer to live in, and it's practically brand-new...

...the marching band wants to give a concert to raise money for groceries and stuff...

...my mom says the Quilters' Guild is planning to raffle off the project they worked on over the summer...

By the time Julie stepped into her classroom, she was smiling.

Kids could be ornery, no doubt about it, but deep down, they cared about each other, as did their parents. This was the Blue

River Julie had known and loved all her life, the community that invariably rallied in the face of trouble, stood shoulder to shoulder, and saw things through to the finish.

"Ms. Remington?"

Julie was only mildly surprised to turn and see Rachel Strivens standing quietly next to one of the bookcases. "Good morning, Rachel," she said, careful not to examine the child too closely or reveal any of the sympathy she felt.

It would be only too easy for Rachel to mistake sympathy for pity.

And pity was the last thing the girl needed.

Rachel wore jeans that didn't quite fit though they were good quality, along with a green sweater set with tiny matching buttons. She gazed earnestly at Julie for a long moment, swallowed and then said, "Do you think you could talk to my dad about—about how folks don't mean any harm by giving us things?"

Julie set her tote bag and purse in her desk chair, took off her coat and draped it over the back to deal with later. Before she could think what to say, Rachel went on.

"He says we don't need charity from the McKettricks or anybody else," she said miserably. "My brothers, they think it's Christmas, because people have been dropping stuff by since the men from the Silver Spur set the trailer down, just in front of the old one. They even hooked up the water and had the lights turned on. Folks bring groceries by the pickup load—clothes—new things, still in the boxes—you wouldn't believe it."

"I believe it," Julie said, with a small smile. She'd been born and raised in Blue River, and she could recall a number of times when the entire town had stepped up. Whether it was a fire, a lost job, a tragic accident or a grave illness—as in her own father's case—the locals invariably wanted to help.

Tears welled up in Rachel's eyes. "Dad's got his pride," she said. "He's already talking about moving on, just as soon as he can get the rig running right."

Julie rested a hand on Rachel's shoulder. The sweater set was soft—probably cashmere. She'd seen Cookie Becker in sophomore English wearing one much like it, and often. Cookie's widowed father didn't own a fancy ranch, practice a profession requiring advanced degrees or own stock in a technology firm or a software company. He worked at the tire store.

"Will you talk to my dad?" Rachel asked again. "I don't want to leave Blue River. Colley and Max don't want to, either. Especially not now that we've got that nice trailer to live in and all these new clothes and good things to eat—"

"I'll talk to him," Julie confirmed. "But that's all I can promise."

Yes, she'd seen the community rise to occasions like this one, some easier, some more difficult, time and time again. Generally, people were grateful, glad to have the help. But she'd also seen folks on the receiving end get their backs up, shake their fists at anything smacking of charity and anybody offering it.

Ron Strivens apparently fell into the latter group.

"Thanks," Rachel said, with more gratitude than the favor warranted, considering success was by no means a sure thing. After all, Julie hadn't accomplished much the *last* time she'd tried to talk to Rachel's dad.

The first period bell rang then, the door of Julie's classroom sprang open and her students poured in, a noisy river of laughter and slang, pushing and catcalls.

Rachel took her usual seat, meeting no one's eyes, keeping her slender back straight and her chin high.

Her father wasn't the only one in the family with pride, Julie thought.

What had it taken for the child to ask for help?

GARRETT WAS SORE as hell, but he saddled his horse anyhow and led it out of the barn, following behind Tate and the gelding, Stranger, into the morning sunshine. A large horse trailer waited in the yard, already hitched to a flatbed truck loaded with spools of barbed wire and various equipment.

Today, they'd be riding the downed fence lines up near where they'd found the dead cattle the day before.

Garrett had suggested taking the plane up again—it seemed like a good idea to him—but Tate refused, maintaining that the rustlers weren't likely to be working in the daylight. The thing to do now, he figured, was fix fences.

Tate was the eldest brother, and he was foreman.

When it came to ranch work, he gave the orders. That was only right, Garrett figured, since Tate was the one holding down the fort while he and Austin ran loose.

Garrett led the horse he'd chosen for the day up the ramp and into the trailer. He secured it among the half dozen others that had already been loaded and he and Tate walked back out into the light together.

Garrett's cell phone rang in the pocket of his jacket.

Tate gave him a wry look, partly disgusted, but offered no comment.

Seeing a familiar number in the panel, Garrett flipped the phone open and answered instead of letting the call go to voice mail, as he might have done otherwise.

"Hello, Nan," he said.

Nan Cox was smiling; Garrett felt the force of it as surely as if she'd been standing in front of him.

"Garrett," the senator's wife practically sang. "It's *so good* to hear your voice." What she meant: *Shouldn't* you *have called me?*

Tate shook his head, turned and walked away, leaving Garrett to hold the conversation in relative privacy.

"How are you?" Garrett asked quietly. "How are the kids?"

"Well, it's nice of you to *ask*, Garrett." *Finally.* "We're all fine, considering that my husband and their father has evidently lost his mind." A pause. "I really didn't expect you to bail out like this. I was counting on you to help me straighten this thing out."

Garrett moved well away from the action surrounding the horse trailer and the flatbed truck. "I didn't bail out, Nan," he said. "Morgan fired me."

"As I said," Nan replied, "my husband is out of his mind."

"I'm sorry," Garrett said. "That you and the children have to go through this, I mean."

"I didn't think you were apologizing for the other part," Nan said, with a sniff.

Garrett said nothing. Tate and the others were ready to head out now; he was holding up the show.

"Garrett," Nan went on, "have you been watching the national news? Reading the papers? Surfing the web? Surely you know what's going on."

He knew, all right.

The party had been pressuring Cox to resign, but the senator was still resisting the idea. According to Garrett's private contacts, who emailed regular updates from various places behind the scenes, the power brokers were getting impatient. Pretty soon, they'd throw the bureaucratic equivalent of a butterfly net over the guy and shuffle him off to some hospital or rehab center.

"I've got a pretty good idea," he admitted, watching Tate, who was watching him back. He knew Nan was calling because she wanted a favor. He also knew she wouldn't bring it up until she was ready, and there was no point in trying to hurry her along.

One foot on the running board of his truck, Tate waved the driver of the flatbed on ahead. Watching as the trailer loaded with horses went by, tires flinging up dust, Garrett recalled what his brother had said about running the Silver Spur with little or no help, and he felt a stab of guilt.

Garrett strode in Tate's direction.

"I need your help, Garrett," Nan said, at long last.

"Short of rejoining your husband's staff," Garrett said, pulling open the passenger-side door of Tate's truck and climbing into the seat, "I'll do anything I can. You know that."

Tate, behind the wheel now, slanted a look in Garrett's direction before turning the key in the ignition.

Nan finally laid it on the line, the real reason for her call. "Morgan is…on his 'honeymoon,' as he put it," she said. "He called me a couple of minutes ago from some swanky ski resort in Oregon, expecting me to share in his joy, I guess."

"Wouldn't that be bigamy?" Garrett asked.

Nan's chuckle was bitter. "Apparently, they decided to throw the honeymoon before the wedding. Morgan says he's going to divorce me and marry Mandy. Morgan and Mandy, married in Mexico. On top of everything else, it's alliterative." She paused, collecting herself. "By some miracle, the press hasn't picked up on any of this yet, but all hell will break loose when they do. That's why I need you to help me."

"I don't work for the senator anymore," Garrett reiterated, though gently.

"I understand that, Garrett. I'm asking you to work for *me*. I'll pay you whatever you were getting before, plus 20 percent."

"That's generous," Garrett said cautiously.

"Think about it," Nan answered, sounding more like her old self again. She was quick on her feet; the daughter of a former Texas governor as well as the wife of a senator, she'd spent a lifetime on the fringes of politics. She knew the ins and outs. "And don't take too long. The you-know-what is about to hit the fan. Besides, there are some other things we need to discuss in person. I've said more than I'm comfortable saying on a cell phone as it is."

Tate's shoulders were tense, and though he kept his eyes on the road and his hands on the wheel, Garrett could *feel* his brother stewing over there on the other side of the gearshift. Clearly, he'd picked up on the gist of the conversation.

"I'll be in touch," Garrett told Nan mildly.

"Make it soon," was Nan's answer. In the next moment, she clicked off.

Garrett shut his phone, tucked it away.

Both he and Tate were silent for a long time.

Scenery rolled by, but the trailer and the flatbed truck veiled most of it in one continuous cloud of road dust.

"What I said before," Tate began gruffly, flexing his fingers on the steering wheel.

Garrett noticed that the knuckles were white. "Yeah?" he prompted, when his brother stopped talking, right in the middle of a sentence. He was always doing that, Tate was, but Garrett did it, too, and so did Austin.

It seemed to run in the family.

"About needing some help from you and Austin, I mean," Tate said, then shut up again.

Winding up this conversation was going to be a delicate process, Garrett figured, like pulling porcupine quills out of tender flesh.

"Yeah," Garrett said, keeping the conversational door ajar. "I remember."

The tires of the truck thunked over the ruts in the road, and then the cattle guard.

"I didn't mind it so much before," Tate confessed. "Before Libby and I got together, I mean, and Audrey and Ava were spending every other week with their mother, but now—" He turned his head briefly, met Garrett's eyes. "I was so lonesome back then, I was glad to put in the hours."

Garrett felt something thicken in his throat. For Tate, who had always played his cards close to his vest, this was unprecedented. "And now?"

"Now, I want a life, Garrett. With Libby, with the kids." He drew a deep breath, huffed it out. "I love this place. It's been in the family for better than a hundred years. But I'd rather sell my share and move on than kill myself trying to run it alone."

"You'd *sell?*" Garrett couldn't believe his ears. The Silver Spur was home. There were generations of McKettricks buried in the private cemetery just a mile from the house, including their parents. Their own kin had fought and died to *hold on to* that ranch for over a hundred years, through droughts and the Dirty '30s, a dozen recessions and two world wars. And Tate was willing to *pull out?*

"Like I said," Tate told him gruffly. "I love this ranch. But I love Libby and the kids a lot more."

"You know damn well some big consortium would buy the place in a heartbeat—open the oil wells up again—clear out all the cowpunchers and their families—"

Tate didn't answer.

They'd reached the place where they had to pull over, help unload the horses from the other truck, mount up and ride in. Once they got out of Tate's rig, there would be no privacy.

So Garrett stayed put.

And when Tate moved to open his door, Garrett got him by the arm and held on, steely-strong.

"I thought better of you, Tate," he ground out. "I really thought better of you."

"What the hell do you mean by that?" Tate snapped, turning to face Garrett straight on.

"You'd never sell your share of the Silver Spur. You know Nan offered me a job just now, and you're trying to goad me into turning it down."

The look in Tate's eyes came as near to contempt as Garrett had ever seen, at least in his own brother's face. "You know what, Garrett?" he asked, his voice low and dismissive. "If you think I operate like that, well, you can just go to hell."

"Tate—"

Tate turned away, shoved the door open and got out.

Slammed it behind him.

Not to be outdone, Garrett slammed the door on *his* side, too.

Charlie Bates, the man who'd no doubt expected to be ranch foreman after Pablo Ruiz died, stood behind the horse trailer, giving orders as the animals were led down the ramp, one after another. His small eyes darted from Tate to Garrett and back to Tate again, and a weird feeling burrowed into Garrett's stomach lining like a red-hot worm.

"You two look fit to butcher frozen beef without a knife," Bates observed. "Is there something I ought to know?"

Tate wouldn't look at Garrett, but he glowered at Bates. "When I feel inclined to discuss my private life with you," he said, "you'll be the first one I tell."

Bates's features seemed to contort a little, but it might have been an illusion, Garrett decided. The man wasn't exactly the expressive type.

Garrett's horse came down the ramp, saddled, and he took the reins from the hand of the cowboy leading the animal and swung up onto its back.

"Let's get this show on the road," he said, echoing words he'd often heard his dad utter, back in the day. "We're burnin' daylight."

Bates got on his own horse, made it bump sides with Garrett's.

"You giving the orders now, Dos?" Bates asked.

Dos. Garrett hadn't been called "Two" since he couldn't remember when, and the reference to his place in the McKettrick pecking order pissed him off, especially coming from Charlie Bates.

"Some of them," he answered, adjusting his hat.

Bates spat tobacco, careful to just miss Garrett and his horse. "And what would those be?" he drawled.

"Well, one of them would be to mind your own business."

"That so?" Bates grinned. Spat again, coming closer this time. "There's another?"

"Yeah," Garrett said. "Clean up."

With that, he rode away, just naturally falling in alongside Tate and his horse, even though they weren't speaking to each other at present.

CHAPTER FIFTEEN

ALL THAT MORNING, the call from Gordon nibbled at the back of Julie's mind, making concentration doubly difficult. Was it true that Calvin had been calling his dad without telling her? And if so, why?

Was something troubling Calvin—how could she not have noticed?—and why had he confided in Gordon, a virtual stranger, and not in her?

Okay, there were things a boy didn't want to tell his mom, but Calvin could have talked to Libby or to Paige. He had a good relationship with Tate too, and Garrett, if he'd wanted to confide in a man.

Why would he choose Gordon?

Julie was burning to speak to Calvin, make sure everything was all right in his small but busy world, reassure him if he was frightened or disturbed about something.

But she still had classes to teach, and the first round of tryouts scheduled for that afternoon and evening. Plus, she'd promised Rachel she'd have a word with Ron Strivens, try to smooth his pride-ruffled feathers, possibly get him to understand the difference between neighborly help and charity.

And frankly, that galled her a little—no, a *lot*.

Men and their damnable pride. She had too much to do already, and now she'd committed herself to yet another task, one that would probably prove impossible.

By the time lunch hour rolled around, Julie was, as the old saying went, fit to be tied.

Even deep breathing, usually her mainstay, didn't help.

Instead of eating in the cafeteria or the teacher's lounge, Julie ducked into her tiny office in the darkened auditorium, got out her cell phone and called Gordon back.

"Julie?" he said, sounding surprised.

"I hope this isn't a bad time," Julie replied, and then wished she'd said something else. *Anything* else. It wasn't as if her ex would be doing her some big favor by taking her call. *He'd* been the one to initiate things, not her.

"I'm straddling the ridgepole on a roof at the moment," Gordon said, with a smile in his voice. "Nailing down shingles."

Julie remembered that Gordon worked in construction now. "I guess I could call back later," she said uncertainly. There was the school day to finish, then the first set of tryouts for *Kiss Me Kate*, then picking up Calvin, getting him through his bath and his prayers.

As much as she wanted to ask her little boy about calling Gordon—it was paramount for Calvin to understand that he'd done nothing wrong by telephoning his father—there probably wouldn't be time or energy for it. Not that night, at least.

"Julie," Gordon said quickly, earnestly, "stay on the line. Please. I'm wearing a headpiece, so I've got both hands free for hanging on."

Julie smiled at that, a smile muted to sadness by memories of another time and place, when she and Gordon had expected to be together forever.

Or, at least, that had been *her* expectation. Gordon's take on the situation might have been entirely different from hers, right from the very beginning.

"I'm here," she said, quietly and at some length.

Gordon's voice was gruff when he replied. "About that phone call this morning," he said. "I'm sorry, Julie. I didn't mean to imply that you were—well—that I think there's anything wrong with the way you're raising our son. From what little I've seen of him—and I know that's my own fault and not yours—Calvin is a great kid."

Julie's eyes burned. Furious heartache rose up into her throat and expanded there, painfully.

Our son, Gordon had said.

The phrase made her feel fiercely territorial, a tigress backed into a corner with her cub, so it was probably a good thing that she was too choked up to speak.

She might not have been able to hold back all the damning questions she wanted to hurl at Gordon Pruett in those wretched moments: *How dare you say* our son? *Where were you when he nearly died of an asthma attack during Thanksgiving dinner? Where were you when he was teething, when he had the flu and couldn't keep anything down? Where were you when he was asking why he didn't have a dad to take him camping and fishing, like his friend Justin does?*

"Hey," Gordon said, when she didn't speak. "Are you still there?"

Julie managed to croak out a "Yes."

There was a pause, then Gordon launched cheerfully into the real reason he'd gotten in touch with her that morning, when she was driving to work. "My folks are visiting Dixie and me next week, and they want to meet Calvin." He paused, reining it in a little. "If that's okay with you, I mean."

Julie straightened her spine. Drew a deep breath and let it out without making a sound. "It depends on what you have in mind," she replied, pleasantly surprised by how calm and together she sounded. Everything inside her seemed to be jostling about, competing for a chance to jump onto a hamster wheel and run like hell. "I think it would be wonderful for Calvin to meet his grandparents."

On her side of the family, there was only Marva, since her father was gone. Marva was an interesting grandmother, in an Auntie Mame sort of way—but there was no getting around the undeniable fact that she was a character.

The one and only Marva.

"But?" Gordon prodded, not unkindly.

Julie sighed, but this time she made no effort to be quiet about it. "But you'll all have to come here, to Blue River. And if I can't be there personally, throughout the visit, then I want one of my sisters to be."

"I'm not planning on kidnapping the little guy, Julie," Gordon said, his tone reasonable, but shot through with some vexation, too. "My mom and dad have never seen him."

Whose fault is that? demanded the part of Julie's brain she was trying so hard to control.

"Those are the terms, Gordon."

"Take it or leave it?" Gordon asked, sadly amused.

"Pretty much, yeah," Julie answered.

"Okay," Gordon agreed. "We'll book a couple of rooms at the Amble On Inn, then, and drive down from Dallas on Friday—Thursday if I can get the time off. I'll let you know when the plans are firmed up."

"Okay," Julie said.

Gordon chuckled. "Julie?"

"What?"

"I know it's hard, adjusting to my being back in your life, but I'm not your enemy. I'm not trying to steal Calvin away, or turn him against you. I blew it, big time, and I'm the first to admit it. You'll never know how much I regret not being there for Calvin and for you, because if there are words to describe it, they're ones I've never learned." A pause, an indrawn breath, a sigh. "I just want a chance to know my son, Julie. That's all. Just to know him."

"And your parents," Julie pointed out, strangely compelled to cross t's and dot i's.

In all the time they were together, she and Gordon, he'd never introduced her to them. She'd wondered, back then and not very often, if it was because he was ashamed, either of dear old Mom and Dad—or of her.

The wild, unconventional girl from Blue River, Texas.

Full of spirit and confidence in those days, either singing and dancing with professional theater companies or waiting tables between semesters of college, always paying her own way, Julie had never *seriously* entertained the possibility that Gordon's folks might not approve of her.

She did now.

"And my parents," Gordon affirmed.

They said their awkward goodbyes then, and, mercifully, the call ended.

Julie had barely caught her breath when Libby dialed in. Calvin, through with kindergarten for the day, would be over at the community center by now, no doubt listening to a story or scaling the walls of the remarkably authentic toy castle Tate and his daughters had donated.

Unless something was wrong.

"Hey, Julie," Libby said.

Anxiety washed over Julie. "Is everyone all right?"

"Yes," Libby was quick to reply. "Mostly, anyway. I just got a call from the school—Audrey and Ava seem to have come down with identical cases of the flu. I'm off to pick them up in a couple of minutes, and I'll be taking them by the clinic, of course, since they're running fevers. What it all boils down to is this—I don't think we should expose Calvin."

Julie closed her eyes for a moment, already shaking her head. "No," she agreed.

"I know you were counting on us to look after Calvin until you get home from the tryouts for the play—"

"Don't worry about it, Lib," Julie broke in. "I'll figure something out. Maybe Paige can help."

"I'm so sorry, Jules."

"Don't be sorry," Julie said. "Just take care of Audrey and Ava. And let me know what the doctor says, will you?"

Libby promised a full report and rang off, only to call again before Julie had even managed to set the phone down.

"Garrett's here," Libby told Julie, without any sort of preamble. "He says he can pick Calvin up and bring him to you or out to the ranch—whatever works for you."

Julie's heart did a funny little flip, and she silently scolded herself for making a big deal out of nothing. "Ask him to please bring Calvin here," she said. "To the auditorium, I mean."

Libby relayed this to Garrett, then asked, "What time?"

"Three?" Julie said. Classes were dismissed at 2:45; this way, she'd have fifteen minutes to "unfrazzle," a term her friend and fellow teacher Helen used, before coming face-to-face with Garrett McKettrick.

Libby repeated the time to Garrett, then confirmed, "He'll be there."

"Tell him thanks," Julie told her sister. "I really appreciate this. And don't forget I want an update on the twins, once they've seen the doctor."

"I won't forget," Libby promised.

Julie speed-dialed the community center, told one of the day-care workers that Calvin wouldn't be riding the bus home with the McKettrick twins the way he usually did. Instead, Garrett would stop by to pick him up.

"This is going to sound real silly," Soliel Roberts said, "since you and Garrett and I all grew up together and everything, but I'm going to need written permission to turn Calvin over to anybody besides you or Libby or Paige, dated and signed. You can fax it over, if you like. The fax number is 555-7386."

"I'll do that," Julie replied gently. "Thanks, Soliel."

Soliel said she was welcome, goodbyes were exchanged and Julie rooted in her lunch bag for the half sandwich she'd packed that morning, in the ranch-house kitchen. She'd already wolfed down the apple during her morning break.

The afternoon passed quickly, and Julie was grateful, considering that the second part of the day often seemed twice as long as the first.

At three o'clock, she was consulting with Mrs. Chambers, the music teacher, and a few of the most dedicated kids were already lolling in the front row of seats, texting each other while they waited to get up on stage and strut their stuff.

Calvin came racing down the middle aisle, his face flushed with excitement and the chill of a fall afternoon. "Garrett came and got me at school today!" he shouted, unable to contain his exuberance. "And it was *just like having a dad!*"

Julie's cheeks stung a little, though she smiled and bent down for Calvin's hello hug. Over the top of his head, she caught sight of Garrett, standing in the shadows at the back of the auditorium.

She couldn't see his face, but that didn't matter.

The familiar jolt went through her anyway.

While Calvin remained at the base of the stage, showing Mrs. Chambers his papers from school, Julie approached Garrett.

"Thank you," she said, peering cautiously at his badly swollen right eye. From a distance, she hadn't been able to see the damage. Up close, he looked as though something with hooves had kicked him in the face. "What happened to you?"

Garrett folded his arms, and his mouth—oh, his dangerous *mouth*—crooked up at one side. "I ran into a door?" he said.

"You were in a fight," Julie guessed aloud, keeping her voice down so Calvin, Mrs. Chambers and the theater kids wouldn't hear.

"You should see the other guy," Garrett joked.

She wanted to touch him. She wanted to fuss and fret and fetch an ice pack.

Which was why she was so careful to keep her distance.

"Does it hurt?" She couldn't resist asking him that.

He chuckled. "A little. Mostly, I'm numb."

"I appreciate your bringing Calvin over from school."

"It might be a long haul for the little guy," Garrett observed. "Hanging around here until you're done, I mean. I could take him on home if that would be better."

Julie glanced back at Calvin, knew he'd be better off at the house, with Esperanza and Garrett, rather than hanging around the auditorium until all hours, either bored out of his skull or creating a distraction or both.

"I couldn't ask you—or Esperanza—"

Garrett silenced her by resting the tip of one index finger against her lips, so lightly and so briefly that afterward she was never sure that he'd touched her at all. "You're not asking," he said. *"I'm offering."*

Julie's heart filled with something warm and sweet, and then overflowed. She hoped Garrett hadn't guessed that, just by looking at her. He'd think she was a sentimental sap if he had.

Just then, Calvin raced up the aisle and leaned against Julie's side. "I'm hungry," he said.

Garrett looked down at him, ruffled his hair. "Me, too," he agreed. "What do you say we go home and see if we can charm Esperanza into rustling up some grub?"

Calvin practically vibrated with eagerness. "That would be cool," he said. Then he looked up at Julie, his little face screwed up with studious concern, his glasses slightly askew, as they so often were. "Aren't you hungry, too, Mom?" he asked.

If she hadn't known it would embarrass her little boy, she would have pulled him into her arms, then and there, and hugged him tight.

"I'll be fine," she said. "Somebody ordered pizza."

Calvin mulled that over. "Harry probably needs to go outside," he concluded at last. "And he'll be needing some kibble and some fresh water pretty soon."

"I'm sure you're right," Julie replied seriously.

"You don't mind if I go on to the Silver Spur with Garrett, then?" Calvin sounded so hopeful that Julie ached. "Instead of staying here with you?"

"I don't mind," Julie said, choking up a little.

Just then, her gaze connected with Garrett's.

"Have you heard anything from Libby? About Audrey and Ava, I mean?" Julie's cell phone was in the bottom of her purse; if her sister had called with news about Tate's girls and their twin cases of flu, she hadn't heard the ring.

"Tate called a little while ago," Garrett said. "It's the usual prescription—bed rest, children's medication and plenty of fluids. The twins will be fine in a day or two."

"But in the meantime," Calvin interjected, with energetic distaste, "they're really *germy*. I could be *contaged* just by being in the same room when they cough or sneeze."

"Sounds ominous," Garrett remarked, giving Calvin's shoulder a light punch, guy-like.

"Let's go," Calvin said, obviously impatient to be on his way, with Garrett.

Inside Julie, sorrow squeezed hard. It would be *years* before Calvin was old enough to leave home. Why was she always so conscious that the clock was ticking?

Garrett ducked his head slightly, to look into her face. "You okay?" he asked.

Julie swallowed hard, then nodded. Smiled. "I'll see you both later—around eight o'clock, I expect."

"See you then," Garrett said. His eyes seemed to caress her, warming her flesh, awakening her tired nerves.

Ten minutes ago, she'd been looking forward to the end of the day, when she could take a warm bath and then crawl into her bed.

Now she was only interested in the bed, and it was *Garrett's* bed she wanted to slip into, not hers.

Julie shook off a cloud of stars, nodded again, then bent to kiss the top of Calvin's head. "Be good," she said.

Calvin gave a sigh that seemed to rise from the soles of his little high-top sneakers. "I'm *always* good," he said. "It gets boring."

Garrett chuckled at that. "Come on, pardner," he said, getting Calvin by the hood of his new nylon jacket and steering him in the general direction of the main doors. "We've got things to do out on the ranch—nothing like doing chores to put an end to boredom—and your mom has things to do here."

"Garrett?" His name came fragile from her throat, shimmering and iridescent, like a soap bubble.

He'd turned away, engaged with Calvin, who was already recounting some incident that had taken place on the playground at school, but when Julie spoke, Garrett turned his head to look back at her.

She moved close to him, unable to help herself, touched her fingertips to the bruised skin under his eye. "You'll tell me what happened? Later on?"

"I'll tell you what happened," Garrett said, almost sighing the words.

Moments later, he and Calvin were gone.

Julie turned back to the task at hand—back to the kids and the stage and Mrs. Chambers's piano-pounding musical style.

Kiss Me Kate wasn't going to cast itself, after all.

UPSTAIRS IN HIS own kitchen, Garrett hoisted Calvin onto the countertop, where the kid could watch the proceedings without being too close to anything hot or sharp. Buzzing with kid-energy, Calvin bounced the heels of his shoes against the cupboard door, stirring the dog, Harry, to a three-legged frenzy of yelping excitement.

"Whoa," Garrett said good-naturedly. "Sit still."

Calvin stopped kicking. Earlier, they'd fed the horses together, out in the barn, and the boy's glasses had fogged over from the cold. Now they were clear again, magnifying his pale blue eyes.

"Do you think the doctor made Audrey and Ava get *shots?*" he asked Garrett, looking horrified at the prospect.

The dog quieted down, went back to his kibble bowl.

"Don't know," Garrett said, peeling the foil off the pan of chicken tamales Esperanza had left downstairs in the oven for supper. Turned out, she had a meeting at church.

"I *hate* shots," Calvin told him.

"Well, now," Garrett said reasonably, taking two plates down from a cupboard, "a cowboy always takes his medicine, if the doctor says he needs it."

Calvin considered that, his eyes wide. "Did you ever cry, when you were little, and you had to have a shot?"

"No," Garrett answered honestly, "but I ran out of the clinic once, when I was about your age, and hid in the men's restroom of a gas station across the street, until my mom walked right in there and got me by the ear."

He grinned at the memory.

He'd barely felt the injection, given a few minutes later, he'd been so impressed that his mother wasn't afraid to march herself straight into a men's room to collect him.

"And she made you get the shot?"

"It had to be done," Garrett said, dishing up tamales.

Plates filled, he hoisted Calvin back down off the counter and set him on his feet.

They washed up, then took their meal to the table over by the wall of windows looking out over the dark range. The boy ate a few bites and then started blinking rapidly, like he had something in his eyes.

Garrett hid a smile, aware that Calvin was having a hard time staying awake.

"You tuckered out?" he asked the little guy.

Calvin yawned widely, set down his fork. "Yeah," he admitted. "But I don't want to go to bed yet, because my mom isn't home and Esperanza isn't either, and this is a big house to be alone in."

He was there, and Austin probably was, too, which meant that, technically, Calvin wouldn't be alone, though he might as well have been, Garrett supposed, considering the size of the place.

"I guess you could stretch out on my sofa till your mom gets back," Garrett offered.

"Would the lights be out?" Calvin asked. "Would you be right there?"

"I'd be right there," Garrett confirmed.

"In the living room, where I could see you?"

"In the living room, where you could see me."

Calvin looked relieved. "I guess that would be all right, then," he decided.

Then, "You wouldn't tell anybody that I'm scared of the dark, would you?"

The earnest expression in the little boy's face touched something in Garrett, caused another shift, one he couldn't begin to describe. It roughened his voice, the strange emotion he felt then.

"I wouldn't tell," he promised.

Calvin pushed his plate away. "I'm full," he said.

"No need to keep eating, then," Garrett replied.

He got a soft blanket and a pillow from the linen closet in the hallway, and made a bed for Calvin on the sofa. Lamps burned at either end, dimmed down to a yellow glow. Garrett switched on the TV, with the volume low, and kicked back in his favorite chair.

The dog immediately started trying to jump up onto the sofa with Calvin. It was a pitiful sight, given that the poor critter was missing a leg.

Garrett got up, hoisted the mutt onto the couch with Calvin and sat down again.

As usual, TV didn't have much to offer, but Garrett had made a promise—he'd stay with Calvin until his mother came home—so he flicked through the channels until he found a rodeo-retrospective on ESPN and settled on that.

His brain immediately divided itself into three working parts.

One level focused on the rodeo unfolding in front of his eyes.

Another, the lovely problem of Julie Remington, her boy and her dog, and all the ways they might change his life.

Still another went over and over that day, out on the range. They'd fixed fences, he and Tate and the other cowboys, but they'd found nothing that might lead them to the rustlers.

Or the sons of bitches who'd shot those six cattle and left them for the flies. The recollection sickened Garrett; it was hard to fathom why anybody would kill a living thing for no reason.

Nan's call had complicated everything, of course.

Fired or not, he knew he'd have to help her straighten out the mess Morgan and the pole dancer were stirring up. Not only had Garrett worked for her husband since law school, his mother and Nan had been college roommates and very close friends.

As far as he knew, Morgan hadn't hired anybody to replace him as yet—the august senator from the great state of Texas had been too busy romancing the pole dancer to do anything about the sudden vacancy on his staff, other than ask other staffers to cover the responsibilities that had been Garrett's.

It was only logical for Garrett to take up the slack.

Besides, he liked Nan. She was mentally, emotionally and physically sound. She knew the issues. She knew the people, cared about what they wanted and what was best for them, not only in the present, but generations hence.

Looking back over the years he'd worked for Senator Morgan Cox, Garrett was astounded at how many dots he hadn't noticed, let alone connected.

Nan was the strong one, not Morgan.

Nan was the force of nature, the skilled politician, the one with A Plan.

Why hadn't he seen that?

The thing Nan hadn't wanted to discuss over the cell phone? She was planning to call in all her markers and run for Morgan's Senate seat when the next election rolled around in a little over two years.

She meant to hire him, Garrett, as her right-hand man.

McKettrick, Garrett told himself, glowering at the TV screen above the fireplace, *not much gets by you. You have the political instincts of a pump handle.*

On the couch, Calvin stirred, made a soft, kid-sound in his sleep.

Garrett's heart actually seized.

He closed his eyes, just to shut out the light for a few moments.

When he opened them, Julie was sitting on the arm of his chair, smiling down at him.

"So," she whispered, keeping her voice down so Calvin wouldn't wake up, "what happened to your eye? Remember, you promised you'd tell me."

Garrett chuckled hoarsely. Julie Remington had no idea how down-home sexy she was. No idea at all.

"Either Tate or Austin punched me," he said.

Julie's wonderful, changeling eyes widened. She moved to smooth his hair back from his forehead, hesitated, then went ahead and did it.

Electricity shot through Garrett; all of a sudden, he was wide awake, every nerve reporting for duty, ready for action.

"'Either Tate or Austin'?" She smiled. Her fingertips rested lightly on his bruises, and he felt some kind of sacred energy surge through him. "You don't know which one?"

Garrett grinned. If the boy and the dog hadn't been sleeping on the couch, just a few feet away, he would have tugged Julie onto his lap. "Could have been either one," he said. "They were about to go at it, and I was fool enough to get between them."

She laughed, and the sound was silvery and pure, almost spiritual, like Christmas bells ringing out over miles of unmarked snow.

"Did Calvin behave himself?" she asked.

God, she was so beautiful. There are perfect moments in life, he thought, and this was one of them.

"He's a good kid," Garrett answered presently, and somewhat hoarsely, with a nod. "Did you know he's scared of the dark?"

"Most kindergarteners are," Julie said.

"I guess you've got a point."

Julie looked over at her son, curled up on the couch with his dog. The perfect moments just kept on coming, and that was fine with Garrett. "Would you mind carrying him downstairs for me?"

Garrett was on his feet. He would have carried the whole *sofa* downstairs, kid, dog and all, if she'd asked him to. He'd have staggered under the weight of just about anything, in fact, just for the light in her eyes and the way she held her mouth, as if she wanted to smile but wouldn't let herself do it.

"Sure," he said. He scooped the boy up, blanket and all.

"Is my mom home?" Calvin asked sleepily.

Julie fetched the boy's glasses from the end table where he'd left them. "Your mom is definitely home," she told her son.

Harry jumped down to follow.

"Keep the dog here," Garrett said, at the top of the staircase leading down into the ranch-house kitchen. "I'll come back for him."

Instead, Julie brought Harry downstairs herself.

The kitchen was dimly lit, and Garrett had no trouble navigating it.

When he laid Calvin down on his bed, his arms ached, objecting to the letting go.

Garrett waited in the sitting room while Julie settled her son in for the night, murmuring mother-words.

Garrett McKettrick marveled.

All his life, he'd wanted to be a U.S. senator and, eventually, president.

Now, incomprehensibly, he couldn't seem to think beyond being a husband, a father and the master of a three-legged dog.

What the hell was wrong with him?

JULIE DECIDED, once she'd tucked Calvin in and kissed him goodnight, Harry properly settled in his place at the foot of the bed, that it would be all right to fuss over Garrett's black eye *just a little*. As long as she didn't get carried away, what harm could it do?

She was pleased to find him still in the apartment when she returned from Calvin's room.

"Now," she said, "let's have a better look at that eye."

"I'm all right," Garrett said, though not with a lot of certainty.

She took his hand—where had her bone-deep tiredness gone?—and led him into the big kitchen.

"Sit down," she said.

Garrett dropped into a chair.

Briskly—*just call me Nurse Julie*, she thought, with a silent chuckle—she found a plastic bag with a zip-top, filled it with ice and approached him.

Garrett winced when she touched the ice pack to his eye, then relaxed with a long sigh.

Julie smiled, overwhelmed by tenderness.

Garrett took hold of the ice pack, lowered it and buried his face in her middle, just long enough to start a wildfire blazing through her veins.

"I'll be going away in a few days," he said, very quietly.

Time itself seemed to stop the instant Garrett spoke those words. At least, for Julie it did.

Why was she so shocked, so shaken? Garrett McKettrick was— Garrett McKettrick. He had another life, away from the ranch, away from Blue River.

Away from her.

"Julie?" Garrett's hands rested on her hips, holding her in place. Not that she could have moved to break away; she was in statue-mode. Frozen.

She didn't answer.

Garrett pulled her down, onto his lap.

She did her best not to look at him; that was all the resistance she could muster at the moment, it seemed.

She'd worn her hair up that day, in what Paige called her "schoolmarm do," secured by a sterling silver clip.

Garrett opened the clip, and all those spirally curls tumbled down.

"So go," she finally managed to croak out. "Nobody expects you to stay."

"Will you look at me?"

"Actually, no. I'd rather not."

He took her chin in one hand, gently, and turned her head. Short of squinching her eyes shut like a child, there was no way to avoid meeting his gaze.

"Senator Cox is about to resign," he said, very quietly. "That's a very big deal, Julie. I have to be there."

"Okay," Julie said.

"I'd like you to come with me."

She blinked, startled. "I can't," she managed, after a long moment of wild consideration. "There's Calvin, and my job—"

"We're talking about one or two days, max," Garrett reasoned. Splaying the fingers of his right hand, he combed them through her hair. "Think about it, Julie."

"I couldn't," she said.

"Just the two of us," Garrett drawled, his voice dreamlike, almost hypnotic. "You and me. Together. Naked a lot of the time."

Julie swallowed hard.

"Think about it," Garrett repeated.

As if she could *help* thinking about it.

CHAPTER SIXTEEN

NAN'S PHONE CALL woke Garrett in the middle of the night.

He sat up, grumbling, and groped for the receiver beside his bed.

"Yeah?" he growled.

"You've got to come," she said.

Sleep still fogged Garrett's head. He'd been dreaming about Julie, the sort of erotic—and thwarted—dream it wasn't easy to leave behind.

"What? Where—?"

"There's been an accident, Garrett," Mrs. Cox replied, and now he could tell that she was struggling to maintain control. "Morgan and the—the woman, Mandy? They were skiing at some resort in Oregon—"

He felt a sickening sense of déjà vu. He couldn't help remembering another call, in the middle of another night, about another accident, of a different kind. That time, the caller had been Tate, and the news was beyond bad.

Their folks had been airlifted to Houston, after a car crash.

Neither was expected to live.

And neither had.

Garrett swore silently and swung his legs over the side of the bed, groping for the jeans he'd tossed aside earlier, after tearing himself away from Julie. God, he'd wanted to share her bed, spend the whole night loving her, wake up with her beside him.

But there was Calvin to consider. He was not quite five years old; he couldn't be expected to understand.

She hadn't said Morgan was dead, he remembered. She'd said there had been an accident. "Exactly what happened, Nan?" he asked. "And how bad is it?"

"As I understand it, Mandy is all right," Nan answered woodenly, sounding detached now, as though she were watching the event unfold on a movie screen no one else could see. Of course she must have been in shock. "Morgan—Morgan is in bad shape. You know what a good skier he was—*is*—but—"

"Nan?" Garrett broke in, firmly but not unkindly. "What happened?"

She gave a strangled little laugh, void of humor and hard to hear. "He was probably showing off for that—that *pole dancer*. Skiing too fast—on a trail too advanced for a middle-aged man, out of shape—" Nan stopped. Made that sound again. Then, "Morgan collided with a tree, Garrett. He's—he's comatose."

Bile scalded the back of Garrett's throat. *Comatose.* He struggled into his pants, wedged the cordless receiver between his shoulder and his ear.

"But he's alive," Nan choked out. "People *do* come out of comas—sometimes."

Garrett closed his eyes, but the images wouldn't be shut out. Morgan Cox had been a brilliant man, a Rhodes scholar. Now, it seemed, he had been reduced to a vegetative state.

"Where are you?"

She named a hospital in Austin. "I asked them to bring him here," she said. "I just hope he makes it, so I can say goodbye, tell Morgan I f-forgive him—"

Nan broke down then.

"I'll be there as soon as I can," Garrett told her, aching inside. "Hold on, Nan." He paused. The question had to be asked. "Are there reporters?"

Another ragged sob burst from Nan's throat. "Of *course* there are reporters," she blurted out. "There are *always* reporters."

"No statements," Garrett warned. It was a real bitch, trying to talk on the phone and get dressed at the same time. He felt like a one-legged man attempting to stomp out a campfire. "Don't say *anything*. I'll handle the press when I get there."

"Hurry," Nan pleaded.

Garrett said goodbye, thumbed the off button and tossed the receiver onto his rumpled bed.

He didn't shower and he didn't shave.

He just pulled on a shirt, socks and boots, grabbed his cell phone, and scrambled out of his room and down the stairs into the kitchen.

Austin was sitting at the table in a pair of sweatpants, shirtless, squinting at the screen of a laptop.

Seeing Garrett, he narrowed his eyes. "What the hell...?"

"Put a shirt on," Garrett snapped. "There's a lady in this house, and a little kid."

The admonition made Austin grin slightly, but his eyes were still troubled. "What's going on?"

"There's been a skiing accident," Garrett said, grabbing the Porsche keys from the hook next to the door leading into the garage. "Morgan isn't expected to live."

Austin gave a low whistle of exclamation, but he didn't say anything.

Even in his distracted state, Garrett noticed the haunted look that fell across his brother like a shadow, at the mention of the word *accident*. Of course, Austin was remembering the night their parents died.

They'd all taken the deaths hard, but Austin, maybe because he was the youngest, had taken them hardest of all.

"Do me a favor?" Garrett asked gruffly, about to go out the door, get in his Porsche and head for his Cessna.

"Sure," Austin said. A news site flickered on the screen of his laptop now, bluish in the dim light. "What do you need?"

"I know you and Tate are getting on each other's nerves and you want to lock horns," Garrett said, choosing his words with as much care as his rush would allow. "But Tate needs our help, Austin. It's not just this rustling thing—he's talking about selling out and moving off the ranch."

Austin's mouth dropped open. He closed it, then blurted, *"Sell-*

ing out?" A pause, rife with blinking disbelief. "He can't be serious."

"I've got a feeling our big brother is *dead* serious, Austin. The
ranch matters to Tate, but Libby and the kids are more important,
and he wants more husband-and-dad time."

Austin still looked as though he'd been sucker punched. "He'd
never do it," he said, pale. Half sitting and half standing now, unable, it seemed, to make up his mind and choose one direction,
up or down. "Tate would *never* sell his share of the Silver Spur!"

Garrett sighed. "We've got a choice to make—you and I," he
said in parting. "Either we step up and help Tate run this place,
or he moves on."

Austin left the table, followed Garrett all the way out to the
Porsche. Stood there, barefooted and bare-chested, while Garrett pushed a button to raise the garage door behind his car and
started the engine.

"I could come along," Austin offered, when Garrett rolled down
his window. "If you need somebody to ride shotgun or something—"

Garrett rummaged up a smile. "Thanks," he said, shaking his
head even as he spoke. "It'll be better if you stay here and help
Tate as much as you can. When I get back, the three of us will sit
down and figure out what to do next."

Austin swallowed visibly, then nodded, stepping back from
the Porsche and giving a halfhearted wave of one hand as Garrett backed out.

He reached the airstrip within five minutes, and after a quick
safety inspection and an engine warm-up, Garrett drove his plane
out of its hangar, lined up the nose and zoomed down the short,
bumpy runway.

Once aloft, Garrett set his mind on reaching Austin.

He'd called Nan back on the drive to the airstrip, given her an
ETA and asked her to have Troy meet him with a car.

In the near distance, the small grid of lights that made up the
town of Blue River twinkled in the darkness.

The river and the creeks looked like black ribbons, snaking
through the night, silvery with the moon's glow.

Tate's place was dark, Garrett noticed.

That gave him a lonely feeling.

He automatically scanned the horizon, though he could have charted the course to Austin or any one of a dozen other places with his eyes shut. And that was when he spotted the snarl of headlights over near the dry riverbed he and Tate had checked out a day or two before.

He banked in that direction, frowning, not wanting to take the time, knowing he wouldn't be able to see much from the air, heading there anyway.

He swung low over the trailer of a semi surrounded by a number of smaller rigs. Several sets of headlights—all but the semi's— blinked out like fireflies going into hiding, but not before Garrett spotted the dark figures of men scattering to flee.

He reached for the handset of the radio, but drew back without taking hold of it. Instead, he fumbled for his cell phone, jammed into his shirt pocket just before he left the house.

He thumbed in Tate's number, then reconsidered and cut off the call.

The rigs below scattered, driving blind. Garrett made an executive decision and stuck to the semi, its trailer probably loaded down with McKettrick cattle.

Tate called him back in two seconds, half-asleep and in no mood to be gracious. "What?" he growled. "You call, you let the phone ring *once*, and then you *hang up?*"

"Sorry about that," Garrett said. "Second thoughts." If he mentioned the semi to Tate now, the damn fool would probably come running out here in the middle of the night, planning to chase the crooks to the farthest corner of hell if he had to—and maybe get hurt or killed in the process.

Below, the semi driver jolted toward the main road, traveling fast, over rough ground.

Garrett hoped the cattle jammed into the back were all right. At the same time, it gave him that old rodeo feeling, tailing that fleeing semi from the air. Even with all that was going on, he could barely hold back a whoop of pure yeehaw.

"You're not getting off that easy," Tate said. "Why did you call me?"

It was easy to tell that he was a man in love, because as pissed-off as he was, he still tried to keep his voice down so he wouldn't wake Libby.

"Garrett," he demanded, in a loud whisper, "are you drunk or something?"

Garrett laughed outright then. It was a broken sound, part tragedy. "No," he said. "I'm not drunk." He was going to have to give up something, he could see that; Tate wouldn't leave him alone until he did. "I'm on my way to Austin," he said. He told Tate what little he knew about the senator's tragic mishap on an Oregon ski slope.

"I'm really sorry," Tate said, when Garrett had finished.

Garrett didn't answer.

Below, the semi pulled onto the main road, heading south.

"Gotta go," Garrett said.

"I could meet you at the hospital—"

Garrett cut him off. "No," he replied, his voice gruff. "Look, I'll call you tomorrow. Bring you up to speed."

The brothers said their goodbyes, and rang off, and Garrett put through a quick call to Brent Brogan. Brent promised to send the state police after the semi, but without a license number or any identifying characteristics other than the direction the rig was headed in, there wasn't much hope.

Just then, there didn't seem to be a whole hell of a lot of hope for much of anything.

Garrett felt a raw and confounding sadness, brief in duration but carving deep, and it had little or nothing to do with the senator's tragedy.

Below, the semi lumbered right, onto a state highway.

The driver could be headed anywhere—Arizona, Oklahoma, or even toward the Mexican border.

Reluctantly, Garrett changed course.

He was needed in Austin.

IT WAS STILL dark when he landed the plane. Troy, the senator's driver, waited on the tarmac, beside the usual Town Car.

The two men shook hands, and then Garrett sprinted around to the passenger side and slid into the front seat.

"Has the senator arrived yet?" he asked, dreading the answer, as Troy settled behind the wheel.

Troy nodded wearily. "He was holding on when I left the hospital, but as soon as they unhook all those machines—"

Garrett's voice was hoarse. "How's Nan?"

"Mrs. Cox is hanging in there."

"Have the kids been told?"

"I don't think so," Troy answered, with a shake of his head. "Mandy, now, she's been spilling her guts to the media. Telling them more than even *they* want to know, probably." With a thin attempt at a grin, he added, "What happened to your *face*, man?"

"I was kicked by a horse," Garrett lied.

Troy's eyes rounded, then rolled. "You are so full of shit," he said.

"I missed you, too," Garrett said, leaning to punch his friend in the shoulder. "How long's it been since we've crossed paths, old buddy? Three days? A week?"

Troy laughed, but there was a note of harsh grief in the sound. "Damn," he muttered. "This is bad, Garrett."

"Yeah," Garrett agreed, tilting his head back and closing his eyes.

"The state police came to the house to tell Mrs. Cox the news in person," Troy said. He lived in an apartment over Nan and Morgan's garage, so he'd be available whenever a driver was needed. Technically, he was on call 24/7, but he had a lot of downtime, too. "I heard a ruckus, so I got out of bed and dressed and scrambled downstairs to find out what was going on." Troy thrust out sigh. "He's not going to make it, Garrett."

After that, there wasn't much else to talk about.

They arrived at the hospital within a few minutes, and Garrett noticed several news vans in the parking lot.

He sighed inwardly.

"You might as well go on home and get whatever rest you can manage," Garrett told Troy quietly, bracing himself inwardly and pushing open the car door. He hadn't missed dealing with reporters during his brief hiatus on the ranch. "However things come down, tomorrow is bound to be a real mother."

Troy hesitated, then nodded. "You tell Mrs. Cox to call if she needs me."

Garrett promised to pass the word, got out of the car, squared his shoulders and headed for the hospital entrance.

As expected, reporters and cameramen were waiting in the lobby, and Mandy Chante, tragic in her black stretch ski pants and fluffy pink sweater, was holding court.

Garrett shook his head, skirted the scene and headed for the elevators.

"That's some shiner, handsome," purred Charlene Bishop, a freelancer who sold mainly to the tabloids, stepping directly into his path. He and Charlene had dated for a while, a few years back, nothing serious. Last he'd heard, she was married to a chiropractor and trying to get pregnant.

Garrett smiled, took the woman lightly by the shoulders and eased her aside. "Nice to see you again, Charlene," he said, moving on toward the elevators. "How's the husband?"

She kept pace, managed to slip into the elevator beside him, along with a guy wearing a backwards baseball cap and balancing a huge camera on one shoulder.

"Turn that thing on," Garrett warned him, "and I'll shove it up your—nose."

The guy grinned. "I've been threatened with a lot worse than that in my time," he retorted.

"You want worse?" Garrett asked. "I can give you *worse*."

"Testy," sniped Baseball Cap.

"Shut up, Leroy," Charlene said, elbowing the guy aside, shifting to stand toe-to-toe with Garrett, so her breasts pressed against his chest. "I need this story," she confided, looking up at him with enormous powder-blue eyes.

Garrett raised an eyebrow. "You didn't notice Mandy Chante in the lobby?" he asked. "You're slipping."

Charlene huffed in disgust. "All she's doing is blowing smoke up everybody's butt," she said, dismissing the other woman with a slight wave of one hand. "Look, freelancing is a tough racket. You know that." She stepped in close, so her breasts pressed into his chest, and wriggled slightly. "How about an exclusive, for old times' sake?"

Leroy crowed at that last part.

Garrett stepped back, irritated, but being careful not to let that show.

The elevator doors opened and he was the first one out.

Troy must have called ahead to let Nan know they'd arrived, because she appeared immediately, slipped her arm through Garrett's and rested her head against his upper arm for a moment.

Her silver hair was pulled back and secured with a barrette, and instead of her trademark designer suit, she wore baggy brown corduroy pants and a heavy beige sweater.

Leroy aimed the camera.

Garrett glared him into retreat.

And Charlene clicked alongside Garrett and Nan, the pointy heels of her shoes tap-tap-tapping on the corridor floor.

"Mrs. Cox," she said breathlessly, "is it true that the senator got a quickie divorce in Mexico and then turned right around and married Miss Chante? She—Miss Chante—says they were on their honeymoon when the accident happened—"

"Charlene," Garrett broke in.

She blinked up at him. "What?"

"Shut up."

"But—"

"Beat it, Charlene. I'll give you a statement later."

Charlene's plump pink lower lip wobbled. "You promise?"

"I promise," Garrett replied tightly.

A security guard was approaching, probably intending to eject Charlene and Leroy from the Intensive Care Unit.

"Where? When?" Charlene pressed, walking backward.

Garrett sighed, rattled off his cell number. "Call me in a couple of hours," he said. "I won't talk to anyone else first. You have my word."

Charlene scribbled down the number, rushed over in a last-minute burst of moxie and shoved a card at Garrett. "Here's my number," she said. "*You* call *me*."

Garrett nodded.

The security guard arrived, taking Charlene's elbow in one hand and the back of Leroy's T-shirt in the other and propelling them both into the elevator.

"Thank God you're here," Nan said wearily.

"How's Morgan?" Garrett asked.

"He died five minutes ago," Nan answered. "His...prospective bride wasn't with him at the time. She was too busy enjoying her fifteen minutes of fame downstairs, it would seem." Her gaze was faraway, and a faint smile, sadder than tears, tugged at the corner of her mouth. "*I* was with him, though. I held Morgan's hand and I told him I understood, and he should just go if he was ready—the children and I would be all right."

Garrett had to sit down. He found a chair over by the wall and dropped into it. "My God, Nan," he rasped out. "I'm sorry."

Nan's eyes swam with tears, but she managed a brave smile. "Me, too," she said, taking the chair beside Garrett's. "The children will be devastated, of course."

Garrett could only nod.

"He wouldn't have wanted to live," Nan went on quietly, resting her hands on her knees. Her spine was very straight, and she held her chin high. "He was much too badly hurt."

Garrett put his arm around the woman's shoulders.

She trembled, allowed herself to lean against him, though just for a moment. "We'll have to make some kind of statement soon," she said.

Garrett nodded again, at a loss for words.

Nan gave a teary smile and tilted her head to one side as she studied him.

"What?" Garrett asked.

"What happened to your eye?" Nan countered.

THE NEWS WAS all over the TV, all over the internet.

Senator Morgan Cox was dead.

His grieving mistress, Mandy Chante, was already angling for her own reality show.

Julie stared at the TV, a cup of Esperanza's coffee raised to her lips. They were in the ranch-house kitchen, Calvin still sleeping, Esperanza watching the morning news as she started breakfast.

Julie felt a jolt of emotion, all of it unidentifiable, when Garrett's head and shoulders filled the screen. His hair was rumpled, his right eye was blackened and nearly swollen shut, his clothes more suited to the barn or the range than national TV. On top of all that, he needed a shave.

Her heart turned over inside her.

I love you, she told him silently.

"Senator Cox passed away at 2:33 a.m.," he said, into a cluster of microphones. He looked weary and grief-stricken and Julie longed to put her arms around him, and hold him, and chase away all the reporters.

All the demons.

"Madre de Dios," Esperanza muttered, pausing to cross herself.

Julie continued to watch Garrett, willing him to be strong.

"Mommy?" Calvin stood in the doorway to the guest suite. He was still wearing his pajamas, his hair was mussed and his cheeks were too pink by at least three shades.

Plus, he rarely called her "Mommy" these days.

She'd been demoted to "Mom" sometime after his fourth birthday.

"I don't feel good," Calvin said. Then, to prove his point, he threw up.

Julie hurried to her son, and Esperanza switched off the TV set.

"He's burning up," Julie told Esperanza, resting the backs of her fingers against Calvin's forehead.

Esperanza rushed to fill a bucket and grab a cleaning rag. "Back to bed," she said. "There can be no going to school like this!"

Calvin vomited again.

"Oh, Calvin!" Julie cried, alarmed by the violence of his illness.

"Am I in trouble?" he asked desperately, blinking as he stared up at her.

"No," Julie said, gathering him to her, mess and all. *"No,* sweetie. Come on, let's get you into some clean pajamas and back in bed."

Calvin cried and then wailed.

Harry, ever sympathetic, whimpered his concern.

Julie swept her son up into her arms and carried him back to their bathroom. There, she quickly stripped him, sprayed him down in the bathtub and bundled him into fresh pajamas.

Calvin had quieted down by then, but Harry cried continuously, the poor thing. He seemed to think his little master was being punished for some horrible misdeed.

Julie had no more than tucked Calvin into bed when he threw up again, all over everything.

Because Audrey and Ava were still sick, and therefore in what amounted to quarantine, she'd planned to take the boy to town herself, drop him off for kindergarten before her first-period class, and bring him back to the high school until tryouts were over.

All that was clearly out of the question now.

While Esperanza changed Calvin, and the sheets and blankets on his bed, Julie showered and changed her own clothes, then made a quick call to Arthur Dulles. The principal wouldn't be happy, since the tasks of overseeing her classes, along with that day's phase of the tryouts for *Kiss Me Kate*, were sure to fall to him.

Julie was relieved to get her boss's voice mail, although she dutifully left her callback information.

Next, she called Calvin's pediatrician.

The office nurse told her to put him to bed, dose him with children's aspirin and bring him in if he got worse.

Discouraged, she got in touch with Paige next, describing Calvin's symptoms.

"I'm on my way," her sister, the RN, responded.

"What about your job?" Julie asked, worried.

"I'm between one and the other," Paige replied. "And this is *Calvin* we're talking about here."

Julie let out her breath, relieved and grateful. "Thanks," she murmured.

She sat with Calvin, who was fitful, until Paige arrived, looking a little frazzled, which was unlike her.

It took Julie a moment to realize that her sister must have encountered Austin when she entered the house.

Paige's expression transformed in a twinkling, though, as she focused her attention on Calvin. "Hey, little buddy," she greeted her nephew, "what's the deal?"

"I spewed," Calvin said miserably. *"Everywhere."*

"It happens," Paige answered matter-of-factly, tossing a wan grin in Julie's direction. "Hi, sis. How about getting me a cup of coffee? I didn't get a chance to grab my usual caffeine fix this morning."

Julie nodded, reluctant to leave Calvin even long enough to pour Paige's coffee, but she knew he couldn't have been in better hands.

When she reached the kitchen, Austin was there, leaning against a counter and sipping coffee from a mug while Esperanza tried to persuade him to sit down and have a good breakfast before he went off to spend the day "playing cowboy."

Disreputably handsome in his work clothes and scuffed boots, Austin hadn't shaved, and if he'd combed his hair at all, he'd used his fingers. He looked pale and deeply weary, Julie thought, and even in her agitation over Calvin, it gave her pause.

Of course there had been an encounter between him and Paige, she concluded, both intrigued and saddened.

He'd been just as rattled by it as Paige.

"You heard about the senator, I guess," Austin said, his voice rough as sandpaper, cocking his head toward the TV. "Garrett will be taking this hard."

Julie nodded. She got a mug and filled it with coffee for Paige. "It's awful."

"Esperanza says your boy is under the weather," Austin said, watching Julie. "Is there anything I can do? Drive to town to fetch a prescription at the drugstore or something?"

Julie smiled, touching Austin's arm to let him know she was grateful for the offer. "Thanks," she said. "Now that Paige is here, I think we'll be all right."

The change in his face was barely perceptible, and he looked away quickly, but Julie saw it and recognized it for what it was.

He still cared for Paige—and he didn't like it.

"I've got my cell phone," he said, glancing briefly at Esperanza before turning his gaze back to Julie. There was a sort of unfolding in the way he moved, getting ready to leave, spend a day outdoors, working hard. "The number's over there on the message board. Call if you need anything."

"I will," Julie promised.

Remembering her errand, she hurried off then, with Paige's already cooling coffee.

"Took you long enough," Paige said, dropping her stethoscope back into her big purse. She was still sitting on the edge of Calvin's bed, and Harry stood with his muzzle resting on the mattress, soulful eyes rolling slowly between Julie and her son.

Do something, the dog's expression seemed to say.

Calvin lay with a thermometer jutting out of his mouth.

He was flushed, and his hair was all spiky, and Julie thought if she loved the child any more than she already did, she'd burst with it.

She handed Paige the coffee.

Paige took a sip, her eyes skirting Julie's.

Julie sat down in the one chair in the room, knotted her hands together.

"So," she said.

"So," Paige agreed, looking down at her watch, then back at Calvin.

Julie waited.

Presently, Paige took the thermometer from Calvin's mouth and checked the numbers.

"One-o-one," she said, ruffling her nephew's hair gently and setting the thermometer aside. "No skydiving for you, bud. And I'm afraid running with the bulls and spacewalking are out of the question, too."

Calvin blinked. He wasn't wearing his glasses, so Paige and Julie were probably blurry. "What about school?" he asked, very seriously.

"No school, either," Paige said, smoothing his covers.

Calvin's lower lip jutted out slightly, and he folded his arms.

Harry made the leap and snuggled up next to him.

"It's my turn to be class monitor," Calvin protested. "The monitor gets to pass out papers and everything."

"Sorry about that," Paige answered, patting his little shoulder. "Try to get some shuteye, big guy. The more you sleep, the faster you're going to recover."

"Read me a story?" Calvin wheedled.

Julie handed over his favorite book, and Paige took it.

Calvin wriggled down into his pillows, pleased.

Within five minutes, he was asleep.

Paige closed the book and she and Julie crept out of Calvin's room, Julie shutting the door softly behind them.

"What do you think?" she asked, worried. "A hundred and one is a pretty high temp, isn't it?"

Paige smiled, perched herself on the arm of one of the sitting room chairs, folded her arms in much the same way Calvin had. "If it goes up, we'll worry. It's not unusual for a child to run a fever, Julie, and this one isn't all that high. And he was vaccinated against the more serious strains of influenza, wasn't he?"

Julie nodded. "Of course," she said. She watched her sister for a long moment, then sat down on the couch, facing her. "I guess you must have run straight into Austin when you got here, huh?" she asked, finally.

The smile faded and Paige looked away. "Yeah," she admitted. "He opened the back door when I knocked."

"I'm sorry," Julie said, very softly.

Paige shrugged. "Don't be," she replied, with a lightness she obviously didn't feel. Finally, her gaze connected with Julie's. "It's bound to happen, with Libby and Tate getting married and you—"

A silence fell.

"And me?" Julie prodded, a few moments later.

"Come on, Jules," Paige said, spreading her hands wide. "I know there's something going on between you and Garrett."

Julie admitted nothing. She just raised one eyebrow.

Paige grinned, though sparely. "You're glowing like you swallowed a strand of Christmas tree lights. Besides, I'm psychic as far as you and Libby are concerned." She leaned forward a little and spoke with quiet drama. "You can have no secrets from me."

Julie rolled her eyes in the direction of Calvin's room, indicating that Paige should be careful what she said.

"He's asleep," Paige said, referring to her nephew. "And, anyway, give him some credit. My man Calvin is a perceptive guy, even if he *is* only five years old. He's probably figured things out by now, and even if he hasn't, it would be better just to tell him that you and Garrett are dating."

"We're *not* dating," Julie whispered fiercely.

Paige widened her eyes in that same mocking way that had driven both Julie and Libby crazy when they were all younger.

"Oh, *right*," she scoffed.

Julie bit her lower lip, stuck for what to say next.

Paige giggled at her discomfort. "What is it with you?" she teased. "Of the three of us, you were always the boldest one. Why can't you admit that you and Garrett are—?" Her voice dropped to a whisper. *"Doing it?"*

"Paige!" Julie protested.

Paige shook her head, and her sleek dark hair gleamed in the thin light flowing in through the windows. It wasn't even October yet, but the weather was wintry.

"You're in love with him," Paige insisted.

Julie thought of Senator Cox, and the dreadful accident, and the look she'd seen in Garrett's eyes when he announced his mentor's death to a television audience.

Tears filled her eyes, spilled down her cheeks.

Paige left the arm of the chair to sit beside Julie on the couch and slip a sisterly arm around her.

"What, Jules?" she asked. "What is it?"

Julie sniffled. Straightened her spine. "I can't fall in love with Garrett McKettrick," she said. "I *won't* fall in love with him."

Paige's voice was gentle. "Why not?"

"Because," Julie answered, groping a little, finding her feelings hard to put into words, "it would hurt too much to fall back out again."

CHAPTER SEVENTEEN

A DEATH IS a complicated thing, and the details took a couple of hours to manage.

Nan's sister and brother-in-law arrived at the hospital within minutes of being summoned and squired her home, where she needed to be. Although the ordeal was just beginning, Nan looked worn through, almost transparent, like the fabric of an old shirt.

Garrett hoped the family would step up, surround her, hold her and the children up until the shock waves stopped coming.

He made calls to various high-level officials, including the president of the United States. He set up a press conference for two o'clock that afternoon, but gave Charlene Bishop the promised lead in the race to break the story first.

Finally, he arranged for Senator Cox's body to be removed to a local funeral home and took a cab to his downtown condo. Overlooking Town Lake and the Congress Avenue Bridge, probably most noted for its periodic eruption of flying bats numbering in the hundreds, the space was large and airy and sparely furnished.

Standing just inside the front door, Garrett took a moment to reorient himself to a place that should have seemed a lot more familiar, given that he'd owned it since he graduated from law school. But he might have lived there in another incarnation, as an entirely different man, for all the connection he felt to those rooms.

He wandered through to the master bedroom, rifled through his closet, chose a suit from his collection and tossed it onto the bed. In the adjoining bathroom, he showered and shaved, but he couldn't quite bring himself to put on the fancy duds, not yet, anyway.

Garrett still had almost two hours before the press conference, so he dressed in jeans and a black T-shirt and boots. He was standing in front of his refrigerator, studying the contents and feeling totally uninspired, when his doorbell chimed.

Custom-designed, the gizmo tripped through the first few lines of Johnny Cash's "Ring of Fire."

Frowning, Garrett left the fridge—there was nothing in there he felt brave enough to eat anyhow—crossed the kitchen and entryway and pulled open the door, braced to face down a reporter, if not a pack of them. Austin wasn't a big city; just about everybody in the news business knew where to find him.

But Tate and Austin stood in the corridor, looking too big for the space, with their wide shoulders and their cowboy hats.

"We thought you might need a little moral support," Tate announced to Garrett, pushing past him.

Austin followed, took off his hat and sailed it onto the surface of the foyer table. "Whether you want us or not," he added, in a drawl, "here we are."

Garrett shoved a hand through his hair, momentarily stuck for something to say. Several possibilities came to mind, but they were all too sappy.

He shut the door.

Tate looked him over as he passed, heading for the living room. "You clean up pretty well," he observed.

Austin got there ahead of them both.

"Thanks," Garrett said, belatedly.

"You even shaved," Austin remarked, making himself comfortable by dropping into the best seat in the condo, a leather wingback chair custom-tooled with the name McKettrick and the Silver Spur brand. "I'm impressed."

Tate set his hat aside and wandered into the kitchen. His question echoed back to Garrett, who was still in the living room. "You got anything to eat in this place?"

"Nothing that might not have medicinal properties," Garrett replied. The situation was still bad, that hadn't changed, but the rest of the day would be a little easier, now that his brothers were there.

Austin took his phone from the pocket of his denim jacket and tapped at the screen a few times with one index finger. "Hey, Pedro," he said affably, after a moment or two, a grin spreading across his face. "It's me, Austin McKettrick—"

While Austin placed an order for Mexican food, Tate meandered back from the kitchen. Looking around, he shook his head.

"Not very homey," he said.

Garrett sighed. "It doesn't have to be 'homey,'" he countered. "It's just a place to shower and sleep when I'm in town."

"Get you," Tate said, with a note of good-tempered mockery. "Keeping a fancy place like this just for a place to crash when you're in this part of the country. You got another one just like it in Washington, D.C.?"

"Extra jalapeños," Austin told Pedro. "Sure, I'd appreciate that," he told the restaurant owner, who happened to be an old friend of the family. "Send the grub on around the corner to Garrett's place when it's ready." A pause. Austin's blue gaze flicked to Garrett, and some of the shine went off him. "Yeah. Yeah, it's a pity about the senator. Yeah. I'll pass the word, Pedro. Thanks."

"I stay in residence hotels when we're in Washington," Garrett snapped, in answer to Tate's question. Too stressed to sit, he paced instead.

"Just like regular folks," Tate joked.

Garrett plunked down on the arm of yet another chair, assessing his brothers. "What do *you* know about 'regular folks'?" he jibed. "Until you took up with Libby and moved into the Ruiz place, you were living pretty high on the hog yourself, over at the main house."

Tate grinned, but his eyes remained solemn.

Except for a slight shrug of his shoulders, he gave no reply.

Austin, evidently bored with the conversation, had taken to scrolling through stuff on the screen of his phone, frowning as though the future of the free world depended on whatever was behind all those colorful icons.

"About that call I woke you up with last night," Garrett began, folding his arms.

"Denzel called me this morning," Tate said, *Denzel* being his nickname for his good friend, Chief Brent Brogan. His tone was flat and a little terse. "Why didn't you tell me you were buzzing rustlers in your plane while we were talking?"

"I figured you'd do something stupid if I did," Garrett replied.

Tate arched one dark eyebrow. "Like...?"

"Like going after them and getting yourself shot."

A muscle bunched in Tate's jaw. "So you just figured I didn't need to know somebody was on the Silver Spur, looting our herd?"

"I figured you didn't need to know it right *then*," Garrett said, grinning. "Thanks to Brogan, you know it now, and I'll bet you've already checked out the scene of the crime. Did you find anything?"

"Tracks," Tate answered flatly. "No more dead cattle, so that's a plus."

"Bates figures the loss at around fifty head this time," Austin remarked, reluctantly dropping the phone back into his jacket pocket. "If that's a 'plus,' then I'd say we're pretty damn hard up for good news around our outfit."

Fifty head of cattle represented a serious chunk of change, but it wasn't the loss of money that galled Garrett. It was the goddamn, brass-balls *effrontery* of cutting a man's fences, trespassing on his rangeland, thieving from his herd.

He swore and looked away. He was developing a headache, and there was still the press conference to get through. Wearing a suit.

The food arrived, delivered by one of Pedro's many teenage daughters, nieces or cousins, the majority of whom seemed to be named Maria.

Austin footed the bill and flashed a grin at the girl as he tipped her.

The poor kid would probably still be blushing come the middle of next week. She was so busy looking back at Austin on her way out the door that she nearly crashed into a wall a couple of times before finally clearing the threshold.

Tate disappeared into the kitchen and came back carrying three plates with silverware piled on top. He'd jammed a roll of paper towels under one arm, to serve as napkins.

"It's good to know he's still got it," Tate quipped, inclining his head toward Austin, who was just closing the door behind Maria, but looking at Garrett.

Garrett grinned. "You were worried that he didn't?"

In the next few minutes, they fell to eating, the three of them gathered around Garrett's table. It was sort of like the old days on the ranch, when the whole family had eaten together almost every night.

Garrett's distracted mind wandered—he thought about the upcoming press conference, the senator's funeral, soon to be held, the inevitable transfer of power—so he snagged on a remark Austin made like a leaf spinning downstream and catching behind a rock.

"—so I open the door and Paige Remington is standing there, big as life, come to take care of Julie's boy—"

Garrett made his reentry into the here-and-now with a jolt. "What's wrong with Calvin?"

"Flu, I guess," Austin said, scraping a cheesy pile of Pedro's unparalleled nachos onto his plate. "According to Esperanza, the poor little guy was heaving like a drunken sailor at the end of a three-day shore leave."

Tate pretended to wince, but he went right on shoveling in the ole enchiladas. "Audrey and Ava are just getting over that stuff," he said. "It's a sumbitch while it's going on, but it doesn't last long."

Garrett frowned, setting down his fork. "How's Julie?" he asked, and by the time he realized what he'd revealed by raising the question, it was too late.

Austin widened his eyes at Garrett, indulged in a long, slow grin before troubling himself to make a reply. "She looked all right to me," he said, letting the words roll over that glib tongue of his like so much butter and honey. "*Better* than all right," he finally clarified.

By then, Garrett was glaring at him. "Paige showed up, huh?" he said, just to get under Austin's hide.

And it worked.

The hinges of Austin's jaws got stuck, or so it appeared, and his eyes narrowed. He looked like he was about to push back his chair, jump to his feet and challenge Garrett to a gunfight, like some old-time gambler in a saloon.

So much for the twinkle and the boyish charm.

"Hey." Tate waved a hand between them. "Do you think maybe you two could get through lunch without arguing?"

Garrett had largely forgotten about his shiner, but now, for no reason he could rightly make sense of, it reasserted itself, aching like hell, and in perfect rhythm with the beat of his heart.

Austin, who had the instincts of a shark scenting blood in the water, relaxed, grinning again. "I'll read a statement for you at the press conference," he offered, "if you don't want the whole state of Texas speculating as to who might have punched your lights out for you in the recent past."

"*Nobody* punched my lights out," Garrett said, through his teeth.

Austin flexed the fingers of his right hand, watching them move as though there were something downright fascinating about it. He had a pretty good scrape abrading his knuckles, Garrett noticed.

So Austin had been the one to hit him. It freaking figured.

"If it's any comfort," Austin said to Garrett, "I was aiming to deck Tate, not you."

"It isn't," Garrett said.

Tate and Austin both chuckled.

Like it was funny or something.

Garrett scowled. "If you'd like a shiner to match mine, little brother," he told Austin, "I can arrange it."

"If we're going to argue," Tate broke in, very quietly, but with the authority that came with being the eldest of the three, even if it was only by a year, "let's argue over something worthwhile. Like whether you two plan on ranching or playing at rodeo and politics for the rest of your lives, like a couple of trust-fund babies."

Silence.

Garrett pushed his plate away. He was riled, but Julie was tugging at the edge of his mind, too. Was she all right? Was Calvin?

Watching Tate now, Austin flushed. "I've still got things to do," he said, his voice low and hard-edged. "People to see. Bulls to ride."

Tate sighed. "So I guess that's an answer, even if it isn't what I was hoping to hear. You're not ready to settle down and help run the Silver Spur."

"I'll hire somebody to do my share," Austin said.

"Don't bother," Tate replied. "No stranger is going to give two hoots and a holler about the Silver Spur." He turned his gaze to Garrett, made him feel pinned where he was, like somebody's dusty science project, a dead bug, maybe, tacked to a display board. "Might be, it's time to call it good, go our separate ways. Hell, both of you have been doing that since Mom and Dad were killed anyhow. Might as well make it official and sell out."

Austin went pale behind his tan. "I'm not selling my third of the ranch," he said.

"Fine," Tate retorted. "Maybe you'd like to buy *me* out, then. The old Arnette farm is up for sale—I could pick it up for a song. Bulldoze that shack of a house and raze the barn, then rebuild. I might even raise some crops."

If they hadn't gone over this ground earlier, he and Tate, Garrett would have thought Tate was just jerking Austin's chain. Since they had, he was pretty sure Number One Brother was serious.

Even if Austin bought Tate's share of the ranch and hired a whole crew of management types to run it, it wouldn't be the same.

"Why the urgency, Tate?" Garrett asked his older brother, genuinely curious as well as quietly alarmed. Who would he be without that ranch? Who would *any* of them be? "The Silver Spur has been in this family since Clay McKettrick bought the original parcel of land a hundred years ago. Now, all of a sudden, you want everything decided and the property lines redrawn before when? Yesterday?"

"What happened to all that talk about how your daughters needed to grow up on the ranch, because they're McKettricks?" Austin threw in. He'd been pale before, now he was flushed.

"Things change," Tate said gravely. "People change."

"And you expect us to believe that *you've* changed that much?" Austin retorted, coldly furious. "Goddamn, if this is what love does to a man, then I hope I die a bachelor!"

Garrett rubbed his face with both hands, realized his beard was already starting to come in again—and it hadn't been more than an hour since he'd shaved. The fatigue hit him between one moment and the next with the impact of a speeding truck.

Back in the day, Tate's temper would have flared up like an oil well set aflame right about then, but loving Libby had mellowed him.

"We can talk about this some other time," he said wearily. He met Garrett's gaze. "I'm sorry," he added. "Austin and I came here to help you in any way we could, and here we are squabbling instead."

Austin let out his breath. Reached over to squeeze Garrett's shoulder without looking at him. "Much as I hate to admit it," he muttered. "Tate's right."

The spread of Mexican food, delicious as it was, had lost its appeal.

By tacit agreement, the meal was over.

Austin and Tate cleared away the debris, while Garrett went into his room and exchanged the comfortable clothes he'd been wearing for the dark suit he'd left on the bed earlier.

Standing in front of the mirror on the inside of the closet door, he straightened his appropriately sedate tie, shrugged his shoulders to make the jacket sit right across his back.

Except for the black eye, he thought, with a rueful shot at a smile that went wide of the mark, he looked dignified enough to be a dead senator's spokesman.

He'd have been a lot more comfortable in jeans and boots, though.

WHEN JULIE HURRIED into her classroom the next morning, moments before the bell would bring a tsunami of first-period English students flooding in, Rachel was already at her desk in the second row.

"I was worried," she told Julie. "When you didn't come to school yesterday, I mean."

Julie felt a pang, even as she managed a harried smile. A glance at the wall clock told her she had roughly thirty seconds before the wave of adolescent humanity would make landfall. "My son didn't feel well," she said. "I had to stay home and care for him."

"Is he better?" Rachel asked.

"Yes," Julie answered, with a sigh of relief. Calvin wouldn't be able to attend kindergarten for the rest of the week, but he'd been well enough that morning to ride into town with Julie. He and Harry were spending the day at Paige's apartment, where they would surely be fed and tended, fussed over and spoiled within an inch of their lives.

Mindful of just how much this child had been through in her young life, Julie trained her full attention on the girl. "How about you, Rachel? How are you doing?"

Rachel shrugged, looked away. "Well enough," she said.

The bell rang.

The doors banged open and students streamed in.

The day had begun in earnest, and Julie didn't get another chance to speak to Rachel until after the last class of the day. Even then, the interlude was brief, because Julie had tryouts to oversee in the auditorium, and Rachel was in a hurry to get to her job at the bowling alley.

"If you need to talk about the fire or anything," Julie said, standing next to Rachel's locker while the girl shoved books onto the overhead shelf and reached for the lightweight jacket hanging on a hook, "I'll listen."

Rachel's spine straightened, and something flickered in her eyes, a sort of shutting-down. "Right," she said, in a that's-what-they-all-say tone.

Kids streamed past them.

"Rachel," Julie said, catching hold of the girl's arm when she would have turned away, "I mean it. We can talk, anytime."

"Really?" Rachel asked, with the first note of sarcasm Julie had ever heard from her. Considering that the girl was a teenager, that was saying something. "Like you were going to talk to my dad, you mean? About how maybe he could set aside his stupid masculine pride for once and let people give us stuff my brothers and I have been doing without our whole lives?"

Julie took a moment before answering. "Rachel," she said at last, kindly but firmly, "I want to help, I truly do, but I've been especially busy lately and, well, the last time your dad and I talked, he wasn't exactly receptive."

All the bluster seemed to go out of Rachel then; she literally deflated. "I know," she said. "It's just that I can't think of anybody else to ask, and Dad's talking about how he's ashamed to show his face in public, what with folks bringing us clothes and food and even a real nice trailer to live in, like he can't take care of his own family—and he's making noises about moving on again, too—"

"I'll try again," Julie broke in gently, laying a hand on the girl's shoulder. "I promise."

"I don't know what we'll do if he won't listen to you," Rachel fretted.

With that, she nodded a farewell, put on her jacket and hurried away.

As Julie had learned that morning, Mr. Dulles had simply canceled the tryouts the night before, instead of putting Mrs. Chambers in charge in Julie's absence or taking over the task himself. That meant, of course, that they'd made no progress at all.

She listened dutifully to every song.

She paid earnest attention to every reading.

And the evening seemed endless.

When the first round of tryouts was finally over, some two hours after they'd begun, Julie was tired and hungry, and she still needed to pick Calvin up at Paige's apartment.

Ron Strivens was waiting outside the auditorium, with Rachel and the boys, when she paused to lock up. Mrs. Chambers stayed close to Julie's elbow, smiling nervously at the ragged little family.

Julie smiled at them, too.

"My girl said you wanted to talk to me," Strivens said to Julie, pushing away from the lightpost he'd been leaning against to stand straight. "Here I am, Ms. Remington. I'm listening."

"Shall I stay?" Verna Chambers asked, hesitating as she pulled her car keys from her handbag.

"No, no," Julie said, patting her friend's arm. "It's all right."

Reluctantly, Verna nodded a good-night to all concerned and headed for her car.

"Would you like to go in?" Julie asked the Strivenses. "We could all sit down—"

"Right here's good," Strivens said, indicating a nearby bench. He turned to his daughter. "Rachel, you take the boys and wait in the truck so your teacher and I can talk."

Rachel did as she was told, though she dragged her feet a little, pulling her younger brothers by the hand.

Julie tried not to sigh as she took a seat on the bench in front of the auditorium. "I know things are very hard right now, for all of you—"

Rachel's father sank down beside her. He seemed weary in every muscle and bone, much older than his years. "Yeah, it's been tough," he said, almost shyly, "without Miranda—that was my wife and the kids' mother—but we've managed."

Julie nodded, full of sympathy, but frustrated, too. "Rachel says you're thinking of leaving Blue River. Where would you go?"

Strivens shrugged. Shook his head.

"People mean well," Julie went on, when he didn't answer aloud. "The stuff they've donated, the food, the clothes—it's not charity in their view, Mr. Strivens. It's just their way of helping you get back on your feet after the fire—like you might do for them if the situation was reversed."

Strivens swallowed visibly, gazing out into the dark parking lot. His shoulders stooped and his hands dangled between the patched knees of his pants. "Folks say it's better to give than to receive," he reflected slowly, without looking at Julie, "and they must be right, though I couldn't say for sure. All my life, I've been on the receiving end." He paused to sigh. "All I want is to do right by my kids, believe it or not."

"I believe you," Julie said. And she did. Being a single parent herself, she knew how rough life could be at times, and how frightening, even with Libby and Paige helping out in every possible way. "It means so much to Rachel to stay in Blue River and graduate," she said. "And your boys—they've probably settled in pretty well, too, haven't they?"

Strivens smiled, but he still didn't look directly at Julie. "So what you're saying is, I ought to swallow my cussed pride?"

"That's *not* what I meant at all," Julie lied.

He laughed. Met her gaze. "Sure it is," he said. "But that's all right. I was thinking—those McKettricks got so much land and money, they can donate a fine single-wide for the use of the needy, maybe they'd have a job for a hardworkin' man, too."

"Maybe," Julie agreed, smiling.

"Reckon we both ought to be going," Strivens said, rising.

Julie did the same.

The man walked her to her car, waited politely until she was inside, with the engine running and the doors locked. Then he waved one hand and sprinted toward his old truck, where his children were waiting.

A few minutes later, Julie knocked on the door of Paige's apartment. Across the street, the cottage looked lonely and dark.

Paige greeted her with a bright smile, and Calvin, ensconced on the sofa in his pajamas, looked almost like his usual self. Apparently, his illness was only the twenty-four-hour stomach kind of thing.

Tears of love and relief and who knew what else filled Julie's eyes.

"You're staying for supper," Paige said, pulling her inside and shutting the door. "And that's all there is to it. No arguments, no excuses."

Paige's place was small, but it was part of a Victorian jewel of a house converted into apartments decades before, and it had charm aplenty—tall mullioned windows with built-in seats, wood floors and a working brick fireplace, among other things. Julie particularly envied the huge claw-foot tub in the bathroom.

Julie sniffled and wiped at her eyes with the back of one hand, hoping Calvin hadn't noticed that she was crying.

No such luck.

Even when he was sick, Calvin didn't miss much.

"What's the matter, Mom?" he asked, with great concern, when she bent to hug him and rest her chin on top of his head for a moment.

"It's nothing," she said. "I just had kind of a long day, that's all."

Calvin took her hand and tugged, and Julie dropped to sit close to him on the sofa. Harry, curled at his feet, eyed her balefully but didn't stir. "Guess what?" the little boy whispered.

Julie smiled. "What?" she whispered back.

"I drank a supersize ginger ale today—every last drop!"

"Did not," Julie teased.

"Did, too," Calvin insisted. "Aunt Paige bundled me up and put me in her car and we went to the drive-through. Harry went with us. He had part of a cheeseburger."

"Wow," Julie said, exchanging glances with Paige.

Paige, clad in jeans and a long-sleeved sweatshirt, made a face at Julie and went into the kitchenette, where she began ladling something savory-smelling into a bowl.

"Beef stew," she said, returning to set the food on the table in the small dining area. "Have some."

"Don't mind if I do," Julie answered. She washed her hands in Paige's spotless bathroom, admiring the magnificent bathtub, then joined her sister at the table.

The stew was delicious, and she felt better after the first bite.

"I didn't throw up even *once* today," Calvin called from the sofa.

Julie chuckled and shook her head, while Paige, seated across from her, smiled over the rim of her teacup.

"Calvin," Julie said, "I'm eating."

"Oops," Calvin replied. "Sorry. I guess you're not supposed to talk about throw-up when people are trying to eat."

"Guess not," Paige sang out. Her dark eyes were gentle as she watched Julie raise and lower her spoon. "You're working too hard," she added, very quietly, for Julie's ears alone.

"Can you suggest an alternative?" Julie asked.

There were so many things she wasn't letting herself think about. Like how soon she needed to have her and Calvin's belongings out of the cottage, so the new owners could move in, for instance.

Like Garrett McKettrick, and how she'd let herself get in deep with him, knowing better all the while.

"You have your share of the money Marva gave us," Paige said, referring to the tidy sum their mother had divided between the three of them before leaving Blue River a few months before. "Why don't you take some time off from teaching, reconsider your options?"

"Options?" Julie whispered back. Calvin was off the couch, gathering his stuff to go home.

Paige propped her forearms on the table's edge and leaned in a little. "Garrett?" she mouthed.

Julie sighed. "Get real," she said. "He's not an option."

"Whatever you say, sis." Paige smiled. "He looked good on TV this afternoon. Nasty shiner, though."

Julie had seen the press conference, along with the entire student body of Blue River High, since Mr. Dulles had called a special assembly for the purpose. Flags all over the state were flying at half mast, too.

Her heart pinched, remembering. Although disillusioned by Senator Cox's recent fall from grace, as he surely was, Garrett had spoken with quiet dignity of his political mentor's years of dedicated service to the people of Texas.

Time tripped back a few notches.

I'll be leaving in a few days, she heard Garrett say. She'd been holding the ice bag to his eye, and he'd pulled her onto his lap...

"He won't be sticking around long," she said aloud, without thinking first.

"Garrett is going someplace?" Calvin demanded, appearing at her elbow, with his jacket on over his pajamas and his glasses crooked. "Where?"

Julie smiled and moved to straighten Calvin's glasses, but he wouldn't let her fuss. He stepped back out of her reach and blurted out, "Garrett can't go away. He promised he'd teach me how to ride!"

"Calvin—"

"He can't go!" Calvin almost shrieked.

Paige didn't say anything, but her eyes were sad as she looked at her nephew.

"Your dad is coming back for a visit this weekend," Julie reminded the boy calmly. "And you're going to meet your grandparents. Won't that be nice?"

Calvin began to wheeze, and then to gasp.

Before Julie could respond at all, Paige had his inhaler out of his backpack and up to his mouth. The familiar puffing sound the device made seemed to echo through the room like a series of small explosions.

"Easy," Paige said, one hand resting on Calvin's small back as he struggled to breathe. "Take it real easy, big guy. You're going to be all right."

Slowly, the little boy's breath began to even out. As soon as he'd had his medicine, Julie hoisted him onto her lap and held him, murmuring, "Shhh," and then, "Shhh" again.

"Garrett can't go away," he whimpered. "It isn't fair if he goes away."

"Hush, now," Julie said, meeting Paige's gaze. She was still standing nearby, still holding the inhaler. "We can talk about this when you're feeling better."

Calvin began to cry then. Since he rarely wept, the sound was especially heartbreaking to hear.

Paige's eyes glistened.

Julie's own vision was a little blurred.

She held Calvin until he began to settle down. Even when the tears had subsided, though, tremors went through his small body, and Julie was afraid he'd have another asthma attack—a worse one, perhaps—one that wouldn't stop when he used his inhaler.

"I want to go back to the ranch," he said, his voice muffled. "I want to see Garrett."

"Honey," Julie told her son quietly, "Garrett might not be on the ranch. He had to go to Austin, remember? To hold the press conference you and Aunt Paige watched on TV this afternoon? I'm sure he has a lot of things to do there—"

Calvin drew back, looked up at Julie. "Don't you want to see Garrett, too?" he asked, with his heart in his eyes. And in his voice.

"Sure, I do," Julie answered, very gently. "It's just that I'm pretty sure he's working, that's all."

Calvin studied her for a long time.

"Maybe you should both spend the night here," Paige said. "It's late and Calvin isn't feeling well. I'll sleep right here on the couch, and you two can share my bed."

It seemed an odd conversation to be having, when the cottage, Julie and Calvin's home for so long, was just across the road.

But the cottage wasn't home anymore.

She and Calvin didn't *have* a home.

Paige was waiting for an answer, so Julie finally shook her head. "You've done enough," she told her sister, giving her a hug. "We're not throwing you out of your bed."

Twenty minutes later, Julie, Calvin and the dog stepped into the warmth and brightness of the ranch-house kitchen, and Julie's drooping spirits were instantly lifted.

CHAPTER EIGHTEEN

GARRETT LAUGHED AND caught Calvin easily when he ran across the big room and launched himself into the man's arms.

Julie's heart stumbled at the sight.

"I saw you on TV!" Calvin shouted exuberantly. "Aunt Paige said you looked good even with a shiner!"

Garrett, wearing jeans, a long-sleeved black pullover shirt and boots, laughed again and stood the boy on the bench that ran along one side of the long kitchen table, so they were eye to eye.

"Is that right?" he asked, finally. He slanted a mischievous glance at Julie. "Your aunt Paige said that?"

Calvin nodded. Then he took a closer look at the shiner in question and frowned. "It's turning green and yellow," he said.

"They do that," Garrett explained easily. "I'll be good as new in a few days."

"That's better, then," Calvin decided, clearly relieved.

Garrett had been resting a hand on either side of the boy's waist, so he wouldn't fall off the bench. Now he raised one to ruffle Calvin's decidedly messy hair. "I heard you were under the weather, cowboy," he said. Over Calvin's head, Garrett fixed that McKettrick-blue gaze on Julie and didn't look away for a long moment. When he spoke to Calvin again, his voice was gruff with masculine concern. "You feeling better now?"

"I *was* feeling better," Calvin replied, "until Mom told me you were going away and you probably wouldn't even *be* here when we got back from town tonight." The child turned his head, gave Julie a triumphant I-told-you-so look before focusing all his attention on Garrett again. "I stayed with my aunt Paige *all day* because I had a fever and I kept *barfing*—"

"Calvin," Julie interrupted. "That will be enough detail, thank you."

Calvin rolled his eyes, and Garrett chuckled.

"I had to use my inhaler, too," Calvin threw in.

Garrett's expression was fond as he looked at Calvin, but there was a certain respect in it, too. "You'll be all right, little pardner," he said, without a speck of condescension. Except for the "little pardner" part, he might have been talking to a grown man. "Sturdy fella like you? 'Course you will."

Calvin all but blossomed under Garrett's quiet certainty that he was All Right. "Sure, I will," the child agreed manfully.

Now that Calvin's worth as a human being had been declared, for all time and eternity, the subject took a new turn.

Julie, standing there in the kitchen, still wearing her coat and holding her purse, had to do some emotional scrambling to catch up.

"Esperanza's in Blue River, playing bingo," Garrett told his pint-size sidekick. "But she cooked before she left, so there's corned beef and cabbage in the Crock-Pot upstairs in my kitchen." He grinned at Calvin before lifting him down off the bench to stand on the floor again.

"We've eaten," Julie said, still dazed. Her remark seemed incredibly mundane, considering the thing she had just realized.

She didn't just *like* Garrett McKettrick.

She didn't just enjoy having sex with him.

She was deeply, profoundly, hopelessly and permanently *in love with him.*

Furthermore, she thought, even more shaken than before, loving Garrett was nothing new. She'd probably fallen for him a long time ago, as far back as high school even. Because they were so different—Garrett the popular rich kid, the high school rodeo star, Julie the drama queen/rebel—she'd repressed the attraction, kept it buried.

That had been so much easier when Garrett was someone she

saw around town occasionally, or at weddings and funerals and other events where the entire community tended to gather.

Living under the same roof, it hadn't taken long to find him irresistible.

A few days.

Calvin gave her a look that was part reproof and part loving tolerance. "Mom?" he said. "Earth to Mom. Come in, please."

Calvin was into retro-TV, so *that* line must have come from *Lost in Space* or *Star Trek*. Julie chuckled, got busy taking off her coat, putting it away, along with her purse and tote bag.

In the guest-suite bathroom, she splashed her face with cool water. Since the small amount of mascara she'd applied that morning had long since worn off, it didn't loop under her eyes, raccoon-style.

Julie straightened, dried her face with a hand towel and remained in front of the sink, squinting into the mirror above it.

Now *what are we going to do, Smarty-pants?* she asked herself silently.

When there was no answer immediately forthcoming, Julie marched herself back to the kitchen. She would help Calvin wash up, tuck him into bed for the night and—and what?

Lie in her bed and stare at the ceiling for hours, probably.

The prospect was dismal, especially after the day she'd put in.

"Maybe you could just keep Austin and me company while *we* eat," Garrett was saying as she rejoined him and Calvin and Harry.

Julie glanced at her watch. Started to decline the invitation.

Spending time in close proximity to Garrett McKettrick, however appealing the idea might be, would only make bad matters worse. That long-ago Julie, the one with the white lipstick and the black clothes, hadn't been wrong about *everything*, after all.

She and Garrett not only hadn't traveled in the same circles back then, they hadn't occupied the same *universe*.

They were older now, and undeniably, they were sexually compatible.

But she and *Gordon* had been, too, though not quite to the same soul-shattering degree.

Still.

Seeing a pattern here, Remington? taunted the voice in her head.

You're two-for-two—you and Gordon wanted different things, and so do you and Garrett, and you might as well face it.

Cut your losses and run.

Garrett was watching her a little too perceptively. "Please?" he said.

"Please?" Calvin echoed.

It took Julie a moment to recall what they were talking about, her son and the man she wished had been his father.

Oh, yes. Garrett wanted them to come upstairs, sit with him and Austin while they ate their supper.

Julie might have been able to refuse Garrett, out of principle and because she needed to draw up lesson plans for the next day and go over her notes from the *Kiss Me Kate* tryouts, but she didn't have the heart to quash the hope shining in Calvin's little face.

"All right," she conceded, "but we can't stay very long."

Calvin punched the air with one fist and whooped, *"Yes!"*

Harry barked, doing a three-legged spin, caught in a backwash of boy-joy, and in spite of everything, Julie laughed.

It was Garrett who carried Calvin up the stairs to his second-floor apartment. Austin showed up just in time to lug Harry.

Julie followed, smiling to herself. Feeling less exhausted, less confused.

Wiser, but a whole lot sadder, too.

"Tough day?" Garrett asked, in his kitchen, when Julie repeated that she'd already eaten at Paige's, and Calvin was okay, too.

He lifted the lid off Esperanza's Crock-Pot and the savory aroma of corned beef and cabbage filled the room.

Calvin and Harry were in the living room, with Austin, with the TV blaring and the fireplace crackling cheerily away in welcome.

"Yes," Julie said. "I did have a tough day, as a matter of fact. But it wasn't nearly as tough as yours, I'll bet."

He gave a crooked grin, carried a plate to the table. "I wish you could stay," he said, very quietly.

Julie sighed and looked away. She wanted the same thing, but it wasn't possible, with Calvin not only at home, but recovering from his illness. And it also wouldn't be smart.

"So what happens now?" she finally asked Garrett, barely resisting the urge to lay a hand on his arm.

She'd asked herself that same question earlier, and she was still waiting for the answer. Maybe Garrett had one.

He didn't.

Garrett looked down at the plate of food in front of him, motionless for the moment. "The governor and some of the state legislators have already been in touch, according to Nan. It looks as though she'll be appointed to finish out her husband's term in the U.S. Senate. She's always worked closely with Morgan—well, until recently, anyway—so she knows the issues inside and out."

Julie nodded. There it was, the handwriting on the wall. "And she'll need your help and advice, of course."

"At first," Garrett said, avoiding her eyes. He wouldn't meet her gaze.

"'At first'?" Julie echoed, surprised.

Inwardly, she braked hard when hope sprang up in front of her like a deer on a dark and icy road.

"Something's happening between you and me," Garrett said quietly. "I'd like to find out what."

Julie thought about Calvin, decided he wasn't listening, because he and Austin were laughing about something they'd seen on TV, and even Harry contributed a few barks of comment.

"Maybe we should just agree that it's been fun and part ways," Julie heard herself say. *Maybe?* jibed the voice in her head.

He set down his fork. Watched her for a long moment before replying. "Why do you say that?"

"Because we're different," Julie said. "You're a McKettrick," she went on, with a slight smile of self-deprecation, "and *I'm* a high school English teacher with a child to raise."

Garrett arched an eyebrow. Dear God, he was good-looking, Julie thought, even with a black-and-purple-and-green eye, streaked with yellow. "All of which means?" he asked, his voice gruff.

"We don't have a whole lot in common," Julie said slowly, and with emphasis.

Garrett grinned at that. "Sometimes that's good," he said. "And there's one thing we *do* have in common."

Julie blushed, looked away.

"Sex," Garrett whispered, close to her ear. His breath was a warm, tingling rush against her skin. "We both like sex."

"Everybody likes sex," Julie said.

Garrett chortled at that. "You *are* naive," he said.

Julie leaned in close. "I'll bet *you've* never had a complaint," she challenged.

This time, Garrett laughed outright. "Thanks for the vote of confidence," he said. "And I have to ask this. Have *you* ever had a complaint?"

Julie blushed. Hard.

"Well, *no,*" she said. "But—"

In the living room, Austin and Calvin hooted in unison. Whatever was playing on TV, they were enjoying it to the max.

Garrett chuckled, but his eyes were solemn. Searching hers, probing deep.

Julie felt as though her very soul had been laid bare to the man.

"There are some things I have to do," he said, after a long time. "I'll be gone for a week, maybe two. Will you be here, Julie—on the Silver Spur—when I get back?"

"Wh-what are you really saying?" she asked.

"That there's something going on between us," Garrett reiterated quietly. "And I need to know what it is before I make any major decisions."

Julie opened her mouth, closed it again.

She had never been at such a loss for words.

It simply wasn't like her.

Garrett raised himself far enough out of his chair to lean over and kiss her lightly on the mouth.

He tasted of Esperanza's delicious cooking.

"Will you wait for me?" he asked, drawing back just a fraction of an inch.

Everything inside Julie was responding to his mouth, to the need for another kiss, for a lot *more* than another kiss. Even Smartypants didn't have anything to say.

"Wait for you? I don't understand."

Garrett grinned and *damn* it was sexy. Definitely an unfair advantage. "I have some things to do in Austin and in Washington," he answered. "Loose ends to tie up. When I get back here, the first thing I'm going to do is take you to bed. The second thing is—well—I'll probably take you to bed all over again. Assuming we ever get *out* of bed in the first place."

"So," Julie said, in a whisper that was barely more than a breath, "you want to have sex again."

"And again," Garrett confirmed. "And again."

Julie raised an eyebrow. And then she asked, only partly in jest, "What's in it for me?"

"Multiple orgasms?" he said, so quietly and so close that his lips were actually touching hers now.

She laughed, wishing she could collect on *that* promise sooner rather than later. "You are *too* cocky, Garrett McKettrick," she murmured, drawing back just slightly. "How do you know I wasn't faking before?"

"You weren't faking," he said, with damnable confidence. "I have the scratches on my back to prove it."

"That could be part of the act," Julie said.

He laughed. "Okay," he replied. "Were you faking?"

"Hell, no," Julie answered, and tasted his mouth, because she couldn't resist.

It was against her better judgment, all of it.

She was merely putting off the inevitable. And there didn't seem to be a damn thing she could do about it, that night at least.

"They're kissing!" Calvin yelled.

That pretty much tanked the moment.

Julie turned and saw her son standing in the doorway between Garrett's kitchen and living room, making quite a picture in his pajamas and Austin's cowboy hat. Since the hat didn't fit, he had his head tilted back a little, so he could see under the brim.

"What?" Austin called back.

"I said Mom and Garrett are *kissing!*"

Garrett rolled his eyes and chuckled; otherwise, he seemed unruffled.

Julie, on the other hand, was mortified. On top of that, her nipples had gone so hard that they ached, and she was damp, too.

She'd already made the mental shift: This thing happening between her and Garrett wasn't going anywhere.

Her body was slower to buy in.

Austin stepped into the doorway behind Calvin and took the boy lightly by the shoulders, turning him around, heading him into the living room again. He glanced back over one shoulder, grinned the grin Paige probably still couldn't get out of her mind.

"Go right on kissing," he said. "Don't let Cal and me bother you."

Garrett had taken up his fork again. He seemed to be enjoying the corned beef and cabbage, since he went on eating, but his gaze was on Julie and it shone with tenderness and comedy and desire and a whole mix of other things that weren't so easily identified.

"Will you wait for me?" he asked again, when he'd finished his supper, carried his plate and silverware to the sink, rinsed them before dropping them into the dishwasher.

"I'll wait," Julie heard herself say. It really wasn't such a noble sacrifice, after all. Unless she wanted to crowd poor Paige out of her bed, forcing her to sleep on the couch, there weren't a lot of choices.

Until the house she and Paige and Libby owned together was habitable, and that might be weeks, she really didn't have any-where to go.

"When will you leave?" she asked, when Garrett stood behind her chair, instead of sitting down again, and began to massage her shoulders.

"Probably tomorrow," he answered. "The funeral will be held in a few days, and Nan has meetings scheduled with the governor and various state legislators."

Julie frowned. "Meetings? The same week as her husband's funeral?"

"She's a strong woman," Garrett said.

Or a cold one, Julie thought, though she immediately decided she was being unfair. Morgan Cox had, after all, been embroiled in an embarrassing and steamy scandal when he died.

She glanced toward the doorway where Calvin had appeared earlier and lowered her voice, just in case he was eavesdropping again. Or still.

"Well, she's certainly a better woman than I am," she said. "If that had happened to me, about the last thing in the world I'd be doing would be jumping in to fill the man's seat in the Senate."

Garrett took her hand, rubbed his thumb lightly, musingly, over her knuckles. "Nobody," he said gravely, "is a better woman than you are, Julie Remington."

"Now," she said, struggling against an insane need to break down and cry, preferably sitting on Garrett's lap, with her face buried in his neck, "you're just flattering me."

He held on to her hand, raised it to his mouth, retraced with his lips the path he'd taken earlier with his thumb.

Hot, shivery shards of wanting poked and prodded Julie from within.

"Don't," she pleaded.

He didn't release her immediately.

She made no effort to pull away.

Austin made a great deal of noise to let them know he was approaching the kitchen; appeared with his plate and silverware and his usual heartrending grin. Coupled with the sadness lurking behind the sparkle in his eyes, the effect was powerful.

"Cal's asleep on the couch," he confided, crossing the room to set the plate and silverware in the sink.

"I'd better get him to bed," Julie said, unable to keep from sighing softly as she rose from her chair. "He has a tendency to get overexcited anyway, and when he's sick..."

A look passed between him and Austin, who lingered at the sink, though he didn't rinse his dishes. He just leaned against the counter, his arms folded, and watched his brother thoughtfully.

"If you need any help while Garrett's gone," Austin said presently, when his brother had disappeared into the living room to fetch Calvin, "just let me know. I'll be glad to lend a hand."

It was a brotherly offer, nothing more.

Julie couldn't help visualizing Paige and Austin standing side by side.

They'd be wonderful together, she thought whimsically. He had pale brown hair, while Paige's was dark. His eyes were the standard McKettrick blue, hers a deep and vibrant brown.

They would have the most beautiful children.

"Do I have something on my face?" Austin asked, with a grin.

Embarrassed, Julie laughed and shook her head. "Sorry," she said. "I didn't mean to stare. I was just thinking—"

Would she have told him what she was thinking—that he and Paige would have made a great couple—if Garrett hadn't come back just then, with a sleepy Calvin in his arms and Harry at his heels?

Probably not.

"Want me to carry the dog downstairs?" Austin asked his brother.

Garrett looked from Austin to Julie and back again. And he frowned, not in an angry way, but in a thoughtful one.

"I'd appreciate it," he said.

Julie, suddenly in a hurry to be on the move, led the way out of Garrett's apartment and down the stairs to the main kitchen.

Garrett followed, carrying Calvin, and Austin came as far as the foot of the staircase, where he set Harry down and immediately retreated again.

She watched from the doorway of Calvin's room as Garrett took his glasses off, put him into bed and gently tucked the covers in around him.

The boy stirred. "'Night, Garrett," he said.

"'Night, buddy," Garrett replied, his voice throaty.

"You going away?" Calvin asked, in a sleepy murmur.

"For a few days," Garrett answered, "but I'll be back." He glanced at Julie, still hovering on the threshold.

"For sure?" Calvin mumbled, as Harry leaped onto the bed to curl up behind his knees.

"You have my word," Garrett said.

Calvin opened his eyes just long enough to look at Garrett and smile. "Good," he said. "That's good."

Garrett lingered a moment, stroking Calvin's hair back from his face with a light pass of one hand. Then, just when Julie was beginning to think she couldn't bear the sheer wonder of the sight of the two of them together for another moment, Garrett stood, crossed to her, steered her out into the hallway.

Very quietly, he closed the door.

When Julie started for the sitting room, though, he stopped her. Pulled her against him.

His hands rested on her backside, deliciously possessive.

Julie whimpered, full of sweet despair, but she didn't try to pull away. She was pretty sure she didn't have the strength—or the willpower—to do that.

And Garrett kissed her.

His lips touched hers, gently at first, then with unmistakable hunger.

Julie still didn't pull away. No, indeed, she slipped her arms around Garrett's neck and rose onto the balls of her feet to kiss him back.

"I'm staying," he told her, when they both had to breathe.

"Calvin—" Julie whispered back.

"We'll be quiet," Garrett said. And he pulled her straight into the other bedroom, the one where she'd expected to spend a miserable and lonely night.

Life was full of surprises.

Garrett was full of surprises.

Julie's heart was thudding away in her throat. "But—"

He closed the door, turned the lock.

"What if we *can't* be quiet?" she asked.

Garrett hauled her shirt off over her head and tossed it aside. Took a moment to trace the round tops of her breasts, rising above her bra, with the tip of one finger.

"We can be quiet," he assured her.

"Speak for yourself," Julie argued, remembering the primitive, gasping *desperation* of the climaxes she'd had the last time she and Garrett made love. He knew just where to touch her, just *how* to touch her.

Garrett chuckled. Then he removed her bra. Weighed her bare breasts in his hands, chafing the nipples to tingling hardness with the sides of his thumbs.

Julie moaned, but very softly, because Garrett muffled her cry with another bone-melting kiss.

She felt a lot of things in the next few moments—confusion and hope and, of course, the fierce and rising need for completion.

Garrett kissed her for a long time, using plenty of tongue, a harbinger of things to come, and then he bent his head and boldly took one of her nipples into his mouth to suckle.

Julie gasped with pleasure, but softly, and leaned back, supported by the steely strength of the arm he'd curved around her waist, giving herself up to him. The more vulnerable she was to Garrett's lips and his tongue, the better it felt.

He turned to her other breast, taking his sweet time to enjoy her pleasure as well as his own, but when he eased her down onto the bed, sideways, Julie knew what was going to happen, knew she wouldn't stop him.

Knew she would soar.

"Shhh," he said, getting her naked. Arranging her on the edge of the mattress, parting her legs, nibbling the insides of her thighs.

She trembled, murmured his name, groped for him with her hands.

"Shhh," Garrett said again. He nipped at her, the way he had that other time, but this time, there were no jeans to serve as a buffer, and no underpants, either.

"Oh, God," Julie whimpered.

He parted her.

"Garrett—"

He slid his left hand up her body, pausing to squeeze gently at one breast and then the other, fondling them.

"Hold on," he said. "The ride is just about to start."

That was when he put his mouth on her, and drew her in, and the pleasure was so great that her hips flew upward, seeking him, wanting more. She covered her mouth with both hands, to hold in cries of frantic welcome, and surrendered.

Garrett put his hands under her, lifted her to his mouth, held her there.

She needed him more and then still more, but she didn't dare move her hands, even to beg, because she knew she'd yell fit to raise the roof.

The build was excruciating—Garrett knew when she reached the edge and he eased up, whispering against her most tender flesh. Then he would tease her a little, with the tip of his tongue, and then—

When, at long last, Garrett let her have the orgasm he'd been taunting her with, Julie's entire body buckled in the grip of it. Grasping at Garrett, tangling her fingers in his hair, she gave a long, low, keening wail of satisfaction.

The climax was protracted, a series of ferocious spasms, and

Garrett granted Julie no quarter. He devoured her, drove her to peak after peak, even when she was sure she couldn't endure the climb again.

The lovemaking that followed was alternately fevered and sacred.

It was very late—or very early—when Garrett awakened Julie from a deep, sated sleep to kiss her goodbye.

She cried, not only because he was going away, because even then she knew that everything would change after this night.

Probably forever.

Three Days Later

THE FUNERAL WAS relatively dignified, Garrett thought, considering the national media attention surrounding Senator Morgan Cox's short, spectacular fall from grace, followed so soon by his dramatic death.

There were plenty of mourners—Mandy Chante being notably absent—and although the press was in attendance, they had the decency to keep their distance, at least until the services were over.

Following the solemn church ceremony, the gleaming, flower-draped casket was lifted into a hearse and taken to the private side of the Austin airport, then loaded into the cargo hold of a private jet. The plane was provided by certain powerful political interests Garrett preferred not to think about.

He was putting one foot in front of the other, that was all.

Showing up and suiting up, as his high school athletic coach used to put it.

Since leaving the ranch, he'd had several job offers, all of which were high profile, but none were more promising than Nan's. She would serve out the remaining two years of the senator's term as an appointee, but all the while, she and the bosses would be grooming *him*, Garrett, to run in the next election.

Young as he was, Nan had reasoned, Garrett was well known in the state, thanks to his time on Morgan's staff. Plus, he was from an influential Texas family.

Garrett McKettrick, United States senator.

It had a ring to it.

And yet he couldn't stop thinking about Julie Remington, her little boy and the Silver Spur.

Some women, he knew, would have been impressed by his shining future in government.

Julie was not one of those.

Then there was the Silver Spur. Austin still didn't want to believe that Tate was serious about either turning the ranch back into the family enterprise it had been since Clay McKettrick founded it in the early 1900s or just calling it quits, but Garrett knew that was a fact.

Tate was as much a McKettrick as any of them, and he loved the Silver Spur.

He just loved Libby and the twins more, that was all.

Garrett couldn't blame him for that.

Nan, buckling in beside him aboard the borrowed jet, elbowed him lightly in the ribs. The kids were all present, the older ones talking quietly among themselves or just thinking their own thoughts, the smaller ones overseen by attentive nannies.

"All this will be over soon," the widow said.

Her eyes were clear, though red-rimmed from private weeping, and Garrett couldn't help thinking what a class act she was. She was, in fact, downright noble.

Garrett managed a smile, patted her hand. He was a good talker, but right then, he couldn't think of one damn thing to say.

"You'll want to find a place in the Washington area," Nan told him quietly. She paused, looking out the window as the jet taxied along the runway, building up speed for take-off. "I plan to spend a lot more time on the job than Morgan ever did."

Garrett closed his eyes for a moment. The woman had just been to her husband's funeral. Her *philandering* husband's funeral. Now, she was on her way to a city where she had many friends, yes, but even more enemies.

"What?" Nan prompted, with gentle humor, and when Garrett looked at her again, he saw that she was smiling.

"We're having some problems on the ranch," he said. "Rustlers, mainly. Tate's getting married at New Year's and he has full custody of his daughters, for all intents and purposes. He's talking about selling out, doing something else with the rest of his life besides running that ranch."

"Maybe that would be a good idea," Nan mused, surprising him a little. "As you know, I kept my father's ranch after he and Mom were both gone. Oh, it's nowhere near the size of the Silver Spur, but I've worried about that place plenty over the years. Sometimes, I think my life—with Morgan, I mean—might have turned out differently if I hadn't been so stubborn about holding on, keeping that land in the family…"

Her voice fell away.

Garrett sighed. He didn't follow her logic, but that didn't mean she wasn't right. "There's not much point in speculating," he said quietly. "Is there?"

She shook her head. "No," she said. "There's nothing to do now but go on. Make the best of a truly tragic situation."

Garrett waited a beat or two before he spoke again, making sure they wouldn't be overheard. "Did you know about Mandy Chante?" he asked.

Her answer took him off guard. "Of course I knew," she said. "Didn't you?"

He bit back a swear word. *"No,"* he said.

Nan broke the news gently. "Miss Chante was only the latest of many, Garrett."

"You seemed so shaken up when he made his little announcement at that fundraiser—"

"I *was* shaken up," Nan told him. "But it wasn't because the news came as any big surprise. It was the *public announcement* that had *me* worried." She craned her neck, scanned the immediate area to make sure none of the children or nannies were listening in. "That was when I knew he was losing it."

Garrett frowned. "Losing it?"

"Maybe it was only a midlife crisis," she said, her eyes luminous with sorrow. "Or stress, or a breakdown, or the beginnings of some neurological disease. Morgan wasn't himself, that's all I meant."

Garrett wondered why Nan or the state politicos thought he was *smart* enough to be a senator. Yes, Morgan had seemed distracted in the days and weeks immediately preceding the Mandy Announcement, but hell, the man held high office. He was up to his ass in alligators most of the time, so why *wouldn't* he be distracted?

"I think," Nan said sweetly, "that that cowboy-idealism of yours clouds your vision sometimes, Garrett. You see what *should* be there, not necessarily what is."

His first impulse was to deny Nan's observation, but he remembered Tate saying much the same thing about his blind loyalty to the senator, only in slightly cruder terms.

He closed his eyes, hoping Nan would think he wanted to catch some sleep.

In his mind, he heard Tate's voice. *Things change. People change.*

Damn if he hadn't changed, too, Garrett thought.

The question was—how *much* had he changed?

CHAPTER NINETEEN

HECTIC.

That was the word Julie would have chosen to describe the last week of her life. Between ferrying Calvin to and from Paige's apartment every day, a full schedule of classes, and the tryouts for *Kiss Me Kate*, she'd barely had a chance to draw a deep breath.

She missed Garrett, and fiercely, but if pressed, she would have admitted there was an upside to his being gone. This way, she didn't have to resist having sex with the man—a tall order, considering that he could arouse her merely by running that earth-from-space blue gaze of his over her. If he touched her, kissed her—well, she was completely lost then.

All common sense deserted her. Instantly.

With Garrett gone, she'd expected to gain some perspective, find the strength to put the brakes on before both she *and* Calvin got their hearts broken.

Seated at a large table in the restaurant at the Amble On Inn that Saturday morning, waiting for Gordon and Dixie and the elder Pruetts to show up for the scheduled visit with Calvin, Julie took a sip from her coffee cup. The little boy sat quietly beside her, coloring the place mat provided, using stubby wax crayons in an odd combination of hues.

Calvin was still a bit too pale for her liking, and he seemed thinner than before, but he was over the stomach flu. Since Garrett's departure, though, he'd been especially quiet.

"Maybe they're not going to show up," he said, lifting his eyes from the printed place mat.

The words punctured Julie's heart, but she smiled. She was very good at smiling whether she felt like it or not. A questionable skill, to be sure, but one that had stood her in good stead since she was a little girl, huddled shoulder-to-shoulder with her sisters on the front porch of the old house, watching their mother drive away with her lover.

"Smile," Libby had whispered to her all those years ago, trying so hard to help. "It won't hurt so much if you smile."

Paige, the little one, had let out a wail of despair and run toward the front gate, sobbing hysterically and calling, "Mommy! Mommy, come back!"

Libby and Julie had rushed to stop Paige from chasing behind the car, both of them trying to smile.

Both of them with tears streaking their cheeks.

It still hurts, Lib, Julie told her sister silently. *Even when you smile.*

"I'm sure they're just late," Julie said to Calvin, checking her watch. "Maybe they had car trouble or some other kind of delay."

Calvin rolled his sky-blue eyes. The lenses of his glasses gleamed with cleanliness that sunny morning, because he hadn't been up long enough to smear them. "They have your cell number," he said.

A lightbulb went on in Julie's beleaguered mind. "Which reminds me," she said. "Your dad told me you called him a couple of times. Is that true?"

Calvin squirmed a little, but there was defiance in his expression, too. "Yes," he said. "It's true."

The door of the restaurant swung open and both of them looked in that direction, expecting Gordon and his wife and his parents.

Instead, Brent Brogan nodded in greeting and strolled over to the counter to order take-out coffee.

"Did you think I wouldn't let you call your dad, if you asked me about it first?"

Calvin considered his mother's question with the concentration of a Supreme Court justice. He was stalling, of course. Hoping Brent would stop by the table to pass the time of day, or the others would arrive, giving him time to frame an answer.

No luck.

Julie waited patiently, her hands folded in her lap.

Calvin sighed, and his small shoulders drooped under his clean T-shirt and lined windbreaker. His hair was slicked down and his face was clean and if Gordon dared to disappoint him—well— Julie didn't know *what* she'd do.

"The other kids at school, they can all call their dad pretty much whenever they want to," Calvin confessed. "I wondered what it was like. So I used Aunt Libby's cell phone when she was babysitting me—she left it on the counter in the kitchen—and I called my dad."

Julie blinked a couple of times, wanting to cry and refusing to give in to the urge. Calvin was going through some big transitions for such a little boy, and the last thing he needed was a weeping mother.

Brent, having collected and paid for his coffee, waved to Julie as he turned to leave. She waved back.

"Was that a bad thing to do?" Calvin asked earnestly, pushing his glasses up the bridge of his nose.

"Borrowing your aunt's cell phone without asking? Definitely not a good thing to do. But calling your dad? That's normal, buddy." She paused, resisting a urge to smooth his hair or pat his shoulder or fuss in some other way. "What was it like?"

He looked genuinely puzzled. "What was what like?"

"Calling your dad, like any other kid."

Calvin raised one eyebrow. "Do you really want to know?"

She leaned in. "Of course I want to know, Calvin," she told him. "That's why I *asked* you."

"It was weird," Calvin replied, frowning at the mystery of it all. "He's my dad, but he's *not* my dad." He blinked at her, confounded. "I know it's hard to understand—"

Julie sighed, smiled. It wasn't an effort this time. "I think I follow," she said.

Calvin opened his mouth, about to reply, but Julie's cell phone rang at just that moment. Gordon's name flashed on the screen.

"Hello?" Julie said.

"Julie? It's Gordon." He sounded happily apologetic. "We got a late start out of Dallas this morning, and then we ran into some traffic, but we're almost there."

Julie smiled, happy for Calvin. Although he tried to act blasé, she knew the little guy would have been crushed if Gordon and the others had been no-shows.

"We'll wait," she said.

"Good," Gordon said. "Mom and Dad are so excited about meeting their grandson. They'll probably want a million pictures."

The voice of an older person sounded in the background on Gordon's end. "A million won't be half enough!"

Julie's heart warmed. "See you soon," she told Gordon.

Barely ten minutes later, the Pruetts arrived.

Gordon's parents were sweet people, delighted with Calvin and cordial to Julie. They'd brought him a pile of presents, all cheerfully wrapped, and Dixie got out her digital camera, the way she'd done on the first visit, and started right in on getting those million pictures snapped.

GARRETT WANTED TO get home, that was all, and the sooner the better.

Even flying seemed too slow.

A flash of something caught his attention, though, and he went to investigate, swinging the Cessna toward the dry riverbed, where he and Tate had taken a look around the other day.

There were at least two rigs parked down there, between the Quonset huts, one of them the property of the Silver Spur. He didn't recognize the other, a sleek white extended-cab pickup, but that wasn't strange. There were a lot of trucks in the county, let alone the state.

It was something else that bothered Garrett, something visceral, almost subliminal. A clenching sensation in the pit of his stomach.

Frowning, Garrett pulled his cell phone from the pocket of his denim jacket, and speed-dialed his brother.

The answer was brisk and businesslike, as usual. "Tate Mc-Kettrick."

"I'm over the old camp," Garrett said. "Did you send a crew out there to do repairs or something?"

"No," Tate said slowly. "I thought you were still in Austin—or even Washington."

"Well," Garrett replied, swooping low over the camp, "you thought wrong. I'm back."

"For how long?"

"That depends. I don't like the looks of this, Tate. Something is definitely going on down there. You'd better call Brent, or even the state police, and get them out here quick—"

"Garrett," Tate interrupted, "meet me at the airstrip. Don't try to handle this by yourself."

Garrett didn't get a chance to answer.

Two men came running out of the Quonset huts, and they both had rifles.

He was in too low and too close to escape; the bullets ripped through the right wing, and the Cessna pitched wildly to one side.

"Garrett!" Tate yelled. "What the hell?"

Garrett's voice was dead calm as he uttered what he was pretty sure would be the last words he ever spoke. "I'm going down," he said. "Don't sell the ranch."

"Garrett!" Tate repeated, sounding panicked.

Garrett didn't reply. He was too busy struggling with the controls.

He was in one hell of a fix. If he managed to set the plane down without the fuel tank exploding, the men with the rifles would finish him off for sure. If he botched the landing or fate didn't cooperate, he and the Cessna would be blown, as the saying went, sky high.

He tilted the nose slightly downward, lined up with the riverbed, muttered a quick prayer and bellied out the plane.

The metal shrieked as it tore away, and cracks snaked across the windshield.

The machine ground to a deafening stop, and then there was silence.

Garrett waited, holding his breath, for the blast.

It didn't happen.

One heartbeat, another.

A cold sweat broke out all over his body.

His head was bleeding, but nothing was broken, as far as he could tell.

Of course the riflemen were still out there, and they would come after him any second now. No doubt Tate was on his way by now, Austin with him, and Brent Brogan must have been called as well.

The figurative cavalry was coming, bugles blaring, but his brothers and the police weren't going to get there in time, no matter how fast they were traveling.

He leaned down, felt under his seat until he found the trusty .357 Magnum he'd never had to use before.

Always a first time, he thought.

A face loomed in front of the shattered windshield.

Garrett gripped the .357, hoping it was out of sight. Let his head loll to one side and waited.

"I think he's dead or knocked out," Charlie Bates told his partner. "Open the door, though. We've got to make sure."

CHAPTER TWENTY

CHARLIE BATES? Garrett thought, playing possum while he waited for the door of the plane to be wrenched open. His palm sweated around the handle of the .357, but he had a good grip and the safety was off, so all he had to do was pull the trigger.

But, Charlie—a rustler? Maybe even the head of a whole *outfit* of cattle thieves?

Shooting a plane out of the sky definitely qualified as a desperate act; the rest was supposition on Garrett's part.

Time seemed to grind by on sticky gears, halting and then restarting again.

Easy, Garrett told himself. *All you need to think about right now is staying alive.*

You have so many good reasons to stay alive.

Julie.

Calvin.

Tate and Austin, Libby and the twins, and the Silver Spur Ranch.
Reasons aplenty, Garrett figured.

Listing them helped him to calm down and to stay focused.

Charlie was no longer looming in front of the plane's shattered windshield—no, he was on the ground now, with his buddy, the two of them cussing and pulling to get the door of the plane open. It must have been dented in good, that door, because they didn't seem to be making a whole lot of progress.

They were creative cussers, though.

In the distance, Garrett thought he heard the faintest sound of sirens, but when the door finally started to give way, the scream of bent metal drowned out every other sound except that of the blood pounding in his ears.

Then Charlie stuck his ugly mug into the cockpit, and Garrett stuck his .357 under the man's chin.

"Don't move," Garrett told him.

The scrambling noise of somebody getting the hell out of Dodge indicated that Bates's partner was already on the run. Of course, there could be more of the sons of bitches out there—he'd only seen two, but that didn't mean the tally was right.

With Tate and Austin, the cops, and half the hands working the Silver Spur on their way, whoever it was wouldn't get far.

And Charlie Bates wasn't going anywhere at all.

Not with the business end of a .357 under his chin.

"You wouldn't shoot me," Charlie said. His Adam's apple bobbed up to the end of the pistol barrel and then back down, and he put on a sickly grin. "Why, I've known you since you were knee-high—"

"You know, Charlie," Garrett said, with rueful ease, "up until a few minutes ago, I would have said pretty much the same thing about you. That you wouldn't shoot me, I mean. But damn if you or your buddy didn't blow my airplane out of the sky with a deer gun."

Charlie gulped again.

"How long have you been stealing our cattle, Charlie?" Garrett asked, to pass the time of day.

He could hear a rig tearing toward the road—it was probably the white extended-cab he hadn't recognized—and there were definitely sirens, coming closer.

Charlie considered denying the charge, Garrett saw that in his face. Or maybe he was just stalling. Either way, he took so long answering the question that Garrett dug the pistol barrel in a little deeper to inspire confession.

"It started out, we'd just take a cow here and a cow there," the older man finally said. "Sell 'em for cheap and pocket the cash."

Garrett nodded. "Go on."

Charlie's gaze shifted nervously to one side; the sirens were almost on top of them now, but someone else had gotten there ahead of the law and the paramedics.

Garrett heard Tate yell his name.

"I'm all right," Garrett yelled back. His gaze was locked on Charlie's. The old rustler stood on what was left of the wing, and his foothold might have been a little shaky. "Watch out for Charlie here, though. I've got a pistol all but jammed down his worthless, thieving gullet, but he might be armed."

"I ain't armed," Charlie whined, sweating now. "I had a rifle, but I set that down when I climbed up onto the nose to see if you were gonna give us any trouble or not."

"Guess you know the answer to that one," Garrett said. There was no pain, but he was starting to feel a little light-headed, as if he'd been riding horseback under a hot Texas sun without a hat.

Tate must have dragged Charlie down off the bent wing, but it was Austin who climbed up and stood in Bates's place.

Eyes scanning the length of Garrett's body before landing on his face, Austin carefully relieved him of the .357. There were other voices outside the plane now—all around—cops, cowboys and God knew who else.

It was over.

"You hurting anywhere in particular, brother?" Austin asked.

"No," Garrett answered honestly, "but I'm sure as hell *numb* in a few places."

"Maybe you ought to sit tight 'til the paramedics can check you out."

Garrett shook his head. He smelled gas and engine oil. "The fuel tank could still go up," he said. "Let's get clear."

Austin nodded, waited a beat, then moved aside.

Garrett made it out onto the wing, but he would have fallen into the stony bottom of the riverbed if Austin hadn't grabbed hold of his arm just as his knees buckled underneath him.

Tate hurried over to help, and each of them got under one of Garrett's shoulders to hold him upright.

Garrett felt it coming.

Either Tate or Austin yelled for everybody to get as far from the plane as they could.

The three of them hadn't covered more than fifty yards when the explosion back-blasted them, sent them sprawling in the dirt.

Garrett swore, turned his head to look back. Heat scalded his eyeballs dry, and he had to avert his gaze again, blink to make them stop burning.

Flaming debris rained down from the sky.

"Shit," Austin said, clearly impressed by the experience. "We damn near bought the farm that time."

Tate was already getting up off the ground. He'd lost his hat, and his clothes were dirty and torn. He put a hand out for Garrett, and Garrett took it, let his brother haul him to his feet. This time, he was able to stand on his own, though he swayed a bit before he steadied himself.

"Yeah," Garrett agreed. "We damn near did."

Brogan approached, shaking his head. He watched the plane burn for a few moments before he spoke. "Either somebody up there likes you," he told Garrett, "or you're one lucky son of a gun."

Garrett laughed. "I figure it's both," he said. "There was another guy with Charlie—in a white pickup?"

"We've got him," Brogan replied, with a smile. He gave the burning plane another glance, shook his head again. *"Damn,"* he said. "That is a sight to see."

Garrett rubbed his chin. He beard was coming in again. "I guess my career as a crimefighter has probably peaked," he quipped.

The chief grinned. "I reckon we can take it from here," he said. "Though there will be plenty of questions for you to answer down the road a ways, after the paramedics check you over and your brothers take you home so Esperanza can fuss over you and all."

The sky tipped, landed at a crazy angle.

Garrett passed out.

When he came around again, he was lying on his back on a stretcher in the back of an ambulance with an oxygen mask on his face.

One of the ambulance attendants—Garrett didn't recognize him, so he must have been new in Blue River—was beside him.

Austin was at his other side and the rig was moving, eating up road at a good clip.

Garrett tried to take off the mask, but the paramedic—Al, according to the name stitched on his shirt—stopped him.

Austin knuckled Garrett lightly in the shoulder. "Relax, cowboy," he said. "We're just taking you to the clinic, so the docs can look you over. Maybe take an X-ray or two."

Garrett nodded and closed his eyes.

THE VISIT WITH Gordon and his parents lasted for a couple of hours, and by the time it was over, Calvin's batteries were starting to run down. Julie explained that he had just recovered from a stomach flu and they all left the restaurant at the Amble On Inn together, Gordon carrying a now-sleepy Calvin, his father lugging all the presents they'd brought.

Since it was a fairly long drive back to Dallas, Gordon and Dixie, along with the elder Pruetts, of course, planned to spend the night in Blue River. It was agreed that they would all get together again for breakfast in the morning, this time at the Silver Dollar Saloon, provided Calvin was well enough.

Julie had planned to leave her son in Paige's care again and spend the rest of the afternoon packing over at the cottage.

The county ambulance, not the local one, streaked past as she was waiting to pull out of the motel/restaurant parking lot, and at the same moment, Julie's cell phone jangled in the depths of her purse.

Julie didn't dig for it.

Tate was behind the ambulance, in his truck, and Libby was with him.

Every instinct Julie had kicked in. Instead of making a right, toward the cottage and Paige's apartment across the street from it, she took a left, and followed Tate and Libby and, ahead of them, the ambulance.

Calvin, buckled into his car seat in back, had already nodded off. He must have been pooped, Julie thought distractedly, not to be awakened by the shrill screech of that siren.

Two nurses and a doctor were waiting at the entrance to the clinic with a gurney.

Tate parked nearby and leaped out of the truck, and Julie pulled up alongside. Libby, seeing her, rolled down the window.

"It's Garrett," she said. "He's all right, really, but—"

Garrett.

Julie's heart seized like a clenched fist. It was actually painful, like being grabbed from the inside.

She turned, saw the paramedics unloading Garrett from the back of the ambulance. Austin jumped out after him.

Julie tried to get a good look at Garrett, but he had something over his face and there were too many people in the way.

She shoved open the door of her car. "Will you look after Calvin?" she asked Libby, breathless.

Libby smiled faintly and nodded.

Julie followed Garrett and the others into the clinic.

"What happened?" she asked, snagging hold of Austin's shirt-sleeve when he would have gone right into the examining room with the rest of them.

"Some rustlers shot his plane down, that's all," Austin said.

And then he was gone.

Some rustlers shot his plane down.

That's all?

Julie swayed.

Libby came in with Calvin, who was baffled, blinking away sleep. "I'm not sick," he said. "Why are we at the clinic?"

Libby squeezed her nephew against her side. "Stay calm," she told Julie, in her cheeriest big-sister voice. Then, after a beat or two, she asked, "Do you want me to call Paige? See if she can come and pick Calvin up?"

"That would be good," Julie said. Anxiety swelled inside her. What was happening to Garrett at that moment?

Was he dying?

Surely he would have been airlifted to Austin or even Houston or Dallas if he'd been so seriously injured, wouldn't he?

On the other hand, the man had been in a *plane crash,* according to Austin. He could be *so badly* injured that there wasn't time to take him to a city hospital. Maybe he needed immediate medical care just to survive.

Maybe it was touch and go.

Life and death.

"I still don't understand why we're at the clinic," Calvin said, looking up at his fretful mother.

Julie didn't want to tell her little boy that Garrett, one of his all-time favorite people in the world, had been brought here—he was sure to freak out and besides, she didn't have enough information to explain what was happening.

"Your mom is visiting somebody," Libby said, as she and Julie exchanged glances. "That's all. Just visiting."

"Oh," Calvin said. "Like when Gramma had to spend the night here at the clinic in a hospital bed after she drove your car through the front wall of the Perk Up Coffee Shop and put you out of business for good, Aunt Libby?"

"Like that," Libby said, giving him a tender smile. Then she bit her lower lip. "Sort of."

Tate came out of the back, and he was so focused on Libby that he might or might not have noticed Julie and Calvin standing there.

"We'll be here for a while," he said to Libby. "They're taking X-rays."

Libby nodded.

"Who?" Calvin demanded. "Who is getting X-rayed?"

Tate looked down at the child, registered his identity, then rustled up a faint smile. "One of my cowboys took a spill," he replied. He was perceptive, for a man, it seemed to Julie, dazed as she was, but then, he was also a father. A good one.

He knew bad news about Garrett might be more than a little guy could process.

She felt a rush of appreciation for her future brother-in-law.

And tears of worry scalded her eyes.

Libby got out her cell phone and went to the other side of the lobby to call Paige.

"This—cowboy," Julie choked out, staring up into Tate's blazingly-blue eyes, "is he going to be all right?"

"We think so," Tate assured her, and he even grinned, though there wasn't much wattage behind it. He was pale beneath his tan and his five o'clock shadow.

Julie nodded, dashed at her eyes with the back of one hand.

"Paige is on her way," Libby said, returning.

Julie just nodded again.

Libby took her by the arm, led her to a chair and sat her down. Tate disappeared into the back again.

Paige came, spoke in whispers with Libby, took Calvin and left again.

Julie felt as though she were underwater, inside one of those old-fashioned diving bells with the heavy brass helmet and only a little face-wide window to look through.

Blood hummed in her ears.

Libby sat down beside Julie, rested a comforting hand on her back. "So," she said gently, "Paige and I were right. You *are* in love with Garrett."

There didn't seem to be much point in denying the fact, especially to one of the two women who had always been able to see right through her.

Julie nodded miserably, knotted her fingers together so tightly that the knuckles ached. A tear trickled down her cheek and dropped onto her right thumb.

Libby hugged her. "It's okay," she murmured. "We can talk about it later."

The wait seemed endless.

Finally, though, Tate and Austin came out of the examination area together. Both of them looked done-in, but they were grinning, too.

"Garrett wants to see you," Austin told Julie, when she and Libby stood to wait for news. "Hell, he hasn't *shut up* about wanting to see you since I told him you were out here."

Julie almost laughed, but it was a purely hysterical reaction. "He's all right, then?"

"Garrett's fine," Tate said, but he moved into Libby's arms, and closed his eyes as he rested his chin on the top of her head. "Just roughed up a little, that's all."

"Come on," Austin told Julie. "I'll take you to him."

Garrett was sitting on the edge of an exam table, pulling on his boots. His clothes were filthy, and so was his hair, but that grin of his was bright enough to knock Julie Remington right back on her heels.

His shiner had lightened considerably.

"Hey," he said hoarsely, drinking her in with his eyes.

"Hey," she replied.

"See you around, Austin," he told his brother, without looking away from Julie's face.

Austin laughed and left the room.

"I love you," Julie blurted out, the moment she and Garrett were alone in the room.

And then she blushed crimson.

"I was about to tell you the same thing," he said. "Nothing like almost getting killed to straighten out a man's priorities. Which is not to say that I hadn't already decided to come back here and ask you if you're totally sure you wouldn't want to be involved with a political animal like me."

Julie went to him. Her eyes were wet and she couldn't seem to speak.

Garrett slid off the exam table to stand, put his arms loosely around her waist.

She lowered her head, but Garrett made her tip it back by tilting his own to one side and catching her mouth in a light kiss.

"I love you, Julie Remington," he told her.

She looked up at Garrett, almost unable to believe she'd heard him correctly. "Really?"

He laughed. It was a throaty sound, all man. "Really," he said. "Will you marry me, Julie?"

She blinked. "Marry you?"

He nodded. "I was thinking we could maybe muscle in on Tate and Libby's wedding, come New Year's, tell the preacher to make it a double."

Julie's eyes went so wide they hurt around the edges. "Yes," she said. Amazed at herself. Amazed at *him.* "Even if it means living in Washington or Austin, instead of Blue River, I'll marry you, Garrett McKettrick."

"Washington or Austin?" He seemed puzzled. His arms were still around her, and he pressed her close, and the contact practically struck sparks.

"Isn't that where you 'political animals' like to hang out?"

"This particular animal," he said, nuzzling her mouth again, getting ready to kiss her in earnest, "wants to live on the Silver Spur with his wife and his stepson and tend to business."

He murmured the part about tending to business, just as his lips touched hers.

Julie's knees went weak.

He kissed her as if he meant it.

"THIS IS GOING to be my room?" Calvin asked, a few days later, upstairs in the ranch house, in Garrett's apartment. "Really?"

Garrett winked at Julie, then put his hands on Calvin's back and gave him a little push over the threshold. "If it suits you," he said, "it's all yours."

Julie looked on, smiling. After giving the matter a lot of thought, she'd agreed to share Garrett's room, and Calvin seemed to be okay with that.

Calvin stepped inside, looked around. Garrett and Austin had moved the old furniture out, and replaced it with Calvin's things from the cottage. There was a flat-screen TV mounted on one wall, and he would have his own bathroom, too.

"Can Harry sleep here, too?" Calvin asked, looking up at Garrett.

Garrett crouched, so he could meet the child's gaze directly.

Julie ached with love for both of them.

"Sure, he can, pardner," Garrett answered gravely, ruffling Calvin's hair. "Harry's a member of the family."

Calvin beamed. "He can even get up and down the stairs by himself now," he crowed, as the dog strolled in to join them, having spent the morning lounging in front of Garrett's fireplace.

"He's pretty handy for a three-legged dog," Garrett agreed, rising to his full height and turning to Julie with mischief dancing in his eyes.

"Ready to go out to the airstrip and check out the new plane?" he asked. Calvin had been promised a flight later on; for now, he'd be staying at the ranch house with Esperanza.

Julie nodded, feeling all shy and warm, and very much in love.

She felt a tingle at the prospect of being alone with Garrett, even in the narrow confines of his Porsche.

He'd be trading that in for a truck soon, he'd told her.

He was just a rancher at heart, and not a politician at all.

Go figure.

They were both content to be silent during the short drive to the airstrip. There, the jet gleamed in the sun, considerably larger than the Cessna destroyed in the crash.

"This is yours?" Julie marveled. They hadn't gotten out of the Porsche.

"Tate and Austin and I bought it together," Garrett answered, looking at her instead of the sleek private jet. "Technically, it's the property of the Silver Spur."

"Pretty fancy for counting cattle from the sky," Julie remarked. Charlie Bates and his accomplice were in police custody, but the case was far from closed. The rustling operation was a big one, and some of the thieves were still at large.

Garrett chuckled. "We'll use a helicopter for that," he told her, squeezing her hand. "Or do it the old-fashioned way—on horse-back."

Julie swallowed hard. "Are you sure, Garrett? That this is what you really want? Living on the ranch, I mean, and getting married? Giving up your crack at being a senator?"

He leaned across the console and tasted her mouth. "I'm sure," he told her. Then he inclined his head toward the jet again. "Come on," he said. "Let's go take the tour."

Julie felt a sweet shiver of excitement. The jet's door stood open, and the steps had been lowered.

Garrett got out of the Porsche, sprinted around to Julie's side and opened the car door for her.

He took her hand, pulled her toward the plane.

At the base of the steps, Garrett swept Julie up into his arms, carried her easily up the incline, both of them laughing.

The inside of the plane was as elegantly simple as the outside. There were eight seats, upholstered in buttery leather.

A silver wine cooler stood on the marble-topped counter separating the small galley from the main cabin, holding a bottle of champagne. Two crystal glasses had been set out as well.

Garrett drew up the stairs, then shut and secured the door.

A delicious little thrill skittered up Julie's spine. "Are we going somewhere?" she asked, almost breathless.

He took her into her arms. "Oh, we'll be going *lots* of places," he drawled, bending his head to nibble at the side of her neck. "Starting with Paris."

"Paris? You mean, right now?"

"No," he said, "I was planning to *make love* right now."

She blushed, but she didn't pull back out of his arms. "Good," she told him, "because I've got Calvin to look after and my classes to teach and a musical to put on, and I don't have the faintest idea where my passport is or even if it's still valid."

Garrett kissed her, thoroughly and for a long time, before he replied. "Calvin will be fine with Libby and Tate for a few days," he said. "Paige found your passport, and it hasn't expired."

Julie opened her mouth, closed it again. So much had happened recently that she could barely keep up.

Tate had hired Ron Strivens, for instance, and he and the kids would be moving to the ranch soon. With a lot of help from Libby and Paige, Julie had managed to pack up the contents of the cottage, most of which were in storage for the time being.

"That still leaves my job," Julie pointed out. "And the rehearsals for the musical."

"You're on vacation, as of today," Garrett told her, "and several of the parents are going to cover the rehearsals."

Julie slid her arms around Garrett's neck, tilted her head to one side. "Well, Garrett McKettrick," she said, "do you *always* get what you want?"

His grin was wicked. "Most of the time, yeah."

"And we're going to Paris? Just like that?"

"We're going to bed first," he said. "*Then* we're going to Paris." Garrett held her a little closer, flicked at her earlobe with the very tip of his tongue. "In the meantime, you might want to fasten your seat belt…"

* * * * *